THE Long Road HOME

ROMANCE COLLECTION

THE Long Road HOME

ROMANCE COLLECTION

Four Romances with
an Enduring Pioneer Spirit

Judi Ann Ehresman & Naomi Mitchum

BARBOUR BOOKS
An Imprint of Barbour Publishing, Inc.

Published by Barbour Books, an imprint of Barbour Publishing, Inc., P.O. Box 719,
Uhrichsville, Ohio 44683, www.barbourbooks.com, in association with OakTara Publishers,
www.oaktara.com.

*Our mission is to publish and distribute inspirational products offering exceptional value and biblical
encouragement to the masses.*

Member of the
Evangelical Christian
Publishers Association

Printed in Canada.

Contents

THE LONG ROAD HOME

The Hand of God, Book One

by Judi Ann Ehresman

Dedication

To my husband and best friend,
Richard Ehresman

And to our children:
Nathan and Ruth Ehresman
Luke and Elizabeth Ehresman

Also in loving memory of
Bonnie Glasspoole, my dearest girlfriend on earth,
who is now home in heaven

Chapter 1

The ground was hard for that time of year. The snows had melted early, and the rains had not been as heavy as usual for March in Indiana. Now that April was here, the ground was already solid enough for Mandy Evanston to walk on without soaking through her well-worn boots.

Even though the day promised to be a pleasant one for April, the sun had not been up long enough to create much warmth. The early morning chill worked its icy fingers up her spine and made her shiver. She pulled her coat closer about her.

Alone. . .alone. . .alone. . .alone. . .alone. Each step she took seemed to stamp out the rhythm of her thoughts, reminding her she was alone. Alone in the woods. Alone for the summer. Totally and completely alone in the world.

"I will not think of it as being alone," she murmured to herself. "With this little one inside me, I am not completely alone. And Ethan said he would be back in August to get us ready for winter, so that is only, let's see—" she pulled one hand free from her woolen pocket and counted on her fingers—"April, May, June, July. . .four months, maybe five. I will keep myself busy these next few months, and time will fly. By the time Ethan comes home, I can tell him about the little one. He will be excited, and then the waiting will not be so long for him."

Once again she was quiet, listening to the sound of her footsteps and the skittering, rustling noises of morning in the woods. The naked trees reached their blackened branches to the sky as though begging for warmth, for the covering of leaves soon to grow on their dead-looking appendages. Mandy breathed deeply of the many scents that formed the one fragrance of the woods. She slowed to a quiet walk. After all, what was the rush, really?

Mandy had felt alone for much of her life. Her parents had died within a week of one another from an illness that had swept through their town, leaving her alone as a young child. She had stayed with a neighbor until her father's brother had been traced. When her uncle came to claim her, she tried to be brave and grown up. He was kind enough to her, but when he took her home, it didn't take long to realize her aunt did not truly welcome Mandy. She resented having to care for another child. So Mandy grew up as more of a servant than one of the family and was always left quite alone.

As she strolled through the woods now, she thought about the time she met

Ethan. He was working in a store in Boston to which she was often sent by her aunt. She couldn't help being attracted to his energy, friendliness, kindness, and handsome looks. Then one day he offered to carry her packages home for her, and she was speechless. For several months he continued carrying her packages, but she always retrieved them just before they got to her aunt's home and sent him on his way. She was afraid that if her aunt discovered she had a friend, she would accuse Mandy of "frittering away her time" and her errands would end. Then she might never have a chance to see him again and would miss their chats, laughs, and brief walks together. She smiled at the warm memory.

One day Ethan started talking of joining a wagon train that was coming through their town as it headed to the unsettled West. He wanted to travel clear out to Ohio, or even Indiana, where land could be had for a song and a man could live off the land and the woods. He shared his excitement about the possibility with her for quite a while until he said he'd finally decided to do it. When he told her he planned to leave in the spring, she couldn't stop the tears from coming.

"Would you miss me?" he asked, gazing at her tenderly.

She hadn't been able to find any words. Her throat was tight, her tongue paralyzed. So she had just looked at him and mutely nodded.

He clasped her arm and steered her into a nearby alleyway behind the livery. "Mandy," he said, his eyes alight with hope, "will you marry me and go with me?"

She hadn't even had to think about it. Again she simply nodded.

Things happened swiftly after that as she helped Ethan plan and prepare for their journey. Each time she went to the store, Ethan had her select goods to add to the wagon he had purchased.

Finally the day came when she packed all of her earthly possessions, wrote a letter of thanks to leave for her aunt and uncle, and slipped off quietly to meet Ethan at the minister's house for a quick wedding ceremony.

Within an hour of the ceremony, Mr. and Mrs. Ethan Evanston were headed to the West on a wagon train.

That was, let's see, this May will make six years. Time had flown. Ethan was such a wonderful husband. Mandy still smiled when she thought about how handsome he was. She couldn't help but notice the way women on the wagon train had looked at him and blushed when he spoke to them. But he seemed oblivious of his effect on women. And now he would be a daddy. Oh, he would make a wonderful daddy! She hoped the baby looked just like Ethan.

Oh, Ethan, why did you need to go away? Why do you think you have to make money on the railroads? Why do you get so restless? Her mind went over and over the questions she'd asked him repeatedly these last few weeks. None of his answers had completely satisfied her, but she was determined not to become a whining, nagging wife like her aunt. So she had tried to cheerfully support his decision, even though she couldn't understand his thinking.

This morning, as she'd walked with him as far as he allowed, she had still tried to change his mind without pleading for him to stay with her. Now, as she walked the six miles back to the cabin, she was content with herself for not using her knowledge of the coming baby to make him stay home. She knew she could make it through the summer, and then when he came home, they would have only a few more months to wait for their baby to arrive. Just thinking about how excited Ethan would be when he discovered he would be a daddy renewed her determination to remain cheerful and patient until his return.

From even before they married, Ethan had talked in a dreamy way about all the children he and Mandy would have and how they would love them, teach them, and be a happy family—something neither had known. They had seen happy families working and playing together, and both had longed for such an experience. But when year after year of their marriage had passed with no babies, they wondered if the best of life had passed them by. Until. . .

Mandy had not wanted to tell Ethan at first, in case she was mistaken. Then, almost as soon as she felt quite certain, that Gerald fellow had talked to Ethan at the General Store and told him how much money men were being paid for laying tracks for the new railroad coming west. From that time on she could sense restlessness in Ethan. No amount of talking could change his mind, and she didn't want him to feel tied down because of the baby. She was afraid he might resent her and the baby, so she had kept her secret. Now she would count the months until he came home, and they could be the family they had always dreamed of being.

She glanced around at the forest, admiring its beauty. Squirrels chattered and scampered; birds sang and called. Mandy made a game of identifying how many different birds she heard and saw. She shuddered as she saw a plump rabbit hop quickly out of sight. Ethan had once showed her how to catch and clean rabbits for meat, but she didn't think she could kill one herself unless she became very, very hungry. She had a difficult enough time wringing the neck of a chicken, but that seemed altogether different than killing a soft, quiet rabbit. Why? She couldn't say for certain, but it just did.

⌒∞⌒

The next day the sun reached in Mandy's window, stretching its long beams over to the bed, draping warmth across her face. As the light gently massaged her eyelids open, she tugged the quilts up around her neck and turned her face away from its brightness. Lazily she reached over to pull herself close to Ethan's warmth. . . .

She sat up abruptly. Then she remembered: Ethan was gone. This was her first morning in almost six years to wake up alone and cold in her bed. Somehow the quilts and bright pillows she had carefully stitched to make their cabin cozy and bright did not hold the same warmth and cheer they had before. In fact, she found herself feeling quite glum.

"I have to stop thinking this way," she told herself. "I will not become melancholy. After all, I still have the baby, and Ethan won't be gone forever."

She swung her legs over the side of the bed but groaned as she started to stand. Every muscle in her body screamed out in rebellion. She chuckled. "Guess I had better pace myself a little better today. But yesterday's work did make the day go quickly."

Yesterday morning, when she'd come back to the cabin, she could hardly stand the loneliness of the empty rooms. Reminders of Ethan and of all the things they had done together were everywhere. So she decided to take a walk around their small farm and form a plan for her days. As she fed the chickens and the few sheep and milked the two cows, she couldn't keep the spring air and the earthiness of the freshly turned sod from filling her with a strong urge to plant her vegetable garden.

She had carried the milk and eggs into the cabin, then taken down her box of seeds. Soon she was planting seeds in the soil Ethan had tilled up before he left. She worked long and hard, planting several rows at a time, then carrying buckets of water from the spring to water the seeds before patting the sod around them. She rested her back from carrying water by planting several more rows, and the cycle started all over again.

By the time she finished, dusk chilled her, and she was hungry and exhausted. After putting away the garden tools in the shed, she was so tired she could hardly walk back up the hill to the cabin. She was thankful she had filled all the water buckets in the morning, because she was too tired to do it now, and she needed to warm a bucket of water for a bath.

Once inside the cabin, she poured water into the big washday kettle and hung it in the fireplace to heat. She built the fire up, selected a large potato from last year's garden, scrubbed it, and put it into the hot coals beneath the kettle. Stretching to ease her sore back, Mandy went out to milk the cows.

By the time she returned to the cabin and placed the washtub by the fire, the water in the kettle was warm. She poured it into the tub, slipped out of her soiled dress, and scrubbed herself clean. The lavender soaps she made were quite refreshing, and as she dried herself, combed out her wet, tangled hair, and donned a clean nightgown, she began to feel much better.

After pouring a cup of tea, she sat down to eat her potato with a thick slice of bread piled high with her homemade apple butter. Eyeing the washtub of dirty water, she decided it could wait until morning to be emptied. The day had flown.

In the morning Mandy reviewed the work before her. Because of her impulsive gardening yesterday, she could hardly move today, yet the planting had made the day pass quickly. She needed a plan for her summer.

After donning a fresh work dress, she straightened the sheets, pulled up the quilts, smoothing the wrinkles out and checking to be sure each quilt laid straight. She smiled as she remembered Ethan teasing her about the fact that she wanted the blankets to lay perfectly straight on the bed. But in spite of his teasing, he often commented to her about how nice she had made their home. She was proud and pleased that he appreciated all the little touches that made their cabin home.

While the water boiled for her tea, she made short work of emptying the bathwater, cleaning out the tub, and hanging it on its peg on the back side of the cabin. Taking out her precious pad of paper, Mandy chose one clean page and, while she ate her egg and bread and drank her tea, started her list.

Mandy listed all the chores she would normally do in a summer, such as keeping the garden up, canning and drying her garden produce, tying up her herbs to dry, washing windows, washing, starching, and ironing all the curtains in the cabin and rehanging them, as well as some projects she had not done before, such as making baby quilts, diapers, nightgowns, and preparing the other bedroom for the baby. She was thankful she'd stocked up on fabrics from the store Ethan had worked in back in Boston before they traveled, not knowing if there were stores or places in the untamed West to purchase such necessities. And there had already been plenty of opportunity to use the materials from her trunks for curtains, quilts, clothes, etc. She added to her list taking everything out of her cupboards and off the shelves so she could thoroughly clean the cabin.

When she saw the length of her list, Mandy smiled. This summer would pass quickly if she was to accomplish all of this, and then Ethan would be home and life would be wonderful again. But, today, she had better stop sipping tea and get some water boiling to wash her garden clothes as soon as the animals were fed and watered, the eggs gathered, and the cows milked.

Chapter 2

One day seemed almost the same as the next now, and Mandy found herself talking out loud more and more. She was so lonely that sometimes she would go to the barn and converse with the cows, mules, and sheep. She'd never before enjoyed cleaning stalls and spending time with the farm animals, but they soon recognized her voice and responded by nuzzling noses or turning a head as she milked or patted them.

Mandy also talked more and more to the barn cat, but Tabby was not as much company as the other farm animals. Other than rubbing herself on Mandy's skirts and shedding hair all over them, she would hardly glance at Mandy. Mostly the cat simply wanted a sunny spot to sleep. But Mandy knew Tabby was about to have her kittens, so she forgave the cat wanting some rest time.

Mandy talked aloud to the baby she carried, too. Sometimes she wondered if it was only her love for the baby or from sheer loneliness. Ethan had been gone a little more than four weeks, and she had not seen another human being in all that time. She desperately craved fellowship.

As the clouds chased one another across the late morning sky, Mandy frowned. It was now the first week of May, and a shower would be welcome, but these looked too far away for rain. The gray sky actually looked like snow. Suddenly she realized that planting a garden the first week of April might not be a good idea in Indiana.

Opening the back door to peer down at the garden by the creek, Mandy felt the blast of cold and knew she'd better do something quickly if she wanted to save those little green sprouts peeking above the rich, dark sod.

Pulling on a heavy sweater as she ran, she first went to the shed for the wooden wheelbarrow Ethan had made for hauling wood. She pushed the heavy thing into the woods, filled it with leaves and pine needles, and trundled each load to the garden, where she pressed armloads of the leaves over each row of tender shoots. Long before she was finished, the snow started falling, but Mandy couldn't bear the thought of losing one precious seedling, so she worked on. Finally, each row was lovingly covered with its mound of warm protection, and Mandy trudged back up the hill with the wheelbarrow.

"We sure had a workout today, Little One. One of these days you'll be running behind me, helping me cover the tiny shoots and getting yourself all dirty in the process." Picturing the scene in her mind's eye, she smiled as she closed the door of the shed.

Since the wind was picking up, chilling the air, Mandy decided to do the evening chores a little early, so she could stay by the fire for the evening. As she finished milking the second cow, the barn door flew open, startling the cows with the noise and blast of cold air, making Bridget kick the bucket and spill most of the evening's milk on the straw. Mandy patted Bridget, talking quietly to her as she rescued what was left of the milk. Taking the remaining milk in the bucket, Mandy struggled to close the barn door against the fierce wind. Finally, the latch was fastened securely, and she hurried back to the warmth of the cabin.

After adding wood to the fire, she stood and turned in front of it for a while, trying to ease the stiffness of her fingers. Then, drawing her rocker closer to the fire, she took up her sewing basket to work on a layette.

Suddenly, she heard a banging and went to look toward the barn—the direction from which the sound had come. The snow was swirling and blowing so hard it was difficult to see, but it looked like that barn door had swung open again. Mandy was puzzled. She knew she had latched it securely.

Donning warm clothes and a cape against the cold, Mandy once again made her way to the barn. Sure enough, the barn door was swinging in the wind. As she tugged on the heavy door to close it, she thought she heard a weak voice say, "Momma," from inside the barn. But surely she was mistaken, and it was merely the soft bleat of a lamb.

Stepping quietly into the darkness of the barn, she listened carefully. Just then a gentle shuffling sounded beyond the cow stalls. Reaching for the pitchfork, Mandy tiptoed around the back side of the stalls. Bridget moved her feet, and Dinah made snorting noises. Perhaps that was all she'd heard?

But when Mandy peeked around the back stall, she saw the back of a black girl huddled low, holding a baby tight against her and rocking back and forth on her heels.

Stunned, Mandy could do nothing for a moment. When she could think, she couldn't decide what to do. Should she be frightened or angry that someone was hiding in her barn? And what was a black person doing in these parts of the woods anyway? No black people lived around here, from what she knew.

But something about the girl touched her heart. Suddenly Mandy wasn't afraid. Putting down the pitchfork, she stepped around the corner and announced cheerfully, "Hello, my name is Mandy."

The frightened girl was speechless as she turned her huge dark eyes with their luminescent whites to stare at Mandy. She was so skinny her eyes looked about to pop out of her head. The child in her arms whimpered as she rocked back and forth, back and forth. Finally, as Mandy squatted to her level, the girl's eyes swam with tears and she cried, "Ah cain' go no futha'! Please don' sen' me back, ma'am. Please don' sen' me back!"

Mandy clasped her arms around the terrified girl, feeling the sharpness of her bones through the back of her thin dress. "You are starved to death. . .and cold," Mandy said gently. "Come into the cabin with me. We'll get you warm and find you something to eat. Then you can tell me what you are doing in my barn." Mandy peeled off her cape, wrapped it around the girl and the baby, and helped the girl to her feet.

As soon as they were in the cabin, Mandy asked the girl to sit at the table. After hesitating, the girl finally did, all the while trembling and staring fearfully at Mandy and hugging the baby. While eggs simmered in a pan, Mandy brought milk, bread, cheese, and some tea to warm and feed the two. Upon seeing the baby more closely, Mandy realized he must be more than a year old but was so skinny and small she had mistaken him for an infant.

When Mandy coaxed her to talk, the girl said her name was Deidre. Between bites of food, Deidre told the story of how she had run away from a plantation somewhere in the South last winter. She had been beaten often there since she could never seem to please the lady of the plantation. One of the slaves had overheard the lady coaxing her husband to sell Jedediah, Deidre's son, so Deidre wouldn't be distracted by caring for her child. The plantation owner had already sold Deidre's husband away from her, and now he agreed to sell her child to make his wife happy.

Tears brimmed as Deidre said she knew her heart couldn't stand being separated from her son, too. So one night, soon after that incident, Deidre had taken her son and fled the plantation. She had walked for weeks at night, sleeping under bridges and in woods during the day, scavenging food anywhere she could find it. They had not found food for days now. When they'd heard the lowing of cows in the barn, Deidre had sneaked in to try to get some milk for her child. With pleading eyes Deidre begged Mandy to not punish her for stealing and, once again, to please not send her back.

Mandy had heard of slaves being owned in the South but had never been exposed to the realities of that sort of life. Her heart went out to the girl, whom she finally realized was no girl but a young woman, married and with a child.

"You're safe now," she promised Deidre. Then she made the exhausted woman a bed of quilts on the large rag rug by the fire, brought pillows, and told her to sleep there with her son. "Tomorrow is another day. We'll think of a plan," Mandy assured her.

Chapter 3

For hours Mandy tossed and turned, trying to sleep. She was wide awake late into the night with the happenings of the day playing over and over in her mind. Several times she had slipped quietly out to put more wood on the fire and to make sure Deidre and Jedediah were sleeping well.

Now, as the morning sun streamed between the curtains, Mandy slowly opened her heavy eyelids. The most wonderful aroma wafted from the main room of the cabin. Just as she sat up to pull on her house socks, there was a tap on her door.

"Come in," she called.

The door slowly opened, and Deidre peeked around it, showing all her beautiful white teeth in a huge smile. "Good mornin', Missus. Ah done made y'all some breakfas'. Ah hope y'all don' min' none."

"Of course not," Mandy replied. "Whatever you made smells really good." Happy to see the woman smiling this morning, Mandy grabbed her robe and followed Deidre into the kitchen.

"Ah seen y'all go down t' the cella' las' ev'nin', so Ah jes 'cided to g'won down an' sees whut Ah could fin' to fix y'all fo breakfas'. Why, Ah jes fin' all kinds of good fixin's, so sets y'all down an' eat y'all some."

Noticing only one place set at the table, Mandy asked, "Deidre, did you and Jedediah already eat your breakfast?"

"Oh, no, Mum. We ain' eatin' y'all's food 'thout y'all's biddin'. Oh, no, Mum. Deidre don' steal. Oh, no, Mum."

"Then let's get more plates on this table so we can eat together."

"Oh, no, Mum, Ah couldna eats at table wit' y'all. Did y'all fo'gets Deidre's a nigga?"

And then Mandy understood. It was because Deidre was a slave. Her heart grew sad at the young woman's plight. "Deidre, my husband is gone on a trip, and I am very lonely. I would truly welcome your company at my table."

"Oh, Mum, y'all sounds jes like Jesus—sayin' come sups at ma table. Ah's glad to keep y'all comp'ny 'thout eatin' y'all's food."

Every time Deidre smiled, her eyes danced and gleamed. She was a beautiful young woman. What would she look like with a little more flesh on her bones? Mandy wondered. It amazed her that Deidre could smile so radiantly after all she had endured.

"Now, Deidre," she chided kindly, "that's plain silly. Where are you going to go, and what are you and Jedediah going to eat if you don't share with me? I was thinking last night of a plan, and if you will sit here and eat this breakfast with me, I will tell you my plan and see what you think."

So they quickly poured another cup of coffee for Deidre and milk for Jedediah and began to eat the wonderful eggs, fried potatoes, mush, and salt pork that Deidre had prepared. Mandy was surprised at how well the woman could cook. She enjoyed every bite of the largest breakfast she had ever seen.

While they ate, Mandy asked Deidre if she would stay on and share the cabin with her. She explained about Ethan's absence, but she knew he would welcome such a friend for Mandy even after he was home. Mandy knew without doubt that Ethan would build Deidre her own cabin once he got home. Until then, Deidre and Jedediah could use the other bedroom next to their own room that Ethan had built for the children who had not yet been born.

Mandy could tell when she mentioned Ethan's name that Deidre was terrified of him already. But Deidre agreed to stay on—at least until Ethan came home. Mandy decided she would have to accept that as the best promise she could get at this point.

After they had eaten all they could hold, Deidre suggested that Mandy get dressed while she cleaned up the dishes. Mandy agreed, and while she quickly dressed and made up her bed, she heard Deidre singing softly to Jedediah. How wonderful it was to have company! Having another woman in the house was such a relief, and dear Jedediah was a sweet baby. Mandy could hardly remember feeling such joy.

Mandy started to plan the day. They would drag everything out of the extra room. Even though it didn't have a bed, they could make a nice bed on the floor for Deidre and Jedediah to share. As the plan formed, she went out to tell Deidre. She talked so fast that the poor woman had a difficult time understanding what she was saying, but Deidre laughed and said to give her orders and she would do her best to follow, to which Mandy tried to explain again that Deidre was no longer a slave, but a friend.

"We'll work together," Mandy explained, "and get twice as much accomplished and have twice as much fun." So together they began.

What fun those two young women had! By evening the clean windows shone in the new bedroom, the walls smelled of damp wood, and all the feathers Mandy had been collecting in the attic made a wonderful feather tick on the floor large enough for Deidre and Jedediah to share and still have plenty of room. Since they used all the feathers that Mandy had collected for the feather mattress, Mandy shared some of the pillows from her room.

Deidre said she had never slept on pillows before, anyway. "But they sho 'nuff do makes the room look bright an' purty," she declared.

Mandy could tell Deidre had not had a bath for a long, long time, so when they were finished with all they could do for that day, they heated some water and dragged the washtub into Deidre's room. Mandy brought some clean towels and her own lavender soap and instructed Deidre to enjoy a bath while she watched Jedediah and made their supper. When Deidre was finished, she asked if she could put Jedediah in the tub.

When they finally sat down to their good supper, Deidre shyly asked if they could thank Jesus for all their blessings. This was new to Mandy, so she watched as Deidre and Jedediah bowed their heads, thanking God for providing so well for their needs and for Mandy, and then began to eat.

That night, as Mandy lay alone in her bed, she pondered over and over Deidre's ability to thank Jesus after all she had been through. Sometime, when the time was right, she would have to ask Deidre about it. But for now she was bone tired and welcomed the soft bed as she drifted into a comfortable sleep, knowing she was no longer alone in the cabin.

Chapter 4

Day after day the friendship between the two young women grew. Thankful for a safe refuge, food, and shelter, Deidre made herself indispensable. Though Mandy had always been an early riser, Deidre almost always was up and dressed first, often already preparing breakfast or bringing in the full water buckets before Mandy awoke.

Together the two made curtains for the sparkling windows in Deidre's room and even some clothes and underclothes for Deidre and Jedediah. Deidre had never had real dresses to wear, only the slave shifts made from feed sacks. She was very shy at first about wearing dresses with tucks and ruffles, so to start out, Mandy made her some nice skirts and several tailored shirtwaists. She was able to convince Deidre to wear them since there was no one around but the three of them.

Deidre looked absolutely stunning in her new clothes but was afraid to work in them at first. However, in a few days, she overcame her discomfort with the beautiful new clothes and settled into the comfortable work routine the two women had worked out.

Mandy was glad to have company. Now the days flew by instead of dragging. The projects she had set for herself to accomplish went much more quickly with Deidre's help, so the two women found they had time to enjoy hikes in the woods, picnics down by the stream, and laughter over Jedediah's cute baby ways. It seemed every day Jedediah learned new words and expressions, and the two women delighted over each discovery. He was a smart, precious child and quickly warmed to Mandy, allowing her to hold and cuddle him.

One day, after washing up the evening dishes and hanging up the towels to dry, Mandy took out her list she had made to see what she still needed to accomplish this summer. As usual, Deidre watched with curiosity, so Mandy handed the list to her. "Which project do you think we should begin next?"

Deidre looked at Mandy with huge eyes. "Ah cain't read. Y'all will have t' read it fo' Deidre."

Mandy had stunned. She'd never considered that her friend couldn't read, and she couldn't imagine what it would be like to not be able to read or write. "Would you like to learn to read? I'm not really a teacher, but I think I could teach you the letters, what sound each one makes, and then the way they fit together to make words. Would you like to try?"

Deidre's brown eyes swam with tears, spilling over and splashing onto the red checkered tablecloth. Her mouth opened, but no words came out.

Mandy sat quietly, waiting. Soon Deidre got up, walked quickly into her room, and returned shortly holding something small and black to her chest. When she sat back down at the table, she slowly and deliberately laid the small black square in front of Mandy.

Mandy could see it was a small book that was quite worn. "What is it, Deidre? Is this yours?" Turning the book over gently in her hands, she read, "*New Testame. . .*" Part of the word had worn off.

"It's a Bible." Deidre spoke softly as though sharing a secret. "A slave woman from our camp done give it t' me jes 'fore she died. She always read t' me from that Bible, an' tol' me t' keep it, so when Ah learned t' read, Ah could read it fo' m'self. Ah strapped it onto m' ches' an' carried it, so Ah wouldn' lose it, an' Ah brings it here wit' me too. Ah wanna learn me t' read so Ah can read me Jesus' words. You can read it, too, if'n ya wants to. We can leave it on th' table an' share it."

Mandy had never seen such devotion to a book. She had attended church with her aunt and cousins on the rare occasions they went, but the minister at their church had not used a Bible, nor had anyone she knew. She assumed it was just another book but could tell it was very dear to Deidre. So she decided that, if it would make her dear friend happy, she would read it to her until Deidre learned to read for herself. When she suggested this to Deidre, her friend was thrilled.

And so it began. Every evening after the evening meal was finished and the dishes washed and put away, the two women sat at the table and worked on reading lessons until they were tired. Then Mandy would read the little New Testament aloud until bedtime. Mandy became so interested in the reading that she would often still be reading after Jedediah had fallen asleep in his mother's arms. Finally they would blow out the lamp and go to bed themselves.

Day after day the words played in Mandy's mind as the women worked on their projects and chores. The more she read, the more she viewed herself in a different light. She had always thought she was a good person, but the more she read of this man Jesus and His teachings, she saw her own faults as they really were—sin. She had always known there was a God out there somewhere but had never considered that He loved her and cared what happened to her. Nor, even more, that He loved her enough to send His Son, Jesus, to die for her. The more she read, the dirtier she began to feel.

One day, while Jedediah was napping and Deidre and Mandy were cleaning out the cupboard, Mandy was unusually quiet as she pondered the things they'd been reading.

Deidre finally said, "Somethin' powerful's been on yer min' lately, an' Ah needs to know if y'all is wishin' Deidre an' Jedediah wasn' here all th' time."

Mandy stopped with a jar in her hand and turned toward Deidre. Climbing down from the chair she had been standing on, she set the jar on the cupboard. Clasping her friend's shoulders, she said quietly, "Deidre, please don't ever think I don't want you here. You are the best thing that has happened to me since meeting and marrying Ethan. You are closer to me than if I had had a sister, and I couldn't bear it if you were to leave.

"Because we are such close friends and I love you so much, I will tell you what I keep thinking about. We read how Jesus told Nicodemus that he needed to be born again. Well, I am just like Nicodemus. I can't understand how we can be born after we are already born. Do you understand what Jesus means?"

Deidre hugged Mandy, then led her to a chair. She began to explain, "God offers us a won'erful gift—t' forgive our sin through His Son, Jesus. . . ."

Mandy listened with awe as Deidre told of Jesus' willing death on the cross. He was perfect, so didn't die as punishment for something He had done, but for the sins of every person. All she had to do was accept His gift by placing all her sins at Jesus' feet and letting Him cover them with His own blood. If she did that, she would be "born" into God's family and become His child. From that moment on she could talk to God about anything, and He would listen and answer.

"Jus' tell Jesus that y'all wants to be His chil', an' He'll do it raht now," Deidre encouraged her.

"But I don't know how to pray."

Deidre smiled. "Talk t' him jus' like y'all talk t' me. God hears ever'thin' we say an' think anyways 'an unnerstan's our hearts, but He jes' wants us t' ask."

So right then and there—in the middle of the housecleaning—Mandy prayed. Soon the joy in her heart filled her until she wept. "Deidre, I've never had such peace. I still don't understand how, but I know I'm now a child of God."

Deidre clapped her hands while she danced around. Suddenly she stopped and said with awe, "Mandy, do y'all knows that now we's truly sisters? God adopted both o' us as His chil'ren, so that makes us sisters!"

They rejoiced together for a while, but soon Deidre suggested they get back to their cleaning, or it would never get done.

In the evenings, as they worked together on the reading lessons, Mandy also taught Deidre correct pronunciations and grammar and refined her use of the English language. The young woman had never known anything but that slaves spoke differently than whites. The white people Deidre had known wanted to keep the slaves as ignorant as possible so they could not break away and make a life for themselves on their own, so they were not discouraged from speaking their own low form of English. But Mandy wanted Deidre to have the dignity of speaking well, understanding the language, and of any education she could share. So as she helped Deidre learn the sounds of each vowel and consonant as well as how to blend the sounds together to complete words, she gently helped Deidre begin using better grammar and more precise diction.

While Mandy taught Deidre lessons in grammar, spelling, reading, and writing, Deidre unwittingly taught Mandy lessons in love, patience, and acceptance. Deidre taught Mandy about being obedient to the teaching in the Bible and about truly serving God with her whole heart.

The two young women became inseparable friends, who could share their very hearts with one another. So, in time, Mandy shared the secret of her own baby she was carrying. Deidre clapped her hands and did her happy little dance that made Mandy laugh. No longer did Deidre talk about leaving when Ethan came home. In fact, they started to make plans for their children to play together. Mandy knew that they had become such close friends that it would be worse than losing family if Deidre ever did decide to go away.

And so the days passed swiftly for Mandy as she worked and played with Deidre—cleaning, sewing, making soap for the next year and storing it away, gathering berries and drying them, and picking her garden produce as it matured and storing it for the family to enjoy during the upcoming winter. But however busy she was, Mandy continued to count the days until Ethan came home and she could tell him about their baby.

Chapter 5

Mandy sat up straight, stretching her shoulders back as far as they would go. Then she reached back and massaged her tired lower back. She turned her flushed face, trying to find a breeze, but the late July sun was hot, and very few leaves stirred. She moved her stool back farther on the porch, trying to find a cooler spot of shade, but the air was still and hot, and there was no escape. She thought for the thousandth time how thankful she was that Ethan had built the steep roof of their cabin to overhang the depth of the cabin by eight feet on both the front and back of the main part of the building, making nice porches to help shade the cabin in the summer and protect against the cold winds of winter.

"Just a few more bunches to tie up, and then we can walk down to the creek for some shade and some cool water." She sighed.

Deidre tilted her head toward Mandy. "Let me finish tyin' up the herbs. Jedediah's hot, too. Why don't y'all go on ahead down to the crik bank and get yourselves cooled off. My black skin don't mind the heat like your white skin does. Besides, you're hotter'n me anyhow just totin' that baby."

Mandy chuckled. "If carrying this baby is what is making me hot, it's worth it all, and I don't mind one bit."

Just as she started to stand, she heard some rustling and twigs snapping in the wooded area not far from the front of the cabin. Startled, Deidre grabbed Jedediah and ran inside. Mandy sat still for a minute and listened. Sure enough, she heard whistling coming faintly through the trees. Her heart seemed to stand still as she peered out beyond their clearing to where the trees separated enough to form a small crooked path deeper into the woods and then out to the world beyond.

As she listened, the whistling came closer, and sticks and pinecones crackled under footsteps. Ethan didn't whistle like that, so she knew it wasn't him. She wasn't sure what to do, so she began to pray. She didn't want to go into the cabin, in case it was someone searching for Deidre or any other runaway slave. She knew Deidre would be listening and watching. If it was someone coming for her friend, Mandy could stall them on the front porch long enough to give Deidre and Jedediah time to sneak out the back and hide.

She reached down to keep busy tying her bunches of herbs to dry. Soon she knew whoever was coming through the woods was headed straight for her cabin.

She tried to stay calm and busy and at the same time keep her eyes on the edge of the woods.

Finally, she could stand it no longer. She stood, leaning the palm of one hand on the porch post, and called, "Hello!" Then a little louder she called, "Hello there!"

"Hello, ma'am," came a masculine voice. And then she could see a man striding through the edge of the woods into the clearing toward the cabin. "I'm lookin' for one Miz Ethan Evanston," he called as he came closer. He carried a bundle tied to a long pole over his shoulder and looked like he hadn't seen a razor or a bar of soap for a long, long time.

"I'm Mrs. Evanston." Mandy didn't move from her place by the porch pillar. She'd never seen this man before, so how did he know her name? She prayed that Deidre would stay hidden and that Jedediah would stay quiet.

"Mrs. Evanston, please accept my apologies. I've been walking for several days, but I came to give these things to you." The man hesitated. "I'm sorry to tell you that Mr. Ethan Evanston was killed a few weeks ago in a railroad accident. I wanted to bring you his belongings because he talked of you, and I knew he would want you to have these." While he spoke he placed the bundle on the ground, untied it, and took out Ethan's coat and gloves.

When he handed them to her, all she could do was take them and stare at them. "What did you say about my husband?" Mandy asked woodenly.

"I said Mr. Evanston was killed a few weeks ago. . .," the man said more softly now, his eyes on her obviously rounded belly in concern.

She couldn't find her voice to ask him any questions or even to offer him a drink of water. Her throat grew tight; her eyes burned.

He cleared his throat, repacked his belongings, then stood, shifting from one foot to the other. "Please accept my deepest sympathy, Mrs. Evanston." When there was still no response, he finally said, "Well, so long then."

Backing away, he turned and walked back the way he'd come until the woods had swallowed him and the world was again silent and still.

Mandy sank onto the porch step and drew Ethan's coat up to her face to inhale the scent of him. The emptiness she felt seemed to have absorbed her thoughts. How long she sat there she didn't know, but the sun moved from overhead to the other end of the porch, and it didn't seem quite so hot.

At last the door opened quietly, and Deidre peeked out. At the sight of Mandy holding a coat and gloves affectionately against her cheek, she slowly closed the cabin door and went back inside.

Sometime later, Deidre came back out to the porch. "Mandy, y'all must eat somethin'. . .for the baby."

Dazed, Mandy looked up. "Deidre," she whispered, "he didn't get to know his baby, and he didn't get to know our God."

And then the tears came.

Deidre's arms enfolded Mandy as she sobbed. Holding her friend close, Deidre slowly rocked her, willing the comfort of her love to fill Mandy's empty heart.

Chapter 6

The work was hard, and the days were long. Ethan Evanston stood in line with the rest of the men to get their pay on Saturdays. Most of the men had little of it left by Sunday morning, but Ethan was careful to tuck his away to take home to Mandy.

Saturdays had become the day he loved best of the work week, because after taking their pay, the men all wandered into the nearby town to spend the evening (and often the night) in the tavern, leaving him with some time alone.

He wondered sometimes why he was here. He and Mandy seldom needed much money because he could usually trade for what little they needed from the store. He had told Mandy he wanted a chance to earn them some money, but deep inside he knew it was more than that. Even though he loved Mandy and their home, he felt restless and unfulfilled. Was it because they had not had children? Was it because they were never around other people? What was it he was missing?

Many times Ethan pondered deep questions. Why was he here on this earth? Was there actually a purpose for his life? Was there really a God? At times his life all felt so meaningless.

After collecting his pay, he usually waited until the other men had wandered into town, and then he would take the old blanket he used for a towel and some soap and go down to the river. He would wash his work clothes and wash himself. Many times he would simply sit on the bank listening to the frogs that seemed to come alive at dusk. Now and again an ambitious fish would jump and make a single splash as it arched back down to the silent deep. Crickets chirped; cicadas sang. It was a noisy world, really, but he was all alone.

After many weeks of spending his Saturday nights alone, Ethan finally found himself being tempted by a card game that sounded particularly challenging. He had played cards with some old guys at the store back East. Now he found himself wondering if he remembered how to play. And he wondered if he were indeed as good as he had thought he was, or if the old men had just allowed the "young pup" to win.

Finally one night he wandered into the town and found the saloon where the men were gathered. He found he still remembered the strategies it took to win the poker games. He quickly became a popular player, and the barmaids gave him extra attention since he usually ended up with the pot of winnings. One of the girls in particular caught his eye, and he was surprised to catch himself watching her more than once. He eventually learned her name was Bess, and she didn't miss the fact that he had noticed her.

More often than not anymore, he wouldn't bother to turn his head as she bent over the table, showing more bosom than he had seen in a long while. Her exotic fragrance lured him. Finally one night the success of his winnings, the quiet way she smiled at him, and the extra beers she'd brought him weakened his resistance until he found himself waking in her arms with the sun pouring in between the silk curtains of her room.

That morning, his guilt overwhelmed him and he hurried back to the camp, spending the day with knots in his stomach and going over and over in his head how he would ever tell Mandy what he had done.

The next weekend he didn't go with the boys, but the week after he went again, determined to only play the poker games and then come home. However, it had been too long since Ethan had been with a woman, and Bess seemed to lure him. Eventually that night he decided that since he had already been with her once, what would it hurt to be with her again? She certainly knew how to comfort a lonely man, and he felt himself drawn to her in a needy sort of way.

The next morning she invited him back on Sunday night, and he surprised himself by agreeing to come. *By now,* he told himself, *what did it matter anyway?*

Ethan tried to stay in the shade of the trees as he scrubbed the railroad dirt from his face, hair, and body. This soap he got from the supply cabin sure didn't clean a person the way Mandy's homemade soaps did. He scrubbed harder, angry that he still compared everything to Mandy. If he really missed her so much, why didn't he go home?

He grabbed the old blanket he used for a towel as he climbed up onto the bank. After dressing, he tried to comb out his hair with his fingers.

As he headed back to the bunkhouse, the perspiration beaded on his forehead. This seemed to be the hottest summer he could remember for a long time. The men, himself included, had stopped wearing shirts while they laid the railroad ties, and the sun had browned his skin, but the perspiration still made him feel sticky and uncomfortable and cross.

It was Friday, and he would see who was going into town. He knew all he needed was a few good belts of whiskey or a few beers and some of Bess's soft kisses, and he wouldn't be thinking of Mandy anymore.

But as he walked, he knew the old restlessness was back. He couldn't seem to shake off the feeling that it had a personality of its own. In his early teens he had run away from an unhappy home to find peace somewhere. His mother was always unhappy, complaining about how worthless he and his brothers were. His dad was always drunk and unconscious or yelling at or beating one of them.

Ethan had run for quite some time before settling down and working as a farmhand. When the farmer's daughter started making her plans for him quite obvious, he ran away again.

He had worked at the store in Boston for several years before the restless itch to move on struck again. In the store he'd heard of the adventures of the wagon trains and also how cheap land was farther west. That was when he decided to marry Mandy if she would have him, settle down and farm, and raise a happy family like some of the ones he saw while working in the store.

From their talks when he accompanied her home from the store, he knew Mandy had also had an unhappy childhood. But she loved children as he did, and he knew they would be content if they had a large family and moved away from the East, where they had both been so unhappy.

For six years now he and Mandy had lived in Indiana. They had found a beautiful spot that he was able to claim and had cleared a good section of trees. There was a stream running along one end of the land, and plenty of room for a good-sized cabin, several gardens, a barn, and the outbuildings they needed.

Ethan had built a beautiful cabin. It was quite large, with a porch clear across the front and the back of it. The main part of the cabin was one large room, and at one end of the cabin he had walled off two rooms to be used for bedrooms. One was his and Mandy's; the other he had planned would be for the babies until they were old enough to sleep upstairs.

Most cabins had a ladder attached to one wall to gain access to the second story, but Ethan had built a stairway so they could easily get to the storage area he had built above the porches on either side of the long center room of the second floor. In the storage areas he had put lots of pegs for Mandy to dry her herbs and vegetables and fruit. She was proud of the comfortable cabin and had worked hard making curtains, quilts, pillows, rugs, and everything needed to make it cozy.

But they had not had children. As one year faded into the next, Ethan felt the old restlessness and sense of failure. Would Mandy soon resent him for not giving her children? He knew she was disappointed that they had not had a family yet.

Then he heard of the railroad jobs. The thrill of adventure tantalized him, and the reality that he could make good money justified in his mind the fact that he was once again moving on. He told himself that he would make some money and then go back to Mandy. But a voice inside mocked him. Who would take over his farm when he was old? Why did he think he was a man when he couldn't even produce sons to share his farm and life with? Without the children for whom they had planned, what would be left for him and Mandy?

So Ethan tried to fill the emptiness inside with money. Every weekend, when the other men went into the town to drink and gamble their money away, they would always try to get him to go along. But he had stashed all his money in an old wallet and stayed at the bunkhouse alone for weeks. Eventually, loneliness got the best of him, and he began joining them on the weekends. Before long, he had met the cute little barmaid named Bess and found he could forget his emptiness, loneliness, and sense of failure for the whole weekend.

All week long as he worked on the railroad, he lived with the guilt of what he was doing. Mandy was such a sweet woman, and he loved her. So why was he here, and why did he continue to spend his weekends with Bess? Finally, he could live with the guilt no longer. He devised a plan that would free Mandy. . .and rid him of his guilt.

He had given Francis, one of the men, a whole week's wages to take his gloves and coat with a wallet full of money tucked into the pocket back to Indiana, along with a story of how he had been killed in a railroad accident. He knew Mandy would grieve, but when she was over that, she would be free to build a new life for herself. Perhaps knowing he had freed her would erase the guilt he felt each time he was with Bess.

So week after week the pattern continued. He'd work all week on the railroad and spend the weekend drinking, gambling, and sleeping it off in Bess's arms in her stuffy rooms above the tavern.

Chapter 7

Week melted into week as hot August trudged slowly into sweltering September. Ethan thought about the farm. Harvesting was always hot, but he could always rest under the shade of a tree for a few minutes when Mandy would bring him a cool drink from the stream. They would spend a little time resting in the shade, talking together before going back to their work.

He remembered Mandy's quiet ways and gentle smile. She was proud of their farm and of the things he built. He hadn't really enjoyed the farm work as much as he had enjoyed the evenings when he would build things for their house and for Mandy. She loved everything he had built for her—the matching rockers she had placed in front of the fireplace, the cupboard and hutch, the table and chairs, the bed and dresser. How she had cherished each piece of beautiful furniture.

One by one he recalled the pieces he had made for their home. Each one had drawn happy exclamations from Mandy, and she had made pillows, rugs, crocheted doilies, and scarves. She'd arranged each piece of furniture to make their cabin as useful as it was cozy. For the millionth time he asked himself why he didn't simply return home.

Today there seemed to be no break from the heat as he pounded the iron pegs into the railroad ties. The sweat evaporated before it could cool him, and he was so thirsty. Always thirsty. The water in his canteen was as hot as the iron pegs. Even though it replenished the moisture his body lost from sweating, it didn't quench his thirst.

⋘∞⋙

The creek that they used for bathing had almost dried up, and what was left was more mud than water. Even though the other men had long ago gone to bed in the bunkhouses, Ethan sat out under a sprawling tree that had already lost most of its leaves from the heat. There was no breeze, but at least the moon was more merciful than the hot sun had been. Judging from where the moon was in the sky, Ethan decided it must be well after midnight. He knew the four o'clock whistle would blow before long, but he still couldn't sleep.

He thought about going back into the bunkhouse. However, the smell of the men's hot bodies, mixed with stale tobacco, had made him feel sick, and the snoring seemed louder than usual. He didn't know what was gnawing at him, but he felt more restless than ever.

As he leaned back against the trunk of the old gnarled tree, he once again looked up at the sky. "God, if You are up there, could You please show me the way out of this mess I've gotten into?" he asked out loud.

Then he thought with a groan, *If there is a God who cares about me, why would I be in this mess?*

But as he got up to head into the bunkhouse, the thought persisted: *Is there a God up there? Does He order our lives? Is He keeping score of all the wrong things I've done? Does He even care?*

∽∾

As Ethan tossed another coin onto the pile in the center of the table, he pushed back his chair until he teetered on the two back legs. The men arguing about the hand they had been dealt were loud and insufferable. Ethan spread out his cards to see again what he'd been dealt, tossed another coin onto the pile, and waited to see what would be laid.

∽∾

Bess stepped over to the poker table, saw Ethan's hand, and went back to bring him another drink. He'd seemed so quiet lately. As she watched him play, the other men at the table broke out in raucous laughter at some joke. Ethan merely laid down his cards and headed up the stairs. He didn't even look her way.

She kept her eyes on the stairs as she took drinks to some of the other tables. It was harder than usual to flirt with the men and laugh when they pinched her. Fear stirred inside as she replayed the past few weeks and the way Ethan seemed to be distancing himself.

When she could sneak upstairs for a break, she headed straight for her rooms. But as she went from room to room, she realized Ethan wasn't there.

Is he with one of the other girls? She wondered. He had been so quiet and mysterious lately. But then she mentally counted and knew that all the other girls were still downstairs since the evening was young. She walked slowly along the hall to go down the back stairway unnoticed, but as she passed the balcony entrance, she noticed the doors were slightly ajar. Stepping to the double doors that opened onto a balcony, she gently moved the curtain with her finger to peek out.

There stood Ethan alone, his hands in his pockets, gazing out across the town.

As the breeze stirred the curtains, Bess ducked back quickly. She couldn't explain it, but for some reason she didn't want Ethan to know she had seen him. After all, she had no right to question him. She tiptoed back to the hallway and made her way down the stairs to the noise and heat of the rooms below.

The night seemed to go on forever. Bess tried to do her job and at the same time keep her eyes on the stairs. She flirted and laughed, but her heart wasn't in it. She recalled what Clara, an older prostitute about the age her mother had been, and the other girls had told her when she started working. She'd assumed their warnings against falling in love were for someone else. Used by men most of her life, Bess knew no other life than this. She loved the pretty clothes and things she could buy that other women only dreamed of, and she knew how to make men happy. But she had never thought seriously about becoming emotionally involved with a man.

Yet here she was, watching the stairs all night. Singing, dancing, watching the stairs. Laughing, joking, watching the stairs. Would the night never end? One by one the other girls romped off up the stairs with their men for the night. She'd had several offers, but she put them off until she ended up alone with Sam, the owner of the saloon, who was wiping tables and sweeping the floor.

As she trudged up the stairs, Bess thought, *Maybe Ethan is in my rooms waiting for me. I didn't see him come back down to join the other guys.* But as she entered her rooms, they were dark, and she knew they were empty. Where was he? What was on his mind? Why did he seem so different from all the other men she had been with?

Bess lit a lamp and pulled back the bedclothes, but instead of getting ready for bed, walked to the window. Tucking back the curtains, she looked out over the sleepy town. The buildings were dark and the streets nearly empty. Her gaze wandered to the cottages along the ends of the street near the edge of town. Some had picket fences and boardwalks up to the front, and she knew late-summer flowers grew by their doors. Now the soft light shining through the crisp curtains in their windows looked cozy and inviting. What was it like to live in a family? She had been raised above the tavern by Clara and the older saloon women. She had never really known her mother, who had never wanted her or had time for her. This was the only life Bess had ever known.

Bess had always been shunned by the other children in town and even by their mothers when she was young. The only thing close to loving she'd experienced was from Clara, the girls who worked in the tavern, and the tenderness Ethan had shown her. As she dropped the curtain back into place and turned toward her lonely bed, her heart cried out for Ethan.

In spite of the late-summer warmth, Bess lay in the darkness, chilled to the bone. Deep inside she knew something was going on inside Ethan's head—something he would never tell her about. And now she was losing something she'd never even admitted to herself she was holding on to and hoping for.

As the morning sun softened the darkness in her room, Bess finally dozed and dreamed that she and Ethan were riding fast horses, their manes and tails flying, across the prairie. She felt so light and so happy. When Ethan said something to her, she laughed and felt completely content until she realized he was getting ahead of her and no longer looked back for her. She spurred her horse to run faster, but the distance between them grew and grew. Finally, as she watched Ethan disappear over the horizon, she screamed and woke herself up with her heart pounding and tears rolling down her cheeks.

As Bess thought of the warning Clara and the other girls had always given her about falling in love, she suddenly realized they were right. But it was already too late.

Chapter 8

Ethan stood on the balcony overlooking the sleepy town and noticed lights in the windows in the church up the street. The windows and doors were open to let in a little breeze. He could hear singing and clapping sometimes; then it became still. He listened for some time before curiosity got the best of him.

Before he really thought about what he was doing, Ethan slipped down the back stairs and let himself out through the door. The darkness hid him as he wandered up the street in the direction of the church.

As he drew close to the building, he realized it was not quiet at all, but that someone was talking, and everyone else was listening. Occasionally the quiet would be interrupted with a chorus of amens, and the talking would continue as though there had been no interruption at all.

Just as Ethan tiptoed close enough to the building to see in the window without being seen, the people started singing again. As he watched, he saw a wide range of emotions. Some people were happy, some were crying, some seemed thoughtful, but all appeared to enjoy being together in that place.

Ethan walked slowly back to the railroad camp, mulling over what he had seen and heard at the little church. He searched for the right word to describe the emotion he sensed—*happy* wasn't quite right. *Joy*. That was it. Even the folks who were crying seemed to be joyful. Ethan had never seen anything quite like it.

All through the night and the next day the experience played itself over in his mind. He would bring up pictures of people in that church—people who had no idea he was watching. He was puzzled by their serenity. Didn't they have problems? Had they not undergone sorrow or loss or rejection or bitterness? How could they be so peaceful? So joyful?

Ethan was so absorbed in his thoughts that when the whistle blew at the end of the day, he was surprised. Now it was Saturday night, and the men were already heading into town. But tonight the nightlife had no appeal at all to Ethan, so he hung back and headed to the bunkhouse.

Lying on his bunk, Ethan thought that it was getting late in October for such a warm Indian summer. He decided to take his soap, go down to the stream, and wash some of his grime and sweat downriver. He scrubbed until it felt he had removed the top layer of skin. Finally he climbed out, dried off, and headed back to the bunkhouse.

Walking up the hill refreshed, he heard singing coming from the town. *They're having a good time at Sam's tonight,* he mused, then realized the singing was different than that at the saloon. As he listened, he knew it was the people in that little church singing again.

Ethan ran back to the bunkhouse to leave his soap and the blanket he used for a towel, then took off for town at a trot. He hardly had time to make the decision before his feet were running in the direction of the singing. Once inside the building, he slipped into the last pew. A few glanced his direction, smiled, and nodded. As they continued singing about heaven, he wished he knew the song so he could sing along.

He watched the people sitting around him. They seemed to know what they were singing about, even though he knew none of them had been to heaven. He could tell they believed the place was real.

Between songs, some people would stand and tell what God had done for them and how thankful they were and how happy their lives were now. Ethan couldn't help thinking that God had never done anything for him, if there even was a God. He thought about his unhappy home. But as he listened, he started to understand that much of the trouble was due to his rebellious heart and independent spirit. He had never thought he needed God or anyone else. . .at least not until recently, when he realized how very badly he had messed up his life.

By this time, a man with a black book in his hand that he referred to as "the Word of God" stood in front of the people and began to teach from the book. He asked the people to turn in their Bibles to Philippians chapter 3. He said that tonight he wanted to read and study verses 13 and 14. And then he read: "Brethren, I count not myself to have apprehended: but this one thing I do, forgetting those things which are behind, and reaching forth unto those things which are before, I press toward the mark for the prize of the high calling of God in Christ Jesus."

"All humans do things that go against the teachings of Jesus for which they are later ashamed. This is called sin," the man said. He taught about accepting God's forgiveness for our sins through Christ and then moving on with our lives. "We will always remember these things," the man said, "but we must remember that Christ took the punishment for them, and we don't need to continue to carry that guilt. As long as we carry the guilt, we are unproductive in our Christian lives and cannot enjoy the peace of God."

Ethan could not help wondering how this forgiveness thing worked. He wanted to have God's peace and wanted to be productive but felt that he had messed up his and Mandy's lives so badly that there was no recourse for him. Still, he was drawn to the kindness of the gentleman who was teaching and longed to know more.

Before they sang again, the teacher invited anyone who had questions to stay after the service and said he'd be glad to talk with them more. Ethan didn't even have to think this over—something deep inside him knew that this was what he'd been missing all his life. When the service was over, he slipped out but stayed around outside the front of the church, waiting for the teacher to come out.

Finally, when the last people had left, Pastor Lewis (as Ethan had discovered he was called) stood alone in front of the church. Ethan approached quietly and cleared his throat.

"Oh, excuse me. I thought everyone had gone," Pastor Lewis said kindly. "Did you wish to talk to me?"

"Yes, if you have a little more time," Ethan said softly. "You see, I've never heard what you were teaching tonight before, and I have a lot of questions."

"Why don't you come home with me? I'll ask my wife to make us some coffee and we can talk as long as we want."

And that's exactly what they did. When Ethan told Pastor Lewis that he didn't even know what questions to ask, Pastor Lewis knew exactly where to start explaining. So he told Ethan about man's sickness called sin and that the only way to be healed from this was to ask God to forgive him. He explained about Jesus taking our punishment for us on the cross, and that it was a gift offered to anyone who cared to accept it.

When Ethan finally understood that Jesus had paid the penalty for his sins for him, he gladly accepted the gift of salvation. He asked Pastor Lewis if they could pray right there, which they did.

When they had finished praying, Ethan knew he was different. His whole life had changed. Pastor Lewis explained to Ethan about the services that were held at the little church each Sunday morning and invited Ethan to attend. Ethan promised he would be there before he headed back to the camp.

He arrived at the bunkhouse long before the other guys dragged themselves away from the liquor and the women. He was glad he had some time to himself, but he had hardly laid his head on his hard pillow when he was sleeping the deep sleep of one finally at peace after a lifetime of turmoil.

Ethan was amazed at how rested he was when he awoke the next morning, and even more amazed at how he had slept at all in all the snoring and bad smells that surrounded him. He quickly dressed and headed into town. He was the first one at the church, so he sat on the front step to wait. As he watched the sleepy little town awaken, he realized how very blinded he had been.

The sun seemed brighter today, the grass greener, the songbirds more merry, and Ethan saw flowers where he was sure none had been before. Everywhere he looked, the world seemed to have vibrant life and new energy. He could hardly wait for the morning service and to be with the friendly, loving people again. But, most of all, he couldn't wait to hear more about God and His Son, Jesus.

Chapter 9

The sun seemed to have spent all its energy on the long, hot days of July, August, and September. As October rolled around, the hours of daylight noticeably shortened. The color of the woods surrounding the clearing was breathtakingly beautiful as Mandy, Deidre, and Jedediah walked the orange, yellow, red, and green carpeted paths into the woods to bring baskets of crunchy red and yellow apples back to the cabin to slice and dry for pies, and to store in the root cellar for the cold, dark days of winter.

They had already stored pumpkins, squash, potatoes, turnips, onions, and carrots in the root cellar, and had dried corn, beans, peas, berries of all kinds, and herbs in the attic spaces. They had made jellies, pickles, and other treats and used up all the preserving jars and most of the sugar that was in the cabin.

Mandy had been concerned for some time about what she should do when her supplies ran out that Ethan had so generously stored up for her from the supply store somewhere out beyond the trees. She knew the general direction of the store and knew he had cleared a wide enough path for the wagon, but she had only gone to the store once several years ago with him, and it was an all-day journey there and back in the summer. Now that the days were shorter and the baby was nearly here, she didn't know what she would do. But she had to do something soon, and Deidre could not go, for fear someone could recognize her and expose her as a runaway slave.

One evening early in the month Mandy told Deidre at the supper table that she would get up very early the next morning and head to the store. Deidre said she would do the chores for the day and pray for her. They planned that Mandy would take some of Ethan's money she had found in the wallet in his coat pocket and buy some supplies for the winter. Both were concerned about the effects of the rough trip on the baby, but they knew it must be done—and as soon as possible.

That night they went to bed before it was even dark enough to light the lamps. Mandy slept as well as possible with the discomfort of her condition.

⁓⁓

The next morning Mandy woke while it was still dark. She was lying there wondering what time it was when she heard the clock strike four from the other room. She quickly picked up a candle and took it out to light it in the coals of the fire.

Bringing it back into her room, she dressed and hurried out to the pantry to get some cold boiled eggs and bread and tea. As she rounded the corner, she almost ran into Deidre, who was busy at the table. There was already a cup of hot coffee beside a plate with fried eggs and biscuits. Mandy thanked her and made herself eat them, knowing it would be a long day ahead and she needed all the strength she could get.

She watched as Deidre spread some biscuits with apple butter and packed them in a cloth-lined basket that already had several things in it. She placed it beside a jug that Mandy knew was full of cold milk.

When Mandy had eaten all she could, the two girls prayed together. As Mandy started out the back door to the barn, Deidre announced, "The wagon's already hitched up out the front, and the mule's snortin' and stampin' and ready to go."

As the two women walked to the wagon, carrying the basket and the jug, Mandy murmured, "You sure have been a blessing from God, Deidre. I'm so thankful He sent you to me."

"And so am I, Miss Mandy, so am I. Just remember, I'll be prayin' every step that mule takes. Y'all be very careful now."

Mandy climbed into the wagon and signaled the mule to go. She knew Deidre was watching her from the porch as she was swallowed up by the dark of the woods.

It seemed the woods stayed dark forever. Mandy bounced and bounced on the hard wagon seat, even though they had padded it with a pillow and quilt. At times the trees were so thick overhead that she couldn't even see the light of the moon. As the mule plodded through the weeds that had grown in the unused path, Mandy could hear the small woodland animals running for cover deeper into the woods.

Once an owl hooted so near that Mandy almost jumped right out of the wagon. "You silly old fool!" She laughed at the owl. "Me. . .that's whoooo." She laughed at herself for talking out loud, then realized it helped her not to feel so alone, so she started talking to God and even to some of the little creatures that scampered out of her way.

One by one the stars twinkled out. As the moon also disappeared from sight, Mandy mused, *This must be what they mean when they say it is darkest just before the dawn. I'm glad I know the morning will come, because I wouldn't want to have to endure this much darkness for very long.*

Just as a little light made the trees again take shape, Mandy thought she smelled smoke. She wondered if someone had made camp in the woods, or if she was nearing the edge. The trees didn't seem to be thinning any, but the smell became stronger and then she saw a little smoke off to the right. Another ten minutes or so and she spotted a clearing in the woods.

She entered the clearing not too long after daybreak and glimpsed a cabin, barn, and several outbuildings. A man, woman, and several children stepped out of the cabin to greet her. They seemed surprised to see a lone woman in the wagon.

After introducing themselves as the Brownings, they invited Mandy in for some breakfast. Mandy climbed down from the wagon to stretch her tired legs and back. She explained her mission and asked if they knew how much farther it was to the general store.

When Mr. and Mrs. Browning said it was another several miles, she saw their concern for her, traveling in her obvious condition, reflected in their faces. Mr. Browning encouraged her to make a list of things she needed and said that he would go get the things for her while she stayed to visit with his wife and children.

"We've been needing to stock up on some groceries before winter as well," said Mrs. Browning, "and Ned can pick up our things while he's there. Why, if we'd known there was a young lady living alone in these woods, we'd have been through to check on you sooner."

Mandy was afraid to tell them she was not alone, because she didn't know how they felt about slavery, so she assured them she was fine and well taken care of.

Edna Browning bustled Mandy inside while Ned watered the mule. Mandy insisted he take her wagon and mule since they were already hitched, but Ned said the mule should rest in the barn to prepare for the trip back home this afternoon.

Soon he came around the cabin with a high-stepping horse harnessed to a light wagon, and Mandy knew his travel time to town would be cut in half with that combination. She herself might have been able to make it from her cabin to the Brownings in not much more than an hour. Her barrels and crocks were already in his wagon, and he stopped in for her list.

As she tried to give him her money, he laughed. "How do you know I'd come back with all that money? No, we'll settle up when I get back. But I will take the nice lunch basket you packed if you don't mind. Edna here will fix you some lunch while you visit." And so saying, he waved good-bye to them, with a few shouted instructions to the children about their chores.

Mandy tried to count the children in her head. From the sound of the things she was hearing there were at least three teenage boys working out in the barn, two slightly younger girls helping in the kitchen area, and three smaller children hiding behind Edna's skirts. *Let's see, that makes eight, I think, if I haven't missed anyone.* They were all beautiful children—some blond and blue-eyed like their mother, and some dark like Ned. The oldest girl was dark-haired, but fair-skinned and blue-eyed, which made a striking combination.

Edna seemed as excited as Mandy to find another woman so nearby. *It's a good feeling to know you have neighbors,* Mandy thought, *and friendly ones are an extra bonus.*

"When's the young-un due, if you don't mind my asking?" Edna posed the question in a gentle way that didn't seem at all bold or probing. "Is this your first one?"

"This is my first, and will be my only one, since my husband was killed in a railroad accident this past summer. The baby should be here in another few weeks, if I have figured correctly," Mandy said with a smile.

"Well, I've never delivered one, but I've had plenty, so I'll come over when your time is near to wait with you and help out with the birthing, if you'd like. The girls here can cook well enough, and Ned and the others will get along just fine for a few days without me. Besides, it will be good company to spend some time with another woman."

Mandy thought about Deidre and wondered how to explain to Edna but decided to wait until the time came and pray about it. Edna seemed like the kind of woman who would love anyone, no matter their circumstances, but still, Mandy would pray first.

Before she realized the sun had moved so far in the sky, she heard the horse and wagon coming into the clearing and Ned's cheerful singing. "What a beautiful voice your husband has, Edna. Why, listening to him sing is better than going to a concert!"

Edna chuckled. "Don't tell him that. If he knows we're listening, he'll stop singing, and I'd miss it terribly. Sometimes, now that the boys are older, he teaches them to harmonize, and it sounds like a choir straight from heaven out there in the barn. We all enjoy music, and it does make the work go faster."

When Ned came close enough that she could hear the words, Mandy heard him singing, "What a friend we have in Je-sus, all our sins and griefs to bear. What a privilege to car-ry. . ."

"Do you all know Jesus, too?" Mandy asked quickly.

"Lands, yes! My daddy is a preacher, and Ned and I met in the church out East. We miss having church so much."

What excitement the two women shared when they discovered they had this in common, too. They were making plans to get together again when Ned came in the door.

"Your mule's hitched, and your wagon is loaded with the supplies. You better get on your way soon if you want to get home in time to get unloaded before dark. The temperature seems to be dropping pretty fast, too. I'm sending our son Thomas with you to help you unload the wagon. We hitched Nelda on the back of your wagon, and he will ride her home. Nelda's been needing a chance to stretch her legs and that will work out fine."

Ned wouldn't listen to any arguments, so Mandy settled up with him, hugged Edna one last time, and climbed onto the wagon. She was thankful for godly neighbors and looked forward to seeing Edna again soon.

Chapter 10

Thomas was good company, for a young boy. Just shy enough to be polite but friendly enough to carry on a conversation. Sometimes they simply enjoyed the quiet noise of the woods as the mule tramped along.

They had been traveling for close to an hour when the first pain came. It was a sharp pain in her lower back that made her stomach tighten enough to make her gasp. Thomas looked at her with concern, but she laughed and said her back must be tired of the bouncing and that she'd be fine. The pain was gone, and she was glad.

She asked Thomas if he would teach her some songs about Jesus while they rode along. It took a little coaxing, but soon he started singing. His voice was clear and mellow, and Mandy thought she could listen to it forever.

They continued on for another fifteen or twenty minutes before the pain occurred again, but this time she wasn't quite so taken by surprise. Mandy began to get an uneasy feeling, however, and asked Thomas if the mule could go any faster. When Thomas urged Flops a bit, he truly did pick up his feet higher, but Mandy didn't think the steps were any quicker. Soon they were plodding on the same as before. Again the piercing pain jabbed and tore at her lower back before they finally stopped in front of her cabin.

Since Deidre was nowhere in sight, Mandy knew she had heard Thomas singing as they were coming through the edge of the woods and had hidden. Thomas helped her down and told her to go rest her back while he carried the barrels and crocks and packages into the cabin for her. Then he unhitched, fed, and watered Flops, and put the wagon in the barn.

When he came back to check on her, she assured him she was doing fine now that she could walk around, so he hopped on Nelda and was gone through the woods faster than Mandy had ever seen a horse run.

Deidre came out of her room as soon as she heard Thomas leave. "Y'all made real good time. Who was the young fella?"

As Mandy started telling Deidre about her day, she suddenly sat down quickly and gasped for breath.

"How long's this been happenin'?" Deidre inquired. When Mandy told her about the pains on the trip home, Deidre took over, telling her to get undressed and into something more comfortable while she prepared Mandy's bed. "Now, don't ya'll worry. Deidre's helped the black midwives deliver lots of babies, and there just ain't nothin' to it. With the time between the pains, y'all still has lots of time before the hard work starts."

Mandy was so comfortable with Deidre that she wasn't frightened at all. Deidre continued to encourage her that this was the most natural thing in the world, and that there was nothing to be afraid of. She even helped her relax by massaging her back and singing some quiet folk songs about Jesus.

Mandy tried to be quiet with her moans, so as not to frighten Jedediah, who played with his blocks of wood on the floor. He didn't seem to think there was anything unusual happening. When it was bedtime, Deidre rocked him and quietly sang her bedtime songs to him, then tucked him into her bed and was back to help Mandy through the night.

∽∞∾

Shortly before dawn the miracle finally happened, and Deidre laid the newborn bundle next to Mandy to cuddle. Daniel Ethan Evanston was the most beautiful baby Mandy had ever seen. Deidre had already bathed him and dressed him in one of the nightgowns they had made for him last summer. Mandy was very tired, but she could not stop looking at him long enough to go to sleep. Her tears wet his downy little head as she snuggled him close.

"Your daddy would have been so proud of you," she whispered, snuggling him even closer. "Oh, how I wish he could know he had a son."

Deidre blew out the candles and lamps and crept into bed to rest a bit before the new day began.

As the sky lightened between the curtains, Mandy thanked God for the miracle that He had given her and prayed for wisdom to raise Daniel to know, to love, and to serve God.

Chapter 11

The days had turned colder, and the wind was sharper now. Most of the leaves had been driven to the ground with the rains, and October was showing the dregs of autumn as it waned and turned to November.

The sun was much slower rising above the treetops in the mornings, and Mandy was glad for the new barrel of kerosene for the lamps. Through the summer they had not needed the lamps much, but now there was not enough light in either the morning or the evening.

She had just finished feeding Daniel and had laid him on his pile of blankets, when she was sure she heard singing. She soon recognized Ned's beautiful voice, so she bustled around to prepare more breakfast and make more coffee.

Soon she could tell Ned was nearing the clearing, so Deidre took Jedediah and went into her room. They had discussed the possibility of telling Ned and Edna about her situation and had agreed that it seemed wise to do so. Both Deidre and Mandy breathed a quick prayer for God's protection for Deidre and Jedediah. Mandy grabbed her shawl and stepped out onto the front porch just as the horse and wagon broke into the clearing.

Edna waved cheerily and hardly waited for the horse to stop before she jumped down and ran to hug Mandy. Mandy ushered her into the house, as Ned climbed down, then started unloading something bulky from the wagon. Mandy told him to be sure to come in for some breakfast and then closed the door.

Mandy could hardly wait to tell Edna about Daniel and show him to her. As soon as Ned came in and sat down for coffee and biscuits, Mandy told the whole story of Daniel's birth, carefully leaving out the part about Deidre.

Edna was amazed that she could have done it all alone, so Mandy explained about Deidre, including the part about the New Testament. By the time she finished, Edna was wiping her eyes. Her first comment was, "Isn't it wonderful how God takes care of His own—a home for Deidre and a companion and sister for you. Even a playmate for Daniel. God is so good!"

"Where is Deidre now?" Ned asked. "Can we meet her, too?"

Mandy went over to open Deidre's door and encourage her and Jedediah to come out and meet the company. Deidre shyly came out with Jedediah wrapped tightly in her arms.

Edna was quick to greet her with a warm hug, and Ned stuck his hand out to shake hers.

"We are glad to meet you and hear your story," Edna said. "It makes us rest easier to know Mandy is not alone out here for the winter. Please feel free to come visit us with Mandy anytime you want. You will always be safe with us. We can have such a great time with three women."

Ned slipped quietly out the front door and returned carrying something big and bulky covered with quilts.

"Oh, I almost forgot." Edna smiled. "We want you to borrow our cradle that Ned made for our young-uns. We don't need it right now, though it's sure had lots of wear. When Daniel outgrows it, we'll take it back."

As Ned uncovered it and stood it by the fireplace, Mandy exclaimed, "It's lovely, and I'm so grateful. I'll take good care of it. Thank you so much."

Ned headed to the door. "You women enjoy your visit. Since we made the trip over, I'll go out to the barn and do your chores for today." And he was gone. Then he stuck his head back in a minute later. "Jedediah, do you want to go help me in the barn?"

Deidre started to decline on behalf of her son, but Edna said in her gentle way, "Deidre, it's good for the child to be around men, too, and there's none better with young-uns than my Ned. He'll have him singing before they come back for lunch."

Deidre glanced questioningly at Mandy and was reassured by Mandy's smile and nod. So Deidre dressed Jedediah warmly, instructing him to obey Mr. Browning, and the two disappeared out the back door. Mandy started to clean up the breakfast dishes, but Deidre insisted she should not be standing so much yet. So while Mandy sat in the rocker with her knitting needles flying, Edna helped Deidre make short work of the dishes and put the bright tablecloth and lamp back on the table. Next Deidre gathered some of their vegetables and placed them in the big kettle over the fire to simmer into a thick soup for their lunch. Then they, too, opened their hand-work and the morning evaporated into thin air as they chatted like old friends.

Soon it was time to set the table for lunch. The soup was making thick bubbling noises and smelled good. They were just pouring the milk into glasses and slicing the bread when they heard two voices singing at the top of their lungs. The women looked at each other, then all broke out in happy laughter.

Edna winked. "I told you he'd have Jedediah singing."

They all ran to the door to see and hear Ned and Jedediah as they came toward the cabin.

While they ate their lunch, Jedediah chattered away. Mandy had never seen the young boy so animated. "Unca Ned said he'd teach me to feesh for feeshes! Unca Ned said I can he'p him work today! Unca Ned said I sing good!" He was almost too excited to eat. "Unca Ned said he din' bring me no bed cuz he din' know Ah lived here. Unca Ned said cud we make me one today?"

Ned explained how quickly he could make a bed with a few of the young saplings from the woods. Of course, permission was granted immediately, so the "men" quickly excused themselves and headed back outdoors.

The afternoon went by far too quickly. Daniel slept peacefully, awakening only to be fed. Before they knew it, Ned was bringing the beds in and asking where to put them. He had made two—one for Deidre and one for Jedediah. They quickly set them up in Deidre's room, using the feather mattress on Deidre's bed and a stack of blankets on Jedediah's until the women could make another mattress for him. Then Ned and Jedediah went out to do the evening chores before he and Edna had to start for home. Edna had been prepared to stay for several days or until the baby was born. But now, with the baby born and seeing the good companionship Mandy had, she was not uncomfortable leaving the young mother.

Before Edna and Ned left, she invited Mandy, Deidre, and the children to come for Christmas. She told how much Thomas loved to drive the sleigh and how quickly the trip would go. They planned that Thomas would come for them on Christmas morning, and then bring them back the day after.

Mandy and Deidre agreed thankfully. It would be wonderful to spend Christmas with their new friends and with all the children.

And so they parted. It was sad watching the wagon disappear through the trees, but Ned's song echoed for a good long while through the woods.

Chapter 12

The wet and dark autumn days flew by and soon turned to snowy winter as Mandy and Deidre prepared for their Christmas Day outing. Deidre had asked if they could make a gift for each of the Browning children, so they planned and worked, and with all the other chores to do, the days passed quickly.

Mandy knitted warm woolen scarves for the three older boys with their initials embroidered on each end, while Deidre gathered small willow branches and reeds and wove a beautiful little box with its own lid for each of the three girls. They lined the boxes with soft cloth and stitched a pretty flower on each of the lids. The flower on one box was pink, one yellow, and one a soft blue. For the smaller boys, they made bright colored wool mittens and caps to match.

For Ned, Deidre found enough reeds by the stream to weave a nice hat to keep the sun out of his eyes in the summer, and for Edna they made some lovely lavender sachets tied with lace and ribbons. They also included in her gift a nice chunk of their lavender soap.

Mandy was delighted to have so much to occupy her time and to not have to be alone, but as the holiday drew nearer, her yearning for Ethan grew stronger. Somehow in her heart she still could not accept that he was not coming back. She found herself listening for his whistle coming through the woods, or as the wind would slam against the door she would look up quickly, expecting the door to open and Ethan to walk in. But she was always disappointed.

While Mandy was busy caring for Daniel, Deidre insisted on doing the barn chores. During the time each day that Deidre was outside, and many evenings by candlelight in the privacy of her room, Mandy stitched away on a warm woolen coat for Deidre. She didn't have enough of any one color of material left in her trunk, but she pieced several colors and a soft plaid together to make a beautiful coat. She had enough pieces of rabbit fur left to make a collar and cuffs, and she even stitched a strip of rabbit fur just inside the woolen hood for extra warmth. She finally finished it by the middle of December, so she knitted Deidre some soft brown gloves to match. Next she made a small warm coat for Jedediah with a matching hat that had flaps he could wear down over his ears. A bright scarf and warm mittens finished her gifts for him only a few days before Christmas.

The last few days before Christmas Mandy and Deidre spent making cookies, candies, cakes, and pies to take to the Brownings'. Mandy went out to the woods where she knew some holly grew and cut several branches with their bright red and yellow berries to decorate their mantel.

On Christmas Eve, after Jedediah was asleep, Mandy went back to the woods where she had earlier that day cut a large evergreen bough and hidden it. While she was making it stand in a bucket of sand, Deidre strung cranberries and popcorn on long cords. They fastened a small candle to the top and tied some bright-colored yarn remnants on to make colorful bows. Finally they stepped back to admire their handiwork. It only stood about four feet tall, but it was very pretty by the fireplace with the holly on the mantel.

Mandy sighed. "I wish so much that Ethan was here to make some toys for Jedediah and Daniel."

Deidre smiled and whispered, "I'll be right back," then disappeared up the stairs. When she returned, she carried a pretty basket with bright-colored reeds running in stripes around the sides. Mandy was admiring it when Deidre said, "Go ahead; look inside." Mandy lifted the lid and saw that Deidre had colored some of Jedediah's wooden blocks the same colors as the stripes on the basket. Also there was a colorful little cloth bag with a drawstring. Mandy took it out and found it full of bright rocks.

"I colored the blocks when I was colorin' the reeds with the berry juices. The rocks I found down by the creek last fall, and I saved them 'til Jedediah was big enough to appreciate them." At that instant Mandy noticed how much clearer Deidre's speech was becoming. She sounded like any other educated woman, and Mandy was proud of her.

So the women arranged the basket beside the decorated branch and tiptoed off to bed with hugs and prayers of thanksgiving.

That night, as Mandy finished nursing Daniel and tucked him snugly in the cradle, she couldn't help but whisper, "Oh, Daniel, if only I had told your daddy about you before he left, maybe he would not have gone and would be with us now. Why do I have to learn all my lessons the hard way? He would be so proud of you and could teach you how to be a man. I miss him so much, but I will teach you the best I can." And she kissed him again and crawled into her cold bed.

Mandy dozed a little but kept dreaming that she was telling Ethan they had a son. When she turned to put the baby in his arms, he was gone. She woke up with a soft cry, her heart pounding in her ears. She quickly got up to check the cradle and found Daniel sleeping soundly. She crawled back into her bed, but sleep refused to return.

Finally, she quietly dressed and went out to the main room. She made a cup of sweet herb tea and sat rocking by the fire.

When she had finished her cup and was no sleepier than before, she decided to make some sweet cranberry muffins and nutmeg custard for their Christmas breakfast. While they were baking, she slipped back into her room and brought out the packages for Deidre and Jedediah and tucked them under their Christmas branch.

Soon after the clock on the mantel struck five, she looked up to see Deidre quietly closing her bedroom door. "I thought I smelled somethin' mighty good out here. Why are you up so early?"

"Oh, I'm worse than a small child," Mandy said with a grin. "I was so excited for Christmas I couldn't sleep."

The two women had a cup of tea together. Then Mandy went over to the packages on the floor, lifted the large one, and placed it in her surprised friend's lap.

Deidre opened it eagerly. When she saw the beautiful coat, her mouth opened but no words came out. She carefully lifted it out of the wrappings and tried it on. When she pulled the hood up around her face, Mandy said, "Oh, Deidre, I had a little of the fur left, so I put that small strip around the inside of your hood to keep the wind out, but I didn't think how beautiful it would look next to your smooth, dark skin. You look just like a china doll."

They laughed and giggled together. Then Deidre jumped up. "Stay right there!" she exclaimed as she ran up the stairs. She came down with a beautiful basket with a lid and a handle. As Mandy delighted over the lovely basket, Deidre said, "Lift the lid and look inside."

Mandy opened the lid carefully. Inside lay a beautiful bonnet. It had a wide brim in front that tapered down to no brim at all by the ears. A wide green sash was fastened by each ear and lay flat against the bonnet behind the brim, with long sashes to tie under the chin. The green sash had a cluster of dried berries, vines, and flowers arranged on it. It was more beautiful than any bonnet Mandy had ever seen in Boston.

"Where did you get it?" she asked Deidre as she gently tried it on.

"I made it just like we always made for the women down South. Do you like it?"

"It's the most beautiful bonnet I have ever seen in my life," she assured Deidre. "I'll wear it today."

Soon Jedediah toddled out of the bedroom, and Mandy went to check on Daniel. Jedediah's eyes were as big as saucers when he spied the decorations. He squealed and pointed. "Oh, it's so purty!"

When Deidre came back into the house from doing the chores she still insisted on doing, they all sat down and enjoyed their muffins and custard. When they finished, they read the Christmas story from their worn New Testament and thanked God for all the blessings He had provided. They each brought their gifts over to Jedediah and showed him how to open them. As he was enjoying his pretty blocks and rocks with his new hat on because he wouldn't take it off, the women cleaned up the table.

They washed and dressed the two babies, dressed themselves, and straightened the cabin. They were packing their treats in baskets when they heard bells jingling and Thomas's melodious voice singing "O Little Town of Bethlehem."

The sleigh ride through the woods went swiftly. Nelda had felt like trotting, and Thomas had let her go. They laughed, agreeing they weren't sure whether she was trotting to get home more quickly or to make the bells ring more. Nelda held her head high, seemingly proud of the bells the Brownings had tied around her neck. Thomas was as good as his father at getting everyone to sing. Before long, they were singing songs they had never heard before, and the woods rang with their laughter on that blessed day.

Edna and the girls had decorated the front door and each of the two windows in the front of their cabin with evergreen boughs and large red fabric bows. The house looked festive and inviting as they drove up to the front. Edna and Betsy, the Brownings' oldest daughter, bustled out to take the babies in to the warm house, and the others quickly followed. As soon as the door burst open, the fragrance of good food filled the air.

The table was set with holly boughs, berries, and apples, making a centerpiece around several tall candles. Touches of evergreen were all about the room. Edna chuckled. She had sent Betsy (her name was really Elizabeth, but she still enjoyed the family's pet name of Betsy best) to get some greens for decorating. Since the other girls wanted to help, they went along. When they came back, they had enough greens and berries to decorate six houses.

"But we just kept tucking it in here and there, and pretty soon it began to look like a real party." Edna laughed.

Deidre and Mandy laid a gift on each plate, and before long it was time for their Christmas meal. As soon as Ned had blessed the meal, Mandy and Deidre encouraged each of them to open their gifts. They started with the youngest and went up by age. They all loved their gifts and thanked the women excitedly.

The dinner was delicious. When everyone had eaten all they could hold, the children politely asked if they could try their new sleds. Permission was granted, so off they went with Ellen and Esther begging to take Jedediah along. They promised to care for him, so they bundled him warmly in his new coat, hat, and mittens, and then they were gone also.

Betsy felt too grown up to sled, so she offered to stay and help with the cleanup. With so much help on the dishes, before long the house was tidy and quiet. Betsy and the three women pulled chairs around the fireplace to chat. They could hear the squeals and laughter outside as the children played. After a while Deidre went out to bring Jedediah in to rest. He was hardly warm by the fire before he fell asleep in her arms.

Later in the afternoon, Ned and Thomas rode their high-stepping horses through the woods to Mandy's cabin to do her evening chores. It didn't take the two of them long to finish, and they headed back through the woods toward home. Mandy's heart swelled with thankfulness for the gift of good neighbors as they heard the men returning.

The afternoon moved lazily into evening, and soon the children came inside to get warmed by the fire. Edna popped popcorn while Ned retrieved some cold cider from the cellar. Betsy, Mandy, and Deidre brought cakes and cookies as they sat around the fire eating goodies and telling stories of past Christmases. Some of the stories made them laugh, and some were poignant and sweet, bringing tears to their eyes. The friendship was so warm and so good that even the quietest children could be coaxed to contribute some memory or story.

When the small children's heads drooped, the older children carried them off to bed and then came back to shyly thank Mandy and Deidre again for their gifts and to say good night.

It was a wonderful Christmas. Before it ended, Ned suggested that the older ones who were still gathered by the fire join their hearts in prayer. Deidre quietly asked if they could please pray for her husband, Jeremiah, wherever he was in the world, and that God would someday reunite them.

When they had finished praying, Ned began a soft song, and all joined in. They sang for quite a while. Ned said to Deidre in reference to her longing to be reunited with her husband, "Whenever the night looks darkest, remember, God will still give a song to strengthen and see us through." And Deidre smiled her gentle smile.

Ned and Edna had given their room to Mandy and Deidre and Daniel. All three snuggled down into the large soft bed and were soon sound asleep.

It felt as though they had barely closed their eyes when they heard soft shuffling out in the main cabin and knew morning had come. They could smell coffee brewing and ham frying as they hurried into their clothes. Ned was moving the straw mattress back up the stairs. He had already done the chores, and Edna and the girls were putting the finishing touches on a large breakfast when Mandy and Deidre came out to help.

After they ate the wonderful breakfast, they had worship together once again. It was wonderful to fellowship with other believers, to encourage one another, and to enjoy that common bond. Mandy and Deidre loved to learn the hymns of the church, and Ned made it easy to sing along. They ended their singing time with a beautiful old hymn that told the story of God's grace. As Ned and the boys harmonized, Mandy listened worshipfully to the words:

"In the perfect world his pride turned
Adam from the Father's face.
It's there I follow in his steps and
seal my own eternal fate.
Here my best is mixed with envy,
selfishness, greed, pride, and hate;
I know the road that I should walk, but
*   take the path through wider gates.*

In God goodness finds its meaning.
He is holy, good and pure.
I am sinful, full of evil
thoughts and deeds—so insecure.
God, the Just, cannot ignore the
sin I must be punished for.
He's jealous of His matchless name.
His name be praised forevermore.

Where His justice and His wrath are
mingled, there my Lord demands
that for my sin my blood be spilled
to pay for guilt that's on my hands.
But oh! His love and grace it was
that took this burden from my head
and placed it on the spotless Lamb
to pay for sin there in my stead.

Praise Him for His mercy that doesn't
end with sacrifice for sin.

Adopted in His family
I'm loved and warmly welcomed in.
Joy and peace He's given me and
conscience clean and cleared of guilt.
Endless days I'll spend with Him up
in a mansion He has built.

I'm an undeserving sinner
but I'm justified by grace.
It's not by things I've done—they're tainted
by my motives and my ways.
It's through grace alone I come with
confidence before the throne
And there cast praises to His name
for Christ has saved me, Christ alone!"

When the hymn was finished, there was silence while they all worshipped in their hearts. Even the babies seemed quieted by the hush over the room. In a bit, Ned closed their worship time with prayer. Mandy couldn't help thinking that heaven must be like this—what glory to sit and worship their loving God!

Too soon Ned was saying they must be on their way home. He and Thomas were going to take Mandy and Deidre and the babies home and do the chores for them, and they hated to make the cows wait much longer. So they bundled up the children and soon were on their way.

After the chores were finished and the men were leaving, Mandy invited them to all come for a visit before too long. When the sleigh was swallowed up by the woods, Mandy turned back to their quiet home. She suddenly felt the loneliness she had been denying almost overwhelm her.

Oh, Ethan, she cried in her heart, *why did you have to leave me? I miss you so.*

Chapter 13

Week after week Ethan could hardly wait for Sunday to come so he could meet with his new friends and hear the teaching from God's Word. One Sunday he was invited to share the noon meal with one of the families from the church. He gladly accepted since he could never get enough of the rich fellowship of the family of God.

As they shared the meal together, he asked something that had been on his mind for some time now. "Do you know of a family in town that would take me in as a boarder if I could find work in town?" He was eager to become a more stable part of the town and wanted to look for a job that would be a bit more permanent than the railroad work. Since he had not yet told anyone about Mandy, they assumed he was a bachelor and assured him they would stay on the lookout for something for him.

They did know of a couple whose children had died of typhoid fever some time back, so they inquired for him. The couple owned the general store in town and were also part of the church. When the Taylors heard of Ethan's query, they were very interested in talking with Ethan and contemplated the possibilities presented by having help in the store and a boarder.

Later in the week, Ethan went to meet them and introduce himself. The store was a large building with a false front, giving the impression of two full stories, when in reality the second floor was simply a loft tucked in under the rafters with a steep stairway leading up from the large room in back of the store. The couple did most of their living in the large room behind the store and the small rooms enclosed to the side. They were glad to offer the upstairs loft area to Ethan.

In the conversation with the Taylors, Ethan mentioned his experience in the store in Boston, and soon the Taylors had the arrangements made. He could live and board with them for free if he would work in the store to assist Mr. Taylor. If he did well, eventually Mr. Taylor would pay him something as well. This would relieve Mrs. Taylor of having to work in the store much at all.

Without delay, Ethan resigned his position with the railroad, packed his few belongings, and moved into the town. His room in the eaves was small, unheated, but very adequate. The Taylors had made a bed for him up there and had placed a crate by the bed for a lamp table. There was an old cupboard tucked in under the eaves that he could use for his personal belongings. Beside it were a couple of pegs for his clothes. The blankets and comforters on the bed were clean and neat, and he smiled to see a small rug beside the bed. Mrs. Taylor and Mandy seemed to have some traits in common.

Ethan enjoyed the work in a store again, meeting people and helping them find the things they needed. He seemed to have a sixth sense of what Mr. Taylor should stock in his store. Business soon picked up as people treasured the friendly conversations with the new help.

Fall soon turned to winter, and the snows came early.

One day Bess stopped in to make a purchase at the store. As soon as she saw Ethan, she turned to leave. But Ethan caught up to her and said he needed to talk to her. They agreed to meet on Sunday afternoon. They set a time that Ethan would meet her in front of the saloon, and, weather permitting, they would take a walk and have a talk.

Bess wanted to be excited because she would be seeing Ethan again, but something deep inside her argued that this was not the same Ethan she had known before. Something was quite different, and she wasn't too sure of herself with this new person. He seemed immune to her flirting smiles and quips, almost as though he could see through to the real Bess inside, the one she kept hidden from everyone . . .including herself.

As the week plodded on, Ethan planned over and over what he would say to Bess. He felt he owed her an explanation of some kind. They had been close emotionally as well as physically, but of course no commitment had been made. She was a prostitute, after all, and he had never hinted that he was married. Not that it would have mattered to Bess. Many of the men who frequented the saloon were married, but he knew in his heart that he had not been honest, implying that he was a bachelor. He sensed that there was an attachment between them that was more than her professional duty. Now that he saw things in the light of his new faith, he realized how very wrong he had been. How could he ever make things right in his messed-up life?

Again thoughts of Mandy pushed their way into his head and heart. He still loved Mandy with all his heart. He longed to be with her and tell her of his spiritual discovery and commitment. But how could he go to someone to whom he had lied in this way—and who thought he was dead? For all he knew, Mandy could have moved back East, or. . .who knew what might have happened to her? It frightened him to think of the possibilities, but he could not gather the courage to go back and try to find her. Maybe someday.

He struggled to push Mandy out of his mind. He had to keep his mind on business and his customers. Many of the new friends he had made at the little church shopped at the Taylors' store, and he truly enjoyed their visits. It felt like the closest thing to an extended family Ethan had ever known. He rejoiced not only in his newfound faith but also in the family of God. But every time he had these thoughts, he soon was overwhelmed with guilt at the huge secret he was hiding from them all. He prayed for God's guidance but was too afraid of rejection if he were to tell them the whole truth. So he struggled on.

When Sunday arrived, he almost didn't look forward to going to church because of the large burden of guilt he carried. He also dreaded his talk with Bess in the afternoon. He had prayed to have an opportunity to tell Bess of the joy and forgiveness he'd found in his new relationship with Christ but was concerned how she would receive the news.

By early afternoon the sun was shining on the snow and made a cheery, if cold, day for a walk. As Ethan approached the saloon, Bess came out, almost as though she knew he didn't want to go into the saloon anymore. After greeting one another, they began to walk, talking very little until they reached the edge of town. It was cold enough to make walking and talking and breathing rather an uncomfortable trio, so Ethan guided Bess to a small cluster of trees not far from the creek where he used to bathe when he worked on the railroad. There were enough trees and bushes to make a small shelter from the cold wind. He asked if she minded sitting on an old fallen tree trunk.

When they were seated, Ethan spoke of his unhappy childhood in an unloving family and of the restlessness that continued to drive him from one thing to another until he finally found the answer in his newfound faith.

Bess listened attentively as he told the whole story—the whole story, that is, except the part about Mandy. He still could not summon the courage to tell that part of his life to anyone.

By the time he'd finished, huge tears were sliding down Bess's cheeks.

∽

As Bess listened to Ethan's story, she was sure she would not be welcome in the little church, but the longing to find the peace and joy Ethan was talking about almost overwhelmed her. Would God ever accept one such as her? Would she ever be able to turn her life around and have a different sort of life? She didn't feel comfortable confiding these thoughts to Ethan, so she just said she appreciated him sharing his story and rose to go.

Ethan was disappointed. He had so hoped Bess also would want to find a new way of life. As they made their way back to town, Ethan decided he would pray for Bess—that she, too, would find new life in God's family.

Chapter 14

The snows eventually melted into early spring rains. Ethan could not help but think of the cabin in the woods and all the things that probably needed to be repaired. He knew Mandy couldn't tap the maple trees in the woods when the sap ran again. But he consoled himself that they had made plenty of maple syrup to last several years before he left last year. He wanted so desperately to go home to Mandy and asked himself over and over why he had done this awful thing. When he thought of what he had done to her, he felt physically sick. No, this was his punishment; he would just have to live with it. He could never face Mandy with his lies and his betrayal of her faith in him.

And so he kept himself busy in the store. He had used his creativity, and the Taylors had learned to trust and appreciate his judgment and let him arrange things the way he wanted. The new displays were as attractive as they were useful, and the Taylors sold more than they ever had before.

During the slow days of winter, Ethan had asked if he could build a cupboard for a display in one area of the room. He had built such a beautiful cupboard that Mr. Taylor had paid him extra and asked him to build one for their home. Ethan had always loved making beautiful things and enjoyed every minute spent doing the fine carpentry work. Before he knew it, the short, dark days of winter had been pushed aside by the longer days and spring rains.

The little church filled a huge void in Ethan's life. The people were very friendly, and often he was invited to share meals with one family or another. At first this was enjoyable, but the more he visited their friendly and cozy homes, the more he thought of Mandy and missed the cozy home she had made for him. Sometimes it was all he could do to keep from telling his new friends the truth, but still fear held him back, so he kept that part of his life locked tight.

Ethan did pray faithfully for Bess. He was concerned about her lifestyle, and that she had no one to care for her. He now knew that she needed to know God, but he also wondered what she would do for a living if she were to change her ways. Still, he continued to pray. From what he'd been learning, he had every confidence that God would take care of Bess's life if she were to turn it over to Him.

One Sunday morning, as they were singing the opening hymn, he heard the door open and turned his head toward it. He could hardly believe his eyes as Bess tried to slide her lace and ruffles and flounces into the back pew unnoticed. She had not seen him, so he quickly pivoted back toward the front. As the songs were sung and the message given, he could hardly hear what was being said for praying for Bess. As the last song was sung, he turned his head slightly to check on her, only to find she had already slipped out and was gone.

He was oblivious to all the friendly chatter and laughter after the service. He knew he had spoken with some people but couldn't remember who or what had been said. All he could think was to pray for Bess. He had no doubt that God loved her too, had a plan for her, and could bring happiness and fulfillment to her empty way of life.

Ethan was surprised but pleased that no one in the church made unwelcome remarks about Bess. He sensed that they really cared about each lost soul and would be praying for her also. He wondered if anyone had had the opportunity to speak with her but didn't feel it appropriate to ask. So he went on his way, determined in his heart to double his effort to pray for her.

As Ethan worked in the store, he found that praying for Bess helped him not to think of Mandy so much. But he also spent time praying for Mandy. He built some new shelves for the walls of the store and a rocker for Mrs. Taylor to rest in by her fire in the evenings. Mrs. Taylor was a quiet, gentle woman probably only six or eight years older than he and Mandy. She had never complained of her sparse furnishings, but now quite frequently commented about how much she enjoyed the rocker for doing her mending and knitting.

She had offered to wash his clothes when she did theirs soon after he had moved into his room in the eaves, which was a great relief for Ethan as he knew he would soon run out of money paying for laundry services. He was so glad he could do something to make her happy in return. He knew she missed their children, but she trusted God's wisdom and never complained. He couldn't help but wonder some-times why God had let a good family like this experience the death of their children, and why he and Mandy had never been blessed with any children at all. He even wondered if it was perhaps better to have never had children than to have them, love them, and then lose them. Much of life was still such a mystery, but Ethan was thankful he now could trust in the all-wise God.

Bess watched out the front window of the saloon as Ethan walked toward the store where he lived with the Taylors. She had never felt so confused. She had never let herself think about her life and what the future may hold for her. Something was changing, she could tell, and she wasn't certain if it was a change she wanted or not. She just knew that, for now, Ethan had found a peace for which she had longed without even realizing she was longing for it.

She had always pretty much stayed away from the other people in the town. She couldn't imagine what they must do with their lives. How boring and empty their lives must be just keeping house and raising a bunch of children to grow up and do the same.

Now, after meeting Ethan and getting to know him, for the first time she understood a little about what being a woman really meant. She daydreamed about settling down with Ethan, keeping house for him, and even raising a family. But then Ethan got involved in that church and stopped coming to see her.

Suddenly her life seemed so empty. So meaningless. What had Ethan said about God and that church the day he had talked to her? How could it have changed him so? Her heart was so conflicted, it was difficult to get from one day to the next. She was always hoping for Ethan to come in and tell her he missed her.

But day after day went by and he didn't come. One Sunday she decided to go to that church and see for herself what it was all about.

After slipping into the back pew, she was handed a songbook by a friendly lady with a warm smile, but the song they sang was nothing like any song she had heard before. She listened to the songs but watched the happy faces even more. Then the preacher began to talk. She didn't quite understand what he was saying, but all the people appeared spellbound by his words. She was still wondering about some of it when they all stood to sing again. Bess decided that this was the best time to slip out if she didn't want them all questioning her, so while they were rustling to stand, she slipped quietly out the back door.

That afternoon, as she was rinsing out some of her clothes and bathing, she couldn't shake the feeling that she was dirty in a way that was deeper than her skin. She had heard them singing about being washed whiter than snow, and suddenly she couldn't explain why she felt so different from those people. Their happiness seemed to come from the inside somehow. They didn't seem to have a worry in the world. Did everything always go perfectly for them? Had they indeed been washed whiter than snow? Like a light flashing on in her mind, Bess suddenly wondered if this was the kind of restlessness Ethan had been talking about. This unsettled feeling, as though something was out of place. . .or missing entirely.

Chapter 15

Monday blew in with such force that even the sun kept its distance in the gray morning sky. The moisture in the air was too cold to be called snow. It was frozen bits of ice being slashed against the glass of the window. The wind seemed to not even realize there was a window there—it came on in and made itself at home, billowing out the curtains and making the room colder than Bess could ever remember.

Bess crept deeper under the comforters for warmth but realized too late that she had forgotten to add wood to her stove before going to bed, and her rooms were colder than she could stand. She knew none of the other girls would be awake yet to share some coals with her, so she huddled under the blankets and tried not to shiver.

Was it the gloom of the day or the gloom of her spirits that made the day seem so dark? Her clock said 7:50 already, but it was not much lighter than the night. She chided herself for letting Ethan Evanston affect her like this. She had been with many men in her short life and could not explain why this one bothered her so. Was it the feeling of rejection since he had stopped coming to see her? Yet he had taken the time to explain why, which was more than anyone else had done. She should be satisfied that he cared enough to want to explain.

"No," she whispered to herself, "it's his reason for not coming back and that church that make me feel as though there is something I am missing and can't quite get my hands on. I have always been content with my life. What's happening to me?"

After trying unsuccessfully to sleep again for about another hour, she finally lifted her eyes heavenward and begged, "If there is a God out there, please help me to find the answers." Then she shook herself, made a dive for her robe and slippers, and dashed down the back stairs to the kitchen to take some coals from the big cookstove and some kindling. While her fire was trying to catch on and make a flame, she returned to the kitchen to take some water from the reservoir on the stove. Hers was so frozen she knew it would be a long time before her fire was warm enough to thaw and warm it.

Back in her room Bess put the water on to heat before once again wrapping in her blankets and watching the flames as they licked the edges of the cold wood. What would today bring? She was glad it was a dark, cold Monday, for business would probably be very slow. She didn't feel like joking and laughing with the rough men who frequented Sam's Saloon. In fact, she decided she would tell Sam she was not feeling well and ask if she could wash dishes tonight. She knew she couldn't get away with that for very long, but maybe for tonight he would agree.

⟨∞⟩

After a few days, Bess got back to work, but for the first time there was no fun in flirting with the men. She was polite and laughed at their stupid remarks and jokes, but her heart was not in it. Somehow the men seemed to sense the change, too, and little by little she had fewer and fewer offers. She knew she had to try a little harder, or Sam would tell her to find a new place. He didn't provide those rooms for free, and he wanted his share of her profits. He had been very patient with her the past few weeks because she had been one of the best workers he had had, but she knew his patience would not last forever.

When Bess did have a man up to her room, she felt soiled and so dirty that she wanted to wash and wash. She could hardly wait to get him out of there. What was different? Was it that song about being washed whiter than snow? She couldn't seem to get it out of her head. Ever since her visit to that little church it was as though she could see herself through some other eyes, and she felt soiled and used. Could God really wash her kind of filth clean and whiter than snow? What did those words mean anyway?

Day after day she pondered the question. How would she ever know? She didn't think she had the courage to go back to that church. She had felt so out of place. She tried to understand why—everyone had been friendly, handing her a songbook, smiling at her, moving over to give her room to sit, but not far enough to not touch her. Why was she hesitant to go back? Was she afraid of seeing Ethan again? Would he think she was just going there to see him? No, she simply couldn't face going back. But then where would she find her answers?

One day Bess awoke to a brilliant sun peeping through her east windows and realized that March was long gone. April had already half spent itself melting the snows into muddy rivers trickling through the ruts in the road and flowing under the boardwalk in front of the saloon. She opened her window and was surprised at how cold it still was, but she was sure she could smell spring in the air. It was enough to give her some hope. Suddenly she had to be outdoors. Could the newness of spring give her new life once again? Then her heart sank. She knew it would take more than a little sunshine and fresh breeze to freshen her wretched life. Still, she felt an urgent need to be outside.

Bess dressed quickly and quietly slipped down the back stairs and out the back doors. After picking her way around to the front boardwalk to walk above the mud, she found herself walking down the street. Soon she realized someone had caught up with her and was walking beside her. She dared not lift her head to look, but she could see a soft skirt and hear the *swish, swish* of petticoats. As she sneaked a peek at the lady's gentle smile, it seemed familiar for some reason, but she knew she did not know the lady. So, as she had been taught, she waited for the lady to speak first.

"Good morning!" came the greeting, accompanied by a warm smile. "Isn't it absolutely heavenly this morning?"

Bess mumbled a surprised "Morning." Usually ladies avoided such as her. What did this lady want?

"We have not had the opportunity to meet before, but we did once share a hymnbook. My name's Rebecca Taylor."

Oh, yes, the lady who had passed her a songbook in the church. "My name's Bess. Guess I don't really have a second name. I always meant to thank you for sharing with me. It was right nice of you."

"Oh, that's all right. I know all the songs without a book anyway. I had always hoped you would come back—you look to be about my age—no, I can tell you're younger, but not by so awful much."

Bess studied the lady for a few seconds. She certainly seemed sincere. She wouldn't have had to acknowledge Bess, let alone walk with her. "I didn't feel like I belonged there. Oh, everyone was nice enough, but I didn't feel like I fit. . ." Bess faltered to a stop, her cheeks flaming hot.

Rebecca was quick to fill the gap. "None of us fits, until we decide to. We would love to have you come again. It's such a happy place!"

"Thanks. It's, just, well, I guess there's so much I don't understand. So much I don't know. I don't want to embarrass anyone. I don't know how it's all done or what it is even all about. I don't even know the right questions to ask."

Rebecca turned and touched Bess's elbow. "Bess," she said gently, "I'm not certain I could answer all your questions, but I'd be glad to try. Or I'd be glad to go with you to Pastor Lewis's and sit with you while you ask him your questions. He is such a wise man and very careful in his study of the scripture. He would know the answers to your questions and would be able to explain it all to you better than I ever could."

They walked on in silence for a while. Finally, Bess surprised herself. "I really do want to find some answers, and for some reason I feel they lie within that church, but I feel so unworthy."

"That's perfect." Rebecca smiled. "Until we recognize our own unworthiness, we can never understand the gift of God. Pastor Lewis lives just around this next corner. Would you like to visit him now?"

Somehow, with Rebecca beside her, Bess summoned the courage to say yes. "But, Miss Rebecca, do you know what I am? Do you know where I'm from?"

Rebecca's beautiful lavender eyes opened wide, and there was warm acceptance in her gaze. "Bess, God knows. And He loves every one of us just the same, no matter what or who we are. Can we, His children, do any less?" And with that she guided Bess up the front steps of a little brown cottage tucked in behind the church.

Chapter 16

Everything had changed so quickly that day. Well, it had been most of the day that they had spent talking with the kind pastor. Mrs. Lewis had brought a lunch and some good coffee in and had taken away the scraps without them even hardly noticing. By afternoon they were all on their knees, and when Bess had finished praying, she knew she was indeed a new person. The old had been washed away, and she truly felt "whiter than snow." No one had coaxed. No one had chided. The pastor simply explained it all to her and answered her questions—even the questions she didn't know how to ask. Such a huge weight was lifted from her shoulders that she felt she could float away.

Mrs. Lewis had quickly offered, "Bess, would you like to stay here for a few days? Our children are grown so we have a spare room, and we'd be glad to have you." That's when Bess realized she could no longer live like she had always lived. What would she do? Where would she go? Who would have her? As doubts surfaced, the Lewises and Rebecca reassured her that God had a plan for her life and would not leave her alone. They were all available to assist her in any way they could.

So it was settled. She moved in with the Lewises, and Rebecca visited her regularly. Bess could hardly wait from one Bible study to the next. She wanted to learn everything she could. Mrs. Lewis taught her some housekeeping skills and a bit about cooking. And Rebecca Taylor became a very close friend.

Bess saw Ethan at the church, but other than a friendly greeting, they had not really spoken to one another. Somehow Bess had lost all interest in men and thought nothing of her lack of conversation with Ethan. She wasn't in church to see Ethan but to soak up all the teaching she could from God's Word, to praise Him with the beautiful songs that were becoming familiar to her, and to fellowship with all of her newfound "brothers" and "sisters." And what wonderful fellowship it was!

One Sunday after the service, when they all stood around talking, a gentleman asked Rebecca to introduce him to Bess. At first Bess was shy about the introduction, but he reassured her quickly. Robert Sheldon was rather shy himself, and Rebecca hurried to explain that Mr. Sheldon's wife was bedridden from polio, and that they were looking for someone to come live with them and help out with the four young children. Delighted with the opportunity, Bess could hardly wait to meet his wife and children. It was arranged for Mrs. Lewis and Bess to go out to the farm to meet the family the next afternoon.

The meeting at the farm was strained at first. Bess had never been around children, but she couldn't help liking nine-year-old Paul's red hair and freckles. Conner had black hair like his dad, dark brown eyes, and another generous helping of freckles. He had just turned eight. Phillip was six years old and had more teeth missing than in, or so it appeared from his shy smile. There was nothing at all shy about Anna. The four-year-old girl was all smiles and dimples and curls and sky-blue eyes.

When she met Anita Sheldon, Bess realized that Anna was a carbon copy of her beautiful mother. The polio had left Anita's legs useless, and the pain she suffered was evident in her drawn face and blue, blue eyes, but only gentle words were on her lips. Bess knew she would have her hands full with an invalid, four energetic children, and a farmhouse, but she longed to be given the position. Though she didn't know the first thing about raising children, much less keeping house and cooking, the arrangements were made, and she soon found herself settled in and running a household.

Chapter 17

After their fun Christmas with the Brownings, Mandy and Deidre settled into their comfortable routine once again. With the little boys to care for, they decided to take turns again doing the chores in the barn. Mandy would do the outdoor chores one day while Deidre cooked and watched the boys, and then they would switch responsibilities the next day. Both women enjoyed the time spent with the little ones, cleaning the cottage, and cooking. Even laundry day was fun with all the baby things to wash and iron. Neither of them was particularly fond of the barn chores but knew they had to be done. This arrangement made life most tolerable for both women.

In spite of the fun times they had together, keeping house and caring for the little boys, both women often felt the weight of having their husbands gone. Mandy wondered what they would do when they ran out of Ethan's money. How would she buy oil for the lamps, sugar, flour, and other staples? Ned had brought them a couple of deer in November that he and his boys had killed, and that meat and tallow had served them well, but Mandy knew she could not always depend on Ned to provide for them. He had his own family to care for.

One day Mandy decided it was time to make soap for the next year. As she began mixing her herbs and oils for softness and fragrance, Deidre commented that Mandy's soaps were much nicer than any she had seen the wealthy women in the South use. She was eager to help Mandy and see how it was done.

An idea formed. "Deidre," Mandy said slowly, "do you suppose we could make soap to sell at the store? My aunt made me make all the soap for the family because she hated doing it. I experimented with the ashes until I learned the best way to make my lye, and I also learned to add salt to my soaps to make them firm enough to cut into bars. Then I started adding fragrant herb oils I had created from the herbs I grew, and soon my soaps were nicer than what could be purchased at a store. Do you suppose the owner of the store here at Canton would buy my soap, or at least let me trade for some of the goods we will need when we run out of money?"

"Oooh, Mandy, we surely could try. Most women would love to bathe with your soaps. They're so soft and smooth on the skin. If they have money, they would surely buy some. And once they have used your soap, they will be back for more, that's certain. Let's make extra soap. Then as soon as it's spring so we can get out, you can take it to the store and ask the man if he would sell it for you or buy some to sell."

So soon the two young women were busy making different kinds of soaps. The entire cottage smelled of soaps and fragrant herbs. After the soap had been cut into bars, Deidre and Mandy went through the scrap bag and cut pretty strips of fabric to tie into bows around each bar. Into each bow they tied a small piece of the fragrant herb used for the fragrance in that particular soap. The soaps were not only fragrant, but beautiful.

One morning Deidre was bursting with another idea. She could teach Mandy how to weave the grasses to make the little woven boxes she had made for the Browning girls for Christmas. They would make each box the same size as a bar of soap, then tuck a soap into each one. What a nice way to sell their special soaps. Mandy learned quickly, and so each day they diligently wove one box after another.

The winter passed rapidly as the two women worked industriously on their soaps and boxes between chores and caring for the boys. By the time they had fifty little boxes made and soaps in each one, spring was just around the corner, and they realized that Daniel was crawling and sitting up and growing from an infant into a pudgy dimpled baby who laughed and cooed and loved to play with Jedediah. Jedediah was a wonderful help sharing his toys and entertaining Daniel while the women worked on their projects.

As Mandy watched Daniel grow, she missed Ethan more and more. She would see Ethan's dimple in Daniel's chin, or Ethan's eyes and brows whenever she looked at her son. How her heart longed after her husband, and even more now, knowing how much Ethan had longed for a son. She realized now how very much she and Deidre had in common. Deidre, too, missed her husband deeply and wondered if she would ever see him again. The fact that Jeremiah had been sold as a slave to another slave owner made it seem even more impossible that he could ever be found.

Once again Mandy ended her ponderings with a prayer of thanksgiving that God had brought the two women together and a prayer for Deidre's husband—wherever he might be. She prayed that God would protect Jeremiah, somehow let him gain his freedom, and allow him to find Deidre and Jedediah. Mandy already had a strong faith that, with God, all things are possible.

Chapter 18

A s Mandy turned the beautiful calendar the Brownings had made them for Christmas to the new month, she realized it was just over a year since Ethan had left to work on the railroad. She remembered how very difficult it was to see him going off through the woods, and how she had longed to run after him, beg him to stay, and tell him about the baby. She couldn't help but wonder if her life would be different today if she had told him. Would he still be with her? Would he still be alive?

She reminded herself once more, as she frequently did, that she had felt right keeping the secret to herself. She also knew Ethan's life was in God's hands. There was nothing she could do to change God's plan for a person's life. It was not for her to understand, but to accept God's will. She squared her shoulders, pushed her mouth into a smile, and turned to start her day. Above all else, she did not want to be a sad, grumpy mother for Daniel. She wanted him to grow up happy and contented, and she knew she would be the influence for the atmosphere of their home.

How often she'd thought as she was growing up in her aunt's miserable, unhappy home that if her aunt could simply have seen the good in those around her instead of always criticizing and degrading them, her home would have been a much happier place. Also, if her aunt had not always complained about everything, the home would have been much more pleasant. Mandy had decided when she was young that she did not want to become like her aunt—unhappy and making all those around her unhappy. *No matter how unpleasant your circumstances,* Mandy had mused, *surely there's always something to be happy about.* So she had tried to always do just that—find the good, the beauty, the gift in everything. But even after all those years of practice, there were still occasional days when she had to remind herself to choose to be happy. And she truly did have so very much for which to be thankful. So she decided not to think about Ethan being gone, but of the happy years they had had together, and of the beautiful gift he had left her, who was going to want his breakfast soon.

Mandy hummed softly as she prepared breakfast. When she heard Daniel gurgling and cooing, she quickly brought him out by the fire, changed his diaper, and was nursing him when Deidre came out to get a cup of hot coffee before heading for the barn. "I'll be finished here soon, Deidre. Why don't we eat before you go out?"

"That sounds mighty good to me. My insides were making so much noise in the bed I was afraid it would wake the children."

By the time Mandy was finished nursing the baby, Jedediah was awake, so they all had their breakfast together.

"I know it's only the middle of April," Mandy said hesitantly, "but what if we see if we can till up the garden plots? I know how to hitch Flops to the plow, but I'm not certain I can guide the plow. It may take several days to get the ground worked up. What do you think?"

Deidre agreed she was ready to start working in the soil as well, so the two decided that as soon as their regular chores were finished, they would try their hand at plowing. Mandy knew it wasn't going to be easy and that the garden would not be as nice as usual, because Ethan had always plowed the dead vines and such under in the fall to let them rot down into the soil over the winter months. This year she and Deidre had not been able to do it with Mandy's advanced pregnancy last fall. She hoped it would still be possible to make a nice garden.

In spite of the chill in the air, the women soon had worked themselves into a sweat trying to hold and guide the plow while not falling down from turning an ankle on the broken-up sod. Soon they devised a way for one of them to walk by Flops's head and guide her that way while the other would follow behind, keeping the plow upright and trying to guide it into straight rows. It was slow work with keeping an eye on Jedediah and carrying Daniel alternately on their backs. They'd had an early lunch before starting the plowing, but before they knew it, the sun was dipping behind the trees. They were far from finished, and it was well past chore time and suppertime.

When they finished the row they were on, Mandy helped Deidre with the chores in the barn. Then both trudged up the hill to the cabin, almost too exhausted to eat. They set out some boiled eggs, bread, cheese, and milk, and used what energy they had left to eat a bite before tumbling into their beds as soon as the boys were taken care of. Just before sinking into a deep sleep, Mandy thought, *We are only about a quarter of the way finished with the plowing*. With a groan she was asleep.

⬧

The next day both women were so sore they could hardly pick up the babies, but they knew the plowing had to be done. They took turns massaging one another's sore muscles, then went out to do the chores together. Afterward, Mandy put some vegetables into the kettle with a bit of venison and herbs to simmer over the fire all day while they worked outdoors. It would taste good to have some stew ready when they came in exhausted at night.

The plowing went even slower the second day. Daniel was tired of being carried in a pack on the back and was teething and fussy. The women took turns plowing and watching Daniel play on a blanket in the grass. When he napped, they would both plow again for a time.

On the third day, as they headed out to plow, they heard horses tramping through the woods with Ned's cheerful songs ringing out loud and clear. They quickly changed their plans and prepared for a visit, deciding that the plowing could wait for tomorrow. They put the coffeepot back on to boil, added more vegetables to the soup pot, and went out on the front porch in time for the Brownings to arrive at the edge of the clearing. Mandy wasn't sure who was more excited for the visit—she and Deidre or the Brownings.

After the greetings were over and the coffee cups emptied, Ned said they had just finished their plowing the day before, and he and Thomas had come to help Mandy and Deidre with their plowing. He was astonished when he heard that they had already been plowing for two days. Mandy was so relieved to not have the heavy plowing to do she felt like crying. Edna assured her that Ned and Thomas were only too glad to help out. And, oh, how they enjoyed taking up the knitting needles and settling into the rockers for a good chat. It was wonderful to feel like a woman again.

Edna told Mandy and Deidre that, since Thomas, Edward, and even Nicholas were old enough to take on a lot of their farm responsibilities, she and Ned almost had time on their hands and were very glad to help out on this farm as well. They were all certain that God had planned their lives to become so close because of the needs both families had, as well as for the wonderful fellowship. Both Mandy and Deidre were speechless with gratitude to God and to the Browning family.

When the sun moved toward the west, Mandy quickly stirred up and baked some cornbread to go with their soup and was just putting it on the table as Ned and Thomas brought the milk in from the barn. They had been able to get the rest of the sod turned and the gardens all ready for planting, as well as doing the evening chores. Mandy felt like a queen not having to worry about the barn and the chores.

As soon as they finished eating, the Brownings prepared to head back through the woods before the sun completely vanished. It had been a wonderful day, and it was harder than ever to say good-bye. Mandy told the Brownings about her plans to sell her soap, so they made arrangements for them all to come to the Brownings' cabin as soon as they were finished planting the gardens. Then Deidre and the babies could stay with Edna while Mandy and Ned went to the store to see if they could find a market for the soaps.

Daniel was rubbing his eyes as the wagon disappeared through the trees. The two women took the boys into the cabin, washed them, and dressed them for bed. While Mandy nursed Daniel, Deidre rocked and sang to Jedediah. Both little ones were sound asleep in only a few minutes and were tucked snuggly into their beds.

While Mandy and Deidre washed the dishes and straightened up the cabin, they chatted and planned and giggled like two schoolgirls. They'd had such a wonderful day, and now all the plowing was done and the gardens were ready to plant. After having the whole day to rest their sore muscles, they could hardly wait to get their seeds sorted and the gardens laid out and planted. They planned to start the very next day as soon as the chores were finished.

It was later than usual when they finally put the last clean dish in the cupboard and hung the broom on its peg in the pantry. In spite of the late hour, Mandy said mischievously to Deidre, "If you'll brew some tea, I'll go get the seeds, and we can get them all sorted tonight so they're ready as soon as chores are done in the morning."

Deidre grinned back. "I was just thinkin' I was too wound up to go to bed. I'll get that pot on right away."

So over cups of tea the women sorted and planned their gardens. After a while the long day caught up with them. Between yawns they told each other good night and went to their rooms. What an exciting, full day it had been.

Chapter 19

In her sleep, Mandy thought Deidre was popping popcorn. Fuzzily, she wondered how her friend could be popping it in her room, and so loudly too. *Must be some large kernels.* Mandy could hardly wait to taste it. *Mmm, I really should see if I can help. . . .*

What? What's that noise? Did Deidre drop something? Mandy tried to pull herself out of her deep sleep.

At the next loud crash, she was awake. It took a few seconds to realize what the noises were. It wasn't popcorn; it was hail, and it had to be huge. But what was the loud crack? There it was again. Thunder so loud the cabin shook and the windows rattled. She pulled a blanket around her shoulders because the temperature had dropped drastically.

Mandy decided she should stir up the fire, put some more logs on, and see what time it was. But by the time she had closed the bedroom door, cold air blasted from the back door, and Deidre was practically blown in with her arms full of wood. She, too, had thought to add wood to the fire, only to discover there was merely one piece of wood in the cabin and a few sticks. With all their plowing and visiting, they had used up all the wood from the back porch, and Deidre had had to go out to the woodpile to bring in wet wood. She was soaked to the skin and shivering.

"Go get some dry clothes while I build up the fire," Mandy encouraged her friend.

But Deidre shook her head. She wanted to bring in more wood before she changed so it could begin to dry before they would need it. She was already soaked, so there was no reason for Mandy to get cold, too. "This storm is goin' to last all day long from the looks of it, so I'm goin' to bring in enough wood to last the day and night. Then I'll warm my body up. Guess we ain't goin' to be doin' any planting for a while. It's dumpin' buckets of rain and hail out there."

While Deidre carried more wood onto the porch and into the cabin, Mandy put the few dry sticks on the coals and carefully propped their one piece of dry wood on top. Soon the sticks were crackling and the flames licking the dry piece of wood. Carefully Mandy laid the wet wood on top of it all in a crisscross pattern to dry out in time to burn and make some heat in the cabin.

By the time Deidre had carried the wood up to the house Mandy had a good hot fire going. She pulled a rocker near the fire, told Deidre to get out of her wet clothes and into something warm and dry, and to come sit by the fire. She heated a cup of milk and had it ready for Deidre to warm up her insides, too.

As they sat by the fire together, both were disappointed that they would be unable to plant the garden—not only that day, but probably for quite a while the way it was raining. It was also going to be too wet to get out for a while. Both sighed, becoming quite gloomy.

Suddenly Mandy looked at Deidre. "We must stop this. We'll turn into two old grouches not fit to be around. Let's think of something good about all this."

"You're right. We don't need to act like the world's endin' just 'cause we can't plant that garden. God's been good to us. We must stop complainin' and start praisin'. Let's think of all our blessin's!"

So together they spoke of all the good things they had and realized even more how thankful they were that Ned and Thomas had come over to finish their plowing. If it had not been finished that day, they would have had to wait a long time before the ground would be dry enough to plow. Before long they were thanking the Lord for all the good things in their lives. They decided to go back to bed and then, after the morning chores, they would declare a holiday and play all day. They hadn't used the chess and checker games that Ned and Edna had made for them for Christmas since Christmas Day. Excited, they returned to their beds and slept soundly while the rain and hail drummed its steady rhythm on the roof and windows.

～∞～

"Mum-mum-mum," Daniel cooed as he sucked his thumb and kicked his blankets. Mandy opened her eyes in the gray light of morning and was sure it was way too early for him to be waking. She waited a few moments to see if he would go back to sleep, then couldn't resist getting up to hug him. She took him out by the fire to change his diaper. When she looked at the clock, she was amazed it was after eight o'clock already. She chuckled. "We sure are having a holiday," she whispered to Daniel as she kissed his neck and ears. "We're going to do nothing but play all day today." And he seemed to catch her spirit as he slobbered all over her cheek.

She was just finishing nursing him as she heard Jedediah climb out of his big boy bed and call for his mommy. She quickly went over to Deidre's door and knocked gently, saying, "Deidre, I'll do the outdoor chores today. You got so wet and cold in the night, it would be better if you stayed in today and kept yourself warm and dry."

Deidre quickly opened her door and took Daniel in her arms. "Then I'll have a holiday breakfast ready for you as soon as you're done. Thanks for taking my turn."

With that, Mandy turned and went to dress in her warmest clothes. Then she

76

trudged to the barn to get the chores over with so they could get on with their holiday.

∞

When Deidre had dressed, she began to make their special breakfast. When the breakfast was ready, she looked out the window to see if Mandy was coming yet. There was no sign of her, so Deidre brought more wood in from the porch to dry out by the fire. She played with the boys a little, and when Jedediah could wait no longer, she let him begin his breakfast while she continued to wait for Mandy. Soon she realized it was getting closer to lunch than breakfast, and still she had seen nothing of Mandy. The knot of fear forming in her stomach would not go away until she had checked on her.

Deidre turned to look at the boys, trying to figure out how to care for them and at the same time go check on Mandy. Daniel was sound asleep on the rug by the fireplace. Carefully she picked up the baby and laid him in the cradle. She hurried to bundle Jedediah, and was pulling on some warm clothes herself when the back door burst open.

Mandy ran in and excitedly laid something small and warm in her arms. "When I got to the barn, I heard the ewe crying," she said breathlessly. "And when I went to check on her, I saw she was lying down trying to give birth. She seemed to strain and strain. I tried to comfort and calm her, but she would only stay quiet for a few minutes. I kept trying to get the milking and other chores done, but she cried and cried until I finally knelt beside her. I knew it was taking too long, and she was tiring, getting weaker and weaker. I had to help her, so I massaged her stomach firmly to try to turn the lamb if it was twisted. She finally gave birth to a little lamb. While the lamb was trying to nurse, the ewe continued to heave and cry. Then I realized she was still giving birth. . .to twins! She never would accept this first little one, and it's getting weaker.

"Take this lamb and clean it up while I go bring in the milk. Then we'll see if we can get it to drink milk from a baby bottle. I brought some baby bottles in the trunk in case I would ever need them. Now I guess I will need them." Placing the lamb gently in in Deidre's arms, Mandy ducked back out into the rain and was gone.

Deidre and Jedediah slipped out of their coats and made a warm bed by the fire for the baby lamb. Deidre washed the lamb with warm water and talked softly to it. When it was clean and dry, the lamb was snowy white. Soon it nuzzled her hands, searching for food. Leaving the lamb in Jedediah's care, she went to find the baby bottles.

As she was warming some milk, Mandy came in, wet and cold. "How's the baby doing?" She shivered.

"Just fine. Go get yourself dry and warm, then come help with this little one."

Throughout the day they continued to cuddle and feed the little lamb until it soon stood on its wobbly legs. Jedediah clapped and squealed. Daniel watched him and then clapped and squealed, too. The women laughed at him. What fun to play with the little lamb and watch and care for it. It was so soft and white they started to call her "Angel."

The day passed quickly, and before they knew it, the time had come to do the evening chores. Mandy was eager to check on the ewe and the other lamb, so she pulled on her coat and wrapped a scarf around her face to shield it from the driving, icy rain. She welcomed the warmth of the barn as she felt her way through the dusk to find the ewe. The other lamb was nursing and being licked by its mother, so Mandy knew it would be all right. She finished the chores as quickly as she could before darting through the driving rain back to the house. As she stepped onto the porch, she realized they had used quite a lot of the wood Deidre had brought in during the night, so she trudged back to carry more up onto the dry porch.

After stacking the wood, Mandy entered the warm cheery cabin to take off her wet, cold coat and scarf. She warmed herself by the fire, thinking again how much she appreciated all that Ethan had taken care of when he was here and how much she missed him and his protection. She was thankful for Deirdre's company and help, but it would never be the same as having her Ethan.

While she was drying and thawing, her nose told her Deirdre had not been idle while she was out in the barn, and her stomach was more than ready to accept some delicious nourishment.

So after thanking God for their many blessings, they ate their meal and talked of their exciting day until it was time to put the little boys to bed. After Jedediah was laid in his bed, Angel began to cry. Deidre and Mandy tried everything to quiet the lamb, until Jedediah toddled out and lay down on the rug beside her. Soon the lamb curled up next to Jedediah, and both fell sound asleep by the fire. From that time on, every evening Jedediah lay down with Angel until the lamb went to sleep, and then the women would push a warmed rolled-up blanket next to the lamb as they took Jedediah off to bed.

Chapter 20

It continued to rain for two more days and nights, and the members of the little household were all quite glad when the sun finally warmed the world with its brightness. Within a few more days, tiny leaves poked out on the trees and bushes, and the grasses started to turn from brown to green.

One day, on her way back from the barn, Mandy noticed a whole mass of yellow, purple, and white crocuses in full bloom. She wanted to walk over to see them closer, but the ground was still soft and mushy to walk on when she stepped off the hardened path. She couldn't help sighing. They still hadn't been able to plant their gardens. Soon her sigh turned into a prayer. "Please, God, let us get those gardens planted soon."

Several days later, the ground had warmed and dried enough that they could begin the planting. They took deep breaths of the fresh spring air. The fruit trees were bursting with blossoms, and the early flowers were breathtaking. Mandy thought she had never seen the world look so beautiful—and expectant.

After they had planted the gardens, she and Deirdre took the boys into the woods, meadows, and down by the creek. They dug up flowers and carried them back to the cabin. They made beautiful flower beds all around their home, adding more to the flowers Mandy already had growing there. They even made a cutting bed out by the barn. Finally they realized they must stop, or they would never be able to keep the beds all weeded and pruned. But they couldn't help admiring the beautiful gardens and anticipating all the rich color.

A few weeks later they decided they must make plans to go to the Brownings' and take the soaps to the store to sell. How quickly the days had passed from winter to spring; soon it would be summer. Once the gardens started to bear their produce, they would need every day to preserve their bounty for winter.

So plans were made, and a day was set. When the day arrived, the women rose earlier than usual to take care of the chores that needed to be done for the day. They packed a breakfast they could eat in the wagon, loaded the baskets of soaps, the children, and Angel. They were on their way just as the sun started to light their path through the woods. Their spirits were high as they ate their bread and jelly and drank their milk bouncing along the trail.

Arriving at the Brownings' home, they were greeted with excitement and warm hugs. Edna said they all had been wondering when Mandy and Deidre would be able to come with their soaps. The family had been planning for the excursion and was as eager as Mandy and Deidre to see if the project would be received well at the store.

Betsy Browning had asked if she could go to the store with Mandy and Ned, and Mandy was glad for the company. Mandy could hardly believe her eyes as they neared the small town. Many new buildings had been built. In addition to the lone store that had been there when Mandy went with Ethan, there was now a hotel, a livery stable, several other buildings, and quite a few houses with a roadway running down the center. Down at one end was a building that looked like a schoolhouse or church—probably used as both. Neither Mandy nor Betsy had anticipated a whole town and were suddenly rather shy.

Ned was quick to assure them that because there was a whole town, the soaps might be more likely to sell. Mandy knew that was true, but she was suddenly conscious of what she was wearing and how long it had been since she had been among other women. However, as she looked about, she saw a woman throwing dishwater out her back door, and she didn't look any more refined than Mandy was. Before long, she relaxed once again, realizing that they were all part of the frontier, and no one would be particularly fashionable.

When they entered the store, the sounds and smells made Mandy remember back to the store in Boston where she had met Ethan. She almost thought she would hear Ethan's voice and warm laughter any minute. She had to shake herself and remind herself where she was and why she was here.

Since the storekeeper was busy with another customer at the moment, it gave her time to look around a bit. Along one end of the store were bolts of fabric and all sorts of sewing notions. She walked over that way with Betsy close behind. How fun it was just to look at all the beautiful things on display.

Soon Betsy tugged at her elbow and whispered, "Look over there, Mrs. Evanston," while she nodded in the general direction of a display at the end of the rows of fabrics. Together they walked down that way and saw lace gloves, ornamental mirrors, perfumes and lotions, and some beautiful filigree fans. "If ladies are buying those things, they surely will buy your beautiful soaps!" There was guarded excitement in Betsy's voice.

Mandy had to admit it did give her more courage to approach the owner. She realized the customer had left and that Ned was speaking with the storekeeper, so with a prayer in her heart she approached the counter. Ned was quick to introduce her and Betsy. When Mandy told the gentleman about the soaps, he waved with a friendly smile toward a door behind him. "You'll have to speak to my wife about those things. She takes care of that end of the store. She should be back any minute. She just stepped out for some fresh air."

At least the storekeeper, Mr. McDonaugh, looked to be a gentleman. He was clean shaven except for a tidy mustache. In spite of broad shoulders that made him look shorter than he really was, he was dressed nicely and had a clean apron on. His eyes crinkled at the corners, and deep dimples almost turned into creases in his cheeks. Mandy wasn't sure if the fair hair made his eyes look so blue, or if it was the freckles, but he did seem to have a perpetual smile, which made her a lot less nervous.

Ned suggested she have her list filled while she waited for Mrs. McDonaugh to return, and then he could fill his while she was visiting with the lady. So, hesitantly, Mandy handed over her list, knowing her funds were very limited. While Mr. McDonaugh prepared her stack of purchases, she heard a door open and close somewhere behind the store.

Mr. McDonaugh excused himself and slipped through the rear door but was back shortly. "Mrs. McDonaugh will be with you in a few minutes."

He continued to fill her order, asking questions occasionally, weighing the coffee beans, sugar, cornmeal, and salt, talking all the time. Mandy was thankful he was such a friendly man. She hoped his wife was as jovial. Soon a plump little woman bustled into the store from the back, looking every bit like a china doll. There was a hint of a flush on her ivory cheeks and again the blue, blue eyes. A few golden curls escaped the combs in her hair and danced merrily on her perfectly shaped neck, almost hidden in soft ruffles and lace. She looked like she had just stepped from the pages of a fashion magazine, but there was nothing reserved about her. She gracefully glided straight for Mandy and Betsy and introduced herself. Eagerly she asked the ladies to join her in the back for tea, so they could talk in private, all the while ushering them around the counters to the door that she and her husband used to enter their home behind the store.

As soon as Mandy was through the door she gasped with surprise. Dolly, as she had asked them to call her, laughed a dainty laugh. "Everyone is surprised the first time they are here, but I just had to bring a wee bit of the old country, and Hiram is very generous with me. Now make yourselves at home. The kettle is on and should be singing any minute." And she bustled through a graceful arched doorway to a room beyond.

Mandy and Betsy stood perfectly still, filling their eyes with all the beauty around them. The room was mostly windows, with flower boxes on the outside of each window overflowing with beautiful red, yellow, blue, and white flowers. Inside were laces and china vases and teapots and plump pillows and soft rugs. It looked like they had stepped into an entirely different world. To one side of the room was a beautiful table sitting in a small area bumped out of the wall with windows on three sides. Each of the three large windows surrounding the table was filled with smaller panes in rows of four, and then draped with lovely lace curtains that spilled into puddles onto the gleaming wood floor. The walls were papered with a pattern of vines, ribbons, and small roses and rosebuds.

The sun poured into the cheery room, filtered by the layers of white lace hanging at the windows. Mandy wanted to walk around the room examining everything but found herself rooted to the spot. After a few minutes, she heard a small gasp behind her. "Just look," whispered Betsy. "Have you ever seen anything so beautiful?"

While they were still standing there looking, Dolly bustled back into the room pushing a tea cart laden with all kinds of beautiful dishes, a steaming teapot, and little cookies and crackers and cheeses. As she set the pretty dishes on the table by the windows, she invited Mandy and Betsy to sit and have tea with her.

As they sat to tea, she inquired why they had wanted to see her. Mandy had almost forgotten her reason for being here. She handed the large basket to Dolly that she had brought in with her, explaining that she was a widow needing some income and wondered if they would sell her soaps for her in the store. "I would appreciate it very much if you would accept one as a gift, and if you like it, perhaps you would be willing to sell some for me?"

Dolly lifted the lid on the basket and reached inside to remove one of the little square baskets inside. Commenting on the pleasant fragrance, she opened the small square basket to see the bar of soap inside tied with a sprig of dried mint. "These smell just like the soaps we used to use at home in Ireland. I can hardly wait to try it." She smiled. "I can't really pay you for all these right up front, but what if we put them in the store, and we will pay you as they sell? Out here on the frontier we have two kinds of women: the kind who work like men and don't take the time to remember that they are ladies, and the ladies who love being ladies. Those are the ones who will enjoy and appreciate something so beautiful and so fragrant."

Betsy spoke up. "There's something in there that makes your skin real soft, too."

Dolly's eyebrows rose as she looked at Mandy.

Mandy smiled and nodded. "I've been making soaps since I was ten years old, and as I had opportunity I would experiment. Because my skin became very dry and would crack in the winter, I wanted to develop a soap that would not only leave my skin soft, but would help it to not dry out. I think you'll find I've been most successful in my experiments."

"I am eager to try them myself," Dolly replied.

The subject changed to flowers and children, and before Mandy knew it, Mr. McDonaugh stuck his head around the doorway to let them know that Ned was ready to return home.

Their good-byes and thank-yous were said, and Dolly invited them back any-time for another visit as she accompanied the women back into the store.

Mandy quickly settled up with Mr. McDonaugh as Ned carried her packages out to the wagon. She was pleased to discover she was able to purchase everything they needed and still had a bit of money left over. Perhaps by the time she came back in the fall, some of the soaps would have sold, and she would have a means to support them all.

That evening, as they made their way back to the cabin, Mandy told Deidre all about the visit and the unexpected tea party, about the McDonaughs, the soaps, the "ladies department" in the store, and all the new, exciting things she had experienced that day. Deidre, too, told about the fun time she and Edna had enjoyed together with all the children. Jedediah had played so hard that he was already sound asleep on a pile of blankets in the back of the wagon with Angel snuggled up tight against him. Daniel was fast asleep in Mandy's arms as Deirdre drove them home. They decided that, all in all, it had been a fun, profitable day.

Chapter 21

Ethan swept off the boardwalk in front of the store, watching the dust swirl into the wind and be blown back in the general direction from which he had just removed it. He worked in the warm spring afternoon trying to make the front of the store presentable. Somewhere in the distance children played. A mother called for her children to come to her. The squeak of a pump handle brought refreshing water to the surface for someone to drink or clean with. Horses stamped and snorted, and a cow lowed in the distance.

He had grown to love this small town and most of the people in it. Many of the families were a part of the church, so seemed family to him as well. He and Mandy had lived in seclusion for so long that he felt he had come back into the light after spending a long time in a cave. But his heart was heavy that Mandy was not with him and even heavier knowing it was he himself who had caused this to come about.

Many were the times he daydreamed of having Mandy in this little town with him. How she would enjoy Rebecca Taylor, Anita Sheldon, and so many of the other kind women here. And he wanted to weep when he thought how much she would enjoy knowing his Lord. Once more he became convinced that he would have to go tell her about God. But always it was followed by a hopeless feeling that she would have no reason to believe him because of the huge lie he had perpetrated. When what he had done overwhelmed him, Ethan breathed a prayer for guidance and forgiveness once more. He would have to trust God to take care of Mandy and to give him wisdom to know what to do. Meanwhile, he would do his best to be patient.

Ethan enjoyed his work in the store because he had always enjoyed being around people and socializing. He loved listening to the farmers as they talked of their crops, the rain, the soil, and their families. He loved watching the children when they came into the store with their mothers. And as he had grown to love Jason and Rebecca Taylor, he was happy to notice they didn't seem as drawn and sorrowful as they watched the children coming and going in the store and in the town as they once had. He hoped they were healing from the sorrow of losing their own children but continued to pray for them.

Often before and after church he would see Rebecca Taylor and Bess talking and laughing together. How he appreciated Rebecca for taking Bess under her wing to encourage and befriend her. It was wonderful to see Bess grow in her relationship with God. Occasionally Ethan and Bess would speak, but only casually and almost as though they were brother and sister. It was a comfortable feeling knowing that Bess was now a child of God and that God was using her to minister to someone in need. He could tell that the situation was not only good for the Sheldon family but gave Bess a sense of satisfaction that she was doing something worthwhile. He could tell the children adored her and that she mothered them as though she had been doing it all her life.

Usually Sunday mornings excited Ethan because of the sharing in the church of God's Word, the learning, and the fellowship with the other families and men of God. However, this morning there was heaviness in his heart that he couldn't understand. Before going downstairs to share breakfast with Jason and Rebecca, he quickly knelt by his bed, asking God to search his heart and reveal to him the reason.

He ate breakfast woodenly, remembering to compliment Rebecca on her light biscuits and thanking her for the delicious meal. He tried to act natural, but it was difficult. He couldn't get away from the black cloud pressing in on him.

Ethan went through all the motions of church, but for the first time, his heart wasn't in it. He couldn't worship. It was as though there was suddenly a thick wall between him and God. He examined his soul to search out the cause but found only closed doors. It was as though there was no light at all in his soul anymore, and Ethan didn't know what to make of it.

While people visited quietly after church, Ethan started to leave. Then he felt a hand on his elbow.

"Is God speaking to you about something, son?" Pastor Lewis quietly said close to his ear.

Ethan turned toward the dear pastor and felt his eyes swim with tears. He could only nod as he tried to swallow the huge lump that prevented speech.

"Would you like to talk to me about it?"

Pastor Lewis was always kind and understanding, but Ethan was amazed at his perception. Ethan could not imagine the good pastor ever being less than loving toward anyone, so he slowly nodded. Pastor Lewis guided him to a small room at the back of the church. The room had a window open on each of two sides, and an old wooden desk and chair were centered under one of the windows. Under the other window was a bench, and along one wall stood a couple of chairs with their backs to the wall. The fourth wall contained the door and a small wooden bookcase with ten or fifteen leather volumes neatly standing in two rows. On top of the bookcase stood a small jar with some flowers. The room seemed empty, yet not desolate, colorless, but not drab, humble, yet welcoming and sacred.

Pastor Lewis closed the door behind them and offered Ethan a chair while turning the other chair to face Ethan and settling into it. The pastor gazed at him for a moment before bowing his head. "Our God and Father, only You can know what is troubling Ethan this morning. I am only Your servant. If I can be of any comfort to this, Your child, then give me wisdom, Lord, and guidance to share it. In the name of Your only Son, Jesus Christ."

As the two waited quietly for God's guidance, Ethan realized the block in his path with God was Mandy. Before he could plan what to say or lose heart, he told Pastor Lewis the whole story, from beginning to end, leaving nothing out. All the while the good pastor looked at him with such love that Ethan finally understood that God had truly and completely forgiven him and so had Pastor Lewis. Peace filled his very being as though liquid were being absorbed into every tissue of his body. And with it came tears. . .slowly at first. . .then a torrent of them.

With the tears came cleansing and Ethan knew without a doubt that God would show him what to do and how to do it. It was such a tremendous relief to have his secret shared by this godly man and to know there was no lessening in the love and respect between them. Pastor Lewis encouraged Ethan to pray for God's guidance and promised to do the same on Ethan's behalf. He seemed to have no doubt that God would show Ethan what he should do, but encouraged him to be patient and not take the situation into his own hands.

Ethan felt as though a huge load was lifted from his shoulders. He was amazed how much lighter the load became when someone helped carry the weight. And so Ethan prayed consistently for God to show him the way.

Chapter 22

The early mornings had become a time of prayer and reading the scriptures for Ethan. As the sun rose early with the longer days of spring, Ethan found he had more time to read his Bible and pray.

One morning he was reading about a young man who wanted his inheritance early in life but took it and squandered it on wild living. After some time the young man realized he had nothing left and no way to earn a living. He was living in a barn eating the slop that was fed to the hogs when he thought of home and his kind father. He decided he had nothing to lose to go home and beg his father to let him be one of his slaves. At least he would have a warm bed and food to eat. But when his father saw him coming, he ran to meet him with open arms and welcomed him home as a son.

Suddenly it was clear to Ethan. He would go home to Mandy, tell her the whole truth, and hide nothing. Ethan knew he no longer deserved to be a husband to Mandy, and he would understand if she could not accept him at all. He would offer to stay to care for Mandy and the farm and make himself a room in the barn. At least if she would speak to him, he would be able to tell her about Jesus. He prayed for God's guidance and leading as to when he should go and then washed and went downstairs.

The day seemed charged with expectation. Even the air was still, as though it, too, was waiting. *Why does today feel so very different?* Ethan thought. *It's as though everything is changed, yet nothing appears changed.* He watched the Taylors to see if they noticed the change, but they acted as though everything was the same as before. People who came into the store talked of the weather, their children, their gardens, even things of the church, as though this were any ordinary day. Yet Ethan could feel the difference.

Throughout the day Ethan found himself glancing quickly over his shoulder. He wasn't sure what he was expecting. It was difficult to keep his mind on his work; restlessness stirred in the very deepest part of his being. He had felt restless before, but this was almost uncontrollable.

After several days, Ethan felt he must talk to someone. After dinner one night, he went for a walk. He headed out of town, finding himself on the riverbank where he used to sit to think when the railroad crew became too boisterous for his tastes.

He wanted to pray but didn't know quite what to pray. As he sat by the water in an attitude of prayer, even though no words formed, he knew he was praying and that God was hearing. Soon he heard a crunch and looked up to find Pastor Lewis standing nearby.

"I felt the Lord leading me, but I didn't know where or why," the pastor said with a gentle smile. "I hope I am not intruding."

"Not at all." Ethan smiled up at the man. "Please sit with me for a while."

Soon Ethan found himself trying to explain what he could not understand himself: the restless drawing and the scripture of the prodigal son that he had read earlier in the week and how he felt he should go back to Mandy. But something felt unfinished here.

Pastor Lewis was quiet for a while; Ethan knew he was praying for wisdom and guidance. Then he spoke. "Ethan, I believe God is telling you the time is here. It is time for you to return to Mandy. And I believe the unfinished part is that you need to tell your church family here first. You have lived a lie among them, and you will not feel free until you allow them to forgive you. It will not be easy, son. But we will be praying for you and God will guide you. I encourage you to be obedient."

In that quiet moment, Ethan knew it was right. He was at the same time overjoyed with the thought of seeing Mandy but full of dread and fear at having to expose his wickedness to her and to these dear friends. He nodded silently.

After praying together, the two men rose and walked with reverence back to their homes. They agreed that Ethan would tell his church family the next Sunday morning during the worship service and then be on his way home on Monday morning.

∞

Sunday morning dawned bright and still, as if the world were hushed and waiting. Perhaps it held its breath in anticipation of the confession that was on Ethan's heart. Pastor Lewis had said he would let Ethan know when the time was right to speak in the service. Ethan equally dreaded and looked forward to his time of confession. It was certainly not normal to expose oneself in their church, yet he longed for the cleansing sense of having his hidden life exposed and not needing to pretend any longer. Ethan knew it would free his spirit to be honest with these dear people. He prayed with all his heart that they would extend forgiveness and not withhold their love from him. But whatever the result, he knew in his heart it was the right path to take. He thanked God once again for the wisdom, understanding, and forgiveness he had received already from Pastor Lewis.

The service started as usual with singing and praising, praying and sharing. And

Ethan waited. Then Pastor Lewis began his message.

"We all know the story of the Prodigal Son. But I would like us to turn in our Bibles today to Luke 15 and start at verse 11. Please follow along as I read the story to you." After reading through verse 32, Pastor Lewis said, "Whenever I have studied this chapter before, I tended to focus on the foolish choice of the young son who ran away from home and squandered his inheritance. Today I want us to think about God's calling the son back home. Yes, the son was foolhardy and unwise. He had gained nothing and lost everything. How many times do we judge this young man, yet we don't look at the part of the story where he admitted his error, picked himself up, and did something about it. He did not blame anyone else but took responsibility for his actions himself. He humbled himself and took a chance that his father might forgive him.

"Now turn to the story of the servants who were forgiven in Matthew 18. We will begin reading at verse 21." And he read to the congregation the story of the servant who was unwilling to forgive the debt owed to him. "How many times," asked the pastor, "must we be forgiven before we are willing to forgive others? In John 8 we read of the woman caught in adultery, and her accusers who wanted Jesus to allow them to stone her because it was the law. What did Jesus say to them? 'He that is without sin among you, let him first cast a stone at her.'

"Today someone among us has a confession to share. I plead that you will hear this confession only in light of your own sins and shortcomings. Let's allow God alone, who sees the heart of man, to be the judge. Ethan, will you come now and share your story?"

Ethan had never experienced the dread that was in his heart now. It was almost a tangible thing rooting him to his seat. But he stood and moved slowly to the front of the church. When he lifted his head to look at the congregation, he saw only love and acceptance among these people. And so he told his story. He told of the restlessness that had been with him since childhood. He told of his precious wife and home he had built, yet the restless spirit still resided in his heart. He spoke of his search for something to quench that restlessness—the money he could gain working on the new railroad. And how, after being away from home for a long period of time and with continual coaxing from his coworkers, he had eventually visited the brothel and betrayed his wife.

Still the searching was not quenched. The emptiness was not filled. The restlessness continued until he was drawn to this little church and found forgiveness and his own relationship and acceptance with his Father in heaven. He explained that now he felt an urgency to share his newfound faith with his dear wife. Fear of rejection had led him to live a lie and keep his secrets among the church folk, but now he felt an urgency to be honest and truthful with those who had accepted, encouraged, and strengthened him in his faith before he left them. He humbly asked their forgiveness and then sat down again.

The church was silent for a few minutes.

Then Pastor Lewis stood. "To close this morning's service I will read to you from Luke 6 starting with verse 37: 'Judge not, and ye shall not be judged: condemn not, and ye shall not be condemned: forgive, and ye shall be forgiven: Give, and it shall be given unto you; good measure, pressed down, and shaken together, and running over, shall men give into your bosom. For with the same measure that ye mete withal it shall be measured to you again. And he spake a parable unto them, Can the blind lead the blind? Shall they not both fall into the ditch? The disciple is not above his master: but every one that is perfect shall be as his master. And why beholdest thou the mote that is in thy brother's eye, but perceivest not the beam that is in thine own eye?'

"Friends, I want to remind us all that there is not one among us today who is without sin. Will you rejoice together with Ethan that he has cared enough for you to ask your forgiveness? Let us not only forgive, strengthen, and encourage Ethan, but let us search our own hearts and confess before God any hidden sin that is there. It is not always necessary to confess it all verbally to one another, but to be open and honest with God and willing to be obedient to Him."

When the service ended, Ethan tried to slip out the side door. But he was immediately surrounded by the loving arms of many of the church family. They reassured him of their love and acceptance, and welcomed him back if he ever wanted to bring Mandy to the community. And most importantly, he was reassured that their prayers would be with him as he went home to Mandy.

Ethan was thankful in his heart for the strengthening he received from these brothers and sisters. But what lay ahead for him was still daunting. God alone could see him through this.

Chapter 23

That evening Ethan had a warm, comfortable time with the Taylors, thanking them for their kindness to him and visiting with them. Both were sad to see Ethan leave and assured him of their prayers for him. They were also quick to welcome him back, should he ever decide to return to the territory. They assured him that as far as it was possible with them, he would always have a job at the store. He asked Rebecca if he could purchase a loaf of bread and some cheese and apples to take with him on his journey.

"Don't worry. I'll have food ready for your journey, and you will not pay for it," Rebecca stated firmly. "It will be a small gift from us to help you on your way."

Before going to bed, Ethan packed his belongings and his beloved Bible so he'd be ready for a swift departure the next morning. He prayed for God's blessing on his journey, as well as on his mission. Something deep inside knew that other church people were also praying for him. Laying his head on his pillow, he slept peacefully.

Ethan awakened as dawn was lightening the sky. As he dressed, he could hear Rebecca in the kitchen below and smell the tantalizing aromas wafting up the stairs.

"I don't want to weigh you down with food, so I have some breakfast prepared that you can eat quickly before you set out." Rebecca smiled and nodded toward the table. He saw a place set for him, and from the steam wafting upwards, could tell the coffee had just been poured and the biscuits had not been out of the oven for long. When his stomach rumbled, they both laughed.

"Guess I can't pass up an opportunity like this!" Ethan pulled out the chair as Jason joined him at the table. While the men ate the biscuits and gravy and drank the hot coffee, Rebecca finished tying up a parcel for him to carry on his journey. And just as he lifted it all to his shoulders, they heard a knock at the front door of the store.

Walking through the store, they could see Pastor Lewis waiting on the front steps.

"I won't keep you, but I wanted to send you off with a blessing and a prayer," he said as he wrapped Ethan in a fatherly hug. Together they all prayed and then sent Ethan on his way with tears and warm handshakes.

As Ethan traveled, he both dreaded and eagerly anticipated the reunion ahead. But because the knots in his stomach were less bearable when he thought about Mandy, he decided to think only about the good things God had brought into his life in the past winter. He shivered. Even though spring was here, today's cold wind let him know that winter had not yet completely given up its grip. He walked as rapidly as he could. He was thankful for the warm new coat and gloves he had purchased last fall. Now and again he encountered rain as he traveled; the cold, gray, and damp filled him with dread. He was thankful it didn't rain the whole day, but neither did the sun ever really shine.

That evening, as Ethan sat by a fire and leaned on a large log eating some of the food Rebecca had packed for him, he could no longer stop himself from thinking of Mandy. It had been just over a year since he had left her home alone. Was she still there in the cabin? Had she made it through the winter alone? It broke his heart to think that she might have been cold or hungry, but he expected that she'd have found a way to stay in the cabin alone, instead of going back East where she was not welcomed and had no place of her own. She was a strong, hard-working woman, but also wonderfully feminine through and through.

He remembered her mouth when she smiled and how she also smiled with her eyes when she looked at him. Mandy was just shy enough that she smiled with her mouth only with most people, but when she smiled at him, her eyes smiled too, and she seemed to sparkle all over. He remembered what it was like to kiss her and thought of her lips and how one of her eyeteeth crossed over the tooth beside it ever so slightly. It gave Mandy's smile so much charm. He loved the little dimple in one cheek only that was not too far from the corner of her mouth. He could close his eyes and see her smile and the way she tipped her head slightly to the side when she teased him. His heart seemed to swell as he thought of her, and he found himself begging God to let her forgive him. He knew he did not deserve her forgiveness, but he prayed for it all the same. He knew for a fact that God was a merciful God and the giver of all good gifts.

Chapter 24

The spring days were growing longer as well as warmer. Mandy and Deidre kept busy with the new animals that had been born to them, as well as planting their gardens and keeping track of Daniel, who wanted to crawl and explore everywhere. He and Jedediah were very good friends already. Mandy was thankful for the way Jedediah helped watch over the baby even though he was not much more than a baby himself.

As Jedediah learned more words and linked the words into sentences, Mandy smiled as she heard Deidre teach him to structure his sentences correctly. She was proud of Deidre's sharp mind and the way she had learned so quickly, no longer speaking the language of a slave but of a free, intelligent woman. Now both women planned to teach their sons together to give them access to any book they could get their hands on and thus all the knowledge they could grasp. But most of all, they read and discussed and put into practice the words of Deidre's little worn New Testament.

Mandy lay in her bed watching the sun rise one morning. Since it rose earlier each day now, she was still awakening right before dawn many days. Today she lay on the edge of sleep—not quite controlling her wandering thoughts—and found herself dreaming about how pleasant it would have been if she and Ethan could have raised Daniel together. With that thought, she was suddenly wide awake. She looked over at Daniel in the cradle as he sucked his fist and made his early morning noises, and was amazed all over again at the strong resemblance to Ethan in his tiny features.

Sighing and reaching for the baby, Mandy felt an unusual heaviness about the prospect of raising her son alone. She was more thankful for Deidre and Jedediah than words could tell, but she longed for the companionship and intimacy of her husband. She missed being loved the way only a husband could love. A new frustration and almost anger rose in her at Ethan for leaving them. But before the mood could get a good hold on her, Mandy made herself stop and pray. It was certainly going to be a discipline to be kind and joyful today, but with God's help, she would do it.

Just as she finished nursing Daniel and put him back into his crib to play while she made breakfast, she heard Deidre putting wood on the fire. Buttoning her dress, she went out to start the day. Before she could say much more than "Good morning,"

Deidre said, "Doesn't today feel different some way? I can't explain why, but it just feels like an expectant day."

"An expectant day?"

"Yes, like the day is expectin' somethin' new. Or somethin' different. Somethin' good, I think. What do you suppose it would be?"

"I don't know, Deidre. But I think you're right. I find myself needing to look for something good in today, so let's name all our blessings throughout the day and watch to see all the ways God blesses us, okay?"

"Sunshine!"

"What?"

"I named the first thing. Sunshine. He has blessed us with sunshine today."

"Oh, okay. Friends."

"Little boys."

"Food."

"Strong bodies. Health. And freedom."

Mandy smiled at Deidre. "I'm glad you can thank God for health and freedom and sunshine and not worry about where your dear Jeremiah is and if you will ever see your husband again."

"Mandy, I have to leave him in God's care. Somethin' in my heart feels strongly that I'll see him again. I don't know where. I don't know when. I just know that I believe God is takin' care of him and will bring us back together someday. God knows where Jeremiah is, and God knows where I am. I believe that from way up there in heaven, God sees a clear path between us. He will bring us together in His own good time. And until He does, I am thankful He has led me to you. And I am thankful for this home for Jedediah. I know God will bless you for the way you have shared with us."

"Oh, Deidre, you have been my lifesaver. Don't ever think I have given to you. It doesn't begin to compare with what you have given to me. We'll just continue in the way that is before us and thank God for providing for us both. And we'll continue to pray for Jeremiah." But Mandy's stomach wrenched again as she thought of the possibility of Jeremiah coming and taking Deidre away from her. In her heart she silently prayed, *Oh, Lord God, please take care of me and my son.* She couldn't help adding, *And please don't let me be left alone again.*

∞

During breakfast, the two women agreed to share all the chores that day instead of dividing them up as was their usual habit. So they finished the dishes together, then took the boys with them to the barn. After the barn chores were completed, they decided to hoe and weed a bit in their gardens before the sun became too warm, so the four went down to the gardens together. Jedediah's most difficult chore was helping baby Daniel stay on the grass and not eat the dirt.

Mandy had brought the little tomato and green pepper plants that they had started in the house earlier in the spring. The women decided to plant them now. They were excited about all the fresh vegetables and could imagine the sweet, yet acid taste of a tomato still warm and just picked from the vine. Mandy loved to rub the hairy little vines with her thumb and forefinger and sniff the tomato smell on her fingers. Watching her do this always made Deidre giggle, even though she said she enjoyed the smell herself.

Now and again, Mandy still sighed. She couldn't help it. But she wouldn't let herself think of Ethan today. It wouldn't work. She just would not let herself. . . .

As Ethan drew nearer and the woods looked familiar, he slowed instead of hurrying. Yes, he could hardly wait to see Mandy again, but he was incredibly tremulous about seeing her for the first time after more than a year and after his horrid deception and lies. How would she react? How should he present himself? Should he have sent someone else in his place first?

Finding a fallen tree, he sat on the log to think and to pray. His stomach was tied in knots, and tension stiffened his shoulders and neck. He prayed over and over, "God, please give me wisdom to know what to say, and soften Mandy's heart toward me and toward You." Tears ran in rivulets down his cheeks as he pounded on heaven's doors.

As the morning turned into early afternoon, Ethan knew he must not tarry. He was out of food today and was feeling hungry and weak. While he sat on the log praying and listening for God's voice, he realized he was hearing a brook. Being thirsty and also knowing he had not been able to wash for a few days, he followed the sound and found a small stream flowing merrily with the spillover from the spring rains. It splashed and danced its way over rocks and fallen logs and was so clear he could see the tadpoles darting this way and that. When he dipped his hands in, the water was cold and clear. He drank thirstily and felt refreshed. He splashed the water on his face and neck, and then, looking around to be certain there was no one in the woods, took off his clothes and waded into the icy water to wash himself completely.

When he was finished washing and lay back in the water a bit before getting out, he noticed the bright sunshine glinting on the water. Then he saw it: a beautiful rainbow shimmering in the sunshine on a small waterfall right above the pool where he was bathing. A rainbow had been God's promise to Noah of a new beginning—a new life in a fresh new world. Was God promising him a new beginning also? Did forgiveness await him?

With faith that God would be with him in this, his new beginning, Ethan climbed out of the stream and shook as much of the water off of himself as he could. He took clean clothes out of his pack to replace the ones he'd been wearing on his journey. He was thankful that when it rained, he had been able to find some shelter by huge rocks or trees and that his pack had stayed somewhat dry. His clean clothes still smelled of the strong lye soap with which Rebecca had last washed them and the spring sunshine from her clothesline. Again he was reminded of and thankful for the many ways in which God had provided for him and directed him. Oh, how he prayed that God had also been watching over and protecting and guiding Mandy. He prayed with all his heart that she would still be in their cabin. . .that she would not have left.

⌒∞⌒

The boys began to get tired and hungry before the garden work was quite completed.

Deidre straightened her back and squinted at the sky. "Mandy, look at that sun. It's past noon already. No wonder the little ones are fussy. Why don't you take the boys back to the house, give them lunch, and put them down for a nap? I'll finish this in an hour or so and then come on up. I ate such a nice breakfast this mornin' that I hardly feel hungry yet, but your little one is goin' to want what only you can give him."

"I think you're right, Deidre. When they're asleep, I'll bring food and water to you and help you finish."

Mandy finished the row she had been working on before gathering up the young ones. Jedediah was eager and danced and pranced at her feet. Chuckling, she picked up Daniel, placed him on her hip, and reached for Jedediah's hand as they started back up to the cabin. Daniel sucked on his muddy fist and tugged hungrily at her shirt. "Won't be long now, wee one. Be patient," Mandy crooned to him as they walked.

While Jedediah drank his milk and ate his bread, jelly, and cookies, Mandy nursed Daniel, who was as sleepy as he was hungry. With talking and bouncing him, she was able to keep him awake long enough for him to finish his lunch, and then she took him into her bedroom to lay him in the crib. When she returned to the main room, she smiled when she saw Jedediah's head drooping as he tried to sit tall and finish his last cookie. She gently removed the remains of the cookie from his chubby black fist and washed each finger carefully, then washed his face and other hand. Picking him up, she carried him into Deidre's room and laid him on his big boy bed. Covering him lovingly with a quilt, Mandy knelt beside the bed to kiss his pudgy little cheek.

What a precious child he is. I will not stop praying for you to find your daddy, little one, Mandy pledged softly.

Just as Mandy was getting back to her feet, she heard a noise near the front of the cabin. She didn't really expect Deidre to be finished so soon, so she left the bedroom expectantly. Was it Ned or Edna or one of their boys? Or was Deidre coming back to the house for something?

When Mandy first entered the main room, she looked toward the back to see if Deidre was coming but then heard a knock on the front door of the cabin instead. Excited about an unexpected visit from their friends, Mandy quickly opened the front door to greet them.

She stopped dead in her tracks at what she saw.

There, standing in front of her, was Ethan! He was alive, and tears streamed down his face.

Chapter 25

M andy couldn't think. She was speechless. Her eyes widened, and one hand covered her open mouth. Finally, she said quietly, "Ethan?" That was all for a moment, and when his head dropped and the tears continued to flow, she said again, "Ethan, is that you? Is it really you?"

"Yes, Mandy. It's me." He paused to draw a shaky breath. Lips trembling, he said, "I lied to you, and I don't deserve your forgiveness. But may I talk with you?"

For what seemed like an hour to Ethan but was really only seconds, Mandy stood still and just looked at him. Then she pulled herself together and, pushing the door open, fell into his arms. "Ethan! Where have you been? What's happened? I was told you were dead. Oh, Ethan, come in, come in. Tell me everything. I can hardly believe it's you!"

Ethan stood still with his arms clasped around his Mandy. While joy bubbled out of her now, he knew in his heart she might not so readily welcome him when she heard that it was not a misunderstanding but a deliberate lie. And when she heard about his life while he was away, what then? While he held her, he shuddered with fear and dread. She must not have heard what he'd said to her. . .that he'd lied.

Suddenly, Mandy straightened and, taking his face in her hands, kissed him. Her hands slid behind his head, pulling him ever closer, and the kiss lingered.

But Ethan felt so unworthy of her kisses that he finally gently moved her away from him. "Mandy, I haven't eaten since yesterday morning. Could I have something to eat? And then we will talk, and I will tell you everything."

"Oh, how foolish of me. Come—I will make you a sandwich of boiled eggs and ham and fresh bread. I have coffee ready for my own lunch, and we will eat together."

After Mandy tugged him inside, she bustled about, bringing food to the table. Ethan lingered in the doorway, scanning the cabin. Oh, it was good to be home, yet he couldn't really allow himself to feel at home here. He didn't deserve to be forgiven and accepted back, and he was unsure how Mandy would react when she heard the whole story.

"Come, Ethan," she urged, "sit down. I have so much to tell you, and I can't wait to hear of all your experiences. Oh, what a joyous day this is!" When she finished pouring the coffee and placing it back on the stove, Mandy laid the dish towel on the cupboard and sat at the table.

Ethan slowly walked over and sat at the place he had always sat when the two of them lived here together.

Mandy was used to thanking God before she ate, but now she hesitated. Deciding quickly that she wanted to tell the whole story in order, she omitted the prayer so as not to cause questions before their time.

"Mandy, I will tell you everything in a few minutes, but I must have food first," he said between bites and gulps.

Mandy just smiled and ate quietly. She could wait forever since he was home. She didn't have much appetite, but she took several bites. Mostly she just feasted her eyes on this wonderful man who had come back into her life. In her heart she kept saying over and over, *Thank You, thank You, thank You, God!*

Finally, Ethan leaned back in his chair. He looked tenderly at Mandy before dropping his gaze. Then, reaching over to the table again, he picked up his coffee cup and drained it. When Mandy jumped up to refill it, she could feel him watching her with a sad expression.

An indefinable dread crept over her. *He's home, so why is he still so sad? Why does he look at me like that and then drop his head? Is he going away again?* Mandy waited with a heavy heart for Ethan to begin.

Finally he said, "Mandy, I want to start my story with how very much I love you. That has never changed, except to grow stronger and stronger. When I am finished with my story, you may not believe me or you may not care, but I want you to know that at the beginning."

"Oh, Ethan, I do love you. I cannot imagine anything you can tell me that will change that fact. But I will be silent and listen while you tell me the whole story. And then I will share mine with you." Her eyes twinkled, and the tiny dimple played merrily in her cheek.

So Ethan began. Slowly at first he told of how he had always felt that something was missing from his life. He always seemed to be searching. When he was young, he thought growing up would take care of that, but it only showed him how little he knew. Then he thought being successful in his job would make him feel fulfilled, but he could never be quite successful enough. When he met Mandy, he figured being married and having a family would complete his search, but it only served to make him feel more of a failure, because he could not give Mandy all that he longed to give to her, and could not even produce children.

Mandy was careful not to smile when he talked of their barrenness. Her heart was putty in his hands, and she only loved him more and longed to tell him of their son. But she would let him have his say first.

Finally he told her he was convinced that if he could earn lots of money and be able to buy her anything she wanted, he would feel he had been a success. So he had gone to work on the railroad.

Then he was silent. He was silent for so long, staring at his hand moving his coffee cup in circles on the table, that Mandy wondered if he expected her to comment.

But she didn't. She sat, waiting. Patiently waiting. Even when she noticed tears splashing on his lap, she sat quietly, knowing he was struggling with some battle he must master on his own.

Ethan looked up at her. "Mandy, I went to the tavern to play cards, but I ended up with a prostitute. More than once. I was so ashamed I made up the lie about being killed and paid a guy to come tell you that story and bring you some money. I thought it would clear my conscience and I would move on, but it didn't. It did serve to show me what a fool I am. And that I needed help.

"Finally I prayed. I prayed that if there was a God out there, that He would find me and show me the way to straighten out my wretched life. And do you know what?" The tears stopped flowing now. Ethan reached into his pocket for his handkerchief. He blew his nose and mopped his wet face. And then he told Mandy of how God found him and drew him with the singing one night as he stood on the balcony of the saloon. He told her of going to the little church, and of praying and asking God's forgiveness.

He told her of the way the church people had accepted him and loved him. About Pastor Lewis and Marita, his sweet wife, about the Taylors, and even about Bess accepting Christ into her heart.

"Mandy, I do not deserve your forgiveness. I love you with all my heart, and I want more than anything in the world to be a husband to you. But if you find you cannot forgive me and accept me back as your husband, will you allow me to make a room for myself in the barn and stay and be your friend and companion? I will work here, and we can live together on this land, but separately. I will still take care of you until the day I die, if you will just allow it."

⨯

Ethan's eyes searched Mandy's face, but he could not read what he found there. What was she thinking? How did she feel? Could there ever be forgiveness in her heart?

Chapter 26

The house was very quiet as Mandy looked from his face down to her hands. A gentle breeze stirred the curtains at the open window by the table. Ethan could smell the fresh earth on the breeze and felt himself longing to help care for this place that he had built with his own hands. He glanced back at Mandy in time to see her raise her head.

Slowly at first, Mandy began to speak. "Ethan, before I respond to your question, let me tell you of my life while you were away. Will you sit and listen to it all? Will you let me tell you the whole story before I give you an answer?"

"Yes, Mandy, I want to hear it all. I will be patient and listen to all you have to say. And Mandy, thank you. Thank you for hearing me, and thank you for talking with me. I truly thank you with my whole heart." He sat back in his chair with his long legs stretched out straight in front of him and his arms folded gently across his chest.

⚬⚬⚬

"First of all, Ethan, when you left, I had been carrying your child for a couple of months."

His eyes grew wide and startled but, true to his word, he didn't interrupt or even move.

"Being my first time," she explained, "I wanted to be certain before I told you. I also didn't want you to think I was using the baby to hold on to you or to tie you down, so I said nothing. Perhaps I was wrong, but it felt like the right thing to do."

Ethan nodded his understanding ever so slightly but still searched her face with his eyes. So Mandy proceeded to tell her story. At one point she heard a noise at the back of the house, but she kept on talking.

She told about her loneliness and about Deidre and Jedediah coming. She told how they had become a family and worked together and played together. She told about teaching Deidre to read and about the worn New Testament. She explained to him about discovering her need for God's forgiveness, about her prayer, and about reading the New Testament and learning more and more about God.

Now a new tenderness and the light of hope shimmered in his eyes.

Mandy also told Ethan about finding the Brownings and about the way the two families would get together and how Ned and Edna had helped her and Deidre out. She told Ethan she had promised Deidre that they would build her a cabin of her own on their land when and if Ethan ever came home.

She told of selling her soaps, of the new livestock born on the farm, but mostly she told about Daniel. Before she was finished, she could hear Daniel cooing and jabbering in the crib in her bedroom. Ethan's head swiveled in that direction, but then turned back to look at her once more.

As she waited for his reaction to her story, she held her breath.

"Mandy," he murmured, "I am so very sorry I have not been here for you. Can you ever find it in your heart to forgive me and allow me to be your husband and Daniel's father?"

As moisture misted her eyes, then transformed into tears that washed down her cheeks, Mandy said, "Oh, Ethan, you have never ceased being my husband. Do you think for one minute that I would not forgive your sins when I have sinned much in my lifetime also? We all have different sins, but we all sin. And God has forgiven all our sins. So we both come back together clean and fresh and new. All I want is for us to be a family. I want Daniel to know his wonderful daddy. I want us to work together. And I want to not have to clean that barn for a long, long time!"

As one they laughed, then stood simultaneously and held each other briefly. They were headed to the bedroom for Ethan to meet Daniel when the sleepy Jedediah peered shyly into the room. His eyes turned wide and frightened as he looked from Mandy to Ethan.

"Jedediah, come here quickly," Mandy said, smiling and extending her arms to the little boy. "You must meet Daniel's daddy. His daddy has been gone for a long time, but he has come home. He can't wait to meet you, too."

Ethan stooped so his tall frame would be closer to Jedediah's height. "Are you the man of this house, son?" he asked as he reached his hand gently toward Jedediah.

Jedediah hesitated, looking questioningly at Mandy's radiant face. He was a smart boy, so Mandy knew it wouldn't take him long to figure that anyone who could make his Mandy smile like that must be good. He walked over and shyly stuck out his hand.

"Hello, sir. I am pleased to meet you," Jedediah said quietly but firmly.

Ethan beamed. "And I am pleased to make your acquaintance also. I have heard about how you take such good care of my son. Would you like to introduce us?"

Jedediah glanced at Mandy. At her smile and quick nod, he looked back at Ethan. "Come right this way, sir." He started toward Mandy's bedroom doorway.

Ethan and Jedediah were headed for the bedroom when Mandy turned her head and saw Deidre duck back from the doorway. She knew Deidre would be nervous about this stranger and what would happen to her and Jedediah. She caught Deidre's eye and gave a quick nod to let her know all was well. And then she followed the "men" into the bedroom.

The mist in Ethan's eyes as he beheld his son for the first time and the way he reached for him with trembling arms was more than worth the long wait.

After the tears on Ethan's part as he held his son had passed, the little family returned to the main room of the house. Mandy went to the back door and saw Deidre sitting on the step with her arms wrapped around her middle, rocking back and forth in a rapid, nervous movement. Mandy slipped out and sat on the step beside her.

"Deidre, did you hear? Ethan is home. He is not dead. It was a mistake. He is home to stay. He will build you a house of your own, and we can all live here in the same clearing and raise our children together. And maybe someday Jeremiah will join us, and we can all be one family. Oh, Deidre, isn't it wonderful? You must come in and meet him. You can't help but love him!"

But Deidre kept rocking. Mandy saw her jaw clenching and grinding; her nails were white from gripping her arms so hard.

Mandy stayed beside her friend and waited patiently. Finally she murmured, "You know, Deidre, that I would never be able to love a man who was not gentleman enough to love my friends. Listen to him talking to Jedediah in the house. Do you think Jedediah is not wise enough to know someone who is not truly kind and gentle?" She paused, then added, "And contrary to what I know you are thinking, Ethan does not care anymore than I do that your skin is dark. To him you are a heroine. He knows I would never have made it through this past year without you. He knows, and he is grateful. Trust me."

Silently they sat together for a few more minutes. At last the rocking slowed. Deidre turned her head to look at Mandy. Mandy smiled and nodded, then rose eagerly and reached for Deidre's hands. Together they entered the cabin arm in arm.

Jedediah ran and threw himself at her legs. "Momma, momma! Come meet Mr. Ethan. Daniel has a daddy, and he is good. Come, Momma!" His little legs stretched behind him as he tugged at her skirt.

Ethan stood with Daniel in his arms and walked to where the two women stood. "I believe I owe you a huge debt, ma'am. I will never be able to thank you enough for all you have done for my family in my absence. I hope you will always be part of our family if you wish to do so. From the looks of things, I think our boys believe they are brothers. And brothers they shall be. Will you please accept my heartfelt gratitude and continue to stay with us?"

Deidre's eyes were huge. Her gaze flickered from Ethan to Mandy and back again. "You're thankin' *me?* Sir, I'll be glad to serve you and your family. I am honored. Thank you, sir!"

"Serve us?" Ethan and Mandy said in unison. "What kind of nonsense is this, Deidre?" Mandy continued. "We are friends, and we work together. You know that. What's this all about?" Mandy wasn't certain if Deidre was joking or had lost her mind.

Ethan quickly reassured them both. "Look, nothing has changed in your role in this household, Deidre, just because I have come. If you live here, you can help with the work just as we will. We all work side by side and play side by side. We all serve one another—out of love, not out of obligation. And we do want you to live here. Even with a husband, a woman needs a friend." Ethan looked briefly at Mandy with a tender smile, then back at Deidre. "And I think we would all find out quickly how much Daniel and Jedediah need one another if we should try to separate them. So again I ask you, will you stay?"

Deidre's eyes swam with tears. "I will find joy in stayin'. And I thank you, sir."

"Ethan! You must call me Ethan, and I will call you Deidre. We are brother and sister, and we must be finished with this 'sir' nonsense. Is that all right with you?"

Deidre didn't say a word, but her beaming face spoke volumes.

⌘

The sun was beginning to lighten the eastern horizon. Mandy lay still, but she was very aware of the warmth and strength surrounding her. Slowly she inhaled the scent of this man who held her close to his heart. She smiled as she remembered his tenderness in the night.

As she listened quietly, she heard the little baby breaths coming from the cradle across the room. She could tell from the sucking sounds that Daniel would awaken soon and find his thumb was not enough. Yet she lay still. Her son would grow to be a man like his father—tall, strong, and handsome. But he would have an advantage that neither she nor Ethan had had. He would hear of his heavenly Father also. He would learn to know and love Him. And he would have parents who loved each other and loved him. Her heart swelled with the joy of it all.

Mandy heard a cheery chirping and turned her head slightly to see the bluebird sitting on the windowsill. He was pecking the log, searching for bugs to feed his own babies. Babies. . .mmm. . .who knew? Maybe in time they would have more. Her mind drifted in future possibilities, but her smile remained as she watched the bird busily pecking.

Ethan's hand gently cradled her cheek and turned her face to his. As she gazed into his smiling eyes, he tenderly kissed her and pulled her gently to himself again.

Yes, Ethan was home. Finally home. It had been a long, long road for each of them, but he was home, and life was good. So very, very good.

ON THE WINGS OF GRACE

The Hand of God, Book Two

by Judi Ann Ehresman

Dedication

To my sisters:

Betty Lou Carter—
who served the best banana tea parties of anyone

Nancy Kay Morgan—
who believed in me when I doubted myself
and always challenges me to be the best I can be

Twyla Jane Burkey—
who loves and accepts me always

And to my mother:
Mildred Michael (Rawley) Nelson

I love you all!

Chapter 1

The hotel had always been home for Bess. It was all she knew. There were several women who cared for her, but she shared quarters with Clara more than the others. When Clara was helping some man to "relax," Bess would stay with another of the women who happened to be "indisposed" for the evening, whatever that meant.

Clara was soft and slightly plump and wasn't quite as loud and mouthy as the other women in their hotel. At least Bess was told this was a hotel. Men came and went, spent the night with the various women in the "hotel" who would "care" for them for the night. It wasn't until she was eight or ten years old that Bess began to wonder why there were never women or children who came with the men that stayed there. When she asked Clara about it, she was told this was a special hotel that only took care of men. So Bess assumed this was just the way things were done and didn't question further.

It was a huge old building with beautiful cherry woodwork, plush carpets, draperies of rich golds and reds, and heavy furniture that glistened and shone. There was a beautiful huge piano that a black man named Augustus played each night until it fairly danced. The women who worked in the hotel were beautiful and always smiled, giggled, danced, and visited with the men who came to the hotel. They would carry drinks to them and bring them food. They would dance with the men and flirt with them until they would coax one of the men upstairs to the hotel rooms with them.

Usually it didn't take much coaxing, but sometimes the girls had to be patient until the men had played their card games. Then Bess noticed that the men either had to go upstairs to be consoled or to celebrate their bounty. Either way, most of those men ended up in one of the women's rooms before the night was over.

Bess could hardly remember a time when she wasn't washing dishes and dipping food up for the ladies to take out to the men. Gertie, the old lady who was master of the kitchen, had no patience with Bess. Bess learned quite young to keep busy, not to make any messes, and not to chatter or ask questions. Gertie had no patience with questions at all. So Bess would drag her stool out from its storage corner as soon as Gertie started cooking in the afternoon and would keep the dishes washed and wiped for her until long into the night.

The kitchen was a large room at the back of the hotel, and it was here that Bess spent most of her days. The ceilings were high and dark. In the summer the kitchen became hot and suffocating; Gertie's face would become red, and she would stand at the back door fanning herself with her apron. These were the times Gertie would be the most cross, and Bess soon learned to ease Gertie's discomfort by offering to fan her and bringing her fresh cold water. These ministrations also helped Gertie to be more tolerant and less cross with Bess, to whom Gertie always referred as "the child" or just "Child."

Sometimes Bess would hear children playing outside. She would sneak out to watch them but was told by the women to never speak to the children and never, never to play with them. In response to her question, she was merely told that she was different. So she would watch them from the windows of the hotel, or occasionally she would sneak out to the big porch at the back of the building behind the kitchen. She could hide behind the stack of wood for the cookstove and listen and watch without being observed by the children.

Bess loved the smell of the outdoors in the spring and early summer—the rich odor of freshly turned sod and the sweet fragrance of grass and early flowers. The sun was warm on her face, and a gentle breeze caressed her hair. All these sensations seemed to draw Bess out of the hotel, but getting caught outdoors by one of the women or Sam, the owner of the hotel, was never a pleasant experience, so she stayed pretty close to the kitchen most of the time.

Bess remembered that another lady had worked at this hotel when Bess was very young. The lady would call Bess "Missy." She was always cross with her and often even slapped her, until Bess didn't care to be around her at all. Bess couldn't remember the lady's name, but she asked her once why she called her Missy and everyone else called her Bess. The lady simply said that, even though her name was Bess, that Bess had been the biggest mistake she'd ever made, so she called her Missy for her mistake.

It was years later, long after that lady moved away, when Clara explained who the lady actually was: Bess's mother. Bess had been given to Clara, since Clara loved her. But a certain sadness always followed Bess because her mother hadn't wanted her.

When she was small, she would wash dishes until she could not stand or keep her eyes open any longer. Then usually Gertie would snap at her to go lay down awhile. She would go rest on the thick blanket that was her special place on the floor behind the big cookstove. She always went to sleep there but would usually wake up in either Clara's room or one of the other ladies' rooms. Occasionally, she would wake in the night and still be on the floor behind the stove, alone in the dark kitchen. Those were the nights she hated. But when she learned that Gertie slept in the room at the far end of the kitchen, it comforted her to know that and helped some way, even though she was too frightened of Gertie to call out or go to her. But it felt safer to know that Gertie was there...that she wasn't totally alone.

Sam seemed to be in charge of the hotel, and Bess was frightened of him. She never was quite sure exactly why she was afraid, but down deep inside she knew she did not want to find out. He was well aware of her but never really spoke to her. If he saw her, he would yell at someone to take care of the child, and his yell was a terrible thing. It would paralyze Bess with fear until one of the women came to her rescue, and then the woman would scold Bess and remind her how fortunate she was that Sam allowed her to stay there, until Bess vowed to never be caught in Sam's presence again.

Once Bess overheard snatches of Sam yelling at Clara that she and the girls needed to keep the child out of places she didn't belong. He was yelling that it was high time the child be put to work to earn her keep. Bess thought of all the dishes she washed and floors she swept (with a broom bigger than she was) and the beds she made and wondered what Sam meant by "putting her to work." They continued to argue for some time, until Clara was able to calm him. Bess was always amazed at how calm Clara could be with Sam yelling at her, when any of the other girls would yell back and end up in tears from his threats.

For a few days after that, Bess noticed that Clara seemed extra quiet. She also noticed that Sam seemed to expect an answer of some kind from Clara. She even caught Gertie looking at Clara with questioning eyes, at which time Clara would nod toward Bess and shake her head at Gertie. Bess wondered some, but since she had always lived in this place with these women and some sense of mystery, she knew not to ask questions. Bess knew if it was something she needed to know, Clara would tell her in her own time.

A day or so later Bess overheard Dinah and Sue Ann, two ladies who lived at the hotel, talking at the table when she entered the kitchen. Sue Ann was saying, "Lord knows I was working and earning my keep long before I was her age."

Then Dinah noticed Bess's entrance and frowned slightly and shook her head at Sue Ann.

Sue Ann pouted and proclaimed loudly, "Well, I don't see why she is treated like the queen bee herself!"

Dinah jumped to her feet, knocking over the bench, rushed over to Bess, and invited her up to her room to see some new bangles someone had given her. When they were leaving the kitchen, Sue Ann was still fuming. Then again, Sue Ann was always fuming.

One day not long after that, Clara awakened Bess early and told her they were taking a picnic for a day and that Bess should dress comfortably and be ready to leave soon. Bess excitedly rolled out of bed, brushed her hair and washed, making her and Clara's beds, and straightening the room as she had been taught. She had never been on a picnic before and had never really had much opportunity to be outdoors and play in the grass and sunshine, so her excitement was almost more than she could contain.

She chattered and teased and flitted around. Clara had said she could wear what she wanted, but Bess was in a quandary as to what one would wear on a picnic. She asked Clara who would be going on this picnic, and when Clara said just the two of them, Bess decided to wear something that would allow her to play, in case that should be part of their day. Clara was just concerned that Bess keep quiet and not wake up everyone in the hotel.

When they were dressed, they went down the back stairway and entered the kitchen before even Gertie was there. Clara made sandwiches and packed some cheeses and fruit into a basket along with a jar of sweet tea, an old tablecloth, and two chipped mugs. Then she handed a rolled-up blanket to Bess as she picked up the basket and headed out the door, again motioning to Bess to be quiet.

It was a late spring day, and the sun was already drying the dew from the grasses that waved in the gentle breeze. Bess walked quietly beside Clara, somehow knowing that Clara did not want to be seen or acknowledged, should anyone notice them walking away from the town.

It was fun, really, walking quietly away from the town. The birds called to one another and flitted busily from tree to tree. Bess had never before noticed how many different kinds of birds there were. She breathed deeply of the fragrant earth. Something sweet wafted past on a gentle breeze, and as she looked at Clara to see if she dared ask, Clara smiled and said, "Honeysuckle."

"What?" Bess asked.

"It's honeysuckle that smells so sweet," Clara explained. "It's a wildflower, and perfumers use it to make some of the beautiful perfumes that women wear."

"Oh, Clara, I love the smell of honeysuckle. Can you show it to me?"

"Sure, honey. See that bush over there at the fence post? It's covered with small white flowers. Do you see that?"

"Yes! It's beautiful! More beautiful than lace! May I pick some and take it with us?"

"No."

Bess looked at Clara quickly to see if she was teasing. She noticed an unusual heaviness in the way Clara walked and in the way she didn't seem to smile like she usually did. Bess was afraid to question, so she walked on.

In a few minutes, Clara looked at Bess and said, as though the conversation was still in progress, "Because if you do, we'll be fighting off the honeybees all day long. The bees love the sweet nectar that is in the center of the honeysuckle flowers. And we must leave those blossoms for the bees. It's all right to pick some when we're taking it indoors away from the bees, but we don't want to take honeysuckle with us on a picnic."

They walked on in companionable silence. Town was now far enough behind them that Bess could no longer look back and see any of it, nor could she hear the town sounds. The world out here seemed so very hushed that it felt wrong to be disturbing the silence with footsteps.

Eventually Bess heard something. She listened carefully and tried to guess what it was. Then she knew. It was water. She could hear it running and splashing, and she could tell they were getting closer. She glanced up at Clara's face, but Clara appeared deep in thought.

The sun rose higher in the sky and felt warmer as they walked. Even the breeze became warmer. Bess felt like she had walked so far from the hotel that she was concerned they might forget their way back.

When Clara turned off of the worn path and entered a lightly wooded area, Bess was amazed at how much cooler it was among the trees. And it was also not as quiet. There was the rustling of leaves, small skittering noises, the calling of birds, and the chattering of squirrels. Now and again they would hear a twig snap, but altogether the noises seemed to make their own type of silence. Bess breathed in the aromas of crushed pine needles and moist earth. The splashing of water grew louder. Now Bess knew they were going toward that water, and she could hardly keep from dancing and questioning.

Eventually Bess could see the brook tumbling and splashing over rocks through the thinning trees. As they came closer, Clara's steps slowed until they stood by the brook. Looking into the water, Bess could see little creatures busily swimming and darting about between the rocks. She crouched on the edge of the bank to see better.

Clara stooped beside Bess. "Look," she said as she set the basket on the grass. She reached over and took the rolled blanket from Bess and laid it beside the basket. Then she reached into the stream. "Feel how cold and refreshing this water is. It feels wonderful to splash it on your face after a long, hot walk."

Bess watched and mimicked Clara's actions. She leaned over, reached into the water, but pulled her hand back immediately. "It's cold, Clara. Really cold."

"Yes, it will warm up later in the summer, but right now it's still cool. It sure feels good on a hot, tired face, though." Again Clara dipped her hands in the water and touched her cheeks and neck with her cold, wet hands.

It didn't take long before Bess was dipping her hands in and splashing in the water herself. Laughter bubbled up from deep inside her, and soon they were both laughing.

Looking around to be sure no one was in sight, Clara whispered conspiratorially, "Bess, take off your shoes and stockings."

Clara started taking off her own shoes and stockings, and Bess followed her lead. Then, lifting their skirts and petticoats above their knees, they sat on the edge of the stream and dangled their feet into the water. Oh, it was so cold, but it felt so good. Together they played in the water's edge. Bess found some smooth stones and made a small pile of the sparkling ones while Clara watched.

After a while, Clara showed Bess how to make a small round stone skip across the top of the water. It was like the stone was dancing its own kind of dance.

Bess tried a few times, but her stones would just go *plunk* into the water without a single hop. She began to get discouraged but noticed that each time hers went *plunk*, Clara would take another one and make it hop across the top of the water. But then, Clara didn't throw hers the way Bess did. She would thrust the stone toward the water sideways, keeping her pitch parallel to the top of the water. So Bess tried again and again until finally hers skipped across the top also. What fun it was!

When their arms tired of skipping the stones and their feet felt like ice, they donned their stockings and shoes and lay back on the soft green grass beside the brook. The clouds resembled huge puffs of cotton floating on a sea of blue. Clara asked Bess if she could find a lamb in the sky, so Bess studied the cloud formations until she saw it. Together they searched for other formations and laughed and giggled like two schoolgirls.

Eventually Bess said, "Clara, this is the most fun day I can ever remember. I don't want to go back, but will Gertie be angry if I'm not there to help her? I don't like it at all when Gertie is angry with me."

Clara turned her head toward Bess. "No," she said sadly, "Gertie has given us this day off to play. We don't have to be back until evening. But the sun is no longer high in the sky, and I'm hungry. Let's open our picnic and see what there is to fill our stomachs."

It should have sounded like an adventure, but it was sounding more like a sentence. Bess couldn't help but feel there was a dread of some kind in Clara's heart, but she knew better than to ask. Silently she spread the blanket on the grass as Clara opened the basket.

While they ate their picnic lunch, Clara told Bess that Sam thought she should begin to teach Bess how to care for the men who visited the hotel, too. Bess had watched the ladies dress in their fancy gowns and powder their faces and their bosoms and perfume themselves; she had played with the cosmetics and combs herself now and again when she was younger. So it was with enthusiasm and excitement that she received the news she was to learn the trade. But she wondered why Clara seemed sad and a little hesitant about it.

After they finished eating, they lay back on the blanket and, looking at the sky, Clara began to explain what Sam expected from the women and now from Bess in order to live at the hotel.

Bess left the hotel that morning a little girl with a spring in her step and a smile in her heart. She returned that evening with a simple understanding of a new reality.

And that was the day the whole world changed for Bess.

Chapter 2

Fifteen years later

It was the strangest evening Bess could remember since she had started working. She had never paid that much attention to one man before, but Ethan Evanston somehow had affected her differently than any other man. Well, maybe it was simply that no man had ever affected her at all before she met Ethan. Suddenly she realized she cared for him, and that frightened her.

She well knew and had been told often that men who used their services had no intention of caring for them in return. But what could she do about her heart? Week after week Ethan had come to visit her on the weekends. He told her how he loved to make things with his hands and of his frustration with his monotonous job at the railroad. She encouraged him to leave the railroad and open a carpenter's shop. He was the first man who actually talked to her. . .carried on a conversation.

But just when Bess felt there might be something between Ethan and her, he started acting differently. He was still gentle and caring but now restless, quiet, and distant. She recognized the characteristic guilt, but Ethan was still different than the others. And then there was the evening he seemed almost completely oblivious of her.

She watched Ethan all that evening until he had finally simply disappeared up the stairs and not returned. She ended up with no man at all that night. She was not up to serving a customer, so she tended to the tables but avoided direct conversations or contact. As she helped Sam clean up, she saw him looking at her strangely, but there was nothing to say so she remained quiet, helping him until his work was done. Afterward she crept up the back stairs and spent the night alone in her rooms.

Early the next morning, before she was quite awake, she dreamed she and Ethan were riding horseback somewhere and eventually he outdistanced her and disappeared. She had awakened in tears and felt there was some truth in the dream. She tried to make herself not care, but it just didn't work. She did care. She cared a lot.

For weeks she didn't see Ethan again. Summer melted into sultry fall, and fall brought in winter before she saw him one afternoon in the general store. She had been taught to never address a man in public, so she looked away, but as soon as she finished her errand and turned to leave, she heard her name and turned to look back.

Ethan was running toward her! When he caught up to her, he explained that things and circumstances had changed for him since he'd last seen her. He wondered if they could meet sometime away from the saloon so he could tell her about his new life.

Bess was totally mystified but too joyous to decline. So they met that next Sunday afternoon and walked out by the stream at the edge of town. Ethan told her all about his change of heart and the faith in God that he had found. He encouraged her to believe in God also and change her life, but he didn't realize how impossible it was to do that. So they had parted.

Several weeks later, Bess had indeed visited the church on a Sunday morning. She had been surprised by the welcome she had received, but she still was at a total loss to understand what was said and done in the service. Before the service was quite over, she slipped out so as not to embarrass herself or anyone else there. She had pondered the things she heard for some time, but finally accepted the fact that what the pastor had said was not for the likes of her. She'd tried to push his message and Ethan Evanston far from her mind.

It was early in the spring one day when Bess felt she must get out of the building. Usually she would have merely wandered a bit behind the hotel, but the snows were melting and the ground was soggy and muddy. So, since it was too early in the morning for many folks to be out, she went to the front of the hotel and decided to walk on the boardwalk that was built slightly raised above the mud and slop of the road.

Bess knew not to look around at folks, so she walked with her head tucked down, simply listening to the sounds, enjoying the warming breeze, and inhaling the smells associated with spring. They were not all pleasant smells, but being part and parcel of the melting and thawing, she took pleasure in them just the same.

She had not gone far when another woman came up beside her. The woman looked familiar, but Bess couldn't think where she had seen her before.

Without hesitation, the lady spoke to Bess. "Good morning! Isn't it absolutely heavenly this morning?"

"Morning," Bess mumbled, surprised. Women like this did not speak openly to a prostitute. It simply wasn't done. "It certainly puts the promise of spring in one's heart," Bess added tentatively.

The lady replied that her name was Rebecca Taylor and that she had shared a hymnal with Bess when Bess had visited the church in the fall. Rebecca wanted to invite her to return. Bess was amazed. Did this woman not understand who she was? Bess didn't quite know what to say, so she said only, "I didn't feel like I belonged there. Oh, everyone was nice enough, but I didn't feel like I fit. . ." She had faltered to a stop.

"None of us fits, until we decide to," Rebecca said.

"Thanks," Bess managed, "I guess there's so much I don't understand. So much I don't know."

Rebecca was swift to reply. "Oh! None of us understands it all. God reveals himself to us a little at a time." She had offered to accompany Bess to Pastor Lewis's home to have him explain some of it to Bess.

They walked on in silence for a while, but then Bess surprised herself. "I really do want answers," she admitted to Rebecca.

Rebecca's eyes had lit up, and she'd led Bess to the pastor's home, right around the corner. Pastor Lewis had clearly explained the whole truth of the waywardness of mankind, Christ's coming to earth and His death on the cross to pay for all of mankind's, and what she must do personally to accept His forgiveness. It sounded so very easy.

And that was the day Bess's whole life changed—for the second time! In light of all that Pastor Lewis explained, Bess did not want to go back to her old way of life. That very day they all prayed together, and Bess knew without a doubt she was a new creation. Her life would be completely different from here on out.

At their generous offer, Bess moved in with the good pastor and his wife that same day. To say that her life had changed was a total understatement. At first, Bess felt at a loss. She had no identity, no means to be independent, and wondered about a purpose for her life. Mrs. Lewis, who asked Bess to call her Marita, took Bess under her wing to teach her and spend time with her. Also, Rebecca Taylor came over often, and the three women visited and chatted together.

Chapter 3

At first, Bess was timid about attending the church services. Marita Lewis and Rebecca Taylor were careful to always sit on either side of her and then to introduce her to others within the church as soon as services were over. Before long, Bess felt accepted and known and loved within that small church. When she saw Ethan, he spoke to her, letting her know he was happy that she had found her answers to life in her faith in God. She knew he was genuinely happy for her, but she also realized he had no real feelings for her other than a casual friendship. For some reason, that was all right with her. She was totally content with her new life with God, since she was trying to read the Bible and understand its teachings and therefore didn't have time to devote to a relationship right now anyway.

Bess had always enjoyed spring with its promise of new life but never had it seemed so overwhelmingly wonderful as it did this year. When she would hang clothes on the clothesline for Marita, she couldn't help just standing in awe and breathing in deeply. The fragrances of new grass, honeysuckle, spring flowers, and fresh air made her heart want to burst with joy. How had she missed all this before? She truly felt like dancing and singing and embracing the world!

One day late in the spring, as Bess, Marita, and Rebecca were visiting with some other ladies after church, one of the men came up to the group somewhat hesitantly.

"Good morning, Robert!" Marita said with a friendly smile. "How is Anita doing today?"

"It's difficult to know for sure. She never complains. But this week I suggested to her that we find someone to come live with us who could keep house and cook for us and help her with the children since she is bedfast. Pastor Lewis thought your friend Bess might be interested." He glanced timidly at Bess, then smiled and offered his hand.

Bess shook his hand but didn't quite know what to say. Should she tell him of her past? Did he know how inexperienced she was with housekeeping?

In the silence Marita replied gently, "Perhaps we could discuss it and then come out for a visit. Maybe when Bess meets Anita and the children she will be better equipped to answer. Would that be satisfactory?"

"Of course! What a splendid idea! Might I suggest tomorrow afternoon, then?"

Bess and Marita nodded simultaneously. "Tomorrow, then," Marita said with another smile.

Over lunch Marita mentioned the conversation to her husband. Pastor Lewis looked at Bess. "When he asked me if I knew of someone, I thought of you immediately, Bess," he explained kindly. "You have learned to cook and take care of a house in the past several weeks with us, and although you are welcome to stay indefinitely, I thought you might want to entertain the possibility. When you meet Anita, you can decide if it is something you care to do or if you prefer to stay on here. Either way is perfectly acceptable to Marita and me." He glanced quickly at Marita, and she nodded enthusiastically.

"We will miss you greatly if you decide to take the position, Bess," Marita said, "but we would not hold you back if you want to do this. It would be a wonderful way to enjoy a bit of independence at the same time you are helping someone in need. You think about it, and we will support you completely, whatever you decide."

Even though Robert and Anita Sheldon were part of the same church Bess attended, she had not yet met Anita since she was unable to attend services. However, Bess was delighted with the possibility of the position.

The meeting at the farm was strained at first. Bess had never been around children, but she couldn't help liking nine-year-old Paul's red hair and freckles. Conner had black hair like his dad, dark brown eyes, and another generous helping of freckles. He had just turned eight. Phillip was six years old and had more teeth missing than in, or so it appeared from his shy smile. There was nothing at all shy about Anna. The four-year-old girl was all smiles and dimples and curls and sky-blue eyes.

When she met Anita Sheldon, Bess realized that Anna was a carbon copy of her beautiful mother. The polio had left Anita's legs useless, and the pain she suffered was evident in her drawn face and blue, blue eyes, but only gentle words were on her lips. Bess knew she would have her hands full with an invalid, four energetic children, and a farmhouse, but she longed to be given the position. Though she didn't know the first thing about raising children, much less keeping house and cooking, the arrangements were made, and she soon found herself settled in and running a household.

The Sheldon home was a very pleasant place in which to work. Bess quickly learned to run the household with Anita's encouragement and advice. The children were a bit shy of her at first, as she was of them, but they all soon learned to love one another.

Bess's life soon took on a contentedness she had never known before.

The fragrance of the lilies of the valley was almost dizzying as Bess cut a large bouquet to take into the house for Anita to enjoy. Anita had commented on the fragrance every time the breeze blew through her window, so when Bess realized how much the dear lady wished to see the dainty lilies, she arranged them in a glass and carried them into Anita's room.

"Oh, Bess, they are even more beautiful than I remembered. I haven't seen them for what seems like forever. This morning I smelled them through the window, and I lay here trying to remember what they looked like exactly, and now you have brought them indoors for me! You are indeed an angel to think of me with all the other work you do. Now I won't long to be outdoors so much. It is wonderful to be able to hear the children playing and know they are being cared for so well. God certainly answered my prayers more than I ever could have hoped or dreamed when He sent you to us."

"Anita, you are God's answer for me. I certainly appreciate the way you and Robert have accepted me and allowed me to be part of your family. This is the first real home I have ever known, and the first privilege I've ever had to be around children. I appreciate your trust in me and patience with me as I learn how to do the housework and care for the children."

As she said all this, she was straightening the bedclothes, plumping the pillows, and trying in general to make certain Anita was comfortable. She was amazed at the way God had given her a love of serving. Her greatest thrill was to make Anita comfortable and to care for those wonderful children. She smiled to herself as she remembered the way she used to think housewives must lead a boring life. She shook her head. There could be nothing more fulfilling than this.

Again she offered her silent prayer of thanks as she hugged Anita and went out to make the bread into loaves and check on little Anna.

Day by day Bess learned how to clean the house, care for the vegetable garden, cook the meals, do the laundry, and care for the children and their invalid mother. How she loved doing the housework to the music of the children's voices outdoors as they played and worked together. What a privilege she had been given.

One day, as she helped Anita sit up a bit more in her bed, she thought how long the days must get for her to be unable to see and hear what was going on in the household. Suddenly she realized that she was probably strong enough to carry Anita outdoors where she could see and hear what was going on in the family.

She quickly went out to place a chair in the shade by the honeysuckle arbor.

Inside she found Anita's kimono and brought it over to the bed. "I have a wonderful idea. I'm going to carry you out of doors today. Would you like that?"

Anita's eyes were large as she looked at Bess. "What if you hurt yourself? I could never forgive myself. Maybe when Robert comes in, he will help you. But, oh, I would love to go out and feel the breeze and be with the children. Do you think it would hurt anything?"

"I think it would be good for you," Bess replied. "Anita, those children need you and so does Robert. Now come on and put your arms around my neck. Try to hold on while I lift you."

It was a bit difficult, but she managed to lift Anita and carry her out to the chair. She took another chair to sit with Anita for a while to catch her breath and get some strength back. Just seeing the happy flush in Anita's cheeks encouraged Bess.

"I must get back to the housework, but I will be out to check on you from time to time." And Bess bustled away. She went out to the garden where the boys were pulling some weeds. "When you finish what you are doing, go to the honey-suckle arbor," she told them mischievously. "There is a treat for you there."

She could hear them trying to guess what was there as she walked back to the house. Anna would wake from her nap anytime now, and she would take her out to her mother. What fun that would be for them both!

All afternoon as she worked she could hear the excited chatter and squeals as the children played with their mother. When she took cold water out to them, she thought she had never seen Anita looking so well. Bess had been right; this was what Anita needed. Bess could hardly wait to talk to Robert about another idea she'd had that very afternoon. No, she decided she would check into that herself.

And so the excitement started brewing. The next time they all went into town to church she pulled Rebecca Taylor aside as soon as she had an opportunity after church and asked if she and her husband could order things for their store from out East.

"Yes, we do it all the time. What is it you need?"

"I want a chair with wheels. I have seen pictures of them. You can sit a person in the chair and move them anywhere you want to. I have some money, and I would like to get one for Anita. Would you help me?"

Rebecca assured Bess that she would look in the catalogues and see what was available. She reminded her that it would probably take several weeks unless she could make the right train connections for shipping. Bess asked her to do what she could and handed her a purse of money. "If that is not enough, I have more. This is really important. Anita needs to be able to get out and about with her family." And with that she hugged Rebecca and went to round up the children so they could get back to the farm, as none of them liked to leave Anita alone for very long.

One afternoon in June while Bess was making some pies, Anita sat in a chair in the kitchen where she had been carried that day. Anita was peeling potatoes into a bowl in her lap while Bess rolled out a piecrust. Anita seemed so much more alive and strong since Bess and Robert had been carrying her into the living room or yard each day. And Bess enjoyed her jolly company.

It was a warm afternoon, and they chatted companionably while they worked. The breeze wafted through the open windows, and a lazy fly came in also and tried to get into the pie. Bess brushed at the fly, then wiped her flour-covered hand on her apron. She reached for a flyswatter. "I'd better get this fly out of here before we have meat in our pie."

"Please do," said Anita. "Flies do not make good meat in pies!" The women chuckled together companionably.

Suddenly Anita stopped with her knife poised and tilted her head. "Is Robert going somewhere?" she asked Bess.

"Not that I know of," Bess replied. Just as Bess turned her head to question Anita, she heard the buggy wheels too. She went to the window but could see nothing from inside for all the shade trees. Quickly she wiped her hands as Anita said, "Go see what it is!" Bess trotted out the back door trying to shade her eyes to see up the lane.

As she watched, a wagon came around the corner and up the lane. It looked like Rebecca's husband, Jason Taylor. And then Bess remembered the wheelchair and ran out to meet him. Sure enough, he had a large crate in the back of the wagon.

Robert jogged up just in time to help Jason lift the crate down to the ground. "What is it?" Robert asked.

"Oh, it's something Bess ordered awhile back." Jason smiled.

Bess was already trying to pull the boards loose from the crate, so Jason and Robert took metal bars and pried the lid off. Jason pulled the chair free from the crate and said, "Sit in it. Let's try it out."

Bess sat in it quickly, because she wanted to make sure it was going to be comfortable for Anita, and was pleased at how comfortable it was. Jason pushed her on the packed dirt of the lane and it was quite easy, but they all decided it would be easier in the house.

Together they all took the contraption into the house to show Anita. Anita was speechless when she realized what it was. "Oh, this will be so much easier for you both. What a wonderful gift!"

Bess and Jason showed her how she could use her arms to move the wheels and would be able to get around some by herself now as well.

One by one the children came running in to see who was visiting and were pleased and surprised by the new chair that would make it possible for their mother to get around. And Bess was pleased when Jason returned some of the money. It hadn't even cost what she had expected. She couldn't help humming to herself as she went back to the work she had been doing. Yes, life was good.

Later as they all sat around the big country table eating the delicious meal that Bess and Anita had prepared, Robert announced that he planned to make board-walks from the doors to the outside so that Anita could get around outside some by herself as well. Anita was so excited by her new mobility that she could hardly finish a sentence. It was wonderful to think that if someone helped her into her chair she would be able to get around by herself and even be able to help out with some of the work from her chair.

Bess's heart was so full she was hardly saying anything. She enjoyed being a part of this family, and for the first time in her life feeling like she really cared about someone and that they cared for her in return.

In the middle of the meal and conversation little Anna slid down from her chair and ran around the table to throw her arms around Bess and whisper, "I think you is jes' wunnerful!" Bess smiled and quickly hugged her back, wiping away the tears with a swipe of her napkin. "I love you, little Anna," she whispered back.

Robert and Anita exchanged smiles and kept on eating. God had certainly blessed their little family, and they were grateful.

That evening, as they were reading the Bible together and praying around the table, Conner prayed, "Thank You, God, for Miss Bess, and thank You, God for giving us our mommy back."

Bess grinned with contentment and joy.

Chapter 4

Bess seldom went to the town anymore except for church. She and Anita would tell Robert what was needed for the household, and he would make the trip into town for the purchases and bring them home for the family. However, the children were growing rapidly, and Anita noticed that some new clothes were needed. So Anita asked Bess if she would go along with Robert on his next trip to purchase the fabrics and threads, buttons and other notions that they would need in order to make new clothes for the children.

Bess agreed, so the two women planned what they would need and made the list. Bess was a bit shy to go back into town and possibly be seen by people who knew of her previous life, but she knew she would need to do so sooner or later, so she convinced herself that now was as good a time as any.

The trip to town did seem adventuresome for Bess, now that she was accustomed to her life on the farm. She and Robert spoke some but rode in companionable silence most of the way. She soon appreciated the bonnet Anita had suggested she wear, even though it was so hot she had not wanted to cover her head. However, because the sun was so hot the shade created by the wide brim was welcome indeed. Yes, Anita was a very wise and knowledgeable woman and good friend.

Besides the smell of the dust from the horses' hooves and wagon wheels, she could smell the nutty aroma of the wheat and barley that was ready for harvest. Now and again as they passed a farm the acidic odor of manure from the barns wafted toward her, and she heard the cattle lowing. Once they passed a house where the children were playing some sort of tag in the yard. The laughter and shouting voices made both Bess and Robert smile. Those would be some hot and dirty children come bedtime, but nothing a little soap and water and a good night's rest couldn't cure.

When they arrived in town, Robert let Bess out of the wagon at the store, while he went to the stables to water the horses. She stood on the boardwalk in front of Taylors' store watching as Robert pulled away and started down the road. She suddenly felt very alone, although the town was busy enough with people and wagons. But she squared her shoulders and went into the store.

Several people were inside. It took a little while for her eyes to adjust to the dimness after the bright sun outside. Several men stood and sat around the stove, even though the stove was cold. She guessed they were in the habit of gathering there in the winter for its warmth, so they still used the benches that were there to meet somewhere out of the direct sun.

Jason Taylor was helping a gentleman and a young woman with some grocery purchases. Over to the left, beyond the crates stacked in rows, she saw shelves along the side wall with bolts of fabrics lining a shelf. It had been months since Bess had been in the store, but not much had changed at all.

Rebecca Taylor was behind the counter talking with a lady who was finding fault with each bolt of fabric. Bess could tell that Rebecca's patience was being tried sorely, but she never stopped smiling and spoke kindly to the critical lady.

To the lady's right another woman was bent over the counter seeming to be very absorbed with something on the countertop. She was certainly transfixed by whatever had her attention. Slowly Bess drew near her, but she couldn't see the object of the lady's attention. Without realizing she was doing so, Bess leaned forward to see, then looked up at the lady.

"Clara!" Bess whispered joyfully. She realized now why Clara had kept her head turned away. It was the way the prostitutes always behaved in public, as they would only end up embarrassed if they were to meet another's eyes.

Clara looked at her, but Bess could see she was troubled. "What is it, Clara? How are you?" Bess wondered.

Clara backed away from the other people in the store until she and Bess were alone in a corner. Again the slight frown. "I'm doing well. How are you keeping yourself? Are you happy?"

"Oh, Clara, God has been so good to me! I have never been happier in my life. I miss you terribly, but I don't miss our life at the saloon. I have real good friends, and best of all, I have met Jesus and He has changed my heart. Clara, come outside with me where we can talk and I will tell you all about it."

"Girl, you don't want to be seen with the likes of me no more. Why would you talk to me?"

"Because I love you, Clara. You have been like a mother to me. Nothing will ever change that. And nothing would make me happier than talking to you again, unless it would be seeing you make the same change I made." Bess was astounded to realize that Clara thought she would not still love her.

The two women headed out of the store, walking down the boardwalk to the edge of town and then down an alley where they could talk out of the hearing and sight of others.

Bess had told Clara about her change of heart the day she moved out of the saloon. But it was all so new to her then that she hadn't really understood completely what had happened to her. So her explanations at that time had been quite vague.

Today, however, she told Clara all she knew. Bess encouraged her to visit Pastor Lewis and ask him all her questions. In fact, since she had to be ready to go when Robert was ready, she volunteered to talk to Rebecca for Clara. She knew Rebecca would be glad to help her.

Clara, however, seemed hesitant.

Saddened by her old friend's lack of interest, Bess determined in her heart to talk to Rebecca and to not stop praying for the woman. She hugged Clara and kissed her painted cheek that was beginning to soften and droop a bit with age. "I will never stop loving you, Clara."

Clara smiled a lonely smile but didn't reply. She merely looked down.

Bess turned back toward the store, knowing she'd need to hurry now or she would keep Robert waiting. But when she returned to the store, she had a few minutes to tell Rebecca about Clara and ask her to watch out for her old friend and help her if she could. Rebecca promised to do so, as Bess knew she would.

Clara stood, alone, as Bess's steps retreated back toward the store. She couldn't help but wonder at the change in dear Bess. But the saloon life was all Clara knew. She had always been content with her life—until Bess's change and the loss of their friendship when she'd moved away from the hotel. The last several months, with Bess gone, Clara's life had seemed empty and heading nowhere.

Suddenly it mattered to Clara that she would die alone in a saloon with no one to care. But she had no idea what to do about it.

Chapter 5

The day was already warm as Bess prepared to help Anita bathe before moving her from her bed to the wheelchair for the day. Anita would be warm sitting in the chair all day long, and a cool, refreshing sponge bath in the mornings helped her feel much more comfortable for the day. Anita was always gentle with her, but this morning Bess thought she felt a slight push as she washed Anita's foot. She looked up at Anita and said, "Do that again."

"Do what again?" Anita asked.

"Push me with your foot."

"I can't push with my foot," Anita replied.

"I know you pushed me with your foot. Just slightly. Try it. See if you can push against my hand."

As Anita tried to obey, she felt nothing, but Bess excitedly said that she could feel the muscles tighten ever so slightly in Anita's leg as she tried to push. Bess encouraged her to try again and again, until Anita was exhausted. Finally Bess laid her leg back on the bed and said, "Okay, we will stop for now and work on it again tomorrow. Maybe we can get your legs strong once again so you can use them. For now, let's not tell anyone in case it doesn't work."

So they agreed. Day after day they worked and worked until Anita could tell she was pushing firmly with her feet whenever she wanted to. Throughout the day she would push on the wheelchair with her feet, until she was actually developing muscles once again in the backs of her legs.

After a number of weeks of this, one day she asked Bess, "Will you help me try to stand?"

"Do you think your legs can hold you if you were to stand?" Bess asked.

"If you hold on to me, I think I can stand for a bit. Will you try?"

"Absolutely. I know you are gaining strength, and it will be good to help strengthen your legs also. Let's try it."

So together they pulled Anita into a standing position, and she stood! It wasn't for very long, and her legs began to sag, but she had stood with her weight on her legs.

Both women were so excited they hugged and cried.

"Now I know how the lame man in the Bible must have felt when Jesus told him to get up and walk," Anita said. "Someday, Bess, I am going to walk again. I just know it!"

Bess had never loved anyone in her life like she loved this sweet woman and her family, and there could be no greater gift than to see Anita be able to walk and do things for herself once again. And so Bess worked and prayed, and worked and prayed.

The two women decided to keep the secret from the rest of the family for a while longer, and they continued to work at strengthening the muscles and bringing some life back into them. The challenge was very fulfilling for Bess. As she became more and more a part of the Sheldon family and stronger in her daily walk with God, contentment became her constant companion.

July was warm as it pressed in on the lives of the happy household. The home so generously shared with Bess was much cooler than the saloon where Bess had lived her life before. Out here there were large shade trees and always a gentle breeze wafting through the open windows. Bess was amazed that she had only moved a few miles to find this whole different world. Her heart was full of joy and fulfillment as she learned to love the Sheldon family and her church family.

Then the hot, hot days of August finally turned to the hotter days of early September. Bess was kept busy with the housework and gardens and care of Anita and the children, but she loved every minute that she labored for these dear friends. Anita worried that Bess was working too hard, and Bess heard her encouraging the children to work harder and help Bess with the chores. But Bess's heart was full of joy with the tasks at hand and the love of this family.

Bess and Anita continued working and exercising Anita's legs, helping her stand and even take a few steps. Finally they could contain their secret no longer. One evening during dinner Anita told the family that she had a secret she wanted to share with them. The family all quieted and looked toward her.

When she slowly stood, Robert's chair fell over backward as he jumped to his feet to catch her. But she didn't fall. He stood beside her as she took a step, and then another. The house was very quiet for a few seconds, and then the explosion of young voices filled the air. Bess caught Anita's eye, and the two chuckled together. Finally Robert made everyone sit down so Anita and Bess could tell the story.

And so Anita told of Bess's encouraging her to press with her feet and then massaging her weak muscles. She told how Bess had exercised her legs and feet for weeks before they tried having Anita stand, and when she did stand, Bess was right there to hold her and help her. Now they had been practicing her steps, and she could not keep the wonderful secret from her family any longer.

Of course the children wanted to help her walk. They wanted to show her everything new on the little farm. While the boys chattered, coaxed, laughed, and talked with their mother and each other, little Anna quietly came to Bess and climbed into her lap, from where she proudly announced, "I think Miss Bess is wunnerful. I love her, and she loves me, too!"

Anita smiled at Anna and then over her head at Bess. "Yes, God did a wonderful thing when He brought Miss Bess into our family. We all love her and are thankful for her," Anita said with a quiet smile.

The two women exchanged looks weighted with their love for one another, and Bess prayed inwardly that God would accept her deep gratitude for the gift of this family. She had never enjoyed such perfect peace of heart in her life.

Each day Anita's legs became stronger. Robert had made a cane for her, but at first she still needed to hold on to someone. However, with work and lots of practice, by the end of the summer she could walk carefully with her cane. Her first Sunday back at the church was a celebration for all. Anita knew they all cared for her, but she was overwhelmed by the shouts of joy from the men and the tears and hugs from the women. Oh, it was good to be back among these dear friends.

Bess was happy for her. Several people had been speaking with Bess and the little group quieted simultaneously as often happens in time for them to hear Anita saying to someone behind them, "Oh, of course we will always need Bess! She is part of our family, and we hope she will stay with us always. I would be lost without her, as would the children. It is her choice, of course, but we certainly intend for her to stay with us, as I will always need her help."

Bess blushed and smiled quietly as she moved to her seat for the beginning of the service. She had wondered if there would come a day when the Sheldon family no longer required her help. Her heart was comforted and joyful to have overheard Anita's comment and Robert's assent.

Chapter 6

Clara missed Bess. There were just no two ways about it. Her life seemed totally barren of happiness when Bess left the hotel. She knew when Bess was staying at the pastor's home, but she sure didn't feel like she dared go there for a visit. And then they moved Bess out of the town to the home of a family that needed her help.

She was truly happy for Bess. She loved the girl like she had been her own and was glad she had found a life where she could have more social contact and be content and happy. But without Bess to nurture and guide, Clara's life suddenly felt very empty and lonely.

Many times she found herself staring out the window and replaying the conversation she and Bess had had while Bess packed her things to move. Bess had seemed like an entirely different person. Something in the very core of that girl had changed. And it was good. Clara was surprised that she could admit that to herself, but she truly saw it in Bess's face and knew with her whole heart that it was good.

Bess had tried to explain it to Clara, but her words didn't all make sense to Clara, so Bess promised to pray for her—when she learned how to pray well. Clara smiled at the memory. Bess's eyes had twinkled like Clara had never seen before. Oh, how she missed that girl. . .

Then she had seen Bess at the store and Bess had tried to explain things more to her. But Clara still didn't understand. She really did want to understand what Bess was telling her, and her heart longed to have the same peace that Bess had found, but she felt so alone and alienated from the others in the town.

Lately Clara had actually started thinking about talking to that woman at the store—Rebecca Taylor. She was curious what could have made such a happy change in Bess. Bess had encouraged her to talk to the Taylor woman the last time Clara had seen Bess at the store, and now Clara found herself contemplating the idea.

Oh, that's ridiculous. She would laugh in my face. Or spit in it! Clara told herself. But immediately she remembered the lady's patience with the complaining patron. *Well, maybe she wouldn't. She does seem like she would be a kind person who would be easy to talk to.* Clara allowed the thought to float around while she watched an orange leaf twirl and dance its way to the ground outside her window.

Falling leaves meant winter was right around the corner. Suddenly the four walls pressed in on Clara, and all she could think of was getting out of the saloon. Oh, how she longed to have a different life—a life where she could hold her head high and smile and chat with other women as they passed by.

Clara grabbed her shawl and was soon walking rapidly toward the general store. Just before she got there, though, she saw some people standing on the boardwalk in front of the store talking. So she turned and walked away, back another street lined with houses on both sides.

As she walked, she heard a mother calling her children to come in for supper. She could hear children laughing and calling to one another. Walking on a bit farther, she saw two women intently talking over a fence between the two yards. The women did not see her, and Clara could not understand what they were saying, but she couldn't help but smile at their chatter and laughter. It all looked so real. So meaningful. So loving.

Suddenly she found herself turning around and walking back toward the store once again. She realized deep inside she was saying over and over, *"Please, please, please..."* Please what? To whom was she pleading? Was she praying? She tightened her lips in a determined expression. Somehow she had formed a resolve, and she wanted—no, needed—some answers.

As Clara reached the store this time, she saw a wagon pulling away from the front, and a gentleman with armbands sweeping the boardwalk in front of the store. Clara hoped this meant the store was occupied only by the lady—Rebecca Taylor.

She pushed the front door open hastily, setting off the clanging of a bell hanging on the back side. She closed the door and gently quieted the bell. Standing just inside, she looked around but saw no one at all. Walking to her left, she peered back into the area where the fabrics and other feminine goods were found, but no one seemed to be there.

She jumped when she heard a soft "May I help you?" Then the lady said, "Oh, I'm sorry. I didn't mean to startle you." Her smile was in her eyes as well as on her lips. This had to be Mrs. Taylor. But Clara didn't really know what to ask. So she simply said quickly that she needed some buttons.

While Mrs. Taylor showed her the buttons, she looked carefully at Clara, which made Clara uncomfortable, so she snatched the first card of buttons she found. Then Mrs. Taylor said joyfully, "I know! Aren't you friends with my own good friend Bess?"

Clara could feel her cheeks flaming as she nodded in a bobbing motion.

"Oh, Bess misses you so very much. She has told me what a dear friend you have been to her. Let's see...is your name Clara?"

She didn't seem to be prying—just caring. So Clara said, "Yes, my name is Clara Johnson. Bess and I have been friends her whole life."

"You must miss Bess. Clara, would you come to tea with me tomorrow afternoon? I would love to know you better."

Clara wanted to ask her, *"Do you know who I really am? What I do for a living?"* But all she could do was nod and say, "Thank you. I would be delighted."

So they set a time. Clara took the buttons she didn't need and left hurriedly as Mr. Taylor stepped back into the store with his broom.

It was a sunny and warm fall day as Clara prepared herself for tea with Rebecca Taylor. Over and over she scolded herself. *What were you thinking? What kind of conversation can you carry with this kind of a lady?* But deep in her heart Clara knew she was going so she could ask about the change in Bess.

After dressing, Clara went down to the kitchen and gathered a small basketful of cookies that Gertie had cooling on a towel. It didn't seem proper to go to tea without some small gift. So she wrapped the cookies in a clean towel and tucked them into the little basket. Then, heart pounding, she headed for the store.

When she arrived, Mr. Taylor was the only one there. He looked up and smiled his question.

"Is Mrs. Taylor in today?" Clara spoke hesitatingly.

"Yes. Are you her friend Clara Johnson?" At Clara's nod, Mr. Taylor pointed to a door in a far corner. "She's back preparing tea for you and asked me to send you on back. Go right through that door and you'll find her easily enough. She's looking forward to getting to know you."

What a strange bunch of people! Did they not know everyone ignored or turned away from women like her? Why were they being so friendly? Was it a trap of some kind?

If it wasn't for her strong love of Bess and curiosity about the change in the girl, Clara would have turned and run. But she forced a smile and ducked through the door to which he had pointed.

Mrs. Taylor was pouring cups of steaming tea as Clara entered. She was a very friendly lady, and soon the two women were chatting as though they had never been strangers. She eagerly answered all of Clara's questions. When the afternoon was turning toward evening, Clara knew she must go.

Rebecca (as she had asked to be called) asked Clara if she would like to borrow a New Testament to read. Then she suggested she come again and talk to her friend Mrs. Lewis also. She told Clara she would be praying for her.

Clara thanked her for explaining so much to her. Clara knew in her heart that she was truly grateful for Rebecca's prayers as she thought about all that she had heard this day. And Clara knew she'd read the little black book and be back with lots of questions for Rebecca and Mrs. Lewis before long.

Chapter 7

Bess enjoyed every day of her weeks now, but Sunday held a special place in her heart because the family went to church together and many times would spend the afternoon with one of the families from the church or invite friends to spend the day on the farm with them. Bess was always considered part of the Sheldon family—by the Sheldons themselves as well as by the other families of the church.

What pure joy it was for Bess to be part of a family! It was not something she'd ever really considered in her young life, but it didn't take long to figure out that God had a wonderful idea when He created the family. She smiled as she thought of Anita. How good it was to see her walking. Bess had noticed that Anita's figure was filling out some too. She was looking healthy and robust.

So it was not unusual for Bess to be humming as she made breakfast for the family that Sunday morning in late September. She had barely started the breakfast when Anita arrived and gave her a friendly hug from behind.

"Good morning to you, too," Bess said to her friend.

"I have never minded mornings in my life, but they are even better when I wake and hear your sweet voice in this house." Anita tied on an apron and grabbed a stack of plates.

"I can't help singing; I'm so full of happiness. I can't imagine anything in the world that could make me happier than I am now in this home with you all. God is so good to me, and my heart just sings."

"Bess, would you like to be part of a secret?" Anita whispered merrily.

"Yes. . .it must be a good one the way your eyes are dancing."

"Well, soon after the first of the year we should have a new baby in our home. My clothes aren't fitting too well anymore, and I wanted you to know and to ask your help in re-fitting some of my clothes next week. I wanted it to be a surprise, but I can't keep something this jolly from you. You know how I love the fragrance of the lilies of the valley? Well, this baby was conceived about the time of the lilies, so I have decided that if it is a girl, we will name her Lily Bess."

Tears of joy sprang to Bess's eyes. "Anita! How wonderful! I just don't know what to say!"

"Don't say anything yet. It might be a boy. And if it is, I haven't even thought of what we should name him. Guess we still have time for that, but something in my heart says this is a sister for our Anna."

Later, as the family was in the wagon on their way to church, Bess started the children singing, and soon Robert and Anita joined in. Bess had quickly learned the songs of the church and sang them beautifully. Joyful sounds floated on the air, preceding the happy family on their way to the church.

As usual, the family arrived at the church a good while before the services were to start. They enjoyed visiting with the other families that they often did not see from one week to the next. It was a beautiful day, and many groups of people stood outside the church. Most of the men seemed to stand near the wagons and horses, while the women tended to stand nearer the church in little groups in the shade of the large old trees.

Today Bess was just climbing down from the wagon when she heard her name called by a familiar voice as Rebecca Taylor hurried over to her. The two women greeted one another with a hug and then reached to help Anita walk on the uneven ground. Bess was happy to see her friend and to be with the other women of the church, but today Rebecca seemed to be nearly bursting with excitement. "Come," she said, tugging at Bess's sleeve.

As they rounded the corner of the church and started over to the trees where the women were standing, one lady approached Bess quickly. Before Bess had time to think, she was wrapped in a strong hug. Pulling back a bit, Bess looked into the smiling face of Clara and immediately knew something was different.

"What is it, Clara? Tell me," Bess said excitedly as she hugged her dear friend back.

"I am a believer, too, Bess! I have been meeting with Rebecca and Marita, and they have helped me read and understand a lot of the Bible. And I have prayed and I now am a believer also. Bess, I have so much to tell you. My life has changed so very much this week."

"Oh, Clara, I was just thinking this morning that I couldn't possibly be any happier, but I was wrong. You have made me so very happy! I am glad for you, and I'm glad for me. It is wonderful to have this new way of life in common with you since you have always been the greatest part of my life and my joy. Tell me, do you still live at the saloon?"

"No, I am staying with the Lewises now, and that's the best news. Rebecca and Marita have encouraged me to fulfill my heart's desire. I have long wanted to run a boardinghouse for families needing a place to stay until they can find a place of their own. Pastor and Marita are helping me until I can buy a place of my own with the money I have saved through the years. I think it will work great, because this town really has no regular hotel or place to stay, and since the railroad has gone in, there are always people looking for a place to stay."

"Oh, Clara, you will be so good at doing that. You are so kind and considerate of other folks. I know you will do well."

"My biggest fear is the cooking. You know that Gertie has done most all of the cooking. I've helped out a little here and there, but I've never really had the chance to learn."

"Clara, I've learned to cook for the Sheldon family. Perhaps I could come in to teach you some of what I know when you get the place. Wouldn't that be fun?"

"Oh, yes, that's a wonderful idea! I'll plan on that."

Bess and Clara continued to chat happily until the bell in the steeple rang. They went into the church and sat together, and several times during the service they hugged one another from pure joy. Bess was contented and happy with her life with the Sheldon family, and now she was pleased that her dear friend would find a better life as well.

Chapter 8

Autumn brought its own special joys for Bess as she learned to prepare a home for winter. Together she and the children would gather the garden produce, as the ground was too uneven for Anita. Bess worked long days cleaning the vegetables and fruit and then preserving them for the winter. She and Anita also cleaned the house thoroughly; hung the heavier draperies at the windows; and washed, aired, and remade the beds with the warm comforters and quilts.

Robert, Paul, and Conner would cut firewood whenever they had time, and the woodpile grew in size and in the promise of warmth in the cold, snowy days ahead. Everywhere on the farm one could hear chatter and laughter as the thankful hearts enjoyed one another and God's goodness to them.

Bess noticed that not only was Anita more energetic and mischievous, but Robert's eyes twinkled with a merry glint that had not been there before. And they often heard Robert whistling on his way to and from the barns.

In spite of being the youngest member of the family and doted on by everyone, little Anna was a happy but often quite serious child. Now and again she would amaze them all with her comments revealing a thoughtful, sincere heart. Bess loved all the family, but knew without doubt that Anna was someone very, very special that God had brought into her life.

One day as she and Anna were watching the birds and commenting about the way God provides for their needs, Anna said, "And God provides for people, too."

"Yes, Anna, God provides for people, too," Bess assured her. "He blessed the gardens and fruit trees and gave us food and shelter for the winter in a warm home."

"And He brought you to us like magic to take care of us. One day we didn't know you, and then God brought you to us and we are happy now."

Tears sprang to Bess's eyes, and she had to swallow the lump in her throat before she could speak to the serious little girl. "Anna, you know that you are God's special gift to me also. My life was very empty before I knew you."

"Really and truly, Miss Bess? You needed us, too?" Her eyes were as large as saucers as they searched Bess's face for truth.

"Really and truly, Anna. You are a very special gift to me, and I love you."

"I love you, too, Miss Bess, and I want to be just like you when I grow big."

Suddenly, Bess thought of her life before she came to this family. In her heart she prayed that when the day came when Anna discovered the truth of her past, that she would indeed not follow in her footsteps in that area, but only to the foot of the cross.

As the cold autumn wind blew a gust of leaves from the nearby tree, Bess saw a vacated bird's nest within reach. "Come, Anna. Look at this. Do you remember the baby birds that cried for food in this nest in the spring?"

"Yes! Are they lost? Did they fall out?"

"No, they grew up and have all flown away for the winter. They will be back again in the spring and will build nests, and each baby will be grown up and start a family of his own." Bess could see the thoughts churning in Anna's little head. "Someday you will grow up and have a family of your own, too, Anna, and it will be nice if you learn some good things from me and from your mommy and daddy also. But the most important thing is to learn the lessons God wants to teach you and grow to be just like Him."

After a short silence when she peered again into the empty bird nest, Anna took Bess's face between her two chubby little hands and said seriously, "I will, Miss Bess. But you must teach me."

"Oh, Anna, dear, I will teach you, and your mommy and daddy will teach you. Learn well, little one; learn well." Bess couldn't help the tears that dropped onto her cheeks.

Anna still eyed her solemnly. Then she carefully wiped the tears from Bess's cheeks. "Don't cry, Miss Bess. I will learn. I promise I will learn good."

∽∞∽

It was late in October when Bess and Anita and the younger children were digging the potatoes. The wind was cold and had a dampness that chilled them to the bone. But it was fun working together. Now and again they would faintly hear Robert's cheery whistle coming from the barns, and the cold wouldn't seem so bitter.

Bess encouraged Anita to stay in where it was warm, but Anita knew they were all cold and since she could help by lifting the loosened potatoes out of the soil, it helped whichever boy was pulling the wagonloads to the cellar for storage. She wanted to help so that they all could get in out of the cold as soon as possible.

Later in the day, little ice crystals stung their cheeks. It was one of those nasty tasks that must be completed but wasn't nearly as much fun as gathering the summer produce.

Bess heard Anita cough a bit; again she encouraged her to go in where it was warm and dry. But Anita would hear none of it, so they toiled on together. Finally, Bess suggested that Anita go in and start a pot of soup for dinner so they wouldn't have it all to do once they came in. This time Anita went inside.

Bess and the children worked on until their fingers felt numb. When the boys complained about the cold, Bess showed them how near they were to being finished. "Let me dig the rest of these, and you go in and warm up a bit now. When I'm finished out here, there will be room for me by the fire," Bess suggested to the children.

Anna was so cold she could hardly speak. "I stay out to he'p Miss Bess. Oo boys go in. Us gulls will finish." Her little nose was red, and her cheeks were rosy and cold.

Bess said, "Anna, why don't you go in and set the table for your mommy? It will help us all. By the time Conner and Philip empty this wagon and come back for the rest, I'll be finished, and we can all go in. Is that all right with you, boys?"

The boys were stomping their feet to stay warm but nodded briefly, grabbed the wagon, and started toward the house.

"Go on, Anna girl. Help your mommy, and we'll come in just a little while, all right?"

So the faithful little girl nodded and turned for the house. Bess dug the rest of the potatoes quickly, turning them up with the sod to be sifted out. When the boys returned with the wagon, they gathered the potatoes from the dirt, and before long Bess heard more voices. Turning, she saw Robert and Paul headed toward the garden.

Together they all finished in short order. Robert sent them all to the house while he took the last wagonload to the cellar. As they started for the house, Paul said, "Philip, where did you get your rouge?"

"Rouge? I'm not wearing rouge!"

"But your cheeks are red and rosy. You look like a lady with rouge."

"I am *not* wearing rouge! Your cheeks are rosy, too."

Bess quickly joined in. "Are my cheeks rosy? We are all wearing rouge! But when our cheeks start getting warm, this rouge will sting and itch. Wait and see."

They approached the house arm in arm, talking about their rosy cheeks and cold fingers. It was a merry but tired bunch that sat quietly at the dinner table that night. Before the soup bowls were even empty, little Anna's head was drooping. The older ones looked from one to another and smiled. Finally, Robert carried her off to her bed.

Chapter 9

Everyone was tired from the hard work and the cold, and sleep came quickly that night. Bess loved sharing a room with little Anna upstairs. The two snuggled close as they slept, while the cold wind blew against the house and the frozen rain scraped hauntingly at the windows and siding.

Sometime in the night Bess realized she had been hearing Anna coughing now and again. She lay quietly and listened, and soon she heard it again. It was a dry, raspy cough. Bess reached out to pat her cheek and was surprised at how warm it was. She held her close for a while and then realized she had been hearing coughing from somewhere else in the house also. And she noticed that Anna's cough was getting deeper and raspier.

Bess half listened to her and to whomever else was coughing through the haze of her sleep. But the coughing outside her room soon had Bess wide awake. She sat up in bed and listened. It sounded like it was coming from downstairs. She knew it wasn't Robert—it just didn't sound like a man. She was pretty sure it was Anita.

Bess slipped out of bed and, pulling on her dressing gown, slipped quietly down the back stairs to the kitchen. She took out a large kettle and filled it with water. Then she took it to the stove that heated the front room and downstairs rooms and placed it on top. She stirred the fire and added more wood. Bess knew if she could get some moisture in the air it would ease the coughing. She hoped some of the steam would find its way into Robert and Anita's room.

Bess went back upstairs and took some blankets from the bed. Lifting Anna in her arms, she carried the child and the blankets down to the front room and, wrapping herself and the child in the blankets, settled down near the warm steam to snooze awhile longer.

By morning, Anna's breathing seemed much better, but Anita's cough sounded much deeper than it had in the night. When Robert awakened and came out of their room, Bess asked how Anita was doing. Robert said she was struggling to breathe. So Bess asked him to carry her out to the steamy front room while she made a bed for Anita on the couch.

All day long Bess cared for Anita and Anna. She made chicken broth and gave them bread soaked in the broth to eat along with warm applesauce. By afternoon, Anna seemed to be feeling some better and even began to talk quietly to Bess between her naps. But Anita stayed quiet all day, and by late afternoon, her breathing became labored. Bess kept the kettle full of hot water and kept the fire hot. Whenever Anita coughed hard, Bess would trickle a bit of brandy down her throat, but it only seemed to help for a short while. Bess couldn't help worrying for Anita and the child she carried.

By evening Robert was nearly beside himself with worry, and Bess was growing concerned also as they listened to the raspy, labored breathing. After the evening meal, Robert announced that he was going into town to fetch the doctor, and Bess was glad to hear it.

While he was gone, Bess prepared the children for bed and read to them. They all prayed for Anita and for Robert and the doctor to return safely and soon.

When the boys were in bed and sleeping, Bess took Anna onto her lap again. She decided it would be best if Anna slept near the steam again. The little girl soon was fast asleep in Bess's arms. Bess found she was dozing, too, from lack of sleep and the warm room, but she would awaken each time the coughing racked Anita's body.

Sometime late in the night, Robert returned with the doctor. Dr. Walker checked Anita's chest and breathing and praised Bess's work of keeping the room steamy and trickling the brandy down her throat. He gave Anita some medicine and told Robert and Bess it would just take some time.

Since the night was half over anyway, Dr. Walker told Bess to go to bed and get some sleep while he kept watch over Anita and Anna. Then Bess would be better able to care for them tomorrow when he was gone.

So Bess went to bed but awakened several times in the night to the sounds of coughing and labored breathing. Toward morning, Bess slept more soundly. No one awakened her, and it was nearly eight o'clock when she awoke with alarm.

Bess dressed quickly and went downstairs to check on the family. Anna seemed to be feeling much better and was hungry. But Anita was much the same.

Bess went to the kitchen to prepare some breakfast and was putting it on the table when Robert came in from the barn. At Robert's questioning look, Bess said quickly, "No change at all. She is struggling to breathe."

"I'll bring in more wood. We must keep the kettle going and the fire hot," Robert said.

"Why don't you have breakfast first, Robert? We still have enough wood in the wood box to fill the stove again. You must keep up your strength, too."

So the family and Dr. Walker sat at the table eating the delicious breakfast that held no taste because of their worry. They all were quiet. The air was compressed with the prayers in all of their hearts. It didn't seem right somehow that someone as dear and sweet as Anita should suffer so much in her life.

Bess took her place beside Anita while Dr. Walker ate with the family. Robert brought in another few loads of wood before leaving to take the doctor back into town and drop the boys off at the schoolhouse. All day Bess watched over Anita. That night she and Robert took turns staying up to keep the fire going and the kettle full.

For several weeks, Anita seemed to hover between being awake and sleeping, but the bright red spots of color from the fever never left her pale cheeks. Each day she appeared more frail than the day before.

Bess tried to keep her quiet because she wouldn't cough as much when she was quiet. But when the doctor visited he explained that the cough was what kept the fluid from filling her lungs. After that, the family actually tried to get Anita to cough, but as she weakened, the coughs became further and further apart. She had stopped trying to talk at all because talking always made her cough uncontrollably.

One evening, as Bess was filling the kettle on the stove, she heard a weak sound behind her. Turning toward the sofa she was overjoyed to see Anita's eyes open and focused on her. Her eyes had been closed for so long Bess was surprised to see them open and focused.

"Did you say something, Anita?" She set the bucket down and went over next to Anita.

"Thank you, Bess. I just said thank you." Anita's whisper was so faint that Bess had to lean close and watch her lips to know what she was saying.

"Oh, Anita, I have done nothing but pray for you. Are you feeling better?"

"I think so, Bess. Just very weak."

"Anita, let me bring in some hot broth and bread. Do you think you could sit if I help you? Would you try to eat?"

"I'll try" was all she said before Bess scurried off to the kitchen to warm some broth and cut a slice of bread and butter it. But by the time Bess returned, Anita was sleeping soundly again, and Bess couldn't rouse her.

When Robert came downstairs from tucking the children into their beds, Bess told him of the conversation and asked if he could awaken Anita so Bess could feed her the warm broth. When they both neared the sofa, they were surprised to see a serene smile on Anita's lips. The drawn look was gone from her face, and she looked so peaceful, they hesitated to awaken her. But when Bess reached to touch Anita's cheek, it was cold. Robert touched her hand at the same time and felt the cold hand as it lay white and still on her breast. The labored breathing had ceased.

Robert gave an agonizing groan as Bess sank to the floor in front of Anita's couch. Robert walked over to stare out into the night, while Bess sat weeping silently on the floor. Both felt too numb to think what to do. Their happy lives had just taken a horribly ugly twist, for which they felt totally unprepared.

Chapter 10

Bess felt numb. Somehow she managed to care for the children and home while preparations were made for the funeral. The boys seemed frightened and lost, but little Anna amazed them all. When the rest of them were thinking of how bereft their lives would be without Anita, Anna was thinking how wonderful it was that her mommy was seeing and talking to Jesus. The child didn't feel sorry for herself at all but was so filled with pure love for her mother that all she could do was rejoice for her. It was the most amazing thing Bess had ever seen.

What alarmed Bess the most was her own anger. All the kind words friends offered, all the supportive phrases spoken to her from her church family flew right over her head and missed her heart entirely. She became so angry in her heart that she could not cry. She felt cold and alone and hard inside.

Bess had known Anita for less than a year, yet Anita had become such a vital part of her life that the loss was overwhelming. She tried to pray but didn't even know what to say. She just kept thinking, *Why? Why Anita? Why did she have to go? There was so much I wanted and needed to learn from her. Why, why, WHY?*

Was God even hearing her groanings and prayers? He seemed so far away, and Bess didn't know how to reach Him. If she was honest, she wasn't sure she wanted to reach Him. What kind of God would allow the death of one so gracious, kind, and giving as Anita and leave this young family without a mother? Why would God give the hope of another child, then take it along with the mother? What could possibly be good about this?

They had the funeral at the church on a cold, sleeting morning. Bess could not even listen to Pastor Lewis's message because of the anger in her heart. She wanted answers, but she wanted them from God. Suddenly it felt like someone had turned off the lights and the heat. The world felt cold and dark, and Bess felt all alone.

Clara, Rebecca, and Marita all tried to comfort her. She went through the motions of conversations and tried to say the right words, but she still felt cold and hard inside. She even tried to reason with herself, to no avail.

As the four friends walked back toward the wagons after the burial, Bess suddenly saw the Sheldon family all together, and she was not with them. She felt she did not belong there any longer. She couldn't stay in that house without Anita. It could ruin Robert's reputation. That's when she realized she had lost not only Anita but her family also.

Bess looked around her quickly. What was she to do? Where could she go?

"What is it, Bess?" Rebecca asked.

Bess turned to look her in the face. "Rebecca, I cannot stay with the Sheldons any longer. I want to, but people would talk about me living there, with Robert not having a wife. With my background I'm afraid that would cause talk about that good man. What am I to do? Where am I to go?"

They had come to the front steps of the church, and Bess sat down hard. Putting her face in her hands, she groaned. "Why has God done this to me?"

The other women sat down with her. Marita said, "Bess, we could put another bed in the room where Clara is staying and you could stay with us."

But Rebecca quickly offered, "Bess, why don't you move back with us? We could even use some help in the store again. Would you be interested in helping us?"

Suddenly a tiny glimmer of light ignited in Bess's cold heart. God was still caring for her.

Almost as though reading her mind, Marita said softly, "Bess, even when we feel all hope is gone and we don't understand the workings of God, He is still working on our behalf. He will never forsake us. We don't understand why He took Anita home, but we can trust Him and know without a doubt that He has a purpose and will work for our good through even this tragedy. He has not left you, Bess. Don't pull away from Him. Just trust Him."

Tears slowly coursed down Bess's face. She had been too angry to cry since she had wept the night of Anita's death. She had not wept during the service and burial, but now the tears came. She couldn't speak. Her mind was numb and icy, but the tears were flowing. It was as though she were thawing from the inside out. She dropped her face into her hands and wept until she lost all track of time. Without saying or thinking a word, she knew she had submitted her heart once again to God's will. And she knew that God knew also and would continue to provide for her.

As the tide of tears subsided, and Bess's mind returned her to the present, she felt small gentle pats on her head. She looked up to see little Anna standing there, with tears running down her pudgy cheeks. "Don't cry, Miss Bess. God will take good care of Mommy. And God will take care of us, too, Miss Bess. Don't be sad."

Bess wrapped her arms around the little girl, pressing her face into the silken hair and soft neck. "I know He will, Anna. I know He will. But we will miss her so."

"You know, Miss Bess," Anna whispered, "every time I miss Mommy, I just thank God that He gave us you. Then I don't miss her quite so much."

The women were all speechless. Such wisdom from one so young. Such a trusting heart. Finally Bess said to the child, "Anna, God has much He can teach me through you. Thank you, sweetheart."

∽∞∾

Robert seemed to be in a daze since Anita's death. Pastor Lewis tried to help with things he needed to remember to do for the children. Robert felt completely abandoned when he thought about Bess moving out, but he knew in his heart it was the right thing for her to do, and he was quick to thank her for the way she had cared for Anita and the family.

Paul was sad and seemed to be burdened beyond his years when he told her good-bye, but Conner and Philip and Anna clung to her. They could not understand why she couldn't stay with them. They loved her, and Bess knew they felt totally abandoned. If it had not been that she cared about Robert's reputation, Bess would have thrown propriety to the wind and stayed to care for the children. But Robert had become a good friend, and she could not do that to him.

However, with Rebecca's encouragement, she told the children that she would come out to their house on Friday to do their laundry and clean the house. Then, if their father approved, they could ride back with her and stay with her until Sunday.

When Rebecca came for her, Bess looked back to wave as they drove away from the farm, but her heart was nearly broken in two by the sad faces of the children as they waved.

Why must life be so difficult? Bess wondered. *Why must we struggle so on this earth?*

Chapter 11

Bess settled into life during her first week with Rebecca and Jason. But she found that, in spite of having people around most of the time, she had never been so lonely. She missed the Sheldon family desperately. Life was good, and she was busy and felt good about helping Rebecca and Jason, but her spark had been snuffed out. The perpetual sadness in her very core was untouched by anything or anyone.

Each day of the week, Bess worked to help out in the Taylors' store. The town was growing rapidly, and Jason and Rebecca had added much inventory to the store, but their space was limited so it had become crowded and disorganized. After Rebecca complained about the inconvenience of the crowded aisles a couple of times, Bess decided to think of a remedy.

She suggested to Jason and Rebecca that they build a couple of half-walls through the main part of the store, with shelves on either side as well as the top. If the walls were only waist or shoulder height, they could stack things on the shelves and still be able to see throughout the store. It would give more organizational options and make items easier to access while not making the store seem closed in and dark.

Jason and Rebecca loved the idea. So that very evening, while Jason was cutting the lumber for the first half-wall, Bess and Rebecca cleared out the space. While they were moving things, Bess organized the goods. Many items could be placed in baskets that would sit in rows on the shelves, keeping things from falling off and keeping it organized also.

They worked late into the night and rose early the next morning to finish organizing that section of the store before they opened to the public for the day. Throughout the day, when she had the time, Bess continued to organize and move items with Rebecca's blessing, making ready for another evening of building another half-wall.

In just a few days, the store took on a whole new look. Jason and Rebecca were very pleased with the easy accessibility of the goods, and the customers seemed to enjoy the changes also. And it actually created a bit more space around the stove for the ones who came in to play checkers and visit there.

The best part was that it kept Bess really busy. She hardly had time to miss the children or count the days until the weekend with them. Jason had a fun idea at one point. He suggested that they pay the children a bit to help them organize and put away some of the inventory. It would give them something to do on Saturday that they could all work together on and would benefit the store also.

On Friday, Bess borrowed Jason and Rebecca's wagon to go to the Sheldon farm. She was eager to be with the children once again and to see how they were getting along.

When she arrived, there was no one at home. Bess assumed Robert had taken Anna with him and taken the boys to the school. So she went on in and started making the beds and boiling water for the wash.

When Robert and Anna arrived sometime later, Bess had opened all the curtains, cleaned the big kitchen, and had a pot of something very appetizing and aromatic simmering on the back of the stove while bread dough was rising in the big crock on the hearth. She was working away at the washing on the big table. The room was steamy and warm, and the fragrance of the simmering soup, mixed with the clean smell of lye soap and the soft sound of Bess humming as she scrubbed on the washboard, felt like a breath of fresh air as they entered the cheery room.

"Oh, Miss Bess, it feels like we finally came home. Our house didn't feel like home all week until you came." Anna was wreathed in smiles and dimples as she ran at Bess with her arms open wide for hugging.

Robert ducked his head quickly as Bess turned toward them, but not before she saw his quiet smile. "Thanks for coming out, Bess. I guess I'll be going on out to the barns now."

"I'm glad I could come to help, Robert. It feels good to be here once again, and to see my dear Anna. And I can hardly wait until school is out, when I can see the boys, too. Lunch will be ready before long if you want some hot soup and warm bread."

Again he ducked his head. He said nothing, but his smile spoke volumes. He was glad for her help also, and Bess was glad she could help them out and be with this family once again.

Years earlier Robert had strung a couple of ropes high across the room in front of the fireplace to serve as clotheslines in the winter months. Bess had all the clean-smelling wash hung neatly on the lines when he came in for lunch. He hung his hat on the peg by the door as Bess took crusty loaves from the oven. Anna hummed as she carefully poured glasses of frothy milk for them all. Bess smiled. She could tell Robert's spirits were lifted, and he ate hungrily.

While they finished lunch, Bess told them all about working at the store. Anna asked lots of questions as Bess shared stories of building the walls and moving all the goods in the store. Bess also asked questions about their week. Robert had learned to cook some things when Anita was down with polio, so they were getting by. But Anna assured Bess that the house felt empty with her gone.

After cleaning up their lunch dishes, Bess suggested to Anna that they make cookies while they waited for the clothes to finish drying. That suggestion met with excited approval, and the two began at once. Anna chattered more than Bess had ever heard her chatter. Oh, it was so good to be together with these dear ones that she loved so much!

When half the cookies were baked, she saw the boys coming from school. She filled a plate with the warm cookies and poured three tall glasses of milk. When the boys entered, they squealed with delight when they saw her and were so busy hugging her they didn't even see the treat on the table.

Oh, what a merry kitchen it was while the boys ate their cookies and drank the milk. They told Bess about the whole week, and there was so much laughter and noise that Bess could hardly think. But she enjoyed watching them and listening to them and just being with them.

While the rest of the cookies finished baking and the boys prepared to help their dad outdoors, Bess took the heated irons and began the ironing. For the rest of the afternoon, she ironed all that needed pressing. When she put the clean clothes away upstairs, she gathered what the children would need for the weekend and went downstairs. She had made a large potpie that was bubbling in the oven and spreading its fragrance throughout the house. A cheery feeling warmed the inside of her as she finished the supper preparations.

Dusk had come quickly, but she was thankful for the full moon to light their way back to town. All the same, Bess felt a heaviness of heart about having to leave this cheerful place. Having the children with her helped, but it made her sad for Robert that he would be alone for a couple of days. When she asked him about it, he reassured her that he'd be fine knowing they'd be back home soon and that they were well cared for and happy. And so they headed back to the town, singing and laughing and talking all the way and just enjoying being together once again.

Chapter 12

Life did settle into somewhat of a busy routine. One day while Bess was working at the Taylors' store, a lady from the town stopped in to chat with Rebecca. The two women had Bess trapped in the corner, so she continued folding and organizing fabrics while they chatted.

Mrs. Tergoza told Rebecca that she and her husband wanted to move to be nearer their married children but had been unable to sell their large house on Main Street. They needed the funds from the sale to build a home when they relocated. She asked Rebecca to mention to anyone she knew who might be interested that they were selling at a very reasonable price.

Bess couldn't think which house it was that the lady spoke of, but she remembered Clara was looking to start a boardinghouse. She wondered why Rebecca didn't mention that possibility, but she didn't want to interrupt or question Rebecca in the lady's presence. So she continued folding and organizing the fabrics until the two ladies moved on.

Sometime later, when Bess and Rebecca were alone for a few minutes, Bess said, "Rebecca, I overheard the lady earlier this morning telling you she and her husband wanted to move nearer their children."

"Yes, Mrs. Tergoza. She and her husband have a large family, but all of their children have grown up and moved farther west. Their father's banking business did not appeal to the children, so they moved to the Dakotas where farmland is rich and plentiful."

"Where do the Tergozas live? She mentioned they had a large house for sale. Do you know which house it is?"

Rebecca looked at her wide-eyed. "Bess, I didn't even consider that you might be interested. I'm so sorry. But I can take you there if you want to see it. Oh, I would hate to lose you from here. . ."

"No, not for me," Bess said with a smile and a hug. "I was thinking of Clara's dream of a boardinghouse. The lady said the house was large and was on Main Street, so I thought it might work well for a boardinghouse for Clara."

"Oh, my, where is my head these days? Of course it might work. It's only a couple of blocks up the street from us, on the other side of the street. Let's go visit Clara and the Lewises this evening and mention it to her. Now that we have the railroad station with a train stopping here, a boardinghouse should have no problem finding boarders at all."

Later that evening Bess and Rebecca walked over to the Lewises' house. Pastor Lewis came to the door with a worried look. "Good evening, ladies." Somehow it sounded more like a question than a statement. "Come in, come in. Is everyone well at your home?"

"Oh, yes," Rebecca said with a chuckle. "We just heard some news today that we wanted to share with Clara."

The sound of clinking dishes and women chatting came from the direction of the kitchen.

"Come on back." Pastor Lewis chuckled as he headed toward the back of the house. "Marita and Clara, you have guests," he announced as they entered the kitchen.

"Oh, what fun! We'll have a bit of a tea party." Clara pushed the coffeepot to the hot part of the stove while Marita uncovered a cake that had about one-third of it missing.

After setting places at the freshly wiped table, Marita asked while serving the cake and coffee, "What brings you out in the cold?"

"We heard about a large house that's for sale on Main Street today. I don't know what they are asking for the house, but it does have lots of rooms and might be just the thing for a boardinghouse," Rebecca said, brimming with excitement. "The location is perfect. We wanted to let Clara know about it."

The women discussed the possibilities while they sipped their coffee and gave Clara what details they knew. She promised to visit the family the very next day.

After a good chat and a nice long visit, Rebecca and Bess left the Lewis home. As they walked home, Rebecca took Bess's arm and asked gently, "Bess, are you happy? Something about you seems restless or at best not quite settled. Is everything all right?"

Bess walked arm in arm with Rebecca in silence. "I miss Anita desperately," she said finally. Tears sprang to her eyes, but she wiped them away quickly with her gloved finger. "I miss the children and caring for that home. Anita and I had become as close as sisters even in the short months I was there, and I feel like a piece of myself is missing with her gone. And then not being with the children breaks my heart also. I wish so much that I could stay out at the farm and care for them. Don't worry. I wouldn't do anything to darken Robert's reputation, but I wish it didn't have to be this way. Rebecca, thanks so much for letting me bring the children to town for weekends. It is such a blessing to me to have them near again."

This time Rebecca was silent for a while. "Bess, before you came into our lives,

Jason and I had three lovely children. When the typhoid epidemic went through the town a couple of years ago, the children and I came down with it. I was expecting our fourth child, which I lost, and all three of the children were also lost to the disease. It felt like such a waste. So useless. I even found myself questioning God. But He was patient with me, and when I accepted His sovereignty and grace, I finally began to heal. I don't know why Jason and I have not had more children since then. We want them very much. But God has filled my life with others like you and Clara who have become very dear friends, and the ache is not as raw as it once was. God has shown me that my life still has purpose. I am praying He will do the same for you, Bess."

Bess sighed. "Thank you for telling me about your hurt, Rebecca. It helps to know that I am not the only one who has suffered loss. And it helps to know that you have been through heartache and loss and have survived, and very successfully too. I pray about the empty spot that was left when Anita died, but I try not to think about it too much. I appreciate being busy at the store and with the Sheldon children. And now, if Clara should open a boardinghouse, we will have our hands full helping her. There won't be so much time for grieving."

"Yes, idle hands are indeed the devil's workshop. And an idle heart is also. Keeping ourselves busy is a healthy way to begin the healing process in a positive way. I will continue to pray for you, Bess."

As the two women walked on, still arm in arm, silence again descended. But Bess's heart rejoiced in the presence of her dear friend.

⁓

Taylors' General Store was busy as usual. The slight hum of conversations was a comforting sound, as was the tinkle of the bell at the entrance as people came and went, taking care of their physical needs as well as their social needs. Often one could hear chuckles and sometimes outright laughter as people of the town sat or stood in small groups around the store.

Bess was noticing the comforting noises and smells of the store when suddenly the front door opened with a hearty bang. At that moment all noise stopped in the store while heads turned to the door to see what the commotion was about.

Totally oblivious to the attention she had drawn, Clara flew into the store, looking around hurriedly for Bess and Rebecca. Catching Bess's eye, she hurried in that direction. "My, the store seems unusually quiet today," Clara whispered as she rushed over to Bess, motioning for Rebecca to join them.

Bess tried to hide her smile while she said simply, "You know, just one of those lulls in conversation when everyone gets quiet at the same time. See? It didn't last long at all."

But Clara didn't even pause to listen to the voices as people slowly resumed their conversations. Instead she gestured again for Rebecca to join them.

Bess took Clara's arm and they started toward where Rebecca was finishing putting away some fabrics. Bess couldn't remember ever seeing Clara so animated.

They had barely reached Rebecca when Clara said excitedly, "Not only did I look at it and love it, I bought it. I bought the whole property!"

"You bought it? Already?!" Bess and Rebecca said almost in unison.

"Tell us all about it," Rebecca insisted as she steered the women through the store to their kitchen behind. Putting fresh cold water and coffee in the coffeepot, she added wood to the stove and pulled the coffeepot to the hottest part of the stove, then joined the others at the gingham-covered table.

Clara could hardly contain herself as she began. "Well, I went over first thing this morning, knocked on the door, introduced myself, and asked if I could talk to them about buying their house and look at the property. Mrs. Tergoza invited me right in and offered to show the house to me right then. When I told her my boardinghouse idea, she also thought it was the perfect location, and the size is wonderful. The way that house is built, it's just made for boarding guests.

"Porches wrap completely around the first floor of the house. You enter through a hallway that divides the downstairs into two halves from front to back. To the right of the front door is a doorway into the parlor. Just beyond that doorway, on the right side of the hallway, is a huge stairway reaching to the second-floor balcony that encircles the center of the whole second floor. There are four large, lovely rooms and a sitting room on the second floor, as well as a smaller room between the two front rooms that can be used for a bathing room.

"Behind the parlor on the main floor is a nice, bright dining room, which can be entered from the back side of the parlor or from the hallway across from the kitchen. The left side of the hallway has a sitting room, another room that will be my bedroom, and a wonderful large kitchen. The sitting room and the other room in front of the kitchen will be for me, while the rest of the house will be used for the boarders.

"Behind the house at the back of the property are a beautiful large stable, a barn, and two outhouses. We can use one for women and one for men. The Tergozas built their house this way to accommodate their large family. They have fourteen children. Six girls and eight boys. So they built a girls' outhouse and a boys' outhouse to keep peace and for convenience.

"As soon as Mrs. Tergoza started showing me the house, I knew it would work perfectly. But I feared it would be way beyond my means. When I finally asked what they wanted for the house and she told me, I didn't even have to think about it. I told her I would be right back with the cash. And now it's mine. And I still have some money left over that I can use to furnish the house and get started!"

Clara had hardly taken a breath while she described the house and grounds. Bess and Rebecca looked at one another and immediately broke out laughing. Oh, how they laughed! And every time they paused to breathe and glance at one another, they laughed again.

At first Clara was puzzled, but when she stopped to think about it, she realized she had been quite worked up as she talked and that she had talked so fast she could hardly breathe. Then she laughed, too, but she was too excited about it all to waste time laughing, so she finally got up and poured the rapidly boiling coffee into mugs for them.

When she sat back down, Bess and Rebecca were wiping their eyes and blowing their noses and trying to regain some decorum. More quietly they sipped their coffee, but not without a few snickers and further smiles.

Finally, Rebecca said, "Well, Clara, I would ask you about it, but I can't think of a thing to ask. I don't believe you left out one detail. But we are thoroughly excited for you. And for all of us. What fun this will be!"

"When will you get possession and be able to move into the house?" Bess was still wiping the merriment from her eyes, but she was truly excited about helping Clara move and plan.

"The Tergozas asked if they could stay until the first wagon trains head West in the spring. Mr. Tergoza thinks there will be a train leaving in March. That should work well, leaving me time to prepare for this huge undertaking and to purchase furnishings and be ready to move in."

"Are they moving all of their furniture? Will they have some things you can buy from them? That might help them as well as you," Bess suggested.

Clara stared at Bess. "I didn't even think of that. What would they do with all those beds since their children are grown? I will go right back over and ask them if I can purchase anything I need that they don't wish to take with them. That will make it much easier than starting with nothing. Oh, Bess, that's a wonderful idea."

"That is a great idea, Bess," Rebecca added with a smile.

The women sipped their coffee for a few minutes, and then Clara said she needed to get her money and return to Tergozas' to see about purchasing furnishings. Rebecca and Bess needed to go help Jason in the store also, so they finished their coffee, put their mugs in the dishpan, hugged the excited Clara, and headed back to the store.

Chapter 13

It hadn't snowed for a couple of days, and the snow that was on the ground, though deep, was packed in the wheel ruts of the roads, making walking much easier than trudging through the deep snow. Bess had risen extra early that Friday knowing that it would take her longer to walk than to drive Jason's wagon. Bess didn't like being responsible for someone else's horses and wagon in this kind of weather, so she had opted to walk to the Sheldon home, knowing Robert would drive her and the children back into town in the evening.

The sun had not yet risen, but the moon gave plenty of light as it shone on the packed snow. There was not much wind, and the cold seemed a bit more gentle than usual. As Bess walked, the crunching of the snow under her boots sounded colder than it actually felt.

But then Bess thought that maybe it was the thought of seeing those dear children that warmed her heart and made her step light. Although the more she thought about the children, the sadder she became thinking of all the things she was missing in their lives by not being with them throughout the week. She even wondered if, in time, they would lose some of their deep affection for her as they spent less time with her. However, unless something happened to change the situation, she planned to continue to spend her Fridays with them, doing the laundry and cleaning for them since Robert and the children really couldn't manage those chores alone very well.

One by one she thought of the children as she walked. Paul was becoming quite grown up in his behavior. He always had watched over his younger siblings with almost a parental care and concern, but now, since Anita's death, he seemed to take that responsibility much more seriously. It saddened Bess that he carried such a burden of responsibility at his young age, but it seemed to come natural for him, and the other children truly benefited from his care.

Bess sighed. Paul would be grown in only a few more years. Bess had to smile when she thought of him as a husband and father. He would make some young woman happy with his gentle ways and tender caring.

Bess's thoughts turned to Conner, who was next in line to Paul. One might expect some rivalry between the two, but Conner seemed to idolize Paul. On more than one occasion Bess had noticed Conner secretly watching Paul and then imitating his actions. She was glad he had such a good example to follow. She would speak to Paul when the time was right and encourage him to give Conner some leadership responsibilities so he could start to learn that role also.

Again Bess sighed. Was it all right for her to take that kind of responsibility with the children still? She and Anita had discussed parenting strategies, and Anita had so willingly listened whenever Bess had ideas. But mostly Bess learned from Anita's nurturing ways. And Bess had always been truly honored when Anita told her she was a natural-born parent. Since Bess had never really had parenting herself or even opportunity to witness it, she and Anita were both amazed that it seemed to come so easily to Bess. But also, having seen some of the prankster children in the town, Bess realized that the Sheldon children were particularly easy to parent.

The snow crunched as Bess marched on. The wind was more biting than she had realized at first. She gathered her cloak about her more snugly and tugged the collar up to shield more of her face. The cold stung her cheeks and nose, so she walked with one gloved hand shielding that part of her face for a while.

Soon her mind wandered back to the children. She couldn't help smiling when she thought of little Philip. With his freckles and missing teeth and wide grin, he looked more mischievous than he actually was. Oh, how broken he was whenever he was scolded—which wasn't often. In her mind's eye Bess could see the way the tears welled up in his innocent eyes when he erred. Just thinking about it made her want to hug him.

And then there was Anna. Bess thought for a minute and then shook her head. No words were adequate to describe that precious child. Anna would one day make a wonderful mother, of that there was no doubt. She already watched over every bird, insect, and brother. Even though she was not quite five years old, she was as serious as though the weight of the whole world was her responsibility alone. She was a happy child, but it was a sober kind of happiness much too mature for her age.

Bess smiled as she remembered Anna bringing gifts of flowers or pretty rocks or broken bird egg shells to her or to Anita. Anna was one small child who had never needed to be taught to share. It seemed to be her very nature.

As the sky lightened, the stars twinkled out. The Sheldon house was now in view. Bess saw light through the kitchen window and knew someone was up. *Probably Robert*, she thought. Then she realized he would be out at the barn now, so one of the children must be up already. Her step quickened as she anticipated the greetings ahead. Her face felt too cold to smile, but she knew she smiled inside.

She could see the smoke coming from the kitchen chimney and wished her legs and feet were not so cold nor the snow so slippery that she could run. She laughed at the childish thought. Yes, she really did feel like running. Anita had been gone for a few months now, and seeing the children only on the weekends was not enough. With that thought she felt her eyes tearing and laughed. *That's all I need—to walk in with tears frozen to my cheeks.*

As she turned to walk to the rear door, she saw the curtain drop back into place at the kitchen window. Who had peeked out? She was sorry she had missed seeing who it was but knew someone knew she was near.

Just as she reached for the doorknob, the door flew open and all the children were laughing and hugging her at once. She entered and closed the door behind her before hugging them all back. All talked at once, and she could not get enough of hearing them and watching them. She tried to respond to a question here and there, but it was lost in the commotion, so she simply held them and listened.

Finally, when things quieted enough, she asked why they were up so early.

"I woke up early because I knew it was the day for you to come," said Paul. "And when I tried to sneak out of the bed, Conner asked if I was going downstairs to wait for you. I told him I wanted to get the fire going so the kitchen would be warm, so he came with me. Then we were building the fire and Philip and Anna came sneaking in, too, as though there was anyone left to be awakened by their noise."

Anna said animatedly, "We all wanted to see you quicker!"

"Well, I was in a hurry to see you, too, and thought that I could get here and get your breakfast made before you even woke up."

"We'll all help," said Philip.

"All right, let's get the table set and breakfast made before your daddy comes in from the chores," Bess said happily, hugging them all once more.

The sausage was browning, but Bess was just putting the biscuits into the oven when they heard Robert stomping the snow off his boots on the back stoop. As the door opened, Anna flew at her daddy to tell him, "Miss Bess is here, Daddy. Miss Bess is here!"

Robert smiled and nodded to Bess as he gathered the child in his arms. "Looks like we're all early this morning. Guess this family gets pretty excited to see our Miss Bess again."

Bess felt herself blush. "You're all just eager to have me do the cooking, I know."

Paul responded innocently, "Yes, we all like your cooking, too."

༄

Bess packed their lunches as the boys finished getting ready for their walk to school in the snow. Anna helped and watched the boys to be sure they were dressed properly and didn't forget anything. All the while they chattered and continued to tell Bess everything that was happening at school as well as in the barns and around the home. They seemed to need to share their lives with her as much as she needed them to. She loved hearing every little detail and asked lots of questions, which kept the conversations animated.

Finally, the boys left for school, and Robert went back out to the barns. The house seemed very quiet. "Well, I guess it's just you and me now," Bess said to Anna.

"I guess we'd better get our work started," Anna said with the maturity of a grown woman. "Daddy already drew the water for you today."

"Oh, my, that was nice of him. Well, let's get some water boiling so we can wash up the breakfast dishes."

Suddenly Anna stopped. Her eyes were large as she turned very quietly toward Bess.

"What is it?" Bess asked with concern.

Anna slowly put her finger to her lips. "Shhhh. . .listen."

"Listen to what?" Bess whispered because Anna was whispering.

But as they stood very still, Bess heard it. Robert was whistling out at the barns. It wasn't one of the frisky tunes he used to whistle sometimes that would dance about in the air creating magic in their feet and fingers, but it was a happy tune all the same and brought with it a sense of contentment.

"I haven't heard Daddy whistle for a long time," Anna said with a happy sigh. Bess realized she had not heard him whistle since Anita had taken ill. She knew this was a good sign. She and Anna hugged because it was the only way they could express their joy.

Bess and Anna worked together doing the laundry, dusting and sweeping the house, and baking and cooking food ahead for the family for next week. It was a busy day, but Bess enjoyed every minute.

At lunch she said quietly, "Robert, are you sure you don't mind the children spending the weekends with me at the Taylors'? I feel bad leaving you all alone out here."

Robert looked deep into her eyes and then back down at his plate. "I won't pretend I don't miss them, but they need a mother, and they love you so much and I know you love them. They look forward all week long to seeing you on the weekends. I would never prevent them or you from this small happiness. Besides, the weekends probably go more quickly for me than the whole week does for you."

Bess smiled. "Yes, you're right. The weeks seem to get longer and longer. I try to stay busy at the store so I don't miss them so much. I really do appreciate you allowing me to continue to be part of their lives, Robert. They feel like family to me."

Robert just smiled and ducked his head again.

"I know! Miss Bess can just move back with us and take care of us like she used to take care of Mother!" Anna presented her cheerful resolution to the problem.

Robert continued to gaze at his plate, but tears sprang to Bess's eyes. *Oh, if life could only be so simple,* she thought. But to Anna she replied, "Then who would help the Taylors at the store? Come on—let's go read a story for your naptime." Bess quickly gathered the child, and together they went upstairs to read before her nap.

Chapter 14

Saturday morning, while the boys still slept on their pallets on the floor, Bess slipped out of her bed without rousing Anna, who had been snuggled tight against her body. She placed her warm pillow next to Anna, then took her dress off the hook behind the door and tiptoed quietly down the stairs to the pantry to dress in private. She built up the fire in the stove in the kitchen and was making the coffee when Rebecca came out of their bedroom still tucking her hair up with hairpins.

"I had an idea this morning," Rebecca whispered with her dimples showing her pleasure and her eyes twinkling.

Bess smiled her question with raised eyebrows.

"Let's invite the Lewises and Clara and Robert to stay for dinner after church tomorrow. Then the children won't have to leave us so early in the day."

"Oh, Rebecca, that's a wonderful idea! I think the children will be pleased. The two older boys love helping in the store. They could work with Jason today while you and I prepare the food with the help of Philip and Anna."

Together they began to plan the meal and how they would get everything made. They decided to write a note to the Lewises and Clara and ask Philip and Anna to take it over to their house and wait for a response.

Whenever the Sheldon children came for the weekend, they worked hard. They always noticed chores that needed to be done and pitched in and completed the chores before anyone had an opportunity to ask. They dusted in the store, swept the floors and the front walk, stacked wood and filled the wood box, and brought in water. They were so helpful that the Taylors as well as Bess missed their help almost as much as they missed the children when they left.

Rebecca and Bess told the children their idea as they sat together at breakfast. The children were excited about the plan and were eager to help. Philip and Anna were proud of being asked to run the errand to the Lewis household, and Paul and Conner felt good about helping in the store in a more official capacity.

Philip said very quietly, "When we get back from taking the note to the Lewises, maybe I could help in the store, too."

Jason was quick to respond. "Absolutely! Those women don't need you in the kitchen as much as I need your help in the store. I don't know what they're thinking."

Surprised, Rebecca and Bess exchanged glances but were careful not to smile. It was strange thinking of Philip as one of the men instead of one of the children. But of course they should have realized he'd feel left out. They were thankful for Jason's quick response and they both readily agreed.

Sometimes during the day Rebecca would be called to help ladies with dress goods or notions, and Bess and Anna would be left to the cooking and baking and cleaning together. Bess found herself humming, and Anna was quick to notice.

"Miss Bess, I miss hearing your humming songs. It is such a warm feeling inside when you are humming. It makes me remember when our family was happy before our mother died." She wrapped her chubby little arms around Bess's skirts and hugged her fiercely. Bess squatted and, removing the girl's arms from around her legs, placed them around her neck and embraced Anna tightly.

"I love you so much, Miss Bess. I miss you all week long and can hardly wait for the Friday day to come again."

Warm tears dampened Bess's shoulder where the curly head rested. Kissing the back of Anna's head, Bess said softly, "Anna, I miss you terribly also. I am so very thankful we still get to see one another and spend time together every week. Let's both try to thank God for what we do have and not think about what we wish we had, all right? And I promise I will hum more often."

"Yes, I will try, Miss Beth. I promise. I will try."

"Oh, the cookies!"

They both made a dash for the stove. . .and the formidable burnt smell.

Opening the oven door, Bess was relieved to see that only one cookie had been placed too near the edge of the sheet, so part of it had fallen onto the bottom of the oven and was burning there. They removed the cookie sheet and quickly scraped the bottom of the oven free of the charred remains of the broken cookie before putting another sheet into the oven.

"Here, Anna, if you eat the half that's left of this cookie, no one will ever know we messed up on one."

Anna grinned up at her, but as usual, quickly broke the piece in two, handing half to Bess. "Here. We can share it. Food is always better when it's shared. Mother always used to say that, and it's true."

Again Bess reached out and hugged Anna. How could one little girl be so very precious? Suddenly she realized she loved the boys just as intensely. *Is this what motherhood is like?* She wished with all her heart she could live at the farmhouse and care for the children all the time. But such wishing was futile, so she tucked the thought far away and got back to the chores at hand.

Before they left for church the next morning, Bess and Rebecca placed all the pans of food in the oven or at the back of the stove, added boards to stretch the table to a larger size, and set the table.

They all left early for the church so they could invite Robert for dinner as soon as he arrived. The children were quite excited as they ran to hug their daddy. They chattered so rapidly that Robert couldn't understand them at all until Jason came over and offered the official invitation.

"I'm delighted to accept." Robert grinned. "But I don't know that I really would have had much choice."

What fun the families had that afternoon. They ate together, laughed together, chatted together, and ate some more. Sometime late in the afternoon, Pastor Lewis said to the group, "I have a feeling we've sampled a little bit of what heaven will be like today."

Bess smiled at the curly head snoozing on her shoulder as she sat in the big rocker by the fire. *Yes,* she thought as she kissed Anna's head lightly, *I can't imagine heaven could be much better than this.* As she scanned the group, she caught Robert's eye and he smiled, too. Yes, it was good to see him smile again.

Monday morning, as Bess folded the blankets and stacked the straw mattresses that they used for the children, she reflected on the weekend and how she loved to be at the Sheldons' house on Fridays. It was a gray February morning, and the upstairs room seemed drab and cold. Looking out the one window onto the street below, she saw only gray skies and muddy, trampled snow. The town looked as barren and cold as she felt at the moment.

Inside, she glanced up at the underside of the store roof above her head. She was thankful for this room and thankful for Jason and Rebecca's kindness in sharing their home with her, but she realized that she had no real life of her own. She had been content and happy working at the Sheldons' and had assumed she would grow old there as part of their family.

At this moment she missed her dear friend Anita very much. Oh, life was so hard. She tried to think of happy things, but the tears started, and she felt helpless to stop the flow. She sat on the side of the bed, put her face into her hands, and cried and cried. She knew she should hurry downstairs and help Rebecca in the store, but for a few minutes she really didn't care about anything at all. Her life felt so very hopeless.

Finally the tears subsided. Bess still had some fresh water in the pitcher, so she poured some into the washbowl and splashed her face with the cold liquid. It felt good on her burning eyes. She held the cold water on her face for a little while to erase some of the puffiness from her swollen eyes. But studying her reflection in the mirror on the wall, she knew she could not hide the traces of her crying.

I need to start making a plan for my life. Perhaps I should ask Clara if I could help her with her boardinghouse. Now that I have learned to cook for a family, I should be able to cook for a boardinghouse also. Hmmm...I know Clara doesn't know how to cook and even hates cooking. I wonder what she plans to do for meals there. That would certainly keep me busy, but I would not want to give up my Fridays at the Sheldons'. I will talk to Clara and Rebecca and see what I can work out so that I have a definite plan for my future. Perhaps that will help me feel like I still have a purpose.

That very afternoon Clara stopped by the store on her way back from the Tergozas' house. "It's official," she said with a grin. "I'm the owner and plan to move there tomorrow. I have purchased quite a lot of furniture from them, as well as some kitchen supplies. But I'm sure I will need to purchase some kitchen items as well as other items from here. But first I must find a cook. Right now I wouldn't even know what was needed in a kitchen."

"Bess is a wonderful cook," Rebecca commented, but then looked as though she wished she hadn't mentioned that out loud. "I sure wouldn't want to lose her from here, though."

Bess was stunned. "That's amazing you would say that. I was just thinking this morning that I would ask Clara if she needed a cook. The only problem is that I wouldn't want to give up my Fridays at the Sheldons' house or my weekends with the children. So I don't know if I would be much help to you, Clara. Rebecca, you and Jason are wonderful to share your home and your work with me, but I can't live off of you forever. I don't feel as though I am contributing much at all here, though I love being with you."

"Please don't ever feel that way. It is so much more fun having you here with us. We truly appreciate your help and creativity, but we love your friendship even more. But, Bess, I realize you have no real identity here. If you need to do something different, I will certainly understand. We will still always be friends." Rebecca's eyes were moist, but her look was sincere.

Bess reached over to hug her, and the two women embraced warmly. Bess remembered how lonely and helpless she had felt only that morning and thanked God in her heart for these two dear friends.

Clara seemed thoughtful. Aloud she said, "Bess, perhaps you could show me some easy things to make on Fridays. Or perhaps you could make a pot of soup ahead or some such that I could serve on Fridays. Or maybe I could find someone else to cook on the weekends. And of course the children would be welcome to spend their weekends with us there. The attic room would make a wonderful huge bedroom for the boys. It's a lovely room with a window at each end."

Bess quietly thanked God for the miraculous ways He provided for His children. And especially that He had accepted her as one of His own.

Suddenly the gray skies didn't seem nearly as gloomy as they had that morning.

Chapter 15

Bess hummed as she hung the sheets on the clothesline. She watched as a couple of robins built a nest in one of the trees. She breathed deeply. The cherry, apple, and pear trees were in full bloom, and the beauty and fragrance filled her heart with joy.

May was nearly half over now, and the boardinghouse had been open for over a month. It had started out slowly, which was nice, as it gave the women a good opportunity to smooth out some rough spots. But all in all, it was going quite smoothly.

The third floor of the house was one large room, with long storage rooms built under the eaves on either side of the long room. Clara had thought she would use the third floor to house the cook and possibly a maid, but instead Bess had claimed the little room behind the kitchen and they used the large third-floor room for the Sheldon boys when they visited on the weekends. They had added a bed for Anna upstairs also, but Anna had looked with such sad eyes at Bess that Bess had quickly offered to share her bed with Anna again.

Anna said quietly, "Or I would even sleep on the floor beside your bed, Miss Bess, but I would love to sleep in your room if I may."

Both Bess and Anna were happiest when they could be together, so it worked out well that way.

As Bess hung out the sheets and hummed, she remembered Anna's delight at her humming. But as she thought about it, Clara hurried out the back door, with Rebecca close behind.

"Bess, do you want to come with us?" Clara was huffing as she trotted toward the clotheslines.

"Come where? What's happened? Where are you going?"

"To the Lewises'." Rebecca was breathless as she stepped up beside Clara. "Pastor Lewis was just in the store and told us that their son-in-law has been killed in some kind of horse and wagon accident in the Dakotas. We are taking a cake over to the Lewises' and want to see if we can help them in any way. He said Marita is taking this pretty hard. They haven't seen their daughter and son-in-law for several years since they moved out West, and she wants so very much to be with her daughter now."

"Oh, my! I hope they won't think of moving West now." Bess stated what was obviously in all of their minds. "I guess that is terribly selfish, but I can't imagine

162

what would happen to our church without them."

Bess finished hanging up the last sheet, gathered the basket, and headed back for the house. "I'll go with you," she said as she untied her apron with one hand. "Clara, I have a large pot of chicken and noodles cooking. Let's dish some up to take to the Lewises' along with Rebecca's cake, all right?"

"That's a great idea." Clara held the door open for the others, wanting them to hurry.

This beautiful day felt suddenly cold.

The women sat around the table in the Lewises' sunny kitchen, but their hearts were heavy. Marita said their two sons had convinced Timothy to move with them when they headed West. All three of the Lewis children and their spouses were very close friends. Therefore, all the grandchildren were more like brothers and sisters than cousins. Rose and Timothy had had three children when they moved West but had added two more in the years after moving that Edwin and Marita had never met. Marita longed to be with her children and grandchildren sometimes, but now more than ever she wanted to have some time with her daughter.

"Are you thinking of moving to the Dakota Territory to be with them?" Bess asked cautiously.

"We have talked about it," Marita said, "but both Edwin and I believe God has us here for this church, and we do not feel free in our hearts to leave. However, this morning Edwin asked if I wanted to ride out with the groups headed West this spring to visit the children for a while. He would stay here, but I just don't feel right about leaving him here alone. So for now, I will pray for Rose and the children and wait to see what God wants from me."

"We would miss you terribly if you did go," Rebecca said thoughtfully, "but please know that we would all help care for Pastor Lewis in your absence."

Clara smiled. "He would probably have more food than he could eat. Everyone loves you all so very much and would be happy to help care for him. But I agree with Rebecca. I don't even want to think about what our lives would be like without you here for a while."

"Oh, Marita, what will Rose do out West with five children to raise alone? Does she have much land? What will she do?" Bess felt the heaviness of Marita's concern.

"Our sons, David and Isaiah, will help, I'm sure. Eddie is fourteen now and has helped his dad with the farming for years. Her two youngest children, Richard and Allen, are ten and eight and will help when they can. They are good with the animals, but I think they would not be able to help much with farming the land yet.

David and Isaiah have their own farms to care for, so I don't know how they will all manage. I find myself trying to imagine, but I don't know how they are actually set up and what the distance between the farms is. I do know their farmlands are adjoining, so I hope this will work out for them. I know God will take care of them."

Marita absently got up and walked to the stove. She took the coffee and lifted the grounds out, walking out the back door to dump them onto the nearest flower bed. Then she came back inside and put together another pot of coffee, set it on the stove, and returned to her seat. The other women watched her without speaking.

"I feel like we are like Job's friends, sitting here in silence," Rebecca commented with a slight smile. Reaching over, she put her hand over Marita's hands that were clamped together in front of her on the table.

"You are nothing like Job's friends," Marita quickly replied. "You have not been critical and have actually been quite encouraging. It helps a lot to have someone ask and care with us. I know you will pray for Rose and the children. She loved that man with her whole heart. Besides their physical survival, I don't know how she will survive emotionally. He was such a good man. He was everything to her."

After a moment of silence, Rebecca said very quietly, "She may never be the same without him, but I do know that time will heal the rawest wounds. There will be scars for sure, but she will learn to survive, and she will heal." A tear slid down Rebecca's nose as she stared into her empty coffee cup. Her hands turned the cup in circles, but she didn't seem to notice what her hands were doing.

Marita regarded Rebecca with sadness. "You do know something about losing loved ones and healing, don't you, Rebecca?"

"I didn't mean to bring that up at a time like this. I have no idea what it would be like to lose a husband."

"No, I know that was not your intent. But I do agree with you, Rebecca, that the same God who healed your wounds will heal my Rose's heart if she will allow Him to. And He will provide for her and the children. I know He is able and that He will do it."

"And I'm sure in time He will heal your heart as well, Marita."

⤜∞⤛

A few weeks later, right before gathering for worship service, the ladies were visiting and enjoying the fresh air. They were clustered in small groups under one of the spreading oak trees at the side of the church when Marita hurried up to them. "I don't have time to tell you now, but Edwin will tell our great news to everyone before the worship service!" Her eyes danced, and her face was flushed with excitement.

There was an excited sense of expectation as they all entered the sanctuary. As soon as the room was quieted, Pastor Lewis stood to make their announcement.

"We received word yesterday that our recently widowed daughter, Rose Ellen Carter, will be arriving with her five children sometime in the next several weeks. Her brothers have agreed to care for her property this summer to give her opportunity to spend time with us. She is thinking of possibly moving back to this area now that her husband is gone. Needless to say, we are excited about the prospect of having our daughter and some of our grandchildren nearby!"

There was a sudden outburst of excited whispering and even some faint applause. The church was excited for the Lewises and all agreed to pray together for Rose's safe travels. It would be quite an undertaking with five children.

When church was over and there was time to chat a bit, Rebecca, Clara, and Bess peppered Marita with questions:

"Will they stay with you?"

"Where will you put them all?"

"Do you need help to get ready?"

"Do you have space?"

Marita calmly told the ladies that she had it all figured out. "The extra bedroom that you stayed in, Bess and Clara, will be used for Rose, plus we have the two rooms under the eaves upstairs. We'll use one for the boys and one for the girls. It should work out fine. We may have a little more difficulty fitting that many around the table, but I'm certain no one will mind if the fit is a bit snug. It will be so good to see them and be together for a while. I'm praying with my whole heart that God will help Rose to heal and to know what is best for their future. I have decided to assume it will be temporary; then if she does decide to go back to the farm, I won't have to deal with my disappointment. But if she decides to stay, it will be a bonus!"

As the women hugged one another good-bye that Sunday, their hearts were lighter than they had been for a while. Bess smiled as she and Clara walked back to the boardinghouse. She was happy for Marita to have some of her family coming home. She was happy for Rebecca that she was feeling fulfilled and content in spite of the loss of her children. She was glad that Clara had been able to save enough money through the years to fulfill her dream of owning a boardinghouse. And she was thankful to have a good place to live and work since she could not be with the Sheldons.

Then, suddenly, her eyes filled with tears. Propriety! It just seemed so wrong that she could not live at the Sheldons' house any longer to help care for them. She knew Robert was a dear friend and that she would not risk smearing his reputation, but it angered her all the same. She had enjoyed living and working in that home more than anything she could have ever imagined. It was as near to being a mother as anything would ever be for her, she was quite certain, yet it was taken away. It was difficult not to feel sorry for herself.

"Time will make it hurt less." Clara put her arm around Bess's shoulders. They kept in step as they walked.

"What?" Bess asked in surprise.

"You are wishing you could stay with your Sheldon family, but you'll get used to being away."

"You're amazing," Bess said with a smile. "Yes, I was resenting the fact that I must not stay out at the farm with them. I miss those children terribly."

"Are you sure it's just the children you miss?"

"No, I miss Anita, too. It was like what I always imagined it would be like to have a sister. I truly loved her with my whole heart."

"I know you loved Anita," Clara murmured. "I'm asking if it is Robert that is causing any of your grief now."

Bess stopped, startled. "Goodness, I do care for Robert, but Clara, I never even considered loving him in any way other than as a dear friend and brother. Whatever made you ask such a thing?"

"I've seen how lively you all get when you're together. I've also seen him looking at you from time to time and wondered if there is something beginning in your hearts for one another." Clara smiled gently.

"Oh, my, I don't even want to think such a thing. Why would he ever care for the likes of me? No, we are friends for the sake of the children, and that is all there is. I don't want to spoil a good friendship by thinking anything else."

"Hmmm...I just wondered."

Clara seemed satisfied. She and Bess walked on companionably, but Bess was embarrassed by Clara's question. Funny, the kinds of things that embarrassed her anymore.

Chapter 16

Bess's mind wandered as she sat in the backyard hulling peas for dinner. She enjoyed her work at the boardinghouse. The sign hanging from a pole by the front walk read CLARA'S PLACE—ROOM AND BOARD. Clara had talked of this dream from time to time as Bess grew up, but Bess hadn't realized that she was saving for it and was really serious about doing it. But, somehow, it all seemed to fit together.

Clara did not like cooking very much at all and was thankful Bess had taken to it so quickly and was quite good at it. In fact, her cooking was becoming known around town, and they had been asked several times about opening a restaurant along with the boardinghouse. But neither of the women really wanted that responsibility, so they continued to cook only for themselves and the boarders who stayed within the establishment.

It felt right to be here with Clara, at least for now. Clara had been like a mother to her, being fifteen years her senior. Bess smiled as she thought of the four friends. Marita was somewhere in her mid-fifties—probably six or eight years older than Clara. Rebecca was much nearer Bess's age, but still maybe six or seven years older. In spite of the age differences spanning nearly thirty years, the four had become good friends.

Bess smiled now as she recalled the good times the four had together in the past year. But, still, something inside her felt slightly out of place. She knew Clara had every intention of Bess remaining with her permanently, encouraging her to do whatever she wanted with her own room and even the kitchen area since Bess was the head cook. Bess was happy enough, but she couldn't quite put her finger on the reason for feeling unsettled.

Setting the bowl of peas on the back step, Bess shook the hulls from her apron into the bucket and took the bucket behind the shed to dump on the compost pile. She knew the bread was probably ready to be made into loaves, and Clara might need help with the dusting. She liked being busy, and there was never a shortage of work.

Bess picked up the bowl of peas on her way into the house and was reaching for the back door when it opened with a *whoosh*.

"Rebecca just stopped by to say that Rose and the children arrived at the Lewises' last evening," Clara said excitedly. "Marita has invited us over this afternoon to meet them."

"Oh, I am happy for them. I'm surprised Marita is willing to share their company already, but it will be fun to meet them all." As they turned to go inside, Bess sighed.

"What? Aren't you excited?" Clara tilted her head toward Bess questioningly.

"Yes, I'm excited for them—and for us all. It will be great meeting their daughter and getting to know some of their family. I don't know why I sighed, really." Bess moved inside and set the bowl of peas on the table in the kitchen. Gazing absently out the window, she said, "You know, Clara, even though I didn't intend to sigh, I think I know why I did. I'm happy for us all, but it seems everyone has a place to fit but me. I keep thinking God has something for me, too, where I can also feel fulfilled. The boardinghouse is yours. It's your dream. Your goal. Marita has her family and knows her place in the church's ministry. Rebecca and Jason have the store. I know they would love to have children again, but at least they have the store, which is their own dream. Me? While I'm very thankful to be part of your dream, something inside me needs to have my own dream. My own place in the world. I had it for a short time when Anita needed me. Perhaps that's all I will get. But I'd like to someday find my own dream once again—whatever it might be."

Clara stood with her hands on her hips, considering Bess in consternation. "I had assumed you'd someday inherit this place and keep it going. How stupid of me to assume my dream would suffice for you." Approaching Bess, she placed her hands on Bess's shoulders. "If this is not what you want, then I, too, hope you will find your own dream—and the happiness and contentment I feel here. But only God knows what I'll do without you."

"Oh, I'll probably be here forever. But don't worry. If there is something else for me, you'll be the first to know, and we'll make sure it works for you, too."

❧

Bess and Clara carried a basketful of cookies as they went by the Taylors' store to pick up Rebecca on their way to the Lewises'. They saw Rebecca watching for them at the window, and then her head disappeared from the window. She came out to meet the ladies before they even entered the store, carrying a small paper sack in one hand.

"What's in the basket?" she asked cheerily.

"Oatmeal cookies," said Clara with a smile. "What's in the bag?" Clara and Bess both regarded Rebecca with eyebrows raised.

"Five peppermint sticks." Rebecca's dimples showed as she fell into step with the other women.

"Oh, that's a good idea." Bess took Rebecca's arm, and they walked along companionably. "That will be a special treat, I'm sure."

"It's going to be a big change for the Lewises to have five children around all the time. I hope it works out well for them all," Rebecca said thoughtfully.

"What are you thinking?" Clara asked.

"Oh, I just know that sometimes life can become quite challenging with children around. Of course ours were younger than the Carter children, but it's still a lot of commotion for a couple who has been alone for so many years. I hope it all works out well."

"That's a good point, Rebecca. Let's all agree together to pray for them every day," Bess said.

So the three women agreed to make that a definite project and commitment.

As they neared the Lewis home, beautiful music danced out of the window as the curtain reached through the open space below the raised pane and billowed on a gentle breeze. All three women stopped as one and stood in silence, listening unashamedly. The notes frolicked in the air, magically making their feet want to tap and even dance. They exchanged surprised glances and, as though in agreement, no one moved toward the door. They closed the gate and stood listening on the little boardwalk that led to the porch of the Lewis home.

Sometimes the music would soften and they'd lean toward the window, only to straighten once again as the merry notes increased in volume and expression. The tune seemed to lift the spirit in such a way that caused an ache in the chest when it ended. Still breathless from the surprise and beauty of the piece, the three women paused another moment to remember where they were and why they had come. Just as they tapped on the door, another tune had begun but was quickly silent.

Marita flung the door wide and motioned animatedly for the women to come inside. "Come in, come in. I can't wait for you to meet our family!"

Behind her, two women who looked like live porcelain dolls were coming toward the front door. Marita reached for the blond woman. "Rose, come meet my good friends." Immediately she reached back farther to include the lovely brunette version of the blond. "Victoria, come! Don't be shy."

Rose put her hand forward and smiled radiantly. "I am so pleased to meet you. Mother has introduced you to me through letters this past year, and it is wonderful to actually make your acquaintance." In spite of the radiant smile that belied any timidity, her voice was soft and shy.

Victoria smiled hesitatingly and nodded at each of the women. She was obviously quite self-conscious.

"We are so pleased to meet you both!" Clara sounded boisterous compared to the quiet voices of the Carter women. "We have heard about you but had no idea you had such musical talent."

The friends had not known which of the two Carter women had been at the piano, but Victoria's cheeks flamed crimson as she ducked her head. "Thank you," she murmured.

Marita hugged her warmly. "Here, here, Tory. You don't need to be shy. These women will be like aunties to you before you know it. No one could ask for nicer friends."

Victoria made a brave effort to lift her head and smile, but her flaming cheeks announced she was still embarrassed.

Rebecca changed the subject to ease her discomfort. "I brought peppermint sticks for you all, and Bess and Clara have brought a basket of cookies." She handed the small paper sack to Victoria as Bess handed the basket to Marita.

"Thank you, ma'am. I'll go find my brothers and sister. Thank you very much." Her smile was finally in her eyes as well as on her beautiful lips.

When Victoria left the room, Rose said quietly, "I am sorry she is so shy. It is something she inherited from me, I'm afraid, but she hasn't worked as long to overcome it. Thank you for your patience with her. She'll be fine, but it takes a bit of time. She really does try to be friendly."

"So it was Victoria playing the piano then?" Bess asked to be sure. "Has she played long?"

"Her dad played, and it seems as soon as she was walking, she was finding tunes on the keyboard. She could barely reach the keys when she began playing tunes she heard him play. He would take her to concerts, and she would come home and play the songs with amazing accuracy. We live too far from any place that she could learn more, so she has not had formal lessons. We are hoping that, perhaps while we are here in a town, there might be some opportunity for her to study. But in the meantime, she plays whatever she hears for the family."

"She plays amazingly well for not having studied. So. . .does she read music at all?" This question was from Rebecca, who made no attempt to hide her amazement. But her question echoed Bess's thoughts as well.

"My husband. . ." Rose's voice broke and tears sprang to her eyes. "I'm so sorry. It's still so fresh," she said quietly. Then, clearing her throat, she began again. "Timothy taught her to read music and the correct fingering. In spite of being a farmer, he was a great musician. But Tory plays mostly by ear since we don't have access to a lot of written music. We are proud of her ability. Actually, all the children play, but Tory is the one who plays most easily and fluently." She smiled warmly.

"Come on into the kitchen," Marita invited. "I'll pour us some coffee to go with these cookies."

The afternoon passed quickly as the women visited and met the other children. Before they knew it, the time had come to get back to their various responsibilities for the evening. So with warm hugs they parted, knowing one more kindred spirit was among them.

Chapter 17

That summer the church decided to have a Fourth of July celebration. There was much excitement, discussion, and planning. Fourth of July was on a Saturday, so they planned for a picnic lunch on the church grounds, followed by games for all that wished to participate. Sometime in the afternoon the men and boys planned to do some fishing in the creek that ran behind the church and hopefully catch enough to provide for a fish fry for the evening meal. It was to be a nearly all-day event with singing in the church in the evening.

A sign was posted in the window of Taylors' store several weeks before, announcing that the store would be closed on the Fourth. The picnic was published for all who wished to attend, whether or not they were members of the church. There were meetings to decide who had sawhorses to donate for tables, who would be involved in the setup and the cleanup, who would be in charge of games, and who would lead the evening sing-along. Such an event had not taken place for quite some time, and anticipation ran high in the town.

The evening before the big event Marita asked Rose to take a stack of clean tablecloths to the church so the men could put them on the tables early in the morning as soon as the tables were put together. In spite of a sunny sky, Rose was still a couple of blocks from the church when the thunder cracked.

"Oh my!" she exclaimed to herself. "I guess it's closer to run on to the church than home." She lifted her skirts a bit in front and trotted as quickly as she could, hoping to get inside the church before the heavens opened.

As the thunder continued to rumble and crash, she took the tablecloths inside and left them with the other supplies for the following day. She hesitated at the front door, deciding whether she should try to make it home before the rain started.

As she was hurrying down the front steps, Robert Sheldon drove up in a covered carriage. Sticking his head out the side, he called out to Rose, "Is your father in the church?"

"He was earlier, but he is at home now helping Mother prepare for tomorrow. You are more than welcome to go over to the house to talk to him." Almost immediately another crash sounded and the heavens opened.

Robert hopped out and held out his arm to Rose. "Climb in and ride over with me so you don't get drenched in this downpour."

Rose smiled her thanks and scrambled into the shelter of the carriage. "You are certainly a godsend today." She laughed as she brushed the rain off of her face. "I hope this doesn't ruin our plans for tomorrow."

"These storms that come out of nowhere are usually very brief. We can certainly use the moisture, but I'm afraid this won't amount to more than enough to tease the thirsty gardens in this community."

Robert was right. The rain had stopped by the time they arrived at the Lewis home, and the sun was shining brightly again.

Bess had taken a large pot over to the Lewis home that Marita had asked to borrow. She was inside when the heavens opened and spilled a shower, but the rain was brief. As soon as the sun came out again, she excused herself to get back to her own cooking for the festive day.

As she and Marita finished their brief conversation on the front porch, a carriage drew up to the front. Robert Sheldon jumped out and stepped around to help Rose out.

As they strolled up the front walk, they greeted Marita and Bess on the porch. After Bess left for the boardinghouse, Robert, Marita, and Rose all went into the house.

As Bess walked to Clara's, she made lists in her head of all that was left to do for their preparations for the big event the next day. She even took time to thank God for the shower. It was enough to settle the dust for tomorrow, but not enough to make mud or to ruin the plans. *God certainly thinks of everything*, Bess thought with a smile.

The rest of the day she worked hard on the picnic preparations. But, strangely, her mind kept straying to the memory of Robert helping Rose out of the carriage. Why did that scene bother her so? And why, in reflecting back, had her stomach tightened for an instant when she saw them together? There was nothing whatsoever improper about it—except maybe that it was so soon after her husband's death. Was it a coincidence that they were together? Was there something between the two?

Bess hated the fact that it bothered her. She loved Rose with all her heart and had the greatest respect for her. And she cared for Robert as a good friend. They had been through a lot together with helping Anita walk and then her death and caring for the children. Was she jealous? Was it possible she felt more for him than she would admit to herself? The questions nagged at her.

That night Bess went to bed more tired than usual. She had cooked for their boarders as well as making lots of food to take to the picnic. It felt like she had been on her feet for a month. Her bed certainly felt good when she finally climbed in, and she thought she'd be asleep before her head was on the pillow. But sleep eluded her. Over and over she relived her surprise at seeing Robert and Rose together.

Finally, long after hearing the clock in the front room chime midnight, she began to doze. In her dream she saw Robert and Rose dancing together. She awakened with her heart pounding and muttered to herself with disgust, "They weren't dancing together. But even if they were, they have that right. Now forget about it and get some sleep!"

Eventually she dozed back to sleep again, and this time she saw them dancing again. Each time they would twirl she could see Robert's children between them. They were all merry and having a good time. Bess called to the children to wave, but they didn't hear her, nor did they even look her way. She thought she'd have to leave the dance before they saw her cry, but the tears began anyway.

When she awakened, she really was crying. And she felt terribly alone.

At last early in the morning she fell into a dreamless, exhausted sleep. When she awakened, she did not feel rested at all. Nor did she feel ready for the day she had anticipated with such excitement. She scolded herself as she made her bed. "If you really love those children, you will want what's best for them. And it would be great for them to have a mother again, someone to be there to teach and nurture them and help provide for their needs. You know it can't be you. You were a prostitute. No man in his right mind marries a prostitute."

Bess sat down hard and gasped while her hand flew to her face. "Was that it? Did I secretly want to marry Robert?" She sat there searching her heart for a while.

Then, being totally honest with herself, she admitted that it had never crossed her mind before now. What was truly bothering her were the children. She did not want to be replaced in their hearts. She honestly had wished with all her heart that they could all continue as they had when Anita was alive. She loved being the substitute mother for the children, and she cared for Robert as a friend, but Bess had no thoughts of taking on the role of a wife. Not now. Not ever. She didn't even want to think about ever being with a man again. There was too much in her past that she had put aside to ever want to try to be a wife.

Finally, Bess admitted to herself that Robert would need a wife and probably would find one at some point. At that time, Bess would no longer be needed in the lives of those children. And if it had to happen, she couldn't wish for anyone sweeter than Rose for Robert's children. Rose was several years older than Robert, but what did it matter, really?

With a heavy heart and tired eyes, Bess tied on her apron and headed for the kitchen to make breakfast for their boarders. She also needed to be sure that the meals were prepared for the rest of the day for anyone who remained at the house.

As soon as she started the coffee and began breaking eggs, Clara came into the kitchen, took one look at her, and exclaimed, "Did you not sleep at all last night? You look awful. Don't worry; you made enough food to feed an army. And your pies and chocolate cake will win the Best Cook Award with no trouble."

Clara bustled around setting the table, but Bess said nothing about why she hadn't slept. When the time seemed right, she might tell Clara about seeing Rose and Robert together, but now was not the day or the time.

Chapter 18

The tables were set up, and people were beginning to arrive when Bess and Clara came with their wagon loaded with food. It was a beautiful day—not too hot, not too cool. A light breeze kept any wayward flies at bay. It was truly a glorious day for a picnic.

Children were already playing tag behind the church and picking wildflowers for the tables as the women started to set out the food. Some of the older girls wove flowers into colorful crowns and necklaces for the younger girls. Bess sighed as she watched the children who had grown up together in this church playing together. How incredible that these children had such happy lives and wonderful opportunities. This is what she had missed as a child. But as she gazed at the children now, she mused, *How can the other women be so busy that they don't take time to simply watch and enjoy?*

Suddenly something or someone slammed into her from behind, nearly knocking her off her feet. "Oh!" she said with surprise. But before she could say anything else, she recognized the chubby little arms wrapped around her skirts. Taking the petite hands in hers, she bent to give Anna a huge hug. She buried her head in Anna's neck and fought hard to keep the tears at bay. She had not taken the children this weekend since they were going to be together all day today at the picnic. But she missed them more than she would have dreamed possible.

While she and Anna were still hugging one another, more arms wrapped around them, and boy-sounding chuckles erupted as Conner and Philip joined in. Paul stood slightly behind with a reserved smile. Bess knew he was feeling too old to hug her in public, yet needed to be reassured of her love also.

"Come," she said happily. "Let's walk down by the stream so you can tell me all about your week. We still have half an hour before we need to finish up the food for lunch. I missed you all last night and can't wait to hear it all. Paul, why don't you start since you are the oldest? You sure look grown up today. Honestly, I think you grow constantly when I'm not looking."

Paul grinned his pleasure, then told her of the new baby pigs and calves born that week. The five of them walked arm in arm toward the creek and away from the rest of the church folk. But the others seemed to understand their special bond and left them alone.

She watched Paul while he talked. She wondered if he would soon feel he was too old for these conversations. He was only ten years old, but Bess wasn't sure when boys began wanting to act like men. It would be interesting to watch him grow. She did hope there would be at least two or three more years that she could be his confidante.

Now and again when Paul was talking, the younger children would add a comment or nod and grin their assent to what he was telling. When they reached the creek, Bess sat on a log while the children crowded around her on the log or on the ground at her knees. They all seemed to want to touch her and be touched by her. She realized they were hungry for a mother's love, so she was careful to touch each cheek, pat and caress their heads, hold hands, or put her arm on their shoulders. But Bess knew it was just as much for herself as it was for the children.

Conner told about the garden and how things were growing. Bess had helped them plant some of the garden earlier in the spring and didn't always have time to check on the progress on Fridays. Conner loved working in the soil and was quick to tell her each detail of the growing things. He reassured her they were keeping the weeds out of the garden and that she would be proud. Bess smiled and praised him.

When it was Philip's turn, he showed her that he had lost some more teeth. They all teased him gently and lovingly about looking like an old man and not having enough teeth to eat the picnic lunch. He enjoyed the teasing and the attention.

Anna seemed unusually quiet. When Bess asked about her dollies, Anna answered the question but didn't add much comment. Her eyes looked sad, and Bess felt her forehead and asked if she felt all right. She smiled at Bess and said she was fine. Finally, when Bess said, "Anna, I miss you terribly," the big blue eyes swam in tears.

"Oh, Miss Bess," she murmured, "it is so lonely without you and our mother. I know Mother can't come back from Jesus to be with us, but I wish you would come live with us again. Every day the sun isn't as sunny as it was when you lived with us, and the birds are sadder and even the bees are sad."

Bess fought tears herself. "Oh, Anna! How do you know that the bees are sad?"

"They don't buzz a happy buzz. Just a sad buzz."

"It's true," Philip added. "She made me listen, and it's really true. And Daddy's soup isn't nearly as good as yours, either."

"And my dollies aren't as much fun because they are sad. They were always happy when you lived with us. They used to tell me fun stories, and now they don't talk at all. I think they cry when I'm not looking."

Bess was stumped to know what to say. How could she explain propriety to these young children? What could she say? "Well, I miss you terribly also. I don't know what Clara would do without me cooking for her boardinghouse, but let's all pray about this, and we'll watch to see what God will do about it, shall we? God knows better than anyone what we all need. He knows you need someone to care for you, and I'm quite sure He has a plan up His sleeve already. Don't you?"

The scene of Rose and Robert getting out of the carriage darted uninvited into Bess's head, but she refused to dwell on it. "Yes, let's all pray about it, but let's not tell anyone else that we are praying. This will be our secret."

All the children, even Paul, had tears in their eyes or running down their pink and freckled noses, but they all smiled and nodded.

"Yes, it will be our secret," whispered Anna loudly enough that they all heard her. The boys nodded their agreement, and Bess was happy to see that Paul did not feel too grown up to be included in the pact as well.

"Now one more hug all around and then we should get back to the picnic, all right?"

They all hugged Bess again, and then, holding hands in a row of five with Bess in the center, they all started back toward the church and the picnic, arriving just as Pastor Lewis was calling them all to gather around for the blessing.

Following the blessing, the children were still gathered around Bess. She searched the crowd for Robert to know what she should do. She was searching intently for him when she felt a soft touch on her elbow and heard a man's voice say behind her head, "Looking for someone?"

"Robert!" she exclaimed. "You startled me. Yes, I was looking to see if you wanted me to help Anna and Philip with their plates. I'm guessing Paul and Conner will manage all right by themselves."

"I would love to have your help, Bess. Why don't we all go through the line together, in case any of the children need help?"

"That would be good. I will eat later with the women who are serving, but I would love to go through the line with you and help fill their plates now."

∾

After getting the children situated on a blanket in the shade with Robert, Bess returned to the tables to help the women who were serving. In spite of the wonderful weather, the bountiful food, the good spirit among the people, Bess's heart felt heavy. She was burdened for the Sheldon children and could not feel as carefree as the others seemed to feel.

As she watched the other families, she noted that Rose also seemed to carry a heavy burden. In spite of her smile, her eyes seemed sad as she guided Mary Rose, Richard, and Allen in filling their plates. The children had already made friends and went to eat with the other children. Rose's parents were occupied as shepherds of the flock, and Rose seemed more alone today than Bess had ever sensed before. So when it was time to fill a plate herself, Bess took hers over to Rose's blanket and asked if she could join her. Rose happily made room and welcomed Bess.

"Are you as lonely as you look?" Bess asked gently as she sat beside her on the blanket. "Or would you rather not talk about it?"

"Oh, Bess, how sweet of you to ask. This is actually the first event we've attended without Timothy. I miss him terribly. I'm actually quite shy—or perhaps timid would be more accurate—and I miss his way of including me and helping me feel at ease. It is quite difficult for me to be assertive, but I know that I need to be friendly if I want friends and if I want to make others feel befriended. Mother was a good teacher in that regard."

"You know, Rose, we all have our. . .hmmm, what shall I call it?. . .infirmities, so to speak. I don't know if you are aware of my background, but I was raised to be a prostitute. My mother was a prostitute, and it was the only life I knew until finding this church and these dear folks. Anyway, now I realize how very wrong that lifestyle is. But God has forgiven me and has given me a wonderful new life. However, because of my past, I really don't know how to be friendly with men without feeling like I am flirting. I'm all right with other women for the most part, but I still feel so new at all this that I fear someone will think I am acting out of place, so even with women I'm somewhat timid. Rebecca has been an incredible friend to me. Her heart is so good and pure that I find myself trying to be like her, but I always feel like I fall short."

Bess gestured toward Clara, who was chatting with some of the other women. "Clara has always been there for me. She also was a prostitute in the same institution I came from. She sort of adopted me when I was born, when my mother decided she didn't want me, and we have always been very close. I am very glad and thankful for the friendship she has with your mother.

"At any rate, Rose, you are probably close to being in the middle of all of our ages, but we don't really think much about age. Our hearts are similar, and we enjoy one another's friendship. I know I speak for the others when I tell you we consider you one of us. There are lots of other friendly women in the church as well. But these are just the ones I have been around the most."

"Thank you so much, Bess." Rose's smile was gentle and lovely, and a tear sparkled briefly in the corner of her eye. She blinked quickly and it started to run onto her ivory cheek, but she reached her handkerchief up and brushed it away. "It's especially comfortable being with you and Clara since you also don't have husbands. Around the others I somehow feel like an extra," she whispered in a conspiratorial tone, and Bess nodded her agreement. "I truly am thankful for you and for your willing friendship." Rose squeezed Bess's hand gently.

The women ate in companionable silence for a short time. Suddenly Anna ran over and showed Bess a grass stain on her skirt. With tears in her eyes she said, "Oh, Miss Bess, is it ruined? I was running and fell, and it got all dirty."

"Oh, sweetheart, I think I can get that washed out with no problem. But you have also torn the waist a bit, so you must be very careful that you don't tear it further. We'll fix your dress together when I come out this week. Don't worry about it, Anna. Just have a good time, but try to remember to be a lady."

"I will. Thank you, Miss Bess. I love you!" Her chubby arms reached around Bess's neck briefly before she ran toward the other little girls again. As Bess watched her, she also glanced around to see if Robert had seen Anna fall. He was watching her and grinned briefly. She realized then that he had headed for Anna but backed away when he saw her run to Bess. When he nodded his thanks, she smiled back and was amazed that she felt herself flush. *Goodness! You'd think I'm a schoolgirl.*

"Those children love you." Rose made the observation with a quiet confidence. "Mother told me that you took care of their mother. It looks like they have adopted you."

"Hmmm, yes." Bess paused. "They need a mother. It's hard for me to see them having to care for themselves. I have come to care for them very much. We had such good times together, all of us. I loved their mother deeply. Other than Clara, Anita was my first close friend."

"Do you think Robert will marry again?" It was an innocent question. Bess searched Rose's eyes but saw only honest curiosity there.

"I have no idea. He loved Anita deeply. I don't know him well, but I do admire him. He is a wonderful father to those children and was a devoted husband to Anita. I don't know why, but it is difficult for me to imagine him with anyone else but Anita, yet the children really do need a mother. I pray for them all. I know we are not supposed to worry, but I confess to considerable concern for that precious family. I'm thankful I am still considered part of their family even though propriety says I can't stay there any longer."

"I will pray with you. I feel like all I do is pray for myself anymore. So it will be good to join in prayer for someone else's needs," Rose said cheerfully.

At that moment Bess knew that Rose understood her concern for the children, and her spirits lifted. Even if Robert should choose to marry Rose, Bess resolved not to be jealous of their good fortune.

Chapter 19

It had been a wonderful day relaxing with good friends and making new friends out of acquaintances. Bess's cheeks smarted a bit, and she realized that, in spite of her bonnet, she had allowed her cheeks and chin to get some exposure to the sun. "How foolish," Bess muttered out loud to herself. "A grown woman with sunburn and freckles. Such nonsense!"

Bess and Clara were carrying the empty pots from the church picnic into the boardinghouse. Clara chuckled when she overheard Bess's complaining. "Oh, stop grouching and look at that gorgeous moon, will you?" Clara stood on the walkway between the wagon and the back stoop, directly in Bess's way.

Bess glanced up. She took a deep breath. Such a glorious night! The two women watched the night sky until Bess started quietly:

> *"The Man in the Moon as he sails the sky,*
> *is a very remarkable skipper;*
> *But he made a mistake when he tried to take*
> *a drink of milk from the Dipper."*

Clara joined in, and they recited the old poem together:

> *"He dipped it into the Milky Way,*
> *and slowly and carefully filled it;*
> *The Big Bear growled, and the Little Bear howled,*
> *and scared him so that he spilled it!"*

Both were silent for a minute, then Bess said, "I remember sitting on the back steps with you when it was too hot to sleep and you would say that poem to me as we looked at the moon. Do you remember?"

"Yes. What a life we lived. But it was all we knew." All was still for a few more minutes. Then Clara said, "Bess, I'm so sorry you grew up in that way of life. I wish I could go back and change things for you. I wish I'd had the courage to take you out of that when your mother said I could have you." Regret made Clara's voice soft. "I thought about taking you away when Sam told me I had to get you started. I just didn't know what I'd do or where we'd go. I'm so very sorry."

"It's all in the past now, Clara. Pastor Lewis says it's Satan that reminds us of our regrets and failures of the past. God has taken it all away. Clara, I don't remember much about the woman who gave birth to me, other than I was a bother to her when I did see her, but I have always been thankful that you were really my mother. I always considered I had a pretty good life—except when I crossed Gertie or Sam the wrong way. Then I wished I were a mouse and could crawl into the nearest wall."

The two women chuckled. They were silent again for a few minutes.

"It sure is a beautiful night," Bess said with a sigh.

"It's been an altogether good day, don't you think?" Clara asked the rhetorical question. "Who would have thought church folks could have so much fun? You know, today I realized that, for the first time in my life, I was really having fun. We've had some good times before, but before we knew God, it never felt like anything was truly fun for me. It merely felt like something was wrong, but I couldn't quite put my finger on it."

Bess tilted her head toward her friend. "Yes, but we've had a lot of good times since that day. Why do you say this is the first?"

"I don't really know," Clara said slowly. "Perhaps today is the first time I have allowed myself to realize I am one of them. I belong. They don't hate me for my past but accept me as one of them. For some reason, I never understood that before today."

"Hmmm. . .thinking back, I think it was Anita who helped me feel like I belonged." Bess was thoughtful for a minute. "I went out to their farm with a lot of misgivings. But she believed in me and was proud of my every accomplishment as I learned with her instruction how to cook and keep house. She accepted me as one of the family. It didn't take long at all to know I was truly forgiven when I was treated like that. God has truly been good to me, and I am so very grateful."

Clara suddenly laughed. "Here we stand with our arms full of pots, and I can't even hug you." She moved swiftly toward the boardinghouse. "But for now, we'd better get some water heated and these things washed. It'll be time to start breakfast before we get to bed, if we don't."

❦

It was late when Bess finally settled into her bed. She was tired, but it had been a good day. Warmth spread through her as she relived the walk with the Sheldon children and their conversation by the stream. She prayed for each of the children and then paused before praying for Robert.

Bess knew it was difficult for the man to care properly for the children alone. Even if she was willing to clean the house and do the laundry for them, it wasn't the same as having a mate there to prepare meals, nurture the children constantly, and support and encourage him. Yet the thought of someone taking Anita's place in his life frightened her—yes, even angered her a bit. Was it merely her love for the children that made her feel this way? No, she finally admitted, it was her love for Anita. There was a jealousy in Bess's heart that she was certain was from her love for Anita, not wanting anyone to replace Anita in Robert's heart.

What a strange one I must be, Bess thought soberly. *Being jealous on someone else's behalf? Is this normal?* She could not answer her own question, so decided to talk to God about it.

"Loving Father, I am told You know my heart. Well, if You do, You are certainly doing better than I am. I am very confused about this whole situation with the Sheldon family. I truly want those children cared for properly, yet I don't want someone taking Anita's place in any of their hearts. I can't do what Clara needs me to do and still go out and care for the family as I'd like to. And I don't really want to be selfish about it, but I don't look forward to another woman taking my place in their affections. I do love those children so. Lord, I am trying desperately to release them into Your care, but I'm afraid. Afraid of losing them, of losing their love to someone else. Please forgive my very selfish heart and help me to trust You completely—for their lives as well as for my own. I truly want what is best for them, but I guess I admit that I want it to be me. I know You can work that out somehow, but I sure don't see how. Please help me to let go of it and be able to rest, knowing the whole situation is completely in Your care."

Finally, Bess rested. She slept soundly and awakened refreshed. She felt lighter somehow. Then she remembered her prayer and felt as though the peace in her heart was from God. He would work for His own good in all their lives.

That very day after the worship service, Rose rushed over to Bess and Clara as they prepared to leave the church. Breathlessly she said, "I need to talk to you. Do you have a moment?"

"Yes, of course we do." Clara spoke for both of them while Bess smiled encouragingly.

"What is it, Rose? You certainly seem excited." Bess was eager to hear what Rose had to say because Rose was so seldom this assertive.

"Well, I've been thinking. I feel rather useless living with Mother and Daddy and having them take care of us, and I was wondering. . .well, I mean. . .I really enjoy cooking, and Timothy thought my cooking was plenty good. . ."

Both Clara and Bess were puzzled. "It's all right, Rose. Tell us what's on your mind." Bess tried to reassure Rose as her timidity got the best of her momentarily.

"I know Bess is your main cook, but I was wondering if I could help out at all. I could maybe cook on the days Bess goes out to the Sheldon farm. Or be of some help. I would love to, well. . ." Again there was a breathless blush as she ducked her head momentarily, then brought it back up and bravely said, "I'd like to earn a small wage if I could and wondered if you could use the help. If you don't need me, please don't feel obligated."

"Oh, my, that's great news!" Bess could already feel a load lifted from her shoulders. She looked at Clara and could tell that Clara was in deep thought.

Slowly Clara said, "Rose, I think that would be a great help to us. Let me think it over and talk with Bess. We'll come over to your house later this afternoon or in the evening to make final arrangements, if that will be all right with you."

"Oh, that will be fine. And Clara, if it won't work out or help you out, then please just tell me and we'll go on being the best of friends. Would you agree to that?"

"Yes, I will be honest with you. But I have tasted your cooking—your potato salad was the most popular dish at the picnic yesterday and your cake nearly floated away. I know the boardinghouse has been a burden for Bess to carry nearly alone since I'm not much help in the kitchen, so I am quite certain this will work wonderfully. And I am thankful you found the courage to speak. I have a feeling this is going to work out great for all of us."

With hugs the women parted. Clara was deep in thought as she and Bess started toward the boardinghouse. Finally she spoke. "What do you think about it all, Bess? Would you like to have the help?"

"Clara, I love to cook. You know that. But I do not really enjoy having the whole responsibility of cooking for that many people all the time. You know I'd love to be free to go to the Sheldon farm more than once a week, and if Rose could help us on the weekends also, it would be wonderful. Can you afford to hire someone?"

"A few months ago when we first started this, I would have been quite hesitant to be committed to pay a salary. However, business has been very good. You know that we keep being asked to open a restaurant also. I think it's a good time for us to hire someone else and perhaps keep that restaurant idea in mind for the future."

"And if she works out well, which I think she will, would you mind if I go out to the Sheldon farm maybe twice a week? Would you feel abandoned if I did that?"

They walked in silence for a short distance before Clara replied. Then she said quite soberly, "Bess, your heart is out there at the Sheldon farm. I would not wish to keep you here. I think I see the hand of God in bringing Rose back here with her parents. I must admit I am concerned for the day she returns to her farm, but God has always been one step ahead of me right along the way, and I know He has a powerful plan that will be for our good—you and me and Rose. Sometimes I can hardly wait to see what He will think of next!"

Chapter 20

Halfway through the month, July turned hot and muggy. It had been two weeks since Rose had started cooking at the boardinghouse, and she was well received. Bess's cooking was delicious, but Rose's meals had a flair all their own. The boarders, as well as Clara and Bess, were delightfully surprised.

As Bess drove out to the Sheldon farm very early on a Tuesday morning, she thought about what a blessing it was to have Rose to free her up for this extra day to help the Sheldons. Their garden was producing well, but the children could not put up the food for the winter. Bess wanted to do that as well as the other household chores. And besides, it felt almost like going home. Oh, how she loved that happy place. She found herself humming a tune and wishing the horses would feel the same urgency she did.

Robert had been delighted with her news when she told him on Sunday that because of Rose's help she could come another day. Bess saw a light in the kitchen window as she drove up. She supposed the children had awakened early in anticipation since Robert was probably out caring for the animals.

She tied the horses to the corner post when she arrived, knowing that Robert would care for them soon, and went into the kitchen to start breakfast for the family. As soon as the door opened she smelled coffee. Knowing the children didn't know how to make coffee, she looked around in surprise.

A cup of coffee sat on the table, curling its fragrance in swirls toward the ceiling. Robert stood at the stove pouring a second cup. He glanced up and smiled as she entered.

"Oh! I thought you'd be at the barns already," Bess said in quiet surprise.

"The children are still sleeping, and I've gotten pretty good at coffee. Here, try some. I'm still not much good at the other food, but my coffee is either getting better, or I'm getting used to it. See what you think." He handed her the cup with a mischievous smile.

She accepted the cup, and he pulled out a chair for her. "Bess, would you sit for a few minutes and talk with me before we start our work?"

"Sure, Robert." She sipped the coffee as she moved toward the chair. "Robert, this is very good coffee. Mmm, I think you're onto something here. This is great!"

After seating her, Robert walked around the table to where the other cup sat. He sat down across from her, smiling, but gazing into his cup thoughtfully. Bess waited silently, sipping the aromatic brew and watching him over the brim. Robert wrapped his hands around his cup, looked up at Bess briefly, then back down again.

Bess set her cup down and leaned forward. "What is it, Robert? What did you want to talk to me about?" She could see he was struggling and had never seen him quite so hesitant. "Is there a problem?" She didn't really think it was a problem since he was still smiling. She waited.

Again there was silence for several seconds. Finally he looked up at her and spoke softly. "Bess, we've been through a lot together. I've leaned on you heavily this past year—first with Anita and then with the children and the home. I believe God sent you to us as a very special gift. We all love you very much." Again he hesitated.

"Yes, I know you all care," Bess murmured. "And I have come to love you all also. You and Anita have raised some very special children, and I have learned to love them deeply. They are a very important part of my life, and Robert, I love coming out here to be with you all."

Her words seemed to give him courage. "Yes, and we would like you to stay. What I mean is. . .well, *I* would like you to stay. Bess, if you would marry me, you could be with us all the time, and you wouldn't have to live in town when I believe your heart is here with the children."

"Marry you?" Bess was so shocked she didn't think she had heard Robert correctly. Her voice was a whisper. Then she said again, "Did you say marry you, Robert? Me? Marry you?"

He searched her eyes for a moment, then focused back on his cup. "Is it such an awful thought?"

"It's just, well, such a surprise. I never thought—but Anita? I mean, how could I? How could you? Marry?"

Robert continued to look down at his cup. "Anita is gone. I have come to terms with that. I will always love Anita, and I think you know that as do the children and, yes, I think Anita knows that also. But, Bess, somehow I think Anita would approve of this. In fact, I think she would approve very heartily. Do you not think so, too?"

"Oh, my!" Bess was silent for a little while. "But I'm—or, I was. . ."

"What? A prostitute? Bess, I know you were a prostitute. I am well aware of that. But that was a whole different life. That was before you knew Christ. That was before you were forgiven. You know that it is all forgiven. And in God's Book, and mine, it's as good as never happened. Look—" Robert jumped up from his chair and reached over to the top of the bookcase for his Bible. Thumbing through the pages, he opened to Isaiah 53:5–6, brought it around the table, and placed it in front of

Bess. "Look what it says right here." He traced the words with his forefinger as he read:

> *"But he was wounded for our transgressions, he was bruised for our iniquities: the chastisement of our peace was upon him; and with his stripes we are healed. All we like sheep have gone astray; we have turned every one to his own way; and the LORD hath laid on him the iniquity of us all."*

Robert left his Bible open on the table in front of her but went back to his seat across from her. "Bess, all of us have sinned. Not just you. All of us. God doesn't see that some sins are forgivable and others are not. Nor does He consider some worse than others. When we truly ask His forgiveness and turn from our sin, He forgives. Simple as that. That is the reason Jesus went to the cross. Our sins were laid on Him. And if God forgives, it's the same as though it never happened. I think it is much more difficult for us to forgive ourselves than for God to forgive us. But at any rate, it's done. It's behind you. Now you must go on about living your new life—your forgiven life.

"Bess, I hope you will understand what I'm saying when I tell you that I have come to love you. It is different than the love I had for Anita, but it is just as genuine. Anita and I were childhood sweethearts. You and I have come to know one another as adults and will have a much different love, but it will be just as real. We have been through a lot together already, you and I. And I can't think of anyone I'd rather have share my home and my life. Do you think you could learn to love me? Will you give it some thought?"

"Oh, Robert, I do care very much for you, but I never even considered anything but a friendship between us. Let me give some thought to this. I will give you an answer as soon as possible. Is that good enough for you?"

"Thanks, Bess. I can't ask for more than that." He quickly drank some of his coffee, then set it down. "I'll take care of your horses now." And he left while Bess still sat staring into her cup. She felt as though someone had snatched her breath away.

What was it Clara had said a short time ago? *"Your heart is out there at the Sheldon farm."* It had startled Bess at the time. Now she wondered if Clara had seen something that Bess had yet to see.

Finally she shook herself and got up to prepare breakfast and ready herself to greet the children as they awakened.

⌘

As the children sat at the breakfast table, they were lively. In fact, they were so excited to have Bess at the farm an extra day that they didn't even seem to notice that she was more quiet than usual. They all chattered about everything that had happened since they had seen her on Sunday.

Robert returned from caring for her horses, took his seat, and prayed. While the table was still silent, Anna said cheerfully and innocently as she reached into the basket for a biscuit and passed them on to Paul, "I knew Miss Bess was here when I woke up because I could hear Daddy whistling at the barns. Daddy always whistles when Miss Bess is here, and I like it."

Bess was holding the gravy, but she locked eyes with Robert. He, too, seemed surprised, as if he was totally unaware that he whistled when she was there. But his surprise was followed by a smug smile and a slight nod. "I think we are all happy when Miss Bess is here. I know I sure like her sausage gravy better than mine," Robert said jovially to the children as though Bess were not within hearing.

The children broke out in laughter. Then Philip joked with a mischievous grin so like his father's, "I like Miss Bess's everything better than yours!" He and Anna giggled.

"So, what's for dinner today, Miss Bess?" Paul asked eagerly.

"Well, I haven't thought that far yet," Bess replied, trying to act as though her whole life had not changed that morning. "Guess I'll take requests today."

No one seemed to notice that Bess hardly ate at all.

Later, as Bess helped the children with weeding the garden and picking green beans for preserving, she noticed Anna copying her actions and staying very close to her side. "Anna, are your dollies playing yet?"

"They are happy today, but they don't feel like playing yet. But it's all right. I need to help you with the work. Will you let me snap the beans again this year?"

"We will all need to snap beans to get this chore done today." Bess smiled at the innocent, expectant face. "I will especially appreciate your help today."

Bess thought about the dollies being happy today and wondered whether the dollies would feel like playing again if she were to marry Robert. Well, she'd certainly give this idea some thought and much prayer.

It was the middle of August before Bess talked to Clara about Robert's proposal. The women were sitting out on the back step enjoying the last streaks of the setting sun. There was not much breeze, but the air stirred ever so slightly now and again. However, Bess was so intent on their conversation she hardly noticed the heat.

"Have you considered it at all?" Clara was never one to beat around the bush.

"That's all I have thought and prayed about for the past two weeks."

"And. . ."

"Oh, Clara, I would love to be a stepmother to those children. You know how much I love them. And I do care for Robert—actually more than I ever realized, or perhaps more than I had acknowledged to myself."

"Then why do you hesitate? What is it, Bess?"

Bess sighed. "Clara, you have always been in my life. You are my closest and dearest friend, but you are more my mother. Until I knew Anita, I had never had a close friend that was near my own age." Tears welled in Bess's eyes and splashed off of her cheeks. She sighed again, then blew her nose and continued. "Something in this feels like a betrayal. I know she's gone, but Clara, she hasn't even been gone a year. I don't know how Robert can even think of another woman already."

"Oh. So that's what this is about. Look, Bess. He needs a wife. Those children need a mother. They already love you, and he knows your ways. It makes sense. It makes good sense."

"Hmmm. . .so I'm convenient? Am I supposed to be pleased about that?"

"Bess, he does care for you. You know he cares for you. And he adores those children. Don't you think Anita would want you, of all people, to take her place since she can no longer mother those children? Do you think she would be happy having them out there all alone with no mother at all?"

Suddenly a loud knocking on the front door of the boardinghouse reverberated through the open doors and windows of the house.

Bess jumped to her feet, moved by the urgency of the knocking. Going in the back door, she trotted through the house to the front, wondering who would be knocking at this time of the evening.

Bess opened the door to see Robert standing there, twisting his hat round and round in his hands.

"What is it?" Bess asked softly. Her heart was pounding. "Are the children all right? What's wrong, Robert?"

"Come out," Robert whispered.

He opened the screen door and stepped aside for Bess to step onto the porch. She looked at him questioningly, still wondering what had brought him to town in the middle of the week at this time of night.

"I realize this is rather unusual behavior, but the children are with you every weekend. They played and worked hard today, and the younger three were already asleep. I asked Paul if he'd be all right with them if I'd go for a ride. So I saddled a horse and came in to see if you would go for a walk with me."

"Everything's all right? You just want to walk?"

Robert nodded, a question in his eyes.

"All right. Yes, that would be good. Let me go tell Clara, and I'll be right back. Do you want to come in?"

"No, I'll wait out here."

When Bess went out back to tell Clara, Clara nodded and said, "I'll pray for you to know what is right to do." Bess had a feeling Clara had already begun praying. Bess gave her a quick hug and returned to Robert.

As they strolled along the quiet street, Robert headed in the direction of the church. They were silent, at first, but it was a companionable silence that felt right. After a short time, Robert began whistling a merry little tune. Bess smiled up at him. When the tune was finished, Robert quipped, "She's right, you know."

Somehow Bess knew what he meant. "She's very bright. Very perceptive. Obviously more perceptive than I am."

"Well, so you know, I also whistle when you're *not* there."

Bess looked at him quickly, wondering why he'd added such a comment.

"I whistle every time I think about you." His eyes twinkled. "I can't help wondering if you've given my proposal any thought." With this comment, he sobered.

Bess sighed lightly. "All I do is think about it."

"And what are you thinking by now, if I may ask?"

"Well, I was thinking that if you asked again, I would probably say yes." This was spoken so quietly that he had to tip his head to hear her.

By now they had come to the churchyard, and Robert steered them toward the large oak tree that spread its boughs like a roof. Several benches scattered beneath its boughs were used by church folk for visiting before and after church.

Robert helped her sit, but instead of sitting beside her, he knelt on one knee directly in front of her. "Bess, will you marry me?" He wasn't teasing. He looked at her intently, with tenderness in his gaze, holding his hat with both hands.

Bess felt herself trembling.

"Bess, before you say anything at all, I want you to know that I would consider it the greatest honor if you would marry me. I think I can teach you to care for me. I know you love the children. It would be the most wonderful thing in the world if you would make our family complete." A tear slid onto his cheek and sparkled there in the moonlight. The moon was so bright it seemed almost as light as day.

"Robert, I am very honored you have selected me," she said in a shaky voice. "I do care for you. Honestly, I have come to care for you more than I had realized. I can't deny that I still have some reservation, but it's not for the lack of caring. It's that I somehow feel we'd be betraying our love for Anita."

Robert searched her face. "But you are still willing to say yes?"

"You're certain it's all right to ignore my sense of betrayal?" Bess felt the need for reassurance one more time.

Robert hesitated only slightly, then nodded thoughtfully.

"Then, yes, I think I can say yes now." For some reason, the trembling suddenly stopped. She had prayed for days and knew that, in time, God would give her peace and confidence that she had made the right choice. She reached out and laid her hand on Robert's cheek. Yes, this was right. She knew she cared for this man. And she knew she could trust God for the rest.

Chapter 21

Life was suddenly full and busy. Robert had not wanted to wait, and Bess saw no need to put off the wedding, either. So they agreed to tell the children together that weekend, and if the children approved, planned to marry as soon as Bess could make arrangements with Clara.

The arrangements had not taken long, after the children's enthusiastic shouts had resounded through the farmhouse, since Rose was very willing to take over the responsibilities of head cook. They had decided to make over the stable behind the boardinghouse into a small home for Rose and the children. Pastor Lewis and a few of the men from the church were doing the construction work, but until it was complete, Rose planned to continue to walk from the Lewis home.

Within two weeks, Robert and Bess were married in a very small ceremony at the Lewis home.

Now it was mid-September, and the garden seemed to own their lives. Working together with the children putting away the produce for the cold days of winter was pure joy. The days were long and hot and tiring, but Bess had never been happier—for the most part.

Within days of the wedding and Bess moving out to the farm permanently, she found Anna playing with her dollies under the grape arbor. As she walked past, Anna called out to her, "Look, Miss Bess, my dollies wanted to play today. I think they are all feeling well now. When I started to leave the room this morning, they whispered that they wanted me to take them with me. I asked them if they wanted to play, and they said yes. It's wonderful they are finally well."

Bess reached down and touched the rosy cheek tenderly, as Anna looked up at her. "I'm so glad they are well. And I am glad they wanted to play with you." She couldn't help the tear that slid down her nose. She quickly squatted and hugged Anna, who hugged her back excitedly.

As Bess walked back to the house, the heaviness she had been ignoring suddenly became a painful knot in her stomach. Why did it bother her that the dollies recovered so quickly? The tears came faster than she could brush them away, so she went into the bedroom where she would not be observed.

She found herself talking out loud. "Oh, Anita, I didn't try to replace you. I really never could. I'm glad Anna is happy, but somehow it makes me feel more guilty than ever. Anita, why did you have to leave us? I don't want the children to ever forget you, but neither do I want to see them sad and uncared for." Suddenly her talking changed to a prayer. "Oh, God, help me!"

Bess fell onto the bed, sobbing quietly into her hands. Her heart continued her prayer, but she felt as though God did not hear. In a little while, the sobs weakened and eventually stopped. She went over to the washstand, poured some fresh water into the bowl, splashed her face, and scrubbed it hard. She pinned her hair back out of her face again and took the bowl of water out to dump on the rose vine by the back porch.

Soon she was working hard again, and she chose to push the questions out of her mind. She could do that most of the time, but she could never get the questions out of her heart. So she'd taught herself to simply ignore her heart, as she had so often in her earlier days as a prostitute. There was always so much to do at the farm that she kept almost too busy to think. But that was good.

<hr>

Bess loved cooking for the family. It didn't matter what she made, they all ate heartily. Robert praised her bread as being the lightest he had ever eaten. She was glad he was so easy to please and that he was happy and content. She wondered sometimes if he was reading her mind when he'd stand beside her as she worked and place his hand on her cheek to turn her face toward his. He would search her eyes and then kiss her tenderly if the children were not around, or sometimes press his hand ever so sweetly on her cheek before walking away. It made Bess feel as though he could see right into her heart.

When he did this the first time, Bess worried all day that he would question her feelings when they were alone. But he never did. He would simply gaze at her with affection and love her gently. Sometimes he would whisper into her ear as he brushed his lips across her cheek, "Thank you, Bess."

Thank you for what? Bess wondered. But she didn't want to ask. She felt so guilty about the marriage that she didn't want to know. So she would simply smile while her stomach knotted.

<hr>

By mid-October Bess found she was truly losing her appetite. She lectured herself about her guilt feelings and the knots in her stomach, but she couldn't seem to make them go away. She still cooked for the family but could hardly eat two or three bites without feeling as though the food would come right back up. Her clothes began to hang loosely on her frame, and she told herself she absolutely must eat.

When it was time to prepare a meal, she would be hungry and think of a delicious meal to make for the family. She would cook it, and they would sit down to eat.

But to her, it would taste nothing like what she had imagined. The family would be delighted with the meal, but she could hardly eat it at all.

Around the middle of November Bess was frying eggs when the nausea hit, and she had to make a quick run for the outhouse. She had noticed the nausea before but never to this extent. Surprisingly, when she came back to finish making the breakfast, it smelled wonderful. And it tasted great. She ate a whole meal, and it all stayed down. *What a strange woman I am,* she mused.

Bess missed having Anna around during the daytime. This was the first year Anna had gone with the boys to the school, and when they all left in the mornings, the house seemed totally quiet. That day, when the children had gone and she was alone in the kitchen washing the dishes, Robert came in, walked over to her, put his arms around her from behind, and began kissing the back of her neck.

"Robert, you startled me! My goodness, what are you thinking?" She couldn't help smiling into his mischievous eyes as she turned herself around in his arms.

Before he said anything to her, he kissed her soundly and passionately on the mouth. "Are you feeling better today?" he asked her tenderly.

"What do you mean?" Bess was truly puzzled by his question.

"I mean that you finally ate a meal this morning. And you didn't even look green around the gills. Are you feeling better about it all now?"

"Oh, well, I don't mean to disappoint you, but today I had to run to the outhouse to empty my stomach as soon as I smelled the food. I don't think it's any better, but something has changed, and my stomach is acting strange still. I'm sorry. I didn't think you had noticed."

"You were sick when you smelled food? But fine after you emptied your stomach?"

"Yes. Why does that make you smile?"

"Mmm. . .don't know. . ." He had pulled her to him and was kissing her hair. Then he held her out from him and gazed into her eyes. There was a mysterious merriment in his twinkling eyes that almost angered Bess.

"What's wrong with you?" she blurted out.

"Well, I remember that happening to Anita also."

She couldn't remember seeing him look so amused before. "Anita got sick, and this makes you happy? Robert, if you didn't look perfectly sane standing there I would be sure you had lost your mind. Will you please stop being so mysterious and tell me what you're thinking?"

"Well, whenever Anita made those early morning trips to the outhouse to empty her stomach before breakfast, then some months later we would have a new little Sheldon to love."

Bess just stared into his grinning face. Was he teasing her? Could it be? Thinking back, it had been more than two months since the wedding and yet ever since the marriage she had never yet. . .

Her hands flew to her cheeks. She leaned heavily into his chest as he held her. "Oh, my goodness, Robert! I think you're right. Who would have ever imagined? Well, what do you know!" Soon she was crying, and he was holding her even more tenderly.

In the next few weeks, Bess's nausea in the mornings continued. She was thankful she could get it taken care of before any of the children were up and wondering. Her appetite was back for the rest of the day, so none of the children really suspected anything out of the ordinary. For his part, though, Robert helped her as much as he could in the early mornings.

Bess found her love for the children growing deeper, and along with it was concern for whether they would accept this new one as one of them. She had heard tales of half brothers and half sisters hating one another. When she looked into the faces of these precious children, she couldn't imagine they could ever be so unkind, yet the worry still needled her.

Bess was glad that it was winter and the gardening and preserving were completed. Her workload was much lighter when she just had the house to care for, the laundry to do, and the meals to prepare. She loved the gardening but was thankful to have a break from the hard work. Especially now that she wasn't feeling as energetic as she had previously. And she continued to feel burdened with her worries and guilt.

Chapter 22

As November became December, Christmas was not far off. Robert had confided in Bess that he was carving a set of horses and a wagon for each of the boys. One day when the children were in school he had taken her out to the corner of the barn where he had a workbench and some tools and showed her. Bess was amazed at the way he could carve. The toys were quite realistic in their shape and form.

The two of them discussed what they could make for Anna. Bess had been knitting new scarves and mittens for all the children, but since the boys would have a toy, they wanted Anna to have a toy also. Finally, Bess had the idea of a tea set.

"Could you carve a teapot and a couple of cups? If you could do the carving, I could paint them. I used to be quite good at painting."

Robert thought the idea was a good one, and then asked her if she wanted to paint the wagons for the boys.

"Sure, I could do that. We can work on the things when the children are in school. It will be fun to give these to them."

Bess was finally feeling well again and found she had more energy than she could remember having before. She was glad to not be nauseated anymore and to feel like taking on a new project.

Robert and Bess worked conspiratorially on their projects. They worked on the toys each morning as soon as the children were gone. Then they would put the toys away and get their regular chores done in the afternoons, so the children did not suspect anything at all.

As Christmas drew nearer, Bess asked Robert if he would mind if they invited Clara out to their house for Christmas dinner. Robert thought it was a great idea. When they told the children, Anna decided they should make a written invitation to give to her. The children had fun planning and creating the invitation.

The week before Christmas there was no school. Bess and Robert had finished the gifts and they were all hidden in the barn, safe from curious eyes. The children and Bess made decorations for a Christmas tree.

Two days before Christmas everything was ready. Robert hitched the big sleigh to the prancing horses and tied the sled he used for hauling fireplace wood on behind. Soon after breakfast they all bundled warmly and crunched across the yard on the hard-packed snow to the sled.

Their voices sounded loud in the silent air that was so still it made Bess feel silent inside. As they spoke, their breath hovered overhead for a few white seconds before dissipating. When they were all piled in the sled and covered with the warm blankets, Robert jumped onto the seat at the front and cracked the whip in the air over the horses' backs, making a snapping sound. As the horses started to trot to the woods, their bells jingled merrily.

"Oh! Daddy remembered the bells!" Anna's eyes danced with excitement. "We always use the bells at Christmas." She craned her neck forward. "Look at the horses dance!"

Paul grinned and said to Bess, "The horses act as though they are very proud when they get to wear the bells. They really do look like they are stepping higher, don't you think?"

Bess watched as the horses bobbed their heads and lifted their hooves high. She wasn't sure if it was the cold snow or the bells that made them do it, but they certainly were prancing as though they were proud. She smiled. "They sure do."

They rode silently for a few minutes before Bess caught the children nudging one another and nodding to one another silently. She looked around at each one and finally asked, "What's all the nudging about? Is there a secret I need to hear?"

The children were silent as though caught in the midst of something. Then all heads turned toward Paul. Bess raised her eyebrows in question. "What is it, Paul?" Her question was quiet, letting him know that she cared about whatever was going on with the children.

"Well, we've all wondered if it would be all right. . ." He glanced around as though to find an escape. All remained silent, so he finally met Bess's eyes. "We wondered if we could call you Mama? We always called our mother 'Mother,' so it would be different, but we love having you as our mother now and would like to stop calling you Miss Bess. Would you mind?"

Tears sprang to Bess's eyes, but she blinked quickly to stop them. She scanned each of the children's faces as they all watched her expectantly. Finally she responded. "I would love for you to call me Mama. We will all remember your mother always, but I would love to be your mama since she is gone."

Again the children were quiet, but Anna had reached over under the blanket and squeezed Bess's hand.

Suddenly Philip started singing, "Jingle bellth. . .jingle bellth. . ." The children joined in. Bess had to cough to cover her giggle at his innocent, toothless lisp. Soon they were all singing merrily.

Bess pointed to the gray and heavy sky. "Look up," she said to the children. "What do you see in the sky in December that you don't usually see in the daytime?"

"Both the moon and the sun in the sky at the same time." Conner was the one who was quick with the answer, while all the other heads turned to make the observation.

While the children were studying the moon and sun, Bess noticed that the sky looked quite heavy. Was Robert aware of it? A needling of worry inched its way in. What if they couldn't get back to the house from the woods?

But she needn't have worried. They found a tree, cut it, and tied it onto the sled behind the sleigh before the first fluffy flakes floated to the ground. She knew Robert was concerned when he snapped the whip twice instead of once in the air. The horses picked their feet high and pranced toward home more quickly. The sleigh bells jingled merrily, and in the sleigh, tucked snugly under blankets, they all sang the old Christmas song lustily:

"Christmas comes but once a year,
let us fill our hearts with cheer,
as we sing along the way,
Christ was born on Christmas Day.

Tiny baby laid in straw,
wise men worshipping in awe,
oh, the mystery so great,
that He was born to bear my fate.

He is worthy of our praise,
let our voice to heaven raise,
let us celebrate today,
that Christ was born on Christmas Day!"

By the time they arrived back at the house, they each had a couple of inches of new snow on their laps, and their noses and fingers tingled with the cold. The smoke puffing up from the chimney looked welcoming indeed as the snow swirled about their heads. The sky was dark and didn't look like a late morning sky at all.

Bess and Anna went into the warm house to make the lunch preparations while Robert and the boys took the horses and tree to the barn. They promised to come in for lunch before making a base for the tree, as the ever-growing Paul had declared he was famished.

What a fun afternoon it was as they decorated the tree together. The snow was coming down thickly and blotted much of the light from the windows, but the atmosphere was so charged with excitement and joy inside the farmhouse that they hardly noticed the dark.

Bess still felt her ever-present sense of guilt, and sometimes felt as though she was someone outside the window looking in on the merry family. But still she observed each personality and cherished this day as a memory she hoped she would never forget. She found herself thanking God over and over in her heart.

That night, when the last child was tucked lovingly under warm blankets and Bess had settled into the rocker nearest the stove with a lap full of mending, she heard Robert in the kitchen, and then the back door open and close. She looked up, wondering if someone had come in or gone out. The kitchen was silent, so she assumed that Robert had gone to the barn to check on the animals. It did seem strange, though, that he had not told her what he was doing. Oh, well, today had been such an unusual day that he probably just didn't think about it. With her lap full of socks that needed darning, she didn't bother to get up and look out the window.

She hummed softly to herself as she rocked peacefully and stitched carefully. How blessed she felt to be here and to be accepted as part of this family. She was just feeling her eyelids get heavy when again she heard the kitchen door open and close.

"Robert?" She could hear him moving in the kitchen again now. "Robert? Is that you?" She kept her voice soft so as not to disturb the sleeping children upstairs.

Suddenly she felt a cold hand on the back of her neck and peered over her shoulder into Robert's grinning, mischievous face. "What are you doing?" Bess asked him innocently before she noticed that he kept one arm behind his back.

He leaned over and whispered, "Put down the socks and empty your lap."

"What?" Bess turned her head so she could see his face better.

Robert was smiling almost shyly, reminding Bess of a schoolboy. "I have a little something for you. I know we'll be very busy tomorrow evening on Christmas Eve, so I wanted to have a few minutes alone with you tonight. Can you put the sewing away?" Why was he acting so timid?

Bess folded the socks together and put the needle through the one on which she'd been working before rolling it and putting it away in the basket with the others. When she sat up again, Robert came around in front of her and handed her a crudely wrapped bundle.

"Open it." His eyes were on the object in her lap. "But be careful not to drop it." He pulled the other rocker over close to her and watched in anticipation.

Bess took off the wrappings to uncover a beautiful teapot. It felt very fragile, as though you could see through it. Lilies and gold edges were painted on it. It was the most beautiful china teapot Bess had ever seen.

"Oh, Robert, it is beautiful. So lovely. I've never seen anything like it!"

"Look inside," Robert said expectantly.

Bess carefully lifted the lid that also had a ring of lilies around the raised loop in the center. Looking inside, Bess saw an envelope with her name on it. She lifted it out and looked at him with a question in her eyes as she opened the envelope. Robert simply sat back and rocked as she read the note:

My dear Bess,

Every day I thank God for you. You brighten every corner of our home and of my heart. Just as lilies are born in the spring when we think the world will stay dark forever, so your love has come to me when I thought my life would be dark forever. When I saw this teapot in Rebecca's display case, I knew I had to have it for you. Bess, besides loving you for bringing joy to my life again, I love the way your joy comes from serving others. As the teapot symbolizes serving, I couldn't help thinking of you when I saw it. I pray that every time you use or see this teapot, you will remember my deep gratitude to you and my constantly growing love for you. I look forward to meeting the child our love and God's mercy has created. And Bess, I offer this simple gift to you in thanks for all the gifts you have brought into my life.

Humbly Yours,
Robert

Bess continued to stare at the page after she had finished reading the note. Tears splashed down her cheeks, and she just wanted to bury her face and cry. She knew she should say something, but couldn't.

Finally she heard Robert say very tentatively, "Are they happy tears?"

"Oh, Robert, I don't even know. I'm so mixed up inside I don't know what they are. I think they're happy tears. I love your note, and I love the teapot. It is beautiful, and I've never had anyone give me something so thoughtful before."

"You *think* they're happy tears? But. . .?" Robert reached over and took the teapot and set it safely out of the way. Then he stood and lifted Bess into the circle of his arms. "Bess, there is more here than happy tears. What is it that continues to weigh on your heart?"

Bess clung to him and sobbed in silence for a while. Finally she said, "Robert, I can't stop feeling guilty for my happiness. For having you when you belonged to

Anita. For having life when Anita lost hers. For carrying this child when you have lost both child and wife. It's such a mixture of feelings. I'm happy, but I'm sad. I'm thankful, but I feel guilty. Will I ever again just be able to enjoy life? enjoy this family? enjoy you? Robert, can you understand that I feel as though I have stolen the life from Anita that she deserved to live and enjoy?"

"Oh, Bess, my Bess, we've talked about this before. I have explained that you had nothing whatever to do with Anita's death. Indeed, if it had not been for you, she may not have lived as long as she did. You did not steal me from her. You never gave me a second look as long as she lived—and even afterwards. I guess I don't know what more to do except to pray for you to find your peace and for you to be able to accept the peace God is offering you. Bess, I will be patient, and I will pray."

Bess looked into his sorrowful eyes. "I am so very sorry. This should have been such a happy moment for you, and I have made you feel sad. Robert, I do truly love the beautiful teapot. I will cherish it and your words always. And I will make every effort to let go of this sense of guilt before it ruins both of our lives." She pulled away, and he set her down.

She found her handkerchief. After blowing her nose and mopping her face, she laid her hand tenderly on Robert's cheek. "I have a small gift for you also. It is not as wonderful as your gift to me, but I do love you with all my heart, Robert. I never dreamed I could love a man like I have come to love you. Wait here for a moment, and I will bring your gift." Bess left him standing there and went into the bedroom. In a few moments she came back, holding a small wooden box in both hands. Shyly she handed it to him.

It was a beautiful but simple little box. As he opened the hinged lid, there, nestled on a bed of green velvet, was a beautiful gold watch on a chain that would clip to his belt so it would not fall from his pocket.

"It's beautiful." He gently removed the watch from the box and opened the lid etched with ivy.

"Look at the back," Bess said timidly.

Robert turned it over, and there in the smooth center surrounded with another circle of ivy was etched: *A time to love...Eccl. 3:8a*. He searched her face. "Then you do love me?"

"Of course I love you, Robert! I have told you I love you more than I ever thought possible. I may feel guilty about it, but I can't deny that I love you with all my heart. And I am very thankful for your patience with me. I am truly trying to get over this guilt."

Robert wrapped her in his arms and kissed her tenderly. Suddenly he lifted his head. "After Christmas, why don't you talk to Pastor Lewis about this guilt that haunts you? Perhaps he can help."

"That's a good idea. I'll do that. When the children go back to school, I will ride into town with you one day. Until then, I'll tuck it back into its corner and try to ignore it." Bess gazed into Robert's tender eyes, and her heart swelled in her chest with her deep love for him. She knew she would do whatever it took to make this wonderful man happy and to enjoy the life with him that God had given to her.

Chapter 23

January was cold and gray, and the winds howled with a vengeance. Other than going to church with the family on Sundays, Bess did not want to venture out into the cold. She told herself she was not as miserable with her guilt as she had been before and convinced herself that it would go away in time. Her life was busy with keeping the household in food and clean, mended clothes. The house was cozy and warm, and Bess really did not relish getting out in the blowing wind and snow.

February came in with sunshine glistening on the mounds of snow. Anna made the cheerful observance that it was actually a yellow sun now instead of the white sun they had seen during January. Bess looked at her with wonder. Such an observant child. It seemed there was nothing she missed.

Bess smiled. "And a yellow sun certainly looks much warmer than a white sun, don't you think?"

"Yes, it looks warmer and brighter." Anna walked over to hug Bess and said quietly to her, "And maybe when you are warmer, you will be happy again."

Her comment startled Bess. "Anna, I am happy. Why do you say that, dear girl?" Bess squatted to gaze into Anna's lovely, innocent face.

"You are happy, but you aren't happy like you were before Mother went to live with Jesus. I miss Mother sometimes, but I know she's happy. I pray every day that Jesus will make you happy like you used to be when we all lived here together." Anna said it solemnly, placing her hands on either side of Bess's face.

Bess stared at the child for a little while, then sighed. Truly nothing escaped this child's observation. Finally she said softly, "Anna, I still miss your mother very much. But I am very, very happy. I love being here with you and caring for you and your brothers and your daddy. Nothing in the world could make me happier."

When the children left for school that day, Bess told Robert that she would like to ride into town with him the next time he went. She told him what Anna had said. "I want to talk to Pastor Lewis to see if he can help me. I thought I was doing well, but that little girl sees to the very core of me every time. Honestly, she sees things I can't see. I can't bear to make her unhappy. So, if it's all right with you, I will ride along the next time you go."

"I can be ready to go within the hour," Robert said in response. He tipped her face up and searched her eyes. "I will do anything it takes to see the smile come back to your beautiful eyes. It is good to see it on your lips again, but I won't be satisfied until I see it in your eyes." He kissed her lips gently before going out.

Bess's lips still tingled from his kiss, even when he was gone. She stood still for a few moments with her arms wrapped tightly around her slightly enlarged waist. She shook her head. It never ceased to amaze her that after all the men she had been with in her life, Robert could make her feel like she had never been kissed before. How did he do that? How did God do that?

Suddenly Bess felt a firm thumping in her stomach. She loosened her arms and laid her hands gently on her abdomen. There it was again! She stood frozen to the spot, afraid if she moved it would quit. There was a pause, and then she felt it again. Tears flowed down her cheeks. Bess knew she should finish cleaning up the breakfast things, but she couldn't move. She didn't want to miss one movement, so she stood there by the back door, waiting from one kick to the next.

Finally she forced herself to attend to the dishes. The kettle was sending steam all over the kitchen and she knew if she didn't get it, her dishwater would boil completely away before she could wash the dishes. She moved slowly, waiting expectantly to see if the movements would continue or stop entirely.

While she poured the boiling water into the dishpan, something changed in her stomach, and then the energetic little movements began again at a different place. She was laughing and crying with the wonder of it as she washed the dishes.

She was putting the last few dishes away, tears still dripping down her cheeks, when Robert came in to see if she was ready. "What? What is it?" he asked with concern.

"Come here," Bess said it quietly, so as not to disturb the energetic baby inside. Bess took Robert's hand and laid it firmly on her stomach. Almost immediately the little one obliged with a firm pounding. The joy that sprang into Robert's eyes was the best gift Bess could have hoped to give him.

"Goodness, he certainly is an energetic little fellow!" Robert pressed his hand more firmly, waiting expectantly. Before long he was rewarded.

"And maybe he is not a fellow at all," Bess said smugly as she untied her apron. "Come on. We must go. I would love to have some time with Clara while we are in town," Bess added as she reached for her coat.

⁓

Bess had asked Robert to stay with her as she talked with Pastor Lewis. When Marita brought them all a cup of coffee, Bess encouraged her to stay as well.

Both of the Lewises were surprised and pleased to hear of the expected child. Marita was very quiet as they all talked, but Bess knew that she wanted to not interfere with her husband's wise counsel. Bess could also tell that Marita prayed for her as she listened to Bess's struggle with the guilt.

Robert sat quietly also and listened with Marita. Bess spoke slowly at first, but soon the words tumbled out. She poured out her heart as Pastor Lewis observed her with tender kindness. When she had told them all about her sense of guilt and unworthiness, she was quiet.

No one said anything for a little while. She knew Pastor Lewis was praying for wisdom and was very careful about his words.

Finally he spoke. "First, let me remind you that none of us deserves the good things in our lives. We all deserve nothing short of death. We are so filthy with guilt and sin that God cannot even look on us. But because of the gift of His Son's life, sacrificed on our behalf, God forgives us of every offense. Your past is just that. It is past. You are forgiven, and in God's Book it is gone. You do understand and believe that, am I right?"

At Bess's nod, he continued. "Did you cause Anita's death?"

"No."

"When Anita was living, did you wish you were married to Robert? Did you wish it was you carrying Robert's child? Did you ever feel that Anita was in the way of you getting what you wanted?"

Bess blinked, startled. "It never even entered my mind. I loved Anita with my whole heart, and I felt she had been cheated to be bedridden. Her heart was so very pure and good. I don't know why she had to be ill. I was very happy when she told me she would have a child. I felt it was the least God could do for her. I know that's not really right to think that way, but it is truly how I felt sometimes. Then she died. And with her, the child. It's truly the worst sorrow I have known."

The tears splashed down her cheeks. She whispered, "Sometimes I feel as though I am carrying Anita's child, not mine. Pastor, I know the right way to think and feel. I don't know where these guilt feelings are coming from."

"They may actually be coming from Satan. Let me show you something here in Philippians." Pastor Lewis reached for his Bible and quickly turned the pages to the fourth chapter of Philippians. "Sometimes, we have to overcome our feelings with discipline. Here, in verses 6 and 7, we are commanded:

'Be careful for nothing; but in every thing by prayer and supplication with thanksgiving let your requests be made known unto God. And the peace of God, which passeth all understanding, shall keep your hearts and minds through Christ Jesus.'

He set the Bible on the table. "Do you see, Bess? God doesn't want us to worry and carry guilt. It's wrong. Instead, we should take these things to Him in prayer and leave them there. If you do that, He has promised He *will* give you peace. He goes on in the next verse to say:

'Finally, brethren, whatsoever things are true, whatsoever things are honest, whatsoever things are just, whatsoever things are pure, whatsoever things are lovely, whatsoever things are of good report; if there be any virtue, and if there be any praise, think on these things.'"

His eyes entreated her. "Do you understand, Bess? It's a discipline. It is not just a gift. We must master our minds and not allow those feelings of guilt and self-blame to win in our hearts. It is the way Satan trips us up and makes us useless to the kingdom.

"From what you have told me, you have done nothing whatsoever for which you should be feeling guilty. I believe it is Satan's way to rob you of the peace God wants to add to all the other gifts with which He has blessed you. He must trust you a lot, Bess, to have given you a loving husband and four children to care for, plus another little one on the way. Very few women are entrusted with so much."

"Yes," she whispered, "I know I am truly blessed. Perhaps that is part of the guilt. I have done nothing to deserve such happiness. In fact, I deserve nothing at all."

Pastor Lewis smiled. "If you deserved the gifts God has given to you, they would not be gifts. They would be payment. Bess, none of us deserves the good that God chooses to bestow on us. But have you ever given someone a gift, and then have them hand it back to you, saying that they don't deserve it? How would that make you feel? Do you think that may be what you are doing to God now? All He wants is for you to accept His good gifts and say thank You. He doesn't want you to try to pay Him."

Bess closed her eyes and nodded slowly. "You're right. That is what I am doing. I am rejecting His gifts to me because I do not feel worthy. And if I was worthy, they would not be gifts. They would be payment. Oh, my." Bess's head bowed as the realization dawned in her heart.

There was silence in the room as that realization took root.

Then Pastor Lewis began praying the very things that were in Bess's heart. "Oh, Lord, our loving God, please hear the cry of Bess's heart as she accepts Your good gifts—gifts she does not deserve, as none of us deserve Your amazing goodness to us. Fill her once again with Your joy, I pray."

As Bess and Robert prepared to leave the Lewis home, Marita asked her quietly if Clara knew yet about the coming child.

"Not yet, but I plan to tell her today. This morning I felt the little one kicking, and suddenly it feels real. I know Clara will be happy to be a grandma."

Marita smiled and hugged Bess. "This is really good news for us all. And I think you might want to tell Rebecca soon as well."

"I thought about that, but I feel so bad for her that I wasn't sure how to tell her."

Marita's eyes glistened merrily. "Oh, I think she'll be happy for you and glad that you told her. I encourage you to tell her today also."

Bess searched Marita's face. "Yes, we are going to stop in for some supplies. I will talk to her." She was puzzled by Marita's insistence but knew the telling would not get easier by procrastination.

It was nearly noon by the time Robert and Bess knocked on the front door of Clara's Place. Bess didn't wait for someone to come to the door but pushed the door open and started back through the hallway to the kitchen.

Rose was slicing bread that had just come from the oven, and Clara was leaning over a kettle on the stove as she lifted the lid to peer inside. When she saw them, she quickly dropped the lid back into place.

"To what do we owe this honor?" She came over and hugged Bess while Robert smiled his greeting before walking to the little table under the windows and pulling out a chair.

"We wanted to talk to you a bit if you have time." Bess looked at Clara and then past her at Rose. "Rose can be included in this chat if she wishes. How about if I help you feed the boarders first and then we can chat when you have a few minutes to sit down. Would that be all right?"

"That would be great!"

Rose handed Robert the heel from the loaf she was cutting and pushed a plate of butter toward him with the tip of the knife. "We'll be back shortly."

When all the boarders were served, Clara dished up bowls of soup for the four of them while Rose brought another loaf of bread to their table. After the blessing, they all looked expectantly at Bess, who blushed beautifully and said, "We just wanted to let Clara know that she will be a grandma in the spring." She took a bite of the soup while Clara's spoon froze in midair.

Rose's eyes were wide and smiling, but Clara just stared at Bess in disbelief. "Grandma? Are you. . .oh, Bess! Really?" She looked first at Bess and then at Robert's smiling face. "It's true, isn't it? You are going to have a baby?"

Clara was so excited that she hardly took a bite for the rest of the meal. She asked lots of questions, and Bess answered to the best of her ability, while Robert ate silently between grinning at the women's animated talk. Finally they left to pick up the things they needed from the store before heading back out to the farm.

But at Taylors', Bess was the one to receive the surprise. Rebecca had taken her back to the kitchen to chat. Bess had no more told her news than Rebecca said glowingly, "Me, too!"

"You, too?" It took a moment to register, and then Bess beamed. "Rebecca! You are expecting a child also?"

"Yes, finally! I thought it wouldn't happen to me at my age. I'm almost forty now, but it's very real. We figure this one will arrive sometime in June. My dresses are already so snug I was afraid you had already noticed."

"Rebecca, that's such good news! We are guessing that our little one will arrive sometime in May. They will grow to be great friends. I am so happy for you."

"And I for you!" Rebecca hugged Bess tightly.

Bess couldn't help but marvel at God's amazing goodness.

Chapter 24

February was soon replaced by a cold, blustery March. The snows continued, but the frozen crystal snowflakes were exchanged for heavy ones. The days seemed grayer and longer than any March days Bess could remember.

She had taken some buckets of good earth to the cellar in the fall, and now she spread it into small containers and placed them in the kitchen's sunny south windows, tucking little tomato and green pepper seeds into the soil. The smell of warm, moist earth filled her with impatience for the winter to end and spring to bring new life once again to the frozen world around her.

She also felt herself getting impatient for the new life growing inside her. Two more months seemed like such a long time to wait. But Robert tried to calm her impatience with reminders that all good things were worth waiting for. She had heard that expectant mothers suffered from fluctuating emotions, but she could not have imagined how true it was.

In the long March evenings, she knitted. She made soft blankets and warm sweaters and booties and hats. She stitched gowns and hemmed diapers.

One day, while the children were in school and Robert was in the barn, she ventured to the attic to see if there was something there in which she could store the baby's clothes. She remembered Anita telling her that the attic stored lots of the furniture that had been in the house when Robert's parents had lived here raising their family. They had planned to go to the attic together some time, but that time had never arrived. Now Bess ventured into the elevated ramparts alone.

Carrying a lamp with her, Bess pushed open the door at the back of the upstairs hallway, entered the stairwell to the attic, and started to climb the narrow steps. She was only halfway up the stairs when she noticed the smell of dust and age. For some reason that aroma enhanced her feelings of mystery. Eagerly, she climbed on.

At the top of the stairs, she paused to catch her breath. This little one seemed to press into the space her lungs were used to inhabiting, and there no longer seemed room enough for a full breath. Breathing heavily, she brushed the cobwebs and dust from an ancient velvet-covered chair and sat down. Leaning her head against the back of the chair, she held the lamp high and gazed around the attic.

There were several small tables, a hodgepodge of wooden chairs, and several trunks. Stacks of leather-covered books were piled in some kind of order on a velvet rug, and cushions were arranged as though someone had come up here to read.

Wooden crates were stacked along one side of the wall, along with vases and pictures. She saw several rolled carpets under the eaves on one side. Dresses were draped on an old overstuffed chair as though someone had just taken them off. Lamps swung from the rafters in several of the gables, hanging there as if waiting patiently for flame.

Getting clumsily to her feet, she walked over to the nearest lamp and swung it a bit. Of course any fuel would have evaporated long ago, but otherwise the wick looked good and ready to light. She must bring some lamp oil up and explore someday.

She found a cupboard, as well as a nice chest of drawers, in one corner beside some piece covered by an old quilt. Bess lifted a corner of the quilt and discovered a large, beautifully made hanging cradle. How lovely! She hoped she would be able to use that for this baby. Behind the cradle, almost as though it were trying to hide beneath the eaves, was a cradle on rockers. That would be nice to keep by the stove for use during the day, and the other cradle could reside in the bedroom where the baby would be close as they slept.

As she lifted the cover from the rocking cradle, she saw a stack of what looked like fabrics. She pushed and shoved the large hanging cradle out of the way so she could touch what was there. When she could reach them, she took the stack out and carried it back to the chair she had used earlier. She set the lamp on a table and sat down with the stack of fabric in her lap.

One by one she unfolded beautiful baby quilts. The one on top of the stack was a mix of blues and greens. The stitching was beautiful, and on a larger square in the center was the name *Paul Robert Sheldon*. Anita must have made this blanket for Paul. Hastily she opened the next one, and on the center square was stitched the name *Conner Eugene Sheldon*. As she expected, the next one spelled out *Philip Edward Sheldon*, and the fourth quilt said *Anna Elizabeth Sheldon*. But there was still one quilt in her lap. Wondering, Bess opened the quilt and was amazed to see the name *Lily* stitched there. The *y* was not quite finished, and that was all that was on the quilt. The needle was stuck into the fabric as though the seamstress had just laid the piece aside for the moment.

Bess sat looking at the quilt, completely puzzled. She knew Anita was expecting a child when she had taken ill before her death. But Bess had been with her daily and had never seen her working on a quilt. Nor had she ever mentioned a quilt. She had confided in Bess that she hoped to name the child Lily Bess if it was a girl, but would she have made a quilt with the name *Lily*, not yet knowing if she carried a girl or a boy?

Bess continued to puzzle over the quilt. It was beautifully made, but obviously not quite finished and never used. When did Anita make the quilt? Why did she not finish it? Was this something she could ask Robert? Her mind rolled one question after another around, but she found no answers. Finally Bess carefully refolded the blankets, laid them back in the cradle, and pulled the cover over to discourage the dust.

Turning back to the chest, Bess opened the drawers one by one. They were filled with lovely handmade baby clothes, with delicate embroidery and dainty stitches. Many looked like they had never been used. What did it mean? Was there a secret here that she should not have discovered? Well, she had indeed stumbled onto a mystery of some kind and would ask Robert when he came in for lunch.

She gasped. *Lunch. Oh, my!* She wondered what time it was. She snatched the lamp and carefully found her way back down the steep stairway. Closing the door behind her, she extinguished the lamp and set it on the hall table, then brushed the dust and cobwebs from her hair and clothes. She must hasten to have Robert's lunch ready by the time he came in from the barns.

She was pouring milk into their glasses when she heard Robert outside the kitchen door stomping the snow from his feet. She gathered the food to the table as he washed in the basin by the door.

Robert was dipping food onto his plate when she began. "Robert, I was in the attic today looking to see if there was something we could keep the baby clothes in."

"Those stairs are pretty steep, Bess. Be careful—since you can no longer see your feet!" The merry twinkle in his eyes made her laugh more than the comment did.

"You'd better not insult the cook. You never know what she might put in your food!"

They chuckled together briefly, but Bess wasn't to be deterred. "There is a nice chest of drawers up there. Could we move it down to our bedroom to store the baby's clothes?"

"Sure we could. Are you wanting to do that already? Don't we still have a couple of months?"

"Yes, we still have time. I was just wondering. . ."

Robert continued chewing. Then he looked up. "Was there something else you wanted? Did you find the cradles? Would you mind using cradles that have been used before?"

"No, Robert. I would love to use the children's cradles. Did you make those? They are lovely."

"I made the swinging cradle. The one on rockers my father made for me when I was a baby. But Anita used it for our children, too."

"Oh, how wonderful! When it is closer to my time, we can move them down, and I will clean and polish them. They have been cared for beautifully already."

Again Bess hesitated. She took a bite and chewed slowly, trying to think how to ask her other questions.

While she looked at her plate, Robert said gently, "What else did you find there, Bess? I can tell there is still something on your mind. What is it?"

Bess looked up, startled as always when he spoke her thoughts. She swallowed. "There was a pile of baby quilts in the cradle. There was one with each of the children's names on it."

"Yes, Anita made one for each child while she recuperated from each birth. I think she was hoping they would be a keepsake for each child, but if you want to use them, you could."

"No, I think we should keep them for the children." Again she paused, studying her plate. Her fork was pushing the food in circles, so she laid it down. Glancing up, she saw that Robert was still waiting. So she pressed on.

"Robert, there are four children, and there are four completed quilts. But there is a fifth quilt that is not quite finished. It has most of the word *Lily* stitched in the center, but the thread and needle are still in it as though it had been interrupted. I know that Anita wanted to name the baby *Lily* if it was a girl. But when did she make the quilt? I was with her the whole time, and she never once sewed on a quilt. Do you know about it?"

Robert sighed heavily before laying his fork on his plate, folding his arms on his chest, and leaning back in his chair. "Bess, I've thought to tell you about this several times since we've been married, but there never really seemed to be a right time. At first I just wanted to help you get over your guilt. Then when we knew you were in the family way, I was afraid to tell you, for fear of causing unnecessary worry. I would have told you at some time. But I guess now's as good a time as any."

Bess could only sit and stare at him questioningly.

Robert took another deep breath. "The year before you came to be with us, before Anita came down with polio, we had a baby girl. We named her Lily Joy. She died suddenly while Anita was still making her quilt, and Anita didn't have the heart to finish it. After she got sick herself, I folded it away with the other quilts in the cradle upstairs. I don't think she thought too much about it until she knew there was another little one on the way. One night she asked me if I thought it would be all right to name the new baby after her older sister who was already in heaven. Instead of Lily Joy, she wanted to name her Lily Bess because of her great love for you.

She remembered the quilt and decided God had stopped her just in time. Now she could finish the blanket with the new baby's name if the baby were a girl." Robert paused and looked down at his plate briefly. "Only the new baby never came." Tears filled Robert's eyes and splashed untouched onto his plate.

Bess moved to the seat beside him and reached for his hand. "Robert, I had no idea you have been through so very much sorrow. I hurt for you, but I don't even know what to say to you. You have lost three. And I didn't know. Oh, my dear Robert, I am so very sorry."

"There is really nothing to say. I won't lie and tell you I am over it all. I may never be over it all. But God gives grace as we need it, and He fills empty hearts with more love than we even know to ask for. I feel like Job sometimes, Bess. He was obedient to God, as I have tried to be, yet God allowed testing. In the end, God gave Job more than he ever dreamed and more than he had had before his trials. I feel so very blessed to have you, Bess. And to have one more little one is more than I could have ever hoped or dreamed for. I will not look at what I have lost, but will focus instead on the blessings God has given to me. I am truly a very blessed man." He laid his hand on Bess's cheek.

Bess pressed his hand gently. "And I am truly a very blessed woman. Do you have any idea how very much I love you, Robert Paul Sheldon?"

She shook her head in disbelief. Who would ever have imagined such a man? Or that he would belong to her?

Chapter 25

There were only two weeks of school left before the children would be able to stay home for the summer. Bess looked forward to having them around more. It was Monday morning, and she could hear the birds singing loudly outside the open window. Robert was stirring. She had meant to be up before now, but her back was hurting terribly, and she had lain still for too long.

Groaning softly to herself, she sat up on the edge of the bed. Why was her back hurting so badly? All she could think was that she had slept in an unusual posture. She rose and pressed on to get breakfast ready and pack lunches for the children. As she worked, hard pains would clamp in her back with force and then ease after a few minutes.

After sending the children off to school, Bess started cleaning the dishes off the table when the pain moved to her abdomen. And then she knew what was happening. She sat down hard in the chair by the table. After a few minutes the pain eased once again, so she continued her work. *Everyone says this could take hours.*

The morning seemed to move more slowly than usual. When Robert came in for lunch, she had not even started preparing the food. He called her name, but she could only groan. Rushing into the bedroom, he saw Bess curled on her side on the bed.

"Please, Robert," she panted, "please get the doctor. Hurry!"

"Are you all right here alone?" His tone was frantic.

"I have to be! Please, just go quickly." Suddenly she blanched white and groaned again, clenching her teeth as beads of sweat stood out on her forehead.

"I'll hurry!"

Robert hadn't been gone more than fifteen minutes when Bess heard Marita's cheerful voice calling in the back door, "Anyone home? Bess? Robert? May Edwin and I come in?"

Bess mustered all the strength she could to call out, "Here, Marita. . .come here!"

As soon as Marita stuck her cheerful head around the doorframe, she became all business, barking orders to her husband.

Within an hour of Marita and Edwin's arrival, Bess held a tiny girl in her arms. By the time Robert returned with the doctor, Marita had the coffee brewing on the stove and Bess was sleeping soundly with the downy little head resting in the crook of her arm.

Robert stood at the foot of the bed with tears streaming unashamedly down his face.

Doc Walker stayed in the kitchen drinking a cup of the strong brew while Marita told what she had done and explained what had happened. Doc Walker chuckled. "Have you ever considered going into midwifery? Sounds like you did a right good job of it. Don't know as I could have done better."

Marita blushed at the compliment.

Edwin chuckled and then commented to the doctor, "You might not have been so bossy."

Again Marita blushed, but the men laughed heartily. "Well, I will go on in and check on the mother and baby as long as I'm here. Give my horse a bit of a rest before I head her home."

While the doctor was with Bess, Robert asked Pastor Lewis to help him move the things from the attic. "We knew we needed to get them out, but we hadn't told the children yet because we thought we still had a couple of weeks. Guess this wee one decided to show up a bit early and catch us off guard."

The house was bustling with activity when the children arrived from school. To answer the unspoken questions, Robert put his finger over his lips and motioned silently for them to follow him. Tiptoeing quietly, they followed him into the bedroom.

There, lying on the bed, was Bess with a baby in her arms. She beamed at the children and said softly, "Would you like to meet your sister? She has been eager to meet you all. I told her all about you, but she wants to see for herself."

All the children stood quietly staring. Finally Anna said, "Is she really our sister? Will she stay with us forever?"

"Yes, Anna, she is really your sister. And we will pray that God will let her stay with us forever and ever."

Suddenly everyone was talking at once. Even the boys were touching the baby and wanting to hold her. Bess welcomed them all onto the bed, and the little family hovered lovingly, examining every finger and toe. The baby's hair curled in swirls over her head, and as she sucked her hand, a tiny dimple appeared in one cheek. Conner discovered the dimple and felt quite proud of himself for finding it first. Her eyes were bright as she looked from one doting face to another.

Finally Paul asked the question. "What's her name?"

All eyes turned to Bess. "Well, I've been thinking for some time that it seems her name should be Lily Grace Sheldon. Because I can smell the lilies outside my window and because I believe a little girl named Lily is supposed to be in this family. Are there other opinions?" She looked questioningly at each child and at Robert.

All was quiet.

Anna was the first to speak. "Mother would like that, Mama. And her little mouth looks just like a lily, don't you think?" Still the room was quiet while Bess awaited other comments. And then Anna added, "We had a sister named Lily once, but she went to be with Jesus like Mother did. I think our other sister Lily would like to share such a beautiful name, don't you?"

It seemed Anna always spoke for her brothers. As though it had been previously decided, they all spoke at once, calling her "little Lily." Over their heads, Bess raised a brow at Robert. The tender look he gave her assured her of his approval.

The gentle May breeze stirred the curtain in the early morning. Bess had finished nursing Lily and laid her back in the cradle, covering her with the now-completed quilt stitched with *Lily Grace Sheldon.*

The birds were singing, and Bess walked to the open window to listen. On the breeze came the fragrance of the lilies of the valley that grew beneath the window. As she inhaled the beloved scent, Bess felt Anita there with her somehow in the fragrance she had so loved. And then she was gone—almost as though Anita had stopped in for a brief hug. In that quiet moment Bess knew she was not taking Anita's place at all, but continuing it. She was right where she was supposed to be, as though she and Anita had shared one spirit.

She could never have explained it, but in her heart she felt peace. She knew Anita was pleased. And so was Bess. Only God could have shown such grace to a poor prostitute and carried out such a perfect plan. As His love enveloped her in the fragrance of the lilies, Bess knew her smile had finally reached her eyes.

WHERE TWO AGREE

The Hand of God,
Book Three

by Judi Ann Ehresman

Dedication

Girlfriends are a special gift from God as we bear with one another
and also help "bear one another up" through the trials as well as joys of life.

In honor of my fictional girlfriends, Mandy and Deidre,
I would like to dedicate this book to two very special friends
that God has brought into my life: Kay Stouse and DeeDee Hart.

I'd also like to thank God for my many other dear women friends
who make my life special every day, of whom I cannot begin to make an
exhaustive list. Please know that I thank God for you and hold you dear to my heart!

Chapter 1

Deidre walked slowly up the worn path to the cabin from the vegetable gardens. The wooden bucket was nearly full from the first picking of the tender peas. She had gone to the gardens to do some early weeding and discovered the bountiful crop ready for picking already. Mandy and Ethan would be surprised. She smiled as she thought of how much the boys would enjoy the harvest.

Stopping to rest for a few minutes, she set the bucket down and straightened her back, breathing deeply of the earth and sun-warmed grasses. She tipped her ebony face up to the heavens and once again felt close to Jeremiah, knowing that somewhere this same sun was warming her husband's rich black skin. Silently she uttered the same prayer she prayed regularly: That God would protect and guide him and somehow bring them back together again.

It seemed unlikely they could ever find one another, with him being sold to another plantation and her a runaway slave, but Deidre clung to the promise that with God all things are possible. She believed with her whole heart it would happen. She had no idea how it could, but she would not stop praying and believing.

She leaned against a tree trunk, listening to the happy sounds that were part of her life now. She could hear her young son, Jedediah, encouraging and instructing Ethan and Mandy's son, Daniel, as they played together. Such love between those two boys. It was a wonder indeed. As she often did, she prayed the boys would never be separated by the hatred of this world that saw the color of the skin instead of the condition of the heart.

As she listened, she could hear the ax chopping and the tall straight trees as they fell. Ethan had offered to build her a cabin of her own, but he also told her he would be glad to build a wing onto their cabin for her if she preferred. Then she and Jedediah would be able to have a little more space of their own while still sharing the main house with Ethan and Mandy. Both Deidre and Mandy preferred having him add the wing to the main house, and they planned to start the building of it tomorrow.

The day was warm, and Deidre enjoyed the shade of the aged maple tree. She sighed. She knew she should soon be going up to the house to help Mandy put the boys down for naps, but she rested yet a bit. A bee lazily droned over the wild daisies across the path, and the gentle breeze that moved too slowly to cool her skin much still brought the fragrance of summer to her. If only Jeremiah could be here with her, life would be as near heaven as it could be on this earth. Indeed, she had never dreamed her life could be so good.

She recalled the many ways God had answered her prayers these past couple of years. She still could never think of it all without tears running down her face and a prayer of gratitude rising from her heart. And, as always, she shuddered as she remembered her life before coming to live in Indiana with Mandy and her family.

Life was hard for all the slaves who worked the Wickner Plantation. Mr. Wickner considered his slaves to be part of his livestock, and Mrs. Wickner acted as though the slaves would contaminate her if she was not careful. The slaves could not please her, no matter how hard they tried. If something was done well, it still was never good enough. And if something was done poorly, she felt it was to be expected (but soundly corrected) because the slaves were so stupid in her eyes.

The Wickners had two sons and a daughter. The sons were becoming as ill-tempered and mean as their father, and the daughter acted as though the world revolved around her and the slaves should know her thoughts before she spoke them. She was becoming even more difficult to please than her mother, if that was possible.

The slave colony on the Wickner Plantation was a community of its own. In spite of the fact that many of the sturdier young ones were taken from their mothers and sold off while still young enough to be trained to serve a new owner properly, their own slave population increased at a steady rate.

Deidre had been with the Wickners since she was young. She was skinny and tall, and Mrs. Wickner particularly took a liking to her cooking, so she had requested her husband to give her Deidre to work in the house. Because Deidre looked somewhat frail, Mr. Wickner agreed to the request, thinking she would more than likely not be much good in the fields anyway.

Deidre guessed she was somewhere around eighteen or twenty years old when Jeremiah was purchased at auction and brought to the plantation. He was handsome, strong, and probably somewhere near the same age as Deidre.

Deidre watched the new slave named Jeremiah as he moved around the slave camp in the evenings. He had a strong back and muscled arms, and Mr. Wickner worked him particularly hard, yet Jeremiah never complained. Around the slave camp, he seemed to always know who needed a hand and who needed encouragement. Even though he worked harder than most of the others all day long, in the evenings he still helped the others wherever he could.

Jeremiah smiled at everyone in the camp. He dared not smile at the white folks, but in the slave camp his smile was constant. His eyes were large and a deep choco-late brown…the kindest eyes Deidre had ever seen. Soon she found herself watching for him, and her own smile came more readily when he was around. And more and more he seemed to be around. Then one evening as she was returning to the camp from her day's labors in the big house, he stopped her, placed his finger under her chin, tipped her face up, and searched her eyes. He didn't say anything for a long time, but just looked into her very soul. She could not tear her eyes away.

Finally he spoke softly. "Deidre, none of us knows what the future holds, or how long we'll be here or if we'll get sold off. All I know is that I believe God brought me here to find ya." He paused briefly, but Deidre remained silent. Then he continued. "Will ya be my wife? If'n you'll say yes, all I can promise is I'll do my very best to buy our freedom so we can be together always. But if'n I cannot buy our freedom, you'll be the only wife I will ever know. That's the best I can promise."

A million thoughts had raced through Deidre's mind, but all were subdued by the thought of being Jeremiah's wife. "Yes, Jeremiah, I will be yer wife and yers only. I believe God will help us. He knows our hearts." And so with the blessing and wit-ness of the other slaves, she and Jeremiah "jumped the broom" quietly one evening, becoming man and wife.

A little more than a year later Deidre could no longer hide that she was expect-ing a child. Mrs. Wickner was furious. She demanded to know how it had happened, so Deidre told her of the marriage. She tried to reassure her mistress that it would not keep her from her kitchen duties, but the woman was still angry. Mr. Wickner was only able to calm his wife with the news that she could have the money from the sale of Deidre's baby when it was born. And to further please his wife, Mr. Wickner promised to soon sell Jeremiah.

Many nights, as Deidre lay in Jeremiah's arms, he promised her that if they ever got separated, he would do all he could to earn or buy his freedom and that he would come take her away from the Wickners. Deidre had prayed fervently they would never have to be separated.

It was the other slaves who told her as she returned to their cabin late one eve-ning that Jeremiah had been taken to the auction that day and sold. Deidre cried so hard that her sobs turned into labor pains. Just as the sun pushed its cold light into what was left of the night, Dodie, who attended all the slave children's births, laid the wee child in her arms. Then Dodie left for a couple of hours of sleep before beginning her day.

Deidre had gazed at her son with wonder the moment she saw him and whis-pered the name she and Jeremiah had decided on, if the baby were a boy: "Jedediah."

The baby had never cried that morning but had taken a gasp of air and just looked at her in awe. He was a beautiful child, and as she held him close he seemed to be memorizing every bit of her. As she stroked his chubby, round cheek, she promised him she would tell him all about his daddy and that one day they would meet. Her heart nearly broke with the longing to lay this tiny treasure in his father's arms. But she would always believe there would be a day the two would meet.

Deidre had closed her eyes just as Dodie had come back into the cabin. "Don' ope' yer eyes, gal. Y' still haf a coupla hour befo' y' haf t' make th' missus' breakfas'. Jes rest if'n y' can a'tall. Ah'll be back t' show y' how t' tie th' young-un onto yer ches' fer th' day. Jes' res' now."

And so Deidre cooked and baked with Jedediah strapped to her chest for the first weeks until he grew enough that she could lay him on a mat in the corner of the kitchen.

Jeddy, as others called him, learned early that he must stay in the kitchen at all times when his mother was there. The child knew no other life than in that kitchen ...until the day they decided to run away from the Wickner Plantation.

Not long before Jeddy was two years old, life suddenly changed for them. Deidre had to make a fast decision when she heard the news from Susannah, one of the slaves who cleaned the house for the Wickners. Susannah had been cleaning outside the library door when she'd overheard Mrs. Wickner complaining about "the kitchen brat" taking up too much of Deidre's time. She was using the whining tone that always caused Mr. Wickner to solve the problem at hand so she would stop whining.

Mrs. Wickner had several voices. It didn't matter so much what she actually said; it was the tone of voice she used. When she barked, she intended to be obeyed immediately. Only the slaves were barked at by Mrs. Wickner. Her helpless voice was used on her children (who were nearly grown). It worked when the children were young, and they jumped to do whatever she bid them. But as they got older, they learned to ignore her completely when she spoke to them unless they wanted something from her, which was seldom. Her subdued voice was saved for Mr. Wickner. Mr. Wickner adored that voice and doted on his wife, whenever she used it. But when she had a problem she needed him to solve, she whined. And when she whined, Mr. Wickner always pacified her.

The slaves all learned to beware of Mrs. Wickner when she whined. Action *always* followed. The fact she was whining about Jeddy was not good. He wasn't even two years old, and the lady had only laid eyes on him very few times. But that day she had entered the kitchen and saw him as he played on the floor.

"Whose child is this?" she had asked sharply. "And what is he doing in this kitchen?"

Jeddy looked up at her with wide eyes. Deidre tried to ignore Jeddy and went quickly to the missus, explaining that Jeddy was her child but that he didn't bother anyone and played quietly there all day while she worked.

"Who feeds and clothes this child?"

"I share my portions with him, Mrs. Wickner. Now, what was it you wanted from me today? Were those biscuits warm enough this mornin'?"

"They were too hot to bite into. They should be cooled slightly before serving." Then she went on to give the instructions she had intended for Deidre. As she left, she studied the child and Deidre feared what she might be thinking.

It was that afternoon when Susannah had overheard the conversation.

As Mrs. Wickner whined, Mr. Wickner became thoughtful. "Wasn't that strapping young buck named Jeremiah supposed to be the father of the child?"

"Yes, I think so. What does it matter? He's long gone now. The important thing is that I need the girl to give her undivided attention to the work she is here to do, and she is wasting time caring for that brat of hers. The quality of the food is deteriorating, and we have that picnic coming up that we want to have done well. . . ." Even her sigh seemed to be part of the whining as her voice grated on his nerves.

"Well, if we keep him, he'll probably grow to be a good worker. But I can sell him if you'd prefer. After all, I promised you the money from his sale before he was born. He will probably bring a good price for a child if he has the same thick arms and legs as Jeremiah. As I remember, his daddy was a good worker and had a strong back. I will look at the child soon and we can decide then."

"You are so good to me," Mrs. Wickner purred. "What would I do without you to solve all my problems?"

There was silence for a short time and then she continued, "Oh, let's just sell him and be done with it. Then Deidre's attention will not be on caring for him, and she can do better work again. Will you sell him, please?"

There had been a heavy sigh, the squeak of a chair, and then indifferently Mr. Wickner had replied, "Oh, all right. I will see to it in a few days."

It was the main topic of conversation in the camp that evening. Deidre knew it would happen. It had happened too many times before. Gerdine, one of Deidre's friends, had come over and put her arms around Deidre. "Honey, I knows y' think if'n y' leave ya'll nevah see yo' husban' agin, but if'n y' stays y'all nevah see neitha' of yo' menfolks. They gonna be ripped away. Ya'll bes' run now an' tak th' chil' with youse befo' it's too late."

Joseph, one of the elders among the slaves, had heard that there was a slave shelter not too many miles from the plantation. He promised to get the details and the directions the very next day. And so the plans were laid.

225

Chapter 2

The next day Deidre prayed all day as she worked. She wanted to take some extra food but dared not take any, even though the leftover food thrown to the hogs on the plantation would have fed her and Jedediah for several days. Still, she would not steal. The God of heaven and earth would provide for her. She struggled inside with the fact that running away was still actually stealing from her owners, but her life felt so hopeless that it seemed to be the only way.

At dusk, when she returned to her cabin, most of the other slaves were waiting there. Joseph had indeed discovered that there was a host family who lived only twelve miles north of the plantation. He gave her careful directions to the house and explained that it would have a quilt hanging on the front porch rails. If the quilt had red patches, she should stay away, because red was a sign that it was not safe at that time. If there were green or blue patches, she should go to the cellar door when no one was around, lift the door, and go inside and wait on the stairs until a family member found her. They would instruct her from there on.

Joseph and Asha told her to sleep for two hours and then start out at midnight. They would keep watch as she slept and wake her in plenty of time. Joseph warned her that she must make it all the way to the safe house before too late in the morning, and if the folks there allowed it, she should stay there until the search parties had lost interest.

The next morning, when Deidre and Jedediah arrived at the designated house, there was indeed a quilt with blue and green patches hanging over the porch rail. They ran across the clearing as quickly as possible and found the cellar doors. They didn't have to crouch on the stairs for too long before the kind folks found them. They gave them porridge and some soft blankets but advised them to stay in the cellar to sleep. They were awakened late in the day with bowls of a savory stew and thick slices of bread with cheese. Both Deidre and Jedediah were hungry and ate heartily.

At dusk they were taken to the barn, laid on straw in a large wagon, and nearly covered with more straw. They would be leaving immediately for another safe house a good distance north of this one where they would be safe to stay for a while.

They stayed at that second house for a couple of months until all search parties were hopefully wearied of the search. But still Deidre was advised to travel as far north as she could and to travel only at night. She was given food to take along, but also the gentleman showed her what nuts and berries and fruit she might find in the various wooded areas to live on until finding a place to settle.

It was a frightening thing when they left the safe house. Deidre and Jedediah walked at night and slept for as much of the day as they could. And most of the time they walked, Deidre carried her son. Once they had discovered a small cave, and Deidre considered staying there and making it their home. However, it was a short-lived idea since there was no good way to provide food there year-round. They did rest there for a few days, but it was too early in the year for berries or apples or fruit of any kind, so Deidre knew they must keep moving north.

In time, Deidre found her way into Indiana Territory and was thankful for the dry, early spring until the day of the May blizzard. She had discovered the nights were quite chilly as she moved north. She and Jedediah had only the clothes on their backs and had run out of any food two days earlier.

Deidre knew she was on someone's property, because there was a lovely log house with smoke coming from the chimney, as well as several outbuildings and a nice-sized log barn. She knew Jeddy was very hungry, and she could hear the animals in the warm barn. So she asked for God's forgiveness for stealing before she even opened the door.

When she opened the door, the wind caught it and tore it from her hand, slamming it against the side of the barn. It made so much noise that Deidre ran to hide behind the barn as she watched the house to see if someone would come out. Instead of coming from the house, a young woman came from the barn itself, carrying a bucket still steaming with warm milk. Deidre had stayed hidden for some time, watching the woman go to the cabin and take the bucket of milk inside. In a little while she saw her come back out to get wood from a woodpile on the back veranda and take it inside. Deidre imagined how warm that snug cottage was as she and Jeddy shivered in the cold.

Finally, when she was quite sure the woman was not coming back to the barn, she carried Jeddy to the door and tried once again to open it quietly. But again the wind tore the door from her weakened hands. This time, when it banged against the side of the barn, she rushed inside and hid behind the stalls at the back of the barn. Deidre crouched low, praying all the while that she would be able to get milk for them from the cows that stomped and snorted in the hay-filled stalls and that they could rest for a while in the warm shelter before moving on.

That was one prayer she was later thankful that God did not answer. Instead, He'd given her much more. While Deidre huddled in the back of the barn holding

Jeddy tightly against her and praying fervently, she listened carefully when she heard the lady return to the barn to check on the cattle and sheep. Deidre was relieved when she was sure the woman had turned to go. However, instead of hearing the barn door close, she heard a sweet voice say softly close to her, "Hello, my name is Mandy."

Deidre had been so frightened to be discovered that she could do nothing but sit and rock Jeddy back and forth while she stared at the young woman. When the kind lady had stooped down beside Deidre, all Deidre could do was cry. She begged to be allowed to rest there and have something to eat. Mandy had wrapped Deidre in her own coat and hurried them to the warm cottage. Mandy gave them food to eat and even made a soft bed for them by her fire for the night.

Deidre had slept hard that night. Jedediah had snuggled beside her on the warm hearth as they slept on a soft pallet of blankets and were covered by more blankets. They had never been so comfortable. She was too tired to even realize that this was the answer to many of her prayers.

She had awakened early with the sun streaming in the window and the coals still glowing in the hearth. While Jeddy still slept in her arms, Deidre had tried to decide what to do. She prayed for wisdom and then planned to make breakfast for the lady and see if the kind lady would help her find a place to live. Again God answered far more than she could have imagined.

Mandy had asked Deidre and Jedediah to sit at the table and have breakfast with her. Apparently, Mandy had no idea how slaves were treated. She truly wanted to be Deidre's friend and asked Deidre to stay and help her on the farm, not as a slave but as an equal.

The two women had become very close friends. They lived as sisters, sharing the cottage and the work. Mandy never asked anything of Deidre but shared everything she owned. It was easy to love Mandy. And it was easy to love her infant, Daniel, who swiftly became a brother to Jeddy.

The next spring, when Mandy's husband, Ethan, came home from working on the railroad, they had both still welcomed Deidre and Jedediah to stay with them.

But still Deidre worried about what she and Jeddy would do next.

Chapter 3

Ethan had been home for a little more than a year, and he and Mandy would be having another baby any day now. Last summer they had discussed from time to time the building of a cottage for Deidre so she could have her own place. Deidre understood that they wanted her to feel a kind of ownership, but the reality was that Deidre was not certain she would be allowed to own a cabin. There was always the fear that federal agents would come along and cast her out as a runaway slave and take away any property she owned. Therefore, whenever the subject came up, she would steer them away from the topic.

In the autumn, Mandy had asked her outright if she wanted to have her own cabin. Deidre finally admitted her fears to Mandy. They agreed to pray about it, and Mandy told Ethan about it also. That was when he suggested building a wing onto the far end of their own cabin for Deidre. Then they could use the bedroom that was beside their own for Daniel, especially with the new baby coming, and Deidre and Jeddy would have more space of their own. All had happily agreed that this was a good plan, but because of Ethan needing to cut wood and butcher meat for the winter, they agreed to wait until the next summer to build it.

Now spring was past and summer was here with its warm sunshine, white fluffy clouds, and long days to store up for the coming winter. Deidre had never really experienced winter before coming to Indiana and had quickly grown to love the distinctness of the four seasons. In the South, one season blended so slowly into the next that there was never a real rush to do anything. Here in Indiana the seasons kept one moving, and they had to plan and prepare to stay one step ahead of the upcoming season. There was much to do, but there was always a distinct sense of accomplishment as well.

Now that the gardens were growing well, Ethan had decided it was a good time to take on the project of building the new wing on the house. Their nearest neighbors, the Brownings, would be coming tomorrow to help him, but he had wanted to get a start on felling logs today. Ethan was a good builder and had made several sketches of what he planned to build for them. Deidre knew that whatever Ethan built would be very nice.

Suddenly Deidre realized that all was quiet. She had been leaning on the old maple tree for longer than she intended. She gathered up the pail she'd been carrying and hurried on up to the house. As she neared the house, Ethan hurried her direction.

"What is it?" she called. "Are the boys all right? Mandy?"

"The boys are napping now, but Mandy said I should get you. Her pains are hard and close now."

"Oh, my! Here. Take this." Deidre shoved the bucket at him as she ran past and up the sloping yard to the cabin.

As Deidre entered the quiet cabin, she shook her head. Mandy was unlike any white woman Deidre had ever known. Not only did she work hard, but she never complained. She had a kettle of water already boiling with the basins standing by and a stack of clean cloths. The door to the Evanstons' bedroom was standing open, and Deidre thought she heard a low groan.

She ran over to the doorway and looked inside. Mandy was curled on the bed, her face red from straining, and her dress still only half unbuttoned. Deidre eased her past the contraction, then helped her get undressed and readied the bed. The two women needed no words. The love and understanding were so great between them that they worked together as one.

As soon as Deidre had Mandy comfortable, she began massaging her lower back and humming softly. She could feel Mandy relax, but it wasn't long before the pushing started again. Deidre knew the time would be short. She had heard Ethan enter the cabin and could hear him pacing back and forth just outside the door. When Mandy was relaxed again, Deidre stepped to the doorway and told him to awaken the little boys from their naps and take them for a walk in the woods.

"Should I go for help?" Ethan was wringing his hands and trying to see past Deidre.

"The only help we need is for you to take those boys outside in case she cries out with one of the hard pains. She's healthy and strong, and we'll be fine. Just take those children and make sure they have a good time. In fact, this would be a great time to take them fishing like you've been promising them. I'll hang a sheet over the porch rail when it's safe to come back."

Mandy was breathing hard, and Deidre turned to go back to her side. In a few minutes they heard the voices of the boys and Ethan as they headed out the back door.

"Deidre, something's different this time. I don't know what it is, but this baby feels like it must be huge. I don't think it's going to take very long at. . .oh!" She doubled over into a ball again.

Ethan tried to concentrate on showing the boys how to fish, but he couldn't. What if something horrible was happening to Mandy? He kept seeing the way she doubled over with the veins standing out on her temples. She said it had started when she tucked the boys into their beds for their naps. They had only been sleeping an hour when he had heard her calling to him from the back porch.

"Go get Deidre. I need some help, Ethan! Please tell her to hurry. It won't be long."

He kept going over it all as he sat on the bank of the stream with the boys. He felt so helpless. Suddenly he remembered that he wasn't helpless at all. He could pray.

So silently he prayed as the boys fished and chattered their innocent questions to him. Occasionally he would look back at the house, but mostly he just prayed and sat quietly with the little boys.

It wasn't very long at all, maybe an hour or two at the most, when he saw Deidre hanging a sheet over the rail of the porch. Could it be? Quickly he gathered the string of fish and the boys and headed back to the cabin.

When they entered the back door, he saw Deidre sipping a cup of tea at the table. He raised his eyebrows when he looked at her. She smiled and told him Mandy was resting but would welcome company.

"Is everything all right?" He seemed hesitant.

"Everything is fine. Go on and see for yourself." Deidre smiled mysteriously as she took another sip of her tea.

Ethan took a hand of each of the boys and headed for the bedroom. As he looked around the doorway, he saw Mandy lying calmly in their bed with a bundle snuggled close to her side. Her eyes were closed, but a definite smile was on her lips.

Quietly Deidre took the boys back into the main room of the house and gave him a gentle shove toward his wife.

Ethan bent to kiss Mandy just as she opened her eyes. "Everything all right?" he murmured.

"See for yourself." Mandy grinned and pulled the top of the blanket back.

Ethan tore his eyes away from Mandy's face and looked at the blanket. Two downy little heads lay cuddled together!

"What?" Ethan didn't quite know what to say.

"We have twin girls!" Mandy seemed quite pleased with herself.

"Oh, Mandy! Two! Oh, they are beautiful. But two?" Ethan stared at the blanket and then at Mandy. Finally, the tears started running down his face. "Oh, Mandy! We have twins. Isn't God good?"

"Yes, He's mighty good. And He's good to have sent us Deidre to help us. I don't know what I would do without her. I want her to be happy, but I do hope she never leaves us. I will never stop praying that we can find Jeremiah and that he will join us here some day."

Chapter 4

Before Deidre got out of bed the next morning, she thought again of what she had overheard yesterday. It made her feel good inside that Ethan and Mandy really did want her to stay. She was even excited about this day, when Ethan and Ned Browning and his boys would build her a wing of her own onto their cabin. She knew they truly considered her part of their family.

However, knowing that her own Jeremiah was still out there in the world somewhere without her made it hard to really allow herself to feel part of this family. It often tore at her heart that she didn't know what sort of life he might be suffering.

She turned her head to look at the small, black, kinky haired head in the bed across from hers. How thankful she was to have this part of Jeremiah with her. She smiled as she thought how very much little Jeddy resembled Jeremiah. Her heart ached with love for this child of theirs.

Quickly she shook herself. There was no time for daydreams and wishes today. The Brownings were more than likely already on their way over for the day, and with Mandy unable to help, Deidre had plenty to do to get food ready for this day.

The sun was brightening the eastern sky as Deidre finished dressing and opened the curtain in the room that had been hers and Jedediah's since living here. "It will be different having windows on the west instead of the east from now on," Deidre said softly to herself. *But it will be nice to have a little more space and privacy,* she thought as she almost bumped her knee on Jedediah's bed.

"Sleep on, little one," she murmured, planting a tender kiss on his fuzzy head. "It will be a busy day for you with all the Browning children to play with as well as Daniel."

While Deidre put wood in the stove for making breakfast, she heard Ethan and Mandy's bedroom door close softly. She looked up to see Ethan running his hands through his hair.

"I'll bring in fresh water," he said as he emptied the bucket in the dishpan and started for the back door.

"Ethan, will you please take the extra bucket and bring two buckets of water for me?"

"Sure. Guess there'll be lots of dishes to wash on a day like today." He smiled sleepily.

"Ethan, how did Mandy and the babies do last night? I didn't hear any crying at all."

He turned and grinned at her. "They didn't have time to cry. I think they ate all night long. I don't know if Mandy got any sleep at all, but they were certainly content as long as she kept them together. We've already learned they do not want to be separated."

"Edna and her girls and I will take them a bit today so Mandy can rest. But she probably won't want to miss out on much of the visiting, either."

Ethan grunted and grinned again. "Hmmm. . .it's going to be a very busy day for us all. I'm glad the birthing is done now. I hope she can rest." He was obviously tired and spoke almost to himself as he headed out the door with the buckets.

Soon the biscuits were baking, the sausages simmering, and the gravy bubbling. The aroma of strong coffee blended all the other smells together to make a fragrant early morning bouquet. Deidre looked up from stirring gravy in time to see Daniel peeking into her bedroom door searching for his sleeping little friend. Deidre smiled.

"Go on in there and wake him up, Daniel." The toddler looked back at her and grinned mischievously before disappearing into her bedroom. Soon she heard the boys chattering and left the stove to go help them get dressed for the day. It warmed her heart to see their friendship. How thankful she was that God had brought her to this place!

⌘

As soon as the boys were dressed, Deidre took a cup of warm milk and a plate of breakfast and knocked on Mandy's half-open door. "Are you awake?" Deidre spoke softly in case Mandy was finally having a chance to sleep a bit.

"We are all awake. Come on in and see the family. Come meet Carolyn and Christina." There was contentment in Mandy's voice as she offered the invitation.

Before Deidre could respond, the door was snatched from her hand, and two little bodies pushed past her into the room.

"See? Babies!" Daniel was showing off the family to Jeddy, who was staring at Mandy.

"Babies for us?" Jedediah finally asked timidly. "Can they play?"

The boys stood beside the bed in awe as Mandy laid the blanket open a bit for the boys to see the two little girls snuggled together inside.

"Can I touch it?"

"*May* I touch it?" Deidre was quick to correct her son. After all of Mandy's help in teaching her grammar and precise diction when she'd first arrived in Indiana, Deidre was determined that her son would grow up speaking properly.

Mandy smiled at them. "Yes, they love to be touched gently." She took his little hand and laid it gently on Carolyn's head. "Jeddy, will you and Daniel take good care of our little girls as they grow up? They will need you to teach them and protect them and help them." Mandy caressed his soft, dark cheek while she asked him.

Jedediah looked from their two downy heads up to Mandy's smiling eyes and pledged solemnly, "I'll do my best, Miss Mandy." Then he looked down at Daniel. "Won't we, Daniel?"

Daniel nodded solemnly. He'd do anything Jeddy asked.

"Now you two go out and wash and get ready for breakfast." Deidre had set Mandy's plate of breakfast on the dresser while she ushered the boys toward the door. "Jeddy, will you please wash Daniel, too?" Turning back toward Mandy, she lifted the bundle of babies into her arms, giving Mandy an opportunity to sit up and prepare to eat breakfast.

"Deidre, I'm so sorry to leave you with all the cooking today. You will have a busy day with all the food to prepare as well as watching the boys. Guess the timing wasn't really good for the birthing, but those girls didn't give us a choice." Mandy sighed happily. "Who'd have thought there'd be two babies? A double miracle!"

"Guess God knew there were two of us needin' a little one to hold. Now I'm wonderin' how we're going to know which one is Carolyn and which is Christina. Have you figured it out yet? They sure look like two peas in a pod."

"Yes, it shouldn't be too difficult, really. Callie—what we'll call Carolyn—was born first and has a little longer face than Christy. She also seems to be a bit more demanding and energetic. Christy's cheeks are a bit rounder, and she also has a freckle on the back of her hand. However, I have a feeling it won't take long to know them by their personalities. Christy seems to be quite passive. I've even had to awaken her to have a turn at eating, or Callie would have eaten it all."

The women cuddled and inspected the tiny girls. "Do you remember we thought we might be makin' too many little clothes? Well, I guess they'll be put to good use now."

"Yes, we may even find ourselves using some of Daniel's things he's outgrown. Now you must eat this breakfast before it's too cold, and I'll tuck the girls down here and get breakfast served up before Ethan comes in complaining."

Both women chuckled at that because they both knew Ethan never complained about anything, and he surely wouldn't start on a miraculous day like today.

Chapter 5

The summer sun shimmered in moving patterns on the painted floor of the porch beside Jeremiah's black, callous feet. How long he sat with his worn hat in his hands, his head hanging low to his chest, he didn't know. His head was swirling with memories and plans, while at the same time it felt as though he was not thinking of anything at all. So much had happened in his young life in such a very short time it made him tired. Yes, today he felt as tired as an old man.

"Always be kind, Jeremiah. Always be kind. People in this world will be hateful and mean, but don't go stoopin' to their level. You jes' smile and be kind. Can't nobody beat kindness outta ya, Jeremiah. It's from God. Jes' let God fill yer heart and soul and always, always, always be kind. It'll pay off in the long run. Jes' watch and see for yerself. It'll pay off. It'll pay off. . . ."

He could still see the sweet smile of his mother's face as she talked quietly to him. He'd seen her beaten. He'd seen her work until she could hardly stand. But he'd never seen her unkind. "They jes' don' understand what they be doin', Jeremiah. They don' mean t' be bad. They jes' don' understand. Always be wise, Son. An' always, always be kind."

He wondered where his mother was now. Had she finished her toiling on this earth? Was she still being kind in the face of adversity? Did kindness ever pay off for his mother? He wished he could let her know where he was and that he was doing just as she had taught him. He wished he could tell her. . .

Jeremiah hung his hat over one knee and put his face into his two large, callous hands. He remembered the last thing he heard his mother saying as he was pulled away from her and led to the wagon to go to the auction. "There ain't no whip that can beat kindness outta yer heart if'n ya choose t' hang on t' it. It's the only way, Jeremiah. Love Jesus an' always be kind."

Jeremiah had stood chained in a row of others, watching, listening, and learning. Some of the slaves led onto the auction block had been surly and mean and had been treated roughly. They all were treated like little more than cattle. But the ones who stood upright and alert seemed to be shown a little more kindness—well, that was stretching the imagination. . .maybe a little less meanness would be more accurate.

When it was Jeremiah's turn to stand on the block, he had quickly surveyed the crowd of bidders. Some looked hateful and mean-spirited. Others appeared curious and some indifferent. But he noticed one thoughtful gentleman in the back who watched him curiously. Jeremiah nodded at him ever so slightly. The man saw and nodded back. It was hard to read what the man was thinking, but when the bidding began, he did not bid at all. Jeremiah thought he would never forget the kind eyes and the curly red hair.

Some of the men had yelled at Jeremiah. Some spat at him. Jeremiah stood silently. Not smiling. Not frowning. In his heart he prayed for strength and for God to guide him. Suddenly he had heard the auctioneer shout, "Sold! Wickner of Devil's Bend Plantation."

Jeremiah hadn't seen the bidder. It was actually another black man who had led him off the block and over to be chained to a wagon nearby.

It didn't take long to understand that Devil's Bend was an accurate name for the sorry plantation to which he'd been taken. Mr. Wickner was mean to the slaves and difficult to please. And Mrs. Wickner was to be avoided at all cost.

The slave camp at Devil's Bend was a good distance from the plantation house and was little more than a field where haphazard, three-sided log shelters had been strewn here and there. The slaves had constructed various types of walls on the fourth side of the huts. Some were not much more than mud bricks, while others were constructed of branches, and still others were nothing more than fabric stretched between pieces of wood. There was one building that housed several young men, and Jeremiah accepted their invitation to join them in their shelter.

Many of the Wickner slaves were sick or hurting from beatings. Jeremiah spent every evening caring for the needs of those who were suffering. Many nights Jeremiah massaged aching backs or dressed the wounds of the beaten slaves. All the slaves were quite subdued each day by the time they returned to the slave camp for the night. Mr. Wickner worked his slaves hard and treated them cruelly.

The nighttime sounds could be heard throughout the slave camp: quiet talking, groans of pain, and the usual sounds of people preparing for sleep. After Jeremiah came to the plantation, his soft songs of comfort were a welcome addition to those sounds. As he sang softly, tired, knotted muscles would relax and tears would dry.

He first noticed Deidre as she walked tiredly into the camp long after the others had settled in for the night the first night he was there, and after that day he was always very aware of her. The children would run to meet her as she approached and walk back with her, telling her of their news and adventures and asking her questions. She was never too tired to chat with the children. And she always checked on the old women before turning into her own hut. Occasionally, she would stop and listen to Jeremiah's singing and turn a tired smile his way before entering her hut.

He had been at the camp nearly a year before he had the courage to speak to her. But it was that night, when he had looked deep into her eyes all the way to her very soul, that he had known for sure she was the one for him. She had agreed to be his wife, and they had jumped the broom and begun their life together soon after.

They had had a little more than a year together. Jeremiah smiled to himself every time he remembered holding her in his arms after a day of work on the plantation. Suddenly he would no longer feel tired. He had felt that with her and for her he could conquer the world.

The news of their coming child had filled his heart with both fear and joy. There is nothing as wonderful as the creation of life from the love of two people on this earth. But the fear of the future on that wretched plantation also twisted his heart with fear and dread for the child. And it renewed his prayerful determination to buy their freedom somehow, someday.

Jeremiah thought of the last time he had held Deidre in his arms. It was just less than four years ago now. That morning they had both awakened early and lay quietly talking until the sun started to lighten the sky. Deidre had told him they should be able to hold their child in their arms within the month. Deidre was such a skinny woman, she hardly looked like she would be a momma. He had prayed that morning in his heart that all would go well with her and that they would have a healthy child to share.

And then, that very day, without even giving him opportunity to tell her good-bye, Mr. Wickner had chained Jeremiah into the wagon and taken him to the auction again.

Jeremiah had stood on the auction block this time not even looking around. He was a grown man, but the tears of frustration at being sold away from Deidre rolled down his cheeks for all to see. While the men yelled and called and bid on him, Jeremiah had turned his face to the heavens and prayed for God to protect and care for his family until he could be with them again. And he prayed with all his heart that he could buy his freedom and theirs, too.

The man who led him toward the wagon that day spoke kindly to him. When they arrived at the wagon, the man had removed his shackles completely and told Jeremiah that his name was Walter Traehdnik, but that Jeremiah could call him Wally. He placed a tender hand on Jeremiah's shoulder and said that he'd be back in a short while.

Jeremiah had not looked at the gentleman until he walked away and left him standing free. What could it mean? Was it a test? Was the man crazy? Jeremiah looked after him and saw a curly, reddish head on broad shoulders, and suddenly he remembered the gentleman who had caught his eye at the auction two years earlier. Could it be the same man?

When the man returned an hour later, he had behind him a fairly bent, old black lady who walked slowly. Mr. Traehdnik matched his step to hers and again removed her chains as soon as they neared the wagon.

"Do you need help up, ma'am?" he said kindly to the black woman. Both black heads snapped up to see if he was mocking, but instead he was reaching to take her arm and assist her to the wagon bed. Jeremiah quickly helped her also and then climbed on after her.

"The straw at this end of the wagon will soften the ride if you care to sit on it." Mr. Traehdnik pointed to a pile of straw covered by an old blanket behind the driver's seat.

"Thank you, sir." Jeremiah spoke for them both as he helped the wizened black lady toward the straw.

As Mr. Traehdnik climbed into the driver's seat himself, he snapped the whip above the heads of the horses, and soon the horses were trotting down the road. When they had passed by the auction area, he turned his head and looked at Jeremiah.

"Jeremiah, is it?"

"Yes, sir, Mr. Traehdnik."

"Jeremiah, I realize it is not the usual way, but I do truly prefer Wally to that long, austere name you've been calling me." He actually smiled. "You'll get used to it, son."

They had ridden on in silence for a spell. Then the gentleman spoke again. "Now, at Rose Hill Plantation you will discover we do things quite differently than at most places. If you will serve well, you may live and work on Rose Hill Plantation as long as you choose. At the end of each year's harvest you will be given a wage. At the end of the fourth year you will have earned enough to buy your freedom if you so desire. I do not sell slaves. So, if you prefer to go your own way after the fourth year, you may turn your wages back over to me, and in return I will give you a document of freedom. At that time, if you choose your freedom, I will take you or see that you have transportation to wherever you wish to live. I recommend all freed slaves either remain as hired people on my plantation or that they move to the North as quickly as possible, because some down here in the South will not take your papers seriously, and you could find yourself back on the auction block.

"Now, should you decide to stay on and work for me after the fourth year, your wages will be your own. You may marry and raise a family in safety on Rose Hill Plantation, and you may stay as long as you are happy." He took a slow breath and then continued.

"I do not believe in chains. You will notice they have been removed and you are free. If you find you do not care to work at Rose Hill Plantation, you are free to leave. However, as I mentioned before, each year you work with us and live at Rose Hill you will earn a wage, so give it some thought before you leave. If you do decide to leave before you have actually earned your freedom, you will not receive any papers of freedom, but I will not track you. You are God's creation the same as I am, and I prefer to think of you as an indentured servant with a choice. I do not consider you to be my property."

Jeremiah had never heard of such a thing as this. Could this be the answer to his prayers? Would he truly be able to earn his freedom and go find Deidre and their child? Could he work here long enough to earn enough to buy their freedom? He had been silent as the thoughts raced through his head. What kind of place would he find this plantation to be?

That had been nearly four years ago. Now Jeremiah was only a few weeks away from having his freedom, but Mr. Wally lay near death's door in the big bed upstairs. Jeremiah was torn inside. Mr. Wally was a good man. His missus, Miss Sue Ellen, and all their children and the servants at Rose Hill needed Jeremiah. What was to come of them all now?

Chapter 6

Jeremiah could hear the rhythmic wailing in the distant fields. All the Negroes were on their knees praying that God would spare Mr. Wally. There was a hush in the house as the whisper of skirts brushed the floors and people moved in silence to accomplish the tasks that must have attention.

He could hear Mammy's soft baritone as she rocked one of the smaller Traehdnik children. He could hear the floor creaking as her rocker massaged the wide wooden boards slowly back and forth. He could imagine several of the children gathered at her knee as she comforted them. For the first time he found himself wondering if Mammy had any name other than Mammy. He'd heard she was born on this plantation and had helped raise Mr. Wally himself. She could have left years ago, but this was home for Mammy, and she wouldn't have even considered leaving "her babies."

No one was working now on the plantation. All work had ceased the minute Mr. Wally had stood on the wagon, then grabbed his head and fallen off. He lay in a crumpled heap among the broken plants until Jeremiah had picked him up in his own arms and ran all the way back to the plantation house. As he passed the stables, he had yelled for Augustin to ride over to Doc Wyndsor's and to not come back without the doctor.

As Jeremiah ran into the front garden, he saw Miss Sue Ellen stand up on the front veranda and start toward him. "What is it? What happened, Jeremiah?" Her voice was a soft whisper as she searched Jeremiah's eyes.

"I don't know, ma'am. He jes' grabbed his head and fell off the wagon in a heap. I snatched him off the ground and carried him home. I sent Augustin for the doctor already."

"Will you carry him up to his bed, Jeremiah?"

"Yes, ma'am. That's where I's headed."

When he laid Mr. Wally on his bed, Jeremiah was relieved to see that the man breathed evenly, even though his eyes were closed and his face was white as ashes. He helped remove his boots and then asked if there was anything more he could do.

"Pray, Jeremiah. Just pray." Miss Sue Ellen laid a soft white hand on his black arm.

So now Jeremiah sat on the porch praying like he'd never prayed before. "Oh, God Almighty, don't take this good man now. His family needs him, and we all need

241

him. Please spare this good man, O God of heaven and earth." He prayed the same prayer over and over in his heart as he held his head in his hands there on the porch with the sun shining as though all was right with the world.

⌇

Darkness hovered over the earth as the sun disappeared slowly below the scraggly surface of the cotton fields to the west of the plantation. Dusk. That was what this moment of near darkness was called. Jeremiah still sat on the porch watching for the doctor to come help Mr. Wally. Dusk described his heart now as it hovered between fear and the calm assurance that God was still in control.

Slowly Jeremiah pulled himself to his feet. Mr. Wally trusted him to watch over the other Negroes and see that all was well. He must go back to the Quarters, but he didn't want to leave here before he knew, before he had some kind of news to tell the black folks who loved this man and served him willingly.

As he leaned indecisively with one hand pressed against the smooth white pillar of the front veranda, he thought he heard a new sound that pulled itself apart from the stillness surrounding him. He listened until he knew it was the gallop of a horse on the hardened sand of the lane leading up to the plantation house.

Jeremiah started down the steps to take the horse as the good doctor flung his leg over the side and ran toward the house in one liquid movement. The horse's sides heaved heavily. Jeremiah laid his hand gently beside the creature's face momentarily to calm him. Then he gently led him over to the cistern and let him drink from the trough before taking him into the barn to be rubbed down and cared for. Soon after they entered the darkened barn, he heard the slower gallop of Augustin's horse as they made their way home.

Jeremiah continued to pray for Mr. Wally and for the doctor as he lit a lantern and cared for the horse. He felt still inside, his whole being a prayer offered up to God. Each step on the straw in the stall sent up the barn odors of aged wood, animals, and warm, clean straw, which altogether seemed to be almost an incense offered with his prayers.

Doc Wyndsor's horse chomped comfortably on the oats that Jeremiah had given him. His sides had finally stopped heaving. Jeremiah knew the animal could handle more water now, but Jeremiah felt frozen to the spot. His right hand rested on the horse's side, his forehead leaned on the horse's neck, and his left hand lay still at the base of the horse's neck. Not since he'd been ripped away from his precious wife had Jeremiah cried real tears, but now they ran down the side of the horse's neck and splashed into the straw. His prayer turned into groans of agony.

He didn't even hear Augustin enter the barn and care for his own horse. As Jeremiah's sobs eventually quieted, Augustin spoke softly behind him. "Is he livin',

Jeremiah? Is there any hope?"

Jeremiah could hear the fear in Augustin's voice. He rubbed the tears from his face with his large hands and turned to the boy. "I think he's livin', Augustin. But somethin's awful bad wrong with him. We must all be prayin'. Miss Sue Ellen needs him and those chil'ren need him, and so do all of us. He's a good man, and I pray God'll spare him for us. This ol' world needs more like him—not less."

"I'll be prayin' jes like ever'one is. They's all prayin', Jeremiah." The young boy looked up with a face full of faith. "Remember what y' tol' us before. Where two or three agree, God'll answer." He was quiet for a couple of seconds. "Listen, Jeremiah. Y'hear them slaves prayin' out there? We'se agreein' and God be hearin'. He'll answer, Jeremiah. He'll answer."

They were silent, listening together to the distant sound of the Negroes as they lifted their voices as one to the heavens.

At that moment Jeremiah felt God's peace spread throughout his being like a warm liquid. He knew God had heard their prayers. He lifted his bowed head and laid a hand on the shoulder of the young man before him. "Yes, Augustin, God'll answer. Don't ever stop believin' that. He may not answer the way we think He should, but He'll answer. That's for sure. Thanks for remindin' me, Augustin. You've been a messenger from God, and I truly thank ya."

The two stood together for a few more moments, Jeremiah's large hand covering Augustin's slim shoulder. Man and boy. Grief, fear, faith, and love were their bond. Jeremiah smiled a slow, sad smile. "God's hearin', Augustin. He's hearin' and He's already answerin'. I know it here." He laid his hand over his chest as he looked confidently into the younger man's eyes.

Augustin nodded. "I know it, too." It was a reverent whisper.

Jeremiah turned thoughtfully toward the big house. "I's goin' up to the house to see what the doctor has to say. Keep prayin', and I'll be back to tell ya whatever I find out."

Augustin nodded silently. Jeremiah turned to go. His steps were heavy and slow at first, but as he neared the house they changed to a hurried walk.

❦

Standing silently in the doorway of the room where Mr. Wally lay, Jeremiah held his hat tightly over his heart with both hands. Miss Sue Ellen and Doc Wyndsor were talking quietly by the bay windows on the far side of the bedroom. Several lamps were lit around the well-appointed room, and the flames flickered, causing quiet movement of shadows and a reverent hush in the room.

As he watched the drama unfolding within that room, Jeremiah knew he was a needed and indeed important part of the future of the plantation. Mr. Wally had entrusted Jeremiah with much of the overseeing and had shown a great respect for Jeremiah's knowledge and ability, leaning heavily on him for many of the decisions.

While Jeremiah watched quietly, Mr. Wally's head slowly turned toward the doorway as though he knew Jeremiah was there. Slowly his eyes opened and in a few moments cleared as they focused on Jeremiah.

The big black man quickly went into the room and knelt by the bed, gazing into the eyes of this good man whom he loved like a father. Quietly, Jeremiah spoke. "I'll take care of things, Mr. Wally. You jes' get well. Don't you worry none."

Mr. Wally looked over Jeremiah's head, just as Jeremiah felt a soft hand on his shoulder. Swiveling slightly, he saw Miss Sue Ellen standing beside him.

"Jeremiah, a couple days ago Wally told me your time with us was nearly up and he suspected you would go find your family. He wants you to be happy. I don't know how we'll get along without you. He was grieving the loss already, but he wants you to be happy."

The silence was thick in the room. They all forgot Doc Wyndsor was even there as the weight of the future lay on all their shoulders—not only the future of the plantation and the family, but of all the Negroes who considered this place their home.

Jeremiah bowed his head while he thought of all his responsibilities. He thought of Deidre and their child. He thought of Miss Sue Ellen and the young family here, as well as the multitude of happy Negroes who lived and served here. He saw in his mind's eye the fields that stretched for miles, the gardens, the stables, and barns. What would happen to this wonderful place if he left now? Slowly he lifted his head and said with reserve, "Don't worry none, Mr. Wally. I won't go nowhere until this place can keep runnin' without my help." His voice became stronger as he continued. "You jes' gets yerself well and then we'll talk."

Mr. Wally's eyes rested on his face for a few moments more, then closed slowly. The slightest smile turned up one side of his mouth ever so slightly, and he breathed deeply.

"I don't know how we'll ever thank you, Jeremiah." Miss Sue Ellen spoke from behind him, and he could hear the tears in her voice. "We'll make it up to you. Of that you can be certain. You are all so good to us."

Jeremiah marveled at that statement all the way back to the tidy village where the Negroes lived at this plantation. He had stopped by the stables to let Augustin know that Mr. Wally was resting well and that they must all work hard while he was ill. Jeremiah knew that every Negro on Rose Hill Plantation would give their own soul for the Traehdnik family. He knew they would keep the place running smoothly, but Miss Sue Ellen's statement about the slaves being good made him smile. It sure was easy to be good to good folks like the Traehdniks. It sure was easy.

Chapter 7

The cabin was warm in spite of the opened windows and doors as Deidre baked and cooked for the hungry men who would be working on building the new wing on the cabin that day. She wanted to get the hottest part of her work done before the sun added to the heat, and she was again thankful for the thick log walls as well as the porch roofs that overhung the windows on the south and north sides of the cabin. Ethan had thought it out well and had built a comfortable home for his family.

Suddenly Jeddy came running into the house with Daniel close on his heels. "They're comin', Momma! I hear 'em. They're comin'!"

Before she could even respond, he had turned and run back to wait on the front steps beside Daniel for his friends to come. She saw Ethan lay down the load of wood he had carried to the porch for her and then head out to the front as well.

Smiling to herself, she thought of how surprised Edna and the girls would be when they saw the new babies in the household. Suddenly her heart lurched as she wondered if she would ever bear another child. Would she and Jeremiah ever find one another and continue their own family?

"Pray, girl. Just keep on prayin'," she muttered to herself softly. She sent another prayer up for her dear husband's protection and that God would guide them back together soon. But something in her heart told her it was not to be yet. "But I'll keep on prayin'." She said it out loud as she firmly placed the last plate on the stack in the cupboard. "I won't quit prayin' until I see his handsome face."

Deidre stood in the doorway wiping her hands on her apron as she watched the Browning children scrambling over one another to get out of the wagon. She smiled as she listened to the happy noise of eight or ten voices all talking simultaneously. The babies would have a noisy first day in this world, she thought. But it was such happy noise that no one minded at all.

Ned reached up to help his beautiful wife out of the wagon. The older girls still held back shyly, waiting for their mother before starting toward the cottage. Deidre saw they had all brought handwork and knew it would soon be ignored when they saw the babies.

As Edna started toward the porch, Deidre noticed how full the woman's slender figure had become around the middle. It looked like they'd be having some news of their own to share on this happy day.

"Is Mandy doing well?" Edna asked as the two women embraced.

"Come on in and see for yourself." Deidre winked at Elizabeth, also known as "Betsy," the oldest of the eight Browning children, over her mother's shoulder. Betsy raised her eyebrows and smiled as Deidre gave a slight nod and ushered them into the cabin.

Once inside, Deidre took the bowls of food they carried and placed them on the table before she motioned for the children to move to the open bedroom doorway. Esther had already gone in, and they heard Mandy shushing her squeals of delight until the others could see the surprise for themselves.

Before she joined the commotion in the bedroom, Deidre checked to see that the little boys were out of the way of the men who would be working on the house. She walked to the door in time to hear Ned telling Clint and Benjamin, the two youngest Browning boys, that they must keep Jeddy and Danny away from the working men, and the four little boys grinned as they looked at one another, nearly bursting with the excitement of a whole day to play together.

⁂

Edna, Deidre, and Betsy had helped Mandy come out to sit in the rocker in the front room when they were ready to do needlework that morning. Now it was time to finish the lunch preparations, so they helped her back into her bed so she could feed the babies and rest for a while, as she looked quite worn out from all the excitement.

Betsy suggested they carry the table out under the shade of a tree for a picnic lunch instead of staying inside on such a beautiful day. All the women thought it was a delightful idea, so Betsy and her sisters, Ellen (or "Ellie" as the family often called her lovingly) and Esther (or "Essie"), managed to set the table up under a large chestnut tree at the side of the clearing. They spread a tablecloth on top and then dragged the wagon blankets over near the table and spread them under the shade of various trees nearby.

A light wind played with the edge of the tablecloth as Deidre set the first of several pots on the table. She paused briefly to savor the cool kiss of the breeze on her hot cheeks. Lifting her face toward the sky, she let it cool her long, slender neck as well. She listened to the sounds of the men's axes as they chopped out the notches on the logs where they would be fitted together. A solid grunt seemed to accompany almost every chop as muscles first tensed and then relaxed and the ax came down with a firm thud. Those men and teenage boys were working hard for her; her heart swelled with gratitude to them and to God for bringing her to this place. She looked around just in time to see Edna bringing more food for the table. She waited to help her friend, and then the two women walked back to the house arm in arm.

"Sure was a surprise to find two babies this morning." Deidre could hear the smile as Edna spoke. "We're expecting another little one ourselves before long. I'm figuring before the summer's over. Maybe in September. God sure has blessed Ned and me. Who'd have thought we'd be blessed with nine children! But I don't think you can ever have too many."

"Yes, children are certainly a great gift God gives us. Such a trust."

"Oh, you're so right, Deidre. It's easy to think of the fun and excitement of another child, but we must take the responsibility very seriously as we carefully guide and teach our children. They learn to know God through our own example. It almost frightens me when I think of it."

Deidre gave a slight chuckle. "I wouldn't worry too much, Edna. You and Ned have done a wonderful job teachin' your children well. Just repeat what you've done in the past."

"And now we even have help." Edna smiled. "It's fun overhearing the older children teaching the younger ones. Often we hear them repeating what we've said and sounding so mature."

"Yes, I've noticed the same in Jedediah as he plays with helps Daniel. They sure catch on quickly."

As the two women drew near the house, Edna stopped and squeezed Deidre's hand. "I don't want to bring up a subject that is heavy on your heart, but I want you to know that I do pray regularly that God will reunite you with your husband. I know it must be hard for you to see Mandy and me both with our husbands and children, and you don't even know where Jeremiah is and if he's well. But we must believe that it will happen."

Deidre's eyes moistened. "Yes, I do believe with all my heart it'll happen. And usually I can be patient and trust God's timin'. Other times it's easy to be impatient and I want to yell at God. But I do know my husband, and I believe he'll find me and come as soon as he possibly can. I do thank you sincerely for your prayers. Please do continue prayin'."

Deidre looked up in time to see the four small boys sitting on the grass playing a game. Daniel was stretched out beside them, looking very near to being asleep. "I also think if we don't serve this meal soon, we'll have a little boy sleeping with an empty tummy." She grinned and pointed in the direction of the boys.

"My, look how dirty those boys are! Guess we'd better get them in and clean them up." Edna gave Deidre a last squeeze around the waist and took off in the direction of the boys.

The Browning girls met Deidre at the door. "What else, Miss Deidre?"

"You girls go tell the men to come and wash up for lunch. Everythin's ready and waitin'. Please tell them there's soap, water, and towels on the back porch."

Chapter 8

Ned Browning and his three older boys, Thomas, Edward, and Nicholas, returned the following day to help put a roof on the new addition. When they finished, Ethan built a lovely wooden floor and divided the new large room into two rooms. Each of the rooms had a real glass window, just like in the main house.

Deidre helped Ethan mix the daubing for between the logs, and she worked at daubing all the walls as far up as she could reach, with Ethan finishing the upper parts. Ethan always enjoyed building things, and what he loved most was making the beautiful furniture that he often created. He was eager to get the rooms finished so he could make furniture for them.

That summer had a pattern and rhythm different than other summers. While Mandy recuperated from the birthing, she watched after the four children, took care of the lighter housework, and made most of the meals for the family. Ethan took care of the animals and barn chores in the mornings and evenings and worked on his carpentry tasks during the hottest part of the day. Deidre worked in the gardens in the early morning coolness, then would work at preserving the vegetables during the hottest part of the day. In the cool of the evenings she and Mandy would sew on the quilts and curtains for the new rooms.

It was a busy summer, but when September came, Ethan decided he must make a trip to the store. The women had also been making soaps for sale, and he planned to take the soaps and get the supplies they would need for the winter.

"Ethan, please stop in and check on Edna as you pass the Brownings'. Her birthing time should be soon now, I believe, and if there's any way we can help, I'd sure like to know." Mandy smiled contentedly as she looked at her two babies lying cuddled together in the cradle.

"Perhaps I could go stay with her until her time comes?" Deidre spoke the sentence as a question, looking at Mandy. "I know she has the girls to help out, but she might like to have a woman to help with the birthin', and Ned might appreciate it this time also."

⁓

Ethan and Deidre left early the next morning, leaving the four children at the cottage with Mandy. As they neared the Brownings' house, Deidre sensed something was wrong. There was no singing and laughter, no shouts of small children at play, no thud of a hoe as it encountered earth.

Deidre pointed silently, and Ethan's gaze followed her finger. Thomas was walking slowly toward the barn with his head low, his feet nearly dragging. The door to the house stood open, but no one could be seen.

While Ethan tied the horses to the fence post, Deidre ran ahead to the house. She knocked gently on the doorframe while at the same time walking quietly through the opened door. The children were all sitting, heads low, at the table quietly. When Betsy saw Deidre, she ran to her and hugged her fiercely. Tears coursed down the girl's cheeks.

Deidre patted her back and realized the other children were crying, too. "What is it? Where's your momma? Your daddy?"

Between sobs Betsy said, "Momma took sick several days ago. She's very hot and thrashing in her bed and talking nonsense. Oh, Deidre, we don't know what's happening with her. Daddy is with her, but he doesn't know what to do either. Thomas rode into town yesterday to find a doctor, but there isn't one around here now."

"Is there fresh water in the house?" Deidre asked softly while taking her bonnet off and tying on an apron almost in the same motion. She looked at Edward. "You and Nicholas go and bring in some fresh water. I must bathe your mother in cool water, and I'll need lots of it."

The young men seemed to be grateful for something to do. They quickly left while Deidre asked Betsy to put on a pot of coffee.

"I'll go check on your momma, and we'll see what we can do. Please let me know as soon as the cool water is here."

∽∾

Deidre stood in the doorway to the bedroom while her eyes adjusted to the dim light. As she made out the forms, she saw Ned sitting in a chair by the bed with his head in his hands. She couldn't tell if he was praying or sleeping. But the form on the bed was very still.

As she walked closer to the bed, Deidre saw that even though the breathing was shallow, Edna was still breathing. She sighed a prayer of gratitude and laid her hand on Ned's shoulder. When he looked up at her, Deidre knew he had not slept well for some time.

When Ned peered over Deidre's shoulder, she turned to see Ethan enter the room behind her.

"She's resting quiet for now." When Ned spoke, his words were thick with exhaustion and unshed tears.

"Ned, why don't you go get some sleep? I'll care for Edna for a while. If there is any change, I'll call you, but you need to get some rest, or you'll be sick, too," Deidre urged.

She was surprised at his nod.

Ethan immediately took Ned's arm, and the two men passed out of the room.

When Deidre placed her hand on Edna's forehead, she was alarmed at how hot her face was. She lifted Edna's hand. It, too, was burning. Quickly she went to the bedroom door and asked Betsy if there was cool water yet. At the same time she saw Edward entering the back of the house with a bucket brimming with water from the well.

Soon she was bathing Edna's face and body with cold towels. She continued bathing her for several hours, but in spite of the cool water Edna began to sweat. Water poured from her body and soaked into the sheets and blankets.

That afternoon, when Ned awakened, he lifted Edna's weakened body so Deidre could change sheets on the bed and freshen it. When they laid Edna back onto the bed, she sighed first and then started breathing the deep breaths of a restful sleep.

"I think her fever is down now, Deidre. She seems to be sleeping better. Do you think she'll get well?" Hope crept back into Ned's voice as he searched Deidre's face.

"We can't know for sure, but I think the worst is over and that she'll get well now. But that was a very high fever, Ned. I don't know what will happen with the baby." Deidre's voice was quiet as she turned her face away from Edna's hearing. "We must continue to pray for her and for this baby."

Ned looked down at his wife and leaned over to kiss her tenderly on her forehead. "Come back to me soon, Edna. We all need you, but I need you most of all. Get your rest now and then come back to us. Please come back to us soon." He placed another kiss on her forehead before turning toward the door. "I'll go help with the chores now." And he walked resolutely out the door.

⌘

Before long Deidre could smell food cooking. When her stomach made noise, she realized they had all forgotten about lunch completely. All was hushed in the main part of the house, as it was here in the bedroom. Deidre could hear the quiet questions of the younger children and the gentle voices of Betsy and Ellie as they tried to answer.

She had learned from Betsy that her mother had been this way for three days now. At first, Edna had just felt very tired and then was cold in spite of the heat of the early autumn days. Soon she had taken to her bed. Betsy and Ellie had tried to keep the family fed as they waited for their mother to get well.

When Ethan returned from his trip to the store, Deidre sent him on his way home, saying she would remain with the Brownings until the baby came and Edna was well.

At dusk, as Deidre rose to light a lamp, Betsy came in through the partially opened bedroom door. "Go have some soup with the others, Deidre, and I'll stay with Momma. I will call you if there is any change."

"Have you eaten today?" Deidre looked into the pale, young face that was turned up solemnly.

"No, not yet, but I will when you are finished."

"Betsy, you go eat with your family, and then I'll eat when you are finished."

Betsy started to argue, but Deidre turned her toward the door and gave a gentle push. The young girl was too weary of heart to argue.

Through the long night Ned and Deidre took turns sitting by the bed and continuing to bathe Edna's face and arms with cool water, even though she breathed much more evenly now and her face did not feel so hot to the touch.

Early in the morning Ned went to the barn to help with the chores. Deidre's head was drooping once again when she heard a weak groan from the bed. When she placed her hand on Edna's forehead, Edna's eyes opened and focused on Deidre's face.

"Are you awake, Edna? Are you seein' me?" Deidre spoke quietly but excitedly.

"I see you, Deidre. Thank you for coming." Edna's voice was very soft as though she didn't have enough strength to push the words between her lips. Suddenly her face tightened as she groaned once again. "I think the baby is coming." Edna spoke the words very calmly. Slowly her hands moved to cradle her distended stomach. "Will you help me, Deidre?"

She barely got the words out before they were followed with a more solid groan. Deidre began the preparation. It was good to hear Edna's voice, even though it was very weak, but Deidre was concerned at the contractions beginning when Edna was so weak. As she ministered to her friend, Deidre prayed urgently in her heart.

Throughout the long day Edna continued to have pains sporadically, but it was in the wee hours of the morning before the limp and blue little girl entered the world. Deidre worked and worked, but the little one never opened her eyes or took a breath. Finally, when Edna was sleeping and the tiny infant was cleaned up, Deidre went to the doorway and called to Ned softly. He looked up hopefully, but she turned back into the room. He followed her and saw the still form wrapped in a blanket in the cradle. Even though tears were running down his face, he looked at his wife quickly and saw that she still breathed. "Is Edna doing all right?"

"So far. I don't think she even realizes the little girl is not livin'."

Ned swallowed hard. "It's probably best for now." His voice wasn't much more than a whisper as he laid his hand on his wife's arm. Then his knees bent and he knelt beside the bed, groaning. Deidre knew he was praying. Quietly she slipped out of the room.

Standing at the front window, she gazed out into the darkened world. The children were all sleeping, but the sadness she felt permeated the home. She couldn't help but wonder if she could have done something differently or if she had failed Edna in some way. She longed to hold her own son in her arms even though she knew he was being well cared for at the Evanstons'.

Suddenly Deidre felt very alone. "Jeremiah," she whispered, "where are you? Are you strugglin', too? Do you miss me?" She looked up to see an almost full moon and remembered that wherever Jeremiah was in the world, the same moon was shining down on him and the same God was watching over him. Somehow she knew that he longed to be with her also.

As Deidre lay on a blanket to rest until morning, she suddenly realized why she felt so alone. It was not only that she missed someone whom she loved dearly. She thought of how Mandy had felt in her heart that Ethan was alive somewhere when she had been told he was dead, and how complete the two of them were now that they were back together. She thought of how lost Ned seemed as he prayed over Edna and tried to go on about the chores and life in general while she lay very ill in that bed. It was as though part of Ned was sick in that bed.

That's when Deidre understood that the longing in her heart for her husband was more than just loneliness. When a man and a woman were joined as husband and wife, somehow, miraculously, God truly joined them as one person and their hearts became one. She was missing that very important part of herself called a husband. But she was reassured that her heart felt quite certain Jeremiah was still living and well.

Chapter 9

Miss Sue Ellen and Jeremiah sat silently on the wide front veranda. It was a hot, still Sunday afternoon. Miss Sue Ellen's fan moved slowly back and forth as they sat companionably in the silence. She was a patient woman. She had asked, and she knew it was an unusual question and that Jeremiah would answer her if she was patient.

∞

Jeremiah looked out over the property. He could hear Miss Sue Ellen's children playing with the Negro children behind the house. He had personally seen Miss Sue Ellen kiss a small, skinned black knee just the same as she kissed her own children's scrapes and bruises. On this plantation they all were considered part of the family, and it was a joy to hear the laughter and giggles and shouts. He knew Mammy sat under a shade tree and would prevent any spats as she pretended to doze, her fan drooping languidly into her lap.

He heard the drone of a hummingbird as it feasted on the nearby roses climbing profusely to the second story on a trellis at the end of the porch, their fragrance blending with the smell of the warm earth. It was a good life here, and he would be content if only his Deidre and their baby could be here with him. He knew Miss Sue Ellen understood his predicament, and her offer was generous. What choice did he have, really?

Yes, he knew he could leave. He'd earned his freedom now. But would it really be worth it to find Deidre and settle down somewhere, knowing this good family needed his help? He knew that by helping them he was not only helping them live a good life, but more importantly, he was also helping free more slaves every year.

She was only asking for two more years (with good pay) and with a reconsideration at the end of the first year. Suddenly his head turned sharply as he heard a child cry out in pain. Immediately he heard Mammy's reassuring voice as she picked the little one up with a grunt. He could picture it all as he heard her murmuring to the child who had fallen. Jeremiah felt his heart tighten as he longed to have his own child here with him, playing with these happy children. Why did life have to be so filled with trials?

He glanced at Miss Sue Ellen. She was lovely to look at, but knowing that her heart was also lovely made it easy to be unselfish. He knew that she depended on him now that her husband was recuperating and unable to run the plantation. God had indeed answered all their prayers and healed Mr. Wally in many ways, but he still could not walk alone and struggled to form sentences. So Jeremiah had taken over much of the responsibility of running the plantation.

Finally Jeremiah spoke. "Miss Sue Ellen, have you noticed young Alexander? Y'all done a good thing teachin' all these youngsters. It's good for even field hands to know how to read a good book and add and subtract. But take Alexander now. He's learnin' to be a right good leader now, don't ya think?"

"Yes, Jeremiah, he certainly is." She closed her eyes as a smile played across her face. He knew she was pleased with young Alexander. Her fan moved again slowly as she waited for Jeremiah to finish his thought.

"Have you noticed that Alexander is sweet on that young Miss Jasmine?"

Miss Sue Ellen tipped her head in a thoughtful nod.

"Well, I'm thinkin' I could teach Alexander all that Mr. Wally taught me 'bout runnin' this plantation. We could work side by side. In another year or so, if he and Miss Jasmine should jump the broom, I'm thinkin' he'd prob'ly be glad to stay on here as foreman and would do a right smart job runnin' this place until yer own youngsters be old enough. Alexander would be a great assistant for Mr. Wally when he begins to get involved in runnin' the plantation again."

"Jeremiah, that is a splendid idea. Alexander takes instruction well and has certainly shown good leadership with the young ones. But would the older Negroes accept him as their leader? Would any be offended to be led by one so young?"

Jeremiah rubbed his hands through his hair to hide his smile. Many would be surprised to find a lady like this who cared how her Negroes felt about the leadership.

"Miss Sue Ellen, all the Negroes know that if they don't like what's goin' on here, they are free to leave. I don't think any of them would argue. We're all thankful to you for treatin' us with respect. 'Sides, if there's a problem, we'll know of it soon enough and can handle it 'fore it becomes a bigger problem."

There was silence for several minutes except for the gentle *whoosh, whoosh* of her fan as it slapped back and forth slowly in front of her face. "Yes, yes, I guess you're right. We won't know if we don't try. I'll keep Alexander after classes tomorrow and ask him how he feels about this plan. If you'll come to the house again tomorrow evening, I'll let you know what he says. Will that be all right with you?"

"Yes, that'll be fine."

They sat still for a while enjoying the peaceful afternoon breeze. They could hear some distant voices from the Negro Quarters. At this plantation it was not called a slave camp because they were not considered slaves. Jeremiah thought about the little "town" in which all the Negroes lived here at Rose Hill Plantation. There were neat little whitewashed cottages in straight rows on either side of pebbled paths. Each person who worked here was given a wage, which made it possible for them to keep their homes up the way they each preferred. Each home was supplied with some furniture and dishes and was quite comfortable and nicely kept. Everyone was encouraged to learn to read and cipher. Jeremiah prayed with all his heart that, as the Traehdnik children grew up and inherited the plantation, the traditions of the past two generations would be continued.

Yes, Jeremiah knew he must stay on for a while. He would have to trust God to watch after his family while he was gone. And somehow, in his heart, he felt that if he could talk with Deidre, she would tell him the same thing. They would be patient. Yes, they would wait.

Chapter 10

Delaney sat by the open window enjoying the slight breeze that moved the summer curtains lazily now and again. The fragrance of the climbing roses on the trellis below the window was heady and sweet. The sound of bees hovering over the red velvety flowers blended with the laughter and voices of children playing somewhere in the large yard under the watchful care of Mammy.

Delaney sighed. Life was good here at Rose Hill Plantation, and she was thankful. Where else were the slaves not only taught to read but welcomed into the library? She caressed the leather cover of the volume in her hands. Oh, how she loved this place! How she adored these people!

She glanced over at the big draped bed. Mr. Wally was sound asleep. Ever since his illness began, they had not left him unattended. She had known he would be sleeping and had volunteered to sit with him while Miss Sue Ellen enjoyed some fresh air. What she hadn't known was that Miss Sue Ellen would bring Jeremiah onto the veranda beneath the window to talk to him about managing the plantation.

Delaney knew that Jeremiah longed to be with his wife. She had heard that he and his wife had a child that Jeremiah had never even seen. He was such a good man. He had become the backbone of the plantation in the past four years, and she knew that the Traehdniks would sorely miss him if he ever left. Her heart ached for them all. She didn't want Rose Hill to lose the leadership of Jeremiah, yet she wanted him to be able to be with his wife and child. Delaney knew God could work it all out, so she resolved to pray about it all.

Mr. Wally snored softly, and then his breathing returned to the deep breaths of one who sleeps peacefully. Delaney watched him for several minutes before she opened the book she held in her hands. Caressing the pages gently, she once again thanked God that she could read and enjoy good literature.

That was another good thing about this plantation. All of the Negroes were encouraged to learn, and education was made available to them if they would work at it. Delaney had studied and worked very hard to fine-tune her speech and to learn all that Miss Sue Ellen could teach her; she hoped that someday she herself could be the teacher for the Negroes on the plantation. Miss Sue Ellen encouraged her to be a teacher and already had her overseeing some of the younger children. But Delaney longed to get more education and someday return to the plantation to teach the other Negroes who wanted to learn. She had already been saving her earnings, but so far had not had the courage to mention her idea to Miss Sue Ellen. Perhaps if she mentioned her dream to Jeremiah. . .

Delaney was still thinking about teaching when she heard a step in the hallway just before the door opened quietly. She looked up to see Miss Sue Ellen smiling at her husband as he rested on the bed. His eyes were open, and Delaney wondered how long he had been awake.

"It's beautiful outside today. Would you like Delaney and me to help you out to the veranda?"

"Yes, yes." Mr. Wally smiled his lopsided smile at his wife and tried to rise. The two women assisted him immediately, and the trio made their way out of the room.

When they had settled Mr. Wally in the shade of the porch where a breeze would keep him comfortable, Miss Sue Ellen sat in the swing that was not too far from where he sat. She patted the seat beside her. "What are you reading, Delaney?"

"Actually, I haven't even started the book." Delaney smiled as she sat beside the lady of the plantation. "I meant to read while I sat with Mr. Wally, but I guess my mind was wandering instead."

"What's on your mind? Anything in particular you've been thinking about?"

Was this her opportunity? Delaney dropped her gaze to the book, then glanced at Miss Sue Ellen's face and then out across the land in front of the plantation house. In her heart was a prayer as she answered, "Been dreaming, that's all. Been dreaming."

The ropes on the side of the swing made a tight, rhythmic rubbing as they moved the swing with their feet. Mr. Wally had turned his head to study Delaney also. They waited a couple of minutes before Miss Sue Ellen asked quietly, "What are you dreaming of, Delaney? Or should I ask who?"

Miss Sue Ellen was so gentle and kind that no one ever thought of her questions as prying. The slaves knew she was genuinely interested in them and that her motives in asking were of the purest kind.

"No, not who." She answered from her heart. "I was thinking how much I love teaching the children and how good you are to allow us all to learn and be taught."

There was another brief silence, then Miss Sue Ellen said thoughtfully, "You are really good with the children, and you have some great ideas to keep their interest. I'm afraid I am depending on you more and more to teach them, now that I am not having as much free time as I once had."

Again they pushed the swing lazily while they enjoyed their individual thoughts. Then Mr. Wally said, "Sue-awn, Miz Noe-man."

They didn't understand what he was trying to say. "What?" Miss Sue Ellen looked at him questioningly. "Who?"

He tried again. "Miz Noe-man. Ball-mo."

"Ball-mo?"

"Ball-tt-mo-rrr." He was trying very hard to say the word clearly.

"Baltimore?" Miss Sue Ellen said.

Mr. Wally smiled and dipped his head in a nodding motion.

"Mrs. Norman? Our friend in Baltimore?"

He nodded more enthusiastically.

"What about her, Wally?"

"T-T-cheech-ah." He worked very hard to make his tongue obey his bidding. He looked at them expectantly.

"Teacher. Yes, she was a good teacher." Miss Sue Ellen turned her head to Delaney and explained. "She was a friend of our family when I was growing up. She was a teacher in a girl's college and helped many young women become teachers. She and her husband had only one daughter, and after the daughter moved West with her husband, Mrs. Norman went back to teaching at the college. I wonder if she is still living. My, she must be nearly sixty years old by now. I wish you could have known her, Delaney. With your heart to teach you would have enjoyed her immensely."

"That would have been wonderful, Miss Sue Ellen. But you're a right good teacher yourself."

As Delaney walked back to her home in the Quarters that evening she smiled to herself as she thought of the conversation. It seemed like Mr. Wally was trying to say something, but neither she nor Miss Sue Ellen could quite grasp what he meant. At any rate, it was nice that she had made him think of their friend who was a real teacher. Was he saying he thought she could be a teacher also? Well, she'd think on it some more and pray.

Chapter 11

The cotton had all been harvested for the final time, and the Negro children were now expected to be in attendance in the brick school in the Quarters. It was a cheery place, and Miss Sue Ellen checked their lessons herself, with the help of Delaney. Delaney was spending more and more time instructing the children with the assistance of a couple of the other young women and one of the young men named Jacob. Jacob loved to learn, and Delaney knew he could be a great teacher himself if the cotton fields didn't demand all his time.

It was a rainy November morning when Miss Sue Ellen sent a note to Delaney to come to the manor when she finished teaching for the day. All day long Delaney wondered what it was about. The rain had stopped by afternoon, and the dry soil looked as though there hadn't been rain for months. But the dust had settled somewhat and the evening was a little cooler as she walked across the fields, taking a shortcut to the big house.

As she entered through the back door, Mariah bustled into the hallway to tell her that Miss Sue Ellen was watching for her. "Go to the library. She's waitin' for you in there."

"Do you know why she sent for me?" Delaney asked nervously.

"Don' know. But Miss Sue Ellen got a letter delivered today, an' as soon as she read it, she been smilin' an' askin' fer you. Hurry up, girl. You don' want t' keep that good woman waitin' now, do ya?"

Miss Sue Ellen and Mr. Wally were both sitting in the library having tea when Delaney stood at the doorway and knocked gently on the doorframe. Miss Sue Ellen jumped to her feet and hurried over to bring Delaney into the room personally.

"Sit down, Delaney. Would you like some tea?"

Delaney knew the offer was sincere, so she said, "Thank you. That would taste very good."

While Miss Sue Ellen poured the tea herself, she smiled. She handed Delaney the cup of tea along with a sweet biscuit on a small plate. Then she sat down and looked at her husband, who glowed with pride.

"How did the schoolwork go today? Are the children working hard at learning still?"

"Yes, Miss Sue Ellen. We all want them to appreciate what a privilege it is for them to live here and have the opportunity to learn. Sometimes I think they should spend a week on another plantation so they can appreciate how good we have it here."

"Well, I pray they never have to know how cruel the world can be. If they can spend all their days sheltered from the evil in this world, that's all the better."

They sipped tea for a minute until Miss Sue Ellen continued. "Delaney, do you remember last summer when Mr. Wally reminded me of our friend in Baltimore named Mrs. Norman?"

"The lady who taught at a teachers' college?"

"Yes, that's the one. Well, he continued to press me until I understood that Wally wanted me to ask her to teach you." Mr. Wally grinned and kept bobbing his head. "I wrote to her soon after and have received a letter this very day in return. She no longer teaches at the college, but she has volunteered to teach you if we can take you to Baltimore to stay with her for a while. She has invited you to come live with her and her husband for a year or so, and she will teach you. Are you interested in doing that?"

Delaney sat very still. She looked first at Miss Sue Ellen and then at Mr. Wally. So many questions flew through her head that she didn't know quite what to say. Finally she said soberly, "Oh, I would love to have that opportunity, but I don't think I've been able to save enough to pay for an education yet."

"No, no, she has invited you to be her guest. She will teach you because she loves to teach and because I told her your heart's desire is to teach the Negroes here. Her husband is a minister, and they both have giving hearts that would look at this as an opportunity to help us out. I told her how quickly you learn and how smart you are. She was excited to have the chance to help you.

"Perhaps if it would help you to feel better about it, you could offer to help her with some housework in exchange for your lessons and room and board. She's getting on in years now. Their daughter and her husband moved out West a number of years ago, so she might welcome some help. What do you think?"

Delaney couldn't stop her slowly spreading smile. "I have so many questions, but I am excited about it. How would I get there? Who would teach the children here? Do I need to buy my freedom first?"

Miss Sue Ellen got up and paced back and forth across the room before looking briefly at her husband. She walked a few more steps, then stopped to look at Delaney. "We can give you your papers—" Mr. Wally nodded happily—"but the way the world is right now, if you truly plan to return, it might be safer for you if you tell folks that you belong to us in case you would be questioned along the way. I believe you will be plenty safe at the Normans' home, but traveling might go easier if you belong to us. If you should decide not to return to us, we can get your papers of freedom to you when you let us know." She turned to her husband. "Don't you think so, Wally?"

He thought soberly for a short time and then nodded. He looked at Delaney. "What you think, D'aney?"

"I don't know what to say. I thank you from the bottom of my heart for your willingness to free me, but I honestly believe God wants me to spend my life teaching here at Rose Hill. That's all I ask—that I can teach the children here at this plantation if you will let me return and live here."

"Delaney, you are as much a part of our family as our own children. We would love to have you spend your days here with us all. You have already given us a great gift, and we are glad this will help you in your endeavor. Now, while you're gone, Jacob and I will do our best to keep the children learning, and then you can take over the school when you return."

⌇⌇

Miss Sue Ellen's brother, Bartholomew Kendall, had business in Baltimore at the beginning of the year, so it was decided that he would personally escort Delaney to the Norman home. Miss Sue Ellen fussed as though she were sending one of her own children away. And everyone at the plantation, both in the house or in the Quarters, helped in every way they could. Delaney promised to send regular letters to be read aloud in the school. Many of the children made little gifts to be tucked into Delaney's carpetbag and trunk.

Delaney was anxious and had to admit that she spent many a night praying for safe travels. She wished they could travel by buggy instead of that loud, fast train, but she knew God could protect them and tried not to worry.

Mr. Kendall was as kind as his sister. He was older and of a larger build, but he possessed the same reddish hair and sky blue eyes, and their smiles were quite similar. He visited the plantation from time to time, and all the Negroes called him "Mr. Bart" with fondness.

Delaney didn't mind making the long trip knowing she was in the care of Mr. Bart. However, she was terrified when she was told upon boarding the train that she could not ride in the same car with Mr. Bart. He insisted they needed to stay together, but the conductor would not hear of it. Since the Negroes could ride only in the last car, Mr. Bart asked if he could ride there with her. It was not to be allowed, but finally he was given permission to ride in the car that was second from the end.

When they finally arrived in Baltimore, Mr. Bart was waiting for her right outside the door of her car when she left the train. Delaney was thankful she had not encountered any problems.

They rode in a carriage to the Norman home. Mr. Bart and Delaney had a jolly time together as they chatted about the plantations they had left behind.

"Your sister and her husband are some of the kindest people I have ever known. All of us enjoy working for them and will probably spend all our days with them. Oh, except Jeremiah, of course."

"And why not Jeremiah?" Mr. Bart asked curiously. "Does he not enjoy working at Rose Hill?"

"Oh, I think he enjoys it plenty. But he has a wife and child at a place called Devil's Bend, and it grieves him terribly that they cannot be together. He has never even seen his child. He was taken away and sold before the child was born."

"Does my sister know this? Does Wally know that Jeremiah's wife and son are in someone else's possession?"

"I don't rightly know. I assume Jeremiah has mentioned it to Mr. Wally, but I don't know that for sure."

Mr. Bart seemed to be in deep thought after that, and the conversation waned until they approached their destination.

Chapter 12

The Norman house was a lovely home that sat within shouting distance of the houses on either side. Across the cobblestone street were more houses arranged in a tidy row just like on this side. The homes were large, and all of them had a small front yard with large trees that reached out to shade much of the street. The Normans had a white picket fence around their property with an arch filled with a rose vine. Delaney could imagine how beautiful it would be draped with summer roses.

Dirty snow lined the sides of the streets. The Normans' yard had patches of snow that were still quite white. Bushes and plants were bent from the weight of the snow. The sky seemed as white as the snow and felt cold and unwelcoming.

The carriage carrying Delancy and Mr. Bart drove into a driveway at the side of the manse. Delaney could see the stables at a distance behind the house as well as some other outbuildings and a fenced-in garden. Everything looked gray and cold, and she could see her breath in front of her face. In spite of the warm blanket tucked over her lap, she shivered.

But when they entered the home, Delaney soon knew the welcome was sincere and much warmer than the weather. The Normans themselves greeted Delaney and Mr. Bart at the front door. Hot tea and little cookies awaited them as they got acquainted in the spacious library. Delaney enjoyed the reminiscing between the Normans and Mr. Bart and far too soon he had to leave. Delaney felt a sudden wave of homesickness as the door closed behind him, leaving her in the strange city all alone with these strangers.

However, the Normans were a jolly couple, and Delaney soon felt very comfortable with them. In spite of city life being completely different from anything Delaney had ever dreamed in her life, she knew she would enjoy her time here.

Mrs. Norman was a very disciplined lady. Delaney assumed it was probably from her years as a teacher in the college for women. But she had a robust sense of humor, and she made life enjoyable in spite of the long days of hard work. Mrs. Norman had smiled at Delaney's offer of help. "There won't be time, child. You are here to study, and we must see that you learn all I can teach you while you are here."

Their days settled into a comfortable, if grueling, routine. Each morning Reverend Norman read to them from the Bible for an hour following breakfast. Then

Mrs. Norman and Delaney would go to the room on the second floor that she had arranged as their schoolroom and they would study hard for two hours until noon.

After lunch they rested briefly and then went back to the schoolroom for three more hours of study. The evenings were free for Delaney to continue her studies and prepare for the following day's lessons.

The Normans' hired help cared for Delaney the same as they did for the Normans, seeing that her room was cleaned, her clothes fresh, and that she had plenty of good food to nourish her mind and body.

Only on Sunday did they vary their routine. Delaney enjoyed the messages that Reverend Norman shared with the worshippers in their church. The songs were lovely, too, but they were not like the songs to which she was accustomed in their church in the Quarters. No one here shouted out their praises or clapped their hands. She knew the worship was in their good hearts, but she longed for the services to which she was accustomed.

On Sunday afternoons Delaney always wrote letters. She wrote to the Traehdniks and to many of the Negroes at Rose Hill, since most of them could read. Many wrote back to her, and she read and reread the letters many times. She came to love the Normans and they were good and kind to her, but the work was hard and in time she missed her home at Rose Hill tremendously.

Chapter 13

"Welcome, home, Brother!" Sue Ellen welcomed her brother with a hug and tender kiss on the cheek he tilted in her direction. "Now, tell me about your trip. Do you think Delaney will enjoy her time in Baltimore? How did you find the Normans? Are they well?"

"Hey, little sister. Slow down. Can't a man sit and wet his dry throat before being bombarded with questions?" He tucked her under his arm and walked onto the wide veranda of the Traehdnik home. "Let me have a look at that husband of yours, and then I'll tell you everything."

As they entered the library, Sue Ellen caught Mariah's eye. "Mariah, will you please ask Eliza to bring us tea in the library as soon as possible?"

"Ah'll he'p her myself." Mariah showed her wide white teeth when she smiled. "Y'all sit yo'self on down an' visit. We'll be in d'rectly." And she bustled off to the back of the house.

Sue Ellen smiled as she listened to the laughter and talk in the room. Her brother knelt on one knee before her husband, whom he loved like a brother. Wally was conversing a bit easier now and was much easier to understand. When there was a pause, Sue Ellen said, "Please tell us everything, Bartholomew. Don't leave out any details."

And so they spent a lovely evening remembering their friends, the Normans, and talking of the wonderful opportunity that was afforded Delaney.

After dinner, as they sipped coffee in the library once more, Bartholomew ventured the question that was on his heart. "Your foreman, Jeremiah. Does he have a wife?"

Both Wally and Sue Ellen looked at him in surprise. Sue Ellen said, "He does have a wife and a child, too, I believe. However, they are at another plantation. Jeremiah plans to try to purchase them when he can."

"Sister, why don't you purchase them and move them here with him? Has he been able to see them since he has been here?"

"Goodness. Not that I know about. We really should ask him where they are, but I wouldn't know how to purchase them with Wally like he is."

"You go fo' me?" Wally's speech was slow but deliberate. But he animatedly poked his finger at his brother-in-law.

"Yes, I would go for you. Do you have funds to purchase another slave?"

Wally's head dropped and lifted in an exaggerated nod. "Haven't been a'le to go auction to buy anyone for long time. Got money, though. You go plantation to ask?"

"I'll talk to Jeremiah, get the information, and see what I can do."

Devil's Bend was a good distance from Rose Hill. Bartholomew Kendall had spent several weeks at his own plantation before leaving for Devil's Bend. As he rode, he thought of his conversation with Jeremiah. In spite of the possibility of having his wife and child with him, Jeremiah had not been overly joyful about his going to Devil's Bend.

"He's a mean man, Mr. Bart, a mean man. And his wife is selfish and unkind. I don't think they'd let her go 'cause Missus Wickner wants only Deidre in the kitchen. If y'all could buy her and our child, they'd prob'ly charge far more than they should. I can't think it will work, but I sho' do 'preciate yer efforts, Mr. Bart. I sho' do 'preciate it!"

Bart had allowed Jeremiah to believe he had been convinced it was hopeless. But in reality that was far from the truth. Bart had decided that if the Wickners were as unkind as it sounded like they were, he would do whatever was necessary to get Deidre and her child away from them.

He looked out across the barren fields and knew that money might be tight for the Wickners as it was for many plantation owners. The sale of last year's cotton was past, and the new crop was just being planted with many weeks before there would be income from it again. It could be that the time was right to make an offer on a slave.

As the carriage passed by some fields, Bart thought it was easy to tell what kind of slave owner owned the various sections of land because of the way the slaves left the land. The land that still had broken-down plants and missed cotton bolls were obviously fields that belonged to a slave owner who was not loved by his slaves. Those slaves didn't really care whether they gathered as much as possible in for the owner or not.

Now and again he passed land that was cleaned and tidily prepared for the next planting. He knew the Negroes who worked there were treated with respect and enjoyed dignity and pride in their work. The more he thought on it, he suspected he knew what kind of fields he would pass when he got to Devil's Bend.

As Bart approached the plantation house called Devil's Bend, he assessed the type of people who worked here. He was convinced it was not a group of colored people that took pride in their work. The Negroes he saw wore worn-out clothes and appeared half starved. If the owner was struggling to keep this place together, he might be willing to sell even a favorite slave. Bart offered a prayer to that effect as he stepped out of his carriage.

The Negro woman who answered his knock looked half scared of him. Bart smiled gently when he inquired after Mr. Wickner.

"Massah Wicknah out t' the stables, sah. Yo wants us t' go get 'im? Or yo wants t' go t' the stables yo'self?"

"Is Mrs. Wickner nearby?"

"Miz Wicknah indisposed today an' she don' talk no bus'niss. Yo wants Massah Wicknah. Yo wants we go call 'im fer ya?"

"No, no. I'll go down to the stables myself. Thanks for your help." Bart tipped his hat at the black lady who stared at him with surprise. Obviously she was not used to being treated with respect. Anger rose slowly from the pit of his stomach, cementing his determination to get Jeremiah's wife and child away from this sorry place.

Not far from the stables Bart saw a man dressed as a gentleman sitting on a horse and surveying the fields.

"Good morning, sir." Bart did his best to sound friendly, in spite of the sour taste in his mouth.

The man continued to stare out across the barren land for a couple of more minutes before turning in his seat to observe the stranger. He scowled. "Do I know you?"

"I don't believe we've had opportunity to meet." Bart looked up at the man still sitting on his horse and shaded his eyes with his hand. "My name's Bartholomew Kendall, and I came to inquire after a slave."

"Ain't seen no runaways out this way. Where you from?"

"No, I'm not looking for a runaway. I'm looking to purchase a slave from you if you're willing."

Greed lit the man's eyes immediately. He swung his leg over the horse's back and dropped to the ground beside Bart. Wiping his hand on his pants, he offered his hand as he said, "Haaman Wickner at your service. Which one of my slaves did you have in mind to purchase? Perhaps we can talk."

"I'm looking for a cook named Deidre, and I believe she has a child also. I'd like to purchase them both if you'd consider such."

Mr. Wickner looked at him long and hard, then scowled and rubbed his hands over his face and into his hair. Slowly he started back toward the house, holding the horse's bridle as he moved. Turning his head toward Bart, he growled, "Don't have such a nigger. She done took the brat and ran away probably two years ago.

We've searched high and low and found nary a trace."

"Hmmm. . .now that is a problem." They walked in silence for a spell. "You still have her papers?"

"Sure, I still got 'em. If she's ever found, I got proof that I've got the right to whup the tar outta her hide. She near broke my wife's heart when she left. I'll whup her good if I ever lay eyes on her again."

Again they walked in silence before Bart finally asked, "Any chance you'd sell the girl's papers to me?"

"What you want her papers for? She's long gone. What good are her papers to you?" He stopped in his tracks and stared at Bartholomew. "You got her? You know where she's at?"

"No, sir, I don't know where she is. But if I had her papers, I could legally look for her, and my sister would like to have her. Would you sell her papers?"

Haaman Wickner appeared to think long and hard. Then greed glinted in his eyes again. "Okay, I'll sell her papers for $1200 cash."

They walked in silence for a little while again. Finally Bart said soberly, "I might pay that much if I were purchasing the girl herself, but I am only buying papers. I will give you $600 cash for her papers and those of her child together."

Mr. Wickner grunted. "No. I have a feeling you know where she's hiding. I say $1200 will buy her and the brat. . .$1200 or no deal."

They were approaching the front of the house now, where Bart's carriage awaited. He headed toward the carriage and called over his shoulder, "Well, I'm sorry then. It was just an idea, but maybe it's best this way. Good day."

Bart stepped into the carriage. As he picked up the reins, he heard Mr. Wickner clear his throat. "If you want to step inside for a drink, we can discuss this further."

"No, thanks just the same, but I'd best be getting on my way." He tipped his hat in Mr. Wickner's general direction.

Quickly the plantation owner stepped up beside Bart's horse. "Look, Mr. Kendall, I could probably sell you the papers for the two of them for maybe $800."

"Done!" Bart pulled gently on the reins and stepped from the carriage. "I might have that drink of tea after all, while you gather the papers."

Chapter 14

Slowly Edna Browning regained her strength and health. By December she was caring for her family once again, but a sadness permeated her spirit and carried to the whole family. She didn't have the same energy with which she had faced her life before.

The Evanstons invited the Brownings to have Christmas at their house this year, and Ned and Edna gladly accepted. Edna didn't know how she would make it through Christmas without spoiling it for everyone, and she was thankful she could be a guest instead of a hostess this year.

Edna realized that the loss of her baby was affecting the whole family one day when she asked Ned why he didn't sing in the barn anymore. "I do sing, Edna. But the songs have changed. I think we buried a wee part of me when we buried that young-un. Something quieted in my spirit somehow."

"Yes, I know what you mean. Everything seems to be much more effort now. I don't know why all of life seems to have changed so. I am praying God will heal us from this great loss."

Ned was thoughtful for several minutes before saying, "It seems I look at each of our eight children with a new love now, Edna. I have always been thankful for each one, but now the thankfulness has grown. I have told myself I must look at all the blessings God has given us instead of feeling the great loss of the child He didn't choose to let us keep."

"Yes, you're right. I try to tell myself the same, but my arms feel so very empty. I guess they were more ready than I knew for the new baby." When tears ran down Edna's face unheeded, Ned took her into his arms. Dropping his face into her neck, he said softly, "I'm so thankful God didn't take you too, Edna. I don't know how I could have gone on without you. I'm so thankful."

⁂

With much help from Betsy, Ellie, and Essie, the Brownings were ready for Christmas Day with their friends. The three daughters seemed to have matured overnight. Edna told them many times she didn't know how she'd make it without them. Together they made gifts for each child in the family. As they knitted the little caps for Ethan and Mandy's twin girls, Edna felt herself grow eager to see the babies again and hold and cuddle them.

Christmas day dawned dark and still. The older boys helped Ned finish the barn chores very early so the family could enjoy Christmas breakfast together. As they packed their food into boxes and loaded them and the gifts into the two sleighs, Edna caught a bit of the spirit herself and sent a prayer of thanks to heaven from her heart.

At first, everyone was quiet as the sleighs started the drive through the snowy forest. But in a short time Thomas started singing softly. Soon the others were humming and singing along. Edna noticed that the singing had changed from previous years. Even the children seemed quieted by the family's loss, and it saddened her and created a new determination to seek God's healing touch.

Christmas was a joyous affair as the families continued their tradition of enjoying the holiday together. This year Callie and Christy were the center of attention. Mandy was concerned that it would act as salt in the wound for Edna to be around her healthy little girls. Instead, Edna enjoyed them thoroughly, confirming Mandy's opinion that there was not one streak of selfishness in that dear woman.

∽∾

With the snow gone now and the ground thawing and muddy, Mandy and Deidre started dreaming of the gardens they would plant. The days were growing longer, and the sun warming the earth sent the longing to get into the garden deep into their hearts. Ethan had built wooden boxes by the windows, which the women filled with earth and planted with tomato and pepper and other seeds. They still remembered with laughter their experiences of trying to plow the earth by themselves the spring that Ethan was gone.

"I'm still thankful every year that Ned came at the right time that year," Mandy said.

Deidre laughed. "Yes, and do you recall the hailstorm we had that night?" They both smiled and nodded as they remembered those hard times that had cemented their friendship.

They were scrubbing the laundry on the washboards when Deidre straightened. "You know, it's so nice today, why don't we hang these clothes outside instead of in here? They would smell so fresh, and we wouldn't have to walk around them in here all afternoon."

Mandy rubbed her back. "Do you think it's warm enough for them to dry?"

"If they don't dry completely, they'll be easier to iron anyway."

"Great idea. Let's do it. Do you think we can get them hung up without being in mud up to our ankles?"

"If it's that muddy, I'll go barefoot and wash my feet after."

"What fun! Barefoot in April. It makes me feel like a child just thinking about it."

Suddenly the women heard baby jabbering from the direction of Mandy's bedroom. "Guess it's time for you to take a break and feed the babies. I might get to hang these out myself." Deidre grinned at her friend. "If you want to feed one of them while I finish here, I'll take her out on my back while you feed the other." Now that the babies were starting to crawl, it was all they could do to keep track of them both.

"Sounds like a good plan." Mandy dried her hands as she walked toward the bedroom. "What would I do without you?" She grinned over her shoulder. "How do mothers of twins ever do it alone?"

By the time Mandy reached her bedroom, both girls were howling shamelessly. She talked softly to them as she changed their diapers, but both continued to cry. Finally she lifted them both and carried them to the main room of the house.

"Deidre, would you mind drying your hands and holding Callie while I feed Christy first? I should have watched the time closer and awakened Christy before they both became so hungry."

As the women rocked the little girls, there was silence for a short time before Deidre said, "You know, every time I look at our precious little girls, my heart feels heavy for Edna. I can't imagine how it must feel to lose a child, but I know her heart has been very sad. It seems to have changed her whole personality."

"Yes, and I wonder sometimes if she has heard from her parents. She dreaded so much the chore of telling them of the loss. Being an only child herself, I know her parents cherish each one of their grandchildren, even though they live so far and can't see them. The last time Ethan saw Ned, they still had not heard from her parents. I hope they have by this time."

"It must be difficult to be a mother and grandmother from such a distance. It would be wonderful if her parents could move closer to Ned and Edna." Deidre tried to keep Callie's attention, but each time Mandy spoke, Callie tried to see her. At last Mandy finished nursing Christy and handed her to Deidre as she took Callie for her turn.

Deidre placed Christy into the carrier the women had fashioned for her back and then went back to finish the laundry. As she headed out the back door, she added one last comment to the conversation. "I know it is difficult to live so far away from those you love. I pray Edna will get to visit her parents before too much longer."

~∞~

The women sat under the shade of the large oak tree. It was late May, and they had just finished planting the last rows in the rich brown earth. The twins were still napping on a blanket beside them as they rested their weary backs for a time before going to the house to start their supper.

Noisy silence surrounded them. Birds busily built their nests and called loudly to one another in the branches above them. Bees hummed frantically as they darted in and out of the daffodils and columbine that grew wild along the path.

Deidre lay back on the grass and stared up at a small patch of blue sky showing between the branches overhead.

Mandy pulled a blade of sweet grass and chewed thoughtfully on the end. "Thinking about Jeremiah?" Her sad tone spoke volumes. She ached for her friend to be reunited with her husband. How hard it must be to never know where he was and if she'd ever see him again. Mandy truly did know what it was like, but she and Ethan had been separated only a little more than a year. Deidre had been without her husband for more than six years now. How very hard it must be.

Deidre was quiet for some time before she turned toward Mandy. "Sometimes I wonder if I should go searchin' for him. I know it would be terribly risky and probably not wise, but how will he ever know where to start lookin' for us? How will he ever find us?"

Mandy regarded her friend with alarm. "You can't mean that, Deidre! The risk would be terrible. Think what could happen to Jeddy. Think what could happen to you. Deidre, tell me you are not really serious about this." She watched her friend's face as she pummeled her with the questions. She knew Deidre really did understand the danger. So why would she say such a thing? Why would she even think it?

Deidre watched Callie as she began to awaken from her nap. Before the baby could wake her sister, Deidre picked her up and held her close, laying her head on the baby's small shoulder.

"I realize it would be too risky to take Jeddy into the South again, and I certainly do not want to find myself separated from him, so at this point I believe my hands are tied. I continue to pray for Jeremiah, but it gets more and more difficult to be patient. I wish there was a way for God to let me know He's workin' on this. I think then it would be easier to be patient. But for now, I will keep prayin' and trustin', even though it becomes easier and easier to doubt."

Suddenly Christy realized her sister was no longer lying beside her; her head popped up and bobbed around, looking at the women. The laughter from the women was spontaneous as Mandy reached for her lonely daughter. Kissing her face and neck, Mandy said quietly, "I'm afraid I'd feel just like Christy if you ever leave here. It probably wouldn't take long at all before I'd come looking for you. But I love you so much that I would certainly never wish to keep the two of you apart. I just don't want you to take any unnecessary risks."

"I know, Mandy. And I do understand. Don't worry. For now I'm not goin' any-where. I believe we will both know in our hearts when the time is right for me to find my Jeremiah. And then God will help us both."

Chapter 15

The snows were muddy, and the days were getting longer. As Delaney stood at the window in her lovely room at the Normans', she finally allowed the tears to fall. The gray, heavy skies matched her lonesome mood. She knew in her heart that she was wrong to cry, because she did love the Normans and was grateful for the opportunity to learn what had been extended to her, but she longed for the companionship of the families at Rose Hill Plantation. She had been in Boston for a little more than a year and was feeling quite homesick.

She scolded herself for the tears. "Delaney, how many Negro girls have the opportunities that have been given to you? You will go home in time, and then you will remember all this and regret that you spent time shedding tears of longing for home. Even though it seems unlikely, this new turn of events may be God's special leading in your life, so look for the good in it and stop moaning over your poor lonesome heart!" Even though she kept her voice low, she spoke aloud and the scolding served to help her put her life back into perspective once more.

"And the good part is that you now get to travel and see sights that very few colored people have ever dreamed of seeing. You'll go home soon enough. You must stop worrying about being lonely and start thanking God for the opportunities He has given you."

A few weeks ago the Normans had received another letter from their daughter who lived in Indiana. She had been expecting their ninth child, when she had suddenly taken quite ill and the little girl had been stillborn. This had happened in the autumn, but their daughter's letters continued to be filled with a sadness that the Normans had never heard from her before. Finally, after this most recent letter, Reverend Norman decided that his wife must go to Indiana to visit their daughter and her family. They had written to the Traehdniks and received permission for Delaney to travel with Mrs. Norman for companionship, since Reverend Norman could not take a leave of absence from their church.

Of course the Traehdniks had responded affirmatively. They reaffirmed that Delaney was a free woman in reality, and that they only kept papers on her to prevent someone from taking and reselling her. They encouraged her to enjoy this experience and thanked the Normans for the opportunity for Delaney. They even enclosed money to help cover her expenses and for Delaney to use as she needed.

As she talked out loud to herself, Delaney realized that she truly was very blessed to have had all the opportunities and experiences that had been hers this past year. And so she decided that she would expect, and be watching for, something very special to happen as a result of this trip that delayed her return to her home.

As she stood at the window this Sunday afternoon, she watched the snow dripping in a steady pattern as it melted from the branches of the large tree outside her window. The black branches looked almost ghostly against the gray skies. Delaney shivered from the dampness.

Suddenly she surprised herself with a thought. *Perhaps it's not as nasty out as it looks. After all, the snows are melting, so there must be some warmth out there in spite of the gray skies.* Grabbing her wrap, she descended the front stairs. She would walk around the neighborhood. Perhaps the fresh air would dispel any lingering homesickness and invigorate her spirit.

Wondering if she should tell someone before leaving the house, she looked back into the darkened home. Both of the Normans enjoyed napping on Sunday afternoons, and the servants usually were not present on Sundays. Seeing no one, Delaney shrugged and slipped quietly onto the front porch, closing the door firmly behind her.

Once outside, she found the air was much warmer than it appeared from inside the house. Standing on the porch, Delaney breathed deeply. She had never smelled anything quite like this in the South, because the ground never froze or thawed. The aroma of the wet earth was laden with another fragrance as well, but Delaney couldn't tell what it was.

She walked down the wide front steps and, looking both ways, decided at the last moment to walk toward the town instead of around the neighborhood. There were brick walkways along the sides of the streets, making walking much more pleasant than having to walk in the streets dodging horse dung all the while.

Again she inhaled the scents around her. The earth was awakening and, as she turned the corner, she saw the origins of the lovely fragrance wafting on the air. Hyacinths. There, before her, was a garden laden with blooming daffodils, tulips, and spears of colorful hyacinths, giving off the heady sweetness she had noticed from half a block away. Wasn't it like God to create such beauty at a time when the earth looked as though it would literally rot in the melting of winter? And wasn't it like God to steer her in this direction on a day she needed the cheering so desperately?

Suddenly Delaney felt like laughing out loud. Seeing that blooming garden reminded her of how near God was and that He did care that her heart was lonely. As she continued to walk, she heard the birds calling and noticed their beautiful colors as they sat in the budding bushes and trees. The longer Delaney listened to the cacophony of sound, the more she realized how foolish she had been to feel lonely. God had called her out into His melting world to show her all the beauty He had created for her enjoyment. She felt His presence all around her. As she turned the final corner, bringing her back to the Normans' home, she was no longer lonely.

She also knew that God had a purpose for her in this trip she was about to take. There had not been words but a quiet assurance in her soul that the trip was not a mistake. Now she looked forward to leaving tomorrow with eager anticipation instead of the heavy dread and homesickness she had endured earlier.

Delaney smiled as she turned the doorknob. No one had even missed her, but she felt as though her whole world had changed in the past hour. She walked quickly back up the stairs with a spring in her step and a fresh eagerness to pack her clothes in preparation for the journey before her.

Chapter 16

Riding a train in the North was much less unpleasant than riding a train coming from the South had been. There was still the heavy smoke that seemed to cover the passengers with its gray, pungent blanket, but at Mrs. Norman's request, Delaney was allowed to ride with her in the comfortable Pullman car. They had brought books to read, but there was so much activity and lovely scenery that Delaney's book lay unopened in her lap.

She felt much like a small child before Christmas. She rode with eager anticipation as she remembered the feeling that God was taking her on a mission. She couldn't help wondering what was before her.

The two women chatted companionably as they rode. Mrs. Norman told Delaney as much as she could about all of her grandchildren. In spite of having only one daughter, she was blessed with eight grandchildren besides the baby Edna had lost in the fall. It had been a good number of years since the two families had opportunity to visit one another, so the Normans had never even seen the five younger children. Mrs. Norman was quite excited as the train drew ever closer to the desired destination. Delaney could sense Mrs. Norman's eagerness in spite of her ever-constant self-discipline. There was a new twinkle in her eye and even a flush to her usually pale cheeks. Delaney smiled and was glad to note that her own homesickness was hardly noticeable in the anticipation for what lay ahead.

What would spring and summer be like in Indiana? Baltimore had been much cooler, and there was much more moisture than what she had known before in the late spring. There had been some flowers and trees, but she really didn't know what the summer would be like in the wooded North, where there was no stench of horse manure in the streets and where the heat was not magnified by the bricked and cobblestone streets. She was certainly learning a lot about geography that she would be able to share with her students when she returned home.

Suddenly she realized that Mrs. Norman was quiet. She checked to see if she was waiting for a response of some kind from Delaney. But Mrs. Norman's head was resting comfortably on the back of her seat and her eyes were closed. The rocking and swaying of the train as well as the constant rhythm of its metal wheels on the tracks had lulled several in their car to sleep. Delaney smiled. Neither of the women had slept well with the bouncing and noise of the train in the night. Now she sensed her own weariness but felt much too excited to sleep. However, she laid her head against the window and sighed deeply, closing her eyes to rest, and soon was also lulled to sleep.

It seemed only minutes but was indeed over an hour later that a loud clanging awakened the ladies from their rest. People bustled about, preparing to disembark. A conductor made his way through the passenger car calling out, "Ten minutes to Brownsville. If you are going to Canton, you must leave the train in Brownsville and finish your journey by carriage."

"Oh, my!" exclaimed Mrs. Norman. "That's where we're headed. I didn't realize we were this close to Brownsville. We must have slept longer than I thought."

"How far is it from Brownsville to Canton? Will we continue our journey yet this evening?" Delaney felt like a child with all her questions.

"It's still nearly two days' journey by coach, so we will find a hotel or boarding-house and rest our weary bones tonight. We'll begin the last phase of our journey tomorrow. I hope they have built a nicer hotel in this town since we visited last."

The two women had already gathered their belongings earlier in the day, so they did not need to be part of the activity in the train car. Delaney was glad she could watch the scenery out the window and was doing just that as the train slowed and pulled into town. She spied a handsome large, white building surrounded with bright tulips and golden daffodils. There was a post by a small path with a sign swinging in the breeze: CLARA'S PLACE–ROOM AND BOARD. The large porches looked welcoming, and a couple of rocking chairs and a large porch swing made Delaney realize how very travel-weary she was.

"Look—a nice boardinghouse. That looks much friendlier than the old hotel where we stayed years ago. I do hope there is a room available for us." Mrs. Norman had seen the same building that had caught Delaney's eye.

Together they picked up their belongings as the train's motion finally stopped. When the conductor stopped to see if he could be of service to the ladies, Mrs. Norman asked about the boardinghouse.

"Oh, it's a lovely place. Miss Clara owns it, but Miss Rose Ellen is the cook, and her food tastes better than any other place along the way. You'll enjoy a pleasant stay if you plan to stay there."

"Will there be a carriage that we can hire to take us to Canton?"

"Miss Clara will know who to ask and how to take care of all your needs. She's a very friendly lady, and you will feel quite at ease with her, I'm sure. Would you like to have your trunks taken to Clara's Place, then?"

"Actually, if we could leave our trunks at the station, we will take only our carpet-bags and have the carriage driver pick up the trunks tomorrow. Is that acceptable?"

"Yes, certainly. Just go to the ticket window and explain, and they will see to your trunks and help you."

∽∾

The ticket master had been quite helpful and had even secured a young man to carry the ladies' carpetbags to the boardinghouse. Before they knocked at the front door, they stopped to listen. Beautiful music was being played inside. The piano and violin seemed to frolic and dance with one another as the women stood on the porch and listened shamelessly.

But when the young man carrying their bags reached around them and knocked, the music suddenly stopped. Immediately they heard the staccato steps as someone approached the front door.

"Good evening, ladies. Are you looking for a place to rest?"

Mrs. Norman collected herself in time to respond. "We need a room with two beds for the night, as well as an evening meal and breakfast. We need to leave for Canton in the morning."

"I have just the room available. Please come with me." Placing a coin in the young man's hands from her own pocket, the lady took the carpetbags herself as she held the door open for the weary travelers.

"I haven't visited this area for a number of years now, and your establishment is certainly a welcome sight," said Mrs. Norman.

"I hope you will know that the welcome is genuine as you stay here. I have been blessed to have this place for only a few years, and to date have had very little competition." The lady speaking was quite lovely, and in spite of carrying the bags herself apparently was the owner of the establishment. "My name is Clara, and if you will follow me up these stairs, I will show you to your room. You will have ample time to freshen up before dinner is served."

As they started up the gently sloping stairway, Mrs. Norman spoke for both Delaney and herself when she said, "We heard lovely music when we approached. Will we be entertained at dinner?"

"Miss Rose Ellen's children were playing their instruments. Victoria plays the piano beautifully, and not long ago Eddie picked up a violin and has been accompanying her marvelously. The children have a wonderful talent, but unfortunately they are terribly shy and seldom perform. I am pleased you were able to enjoy their talents for a little while."

"Miss Rose Ellen?"

"She's the cook. And she cooks every bit as well as her children play music. You are in for a treat for sure."

Clara set their carpetbags on a cedar chest against one wall of a lovely rose-patterned room. There were crisp white curtains at each of the two large, latticed windows, and a beautiful hooked rug covered most of the wide plank floor. The two beds were parallel with one another and boasted beautiful matching quilts. The small stand between the two beds held an oil lamp with a polished globe and a Bible next to the lamp. The windows were on the two outside walls, with a pair of rocking chairs and another small table in the corner between the windows. Along the wall on one side of the far window was a washstand with a large pitcher and bowl on top and a small stack of clean towels. It was a very simply furnished room but quite welcoming and restful to the weary travelers.

Clara walked to the washstand and lifted the large pitcher. "Please make yourselves comfortable. I will be back shortly with fresh water for washing. There is a small room outside your room that all the guests use for bathing. It is available for thirty-minute intervals; you may check the schedule downstairs if you care to sign up for a time to bathe in a tub. Soap and towels are available in the bathing room." With that Clara smiled warmly and left with the pitcher, closing the door gently behind her.

Delaney looked around with much appreciation. "What a lovely room! It will be restful and enjoyable to stay here, I believe."

"Yes, it is certainly lovely. And I, for one, look forward to a bath in a tub this evening. Do you plan to bathe also?" Mrs. Norman sat wearily in one of the two rockers.

"Oh, I would love to, but. . .is it acceptable for a Negro to bathe in the tub also?" Delaney was hesitant.

"Why, I can't imagine why not. I'm certain Clara would have offered something different if it were not allowed. I think you should enjoy the tub also. We will each sign up for a bath when we go downstairs. I brought some lavender bath salts that we can both use. It will be quite relaxing."

Just then there was a gentle knock followed by Clara's voice again. "Ladies?"

Delaney quickly opened the door as Clara stepped inside with a full pitcher of water in one hand and a bucket in the other. "When you have finished with a basin of water you may pour it into this bucket. Rose Ellen's boys will collect the used water later for the gardens and will keep your pitcher filled. Now, is there anything else I can get for you?" Without waiting for a response she continued, "Dinner is served at seven; you are welcome to rest on the porches or in the front parlor at any time." With a smile and a nod, she disappeared, again closing the door behind herself.

As soon as the door had opened for Clara's departure, the ladies could smell the fragrant aromas of dinner, and almost immediately Mrs. Norman's stomach growled.

She looked up, surprised. "Well, I don't know which I want more—a bath, dinner, or this bed."

Delaney's eyes sparkled with her excitement. "Well, in whichever order they happen, they all sound delightful to me!"

At breakfast the next morning Clara told the ladies no one else in town needed to go to Canton, but there was a carriage they could hire for the trip if they wished to do so. They would travel approximately forty miles the first day, spend the night in a small town, and finish the final thirty or so miles the following day. Since the driver of the carriage preferred to stay one more day in Brownville, they could leave very early the next morning. Rose Ellen promised to send them on their way with a basket of food for the day's travels.

Before daybreak the following day, the carriage waited in front of the boarding-house with the ladies' trunks already loaded. It was a small carriage, but since the two ladies were the only passengers, they each enjoyed a seat to themselves. As the carriage rolled noisily away from Brownsville, the sun was just lighting the eastern horizon. Delaney was excited and watchful, but Mrs. Norman had ridden in carriages before and knew that a long two days and a hard ride were before them.

When finally they arrived in Canton, it was late afternoon. Both ladies were tired and sore but still eager to reach their destination. Since there was no hotel in Canton, the carriage driver took them to the general store, where they inquired about a place to stay or a possible ride to the Ned Browning home. The store owner, a very friendly fellow, was sweeping out the store to close for the day. He invited the ladies to stay and have dinner with him and his wife and then said he'd take them himself to the Browning home in the evening.

In spite of their weariness, both ladies were delighted to finish their journey the same day, so accepted the invitation with gratitude.

Chapter 17

It had been a long spring day for Ned and Edna, but the children were tucked into their beds. Ned was whittling a bedpost for a new bed frame while Edna worked on her endless stack of mending. The day had been unseasonably warm, so they sat out under the large maple tree that stood near the front of their house. Daylight was waning, and Edna was having difficulty seeing her stitches. Her hands rested in her lap, and she laid her head against the high back of the chair with a soft sigh. It had been more than eight months since they had buried the baby, yet Edna still did not feel recovered. Sadness weighed on her heart like a heavy load that she must carry.

She looked over at her husband. He had not glanced up, but she knew the moment she had sighed that he was aware of her burden and ached with his own loss. His shoulders seemed more bent than she remembered, and his blond hair was turning noticeably white.

Closing her eyes, she prayed as she had many times before: *Please God, please lift this burden that we carry. Please replace our sorrow with joy once more.* A tear slid down her cheek, but she stopped the sigh that wanted to escape before it was audible. Aloud she said, "A good breeze would feel good right now."

"A good breeze as well as a good rain," he replied. Ned stopped carving and gazed at his wife.

She knew that he knew the conversation was not about the weather. It was her way of letting him know that life goes on and that she was trying not to let the grief weigh her down. He observed her closely, then sat back and spoke gently. "Edna, I've been thinking a lot about the loss we've had. Yes, I grieve for the loss of our daughter, but I grieve even more for the sorrow in your eyes."

He took a deep breath. "I've been thinking that it might help you to heal if you could see your mother again. It has been a long time. We have too many young-uns now to make the trip together with the family, and I don't think we'd either one be easy in our hearts to leave them here alone if we went together, but I'm thinking that perhaps it would be good for you to take the little boys and maybe Esther, too, and go spend some time with your parents this summer. I believe the older children and I can keep things going around here until you return."

Ned leaned closer. She knew he was studying the lines on her face that weren't there previously and the dark circles beneath her eyes. "I'll miss you terribly, but I would be happy knowing you might get a comfort," he added.

Tears splashed down her cheeks, but she smiled at him. "Oh, Ned, how I would love to see my mother for a little while! I have told her everything in letters, but just to chat with her face-to-face would be so wonderful. I can't bear the thought of being away from you and the children, but perhaps it truly would help a bit. I will think on it."

Suddenly something large moved through the trees, and they both turned toward it. It was a very unusual sound at dusk unless it was a large animal. Edna began gathering her mending and sewing supplies and then stopped in surprise. She could tell now it was horses…and a wagon. But who would be traveling at this time of day?

Soon they could hear voices above the clatter of the horses' hooves. The wagon approached, slowing in front of the house. They recognized the storekeeper, Hiram McDonough, as he climbed down over the wagon wheel, but the two ladies' faces were shadowed by their bonnets and the dusk. All the same, Ned and Edna approached the wagon.

Hiram helped the younger woman down first. She was a Negro girl, a total stranger to them. Next the older woman climbed down with Hiram on one side and the young woman on the other, steadying her. As soon as the older woman was standing firmly on the ground, she walked toward Edna. "Edna," she called softly, arms reaching out.

"Mother!" Edna whispered and was immediately lost in her mother's embrace. Both women were crying and laughing at once. But soon Mrs. Norman pulled back slightly and smiled at Ned. "Blessings on you, Son!" She moved to hug him as well.

Ned and Edna were nearly speechless with joy, but their eyes looked questioningly at the young Negro woman who was traveling with the older woman. "Oh! Where are my manners?" Mrs. Norman exclaimed as she reached for Delaney. "Please meet my friend who has agreed to accompany me on my journey. This is Delaney from the Rose Hill Plantation in South Carolina, about whom I have written. I am certain you will enjoy her company as well."

Delaney smiled hesitantly at Ned and Edna, but she was soon wrapped in Edna's warm embrace. "Oh, thank you for accompanying my mother and making this trip possible for her. We are delighted to have you stay with us."

Mr. McDonough cleared his throat slightly. "Ned, if you'll help me with these trunks, I can leave them here and still get home before the darkest part of the night."

Over coffee and cookies the women talked quietly while Ned watched his wife's face. The smile on her face matched the one in his heart. He had been right. A visit with her mother was just what Edna needed. He silently thanked God that he had not had to be separated from his wife for them to visit one another. Soon he noticed that Delaney was struggling to stay awake.

"Edna, these women must be exhausted. I'll take a blanket and sleep in the fresh hay pile in the barn. And I'll awaken Thomas, and he can sleep with me. Then Delaney can have the small room behind the kitchen where Thomas sleeps, and you and your mother can share our room. Would that be acceptable to everyone?"

"Oh, don't wake the boy. I will gladly sleep on the rug here in the sitting room. I am so tired I believe I could sleep fine even in this chair," Delaney said warmly. "Truly, I would feel very bad for you to awaken anyone on my behalf."

At that moment Thomas came sleepily around the corner. "What's all the noise out here? Is everything all right?" He was still trying to open his eyes when he spoke, but soon he said hesitatingly, "Grandmother?"

"My, Thomas, how you have grown! You are a man. I still think of you as a little boy." Mrs. Norman hugged her grandson as they all explained at once about the surprise.

When things settled down once more, Thomas asked, "Miss Delaney, would you care to sleep in my room? I will sleep in the fresh hay in the barn with my father."

Ned put his arm on Thomas's shoulders. "Come on, Son. Let's hit that hay before the cows want their morning milking." Grinning, the men walked out calling over their shoulders, "Good night, all."

Chapter 18

Bartholomew Kendall felt like a young boy at Christmas. His horses seemed to sense his excitement as they trotted briskly. There was still a chill in the warm spring air, but the colors of the early flowers and the sounds of the nesting birds appeared totally in sync with his spirits. He couldn't help smiling at the bulky envelope peeking out of the velvet pocket in the front of the carriage. He was glad he could give this to his sister and her husband; he knew they would be pleased.

He suddenly realized he had been humming, so he broke into a lusty song. The tune he'd been humming had been put to a couple of verses of Psalm 25 that they often sang in his church. As he sang the song now, he realized how very much he had trusted in God, his hope and his Savior, on this mission.

The countryside was still as the horses pranced out the rhythm of the song with their hooves. Bart sang out with his resonate baritone into the hushed silence:

"Show me Your ways, O Lord;
teach me Your paths;
guide me into Your truth and teach me.
Guide me in Your Truth;
teach me Your ways,
for You are my God and my Savior, my Hope.
I trust in You all day long."

As he sang, Bart felt as though he could actually feel God smiling on him. His heart rejoiced with the success of his journey, and he eagerly looked forward to giving his sister his news.

Bart adored his sister and her family, and Bart's dear wife enjoyed them as well. Bart thought now of the way God had blessed the Rose Hill Plantation, and he thought of all that he had learned from his generous-hearted brother-in-law. Since he and Adele had been unable to have children of their own, they intended to make Wally and Sue Ellen's second son their heir. They felt good knowing that their own plantation would continue in good hands, in the tradition of Wally himself.

As he drove, he suddenly decided to stop at his own plantation, Windy Oaks, before going on to Rose Hill, and take his wife with him to Rose Hill for a visit. He knew his sister would enjoy the visit, as would his lovely Adele.

In his mind he compared the two women he loved most in the world. His sister, Sue Ellen, was a lovely and graceful woman, but quite capable in all her undertakings. She had taken over the running of the entire plantation since her husband had taken ill and had done a very good job of keeping things running smoothly. He knew she depended heavily on the help of Jeremiah, but the bulk of the responsibility rested on her own shoulders.

His Adele was a small, fragile-looking woman. She was rather timid and quiet and had never quite mastered the running of the plantation home. However, they had been blessed with the gift of Adele's personal slave, who had been given to her as a small child. Her name was Maddie, and she had grown to be tall and strong of body and mind. Bart had learned from his brother-in-law to give all their slaves their freedom, and like Wally, most of his people had stayed on to serve willingly and be part of the family. So Maddie was hired not only as Adele's helper, but she quickly picked up the task of running the household for the Kendalls in Adele's place.

Maddie's marriage to their overseer, Jasper, had been a very happy occasion on the plantation, and the union had produced four precious boys in the past ten years who quickly won Adele's heart. Bart smiled as he thought of the small boys. They were growing wise and strong under the care of their two mothers: Maddie and Adele.

He knew Adele would not want to go away without taking the four boys. Maddie wouldn't mind, and it would be a great adventure for the boys to visit Rose Hill with them. Adele would enjoy the visit with Sue Ellen, and Windy Oaks would be in good hands with Maddie and Jasper. As the plan developed in his mind, Bart became more and more eager to get home and share his idea with his wife. They could leave first thing in the morning and be at Rose Hill before noon. Sue Ellen would be happy to see them all. Again he smiled as he thought of the joyful news he would share with Wally and Sue Ellen. He felt certain Jeremiah would be pleased with the news also.

⌘

The huge live oak trees lining the sides of the winding driveway up to the Windy Oaks main house were a welcome sight. Their branches were gnarly and often were the place the boys would be found playing. As he drove between the spreading boughs, Bart looked carefully into each tree and was not disappointed. He smiled as he called out to Clifton, who was cradled in the arms of the spreading boughs, his legs swinging happily while his face was buried in a book. Apparently Clifton had been so wrapped up in the story he was reading that he had not even heard the carriage.

His dark face popped up above the top of the book, and his face lit as he saw

Papa Bart slowing the horses. Scrambling down the tree, Clifton held the book carefully protected with his finger marking his spot. He darted toward the carriage as it came to a stop near the base of the favorite tree.

Clifton climbed swiftly into the carriage. "We didn't expect you yet for several days. Did everything go well on your journey, Papa Bart?"

Bart smiled at the boy. "Everything went very well. I still need to go to Rose Hill for a few days. . ." Before he could even finish his sentence he saw the boy's smile fade to show his disappointment. Bart continued, ". . . so I thought I'd stop here and take Mama Del and you boys to Rose Hill with me for a visit."

The small dark face lit up like a jack-o'-lantern. "Really, Papa Bart? We can go, too? Really?"

"If your mama and papa say it is all right with them. We may be gone for several days or even a week. Are you sure you want to go?"

Clifton didn't even answer the question. "Oh, I haven't seen my cousins Nate and Luke and Ruth Elizabeth for ever so long. Oh, I can't believe it. You know, Papa Bart, Ruth Elizabeth isn't really like a girl. She's my very best friend. She loves to read books, too, and she knows where all the baby birds' nests are and she lets me hold the kittens and she's not a sissy at all. She's not afraid of nothin'!"

"Anything. . ."

". . . of anything and we know where all the best turtles hide in the creek, but we don't tell anyone. I can't wait to play with her."

Bart stopped the carriage at the front gate as Jasper appeared and reached for the reins. "We'll need the carriage in the morning to go on to Rose Hill. Do you mind if the boys ride over with us for a few days?"

Jasper smiled at his son as Clifton climbed out of the carriage, guarding his book carefully. "His mother will want the final word on that, but I'm sure it can be arranged." Looking at his son, he said, "Do you remember where you put the present you made for Ruth Elizabeth?"

"Yes. And Mama will help me wrap it, I know. No, I want Mama Del to help. She makes prettier bows." Clifton ran happily up the steps of the house calling, "Mama Del! Mama Del!"

Bart looked at Jasper and chuckled. "Well, I guess I won't be the one to break the news about the trip to Adele after all. Although I may have to do some explaining." As he handed the reins into Jasper's ready hands, he said, "Thanks, Jasper. Thanks for caring for the horses and carriage, and thanks for sharing your boys with us."

"Yes, sir. Maddie and I appreciate very much that you and the missus love our boys like you do. They don't really know what it's like to be a Negro in the South, and for that we'll always be grateful, sir."

"God has been good to us all, Jasper. Let's just thank Him faithfully."

Chapter 19

Morning dawned slowly the next day. Thunder rolled across the heavens and dark clouds blotted the sun. But the large, old plantation house was bustling with happy noises in spite of the spring rain that pelted the windows.

After their marriage, Jasper and Maddie had been asked to move into the east wing of the house, so the boys had grown up as part of the family in the home. It was truly an unusual situation, but they were all comfortable with it, and Bart and Adele were glad to not be alone in the huge old estate.

Breakfast was a riotous affair, as was the packing and loading of the carriage. When finally all were inside and the baggage was properly covered for the wet ride, Bart began to wonder what he'd been thinking to suggest such a thing. But one look at his wife's joyful face and he knew he would not regret it in spite of the dreariness of the day. However, he was glad he had sent a messenger over yesterday afternoon to prepare his sister for the commotion that was coming. Bart smiled as he remembered his sister's happy reply. He knew her household would also be bustling with happy preparation.

Suddenly there was the rustle of a page turning. Bart turned and looked behind him to find all three older boys with their noses in books. "Are you afraid of being bored that you brought along your books?"

"No, sir," Afton replied politely. "We brought books to make the trip go faster."

Boren, the smallest boy, sat between Bart and Adele. They looked at one another over Boren's head and smiled. They were quite proud of their boys and were thankful for their keen minds.

Ezra spoke up quietly, "Don't worry, Papa Bart. We won't lose or damage the books."

"I know you won't. I'm glad you enjoy reading." Again he glanced at Adele and smiled. Her arm was around Boren, and she hummed softly. In spite of the rain, it was a very pleasant drive.

❧

By midafternoon the rain had ceased, but a late spring chill hovered in the air. After dinner at Rose Hill, and getting the tired children settled into their beds, Bart and Adele retired to the library to enjoy coffee with Wally and Sue Ellen. Sue Ellen spoke for her husband, too, as she immediately inquired as to the results of Bart's trip to Devil's Bend.

"So were you unsuccessful then, Bart? Did you find out anything about Jeremiah's wife?"

Bart grinned as he stirred sugar into his coffee. "Not as successful as we had hoped, but I believe the news is somewhat good all the same." He laid his spoon on the saucer thoughtfully. "She escaped four years ago and took the child with her. Mr. Wickner said they searched for over a year, but to no avail. It's as though the ground swallowed the two of them. They were gone without a trace.

"Now, I have heard from my people that there is a safe house not far from Devil's Bend. My guess is that she made it there and then was aided on her trip to the North. I'm certain she is safe or there would have been something found of them if they had not made it to safety. I think Jeremiah will be relieved to know that she is safe."

Sue Ellen sat on the edge of her seat, her coffee forgotten on the table beside her chair. "Has Mr. Wickner stopped searching for her, then?"

"I believe he had pretty much given up the search. But I bought her papers so he cannot pursue her any longer. I was fairly certain you would want to do that. If not, I will pay for them myself."

"Oh, yes!" Wally's head bobbed happily. "Thas good. We give th' papuhs to Jeremiah. Yes. Thas good."

"That was what I thought. As soon as he can get away, Jeremiah can probably discover the direction she took by visiting the safe house. He will be pleased that she is no longer living in those terrible conditions."

◈

By morning the sun shone brightly on the freshly washed world. The children played noisily as they enjoyed knowing they had the whole day together. Adele and Sue Ellen smiled as they sat together on the veranda and listened and watched.

Bart was helping Wally walk toward the stable, where they planned to take a cart to the fields to chat with Jeremiah. However, they found Jeremiah in the stable, so they all sat on hay and visited. Finally, Wally looked at Bart and said, "Tell th' news, Bart."

Bart chewed thoughtfully on a piece of straw. "Jeremiah, I rode over to Devil's Bend several days ago, to try to purchase Deidre and your child. However, Mr. Wickner told me she had taken the child and run away about four years ago. I was able to purchase her papers, though, so if she can be found, she is a free woman now."

Wally pulled the papers from his shirt pocket and pushed them toward Jeremiah. "Is good news, Jeremiah?"

Jeremiah was silent as he stared at the folded papers in his hand. He was not certain if he was happy or sad. He was glad that she had escaped from Devil's Bend, but where was she now? How would he ever find her? His mind whirled with more questions. Was she safe? Was their child alive? He was silent so long that Bart spoke again.

"Jeremiah, perhaps you could ride over to the slave quarters at Devil's Bend and inquire there. Maybe one of the Negroes will know where she went. They would never tell me, but perhaps they'll tell you?" Even though it was a statement, Bart spoke it like a question. They were watching Jeremiah's face.

Jeremiah looked up slowly—first at Wally and then at Bart. "I'm glad she's gone from that place." He swallowed. "I will trust that they are safe."

Bart spoke up quickly. "Mr. Wickner had people searching for her for over a year, and they found not a trace. I'm thinking chances are real good that she made it to the North or they would have found her or some trace of her. We won't rest until we find her. I believe with all my heart that God is protecting her and keeping her for you."

Jeremiah nodded. "I'll believe that, too. And I'll pay you for these papers as soon as I can."

"No!" Mr. Wally spoke quickly. "It's gift. Owe you for all you've done here. You keep papers. Gift for you."

"Jeremiah, look at the papers. Do you know if you have a son or a daughter? It should say on the papers, don't you think?" Mr. Bart seemed curious and excited.

Suddenly tears streamed down Jeremiah's cheeks. His big hands shook as he opened the roll of papers. It said *Deidre and son, Jedediah* on the papers. A son. He had a son! He would now be able to think of him as a person—with a name. *Jedediah.* A good strong name. The lump was so tight in his throat that he couldn't talk, so he shoved the papers toward Mr. Bart and Mr. Wally. Both men looked at the words, then smiled happily at Jeremiah.

Bart thumped Jeremiah on the back and laughed loudly. "A son. We should celebrate. Jeremiah is the proud father of a. . .a six-year-old son!"

Wally smiled happily. "Yes. Is holiday. We mus' celebrate. Le's go, Bart. Tell all the people, Jeremiah. Today holiday. We be celebrate tonight." As he struggled to get to his feet, Bart quickly stood and took his arm. Helping Wally out of the stable, Bart said, "We must tell the women quickly. There will be lots to do."

Suddenly Wally stopped and looked back at Jeremiah. "Jeremiah, tell all people to meet at house in an hour. They stop work in fields now. We get ready today and celebrate all day tomorrow. Everyone mus' help get ready!"

Jeremiah hadn't seen such joy on the old gentleman's face for a long time. In spite of the fact that it was a tradition on this plantation to have a day of celebration whenever a baby was born (black or white—all were equally celebrated), Jeremiah had not seen this much excitement and joy for a long time. He was ever thankful that this family all shared his joy.

Chapter 20

Jeremiah's eyes opened to the darkness suddenly. He lay very still wondering what had awakened him. The birds were not even singing yet, but he could hear a few chirps so he knew morning wasn't far off. But what had awakened him?

Then he heard it. Very faintly, off in the distance, he could hear the dancing bows of a pair of violins. Lem and Dennel must be practicing for the celebration. There was no mistaking their unique style of fiddling. But what were they doing playing at this hour?

Jeremiah lay still for a few minutes longer. Deidre was safe. And the baby—Jedediah. He must think of Jedediah as a little boy now instead of a baby. A slow smile played across his face in the dark. He hadn't been thinking of the baby as a child before. For some reason he had continued thinking of their offspring as a baby.

He wondered what Jedediah looked like. And what his personality was like. Was he like his mother? like Jeremiah? Was he a good boy? a happy child? And where were they? Did they have a place to live? food? clothing? Were they safe?

Before long he was praying earnestly for them. He knew his Deidre was a strong woman and would do her best to take good care of the boy until they could be together again. As he prayed, he noticed the room beginning to get light. Going to the window, Jeremiah saw the sun as it pushed over the horizon. Suddenly he thought that somewhere this same sun was shining on Deidre and Jedediah, and he would trust God to take care of them and to someday bring them back together again.

Jeremiah knew Deidre was also praying for him and for God to bring them together soon. Well, he would pray the same and watch God work, because he remembered the verse of scripture that said that when two or three agree on anything as touching heaven, that God would hear and answer.

The violin music stopped. Jeremiah could hear the stirring of excited people getting ready for a day of celebration. He washed and dressed quickly. There would be tables to set up and benches to put together and awnings to stretch while the women prepared the feast. More than ever he wished Deidre could be here, but he intended to celebrate God's goodness to him and trust God for their future.

⁓

It was a beautiful day for a celebration. The front pasture was used for parties such as this, and all the little boys had been cleaning out the cattle droppings all morning.

292

The grass was the beautiful yellow-green of late spring, and the violets were in full bloom. A gentle breeze stirred the tassels that hung from each pole that supported the large awnings erected for shade over the tables.

Augustin had been sent yesterday afternoon to tell all the people at Windy Oaks to come for the celebration. Now the people from both plantations were gathered together and the tables were laden with food. Silence reigned as Mr. Bart and Mr. Wally rose to give thanks before the feasting began.

"Greetings to all you here today to celebrate the birth of Jeremiah's son, Jedediah." Mr. Wally spoke slowly, but was speaking better than he had for a long time—ever since his stroke last summer. He still leaned on his cane, but his voice was strong. "As is our tradition, I will pray for the baby, who in this case is no longer a baby, and for the parents before we partake of our feast together. But before we do that, we have received a letter just this morning from Delaney, and I have asked Bart to read it to you all."

All the people knew about Delaney studying with Mrs. Norman from Delaney's previous letters, and her travels and experiences excited them all. There were exclamations and low murmurs of anticipation as Mr. Bart took a piece of paper from an envelope and unfolded it with much ceremony. After clearing his throat, he began reading:

"Dear loved ones at Rose Hill Plantation,

How I long to see your faces and hear your voices again. You are still such a part of me—all of you—that I think of you often and am reminded of you all in everything I do. My heart is ever grateful for this opportunity afforded me, and I continue to work hard to learn all I can so I can return and enrich your lives, too.

Our train trip here to Indiana was much more enjoyable than my trip to Baltimore, because I was allowed to ride with Mrs. Norman, and we enjoyed conversation and fellowship all along the way. The scenery as we rode was lovely, even though the train sped so fast it was impossible to focus for long on any one thing. It is ever amazing to me that we could travel nearly halfway across a continent in a few short days. Times are changing quickly. I am reminded we are in a very industrious century that is making leaps of advancement.

We are staying on a farm here in Indiana. It is much different than the plantations in the South. The most noticeable thing to me is that the ground in the freshly plowed fields is not red clay or brown dirt but rich, black soil. The family does all the work themselves—there are no servants at all. They work hard, play hard, and laugh hard. It is a merry family, and I enjoy being with them.

Mrs. Norman's daughter, Edna, is a precious lady and as gracious as her mother. She and Mr. Browning have eight beautiful children, and they have all been taught very well. They are well-spoken and industrious children, but the whole family is quite jolly and talented. I have found myself to be quite contented here. (No, do not worry. I will return to Rose Hill and you all as soon as possible.) But while I am here, I am enjoying every minute with this precious family.

The Browning family often talks of a family who lives only an hour's journey from them. I understand that each month the two families meet together to worship and enjoy a meal together at one or the other's home. This next Sunday is the day, and we will travel to the Evanstons' home and worship there. I look forward to our time of worship together and also to meet the Brownings' friends. They have told us that a young woman and her son who have escaped slavery in the South and traveled alone to Indiana live with the Evanstons. It will be interesting to meet her and hear of her experiences.

Mrs. Browning (Edna) has been much encouraged and uplifted since her mother has come to spend time with her. And I am grateful to you all that this opportunity has been afforded to me as well. Until next time, I will remain,

Your dear friend and future teacher,

Delaney"

There was a brief hush as everyone took in the experiences of Delaney, and then they clapped and cheered lustily.

Jeremiah thought of the lovely young woman who had such a tender heart to teach the Negroes here on the plantation, so they could be prepared for the world and hopefully help to change the world for the better. He looked around and saw many of the children she had taught. He could tell that they loved her and looked forward to her return. In his heart he prayed that she would indeed return to teach here and that she would not be tempted to stay in the North even though he knew she was free to do so if she desired.

And then, before Mr. Wally prayed for Jeremiah and his family, Mr. Bart offered encouragement from God's Word to all the folks gathered here. "In Job 23, verse 10 we read, 'But he knoweth the way that I take: when he hath tried me, I shall come forth as gold.' And Psalm 66, verses 10–12 say: 'For thou, O God, hast proved us: thou hast tried us, as silver is tried. Thou broughtest us into the net; thou laidst affliction upon our loins. Thou hast caused men to ride over our heads; we went through fire and through water: but thou broughtest us out into a wealthy place.'"

Mr. Bart paused briefly, then continued: "We don't know why you have all had to go through some of the hard trials you have endured, but we do believe you are being refined into men and women who will be used of God to change this world. I would caution you all to have hearts of compassion and forgiveness as you remember those who have caused you pain, just as Jesus forgave those who hung Him on a cross to crucify Him. And now we are especially thankful today that Jeremiah's wife and son are freed from their suffering. We pray for them and for God to reunite this family."

Suddenly Jeremiah heard Mr. Wally call out his name. Jeremiah walked forward alone to stand before him as Mr. Wally prayed for him and his family. It was a tradition here at Rose Hill. Jeremiah was grateful, but he wished with all his heart he could stand proudly with Deidre and his son by his side as Mr. Wally prayed for them all.

Jeremiah could feel the slight tremor in Mr. Wally's hand as he laid it on Jeremiah's head, but his voice was strong. Jeremiah rejoiced at the healing that was taking place in the man. There was complete silence as Mr. Wally began to pray:

"Oh, Lord, our Father, we humbly present to You this day our prayers and petitions for Jeremiah and his family. We thank You for blessing the endeavors to purchase his wife, Deidre, and son, Jedediah. And now we pray that You would work in such a way that Jeremiah could someday be reunited with his family, as was Your intention from the beginning of creation that a man and wife should live together as one and multiply to replenish the earth.

"Lord God, we know from Your Word that You work all things together for our good if we trust in You. You have also told us that You know what we need before we even ask. Today we are trusting that You are working to bring these two young people back together as one. We don't know how; we don't know when, but we are trusting that You will do it. We know that we will not be disappointed, for You never fail to keep Your promises.

"Father, we thank You for the way You so bountifully provide for our needs, and we thank You for this food and for this celebration. Let us ever honor You as we partake together this day. And we thank You and praise You for hearing our prayers that we offer in the name of Your Son, Jesus Christ. Amen."

There were many "Amens" shouted from among the people. Jeremiah realized, among the clamor, that a miracle had already taken place. God had allowed Mr. Wally's speech to be completely his old self in the prayer.

Clearly, Mr. Wally knew it, too, for moisture misted the kindly gentleman's eyes, and he lifted his face heavenward for a moment. Then, smiling at the group of people, he announced, "I believe food is ready, and I also believe you all know what to do!"

The afternoon proceeded in celebration with the meal being followed by games, and then the fiddles tuned up to play for square dancing as well. The Traehdniks and the Kendalls all shared in the merriment for a very pleasant day.

But Jeremiah's heart, although grateful, was not in the celebration. Instead he was praying for the future reunion with his family. He couldn't help feeling he must wait to celebrate until he and Deidre and Jedediah were reunited as one family.

Chapter 21

Delaney quickly learned to love the mild summer weather in Indiana. The days were sunny and bright but quite comfortable, and the nights were cool. Often the rain that came in the night was gone by morning, and the world was refreshed and vegetation grew lustily.

Today was Sunday. Before the sun rose, she heard excitement and commotion in the main room. She eagerly hopped out of her bed and washed quickly, knowing the Brownings anticipated a fun day ahead and that they could use her help in preparation.

Dressed in her church dress, Delaney entered the kitchen to find the family already busily brushing and braiding hair, making breakfast, setting the table, packing baskets with food and generally bustling in every direction. She took over the setting of the table so Betsy could help her younger sister fasten her dress and tie her shoes. She could hear Ned and the older boys as they tied the horses and wagon outside the front door, getting them ready to load.

"I'm glad we made our food for taking yesterday." Mrs. Norman was tying on an apron as she entered the room and prepared to help.

"Good mornin', Mama. Yes, with all these young-uns I've learned I have to plan ahead. But I'm thankful for all the help I have in the kitchen, too. Betsy's getting to be a better cook than I am, I do believe." Edna was pouring steaming mugs of coffee while she spoke. Betsy looked up at her mother and blushed with pleasure.

Ned, Thomas, Edward, and Nicholas came in through the back door looking freshly scrubbed from the basin on the back stoop. They quickly reached for the towel that hung behind the door. Nicholas swiped the towel across his face and started toward the smaller children, but Ned grabbed his collar. "Whoa, there. There will be no breakfast until that head of hair is combed."

Nicholas grinned mischievously, turning to the small mirror and reaching his hand toward his dad for the comb.

As they all finally sat around the large table to eat breakfast before heading for the Evanstons' for the day, Delaney couldn't help thanking God silently, not only for the meal but for the fellowship and love of brothers and sisters in the faith. Even though she was many miles from all that was familiar to her, she felt as though she was part of all that was going on today and the others who would worship together shortly. She was thankful for the peace and joy within her heart.

The ride through the woods was joyful. Ned's singing voice was as lovely as any trained voice Delaney had heard, and he had taught his children well. They sang many hymns in four-part harmony as they rode through the forest. Even though some of the songs had words unfamiliar to Delaney, she could soon hum the tune along with the rest.

Delaney smiled as she watched her dear teacher, the formerly somewhat re-served Mrs. Norman. As she sang and cuddled and teased with the children, she seemed to be twenty years younger than she was before this trip. Delaney had also seen a tremendous change in Edna Browning as well. Yes, the proverb was certainly proven true that said, "A merry heart doeth good like a medicine."

The singing and laughter and chatter along the way made the trip seem much shorter than Delaney had anticipated. Before she knew it, they were being introduced to the Evanstons and to Deidre and Jedediah.

The families visited and played for a short time while the women warmed the foods and prepared the combined feast. Soon they joined one another around the enlarged table. When there was room for not one more bite, the women cleared the tables, while the men set up chairs and benches for their worship time.

And what a time of worship it was. With Ned leading, they sang many hymns of the church. They prayed together and read scripture together. Even the children shared insights and stories of what God was teaching them in their lives.

After more singing, the children were excused to play together for a while before starting the trip back to the Brownings'. The women enjoyed playing with the Evanston twins and watching all the new things they could do as they were now crawling and pulling themselves up on chairs. It was fun watching how dependent they were on one another. It was difficult at first to tell the two girls apart; they were so identical. However, in time Delaney could tell by their personalities. Callie dominated and Christy followed. They were adorable babies.

"Do you mind if I go look at all your lovely flower gardens?" Delaney asked Mandy when there was a pause in the conversation.

"Not at all. I hope you enjoy them like I do. Deidre has actually done as much of the transplanting and dividing as I have, so they are certainly not my gardens."

"Want some company? I'd love to take a little walk, too." Deidre looked at Delaney questioningly.

"Oh, yes. Please join me, Deidre. I'd love to have you tell me about the gardens and flowers. Would anyone else care to join us?"

Betsy picked up one of the twins. "Not me. I want to play with this baby doll while I can." The other Browning girls nodded their agreement with Betsy, so Delaney and Deidre went out alone.

As they walked, they soon began to share about their lives. Deidre was very interested in the sort of situation Delaney experienced in the South. Delaney was glad to tell her of the unique plantation on which she worked and participated willingly. All the white folks whom Deidre had known in the South were adamant about keeping the Negroes as ignorant as possible. It was hard for her to imagine a home where the Negros not only were allowed an education but were even encouraged to learn and improve themselves.

Deidre also told Delaney how Mandy had taught her to read and encouraged her to learn and speak as an educated person instead of using the slave slang. The two young women were actually close in age and quickly became friends, looking forward to more visits in the upcoming weeks.

Mandy and Deidre stood on the front porch, each with a baby girl on one hip and their free arms around each other's waist, after the rattle of the departing wagon could no longer be heard.

Mandy sighed. "How good it is to have such good friends and such sweet times together."

"Yes, it is. . ." Deidre's voice was quiet.

Mandy turned to look at her friend. "Is anything wrong?"

"No, just thinking. As they were pulling away, I wished I had asked Delaney if she had ever heard of my Jeremiah. She seems to get out more than most Negroes in the South. It is highly unlikely, I know. The South is a huge place. But I just wondered. Perhaps next time we're together I will have the opportunity to ask her."

"It certainly couldn't hurt to ask. Yes, I think you should definitely ask her. Why did we not think of that today? In fact, you could ride over in the next few days and ask her if you want. Why don't you?"

"Hmmm. . .I'll think on it." Deidre straightened her back. "Meanwhile, we have two sleepy boys and two completely worn-out little girls needing our attention." The girls were rubbing their eyes and chewing on their fists.

"Yes, we'd better take care of them before they begin howling." With that, Mandy placed a kiss on Christy's head and turned toward the house.

Monday evening the Browning family was sitting at the supper table passing the bowls of food when Edna said to Delaney, "I am so glad you could spend time with Deidre, Delaney. She misses her husband so. I have a feeling that just talking with you, being from the South yourself, helped her feel connected to Jeremiah once more in a small way."

Delaney's eyes opened wide, and her hands froze as she turned her head toward Edna. "To whom?"

Edna looked at her, a bit puzzled. "To Jeremiah. Her husband. He is still in the South somewhere. She doesn't know who bought him when he was sold from Devil's Bend."

"Jeremiah?" Everyone became very still, looking at Delaney. Then she shrugged. "No, it couldn't be. . ."

"What is it, dear?" Mrs. Norman questioned Delaney.

Delaney took a scoop of fried potatoes onto her plate and passed the bowl before saying, "The overseer at Rose Hill Plantation. His name is Jeremiah. He has a wife and baby somewhere and he misses them terribly, but Deidre's child is not a baby, so it couldn't be."

"How old is his baby?"

"I don't really know. It was born sometime after he came to Rose Hill. He doesn't even know if it is a boy or girl. He doesn't talk about them much, but he obviously misses them terribly and is devoted to them. He had mentioned once that when he earned his freedom he planned to stay at Rose Hill until he earned enough to buy his wife's and baby's freedom and bring them to Rose Hill to live with him."

Everyone began to eat again, all but Edna. She became very quiet. In a little while she said, "Delaney, how long has Jeremiah been at Rose Hill?"

"Well, it's been a few years now. I don't recall for sure, but probably. . ." She stopped to think briefly. "Nearly five years now. Maybe six."

"And his child was born after he came to Rose Hill?"

"Yes."

"Then the child would be five or six years old, not a baby. Jedediah just turned six years old not long ago."

Everyone at the table became very still. The wonderful meal was forgotten momentarily as their minds worked on the possibilities.

"Oh, my. That would be utterly amazing!" Ned acted as though he could hardly sit still. "Delaney, tomorrow we must go back to the Evanstons' and talk more with Deidre. We have to know. We have prayed for her to find him for many years now, and we must do our part to find out if this is God's way of answering."

Clint, who was seven years old and adored his friend Jeddy said, "Daddy, did we find Jeddy's daddy?"

"We don't really know, Son. But we must do whatever we can to find out if we can find him. Let's all agree to pray for God's guidance, and tomorrow Delaney and I will go to find out what we can."

"I'll pray, Daddy," Clint was quick to volunteer.

"I will, too." Benjamin added his support as well.

Chapter 22

Edna carefully covered the gooseberry pies with a dish towel before she placed them in the basket. There was an unusual hush over the household as they all prepared for the trip to the Evanstons'. Even the young ones seemed to feel the awe of the possibility of finding Jeddy's daddy.

"Now you children take good care of your grandmother today." Edna leaned down to wipe some breakfast from Benjamin's face. "That means you, too, young man." Her voice was gentle as she smiled at her youngest child. She gently caressed his cheek before standing.

"We'll be good, Mama. We'll help real good, too."

"Yes, I know you will, Son."

Delaney was still wiping dishes at the sideboard when Ned pulled the wagon up to the front of the house.

"Come, Delaney. The girls will finish that. Let's be on our way."

Ellie quickly took Delaney's dish towel, and Essie handed her the bonnet she had laid on the table. Both girls hugged Delaney quickly. Mrs. Norman walked over and laid her hand on Delaney's shoulder. "God be with you, Delaney. I hope this could be Deidre's answer to prayer."

Edna tugged at Delaney's arm. "We do, too, Mama. And now we must be on our way."

The family stood at the front door waving as the wagon carrying Ned, Edna, and Delaney disappeared through the woods. Mrs. Norman was quiet and thoughtful when Betsy said quietly, "Mama hasn't been this excited since she took sick last fall."

"What?" Mrs. Norman looked at Betsy thoughtfully. "You know, that could be it. It may be exactly what your mother needs to heal her wounds—to see another family healed." She put her arm around Betsy's shoulders as they turned back into the house. "Yes, that could just be it."

❧

Ethan was chopping at the stumps left from the trees he had felled for Deidre's wing to the house last summer. They had rotted some, and he dug and chopped at them more as he tried to clear the area for growing hay for the cattle.

Mandy and Deidre worked in the garden, planting late green beans and picking the last of the peas. They had dried what they planned to dry for winter, and these late ones would taste good fresh for their lunch. The little girls were crawling all over the blanket spread for them in the shade, and Jeddy and Daniel played quietly nearby while they kept an eye on the babies also.

Deidre stood and stretched her back, shading her eyes as she looked into the blue sky. "I think it is only goin' to keep gettin' hotter and hotter now." She took off her straw bonnet and fanned herself with it. "I don't know which is hotter: wearin' the bonnet and feelin' no breeze, or takin' it off to feel the breeze and gettin' the hot sun along with it."

Mandy didn't respond, so Deidre turned her head to look at her. She had set down on the blanket to nurse the babies while she hulled some peas, but was leaning her face into her hand.

"Mandy, are you all right?" It wasn't like Mandy to ignore her comment.

Mandy looked up slowly. "I'm so warm I feel as though there is not enough air to breathe. I must rest and cool off a bit." She wiped her forehead slowly with the corner of her apron.

Jeddy looked up quickly, and Deidre said quietly, "Jeddy, you and Daniel go fetch a bucket of cool water from the well and bring it to us with a dipper."

"All right, Momma." He stood and reached for Daniel's hand.

Daniel grinned mischievously. "All right, Momma; me, too."

Deidre grinned back at the boys while she took her bonnet over to fan Mandy's face. Mandy motioned for her to sit beside her. "I think I stayed in the sun a bit too long. It seems unseasonably warm to me, don't you think?"

Deidre didn't mention that she had just said something similar. But as she sat beside Mandy, she said, "Yes, it's very warm. Some cool water will taste right good."

They were still while they waited for the boys to bring the water. The ringing of Ethan's ax as he chopped at the stumps was rhythmic in the distance. Between blows of the ax, they could hear the chatter of the boys as they obeyed. And then they heard other voices talking with the boys.

Deidre looked around. Visitors? In the middle of the week? Soon Mandy took notice, too.

Deidre was the first to speak. "It sounds like Ned. Why would Ned be here? And who else?" She paused for a few seconds while they listened; then she said as she laid a hand on Mandy's shoulder, "Stay here with the girls, and I'll go check."

She hadn't gone far up the path to the house when she saw a merry group coming toward her on the path. Ned was walking with Jeddy on his shoulders, Ned now carrying the bucket of water. Edna and Delaney were following him, holding Daniel's hands.

"We couldn't find anyone in the house so we came hunting," Ned said. "My wife has made some great gooseberry pies this week and we thought if you have time to come to the house we could all have a piece of pie."

Deidre and Mandy were both dumbfounded. Ethan had heard voices and was wiping his face and neck as he joined them. "You drove clear over here for a piece of pie?"

"Well, we thought we could visit a bit, too."

Mandy spoke up. "Is everything all right? Is there news of some kind?"

"Nope. Just wanted to visit with our neighbors a bit. 'Course, if you're too busy. . ." Ned's eyes twinkled.

Edna spoke up. "Ned, stop teasing. We actually do have something we want to talk to Deidre about. Well, Delaney wants to talk to her. Won't you come to the house and have a piece of pie while we chat?"

Everyone helped gather the tools and vegetable buckets. Edna and Delaney each picked up a little girl. While the group headed toward the house, Edna said, "I hope you don't mind; I put a pot of coffee on to boil before we came down to find you. It should be ready soon."

The women stopped at the outside basin to wash the dirt from their hands and faces. Ethan did the same. The boys were chattering with Ned as though they hadn't seen him for a month.

When they entered the house, there was much commotion cutting the pies and pouring the coffee, putting milk on the pie for the boys and getting the girls settled down. Finally sitting at the table, they all looked at Delaney.

"Well, this may be nothing at all. I don't know why I didn't think of it on Sunday when we were together, but, well. . ."

Everyone was silent while they waited for her to say what was on her mind. Finally, she laid down her fork and looked at Deidre. "I hardly know where to begin. The foreman at Rose Hill Plantation is named Jeremiah. He is a large Negro with wide-set eyes. He is very kind and gentle, in spite of being large. He has said that he has a wife and child at the plantation he worked previously. I've never asked where he was before he came to Rose Hill. I don't know if his child is a boy or a girl—it was born after he was taken from there. He doesn't talk about himself much. I just didn't think about the possibility when we were here on Sunday. Should we write to him and inquire?"

Deidre's eyes were huge, but she sat very still. Suddenly tears slid down her cheeks unheeded. Quietly she asked, "Does he have a space between his two front teeth? and a dimple on the side of his chin when he laughs?"

Delaney gasped. "Yes! He most certainly does! A noticeable space. And an unusual dimple."

Jedediah quietly slid off of the bench and walked around until he leaned on his mother while he listened carefully and looked at her questioningly. Deidre wrapped her arms around him and held him. There was a hush in the room except for the gurgles of the twins.

Then everyone seemed to talk at once.

"What should we do?"

"It can't be a coincidence."

"It must be him!"

"What can be done?"

Deidre sat with her face in her hands.

Finally Ned got their attention above all the commotion. "All right, let us devise a plan. Shall we have Delaney write to him and ask his wife's name?"

Mandy quickly responded, "I think we should be careful about telling too much about Deidre since she ran away. You never know into whose hands a letter might fall."

"It will be safe at Rose Hill," Delaney said confidently. "Mr. Wally and Miss Sue Ellen are very concerned for all the Negroes who work there. They refuse to call us slaves, even though they bought us. They give us a wage each year from the profits of the plantation, and after four years we can have our papers and be freed. Most of us have nowhere else to go, so we remain and work for a wage. We have built our own little village on their land. We have a good life there. They are unlike anyone else I know. We all know that if we work hard and help them earn as much as possible, they will use the money to free more Negroes. Miss Sue Ellen told me once that Mr. Wally would like to see all Negroes freed and independent some day. They educate us so we can live on our own and do well if we choose to do so.

"Jeremiah was actually free before I left, but he planned to stay and earn as much as he could so he could buy his wife's and child's freedom as soon as possible. I believe Mr. Wally was paying him extra money so he could save enough, but I don't know that for sure. The Traehdniks depend on Jeremiah a lot, but they will want him to be happy and find his family."

Mandy asked thoughtfully, "But if the letter should fall into other hands along the way?"

"It is not likely, but don't worry. I will be quite discreet in my writing."

"If you write your letter tonight, I will take it to Canton tomorrow. None of us have peace until we know for sure," said Ned.

Ethan had been very quiet, but now he spoke. "Why don't we join our hearts together and pray right now that God will send an answer swiftly?"

And so they did.

Chapter 23

July was hot and dry at Rose Hill. The fields of cotton were looking very good. The workers were meticulous about keeping the weeds out and keeping each plant growing well. Jeremiah had divided the land into sections, and each Negro was given a section to work as his own. Jeremiah had talked this plan over with Mr. Wally, who approved heartily.

Each Negro planted and cared for his own section of land and was allowed to be responsible for as many sections as he wanted. This year, instead of the workers being given a wage, they would work on percentages. Each Negro was to receive 25 percent of the profit from his section or sections. Obviously, it was of benefit to a worker to make his land as productive as possible.

Mr. Wally had offered an even higher percentage, but after meeting with all the workers, Jeremiah was able to report that they preferred to receive 25 percent, and that Mr. Wally could use any extra funds to purchase (and free) more Negroes.

Thus, everyone on the plantation was content and worked hard. The fields of cotton were neater and more productive than any others around. Jeremiah worked his own plot of ground but received an extra wage from Mr. Wally for overseeing and being available to help wherever help was needed. All in all, the people were all quite happy and content.

Miss Sue Ellen helped with the housework as she could, but there were plenty of Negro women who were glad to work in the house and kitchen gardens instead of in the cotton fields. They were paid a wage instead of a percentage.

Today was an exceptionally hot day. Mr. Wally and Miss Sue Ellen were sitting on the shaded front veranda in the late afternoon when a rider came up the driveway with a letter.

"Oh, Wally. It's another letter from Delaney. We must gather everyone together to read her letter to them." Miss Sue Ellen continued fanning herself slowly. In a few moments she said, "It's so hot I don't even feel like walking to tell the others. Perhaps we could read it and then share it with them tomorrow when everyone meets for worship?" She looked at Wally to get his opinion.

"Yes, read it. It is always good to hear from Delaney. God has been good to her." Wally still spoke deliberately, but he smiled happily at his wife as she gently slipped a hairpin under the seal and opened the envelope carefully. As she turned the envelope over she looked a bit puzzled.

"Delaney usually addresses her letters to 'All my dear friends at Rose Hill Plantation,' but this letter is addressed only to 'Mr. and Mrs. Walter Traehdnik.' Perhaps it is not to be shared at all." She carefully unfolded the pages and read quietly for their ears only:

"Dear Mr. Wally and Miss Sue Ellen,

The most unusual thing has happened, for which I need to ask your help. We recently visited with good friends of Ned and Edna Browning here in Indiana. They are a white family who have a Negro woman and her son living with them. I have just discovered that the Negro woman (her name is Deidre, and her son's name is Jedediah) ran away from a plantation in the South called Devil's Bend because of severe mistreatment and a pending sale of the little boy.

As we spoke together, I told her about our Jeremiah there at Rose Hill. As she described her husband, they certainly sound like one and the same. How many large, black Jeremiahs could there be with a space between his two front teeth and an unusual dimple on the side of his chin?

I am writing to you to inquire what we should do about this situation. Deidre fears coming back to the South since she is a runaway and could be punished severely should she be discovered. But she loves her husband and longs to be reunited with him.

When the harvest is completed this fall, might you be willing to send Jeremiah to Indiana to meet her? Or do you have another idea?

She is very wary about me disclosing her information to you, but I reassured her of your heart for all people to be free and for families to be reunited. If you tell Jeremiah, please reassure him that they both are loved and well cared for in the Evanston household, and that they are happy except that they miss him very much and long to be with him. We will together be looking for a letter of advice and information from you.

I continue happily in this household until such a time that we shall be reunited.

Delaney"

Sue Ellen dropped the letter into her lap. She didn't know what to say or think. She stared at her husband and could tell that he was deep in thought, too.

Finally he looked over at her and said quietly, "Let's pray for wisdom, Sue Ellen. And for guidance."

"Yes. Let's go into the library and pray. I don't really want word getting around until we can talk to Jeremiah ourselves."

"Yes, that's good." Wally slowly pulled himself to his feet, reached for his cane, and walked with deliberate steps into the house, with Sue Ellen right behind him.

The Traehdnik household had an understanding with all who lived on the plantation. For the most part, the library door remained open. But when it was closed, it was generally for prayer for one thing or another, and no one was to enter unless it was for something very important. All the servants as well as the children respected that completely.

After a time of prayer together, Wally and Sue Ellen discussed what should be done about the situation. After considerable thought, they decided to call Jeremiah in and let him read the letter and ask what he wanted to do.

Jeremiah was hoeing the ground in his plot of cotton. The afternoon was very warm, but the sky was clear and he was taking much pride in the many lovely fields full of cotton on this plantation. His idea of having all the workers take care of their own patch of ground was working well, because they would make only as much money as they were each willing to work for. They all knew that Mr. Wally would indeed give them their share of the earnings. It certainly made working the field a pure pleasure.

Jeremiah felt good as the sun warmed his large shoulders and black head, and the freshly loosened earth cooled his feet. The cotton flowers were mostly gone now. The bolls were growing and would soon be bursting with the soft white cotton fibers. He knew they would have a very good crop for Rose Hill this year, and all the Negroes would profit as well.

Jeremiah took a moment to lean on his hoe and study the fields surrounding his. Yes, the others were taking pride in their plots also. He breathed deeply. He loved the scent of the freshly turned, warm earth and closed his eyes to savor the moment.

Then he opened his eyes quickly. He heard running footsteps and then a child calling, "Jeremiah, Jeremiah!"

His heart stopped as he thought of Mr. Wally being in trouble again. Then he saw Mr. Wally's son Nate running crazily through the fields in his direction, motioning with his hand as he ran.

Jeremiah dropped his hoe and ran toward the boy, filled with fear and unspoken prayer. But as he neared, Nate said breathlessly, "Daddy and Mama have asked you to come to the house to talk to them as soon as you have time."

"Is everyone all right? Your father?"

"Yes, everyone is fine. Mother just came out to where we were playing and asked me to run to tell you that they need to talk to you when you have time."

"Thank you, Nate. I will gather my tools and come with ya now."

"May I carry your hoe, Jeremiah?"

"Of course you may." Jeremiah handed the hoe to the boy and walked toward the house with his hand lovingly on the boy's shoulder. "You'll be a man soon, Nate. And you'll make a fine master of the house."

The young boy looked up at the man with a question in his eyes. "Do you really think so, Jeremiah? Do you think I will be good like my daddy?"

"I hope so, Son. I pray ya will, and if you try hard and trust in God to help you, I know ya will."

Nate walked quietly by his side. Jeremiah couldn't help loving the boy. His own son would be half the age of Nate by now; Jeremiah also wondered what he was like. Putting his hand on young Nate's head, he said, "Always be kind, Nate. No matter what people say or do to you, always be kind. If you decide to keep kindness in yer heart, there is nothin' anyone can do to ya to steal it out. And you'll always have a friend if you are always kind. You'll be just like yer own daddy."

Nate gazed at Jeremiah with admiring eyes. "I will, Jeremiah. I will."

As they passed the toolshed, Jeremiah stopped to clean his hoe so it would be ready for another day. While Nate watched intently, Jeremiah said, "Always take good care of yer tools, Nate, and they'll serve you well. If you leave 'em out in the weather to rust and rot, you are throwin' yer money away. You must take good care of 'em to get the most out of 'em."

Nate grasped the oilcan and an old rag that hung on a nail and handed it to Jeremiah after he had washed the dirt off his hoe. Jeremiah rubbed the metal with the oiled rag before hanging the hoe on the nail on the wall. "That's good, Nate. The oil will keep the hoe from rustin'. You're learnin' well."

The boy smiled proudly.

As they neared the house, Jeremiah could smell the good aromas of dinner. He knew he would be invited to participate in the meal with the Traehdnik family. He could hear Mammy as she talked with the children somewhere not too far away. Nate said a quick good-bye and ran to be with the other children.

Miss Sue Ellen stood looking out the screen door as he climbed the steps to the wide veranda. "Good evening, Jeremiah. It's good to see you."

"Thank ya, ma'am. I got word that you wished to speak with me?"

She held the screen door open for Jeremiah. "Mr. Wally and I wish to talk with you about a letter we just received from Delaney. Won't you join us in the library?"

As soon as Jeremiah sat down, Miss Sue Ellen offered him a frosty glass of sweet lemonade. The lemons had done very well this year, and the lemonade tasted exceptionally good. He drank thirstily, and Miss Sue Ellen refilled his glass before she even sat down.

When he smiled at her, Mr. Wally spoke. "Jeremiah, we received a letter from Delaney that we wish to have you read. Then we will discuss the possibilities."

Jeremiah looked at him questioningly, then at Miss Sue Ellen, but she just smiled sweetly as she handed him a folded sheet of paper. She sat down and waited while he read. Jeremiah had only learned to read in the past few years here at Rose Hill and was still somewhat slow at the task. But soon he raised his head in awe. Quietly he said, "Could it be? Could it really be?"

"Jeremiah, of course it could all be a mistake. But it certainly does sound like it is for real. Mr. Wally and I both think it sounds like a good possibility that Delaney has found your wife and son." Mr. Wally was nodding happily.

Jeremiah was speechless. Many questions ran wildly through his head. Indiana? How far was that? How would he ever get to them? When could he go?

When he didn't say anything, Miss Sue Ellen continued. "Mr. Wally and I thought that perhaps we could make the trip to Indiana together—the three of us. Then, if it is truly your wife and you wish to stay, he and I would come home together. Or if you wish to bring her back here with you, we would make arrangements for us all to travel home together. The fields are planted and growing well. Do you think Alexander could oversee everything here now until we returned? Your idea of everyone having their own field was excellent. The crop is looking better than it ever has before. I think the time to take a month or two away is now, don't you?"

"Yes, I suppose we could," Jeremiah responded. "That is very generous of y'all. I would love to go to see if this is really my Deidre. Do you really think we could? When do you think we would leave?" Suddenly Jeremiah had more questions than he knew how to ask.

When they were called to dinner, they continued to discuss the options and the plans while they ate. After dinner they went back to the library to finish their plans.

As Jeremiah walked back to his little house under the full moon that night, he looked up at the moon and smiled at the face he saw there, thinking that somewhere out there, Deidre might be looking at the very same moon. And the path between them was getting suddenly much straighter.

Chapter 24

There was much to be done in only a week's time before they left for Indiana. Jeremiah worked diligently with Alexander. The young man wrote volumes of notes as he listened solemnly to everything Jeremiah had to say to him. He was a very smart young man, and Jeremiah was confident that he would serve the Traehdniks and all the Negroes fairly and well.

Jeremiah stressed to him that he should never forget from where he came. Just because God had seen fit to give him some administrative abilities did not make him any better than the ones to whom he was giving guidance.

"And remember. That's all you're here for: to give guidance. Let each man work his land the way he sees best to do it. If his crop is not as good as it could be, he will learn and do better next year. But if'n ya force him to do it yer way—even if it is a better way—you're stealin' his freedom just as though ya were buyin' him on the auction block. Respect each man's personality and abilities. But any way ya can see to help out, be willin' to work at it and help all men. You will never be sorry if you help someone improve himself or pick up slack where there is a need."

Alexander continued to write in his notebook. Jeremiah chuckled. "Will you know where to look in your notebook each time you have a question?"

Alexander didn't smile but said very soberly, "I will read the notes over and over until I become as good an overseer as you are, Jeremiah."

"Well, just never forget to pray and seek God's guidance. And never be too serious to laugh. Laughter is good for your soul. The Bible says so. Did you know that, Alexander?"

"Do you mean Proverbs 15:13 that says, 'A merry heart maketh a cheerful countenance?' or Proverbs 17:22 that says, 'A merry heart doeth good like a medicine?'"

"Yes, both of those teach the same lesson. It is a good thing to be jolly."

Alexander still did not smile but continued to write rapidly in his book. Jeremiah observed the young man, shook his head, and ran his hands through his hair, and stood to go. "And don't forget that you can ride over for help from Mr. Bart if you have any questions."

Jeremiah had a little money tucked away that he had been saving to buy Deidre's freedom. Now that he had been given not only Deidre's papers but Jedediah's also, he felt the money could be used as he needed. He really did not know how much the trip would cost, but he did know that he needed some new clothes.

The Traehdniks were very generous with the Negroes and encouraged them to dress nicely. Jeremiah had been very conservative with his money, hoping he could earn enough to purchase his family, so had worn his clothes as long as possible. His clothes were faded and worn, although still serviceable as work clothes, but he wanted to look nice as he rode the trains and when he saw Deidre.

He rode into town to make some purchases for himself. He had spent very little time in the town, knowing that Negroes were not welcome most places, but he was certain it would be different if he had money to spend. He was eager to bring his family to his nice little home, so he wanted to know a bit more about the town where they would go to buy their supplies.

After leaving his horse at the stables, Jeremiah first walked along the street to look at the various stores. Soon he noticed that folks pretended he was not there, and they would not speak to him. He looked into the store windows but was ignored by the white folks inside.

When he saw a store with ready-made men's clothing, he decided to go inside and inquire about the clothes. There were several people in the store, and he could hear conversation as he opened the door. But when he stepped inside, the store became suddenly silent. Jeremiah looked around and noticed that everyone was staring at him. One gentleman came up to him abruptly and said in a businesslike tone, "May I help you?"

Still everyone in the store was silent. All heads had swiveled to stare at Jeremiah. He cleared his throat and spoke softly to the man, "I am going on a trip and need some clothes."

"I'm sorry. We don't serve niggers here."

Jeremiah was expecting some rude treatment, but this completely surprised him. He was speechless momentarily. Before he could think what to say or do, the man spoke again.

"Did you hear me? There's nothing for you in here. You'll have to get your fancy clothes somewhere else."

Jeremiah dropped his head and turned to leave. He walked out of the store without speaking a word. On the sidewalk he turned back toward the stables. There had been a Negro who had taken his horse. Perhaps he could ask him where to purchase new clothes.

At the stable, Jeremiah waited until there was no one else around and asked the man there where he could buy some clothes.

"They ain' nowheres in this here town that a nigger can shop. Wher' you from?"

"I live and work at Rose Hill Plantation."

"Why cain't ya git yer clothes out thar?"

"Well, I do get my clothing there for the most part. But I'm leavin' on an important trip and was hopin' to purchase a tailored suit and some other things and thought it would be quicker to get some things ready-made."

"Well, it ain' gonna happen in this here town fer sure. Better git—"

His sentence was cut short by a carriage pulling up to the stables. Looking around, Jeremiah was surprised to see Mr. Bart jump down. At this point Jeremiah was so confused he didn't quite know what to expect, so instead of greeting Mr. Bart, he stood quietly to see if he was spoken to first.

Mr. Bart came around his carriage and handed the reins to the man to whom Jeremiah had been speaking. Suddenly his face broke into a large smile, and he reached for Jeremiah's hand. "Well, look who's here. What brings you into town on this fine day, Jeremiah?" He clapped Jeremiah soundly on the shoulder in his joy and began walking out of the stables with Jeremiah at his side.

Jeremiah stopped outside and explained what had happened to him.

Mr. Bart's face turned red and he looked at Jeremiah seriously. "How badly do you need a suit of clothes, Jeremiah?"

Jeremiah told Mr. Bart about the letter and the pending trip and why he had wanted to purchase new clothes. But he turned back toward the stables with heavy shoulders. "Guess it doesn't really matter. I'll see what Claudette and her girls at the plantation can get stitched up for me before we go."

"Yes, it does matter, Jeremiah. It matters a lot. Come with me, and let's see what we can do about new clothes for you."

"Nah, Mr. Bart. I don't want to cause any trouble."

"You're not the one causing trouble, Jeremiah. You come with me and let's see what we can find for you."

Together they turned toward town, but Jeremiah hung his head reluctantly. He really didn't want to cause a disturbance, and he sure didn't want to smudge Mr. Bart's good name.

Mr. Bart steered him toward the same store from which Jeremiah had come. Mr. Bart entered and held the door open for Jeremiah. Jeremiah was reluctant to enter, but Mr. Bart called out loudly to the owner while continuing to hold the door for Jeremiah, "Donald, my friend here needs some clothes for an upcoming journey. Do you have some things that will suit him? Or will I need to take my family's business somewhere else?"

The same man who had spoken to Jeremiah earlier came over and looked at Mr. Bart somewhat apologetically. He hung his head slightly and murmured, "Now, Bart, you know we serve good people here, but we don't serve niggers in here. If there is something *you* need, I'm glad to help you, but tell your friend to go back out to the farm to get his clothes."

"Donald, I've purchased a good amount of clothing from you, as has my brother and many of my friends. I'm afraid if you refuse to sell to my friend here, I will have to take my business elsewhere. I'm certain you will miss the business of my family, Wally's family, and our friends. By the time I'm finished with you, you may even have to open your store in a different town."

"Well, now, we don't mean to be difficult. I suppose if he's a friend of yours. I just don't want those people to start thinking they can come in here anytime they want." He looked at Jeremiah and moved toward the clothing. "How was I to know he had money? And where did he get his money? What sort of clothes does he need?"

Mr. Bart motioned for Jeremiah to come farther into the store, and Jeremiah did so reluctantly. Mr. Bart spoke again to the owner with exaggerated patience. "Well, I guess if you want to know what he needs, you will just have to ask him, don't you think? And where he got his money is his business, not yours or mine." Mr. Bart shook his head subtly at Jeremiah to indicate he should not respond until the man spoke to him.

Jeremiah caught himself before he smiled at Mr. Bart. This might be fun after all.

⟶∞⟵

After they left the store, Mr. Bart headed back toward the stables with Jeremiah, who was carrying his new clothes. They continued their conversation about the letter.

Mr. Bart looked at Jeremiah thoughtfully. "Isn't it great the way God works? I am so thankful that we were able to purchase Deidre's papers this past spring. Now the two of you can decide together how and where you want to spend the rest of your life." He paused briefly, but Jeremiah knew he had something more to say, so he waited. In a short time, Mr. Bart continued. "And Jeremiah, I want to tell you that I know my brother-in-law and sister will miss you terribly if you decide to stay up North, as would Adele and I and all the folk on our two plantations, but you must realize that things are only going to get harder for the Negroes in the South. What we experienced this afternoon is only a sample of what is to come. What we all want for you is what is truly best for you and for your family. Think about it and pray about it before you decide."

Mr. Bart stopped in the street. His eyes met Jeremiah's squarely.

Jeremiah nodded solemnly. "I guess things are changin'. I'll pray about it, Mr.

Bart. Yes, I'll pray about it."

They stood for a moment in companionable silence, and then Mr. Bart said, "I really didn't have anything important that I need to do today. I think I'll ride out to Rose Hill with you. Let's tie your horse on behind and you can ride in my carriage. The clothing will ride better in the carriage than on horseback anyway. And I could use some of Eliza's good lemonade."

Chapter 25

It was on the train that Sue Ellen realized that she had not taken the time to respond to Delaney's letter. No one knew they were coming to Indiana! Things had happened so fast on the plantation that she had not even thought of it.

When she told Wally, he patted her hand and smiled. "Well, perhaps it's best this way. Just in case it really is the wrong woman, we will not have raised her hopes needlessly."

"Yes, I suppose. But I don't know how it could be the wrong woman. And I think Jeremiah feels the same way. There are too many indications to be a coincidence. I believe I feel the hand of God working, don't you?"

Wally smiled. "Yes, I do feel the hand of God in this. And I do believe that Jeremiah does also." He sighed heavily. "I wish so much that he could have ridden in this car with us. There's just *no* good reason that he can't. I am going to put up more of a fight to get him up here with us. I'm going to miss that good man if he decides to stay in Indiana, but I do believe Bart is right. He and his family would be better off there than in the South. I fear some hard times are coming in the South, and I believe he'll be safer in the North. Did you know that in Indiana all blacks are free? I hope I live to see the day when it is that way everywhere. And that it will not be profitable to be bringing them over from Africa anymore. I hope I live to see the day."

"I am thankful that God gave you the heart and the ability to free as many as you have through the years, Wally. And that you teach them to be independent and how to live in this country as free people."

"I am thankful that God has blessed us in such a way that we have the means to free as many as we have. And I pray that we can continue to do so in the future. It never fails to amaze me at the way God has blessed our land and crops since we have been doing this. I am convinced that He is making it possible for us to free more and more."

They were silent for a little while, and then Sue Ellen spoke again. "I am thankful that God has blessed us with this trip. I feel like Jeremiah is one of our own children. I'm happy that we have the opportunity to meet his wife ourselves and know what kind of family he will have. I do hope she is as good a woman as he thinks she is."

Wally looked at his wife's face. "You are worrying like a mother hen over her baby chicks." He smiled. "Better stop it, or you'll soon be fretting over those wrinkles between your brows." He paused while she smiled and then added, "I pray he has made as wise a choice for a wife as I have. And I hope he will be as happy as I am."

Sue Ellen kissed her husband and then patted his hand.

Suddenly there was loud clanging, and the conductor entered their train car. "We are stopping at this next station if anyone needs to get off the train to refresh yourself or get some fresh air. There is a store around the corner from the station if you wish to purchase snacks and a restaurant on the other side of the store. We will be loading some freight at this stop, so we will be here for one hour before leaving. Please be certain to be in your seats and have your tickets available for checking in one hour. Are there any questions?"

Sue Ellen nudged her husband and whispered near his ear. "Where are we?"

Wally cleared his throat and asked the conductor, "Where are we and how much farther to Brownsville, Indiana?"

"We have just entered Ohio Territory, and will be in Brownsville in approximately ten hours." He glanced briefly around the car. Apparently satisfied he had answered all questions, he left the car.

Sue Ellen whispered to her husband again. "I have a plan. Let's get off the train and watch to see if there might be a change of personnel. If there is, and if we can find Jeremiah, let's suggest to him that he get on our car for the rest of the journey. Isn't Ohio a free territory?"

"Hmmm...well, that might not be a bad idea. What can it hurt to try? But we'll ask Jeremiah what he thinks of the idea. More than anything I don't want to cause further embarrassment or harassment for him."

"Yes, of course you're right."

Soon they were stepping into the warm sunlight of the late afternoon. There was a nice breeze and the air felt refreshing. They stood together for a little while watching the train and soon saw their conductor leaving the train and even leaving the station. They were debating whether to go to the restaurant for a snack when they saw Jeremiah walking toward them. Sue Ellen motioned for him to join them so she could tell him about their plan.

"I don't want to cause any trouble, but I'm willing to do whatever you all want. It certainly would be nice to have the time to visit and be together."

Wally interjected. "I think since we've seen the conductor leave that you should just get on with us and we won't ask any questions. If they make us separate, we will and not cause any trouble, but how will the new conductor know but what you are supposed to be in our car?"

After enjoying dishes of cold custard and fruit, they returned to the train. They were encouraged by the fact that Jeremiah had been served at the restaurant at their table and no comments had been made at all. They had seen two other Negroes eating at the establishment, so apparently it was not an unusual sight in this area.

When they reboarded the train, Jeremiah retrieved his bag from the car he had ridden previously and got in the car with Mr. Wally and Miss Sue Ellen. Before long other people began filling the car, and there were a few new faces. Soon the new conductor began making his way through the car checking the tickets. When he checked their tickets he looked at them and asked, "Are you traveling together?"

Wally responded in a friendly vein, "Yes, we are visiting some friends in Indiana."

"Indiana is beautiful," the gentleman replied. "I trust you will enjoy your visit." And with that, he moved on to the next group of seats.

Sue Ellen nudged Wally's ribs gently, while Wally and Jeremiah smiled at one another. This was the way it should be. As they rode, Sue Ellen realized that she really wanted this for Jeremiah. Even though she and all of Rose Hill would miss him terribly, they longed to see him be treated with the respect that he should have. Her heart swelled with the fear that Jeremiah might be moving away from them permanently, but her great love for him would not allow her to wish him back to the way he would always be treated at home.

Chapter 26

Deidre smiled as she finished stitching the binding on the blue and yellow quilt. Her wing of the house was looking very lovely. Ever since her conversation with Delaney a few weeks back, she was filled with hopes and daydreams of someday bringing her Jeremiah here to live with her. It seemed each day her heart grew lighter.

She had never been as happy as she had been since coming to live here with Mandy and Ethan. She had felt content, but always there was that nagging concern in the back of her heart—that sense of loss at being so far from Jeremiah. Now, to quiet her heart, she tried to reason that the possibility Delaney knew *her* Jeremiah could all be a mistake, but still something told her to have faith. Was God really answering her prayers? She had thought she had faith, but why was she so surprised at God's ways?

Ethan had placed windows on two sides of her room. This afternoon as she completed these final stitches, she sat in the rocker, which she had moved away from the fireplace to catch the breeze between the two windows. Mandy had been helping her but had left to feed the girls and tuck them into their bed for their afternoon naps.

Deidre paused and looked toward her windows. The white lace curtains that hung there fluttered in the afternoon breeze. How lovely her room would be when she finished the quilt and put it on her bed. Throughout the past winter she and Mandy had braided a beautiful brown and blue rug that she kept by the fireplace and another like it by her bed. Yes, this quilt would be the finishing touch. Oh, if only Jeremiah could share this place with her!

Her hands stopped sewing and rested in her lap. She leaned her head against the back of the rocker, closing her eyes as she thought of her husband. She believed with all her heart that God would answer her prayers. Being patient was the hard part.

"Is it finished yet?" Mandy's cheerful voice preceded her into the room. "Oh, did I waken you?" She had a cold glass of apple cider in each hand.

"No, just woolgatherin'." Deidre glanced up and smiled. "Oh, that looks good."

"Yes, I'm glad Ethan tried making it with the drop apples. It's not as good as fall cider, but it sure is a good reminder of what's to come."

"Come sit with me while I finish. There isn't enough left for both of us to sew, but I'd love to have your company while I finish."

"Deidre, didn't you have a piece of that blue fabric left over?" Mandy pointed to the piece in the quilt that had small yellow flowers on a blue background.

"Yes, there was a good-sized piece."

"Why don't I make a small tablecloth that we can edge in the yellow gingham for on the small table that sits by your window?"

"Oh, that's a splendid idea." Deidre set her glass on the windowsill near her elbow and got up to get the material for Mandy. Looking back over her shoulder as she opened the bureau drawer, she said, "Mandy, Ethan has spoiled me terribly with all this lovely furniture. I feel like a queen every time I open the bureau drawers or sit in the rocker or dust the little table or lay in my bed. Who would have ever thought I'd have such a life?"

Mandy giggled. "We truly do have lovely furniture, thanks to my husband's talent. I am certainly glad he loves making things with his hands. We both get to benefit."

Deidre laid the piece of fabric in Mandy's lap. Mandy fingered it lovingly and then sat still, drinking her cider slowly. The two women sat together enjoying the cool breeze, the sweet cider, and the contentment of friendship.

Deidre's eyes opened slowly. Something had awakened her, and she tried to get her bearings to determine what it was. Then she heard it. At night she often left the door between Jedediah's room and hers slightly ajar. She smiled to herself as she heard the whispers next door that had awakened her.

Often since she and Jeddy had moved to this side of the cabin, Daniel would sneak over and crawl into Jeddy's bed as soon as it was light, and the two would whisper and giggle like two teenage girls. How precious it was to see the love between those two friends in spite of nearly a three-year age difference.

Deidre smiled as she thought of the way Jeddy loved and protected his little friend. He could be quite solemn, taking Daniel's side if he thought there was any injustice being served to his friend. Daniel looked to Jeddy for the final word on any decision or thought. Their friendship was indeed a thrill to a mother's heart. And Deidre knew that Mandy enjoyed watching it grow as much as she did.

Soon Deidre was dressed and pulling up the new quilt on her bed when she heard thunder rumbling in the distance. "Oh, no," she groaned. "I wanted to weed and prune the flower gardens today."

Mandy's head came in the doorway. "I was just walking by—what did you say?" She bounced Christy on her hip, holding Callie's hand in her other hand. The girls were just over a year old now and were walking everywhere, but Christy still preferred to be carried.

Deidre smiled. "I was grumblin' because I heard thunder, and I had wanted to work in the flower gardens today."

"You must have slept well last night. It rained all night and thundered and lit the place up with lightning. You didn't hear it?"

Deidre dropped the corner of the quilt she'd been holding, staring at Mandy's grinning face in consternation. "No, I didn't hear any thunder. Mandy, are you playin' with me?"

"I am not. Look outside for yourself. I think the rain is past, and by the time we're ready to go outdoors it should be an excellent day to work in the flower gardens. The ground will be soft, and I think the rain lowered the temperature considerably."

Deidre had walked to the window while Mandy spoke and was shaking her head. "Things sure are different on the west end of the house. I did not hear that storm at all, but the world sure looks washed clean and fresh. I love it when it rains at night and the world is fresh in the mornin'."

The two women left the bedroom together. Deidre turned back at Jeddy's doorway. "You boys should get your clothes on and get washed. Breakfast will be ready before you know it."

"We will, Momma." Jeddy was quick to obey.

"We will, Momma."

Deidre stuck her head in the doorway in time to see the two boys giggling at Daniel's imitation of his friend. She grinned as she walked to the kitchen. "That Daniel is getting to be quite a tease."

"Is he mimicking Jeddy again?"

Deidre smiled. "It really is so precious."

"Hmmm, I'm just worried he will carry it too far." Mandy's brows were drawn together.

"I will talk to Jeddy about teaching him respect. It might be much easier learnin' it from his friend."

"That's good, but I'll have a talk with Daniel also. Or perhaps Ethan should."

Deidre hung the dish towels on the peg beside the cupboard while Mandy finished wiping the table and spread the cloth on it. Deidre brought the jar of flowers for the center of it and was picking out the dying flowers as Mandy threw the dishpan of water on the flowers outside the back door.

"Guess they don't need the water so much today, but the lye soap will help keep the bugs off the leaves." Mandy wiped the dishpan and hung it on its peg on the side of the cupboard.

Deidre started for the back door, scooping Christy into her arms as she went. "We'll go to the shed and bring the garden tools if you and Callie want to go ahead and head for the garden."

She walked down the path to the shed that Ethan had built near the gardens, breathing in the freshly washed air. The ground was soft enough to be easy to work today, but not pure mud. Deidre couldn't help humming as she walked, and soon Christy was humming, too, albeit a different tune altogether. Deidre grinned and kissed the baby's tender neck, making her giggle. She felt as light as a feather today. Deidre couldn't help thinking that perhaps Delaney would receive a letter today.

Chapter 27

Delaney had stepped outside the front door to shake the breakfast crumbs out of the tablecloth when she heard what sounded like a horse and carriage. She stood still and listened carefully, and soon she was certain it was coming their way. However, she knew it was not coming from the direction of the Evanstons' home but from the direction of the town.

Indoors the Browning family was chattering and scurrying around cleaning up from breakfast and making preparations for their day of chores. Delaney knew there was too much commotion for them to hear the visitors coming. She never knew why she stood there watching instead of telling the family, but something held her to the spot until the carriage came into view.

A large black man was driving the carriage and the couple inside looked amazingly like her dear friends, the Traehdniks. How many couples had that color of hair? She was frozen to the spot until she was sure. It really was!

Throwing the tablecloth over her arm, she ran to meet the carriage. As soon as it stopped, Miss Sue Ellen jumped down as though she was still a teenager, and the two women hugged and cried. Mr. Wally stood slightly behind his wife, leaning on his cane and grinning as though he had conquered the world.

Delaney greeted Mr. Wally warmly too, just as the Negro came around the back corner of the carriage. "Jeremiah! Oh, you came! Oh, Jeremiah, I didn't know you all were coming. I am so glad to see you." She was jumping up and down and clapping her hands.

Soon the Brownings became aware that someone had come and they all came outside to greet the visitors. Breathlessly Delaney explained and introduced them all, while Edna invited them all in for coffee.

As they sat around the table, they told the story of their trip in response to Delaney's letter. Sue Ellen explained about their rush to get ready for the journey and forgetting to let them know they were coming.

Finally Ned said what Jeremiah had been longing to hear. "Let's not waste these people's time. Let's take them over to the Evanstons' so they can see Deidre and Jedediah. We'd all like to be there to witness this, but I really think these young people need to meet without a crowd. Why don't Mother and I stay home with the children while the rest of you go?" Edna looked at her husband for his opinion.

Ned turned to Delaney. "You know the way by now, don't you? Why don't you go with them and the rest of us will stay here? You can tell us all about it later."

Jeremiah looked at Mr. Wally, who spoke slowly. "Well, then, we'd best be on our way. I know that Jeremiah has waited a long time for this day, and I trust he will not be disappointed."

There were several mutterings of affirmation while the Traehdniks rose to their feet. Sue Ellen tilted her head toward Mrs. Norman. "Before we leave the area, we must have some time to visit together, too."

Mrs. Norman grinned. "Yes, my friend, I look forward to visiting with you as well." She gestured toward the doorway, where Jeremiah stood with his hat in his hands. "But now is not the time."

Everyone laughed merrily, while Jeremiah ducked his head. Ned went over and patted Jeremiah's large shoulder. "You've waited a long time for this day, son. I'd be in a hurry myself. And I do pray it will be a day of success for you."

⌒◦⌒

The carriage they had rented was light, and the horse was a lively young filly that loved to trot. Jeremiah wanted to make the horse run but tried to be thankful for the lively trot. The same prayer went over and over in his mind: *Please, God. . .Please, God. . .Please, God!*

Delaney and the Traehdniks were busily talking and listening as they each shared what had happened in their lives since they had seen each other. Jeremiah tried to listen. He really was very happy for Delaney to have this opportunity. He knew she loved the Traehdniks and longed to help all the Negroes at Rose Hill to become educated so they could have a good life if they should ever leave Rose Hill Plantation.

Jeremiah also was pleased that Delaney was learning so much so that Jedediah could have a good education when he brought his wife and son home with him. He smiled as he thought of his nice little home at Rose Hill. And he thought of the community of dear friends with whom he worked and lived. He was eager to show his Deidre and Jedediah to them all and eager to have them where he could care for them.

"It's not far now!" Delaney seemed almost as excited as he was.

He turned to smile at her and saw the eagerness on Mr. Wally's and Miss Sue Ellen's faces. *Thank You, God,* he prayed in his heart. So much of his life he had been alone or afraid. It was more wonderful than he could express to know he was loved and safe. And then he also prayed, *Thank You, God, for healing Mr. Wally. It is good to see him almost back to normal once again.*

"Can you see it?" Delaney sounded like a small child in her eagerness. "Can you see the clearing? Their house is just around that bend. They've probably heard us already."

Mandy heard the carriage soon after she started working in the flower garden. Jeddy and Daniel were playing on the front porch. Callie wandered around the clearing, but soon heard the commotion and began running for her mother. Mandy scooped up the baby and stood watching while she rubbed her hands on her apron. Deidre and Christy had not yet returned from the garden shed.

It didn't sound like the Brownings' horses and wagons. And it couldn't be the Brownings, because no one was singing. While Mandy was thinking this, Ethan came around the house and walked over to where she was standing. She eyed him questioningly, but he looked puzzled too.

"I can't think who it would be, Mandy, but I guess we'll find out soon enough."

Mandy was thankful for his presence and remembered with a shudder how she had felt when the stranger had come through the woods years ago to tell her that Ethan was dead. She gazed at his thoughtful face again and smiled at him. He gave her waist a slight squeeze as the horse and carriage came into view.

Mandy was disappointed when she didn't recognize the carriage or the people inside, but she was still happy to have visitors. When she looked again more carefully, she recognized Delaney. But who were the others? Before she had much time to think about it, they had stopped and were climbing out of the carriage. Ethan had taken the horse's bridle to tie it to the fence.

Delancy quickly spoke. "Mandy, Ethan, this is Mr. and Mrs. Traehdnik from Rose Hill Plantation where I live, and this is Jeremiah!"

Since Jeremiah was standing politely behind the others, Ethan and Mandy reached to shake the Traehdniks' hands first. But almost simultaneously they looked up at the tall black man. When he smiled at them, they both gasped. He was obviously an older, much larger version of Jedediah. Mandy's hands flew to her face as tears began to stream down her cheeks.

The Traehdniks quickly stepped aside as Mandy reached for Jeremiah's hand. "Oh, my. . .you *must* be Jeremiah!"

When he nodded, Mandy quickly looked toward the porch, where the two boys were watching the visitors from behind the railing. Mandy turned back to Jeremiah and laid her finger across her lips. She wanted him to see Deidre first, but he had already seen the boys. He looked back at Mandy, then at his son again as tears trickled down his dark cheeks.

"Come." Mandy took his hand. "Come, and I will take you to her."

The others stood back silently smiling as Mandy led Jeremiah around the house and down the path to the garden shed. Just before they reached it, they heard Deidre humming. Turning the corner in the path, Jeremiah stopped dead in his tracks as he stood face-to-face with his wife.

Mandy scooped Christy out of Deidre's arms as the couple continued to stare at one another. Swiftly turning, Mandy hurried back to the house to welcome their other guests.

Chapter 28

Deidre did not move, staring at the big man who stood in the path in front of her. Her heart leaped as she realized it was not her imagination. It truly was Jeremiah, and he looked just as she remembered. She reached one hand to touch his cheek. The tears brimming in his eyes overflowed.

With trembling hands, Jeremiah gently cupped her face and gazed deeply into her eyes. "Deidre. Is it really you? I was afraid to hope." His voice was no more than a whisper.

She didn't speak. She couldn't speak, for her heart was overflowing. At last she whispered back, "Jeremiah, my Jeremiah. God has brought you to me." And with all the longing she had stored up all these years, she embraced him.

Deidre had no idea how long they stood there, together, wrapped in each other's arms. She only knew, once again, the contentment she'd always felt as she nestled close to Jeremiah and felt his heart beating joyously for her.

At last she drew back and touched his lips with her finger. "Come with me. Let's sit by the stream and talk a bit before I take you to meet Jedediah."

He followed her as she walked down the well-worn path to the gurgling stream. They sat under the spreading boughs of a large maple tree and told of their experiences as briefly as they could.

Jeremiah explained to Deidre about Mr. Wally buying him at the auction and taking the chains off right away. He told of the kind Traehdnik family and the way they bought slaves regularly at the auction so they could free them. Deidre marveled that there were truly some good people who bought slaves at that auction. Jeremiah explained to her about the way the Traehdniks allowed each slave to purchase their freedom and to earn a wage if they wanted to work at the plantation. And that their work in turn enabled the family to purchase more slaves and that they could then earn their freedom and so on. He told how they worked to educate the Negroes so they could earn a wage and live independently when they left the plantation.

Deidre shared her experiences at Devil's Bend and why she had felt the urgency to leave with their son. She told of the long, long walk they had taken to finally arrive here on that snowy May day, and of Mandy finding her and offering her a home. She told about her life here with the Evanstons and how happy they were together.

Together they marveled at how God had worked in both of their lives in the past six years to bring them to this point.

Deidre sighed. "It makes me think of the verse in Romans that says God works all things together for our good if we love Him. Even the bad things we went through in the past served to bring us to this place. God is always faithful to keep His promises—even when it seems impossible!" Again Deidre snuggled tightly against Jeremiah's chest, and he had to lower his head to hear all that she said.

In a little while Deidre jumped to her feet and grabbed his hands. "Come, Jeremiah. You must meet your son. He looks just like you. And his heart is just like yours, too."

They hurried up to the cabin and entered through the back door to find the others all drinking coffee and eating cookies around the table. Jedediah was sitting silently beside Daniel on a bench at the back of the table. Both heads swiveled to stare at Jeremiah soberly; then Daniel looked at his friend.

Deidre greeted everyone and then turned to Jedediah. "Jeddy, come and meet your daddy."

Jedediah stood obediently and started toward his mother. Daniel stood with his friend and stayed by his side until Mandy lifted Daniel suddenly into her arms. While she was standing, she looked at the others and said, "Why don't we move out to the front porch where there is a breeze and continue our visit out there?"

Everyone was quick to agree. Chairs scooted noisily on the wooden floor as they hurried to give Jeremiah and Deidre and Jeddy time alone.

The door stood open to allow for a breeze, but the little family finally reunited didn't even notice.

"Jeddy," Deidre said softly, "this is your daddy that I said you'd meet someday."

Jeddy put his hand into the large hand of his father and regarded him solemnly. "I am pleased to meet you, sir. I have done my best to take care of Momma for you."

Jeremiah grinned. "Looks like you've done a mighty fine job of it, too, young man. I'm glad I could trust you to care for her so."

There was a slight pause while Jeddy looked first at his daddy and then at his momma. Then, addressing his daddy, he said, "Are you goin' to live here with us now?"

Jeremiah glanced quickly at Deidre. "Well," he spoke slowly, "we will for sure live together somewhere—either here or back at Rose Hill Plantation." He looked again at Deidre. "Your momma and I have to discuss where we'll live."

"But if we move away, how will I take care of Daniel? He's my friend, and I must take care of him and teach him right and wrong."

"Ya know, Son, we'll pray about it, and God will show us what is the right thing to do. God loves Daniel, too, and will want what is best for him as well as what is best for us."

"Yes, Daddy," Jeddy said confidently. "That's what Momma and I always do. We will pray about it."

Ethan had built a large home, and now with the extra wing for Deidre it was quite spacious. He and Mandy had invited the Traehdniks and Delaney to stay with them a few days until Jeremiah and Deidre knew what they would do.

The next morning Jeremiah awakened early. The sun had not yet risen, and the birds were silent still. He slipped out of the bed while Deidre slept soundly and went to the back porch to sit on the steps alone.

He hadn't slept well at all. He had been so certain that he should return to finish his commitment at Rose Hill and perhaps to stay there and continue working to free more Negroes from their bondage. And yet, how could he take his son away from the only home he could remember and from his dear friend? How could he pull Deidre away from Mandy? They were obviously closer than sisters. What was the right thing to do?

He sat with his elbows on his knees, his head in his hands, cradled in the darkness of the predawn. The world was silent around him, and he could smell the rich earth and the growing things that surrounded this home. In the hush his heart sought the heart of God.

He felt a hand on his shoulder. Lifting his head, he realized that the sun was rising, and Mr. Wally had slipped out of the cabin to stand behind him.

"May I join you, son?"

"Of course. You're always welcome. Perhaps you can help me know what is best to do."

"Well, Sue Ellen and I have been praying for wisdom for you and for all of us. And she said I should come tell you some things we've been discussing." Jeremiah waited silently while Mr. Wally sat on the step beside him. "Jeremiah, you know that we love you like our own son. We will always consider you to be part of our family. But we think you should stay here with your family instead of taking them back South with us.

"They are obviously at home here. Mandy and Deidre truly live as sisters as much as Jeddy and Daniel believe they are brothers. We think it would be devastating to pull them away from this home. And you know that Ethan and Mandy are sincere in their invitation to have you live here also.

"We also believe troubled times are coming soon in the South—especially for the Negroes living there. We have been hearing rumblings, and I believe the treatment you received at the store the other day is only a mild sample of what is to come. I think it could be devastating to take your family into all that when you can live here in Indiana together as a family should. Sue Ellen and I brought all your papers with us, so you and Deidre and Jedediah can truly live here as free people with no fear."

Jeremiah was silent while he thought it all over. Finally he spoke. "Mr. Wally, thank you. Thank you for all you've taught me. And for trustin' in some of my ideas and givin' me the freedom to try them. I thank you for lovin' us all and for treatin' us with respect, for believin' in us and carin' that our lives are good and fulfillin' and profitable for us and for others. I've never met a man like you before and doubt I ever will again. I thank God regularly that He allowed me to be one of the Negroes you purchased and freed. I will always be indebted to you.

"As I prayed this morning, I felt I needed to stay here instead of pullin' my family away from the only real home they've ever known. But I didn't want to break a commitment that I made to you and to all the people livin' at Rose Hill. And now you come out here and release me. It truly is amazin' to see the way God works."

Breakfast was a joyous affair. Jeremiah announced that if Ethan and Mandy were truly sincere in their offer to let him stay until he knew what they would do, he would gladly accept. Mandy and Deidre both sighed in unison as though they had not breathed all morning. Immediately there was laughter around the table.

When the laughter subsided, Jedediah said very seriously, "Now we are finished."

Everyone looked at him questioningly, since his breakfast was barely half-eaten, and everyone else was still eating.

Ethan spoke first. "What do you mean, Jeddy?"

"Our family is finished. Mommy and Miss Mandy have each other, Daniel and I have each other, Callie and Christy have each other, and now you and Daddy have each other. We are finished!"

Everyone chuckled as Deidre corrected, "By finished I believe you mean completed."

Mandy and Deidre looked at one another quickly before Mandy spoke both of their hearts. "Our family may be completed, but hopefully it is not finished yet."

Almost on cue, Callie looked at Christy and spoke her first real word. Pointing her finger at her sister, she said quite clearly, "Bay. . .bee."

The laughter that followed was only a taste of what was to come!

About the Author

Judi Ann Ehresman married the love of her life, becoming a pastor's wife and, in time, the mother of two sons and a grandmother. But she's never lost the love instilled in her heart by her high school English teacher: writing.

After her children married and started their own homes, she finally concentrated on fulfilling the dream of many years. She finished her first and second books—*The Long Road Home* and *On the Wings of Grace*—while doing freelance work for the local newspaper in Indiana. Then, suddenly, her husband's job moved them across the country (but nearer to where the children had settled), and she began the third book in The Hand of God series—*Where Two Agree*.

"I want to write good books that will stretch the reader to be all God wants her to be," says Judi Ann. "There is enough wickedness in the world, and I'd much rather fill my mind and heart with the things that are good and true and pure and sweet, for I find that whatever I put into my mind and heart is what I become."

She has owned and managed several businesses, has worked as a freelancer for a local newspaper, writes a well-received, encouraging blog, and is a popular oral reader of her short stories and poetry at children's and women's banquets and teas. Judi Ann is also the author of *The Ride* and *The Hidden Legacy* (both OakTara).

judi.ehresman.org
www.oaktara.com

THE RELUCTANT IMMIGRANT

by Naomi Mitchum

Dedication

For my husband, Bob,
and my family of Guadalupe River paddlers,
whose canoes and kayaks live near New Braunfels.

My thanks also to:
*Dorothy Sinclair, friend and mentor, for her faithful
encouragement and crystal-clear writing advice.
*Paul Mitchum, for his focused editorial critique.
*Texas libraries and historical archives in Port Lavaca, Victoria,
Sattler, Galveston, Houston, and New Braunfels,
and especially to the Sophienberg Museum in New Braunfels.
*The Port Lavaca Historical Society for valuable information and for inviting
me to view the model of a ship that carried immigrants to Indian Point.

I would like to acknowledge the courage and tenacity of the Germans who
forged a trail to and settled areas in the Hill Country of Texas. My thanks
for their diaries and for historians who recorded details of everyday life.

Chapter 1

It was sunshine and shadow. On the day I became a Texan, I met a handsome stranger who made me feel important, left me speechless, and made the horrible trip seem almost worthwhile. But before the sun dipped into the Gulf of Mexico behind the ship's mast, I was threatened by two ugly criminals who would become shadows in my life.

Lifting the hem of the clean blue skirt I had saved for this exciting day, I stepped up the hatch onto the polished deck of the sloop cutter *Naghel*. For the first time in weeks I relaxed and walked along, listening to the soft sighing of the wind in the sails, their square, white riggings unfurled against a clear blue sky.

Only when I found a secluded, shady spot of lashed crates of machinery did I dare open the blue reticule Oma had given me the day we left Germany. It held my two secrets. One was a red velvet diary with a little pencil stuck in the cover. Lately there had been no privacy for writing, so I took out the pencil and wrote:

April 20, 1846

> *The 75-day ocean trip that brought us from Germany to Galveston, Texas, on the sailing ship* Franziska *now seems like a bad dream with its bad weather, bad food, and crowded conditions. I am now four days out of Galveston on a smaller boat that is clean, the weather is good, and I am not seasick. We should be at Indian Point by evening, and I will see my friends who came on earlier ships. They haven't seen me since I turned sixteen and started wearing long skirts.*

The diary's musty smell stung my nose, and I was about to spread it to air in the sunshine when I heard angry voices that made me step deeper into the crate's shadow.

"Well, so far nobody's noticed," said a booming deep voice.

"Be still, Lucas," said a raspy, high-pitched voice. "Don't you know the crates have ears?"

Something sinister in their voices made a circle of fear tumble through my head. *If I leave now,* I thought, *they'll know I've been listening. If I run for the steps, they might hear me.*

"What could crates know?" the deep voice asked.

"The crates know nothing, but I keep glancing over my shoulder expecting to see a Silesian parent hiding there."

"Relax. These *Dummkopfs* are from Bremen. They won't know you," growled the one called Lucas. "But you shouldn't have falsified the records to get that teaching job in the first place."

"I'm a good teacher," said the raspy voice. "Can I help it if the kids failed the tests? They should have given me another chance."

"That's what you said when you got caught with the payroll in Berlin. No more chances. I told you I was watching you then, and I'll be watching you now, Otto Mellinghoff!"

The raspy voice betrayed his disgust. "And remember that I'm watching you, too, Lucas Beck. Part of that money from the bank in Oldenburg belongs to me. I'm the one who got it exchanged to Texas currency. I'm the one who got you on this ship, and don't you forget it."

"Not likely you will let me forget, you *Rabbelkopf*."

"I want to see that money every day," said Otto, "to make sure you aren't putting your sticky hands on it."

"All right, Otto. Just don't crowd me. I like my space."

Heavy footsteps came my direction. My heart pounded wildly, and my fingers fumbled with the diary, trying to clutch it tighter. I heard it hit the floor. I stopped breathing as the footsteps stopped near me, and a huge black boot kicked the diary out of sight toward the mast. I looked up into black bushy eyebrows running into each other in a frown and broad shoulders hunched for action. A scream stuck in my throat as a big, hairy hand grabbed my wrist.

"Don't say a word, you spy." With one hand he kept a painful grip on my wrist; the other he drew back to hit me. "You're dead if you tell what you heard."

The little man appeared behind the hunched shoulders, his small frame almost obscured. "Wait, Lucas, don't hit her! You want to get the ship into an uproar?"

Lucas checked the forward motion of his hand, merely grazing my cheek. I turned to flee. The vise of his big hand tightened. "Who are you?"

I tried to think of a name, any name, of a girl back in Germany.

"I asked you a question." Lucas twisted his grip.

"I–I'm—I'm Sarah Ann Martin," I whispered.

"Well, listen, Sarah Ann, I'll be watching you. One word about this and I'll enjoy feeding you to the sharks." His tone was icy.

"Not one word. Understand?" Lucas shook my arm.

I nodded but couldn't say anything.

"Understand?"

I cleared my throat. "Yes, sir." Then I plunged into a bluff. "What's all the fuss about? I only came out to get some sunshine. Why do you want to hit me?"

Otto moved closer to Lucas and rasped softly, "Maybe she didn't hear us."

"Of course she did. Move, girl. Get out of here and remember that both of us will be watching you all the time." Lucas released my wrist and shoved me out into the sunshine toward the diary. "Pick it up and get out of here."

I groped around the halyard rope where he had kicked the diary.

Lucas followed and growled right in my ear, "I said, get it and get out of here!"

I grabbed the diary and ran up the promenade deck, my heart still pounding. I could still feel his hot breath and smell the rum he had been drinking. Hands trembling and my knees shaking, I sat down to keep from falling. I looked around to see if anyone had witnessed what had happened, but the deck was empty and only the gulls circling the ship chattered noisily among themselves.

I sat there thinking dark thoughts. *They could have killed me, and no one would know what became of me. If I tell, they will know. If they even think I've told someone, they'll get rid of me in some awful way.* I wondered about the money they talked about. Where was it? I sat on the floor a long time thinking in circles and longing for wise Opa, who would know exactly what to do and when to do it.

"Fr-Freder—r-oh-Reeka, where are you?" My five-year-old sister, Sophie, skipped toward me. "O-o h, t-there you are," she uttered. "I've b been c-calling all over." She was pudgy, awkward, and a general nuisance; nevertheless, her blond bouncing curls were, for once, a welcome sight. "Come back to the cabin. Mutter w-wants you to help ch-check everything in the trunk." When I didn't move, she said, "W-well, c-come on."

I tried to get up but couldn't. "Give me your hand, Sophie."

"What's the m-matter? You s-sick? You look w-white."

"No, I'm not sick."

"Well then, c-come on." Sophie helped me up, and we went to the compartments at the front of the ship. "M-mutter says we'll be at Indian P-point by night. Y-you think Marianne or Chris will m-meet us?"

The feel of Lucas's big fingers still burned on my wrist. I felt too weak to think about Indian Point so answered automatically. "Of course."

The cabin we shared with another family was crowded and cluttered. Mutter was carefully neat and expected us to be the same way. In the face of clutter, trouble, storms, anything hard in life, she always had the same answer: "Find a way." So Sophie and I cleared a space in the midst of the crowded quarters for the trunk so we could help Mutter pack our belongings. Before wrapping the tissue paper around

Glorianna, her beautiful doll, Sophie ran her fingers around the doll's black wavy hair, bright blue eyes, and smiling pink lips. Then she felt Glorianna's leather hands and fingered the pink-flowered dress with its soft, white lace.

"W-when can I k-keep h-her?" Sophie asked.

"When she gets safely to New Braunfels," said Mutter. "Wrap her carefully, now, so she won't break, and get on with sorting the rest."

Sophie lifted the worn leather Bible onto a stack.

"Leave it on top, Sophie," Mutter said. "I read it every day."

It was true. I'd watched her morning ritual all the way across the Atlantic. Even when she was seasick and weak every day, Mutter reached for what she called "the sustaining" book. "It helps me find the way," she had often said.

We sorted the rest into piles. I was thankful the cookstove and heavy farming equipment, all purchased and crated in Galveston, were lashed to the main deck. At least we didn't have to move that.

"Hand over the seeds and kitchen tools," said Mutter.

Sophie found the seeds and I handed the pots and pans and other kitchen tools.

"Now the medicine box and recipes and sewing things."

Mutter checked them on her list. We continued with stacks of music and a flute and clarinet. I fingered Emil's shiny trumpet and ran my fingers over the pebbly brown leather friendship book that my friends signed the week before we left. Next I handed over the pewter dishes for which Mutter had traded our beautiful china dinnerware.

Mutter looked at the pewter a long time before she checked it on her list. She missed the dainty flowered china, too.

Sophie found the blue silk family album cornered in silver and wound the music box in the back cover. The lively waltz tore at my memory, and once again the enormity of leaving Germany for an unexplored part of Texas washed over me like one of the ocean waves I had been watching. The familiar tight feeling of dread tore at my chest, and the knot in my stomach that I'd endured for days twisted tighter.

Mutter handed me a package. "Here, put this bread and cheese in the trunk so I won't have to carry it."

I did as she asked without answering, remembering our silver platter with a fat goose resting on it and dumplings in a side bowl. Now we must eat stale bread and cheese.

"Mutter, there must be nothing in this awful land. The closer it gets, the worse it seems."

"We've been over this before. You've been disagreeable about it ever since your

Vater decided to come." Mutter lowered her head and crossed the music box from the list. "I know it's hard, but you should try to adjust and. . ."

But I didn't want to hear one more time about being the reluctant immigrant who had to adjust. I'd heard it all the way across the Atlantic while we were crowded into our tight, make-believe room in the midst of the noise and peering eyes of the other 208 persons in the hold. I'd heard about it for 75 days on the dirty, sour-smelling ship *Franziska*, with its spoiled food and stagnant water. Plagued by seasickness due to rough weather most of the way, I had complained every day until Mutter, also seasick, had lost patience with me. Now I ran from the cabin and didn't stop running until I reached the foredeck, where I leaned back into the shade of the deckhouse and made myself take deep breaths of the balmy gulf air.

"There she is!" My brother, Emil, and a friend came toward me. "We've been looking for you." Then he said in broken English, "Goot aafternoon."

Emil's friend clicked his heels together and bowed. He stood tall and straight in the blue uniform of his German state and wore black boots so shiny I saw the sky reflected on the toes. His skin was browned and clear, and brown curly hair showed from under his military cap.

"Good afternoon," the stranger said in German.

"Good afternoon," he repeated.

I kept looking at his sparkling eyes.

"Goot aafternoon," Emil repeated in halting English.

"What did you say?" I asked Emil.

He replied in German. "I said, good afternoon, and I said it in English."

"But where did you learn that?" I asked.

"From me," the stranger announced in German. He held out his hand to shake mine.

"Sis, this is Karl Behrens, who comes from Oldenburg, and who learned English in only two months in Galveston."

When I took the offered hand, a surge of energy flowed into my arm and up to my shoulder. "I'm very pleased to meet you." I tried not to blush, but I had a feeling my cheeks were blazing red. I made myself take a deep breath. "Did Emil tell you that we're from Delmenhorst—only thirty miles from Oldenburg? We were practically neighbors."

"He told me we are all bound for New Braunfels, and that your father has been there since October." Karl moved back into the shade of the raised forecastle to avoid the blazing afternoon sun.

"We can't wait to see him," I said.

"You're lucky he came ahead to get things ready for you."

"He didn't actually come ahead for that. You see, our little sister was so sick the day we were to leave that they wouldn't let her onboard ship. The money was already paid, and we couldn't afford to lose it, so Vater came ahead while we stayed with Aunt Eva and Uncle Herman." I suddenly realized that I was rattling on and on, and took refuge in looking down at my ugly brown walking shoes.

"That must have been hard for everyone." Karl smiled at me. "But you must feel joyful that you will be in New Braunfels soon."

Emil looked at me, and a deep, gurgling laugh escaped. "I doubt it," he said. He had heard my complaining day after day as we crossed the entire Atlantic.

I couldn't bear to look at anyone. I kept looking down during a long moment of silence.

"Don't worry, Rika. You'll grow to like it." Karl was cheerful. "Here's your first Texas present." He pulled a small, folded newspaper from inside his jacket pocket and handed it to me.

I unfolded it and scanned the front page. "But it's not in German. I can't read a word."

"Ah, but you will. What do you want me to read for you?"

I pointed to the words just under the masthead.

"That's the motto of the newspaper. It says, 'The Will of the People Should Rule.' Above that it says *The Galveston News.*"

"You mean they print those words on every paper?"

"Yes."

"Do you think they mean the will of the people will really rule?"

"Yes, this is a free country. It's not just a lot of talk like the revolutionists in Germany, it's really free." I could hear the excitement in his voice. "I think we will all like the freedom, and we. . . ."

I didn't hear the rest of the sentence. Short Otto and the tall Lucas were walking slowly toward me. Lucas still wore the rumpled black suit and messy white shirt, but he had added a tall, black hat that made him seem even bigger. Short Otto, dressed in a tidy brown suit, seemed smaller than ever beside Lucas, whose huge shadow fell onto Emil. Before I could turn to leave, Otto slid from behind Lucas, attempting to mold himself into the group.

"Good afternoon, Sarah Ann," sneered Lucas.

"Afternoon. How are you, Sarah Ann Martin?" Otto stepped in front of me. "Introduce us to your friends."

Chapter 2

I glared at the men. How dare they ruin the only bright spot of the entire trip?

"Well?" Lucas said near my ear.

My anger turned to a web of fear. I could barely speak. "This is Emil. . .and . . .Karl, two friends of mine." My voice sounded far away.

Emil and Karl stuck out their hands in good faith and in turn Lucas and Otto shook them.

"Your friends are ours," said Lucas. He leaned toward my ear again. "Remember nothing, Sarah." Then he strode down the deck and out of sight, followed by Otto quickly short-stepping behind, trying to keep up.

"Sarah Ann?" asked Emil. "What was that all about?"

I leaned against the wall for support. What could I say? Explaining could put my life in jeopardy.

"Well, who are they? And why do they call you Sarah Ann?" Emil stared at me. "And why am I suddenly just a friend?"

"It's hard to explain."

"Try!"

"I met them walking on deck. They seemed forward, so I just told them the wrong name." The words tumbled out too fast. I could see in Emil's eyes he knew I was lying.

"A very smart thing to do, if you ask me," bragged Karl. "A lady can never be too careful."

I felt my spirits soar. He believed me! And no one had ever called me a lady before!

Emil glanced at my clenched fists and looked at my eyes. "But why are you so frightened?"

"They're ugly characters!"

"Right," said Karl. "Forget about them. Tell me what your father said about New Braunfels."

I sighed and relaxed a little, but a twinge of guilt pulled at me. I had never lied to Emil before.

"We had one letter," answered Emil.

"Does your Vater have a farm?"

"It was assigned, but there's been no time to farm it," Emil said.

"Vater only said he was a farmer to get a place on the boat," I explained. "He's really a music teacher."

We talked of New Braunfels until we had to move to the shady side of the deckhouse. Then we talked about friends left in Germany. Karl told about the military service he disliked so much he left Germany. He spoke of family left behind and his hopes for adventure in unexplored Texas. Emil described his apprenticeship to a tailor and shared his hopes for opening a tailor shop in New Braunfels, where there were no trade guilds.

One of the American sailors called to Karl that we would soon be unloading at Indian Point.

Karl surveyed the shoreline. "Where's Indian Point?" he asked the sailor.

"Can't see it yet. The *Naghel* can't go on into Indian Point because the water is too shallow. We stop in the bay outside the sandbar and wait for a small boat called a lighter to take our cargo across the shallow water to Indian Point." The sailor ran off to his ropes.

Karl translated the information into German for us, and a crowd gathered around, requesting another translation.

Hands pointed to the west, and calls of "Land! Land!" echoed across the ship. Passengers gathered along the railing, peering into the sun's dazzling reflection on the water for the first glimpse of the new land. When they saw the sandbar, cheers of joy went up and people danced around, hugging each other and hopping up and down. I was jostled and crowded, yet I had never felt so alone. I blotted my eyes with the handkerchief from my reticule and stood fingering the blue embroidered *F* and the lace ruffle on the linen.

"F-Freder—Rika, we're here!" Sophie tugged at my skirt. When I looked at the joy on her face, I was surprised to feel at least a little thankful that the long trip was over and welcoming friends were near.

⁓

The next few hours were filled with hectic preparation for boarding the small lighter. Finally, families bunched together, surrounded by their trunks and satchels of belongings. Everyone watched silently as the first three families and their belongings were lowered onto the lighter and disappeared across the bright water into a small speck on the horizon.

As the lighter returned from the third trip, clouds covered the sun, and a sudden wind tossed the boat like a piece of paper. Sturdy arms strained at the oars, and the tillerman barked commands to keep it from swamping, and the little boat arrived back at the ship ready to take more of us ashore. The wind whipped my skirt and tangled my hair, and it plucked the handkerchief from my hand and sailed it high into the graying sky. I watched it disappear into the water while the crowd watched in silence. Was it an omen? The little knots of persons and their possessions pulled together tighter, daring the wind to take anyone or anything that belonged to them. Mutter, Sophie, and Emil pressed even closer to me.

"Mueller! Ikert! Kessler!" The names were barked into the wind.

"Mueller family, here!" called Emil.

I felt myself swept toward the gap in the ship's rail. The Ikerts, who loaded first, were kept waiting on the lighter when the tillerman refused to take an animal. Herr Kessler argued with the captain about his cow. Any animal that could stand the trip from Galveston was by now a family pet, he said, and deserved to board with the family. Besides, he argued, did the captain actually want to keep a balky, seasick cow? Finally, the bawling cow was tugged to the rail, the sling put under her belly, and she was lowered to the small boat, her bawling carried away by the wind.

When it was our turn, we were lowered by a wildly swaying sling onto a thrashing boat. I swallowed hard to quiet my fearful, retching stomach.

Underway on the raft-like lighter, the wind grew warmer and less fierce, but cold waves washed over us again and again. I trembled and clenched my teeth to keep them from chattering. Mutter's eyes were closed, but her lips were moving. I closed my eyes to pray also, but such blackness engulfed me that I opened them again and stared into the stinging wet wind, afraid to blink.

After what seemed an eternity, the bay settled, and the sailors stopped rowing and rubbed their tired arms while only the tillerman kept a steady hand to guide the small boat. We and the other immigrants touched each other and wrung water out of clothing. People called reassurances to one another. Farmer Kessler examined his seasick, swaying cow, and his children reached up to pat her.

The oarsmen pointed to the fog bank ahead and argued among themselves. Finally, they began cadence counting—1-2. . .3-4. . .1-2. . .3-4—then dipped their oars again, and the little boat moved ahead into a fog bank.

"I'm scared!" Sophie turned loose of my hand and threw her arms around my waist.

I couldn't say a word, but Emil said, "Don't worry, little one, we'll be there soon. Just think of Marianne there to greet you."

Although I knew the fragile lighter was taking us toward land, when the curtain of fog closed in behind us, the world ceased to exist. It seemed like a dream. Only the rhythmic pitch of the lighter, the sound of water and the tightening grip of Sophie's arms around my waist made the dream real. I sat frozen with fear until much later when the boat scraped sand and came to a sudden halt.

The oarsmen jumped into the water, and began the backbreaking job of unloading the Kesslers, their trunks, and the balky cow from the bobbing lighter. I heard the Ikerts slosh through the shallow water to safety, but when it was my turn to step over into the water, I felt that I'd rather die than take those last steps into Texas. When I did, the water was ankle deep and cold, and seeped down inside the clumsy brown shoes, making them even heavier.

When we were safely on dry land, the German oarsman explained that our crates left on the boat would be unloaded the next morning. He told us to camp well out of the incoming tidemark, wished us luck, and disappeared back into the fog.

Under Emil's direction we opened the trunks and were soon set up under a low, makeshift canopy of sheets and spread dry sheets and pillows for sleeping. As the gray light turned to dark, in silence we ate wet bread and the last hunk of cheese.

With darkness came thicker fog and air that was strangely heavy with a warmth I'd never felt in Germany, yet the sand beneath felt clammy and cold. Emil found his flint and lit a candle, giving a cheerful yellow glow to our strange, tiny tent. In tired voices tinged alternately with bitterness and hope we discussed what might have become of the Indian Point wharves and wondered why our friends hadn't come to welcome us. But there were no answers.

Mutter, optimistic as usual, told us our questions would be answered tomorrow. The answers, she said, would be a pleasant surprise.

But she sighed with resignation even as she said it.

Sophie whined again and again, "Where are all the people?"

Finally Mutter yelled at her, "Go to sleep!"

Emil felt sorry for Sophie and started to explain once more that we didn't know, but Mutter became angry with him and yelled at him to be quiet and go to sleep. Emil quietly left the lean-to without realizing that his slight movement made the candle flicker and go out.

I sat in the dark thinking. It had been years since Mutter sounded cross with good-natured Emil. A dark realization crept over me: *Texas has a dreadful aura, one that makes us mean with each other. This awful place smells like fish. It's so bad no one lives here—not even a person who could come down to meet us.* Angrily I pounded my pillow. Sand flew into my mouth and gritted between my teeth. I wondered how any place could be more miserable.

As if in answer, I heard the faint buzz of a mosquito, then two, then three, then thousands that filled the sheet-tent with humming. I slapped at them wildly as they bit my arms and face relentlessly. "Mutter! Mutter!" I called. But mosquitoes flew into my mouth. I had to cover my nose to keep from breathing them.

Sophie scratched and cried hysterically until Mutter covered her from the top of her head to her toes with a sheet. Mutter sat very still hugging Sophie tightly, and I imagined the mosquitoes feeding on her, for I could hear her crying.

I'd heard Mutter cry only once—the night before Herr Dittman came to get the furniture to help finance the trip. I had watched from the shadows as Mutter walked from room to room, slowly running her soft hands over the smooth, oiled furniture, caressing each piece, saying good-bye to the treasures that had been part of her dowry. It had been a time of deep sadness and quiet tears.

I felt a great longing to flee from the sad memory and from the present terror and disappointment. With my hand I covered my mouth and called to the returning Emil, "Where can we go to get away from the mosquitoes?"

"No place. Everyone's in trouble. And some of the families didn't even get to shore."

In the desperate dark came a guilty glimmer of hope. Perhaps Otto and Lucas had drowned.

But what about Karl?

Chapter 3

L aughing sounds awakened me the next morning, and I crept stiffly from the sheet-tent into the blinding sunshine to see who it was. Black-headed gulls with shimmering bodies circled then dipped to shore for small fish, laughing as they dived. Farther down the beach, brown shore birds wearing white bibs walked like miniature men on stilts in the shallow surf. Stiffly they tipped their beaks into the soft, white foam searching for breakfast.

Sparkling flat stretches of buff-colored sand, damp in the morning sunlight, caught the reflection of glassy, blue surf. Behind the flat beach, grasses and tiny yellow flowers bloomed on mounded dunes. My spirits soared. I had come to a wonderland, a picture from a fairytale. I stepped back into the tent and shook Emil's shoulder.

His eyes opened slowly. "What's the matter?"

"Shh." I pointed to the exit. Emil got up slowly and followed me.

"I don't believe it." The bright blue water glistening in the sunshine made him shield his eyes. "How could it change just overnight?"

"It's a miracle!" I burrowed my feet into the warming sand. "This feels good. Try it."

Emil dug his feet in, then kicked dry sand into the air and walked the few feet to wet sand where the tide was going out. "See this little hole? A crab lives there."

Just then a strange creature with many claws and a set of fierce-looking pincers came out of the hole and scampered sideways down the beach. I jumped back. "Does it bite?"

"No."

"How do you know?"

"Karl told me he caught them on the beach in Galveston." Emil watched other crabs move down the beach. "Have you seen Karl this morning?"

"No. Maybe he's down the beach. Lots of bundles and stacks down there, but no one's awake."

Emil pointed. "Look, something's moving."

"It's the Kesslers' cow!" I ran down the beach to the cow and threw my arms around her sandy neck. Suddenly, the Kesslers appeared from all directions, everyone talking at once. Frau Kessler asked about Mutter and Sophie, and we compared our frantic, mosquito-ridden night. In the midst of the happy confusion, the cow started to bawl. Herr Kessler found his milking bucket. Frau Kessler sent me back to get a pan for some milk, and as I walked past the milking, I heard Herr Kessler coo, "Oh, Wilma, you lovely creature. Oh, Wilma, you are a beautiful cow."

I burst into the tent. "Herr Kessler is milking Wilma, and I need a pan from the trunk."

Still wrapped like a mummy, Sophie tried to stand but fell over, helpless, until I unwound the sheet. "Sophie, look outside. It's so beautiful you won't believe it." She took off running into the shallow water, laughing with glee every time she frightened a group of shore birds into flight.

"Mutter, are you all right?"

She looked pale and had dark smudges under her eyes, and the red welts on her face and arms were swollen and inflamed. The usually neat bun of blond hair at the back of her head had come loose and long strands hung around her shoulders and shorter wisps clung to her face. She had lost weight from seasickness, and this morning her damp, oversize clothes hung limply against her.

Mutter's eyes met mine for a long second. "Oh, yes, Rika, I'm fine." She continued searching the trunk for a pan. "Although I do believe the mosquitoes have more blood this morning than I do." She handed me the pan. "Please tell Wilma she is beautiful, and I love her."

"What about Frau Kessler?"

"Tell her I'll come calling as soon as I've had a bath and cleaned the house." Walking down the beach with the pan I felt an unexplainable pride in my optimistic Mutter.

⌒∞⌒

It looked like mass confusion that morning, but when I wrote about it later in my diary I found that it did have a sense of order. Mutter washed her face in seawater, stoically enduring the sting of the salt against the raw mosquito bites. Only after she brushed and coiled her long blond hair, straightened her blouse and skirt, and read her morning passages from the Bible did she close the second trunk and make her way with dignity down the beach to thank Frau Kessler for the milk.

Emil returned with the news that we should move south and eastward down the beach to Indian Point; that, he said, was less than a mile. We suddenly became giddy with optimism and gladly blamed the fog for our misadventure on the beach. I couldn't wait for civilization. Houses with windows, welcoming open doors, and friends from Germany would reassure me that Texas wouldn't be as bad as I had dreaded. I wondered if Karl was among the seven families camped along the beach toward Indian Point.

Mutter was optimistic. "Such a fine, handsome young soldier surely knows how to care for himself. Why, he's so handsome I'll bet he is already eating a fat breakfast with some beautiful lady who spied him on the beach."

"Sorry, Sis." Emil grinned. "You may have to stand in line to talk to him."

"Who said I wanted to talk to him?"

"Well, you're worried about him," said Emil.

It was true. I couldn't stop thinking about him even in the flurry of activity to leave for Indian Point.

The long walk to Indian Point became festive as other families joined us along the way, calling greetings and encouragement. As our numbers grew to nearly forty, we collected explanations for the miserable arrival and lack of welcome. Expectantly we walked faster and faster.

At first Indian Point was just a speck in the distance; then it grew to lumps and heaps resembling buildings. But as we walked down the town's one beachfront street, I was puzzled and dismayed. Then a gnawing fear took over. Hundreds of tents and sod houses, some with brush roofs, some with no roofs, some partially made of scrap wood, huddled along the beach, looking like they grew close together for protection. Between the houses stood skeletons of rusty farm machinery, stoves, and rusty buckets. Occasionally a thin, unkempt child waved from the doorway, but there were no welcoming calls, no invitations to celebrate our arrival. I studied each makeshift doorway looking for Marianne. Sophie darted toward a child she mistook for Chris, but the child silently fled into a dark hut. Stunned by the sight of shacks and tents and the unfriendliness and lack of activity in the town, we walked slowly and silently on.

At the end of the main street, the business section looked as unkempt and disappointing as the huts and dwelling tents. Various large business tents displayed crudely lettered signs offering everything from clothing to harness to home-cooked meals. Even the *H. Runge and Company, Bank* sign was roughhewn and hung over a sagging tent. We reached a large square wooden building bearing a sign *ADELSVEREIN* and poured inside to escape the scorching sun.

Adelsverein, the sponsoring society of German states who had planned the settlement of central Texas, made many promises to us before we left Germany. Inside the building we hoped to find these promises fulfilled or to find answers to questions about our arrival and cold reception at Indian Point. Herr Kessler, followed by his family and our family, boldly led his precious cow through the door and to the front of what looked like a meeting hall, where two officials sat behind a table. When no one spoke, Herr Kessler announced himself and the arrival of the sloop cutter *Naghel*. Reluctantly, the larger of the two men rose and told the group that other immigrants from the sloop had landed on the other side of Indian Point and were already headed for the pier, where their crates would be unloaded.

I caught my breath. Was Karl with the other group?

Emil must have read my thought, for he smiled.

Herr Mieckle, a short, round, little bald-headed man with a mustache and a spokesman for the German immigration society, stood up behind his heavy table to give us an official welcome to Texas. First he commended us on our courage in landing in the fog and spending a miserable night on the beach. Then he told us about the bank and mercantile tent. Next, and he lowered his voice almost to a deep whisper, he told us that the United States was preparing for war with Mexico over a boundary dispute.

There were mumbles among the immigrants that they came to Texas to find freedom, not get involved in a war.

Herr Mieckle held up his hands for silence. He told us we were not in danger from the dispute, but that most of the wagons and teams that would have transported us inland had been conscripted by the army, and the owners and drivers of the rest had received better wages from the army. He apologized on behalf of the Adelsverein and announced that although the Verein, the Texas nickname for Adelsverein, was having financial difficulties, there would be plenty of food for as long as we had to wait for transportation.

"Water is, however, rationed here," he announced, "so you will need to talk to your neighbors about how to conserve it. Lots are for sale for $3,000 each, but most of you will want to just camp on any available spot until you find transportation inland." Without waiting for questions he turned sharply and walked out the back door of the crude warehouse, leaving the door swinging crookedly on one broken hinge.

I felt trapped in a bad dream. I hadn't wanted to come to a land of log houses and farming and political freedom. That was my Vater's dream; that had been bad enough. Now this man had just told us we were trapped on a mosquito-ridden beach with no water. I wished the new life to be a dream. I wanted to wake up in my beautiful bed with roses on the walls and to inhale the aromas of breakfast.

A buzz of conversation filled the small room, bringing me back to reality. It spread to those waiting outside as the news was told and retold. With each telling the voices grew louder and angrier, and the crowd surged toward the remaining minor official of the Verein. At exactly the right moment before he would have been mobbed, he climbed on top of the table and announced that the lighter was unloading crates at the pier. He barked instructions for collecting the day's ration of meat and water after everyone was settled.

Without thinking, I shouted bitterly the question in everyone's mind. "Settled in what?"

Quiet descended over the room. No answer came from the remaining official.

Finally, Mutter lifted her chin and replied loudly, "Settled in our new house of course." Dragging Sophie by the hand, she pushed her way through the crowd toward the door.

I was so filled with anger I stood frozen, unable to move. Hadn't she heard what the man said? Hadn't she seen the shacks, the huts no one could call a house? But Mutter, head held high, chin up, looking straight ahead, walked resolutely out of the hall into the sunshine with the crowd falling in behind her. Halfway out the pier she stopped and stood regally and silently waiting for the lighter to arrive with her precious cargo. And there she waited in the boiling sun until three hours later when it was unloaded. Sophie, near exhaustion from the long walk to Indian Point, lay down at her feet and went to sleep in the shade of her skirt. I chose to wait in the shade of the hall.

While I waited for Emil to find wagons to get our trunks, I looked at my slender, white hands, the hands of a musician and student. Would those hands become brown and calloused from living in a tent and cooking over a campfire? I felt the stinging welts of mosquito bites on my neck, and ran my fingers through my long, blond hair, now gritty with sand.

We will live in filth!

I felt the final death of my dreams and my ambition to do something important with my life slip away into the sand. What could I do? The smoldering, controlled anger I had felt for so long boiled, out of control, to the surface. I thought I'd explode with the hot fury that engulfed me so completely that it made me afraid. I had never felt such anger. I dared not scream. I couldn't cry. I wouldn't hit anyone. What could I do?

I felt totally helpless until I took control. *But why should I do anything?* I wondered. Around me, people scurried here and there in the oppressive heat. *It was their idea to come here. Let them manage! I'll just sit.*

And so I sat, in the shade of the Verein warehouse. I straightened my blue skirt and white blouse and imagined myself looking poised and pretty. After a while, sweat trickled down my neck and my damp clothing wilted. So did I.

Much later Emil drove up in the borrowed wagon loaded with our belongings.

As we drove up the beach, a familiar voice hailed us.

"Rika! Emil! Wait for me."

Karl ran up to the wagon, heaved himself over the side, and sat on the floor as if no time had elapsed since our last conversation. "Is this to be your location, then?"

Emil heaved the horses to a stop. "Our location was suggested by the driver, who loaned me his wagon. Up beach is filled with sickness and even more mosquitoes. Half the people in town are sick, and hundreds have died."

I gasped. "We're to die here?"

"Don't be silly. It's only temporary," said Karl.

"We must buy this wagon and go on to New Braunfels by ourselves," I declared.

Emil's answer made me feel stupid. "That kind of trip requires the protection of a group. We could never make it alone."

"I know we could." I defended the idea.

"According to Vater, it's 240 miles, too far to go alone."

Karl placed a grimy hand on my shoulder. "It's not a good idea, Rika." His voice became placating. "I'm just glad you're all right."

I tried to act casual, even though I felt rebuffed. The warmth of his hand sent currents of tingling through my arm. "I'm glad you're all right, too, Karl."

By late afternoon the crates and trunks were sorted, and all the families were grimly building impromptu shelters. One by one, as they worked, the families' spirits lifted, and from a distance I could hear cheerful calls of the ever-present German proverbs: "Work makes life sweet" and "Laziness makes your limbs stiff." When Karl added his version, "Laziness strengthens your limbs," we all laughed, including Mutter, who had suffered a painful sunburn from standing hours on the pier. She was lying in the shade of a suspended sheet, watching Karl and Emil dig an oblong, shallow pit. In the middle of the pit they placed our trunks. Then they uncrated the farm machinery and the stove, and used the wood to build walls for the house. They drove the staves into the ground around the edge of the pit and nailed the last few boards across the top to form support beams for a low roof. But there was no wood for a roof.

Karl arranged the remaining machinery outside the strange pit-house to form a private necessary room, into which Emil with great humor and ceremony placed the chamber pot. Sophie pointed to its painted pink and yellow flowers and clapped her hands over her mouth to suppress a giggle. We all smiled, but no one had the heart for humor except Mutter, who laughed and said, "Flowers, but no wood for a roof." Then she did something I will always remember. She handed Emil the sheet under which she had been resting, and said, "Here, use this."

"You know we have to nail this to the roof supports, don't you?" Emil fingered the cutwork and embroidery along the hem and looked at me. I knew what he was thinking. When we were little, for a special treat Mutter would invite us to her big, carved walnut bed for a bedtime story. As we got sleepy, we traced the cutout scallops and embroidery stitching of the sheet's edge with our small fingers until we went to sleep.

"Oh, yes. Go ahead and nail it," she said. "It's just an old sheet." Mutter didn't falter, but I noticed when Karl put the nails in, she turned away.

Karl offered his army blanket to finish out the roof, and it was decided that he should stay with us since he owned half the roof. I felt such unexpected joy well up inside me that I had to leave.

I walked along the beach asking myself questions. *Why am I so excited when Karl is near? What makes me feel so happy when things around here are so terrible? Is it because of Karl? Is it obvious to the others that he makes me feel this way?*

I stood for a long time looking out over the water, listening to the gentle swish of waves, and thinking about myself. A sense of uneasiness crept over me when I tried to picture how I'd act with Karl as a member of the Mueller family. Who ever heard of the boy you wished to court actually living with you? *Mornings he will see my tangled hair. He'll hear me argue with Sophie, and, worst of all, he can't miss the childish directions Mutter still gives me even though I'm sixteen. And how can I dress in the same quarters with Karl?*

Then I thought of walking along the beach with him at sunset and making jokes with the family, and I smiled to myself. *Yes, Rika, you can manage.*

"Frederika! Frederika!" a raspy voice called.

I looked with disbelief at the little man in the brown suit coming down the beach. Why couldn't they have drowned off the lighter?

Otto Mellinghoff smiled his liquid smile. "Hello, Frederika. I'm so glad to see you."

"How do you know my name?"

"Silly girl. I saw you in the crowd this morning. Everyone knows about Frau Mueller, who led the pack to the pier."

"You stay away from me."

"Silly girl. You know we can't do that."

Chapter 4

I wanted to go back to the hut, but my feet froze in the warm sand. "I have nothing to say to you and nothing to say about you."

"Good. Let's keep it that way. And, by the way, here." Otto pushed a pail of water toward me. "Money buys extra rations."

I pulled my hands back as though the tainted pail was scalding hot.

"You pay attention," Otto demanded. "Pay attention right now. We know who you are. One word about our secret, and that precious little sister of yours just might come up missing. Understand?"

I took the pail and fled.

Emil met me. "Wasn't that the weasly little man from the boat?"

"Yes." I was trembling inside; my voice sounded tight.

"What did he want?"

"He brought us some water." I took a deep breath and cleared my throat.

"Where did he get it?"

"Didn't say."

"And why would he give us water?"

I thought for a minute before answering. "He admired Mutter today on the pier and wanted to show his appreciation." The lie burned in my throat.

He considered the answer for a long time. "Rika, is there anything you want to tell me about those two men who call you Sarah Ann?"

"No, there's nothing I can tell you." I ducked under the low roof and disappeared inside.

⚬

It was an unsettling first night in the tent home. I wrapped and unwrapped my body over and over, alternately hot and sweaty from the damp air and shivering cold from the clammy, damp sand. Mosquitoes buzzed incessantly, and during my uncovered times, they raised stinging, itching welts on my arms and legs. Sophie talked in her sleep. Emil thrashed his legs, bumping Mutter, who sat up most of the night. Only Karl slept soundly.

When finally I heard the laughing gulls announce daylight, I tiptoed over the sleeping bodies to the door and walked along the beach to watch the sun come fully into orange and pink streaks. It became my morning ritual, for I discovered that the privacy of getting up before the commotion of the day was a treasure. I liked time to ponder what wise words Professor Hinterwinkler might have had for surviving in the crowded hot hut. Sometimes, off where no one could hear me, I practiced singing scales.

As the days wore on, living in a hut became less unusual, and we fell into a system of sameness. There was a monotony about my arguments with Mutter over washing dishes and linens or smoothing the floor of the hut. When she asked me to help, I simply walked to the edge of the water and sat down. There I sat through pleas, shouts, threats, even prayer. Sophie had to do all the chores and began calling me "pain in my neck." I didn't really mind, for, after all, I hadn't asked to come on this trip; it was their doing.

Until one day my hair and clothing felt so gritty I couldn't stand it. I had to wash. Fresh water, which the Verein collected in huge cisterns and rationed to each person, was precious. After three weeks of spilling and wasting, I learned how to use it. Besides drinking water, the small amounts meted out were used for taking a pan bath about once a week. I saved this water to wash my feet about twice a week, and then saved it to wash delicate clothes. The very little dirty water left after many uses was finally given to Wilma with the understanding that the Kesslers would occasionally share Wilma's rich milk.

Hope for transportation inland was displaced by despair, and as the idle days wore on, even the guessing games we played took on a sameness. If we stayed outside too long, we would get heatstroke like Frau Schmidt. As we stayed inside day after day we became weaker and more irritable, more grouchy and touchy over the least detail of daily life.

Finally, one day Emil jumped up as if he would burst. "One more day like this and I'll go crazy."

Mutter straightened her back and leaned against the trunk. "Do you have a suggestion?"

"I'm going to get a job at the pier."

"In that boiling sun every day?"

"Any other suggestions?" He looked from Mutter to me then to Karl.

There was no answer. So Emil went to the pier. Sophie and Mutter went to the dunes to look for flowers, and Karl stopped writing in the sand and asked me if I still had my copy of *The Galveston News*. I nodded, hoping he didn't notice the blush of pleasure spreading across my cheeks. I got the paper and followed him outside.

"We'll start at the top of the page. I'll read; you follow where I point." He read, "*The Galveston News*, The Will of the People Should Rule, March 3, 1846." He paused.

I repeated in halting English, "*The Galveston News*, The Will of the People Should Rule, March 3, 1846." I looked at the rest of the strange words. "What else does it say?"

"Here's an advertisement for lemon syrup, another for Sappington's Pills and Brandreth's Pills and Bateman's Drops at a drug store."

"What else?"

"There's a notice of the Sloop Cutter *Naghel* leaving for Port Lavaca—that was us, you know—and an invitation to stay at Tremont House for $30.00 a month board and lodging."

I longed for the place called Tremont House with real beds and tables and chairs.

"Hey! Here's an advertisement you should answer," said Karl. "Mr. J. M. Habich wants music students on Fortepiano."

A sense of absolute joy took hold of me and I jumped up, shouting, "Amazing! Absolutely astounding!"

"What's so amazing?"

"Texas has pianos! Can you believe it? This place is civilized after all!" I suddenly felt that I must look silly and sat back down in the sand.

"Why is a piano so important to you?"

"I want to do something important in music. But it's a secret."

"Come on, tell me."

"You won't laugh?"

"Of course not."

"I've been thinking about freedom. If I'm free to do what I want, then I want to be a music teacher. What do you think?" I watched his face and prodded him when he didn't answer. "Well, what do you think?"

"It's a good idea, but. . ."

"But what?"

"But you don't know how to do it."

"Oh, is that all? I thought you were going to say a woman's place is in the home."

"Perhaps it is. But that's not what I meant. I meant you would need some sort of training to become a teacher. Do you see any schools nearby?" He waved his hand toward the sand dunes and warehouse.

"No, but I left two perfectly good schools behind me in Germany."

"How did you get in two schools?"

"Oma Gruenwald, Mutter's Mutter, took care of me when Sophie was born. And she said I—said I—" I hesitated, thinking I sounded conceited.

"Well, come on, said what?"

"Said I had more musical talent than Vater when he was small, and Vater is a music teacher. She made arrangements for me to go to a special school, mostly for boys, where I studied mathematics and composition. The boys all grumbled because I was quicker than they, but finally some became my friends. I also attended a music academy one day a week."

"Do you play an instrument?"

"I can play Emil's trumpet, Vater's horn, the pianoforte, and a flute. But my first love is singing. Always singing."

"Why haven't I heard you sing?"

"I go off alone to sing. Besides, there's not much to sing about."

"How about a song about Wilma or mosquitoes?"

"You start it and I'll join in."

Karl stood and then marched down the beach singing, "Moo! Moo, moo! Moo!" We began to act silly, singing in proverbs and mixing in words about our sunburns, foot washing, and Wilma and Frau Schmidt. Sophie and Mutter came back from the dunes and added verses about crabs, snakes, and mosquitoes. We sang and laughed and marched until, exhausted, we fell into the rim of shade around the hut. Mutter, drenched in perspiration, blotted at her sunburn with her sleeve.

"In the army we put butter on sunburn. I'll go ask the Kesslers." Karl was on his feet.

"Please, no," insisted Mutter. "Butter is one of the few nutritious foods we have. Leave it with them."

It was true—there was very little good food. We sat with our backs to the rough wood in the shade, comparing good food we had eaten in Germany to the food at Indian Point. I told how Vater in his only letter to us described the food provided for the inland trip, food he had shared with people who helped him get to New Braunfels. He had 43 pounds of beef, more than he could eat, smoked bacon, dry vegetables, peas, beans, rice, bread. The list went on and on. He said he missed coffee, but most of all he missed Irish potatoes, the German life staple.

"What do you suppose happened to all those supplies?"

"Finances have changed, but," I said, "we have plenty of beef and corn."

"But *corn*. Ugh! In Germany we fed that to cattle."

"Pretend you're an animal, then," I told everyone. "We're having cornbread and beans for lunch. But first you all need to find some cooking wood."

Sophie's eyes grew wide with surprise. "*You're* cooking?"

"Of course," I said. "Anyone can cook." I'd watched Mutter do it a hundred times. When the cornbread was finished, Sophie declared that we had rockbread with beans for lunch. Karl chewed away on his small piece and declared that it was delicious. Mutter said nothing, just nodded and smiled as she chewed. Deep inside I felt a little strange. I had broken my resolve not to help. But I hadn't done it to help. I had done it to impress Karl. However, to my surprise I also felt like smiling. The cornbread wasn't good, but at least I had *done* something.

Just before dark Emil came trudging down the beach. His shirt tail was out, and he was covered with grease and sand, but triumphantly he carried three pieces of wood for our roof. About ten steps behind him, like a shadow hurrying to catch up, was a short, egg-shaped little lady wearing a pink gathered skirt that made her look even rounder. She wore tiny, thick, round spectacles perched upon her upturned little nose. Her thin gray hair, rolled into a skinny bun on the back of her head, had wiry wisps sticking out that made the bun seem ready for flight. Her round face was red from sunburn except for little white rings underneath her glasses. On one arm she carried a heavy bucket. With her other hand she dragged a huge black valise that moved so fast fantails of sand flew out behind it.

Emil deposited his load of wood and wiped his sunburned face on his grimy sleeve. "I've brought a guest. Or, to put it bluntly, a guest has brought me."

I couldn't believe it. How could he bring a stranger into our already packed hut? I looked him straight in the eye. "We're already crowded."

But Sophie hugged the little round lady and declared that she looked like Oma Gruenwald in Germany.

"Good evening. I am Frau Anna Gunkel, once removed from Hamburg." She bowed low, set the bucket down near the stove, opened the valise, took out an apron, which she tied around her bountiful middle, closed the valise, and put it inside the house. "Your dear Emil spotted me stumbling off the lighter and gave me kind assistance. He assures me that this is the best end of the beach for a house, so I announce my intention to build one tomorrow." Out of breath, she paused to look inside the cold stove as the assembled group looked on in amazement.

Karl leaned close to my ear and whispered, "We have been invaded."

"You have, indeed," agreed the Frau Gunkel, whose hearing we discovered was excellent.

Mutter stepped forward. "Welcome to our tiny home. We haven't much, but it is partly yours. Please call me Anna." She held out her hand. ·

But Frau Gunkel opened her arms and enfolded Mutter in a tight hug. "My name is also Anna," she said at last as they disentangled from each other.

"You're Oma," declared Sophie, running into the open arms.

Like an invading whirlwind Oma Gunkel began supper. From her bucket she took four oranges, two huge pieces of jerky, a small loaf of white bread, and a small bag of jelly tart candy. When asked how she came by such delicacies, she simply asked if from the looks of her we thought she would leave Galveston without extra supplies. She told us she had found that Texas jerky, made of dried beef or deer, would keep indefinitely. One thing, though, she cautioned, "Jerky does make you thirsty."

I remembered her caution later when Sophie collided with me as I lifted our pan of water. I watched the precious drops disappear into the sand. "Sophie, you dummy, look what you made me do!"

"M-made you do? Y-you did it. Y-you spilled the w-water!"

"But it was your fault. You bumped into me."

"No harm done," said Oma Gunkel.

Who was *she* to say such a thing? *She* hadn't been here for weeks going thirsty. "No harm done? That was our drinking water for tonight and tomorrow!" I said angrily.

Sophie sobbed, stuttering her apologies over and over until Mutter grabbed her shaking shoulders in a big hug and held her tightly. "It was an accident. Don't worry, honey. We can get by."

But Sophie sobbed until she fell asleep, and we all felt our spirits dip as, thirsty from the jerky, we sorted ourselves out for another crowded night with the added bulk of Oma mounded in one corner of the hut. My mouth was so dry my lips cracked, and my back was crowded uncomfortably against a trunk. I felt my tangled hair, imagining that it represented my tangled life. I didn't like Texas; I was mad at Sophie. I resented Oma Gunkel's intrusion in our crowded hut. And I was afraid we would get sick.

Worst of all, I feared for Vater. Could he possibly be all right in such a harsh land? Could he even be alive after all this time? For hours I tried to untangle the web of worries.

Chapter 5

Although she had recruited him to build her hut, Oma hovered over Karl's every move. It took two days to complete the hut, partly because of her interference and partly because he knew nothing about building. The walls caved in, or the floor filled up with water, or the doorframe leaned precariously. I had drawn a plan the first day, could have organized the project better, and several times started to the building site to make a suggestion, but each time Mutter called me.

"Rika, help me find the needle I dropped," or, "Here—try on this bonnet," she called again and again from our doorway. Finally, she came straight to the point. "I want to talk to you. Sit close. What I want to say is private, and nothing is private at Indian Point unless it's whispered."

I sat on the floor next to her.

"He's attractive, isn't he?" she asked.

"Who?"

"Kris Kringle, of course." She laughed. "I think Karl is a very nice young man. He has good manners."

"You noticed that, too?"

"Noticed it first thing," she said. "I also noticed the ripple of his muscles, the slight swagger in his military walk, and the way you smile at him."

"He smiles at me, too. Do you think I'm flirting with him?"

"No, not too much. It's very natural for you to talk to him. After all, he lives with us, and. . ."

"And?"

"And you are a very pretty girl, one of many pretty girls Karl has been near." Mutter hesitated to go on.

"And?"

"And you are a bright girl with unusual education for your age. You know how to figure facts, and you think, in many ways, like a man."

"And?"

"And, Rika, you will have to be very careful if you wish Karl to admire and feel something special for you."

"Why are you telling me this, Mutter?"

"Because I think you are falling in love with him, and before you go over there giving him advice on how to build a house, you need to stop and remember the proverb: 'Talk is silver; silence is gold.' You must think of silence as a golden duty." Mutter twisted the sunbonnet sash in her hands.

"What does that mean?"

"You have noticed that only Emil may go for our food and water rations. Men do that." Mutter now worked furiously at the wrinkles she had put in the sash. "Men build houses. They do that. If the houses fall in, the men learn from that. But no woman may insult a man by telling him how to do his job."

"But I figured it out on paper. Here." I pulled out the scrap of paper on which I had drawn the hut with the dimensions noted for each wall.

Mutter looked at the paper a long time. "If you give this to Karl, he will be put down. Never put a man down. This is a military man filled with pride and self-confidence. Silence is a duty that doesn't take those things away from him."

"But I could help."

"That would subtract from his sense of worth. You sit in here and think about it. If you go out there and talk too much, you'll come up with a mouth full of sand that grits in your teeth, maybe for a long time." Having finished her motherly duty to me, she gave me a self-conscious hug, put on her bonnet, and left with a threaded needle still stuck in the lapel of her blouse. I sat on the sand floor thinking.

Without my help, the hut was finished, and we gathered to admire it. Oma complimented Karl and announced that since he had worked so diligently on the house, she had invited him to share it with her. And, she said, proudly hugging his waist, the part of him she could reach, he had accepted. I felt as if someone had slapped me and opened my mouth to say that he belonged in our house, but Mutter placed a finger across her lips to signal silence.

"What do you think of the house?" Karl asked me as the two Annas and Sophie went inside to arrange things.

I looked at the low-slung little hut with a funny, lopsided wide-enough-for-Oma door. The walls were made from raw, splintery crate boards, and the crooked peaked roof was of smoother sawmill lumber from the warehouse. It looked like a bald-headed porcupine. I wanted to burst out laughing, but in a flash Mutter's words, "Silence is a duty," came to mind.

It took me a minute to think of something to say: "Why, I think it's the most beautifully unusual architecture in the world. The door is just right for Oma." Then, unable to control myself, I broke out laughing. "But how will you ever get in?"

Karl looked crestfallen, then examined the door objectively and also began to laugh with deep guffaws. When he had recovered, he said, "Why, I'll just bend over."

I laughed until tears flowed down my cheeks. I imagined short, plump Oma going in the square door dragging her valise with the fantail of sand spewing out behind, and next to her, folded double, ape-like, to get in the door, was Karl.

For the next few minutes Karl walked ape-like, bent double, hands dragging in the sand.

Sophie came out of the ridiculous house, joined the fun, and when she fell exhausted on the sand, said, "Texas is really a funny place."

We knew that Sophie would never know why we were laughing, and it started all over again.

∞

That night, for the first time in a week, I slept well. It was a relief to have more room in our house. I watched the shadow of Oma's campfire on the tent roof and realized Karl had struck it rich. For indeed, Oma had money, and she had used some of it to buy wood to burn for cooking and warmth. People all around were struggling to put up a roof, and Oma Gunkel appeared extravagant. But I liked her spirit.

The next morning Karl met me at the water's edge. "That woman is cuckoo," he said.

"What do you mean?"

"After we ate our stew, I started down to the water to wash the dishes, but Oma said, 'No, don't do that. I'm expecting company.'"

"Company?" I asked. "Who?"

"Well, we sat by the fire, and Oma crossed her arms, closed her eyes, and started to rock back and forth. After several times of doing that, she began to say, 'Yes, yes, yes.' Then she rocked back and forth and said, 'Yes, yes, yes.' After several times of repeating it, she opened her eyes and laughed and laughed, then closed her eyes, folded her arms, and rocked back and forth."

I liked her, admired her spirit, and didn't want to think ill of her. "You think she is crazy?"

"I said she was cuckoo, didn't I? But you haven't heard the end yet. After she quit rocking, I told her I was going to bed and asked if she still expected company. She laughed and said, 'Oh, didn't you enjoy his visit?' When I asked whose visit, she became indignant. 'Whose visit indeed! Why Gustav Gunkel's, of course.'"

"What did you say to that?"

"What can you say about a man who has been dead three years? I said, 'Good night, Oma' and went to bed."

361

The days passed. Somehow I idled away the time watching Mutter shake out the sheets and wet down the sand floor. Karl and I read *The Galveston News*. I rescued Sophie from one of the fighting Kessler boys who socked her in the eye. Every evening at sunset I met Emil up the beach when he came home from the pier. We shared news of the day.

When told of Oma Gunkel's long-departed husband, Emil became protective.

"The woman's crazy, so stay away from her. And keep Sophie away from her. There's no telling what she will do next."

I shrugged, planning to keep an open mind. I liked her independent spirit, one very much like mine.

I looked at the sunburned and peeling protective brother who had been my playmate, teasing brother, friend, and now confidant. There was something about the way he held his teeth together tonight that made him look different, and for the first time I realized that the responsibility of getting the Mueller family safely to New Braunfels was taking its toll on Emil. His shaggy hair, the ragged tears in his pants, and the patched places in his shirt where the heavy crates had ripped the sleeves told of his character. I felt swollen with pride at the way he handled this horrid place. At least he was doing something important with his time.

Paying only a minute's notice to the tinge of guilt whirling in the pit of my stomach, I touched his shoulder. "Emil, I really admire you."

"Why?" He shifted the three pieces of rough wood he had brought home.

"Because you never complain, and you are very responsible. You work harder than anyone. I don't think we could survive this short layover at Indian Point without you."

He stopped walking, started to say something, decided against it, and moved on toward the house. "Thanks, Sis. I'd say nice things about you, too, but I'm just too tired to talk." Wordlessly, he placed the three boards on top of the draped sheet roof, then ducked his head and entered the house.

During supper Emil ate automatically, constantly looking from Mutter to Sophie, then me. I asked him what was wrong.

"Nothing."

"Then why do you keep staring at us?"

Sophie looked at Mutter. "Be-because Mutter looks awful."

Mutter forced a smile. "The heat bothers me. So do the mosquitoes."

"You should talk about awful, Sophie. Look at your black eye! You've been in trouble with every kid on the beach," I said.

Sophie defended herself. "Y-you should t-talk. Y-you're just a pain in my n-neck. A-all y-you ever do is sit a-around."

I couldn't defend myself. It was true.

Emil sounded tired. "I'm worried about your thin bodies. I hate seeing you grimy and sunburned."

We sat in silence. Finally, Mutter spoke. "Virtue has its own reward. We are doing what we must do and will be rewarded."

I tried to cheer Emil. "Besides, it's only temporary."

"No! I have to tell you. . ." Emil's voice was scarcely audible as he folded his arms across his knees and put his head down on his arms. "The news at the warehouse is very bad. I'm glad you have stayed away from there. Everyone is sick. And on the other side of Indian Point they are burying dozens every day."

"But we're not sick, and any day we'll leave for New Braunfels," Mutter insisted.

Emil raised his head and looked wildly from one to the other. "That's just it. We may be here for months. Most of the wagons returning from New Braunfels have been conscripted by the army. There is no one to help us here, and no way to go inland." We sat in silence. "And we're out of money."

After a little while he continued apologetically, "I'm sorry. I'm so sorry." He put his tired head down on his arms again.

We couldn't take it in. No money. No transportation for months. How could we survive Indian Point? How long before hunger, malnutrition, or disease hit our family? Even sassy Sophie said nothing.

Chapter 6

Oma would not believe the worst. She talked gaily about the forthcoming trip to New Braunfels, chatted with Karl, and kept her nightly laughing vigil with long-departed Gustav.

Big Lucas Beck and his shadow, Otto, continued to walk at the water's edge every day, making certain I saw them. Feigning politeness, Lucas lifted his big, black hat. With a guilty black feeling in my soul, I wished both of them would catch the fatal typhus sweeping Indian Point.

Mutter cheerfully kept her daily routine, and with enduring optimism encouraged all of us. Each day she sat in the shade of the hut teaching Sophie the well-known proverbs that were the basis of all German education. I had heard them all again and again since I was three. What's more, I had believed them all. But where had the proverbial honesty, hard work, and cooperation brought me? Grudgingly I admitted that I still believed in honesty but knew I wouldn't participate in hard work and cooperation.

I divided my time between learning English with Karl and reading music from the trunk. With music propped against the water bucket, I practiced fingering a Robert Schumann song on my imaginary pianoforte. As I became more bored, I argued with Mutter every day about playing Emil's trumpet or Vater's flute. She forbid taking the valuable instruments out of their wrappings because, she said, the salt air would corrode the valves. I knew she was right, but even the arguments were diversions and gave me the chance to vent my anger at Vater for bringing us to this place.

Karl paced up and down the beach and trudged along the dune crests every day. Watching him, I began to understand the meaning of the term *itching feet*. He longed to move on. Finally, he went to Runge's Store and meagerly outfitted himself for the trip. It was a gamble because the expenses of his trip inland with the Verein had been paid in advance in Germany. He said he still had some savings but could see no future in waiting at Indian Point. Every morning before daylight he hiked the trail toward Blind Bayou, where he waited for the chance to join an occasional group of immigrants leaving for Victoria or Cuero or Seguin or, as he said, "Just anyplace out of this God-forsaken mosquito-ridden pesthole."

Every day he returned, having eaten a few supplies from his duffel, for no one in any part of Indian Point would share food with him. An eerie mood of selfishness prevailed. While there was plenty of food and liquor, a scarcity of water and the probability of catching any one of the dreaded diseases made everyone leery of strangers and downright unfriendly. The Kessler's cow, Wilma, lacking proper food and water, had begun giving less milk, and the Kesslers quit sharing with us. And Oma, quick to share in the beginning, now felt our withdrawal and kept to herself. She was right. Emil pleaded with us to stay away from the crazy lady with the present dead husband.

As the days went by, I missed Karl and our daily English lesson. Even music held no charm. Only the weather varied when a blue norther blew in, and the temperature dropped from blazing hot almost to the freezing point. With chattering teeth we opened the trunks and dug deep for woolen clothes, but Emil was working when the temperature dropped and came home sneezing and coughing.

He insisted on working the next day. There were, he said, at least three dozen men waiting to take over his job. But that evening he staggered up the beach and collapsed just inside the door. Mutter and I dragged his limp, hot body to a small rug in the corner, took off his shoes, and loosened his belt.

Sometimes he chilled until his teeth chattered and his body convulsed with shaking. Then he burned with fever. All night we bathed his face and arms with damp cloths until the water was gone. The tallow candle flickered over into a puddle and we sat helplessly in the dark, listening to him groan.

All night I held Emil's hand and worried.

By sunrise I rummaged through a trunk for something to read, anything to take my mind off Emil. All I could find was a pamphlet widely circulated in Germany by the United States government called "Special Report on Immigration." It told of the healthy climate of Texas, employment opportunities, the ability to market produce, and the liberties unrealized in Germany. I examined the Adelsverein papers, which in exchange for 240 dollars had promised land to cultivate, a log house, transportation to the interior, and food for the trip plus public services such as mills, gins, hospitals, churches, and schools—all to be built at Adelsverein expenses.

I couldn't help but wonder. *Were all these promises lies? Will there be land or food or transportation, or will we all die here in the filth and heat?*

I flung the pamphlet to the ground and went back to watching Emil.

It was the first time I had nursed anyone, and I found the constant bending and the wringing of cloths and the stifling, moist heat in the tent oppressive. After a few hours, I staggered out of the house and plunged headlong, clothes and all, into the foaming, cool surf and lay there a long time thinking about Emil. A fear gnawed at

365

me. *What if Emil dies? How could we bear living without him? How could we survive without our leader and caregiver?*

But Emil didn't die, and in the midst of nursing him I made the discovery that it felt good to help. The crack in my resolution against helping made me feel uncomfortable. For a fleeting minute, I considered helping with the dishes and laundry, but glancing around the littered beach Vater had brought me to made me stiffen my back and lift my chin.

After four days of worrying about his job, Emil dragged himself to the warehouse. He was gone less than an hour. Adolph Stein had been given his job.

"But," he announced proudly, "I have found a way for us all to survive. I have joined the Texian army. My pay will be sent to you here."

We sat in stunned silence. Finally Mutter uttered a soft protest. "Oh, no!"

"But, Emil, you're the head of the household. How shall we get along? I don't want you to leave." I clung to Emil's arm.

"Don't do it, Emil," said Mutter. "You should have talked it over with us. You could be killed! Don't do it; everything will be all right. You'll see."

"All right?" Emil shouted. "Look around you. We're stranded in the middle of a nightmare!" He pounded the doorpost until the hut shook. "We could die here!"

Sophie cried, holding up her arms to be lifted. "D-don't g-go, Emil!"

Mutter and I pleaded with him, using every argument.

"Stop!" yelled Emil. "It's the only way."

It was true, and we knew it.

⸎

A black feeling of despair pressed down on all of us the next day as we watched the small band of recruits walk out of sight toward Victoria. I tried to comfort Mutter and Sophie but gave up and spent the rest of the day on the beach crying and talking to myself about the unfairness of life.

By evening, limp from grief, eyes red and swollen, I moved into the foaming shallow water and let it wash over me. As the tide went out, I lay on the cool sand with my eyes closed, listening to the mockery of the laughing gulls: "Emil's gone, ha, ha, ha. Emil's gone, ha, ha, ha."

"R-reeka, get up and s-see what K-karl has brought us!" Sophie pounded on my shoulders.

I opened my eyes and found myself looking into the eyes of a square-nosed, snorting creature that stared down at me a few inches from my face. It nuzzled my chin, and I tried to slide from under it.

"Don't worry. It's tame as a lamb." I saw that Karl was holding it with a rope.

I sat up to look at the rest of the horse. It was huge, except for its head, which should have been on a smaller horse. It was chestnut-colored, except it looked as though someone had spilled a bucket of milk over its back. It had a long silky tail, except that someone had cut part of it away. Its limpid brown eyes looked sleepy, and there was an aura about the animal that said, "Don't bother me. I'm resting."

"H-his name is B-baya," announced Sophie. At the mention of his name, Baya swished his half tail and laid his ears back. His nose twitched.

Karl handed me the reins. "I bought him from some Mexicans who were sick and tired of transporting Germans."

I was speechless.

"And he bought a w-wagon and a t-team of oxen."

"Say something, Rika. Aren't you pleased?" asked Karl.

What could I say? "*How wonderful that you spent your last dollar and got us transportation.*" Or should I yell, "*Why didn't you get this yesterday before Emil joined the army and went off to get killed?*"

Finally, throwing my arms around his neck and blinking back hot tears, I said, "It's ironic and wonderful. You did it!"

Karl grinned. "You knew I would."

I hugged him again until a stern voice interrupted. "Rika! Come here!" My disapproving Mutter stood by the wagon wearing a scowl. She would have much more to say later about the hugs, but for now I was drenched in joy.

Chapter 7

The argument had been going on for hours while they loaded the wagon with our trunks, the crated plough, an anvil, and the heavy black stove. Mutter said no proper young lady would ride in a man's saddle, and Karl countered that we didn't own a sidesaddle. Mutter said it was unthinkable for her own daughter to be seen riding astride a horse, and Karl said it was unthinkable for me to walk and drive the oxen team, and she certainly couldn't do it.

"You and Sophie must ride. I must walk, and Rika must ride the horse, and that's final!" Karl announced.

But Mutter wouldn't let it rest. They didn't ask, but I could have told them I wanted to do neither. Much as I hated Indian Point, my hut home was a known quantity. The impending change churned up new fears, and I looked across the sand dunes, the quagmires of sinkholes, and the mudflats with a gnawing feeling in the pit of my stomach. How would we ever last the distance? And how far would it be? Some said 150 miles. Others said as far as 250 miles.

Finally, Oma Gunkel, who had been hovering around her front door, stopped the argument. She came directly to me. "Take off your petticoat, and put on an extra skirt. I'll show you how to tie the underskirt into protective pants."

Wordlessly, I stepped out of sight behind the wagon, took off my petticoat, rummaged through a basket for my other skirt, and put it on.

"Get on the horse," she said.

I struggled for a foothold on the wagon axle so I could mount, one of the few things Karl had taught me the day before. The riding lesson had left me sore in every muscle and sure that Baya, the comical looking, mixed-breed horse, was deceptive, stubborn, scheming, unruly, anything but funny. Now, as I threw my leg over his back, he sidestepped away from me, leaving the leg dangling in midair.

"Haw! Here, haw!" Oma called in a big, guttural voice that surprised me. It surprised Baya, too, and he allowed Oma to keep a tight grip on his bridle, holding him still, until I was seated. Oma told me how to shorten and gather the underskirt and tie it in a knot, making something like culottes. I wasn't comfortable and couldn't imagine sitting like that for 200 miles, but when I pulled the voluminous top skirt down over my legs, at least I looked presentable.

From my perch on Baya, I watched Oma plant herself between Mutter and Karl.

"She has to ride, you know," she said into Mutter's face. Then she hugged her beloved Karl around the part of him she could reach and, with tears welling under her little round glasses, she fled.

"B-bye, Oma," called Sophie. "W-we'll miss you."

Oma stopped. "Miss me? You've avoided me for weeks. Why?"

No one spoke. Finally, Sophie said, "C-cause Emil told us to. It's because of Gustav, I-I think."

"Emil's been gone three days," Oma said sadly, hurrying through her lopsided, square door and out of sight.

Later we would remember that someone should have gone after her, but we were pressed for time. At the last minute, our wagon had been permitted to join a group of ten others leaving at noon, and we were late for the assembly. As we pulled our wagon into place, the group finished singing the rallying song of all German immigrants, *Das deutche Lied (German Song)*, rolling a renewed wave of homesickness over me like a fog. I barely heard the already elected leader, Frederich Mittendorf, review the rules of the road. However, he got my full attention with the last two rules.

"Most of the halting places have been set. But, depending on traveling conditions, others will be needed. There will be no argument about the campsite selection," he said. "Peter, Hugo, and I will find sites having water, grass for the animals, and wood for cooking. The remaining men and the boys over twelve years old will be responsible for Indian protection."

A chill ran down my back. I hadn't believed the rumors of raids by the Karankawas who ate human flesh. Goosebumps tightened my skin and my body was seized with shakes that frightened Baya. He pumped his head up and down and looked around wildly.

"Are you ill?" called a voice from the next wagon. His voice was musical and his eyes bright with excitement.

"No," I said.

"But you're shivering."

"It's only terror." I hung my head, continuing to shake.

"Don't worry. I, Engel Mittendorf, son of the wagon leader, promise you a good trip. No Indians. Only sunshine and fun." Engel grinned at me.

"Engel! Mind your own business." His mother from next to him on the wagon seat eyed my strange riding habit and smirked disapprovingly at the small-headed horse.

"Good promise, young man," said Mutter from her seat on our wagon opposite the Mittendorfs. "See that you keep it." She handed me her shawl. "Rika, would you like me to hold your reticule while you wrap up?" I couldn't mistake the pride in her voice as she emphasized *reticule*, the height of fashion.

"No, thanks," I said, pushing the strap tightly up to my shoulder. Already this morning I had rescued it from Sophie, who was about to show Karl my diary. If Mutter found out about my secret lump under the diary, she would be angry. After all, she had forbidden the dancing shoes. Oma Gruenwald, my favorite grandmother, had hugged me the day before we left Germany and whispered, "I usually don't hold with fashion, but for once these newfangled reticules make sense." She had draped it silently over my arm.

The large blue and gray tapestry bag held my diary and my secret. "You can't take those frilly dancing shoes to Texas," Mutter had said. "You need sturdy walking shoes." So into the trunk went a pair of ugly brown walking shoes, and on my feet went an identical pair. But wrapped in soft white paper and hidden under my diary rested my secret, my satin shoes with bows and rosette trims. Surely somewhere in Texas there would be a floor for dancing.

As the wagon train began to move, I draped the shawl tightly around my shoulders, waving automatically to the few well-wishers lining the rutted trail out of Indian Point. Suddenly, a weight lifted from my shoulders. Among the well wishers was Otto Mellinghoff, waving his hand, while Lucas Beck, tall in his black hat, shook a clenched fist at me. At last I was free from them. Perhaps I would also be free from the green stinging flies, coral snakes, houseflies, and sand fleas. Such small things, but surely our leaving them was an omen of better things to come. I straightened my back and took a new interest in the wagon train, occasionally stealing glances at Engel Mittendorf. He was very good looking.

Skirting the mudflats surrounding the north rim of Powderhorn Lake, our leader followed the rutted trail left by previous groups of wagons. Heading northwest, we traveled at first on wet, hard-packed sand, finally veering through a small passage between shimmering, jelly-like mudflats.

The sun stood overhead when we cleared the last yellow-flower-covered sand dune and entered the deceptive salt marshes. As far as I could see, the familiar black mangrove dotted the sea of an unfamiliar needle-like grass that looked black and stiff. There were shorter grasses I hadn't seen before, some of them accented with colorful star-shaped flowers. I soon found that the plants were sometimes growing in water when I let Baya wander. His front feet sank, and I was barely able to pull him free, and his hoof prints filled with water before we turned back to the trail.

Flocks of redwing blackbirds darted in and out among the mangroves, and down behind our trail they nabbed insects from the short, matted grass.

I shifted in the saddle, wondering how much longer I could stand the pain of sitting, and strained to see Mutter, whose chin bobbed on her chest. Her drooped shoulders told me that even in the rough-riding wagon she was asleep. Riding next to her, Sophie clutched a fold of Mutter's skirt. . .as a sort of real comfort blanket, I guessed. Over Sophie's shoulder I glimpsed Karl's tilted cap bobbing as he walked next to the oxen.

Our wagon, a bargain for only 45 dollars, was a curious mixture of Mexican, German, and American design, resembling a two-wheel Mexican cart with solid disks for wheels. It qualified as a wagon because it had four wheels and high wooden sides. Swinging from hooks and ropes on its sides were a lantern, water bucket, a bucket of cornmeal, a plank Karl insisted would make a table, and a lidded bucket of oats for the oxen. Tied to the back of the wagon was a square salt lick just out of Baya's reach, but not out of his intention. My arms were sore from holding him away from it.

All morning I scanned the horizon for the dreaded Karankawas, but as the noon heat burned into my face and shoulders, I loosened the shawl and slumped in the saddle, turning my attention to the ragtag collection of wagons creaking and squeaking inland. All the wagons except ours were pulled by horses. Eight of the drivers were Germans wearing the traditional dark woolen caps, and two drivers wore colorful, sun-shading sombreros. These I figured to be hired Mexican drivers. We were next to last in the chain of wagons, directly in front of a Mexican driver who shouted incessantly at the horses in Spanish.

We traveled for several hours, stopping midafternoon to rest the livestock and eat a cold lunch. Every bone and muscle in my body ached, and Karl and Mutter had to help me off Baya.

Mutter felt the effect of the trip, too. Underneath the shade of her big sunbonnet, her eyes had a glazed, burned-out look. When Sophie hurried off in search of other children, Mutter touched my arm and pointed after her. Through parched lips Mutter said softly, "Take care of Sophie. I don't feel well."

Stiffly, I hurried after Sophie, yanked her by the arm, and lectured her all the way back on the lurking evils of the marshes and the probable dishonesty of people on the wagon train. For once, Sophie was too tired to argue.

Remounting Baya was an ordeal I would learn to endure. He was a stubborn, disgusting horse with a fiendish streak running from sidestepping when I mounted to backing me sideways against anything handy. He ignored all my commands, doing just what pleased him except when I kept a painfully tight rein on the bit.

People stared as I struggled to mount, and I wondered if they were staring at the strange horse with the small head and half-shorn tail or the sunburned girl with the strange riding habit mounting a man's saddle. I returned disdainful looks to all who stared and tilted my nose skyward in an imitation of Mutter, who silently endured the hard wagon seat.

As we rode toward Chocolate Bayou, I wondered if I would make it all the way to New Braunfels. Angry as I was at Vater, I missed our long conversations about music and people, and for the next few hours I replayed in my memory the sound of his music lessons and listened to his ideas about the new composer, Carl Maria von Weber. After several hours I lost my sense of place and felt suspended in a dream. I looked with longing back toward Indian Point, now out of sight and miles away.

The Mexican driver, evidently mistaking my looking, lifted his sombrero and smiled.

Abruptly I turned a stiff back toward him.

Chapter 8

From my view on the strange horse, I noticed the vegetation change when we left pure salt marshes. Now we could see small flowering stalks as well as leafless spike plants on which, to Sophie's delight, muskrats and waterfowl fed. The brackish marshes with slippery mud were treacherous. Several times I saw Karl fall and struggle back to his feet, and the horses and oxen lost their footings and had to be helped. Because of the delays and the extra rests our oxen required, we wouldn't make Chocolate Bayou by dark, so a new halting place was scouted.

We circled our wagons and began a frenzy of activity, trying to decide what to do first. Eventually we would establish a routine, but for now everything was disorderly. Finally, Karl unyoked the oxen and led them off to the creek calling over his shoulder, "Rika, you take care of Baya."

Every bone in my body ached, and I could barely stand. "I'm too tired," I muttered. "Besides, I hate that horse. Let him starve."

Karl's eyes burned with anger. He started to retort, closed his mouth, and after a moment's silence said, "You'll have to do it anyway."

Mutter turned from rummaging in the food box. "Let Emil do it."

"Mutter, Emil isn't here."

"Yes, he is."

"No, he joined the army."

For a moment she remembered. "Oh, yes. That's why I feel hollow."

I noticed her repetitious, unthinking movements, dull and lifeless eyes, and her frozen expression. In one day, the life had gone out of her. Or had it been only one day? I recalled the unusual sarcasm and general grouchiness as we packed for the trip. Of course, I had earned the sarcasm. A little guilt crept over me. Perhaps I was partly the cause of her hollow feeling.

"Let me help you find the cornmeal," I said.

She wandered aimlessly away from the food box without answering, drifting toward the oxen, then to a tree, and staggered back to the wagon.

"Sit here." I led her to a shady spot near the wagon.

Her body was limp as a rag doll; her eyes stared ahead vacantly. She was no longer grouchy, just docile.

The little scene had been played out before a silent Sophie and Karl, who still held the oxen's lead lines. His eyes met mine.

"You help here," he said. "Later, I'll show you how to groom the horse." Our eyes lingered for a minute, and he opened his mouth to say more, but, with a jangle of harness, he left.

I sent Sophie to hold Mutter's hand to keep her from wandering, then tried to organize myself to get supper.

But my mind kept going back to Karl. What had he wanted to say to me but couldn't? I hadn't heard him laugh all day, and he seemed changed in ways I couldn't quite name. Was it the long, hard walk? the unasked-for responsibility? the money? Although we would repay him when we got to New Braunfels, he had spent all his money for Baya, our wagon, and the oxen without knowing that we had no money to repay him at Indian Point or that Emil would be gone. Suddenly the carefree soldier of fortune who had come to Texas for excitement and freedom, like the oxen, had been yoked with heavy responsibility. His situation was probably terrifying. A lump came to my throat as my heart reached out to him. I knew exactly how he felt. I hadn't chosen to be here, either.

Somehow I got a meal together with the help of Engel Mittendorf, who urged me to thoroughly cook the dried vegetables Mutter had cooked the day before. His comical pantomime of how sick he had been from eating spoiled vegetable mush made us laugh, and Sophie's giggles got louder and louder.

"Engel, get over here this minute!" his mother squawked like a frightened hen.

Engel flapped his arms imitating a chicken and silently went back to his own campfire, leaving me with a smile on my face.

❦

Morning brought cheerfulness, and as we packed to leave, the usual German proverbs were called from wagon to wagon: "Well begun is half done," "A sleeping fox catches no hens," and "No rose is without thorns." Karl told me more than I wanted to know about oxen as we carried extra water from the creek for them. Oxen do well on low-grade food and pound for pound can pull more than a horse, but they can't sweat so they become overheated and have to be rested until they cool off. This had slowed the wagon train, so Karl's plan was to carry extra dousing water to help with the cooling down. Of course, the water made the load heavier, slowing the oxen even more, but it was the best we could do. If this didn't work, we had been warned by Frederich Mittendorf that our wagon would be placed last in line. If we lagged behind, we would be unprotected.

We were already lagging as the wagons pulled into line. I had been told that an authoritative tone and a short grip of the reins would discipline Baya. So, clutching the reins up short, I stepped one foot on the wagon's axle and threw my other leg up toward Baya's back. In an instant, his tail swished violently, his head and neck pumped up and down, and he sidestepped, leaving me with my leg dangling. I screeched angrily. Eyes wide and angry looking, Baya turned his head and nipped the front of my blouse with his sharp teeth.

My face burned with embarrassment as I tried to ignore the laughs around me. I glared at the rear driver who then lifted his hat, smiled, and said, "Senorita!"

The wagon train moved away from us, and finally I walked Baya until we caught up with the Mittendorf wagon. Engel jumped down to walk with me.

After a while I asked, "What wise proverb have you for this horse?"

"The egg often claims to be smarter than the hen," Engel said.

"So now I'm a hen?" I laughed.

"No. In your case the best proverb is: 'The wisest one gives in.'"

"That's not supposed to mean with horses," I denied hotly.

"All right. Try this one. 'Must is a hard nut to crack.' You *must* ride the horse."

"Would you call this nut a pecan or a walnut?"

With that we both convulsed with silly giggles until Frau Mittendorf cackled, "Engel! Get back up here this instant."

Engel flapped his arms and clucked like his mother hen. Then he grabbed the bridle, stared into Baya's eyes, and shouted, "Whoa, Baya! Stop right now, you stupid animal, you *Dummkopf* of a horse, you walnut and pecan of a horse. Let this girl on your back! Do you hear me, horse?" He offered his knee for my foot, and I clambered on to the surprised horse.

But Baya had the last word. Tail swishing and head weaving, he sidestepped into every bush or small tree he saw all morning. By the first rest halt I was covered with scratches and leaves but dared not get down to help drench the oxen because I feared getting back up. Karl watered the oxen and brought Baya a handful of hay. In return, Baya laid back his lips and nipped a hole in Karl's uniform shirt with his razor-sharp teeth.

Karl swore a string of soldier words I had never heard. Everyone within earshot gasped. Except me. I wondered what they meant.

The Spanish driver behind me laughed, and I glared at him. He dipped the big brim of his sombrero and smiled. "Señorita. Señora."

The misery of sweltering in the August heat and trying to outsmart Baya took concentration, so I didn't notice Mutter huddled in the floor of the wagon seat until the oxen lurched out of line and fled toward the shade of two small trees. Karl ran alongside, whacking their backs with a stick, but it had no effect until they reached the cool shade and stopped so abruptly that Sophie and Mutter were shaken and bruised. That's when I noticed she was wrapped in her shawl and two blankets.

"Tell Emil to help Sebastian get my feather comforter," she said. "I'm so cold I've turned blue."

Sophie's eyes grew wide. "D-don't you know Emil is in the army? What's the matter?"

"Nothing is the matter. I'm just cold," Mutter said.

Nevertheless, her pallid skin, dazed eyes, and wandering mind told me she was very ill. I felt useless. I had no idea what to do for her.

The Spanish driver nodded his huge hat and called "Senorita" as he followed the wagon train out of sight. We had been warned to keep up, and now we were alone on the vast plain. I scanned the horizon for Karankawas and felt goosebumps all over my body as I imagined a flesh-eating Indian behind every bush.

After much nudging and calls of "Haw! Haw!" Karl headed Buck and Bright up the trail. I followed, leading Baya. Walking churned my anger at the uncaring people on the wagon train.

"What kind of people go off and leave us to the Indians?" I yelled to Karl, who didn't answer.

"And what about the sneering Mexican pulling off and leaving us?"

"You mean the m-man in the b-big hat who s-smiles at you?" called Sophie.

I didn't answer.

"And you, Baya, why do you step me into bushes and trees?" I shook his bridle angrily, and he swished his half tail and pumped his head up and down, flinging hot, rancid sweat on my clothes, a stench my nose would endure for days. I tried to remember some of Karl's angry, dirty words.

The afternoon marched angrily on with Karl shouting orders to the oxen while I shouted accusations at the strange, wild horse, and Sophie shouted, "Do something for Mutter!" every few minutes. But as we scanned the horizon and watched the packed trail we were following, we knew we had to keep moving.

The sky was streaked red and pink with sunset as we pulled our wagon into the circle at Agua Dulce. After Karl unyoked the oxen and hobbled their front legs with rawhide thongs, he showed me how to unsaddle and brush Baya. Reluctantly I took care of the wild horse because, as Karl explained, the animals were our future. Only then could I turn my attention to Mutter.

By this time she cried out with leg cramps and begged for more and more water. When I talked to her, she didn't understand me, and her answers to my questions made no sense. I looked down at her pain-wracked, shivering body, and wondered what to do. More water? More blankets? Or would the water set off a cycle of more fluid loss? I wished for Oma or Aunt Eva or, even crazy as she was, Oma Gunkel. I felt helpless and stupid and swollen with fear.

In a panic, I ran to the next wagon and asked Frau Mittendorf what to do. She stepped back from me a few paces and hurled her answer. "Don't come over here spreading your disease, young woman," she squawked at the top of her voice.

I felt like someone had punched me in the stomach. I couldn't get my breath, and the pain of realization felt like thousands of needles sticking in my skin: *Mutter is contagious! No one will help us, and we will all die from the disease as so many did at Indian Point.*

"Rika—hey, Rika," a voice whispered from behind the Mittendorf wagon. "Come here." Engel kept his distance but quickly said, "Frau Kellerman in wagon four has nursed a lot of people. Ask her what to do."

"Thank you, Engel," I said quietly.

"Engel! Get here this minute," his Mutter cackled.

Engel flapped his chicken arms and grinned. "I'd help you if I could." And he was gone.

Chapter 9

I found wagon number four and in the gloom of darkness stood just outside the ring of light from Frau Kellerman's fire while I studied the shadowed angles of her face. She was tall with blond braids coiled around the top of her head. A shapeless, patched dress covered her thin, angular body. She bent to stir a pot full of thick gruel that sent steam spiraling into her face. Something about the ramrod straightness of her back made me hesitate. Could I trust this stiff-looking woman? Would she, fearing sickness, send me away? If she agreed to talk to me, could I trust what she said? I had trusted Vater, and he had brought us to this terrible place. I had trusted Oma, and she turned out to be crazy. I had trusted Emil to take care of us, and he went off to get killed. But Mutter's life hung in the balance.

"You, in the shadows, come on in." Frau Kellerman motioned.

I ran to the fire and, like a small child, blurted out my predicament.

Frau Kellerman stopped stirring the contents of the pot and studied me. The delicious smell of oatmeal made my mouth water. I had last tasted oatmeal in Galveston. I scuffed my heavy shoes, nervously waiting for her answer.

"You're the courageous girl on the strange horse."

"Strange horse, but I'm very lacking in courage."

Frau Kellerman reached for a bowl, spooned in a generous serving of oatmeal, and poured molasses over it. As I ate, she removed the pot from the fire and handed her husband the spoon. "Herman, this pretty girl needs help. Will you serve yourself tonight?"

"Of course. God go with you."

Why was Herman not surprised?

"Do you do this often?" I asked as we walked toward our wagon.

"Yes."

"Are you a doctor?"

"Oh, no. I once worked in a hospital in Bremen."

"You're a nurse then?"

"No. I merely changed linens and cleaned messes."

My silence betrayed my disappointment.

"Don't worry. I learned a lot by watching and listening. I can at least help you find out what is wrong with your Mutter. Then you will know what to do."

"But I don't do anything." My voice trembled. "I don't know how."

"You must learn."

Once again the words of a proverb came to mind: "Must is a hard nut to crack." But this time, with all my heart, I wanted to learn what to do. Mutter's life depended on it.

Confidently, as though she had done this a thousand times, Frau Kellerman made the diagnosis. The low body temperature, blue skin, leg cramps, and acute thirst, she said, indicated the first stages of cholera, which Mutter had probably caught from contaminated food or water. Within the next two days she would probably worsen with diarrhea, vomiting, and complete body cramps.

"W-will she d-d-die?" Sophie stammered.

"We don't really know. But we will do our best."

Without looking up, Karl poked the ashes of our fire and said, "We ate and drank most of the same things."

For a long time only Mutter's moaning filled the silence.

"It's entirely possible you won't have cholera," Frau Kellerman said finally. "We must not think that way. Fear has a way of paralyzing us."

Frau Kellerman comfortably slipped her arm around Sophie's shoulders, hugging her close. That's when I noticed she had no hand. She dismissed my stare as nothing and continued, "We must do our best and pray a lot."

Clusters of crudely made crosses marked the trail we had traveled so far. Had the loved ones of those persons done their best and prayed a lot? Suddenly the balance had gone out of everything. A dizzy panic swelled behind my eyes, and my knees felt weak. *Lord, help me,* I prayed silently.

Then, leaning against the wagon, I asked weakly, "What must we do to help her?"

Frau Kellerman told us, and doing it took most of the night. Quietly so not to awaken our neighbors, we rearranged the contents of the wagon to make a bed. The anvil had to be left behind, along with a large black cooking pot that just wouldn't fit. We boiled water and cooked a pot of watery corn gruel, and, in the dark of night, I went to the creek to wash Mutter's clothes. Dunking my hands in that cold, black water was almost as hard as taking the last wet steps off the lighter into Texas.

"Don't be afraid. I know you can do it." Frau Kellerman stooped beside me to help.

"How do you know that?" A tinge of defiance must have been in my voice.

"I've been there," she said simply. "I have come through the blackest time of my life." She paused, seeming to gather courage. "Four months ago at Indian Point our two children died. How I survived I do not know. But I did, and you can."

"But I don't know how to cook or take care of Sophie or even ride that horrible horse."

"Frederika, you can do it. What is, is. What you must, you will." We had finished wringing the clothes. "Straighten your hair and blouse before we go. That handsome soldier is waiting by the fire to be fed."

It was when I bent to stir honey into the cornmeal mush that Karl chuckled.

"Is there anything funny?" Sarcasm tinted my voice.

"Nah, I was just thinking that you may become the fat *Housefrau*."

"What I intend to do in Texas certainly does not include becoming a fat *Housefrau*. I have other plans."

But later, as I handed Karl another bowl of mush, my hand stopped in midair with surprise. Although I enjoyed feeding this handsome soldier who made me feel all tingly inside, I felt trapped by responsibility. This was my family, and I had indeed become the *Housefrau*.

❦

The next morning Karl made all the arrangements. First he convinced Frederich Mittendorf that if we isolated ourselves to lagging last on the wagon train, the others wouldn't become contaminated. Next he had to convey this message through a series of gestures to the Mexican drivers behind us. Before they pulled away, they loaded the cooking pot and anvil on their wagon.

The larger driver tipped his sombrero, smiled at me, and said, "Thank you, Senorita."

I glared at him. Imagine taking advantage of our misfortune!

"Wait!" called Karl. "You speak English?"

"Yes, hombre. You also?"

I couldn't understand most of what they said, but they laughed a lot and pointed at the horse. Karl was laughing when he turned back to me.

"His name is Carlos. We have twin names," Karl said. "Carlos says that unless he has to discard the anvil because of its weight, he will return it in New Braunfels. He also says *Baya* in Spanish means 'berry.' The horse is well named." He laughed again.

"I see nothing funny about it," I said.

"But he earned his name from backing people into berry bushes."

"So?" I said acidly. "How does that help me stay out of bushes and trees?"

"Don't you see? His name is Spanish for his bad habits. He is known in Spanish, and he knows Spanish. Baya is a Spanish-hearing horse. You speak German."

"So, I don't know Spanish."

"But Carlos will teach you."

I glanced back at Carlos, who lifted his sombrero and smiled, showing his straight, white teeth.

"Quit scowling at him. He has already nicknamed you 'the dragon baby.' At least smile and nod. We need his help."

I smiled and nodded.

There were calls back and forth in English and Spanish with explanations in German and my trials of the Spanish words that brought howls of laughter from Sophie and the men. I hated it, but I had to conquer Baya before he conquered me.

I tried again and again. The Spanish words felt uncomfortable in my mouth, asking my tongue and lips to do strange rolls and swallows. Finally, I learned *parar* for "halt" and *¡andele!* for "get a move on there." My mind could not comprehend getting the horse to hold still, *estarse quieto o callado*, which I yelled again and again at Baya. The wagon train was moving out of sight when Carlos called to Karl with instructions for a verbal shortcut: Slap the horse on the rear with my hand and yell, "*Aquietarse!*"

It worked! I soon found myself arranging my strangely tied skirts on the even stranger horse.

Despite the scorching heat, Mutter grew colder, and her skin turned a deeper blue. From time to time Karl gave her water, and I helped her with the frequent toilet stops. Our wagon lagged farther and farther behind. Fearfully I watched the occasional solitary groves of six or eight trees for signs of lurking Karankawas. To give her something to do, I asked Sophie to help me play "I Spy" for Indians. It was a mistake. She became more and more fearful and kept asking if an Indian would eat her. As I scanned the trees, a tingling sensation played up and down my back as I wondered the same thing, but each time we passed safely.

Following the prints of the wagon train, we made our lumbering way mile after mile, halting for rest and food where the others had stopped. At one stop we found a little bucket of berries between the worn wheel ruts. Another time a tin plate of corncakes and dried beef was placed on a big rock between the wagon wheel marks. I knew who was responsible and imagined her picking the berries. How did she hold the bucket? And how, with only one hand, could Frau Kellerman pat out the corncakes? Considering her thin body in the patched, shapeless dress, how could she afford to share with us? Suddenly I was warmed with respect for this woman I didn't know. But perhaps I knew the important thing about her. *She cares.*

Frau Kellerman's surprises were the only glimmer of brightness in an otherwise painful day. Although Mutter was freezing under her blankets, my head was on fire from the relentless burning sun. Even the part in my hair was burned and blistered. That morning Baya had sidestepped me into a bramble tree, and when I finally freed myself, I was so distraught I hadn't even missed my blue-flowered sunbonnet that was probably still dangling from a bramble.

⁓⁓

It was dark when we caught up to the halting place. Carlos motioned us to a fire burning near but not in the circle of wagons. Over the fire hung a big cooking pot bubbling with beans, and stacked neatly on a hot rock near the fire were steaming tortillas. Carlos smiled, lifted his hat, pointed to the beans, and disappeared to his own fire. The surprise gesture, especially from someone I thought had been leering at me for three days, overwhelmed me to tears, and I fled out of sight in back of the wagon. Exhausted and afraid, I leaned over the salt block and gave in to silent tears.

The day had sent too many assaults on my senses. Mutter had lost so many body fluids her skin looked like a dried prune, and the smell of her even now left my stomach queasy. My entire body ached from the part of my hair and my eyeballs to the blisters on my ankles. All day Sophie had whined and cried and Karl, though hotly denying he was hurt, had limped and his shoulders had the same droop of fatigue I had seen when Emil came home from working in the warehouse.

My silent tears turned to sobs as I remembered the mounds of dirt with crude wooden crosses at Chocolate Creek. Next to them had been no longer needed possessions. And along the trail at a distance we had seen sheets and clothing covering mounds of what I guessed were partly decomposed bodies. Would we become wooden crosses or lumps under covers?

Just then the stump of an arm rested on my shoulder, and a husky voice said softly in my ear, "Texas is hell."

I flung my arms around her neck and wept my gratitude and fears onto Frau Kellerman's thin, bone-sharp shoulders.

⁓⁓

Mutter's only chance for survival would be a doctor, and the nearest doctor would be in Victoria. Frau Kellerman said if all went well, the wagon train would arrive at Spring Creek the next evening. It was rumored to be only two or three miles from Victoria, a Spanish town in which a group of German immigrants had settled. We would look for a doctor who spoke German. I had to leave the wagon train. There were things I must do, like them or not. First, I had to deal with my frightened sister, who was clinging to a lifeless-looking mother. I opened the trunk and took out Sophie's doll.

"Sophie, I think Glorianna is feeling sad. Why don't you hold her while we travel. She would feel much better."

"R-r-really? You m-mean it?" She hugged Glorianna.

"Yes, I mean it. Just keep her away from Baya, or he will bite her clothes. Why don't you take her to bed with you tonight?"

Sophie squealed with delight. "Glorianna, you have n-never s-slept under the s-stars. W-wait until you s-see them."

The next morning Karl called me to help him yoke the oxen. As we worked, he said, "You must know that without these oxen and the horse you dislike, we will never make it to New Braunfels. They deserve your best care."

"I'll help you take care of them," I said.

Karl looked at the ground as he spoke. "You'll have to do it alone. I am going on to New Braunfels with the others."

My breath caught in my throat, and every muscle in my body tensed. *What could I say?* Angry thoughts tumbled through my head. He was deserting me when I needed him most. *I can't manage the oxen. In fact, I can't manage anything.* Then I remembered that he had spent the last of his money for us and had been yoked with such grim responsibility that the carefree soldier had disappeared. To be fair, I shouldn't make him feel guilty.

I studied the face of the grimy, unshaven person before me and said the only phrase that came to mind: "Texas is hell!" I could feel my face go hot and red.

It was out of character for me and made him laugh. I laughed, too, and we both laughed for a long, long time, but it wasn't really funny. We only covered our tension.

Between stops to help Mutter, when Baya was plodding along behaving himself, I tried to untangle the anger I kept feeling. I could be enraged at Emil for leaving us. Or I could hate Karl for not even considering what would become of me. For a moment, I even played with loathing myself, but it was too painful. By nightfall, as I climbed off the hated horse and faced another sleepless night, I was able to focus my genuine anger at Vater. He was the only one who had wanted to come to Texas.

There weren't many choices after I pulled away from the wagon train the next morning. All I could do was try to hold the oxen to the packed dirt leading toward Victoria. When the oxen behaved themselves and everything was calm, I remembered our departure. At the last minute everyone had given me instructions until I had become totally confused. My mind became numb, and I couldn't remember anything. Finally, I had written down Spanish words for Baya, commands for Buck and Bright, the amounts of feed for the animals, Frau Kellerman's instructions for Mutter's sanitation and care, and the name of Dillman Mantz, whom Engel had met at the Galveston Verein compound. I got it in writing, but I was in a fog and strangely couldn't feel anything. My body seemed detached and just going through necessary motions. . .until something happened that I would replay in my mind for days to come.

As we said good-bye, Karl reached for my hand, slowly interlaced his fingers with mine, and pulled the hand close to his chest. My hand tingled, and my heart raced as our eyes met and the back of his other hand tenderly brushed my cheek. I couldn't breathe.

"You're very special," he whispered. Then he pressed his lips to mine in a long, mouth-tingling, body-jangling, good-bye kiss. My lips responded. Surprised by our reaction to the kiss, neither of us spoke. We just stood there slightly apart, looking at each other.

In the background, Sophie had cried and begged him not to leave her with me, the old "pain in my neck." But after promising to tell Vater we were in Victoria, he waved and walked away.

"You can't leave us," Sophie called, "you're family."

But he kept walking. It was true he had become one of the family, but I had hoped for more. Frau Kellerman knew it. And she knew me. As I struggled to get Baya and the oxen moving at the same time, I had heard her call, "You can do it. You can do it."

It took us most of the day to get to Victoria in the zigzag course the oxen took. As we entered the town, people stared at the strange horse tied to the strange wagon with a sheet tent tied over Mutter, and I felt their eyes intent on the sunburned, grimy girl driving, of all things, oxen!

But there sat Sophie on the wagon's seat, clutching Glorianna and smiling and waving to everyone as if she were in a parade. Soon the stares turned to words of welcome, and by the time we reached the Street of the Ten Friends at the square, a few people offered to help. I was wary. Everyone looked strange with handkerchiefs covering their lower faces, and we could barely see their eyes. Then I noticed that the square had been dug into a mass grave. Across the square, a large man was unloading stiff bodies into the pit. I looked away.

"What's going on here?" I called to a man.

He shrugged, said, "English?" and walked away.

From the shadows of a doorway stepped a tiny lady whose straw hat perched on top of curly gray hair. "German?" she asked.

I nodded.

"You are welcome here, but if I were you, I'd turn that wagon around and leave. People have died of cholera," she said in her high-pitched voice.

All hope evaporated. My shoulders slumped in defeat. "But I can't leave," I said softly.

The little lady came nearer. "There is the blackness of death here. See?" She pointed across the square to the man unloading corpses. "We call him Black Peter. Day and night he unloads bodies. And here"—she pointed to an approaching wagon—"is Dillman, his helper. I watch them from my window day and night. You must leave."

"I have brought my sick mother to a doctor. She has cholera."

The petite lady stepped quickly away and fled across the street to her house, slamming the door behind her.

"Dillman! Dillman!" I shouted at the approaching wagon that halted near where I stood. "Are you Dillman Mantz?" I directed my gaze at his eyes, trying hard not to look at the corpses piled high in his wagon.

Sophie threw herself into my arms. "They're all d-dead!" she cried hysterically.

Dillman remained calm. "Yes, I'm Dillman Mantz. Do you have a body for me?" He eyed the prostrate form of Mutter.

"N-no! N-no! N-no!" Sophie cried shrilly.

I continued looking at his eyes, afraid to look at the bodies. "Engel Mittendorf said I should find you."

Dillman's eyes brightened, making him look instantly younger. He seemed my age with blue eyes and long, straight blond hair showing under the black hat that matched the rest of his black clothes. Quickly I told him my story, and he directed me to the doctor's small house a few blocks away, saying he would meet me there later.

A crowd of worried people gathered around the front door of the doctor's house. They shifted restlessly, some talking softly to companions, others staring into space, concern showing on their faces. They scarcely noticed when I pulled my strange wagon to a halt.

"Excuse me. Excuse me." I tried to get through the crowd, but they were locked in their own world of concern.

Sophie charged ahead. "M-m-move," she shouted.

A path opened before us.

Inside, the doctor's house was chaotic. There were beds everywhere, with many pallets made on the floor, all filled with people moaning from various symptoms of being sick. The stench made my stomach churn, and I put my hand over my nose and mouth. Loud moans made talking to the doctor impossible. The doctor turned from a patient and followed me outside.

"Pretty bad," he said. He was gaunt and unkempt with a face that told me he had seen too much suffering. Also, he was dirty, and I thought of Frau Kellerman's sanitation instructions. But he was Mutter's only chance. After he examined her, he said that it seemed she had survived the worst stages of the cholera but had rattles and rales of pneumonia. She also showed signs of malnutrition and dehydration. Without nourishing broth and medicine, he said, her chances for recovery were not good. I spent my last small coin on tonic and medicine but declined his offer to keep Mutter at his chaotic, sour-smelling house. Leaving her in such filth would be a death sentence.

But where would Mutter go? We couldn't live in the wagon without food and water. And Mutter needed rest, broth, and peace.

In the end, it was Dillman Mantz who became my hero, riding up in his empty, rattling wagon. His aunt, whom he described as ancient but able-bodied, might take Mutter in.

And she did. Two people had been nursed to health under her care. There was a catch, of course. She demanded professional payment. She stood there filling the kitchen doorway with her plump, busty frame on which was draped a faded but clean dress and long, starched apron. There would be no admittance until finances were arranged. We haggled, my temper flared, Sophie cried, Dillman pleaded, but she was immovable. Mutter was carried to a clean bed only after I brought out Emil's gold trumpet and some of our pewter dishes. Until I thought of how much it would cost to care for Mutter, I considered Dillman's Aunt Mathilde a swindling crone, but after I paid her, she turned friendly, even fed us fried chicken, mashed potatoes, and gravy for supper. We gloried in eating real food.

"This was my hospitality," Aunt Mathilde said in her ancient scratchy voice. "It is all. I cannot board all of you or feed your animals."

I am a pauper, I thought, *with a child to care for. And I'm trapped in a dying town.* I became suddenly chilled with fear. Shivers made my hand shake as it stroked Sophie's hair.

"I don't know what to do," I said simply.

"You probably think me a hard woman," Aunt Mathilde said, "but desperate situations call for desperate decisions." She cleared away the dishes as she talked. "How did you get yourself into this situation?"

"I didn't," I said bitterly. "My Vater got me here." Too tired for emotion, I simply poured out the story, leaving out nothing, even my disappointment when Karl abandoned us.

Aunt Mathilde wrung out her dishrag, carefully hung it on a wooden drying rack, and turned her wrinkled face toward me. I felt her bright eyes were seeing to the core of my being.

"Will you listen to the advice of a 70-year-old ancient aunt?"

I nodded my agreement.

"You must go back to join another wagon train going to New Braunfels. Their supply wagon will feed you, and men will help with your wagon."

The thought of leaving my wonderful Mutter behind brought a ringing to my ears, and I thought I would faint. *What would Vater want me to do? What about Emil? Would he leave Mutter behind?* I asked myself. *But they aren't here. What would Mutter want me to do? Burning with fever and unconscious, she couldn't make her wishes known. If she lived, would she think I had abandoned her to death?*

Frozen to the chair with fear, I thought so hard the ringing got worse. I pictured Mutter bravely standing on the dock in the burning sun and again stoically bathing and saying her prayers and reading her Bible in our makeshift beach home. I thought of her selling her dowry furniture to finance the trip. "Find a way," Mutter would say. But what way?

"I can't leave Mutter," I said to the piercing eyes of Aunt Mathilde.

"But you must. Live or die, out of her head as she is, you must leave her. Think of Sophie and yourself and get out of Victoria before you get sick. You must move quickly."

"I feel frozen in the chair. I can't move."

"Do you want to live?"

"Yes," I answered.

"You are well-educated and intelligent."

"Yes." I sat up in the chair, wondering where she was going with the questions.

"You have dutifully obeyed your parents in the past, haven't you?"

"Yes. Except for being lazy at Indian Point. I'm ashamed of that."

"That is the past. In the present, here in my crowded kitchen with death in the wind and no one to tell you what to do, you are in charge. You must make the decision. Whatever you decide has consequences for your entire family. Which consequences are the most promising?" Never once did Aunt Mathilde's eyes waver from mine.

We sat in silence.

Finally I said, "I choose to go to the wagon train. It's our only chance."

"A good choice," said Aunt Mathilde, hugging me. "You are strong, and you will make it."

Chapter 10

B y the time Sophie woke up the next morning, still dressed and clutching Glorianna, Mutter's bedding and soiled clothes had been burned, and her clean clothing was moved inside. As I repacked the wagon, I set aside items Mutter might use when she got well, including some sewing supplies, our beloved family album with the music box, and a heavy plow she could sell for her keep with enough money left for transportation to New Braunfels.

Under the watchful eye of Aunt Mathilde, I yoked the oxen and tethered Baya to the wagon's side. The animals sidestepped and shifted back and forth, apparently as nervous as I was, especially Baya, who reached his razor-sharp teeth toward the buttons on Aunt Mathilde's blue blouse. She ducked backward just in time and slapped his nose. "Keep your teeth to yourself, you deceitful animal."

Wide-eyed, he pumped his head up and down as if to say, "Getcha next time."

"This is a Spanish-hearing horse," I said. "You're wasting good German advice."

Aunt Mathilde laughed. "He understands. Especially the slapped nose. Be firm, Rika, but be careful."

I struggled to hold the nervous oxen steady.

"Here let me hold the yoke while you say good-bye to your Mutter." Aunt Mathilde stretched out her muscled arms and grasped the yoke with such authority that the oxen stood still.

As I looked at Mutter in her clean bed, my heart broke. Eyes closed, lips clenched against painful cramps, purple skin wrinkled and sunken against her thin bones, she gave the appearance of death, and except for an occasional moan, she seemed to be slipping quietly out of my reach. I had never been near to death before and was surprised to find it strangely silent. I was also surprised to hear myself whispering to God, asking him to help Aunt Mathilde keep Mutter alive. Almost as a postscript, I said, "I am such a mess, God. Everyone says I can do these hard things, but I don't feel like it. I need your help. How will I ever do what I have set out to do?"

In spite of the lump in my throat and weakness in my knees, a sense of calm washed over me as I left the safe haven of Aunt Mathilde's clean, little house and silently charged the oxen onto the trail toward New Braunfels. I dared not look back, say another good-bye to Aunt Mathilde, or even turn to wave for fear of losing my nerve. Alone and completely in charge of everything, I fought to remain alert to the dangers of Indians, wild animals, and sinkholes, but my mind wandered to the picture of my silent Mutter. *Leaving her was my only choice*, I kept telling myself.

The morning sun burned my face and sweat ran into my eyes as I trudged on and on. Never had the ugly brown shoes felt so heavy.

Sophie cried all morning, great, wracking sobs that exhausted her until she fell asleep. I felt the same way. Grief for Mutter burned behind my eyes, but her usual words, "Find a way," meant complete concentration on the oxen and the devious horse, Baya, who tried to rush off to any berry bush or low tree.

By early afternoon we approached McCoy's Creek.

The McCoy Creek halting place was at the bottom of a low, sloping hill, the first hill I had seen in Texas. Along the creek grew giant oak trees, dripping gray swags of what I learned later was Spanish moss. There were also small yaupon trees with red berries, huge walnut trees, and giant pecan trees from which hung long twists of grapevine.

Nestled under the oasis of tall trees stood three blacksmith shops, backed by three adobe and timber houses that spewed dogs and children as soon as we were in sight. Besides a few crude outbuildings, there was nothing else to notice except a large stone well. I persuaded the oxen toward the well and halted. Sophie awakened when she heard the children, and she climbed down into the midst of chattering, friendly children whose dogs barked and licked her face and swished circles around her.

I stood still in the midst of the pandemonium and the green paradise that was McCoy Creek. Tired, thirsty, dirty, with tears still burning behind my eyes and memories of dead bodies in wagons seared into experience, I felt relieved and proud. I had made it this far. I could do it! *Frau Kellerman is right*, I thought. *She said I could do it. Whatever "it" is.*

That night I slept in a bed. And the next night. And the next. I washed our clothes and our hair, and we slept in beds night after night waiting for the next wagon train.

Our food supplies dwindled. I knew we had to go with the next wagon train. It was now or never.

∽✇∾

A maximum of ten wagons always made up the next north-bound caravan. Every day I silently rehearsed the little speech I'd make to the next wagon master, trying to convince him to take eleven wagons. My only hope was to convince him before he saw my strange livestock and the weird Mexican cart that really wasn't a wagon. But when the caravan moved in, the wagon master, Herr Schmidt, a strong, hulking man in heavy boots, was not impressed with me, a thin, tall, blond woman with well-kept hair and clean clothes. He was even less impressed with what I proposed to drive. He laughed and ridiculed me. Other drivers gathered around into a tight group, waiting to hear the outcome of my plea and to stare at the strange young woman who dared to consider herself their equals. In the end, they laughed, too. Until a tiny lady with round spectacles perched on her nose, dragging a black valise that made fantails behind her in the dirt, hurled herself into the discussion circle.

"Hold on!" she called.

The men stopped laughing. Sophie flew into Oma Gunkel's arms.

"I know this woman," Oma explained. "She is hard-working, cooperative, deserving, and she has muscles of steel."

Sophie's eyes widened. "R-r-Rika?"

Oma squeezed the breath from Sophie so she could say no more. "Frederika Mueller is a victim of circumstances. I will help her. And my driver, Kurt Kessler, will vouch for her. We are all friends."

I held my breath. Emil had warned me to stay away from the crazy Oma Gunkel, but here she was, about to save my life. *What would Emil want me to do?*

I wondered how Kurt got involved with Oma. I wondered how I could accept her help and not get caught in her craziness. And I wondered if I could possibly live up to her assessment of me. I held my breath as the wagon master considered. Then I noticed him staring at my ugly, worn, and dusty brown shoes, barely visible under my clean skirt.

"I don't know you," the wagon master said, "but your shoes tell me much. You and your strange livestock may go with us. I know a few things about oxen, though. They overheat. You carry extra water to avoid delays. We will leave you if you lag behind."

"Thank you," I said. "I'll work hard to keep up." Then I gave Oma a big hug and whispered in her ear, "I'm not any of those things you said."

She whispered back, "Oh, but you are. You just don't know it yet."

Her confidence overwhelmed me, and I felt my spirits soar. Maybe I could do it. Suddenly I felt happy. "I'm really glad to see you, Oma. And I'm glad you got out of Indian Point so quickly."

A raspy voice behind me said, "And we're really glad to see you, too, Frederika. I'll vouch for you. And we will also be watching over you."

My heart turned in terror, and I clutched Sophie's hand protectively.

I turned to glare at Otto.

He sneered. "We are watching Sophie, too." Before I could reply, Otto and Lucas walked away.

"Tell me about the terror I see in your face," urged Oma.

"I can't tell you," I murmured.

"Or they will hurt you or Sophie? Right?"

"Something like that," I said.

"Who's g-going to hurt me?" asked Sophie.

"You're safe as a bug in a rug, Sophie. No one is going to hurt you. Frederika looks out for you all the time," said Oma.

Sophie giggled. "A b-bug in a r-rug?"

Elise Schmidt, the wagon leader's wife, came to wish me well the next morning. As she spoke, her eyes roamed the oxen's yoke and checked the tether on Baya, who was tied behind the wagon. However, she seemed friendly, and I couldn't blame her for running a safety check. "Would Sophie like Catherine, who is five, and Phillip, who is six, to come sit with her this morning?"

"Y-yes, y-yes!" squealed Sophie.

It was arranged, and Elise brought them. Before they climbed onboard the wagon, she made the three of them run around the wagon fifteen times, one for each year of their ages. She said the running would keep them from becoming restless on the long ride. Then she made them go to the outhouse, the last one we would see for days.

While they were gone, she confided in me. "I know this responsibility is new to you. I'm sorry for your situation. The women will help you any way they can, but I have to say the men all have bets on how many miles you will last. I'm betting on you." She glanced at my dirty, heavy, brown shoes. "The men who walk with the animals all wear two pairs of socks. It prevents blisters."

I found another pair of socks and relaced the dreadful brown shoes just as the wagons pulled into order. The socks felt soft and my spirits soared with confidence as I pulled our wagon into last place, a dangerous spot for one likely to lag behind, and took my place walking next to the oxen.

I thought of Frau Kellerman and her two lost children and how she managed with part of an arm. She had said I could do "it." And Aunt Mathilde's voice rang in my ears: "You are strong, and you will make it." Now the crazy woman Emil had warned me against, Oma Gunkel, had turned up telling everyone I was hard-working and had muscles of steel.

They might be right, I thought, *but how can I ever carry these heavy brown shoes over a hundred miles?* I was yanked back to reality when Bright lunged off, and I quickly flicked him with my stick and called his name. He lunged against the yoke, dragging

Buck along with him.

Although the men had doubts about my making it to New Braunfels, at least one man at the McCoy Creek station had taken me seriously. Bart Creedon loved animals and thought that everyone should. When I hurried through the feeding of the oxen and Baya one morning, he had chastised me. "Treat them with care, and they will work hard and obey you. Well, almost obey you," he admitted. "They're stubborn creatures. Get to know them. Touch them. Talk to them."

"Talk to them? What would I say to an ox?"

Every morning Bart came to tell me exactly what to say and when to say it. All oxen have the same names related to how they are yoked. Buck is in the left loop, and Bright the right. Oxen lunge forward in the yoke rather than pulling in harness as horses do, so guiding them meant walking to their left and controlling them verbally.

Bart, who had immigrated two years before, had learned English, so he was able to instruct me in the English command words: *Gee* meant "turn right," *haw* meant "turn left," and *whoa* meant "stop." Bart said that sometimes when one or both oxen got out of control, all the driver could do to stop them was jump up and down and swear. Would I like him to teach me some English swear words? he asked.

Since stored in the back of my mind were the Spanish commands and swear words I was to use on Baya, I figured they would all come out a jumble, so I declined.

"Whoa! Whoa!" I yelled as Bright moved away from me. Frantically I searched my English vocabulary learned from *The Galveston News* for words the oxen might know that would bring them to a halt. Bright lunged on, dragging the struggling Buck.

As loudly as I could muster, I yelled, "J. M. Habich wants music students on pianoforte."

Bright lunged on.

"Sappington's Pills and Bateman's Drops! Sappington! Bateman! Whoa!" I switched to Spanish. "*Parar! Parar!*"

Tossing wildly, and hanging on for dear life, the children in the wagon began German namecalling: "Rattle buck! Rattle buck!" They switched to, "*Dolt! Dolt!*"

Suddenly Bright slowed his gait, Buck steadied in the yoke, and when I called "Whoa," they halted.

Even with a big bruise on his chin, Phillip thought the ride a great adventure, but Catherine and Sophie were crying and shaking as I climbed up to the wagon seat and took them in my arms.

"Did you see the snakes?" Phillip asked.

"What snakes?" I asked.

"The ones on the trail that Bright went around."

"Snakes!" My heart that had been beating faster than a drum suddenly stopped, and my skin went cold and clammy. I thought I'd faint. I put my head on top of Sophie's and Catherine's and wept.

After the oxen were watered down, and the children settled, I hugged Bright's neck and told him very complimentary things in German. When I took my walking place next to the oxen I discovered that the brown shoes rebelled against taking one more step. My legs felt loaded with lead, and I heard a strange buzzing in my head. Totally unequal to my responsibility, I did something I hadn't done in a long time.

I closed my eyes and prayed: *God, help me. I'm nothing. I don't know oxen. I hate the horse, and I can't cook. Most of all right now, I'm tired and afraid, and the children are scared. The wagon train is out of sight. Father in heaven, please save us from the Karankawas. Oh, help. . .*

When I opened my eyes, it hit me. *I have just been delivered from snakebite. All blessings come from God!*

I yelled the oxen forward, and launched into joyous song:

"*Praise God, from whom all blessings flow;*
   praise Him, all creatures here below;
   especially you, Bright,
   praise Him above, ye heavenly host;
   praise Father, Son, and Holy Ghost. Amen."

The blessing of deliverance from the snakes on the trail made even the dreadful brown shoes lighter on my feet. As I walked the next few miles, I scanned the packed ruts in the dirt and grass for other snakes, only occasionally glancing at the trees for signs of Karankawas.

About noon we found where the wagon train had halted for lunch. Between the wagon ruts in a clearing near a small stream someone had placed a tin of biscuits and jerky, Oma Gunkel's favorite meat. As we ate, I asked myself some silent questions: *How can I keep moving when my head is spinning from fatigue? Why did I accept two more children for my responsibility? Will I ever catch up with the group, or will they abandon me here?*

Suddenly a light turned on in my head with some answers. Phillip and Catherine will not be left behind by their father, and their mother knew that. That's why she let her children ride with Sophie. This tiny encouragement made me spring into action.

"Phillip, you're the oldest. I shall give you the most important job. I am going to lie down on the grass and rest until you count to five hundred," I said.

"Why is that the most important job?" asked Phillip.

"I'm dead tired. My head is spinning, but if I go to sleep, we will be left behind."

"R-rika, what can I do?" asked Sophie.

"You and Catherine stand in front of the oxen and talk to them. Keep them steady and happy, and whatever you do, don't scare them."

I took off the hated brown shoes and aired my toes; then I lay on the cool grass. Phillip must have counted to at least six hundred, for when I closed my eyes to rest, I was instantly asleep. It was a foolish thing to do, but I honestly think I would have died of fatigue if I hadn't rested. In a few minutes Phillip awakened me, and we were on our way, refreshed and in a cheerful mood.

⸙

When the sun went down and a darkening haze covered the countryside, I spoke reassurances to the children and the oxen, partly to cover the fear growing inside me that Karankawas we couldn't see would pounce at any moment. Also at any moment, complete darkness would hide the wagon ruts I was following, and we would be lost unless we stopped for the night.

As I peered at the barely visible trail, I tried to plan what I would do alone for the night with three children and livestock to care for. What would Emil do if he were here? And how would Mutter calm the children? Who would calm the flutter of fear in my heart and ease the aching of my tired body? To bolster my energy and opinion of myself, I recited my encouragements: Oma Gunkel had said I had muscles of steel, Aunt Mathilde had said, "You are strong, and you will make it," and Frau Kellerman said I could do it. Could they all be right?

I trudged forward, peering into the distance for a direction marker, and my heart leaped with joy when finally I saw bright fires far ahead. As we got closer, against the light, I could see Elise Schmidt walking toward me.

Her only greeting, "I wasn't worried. I knew you'd make it," brought a lump in my throat as she guided me to the space saved for our wagon. Catherine and Phillip jumped from the wagon and were all over Elise with hugs and all-at-once jumbled stories of the oxen, snakes, how they helped, including my 500-count nap.

Elise looked startled, then said in a loud voice, "A very smart thing to do. You were all very brave." She left with her two happy children in tow.

In a way, I was happy, too. Barely, just barely, I had made it. Oma Gunkel appeared from the shadows and announced supper by the nearest campfire, and I heard a rustle of harness, making relief flow over me, until a voice said, "We will take care of the livestock."

There was no mistaking the insinuating voice of Otto as he walked past me in the darkness leading Baya, and there was no mistaking the towering, dark form of Lucas unyoking the oxen. A tremor of fear snaked down my spine. They were keeping their promise of "We will be watching you." Instinctively I reached for Sophie's hand, for they had promised to watch her, too. But I was too tired to protest, and I let them lead the animals away to grass and water as Oma Gunkel guided my arm toward her fire and hot food.

Oma had done strange and tasty things to the dried beef jerky and hominy with herbs from her little bottles, and I could feel myself relaxing after eating the warm meal. I sat on the ground leaning against a wagon wheel while Kurt Kessler and Sophie cleaned the dishes. I felt myself nodding off.

"Don't go to sleep yet," said Oma. "Gustav will be here soon." Karl had told me about Gustav, and Emil had warned me to stay away from Oma. I moved to leave.

"Don't go, Rika," Oma said. "He's harmless, but very entertaining."

"But, Oma, he is dead," I replied.

"Only his body," said Oma. "His spirit gives me laughs and comfort. Don't be afraid. He likes you."

Sophie came to sit by me, and Kurt winked at me as he sat near the fire. Oma had brought out her rocking chair and was rocking vigorously next to the fire.

Oma rocked and chuckled, chuckled and rocked. She slapped her knees and rocked some more. Then she rose and danced around the dwindling fire, kicking up her heels and sashaying this way and that, her face wreathed in smiles. Falling breathlessly back into the rocker, she fanned her hot face and wiped her small round glasses and the bridge of her nose.

"Gustav always swept me off my feet with dancing," she said breathlessly. "Tonight he was dressed in his fine velvet suit, the one he wore the last time we danced. I was the envy of everyone there, for all the women loved to dance with Gustav. He said he would have danced with you, Rika, but he knew your feet hurt, especially in those awful heavy shoes."

I felt under my petticoat for the bulge of the reticule and its contents, and wondered if Gustav could know about the dancing shoes. I shook off the thought, realizing that my thinking sounded as crazy as Oma's. "Did Gustav say anything?" I asked.

"Oh, yes. He had a message for you. 'A fine mess you're in,' he said. . . .I guess referring to the big guy and the little guy. He said that you're so smart, you'll probably use them all the way to New Braunfels."

"Use them?" I asked.

Oma's tone became confidential. She rose from the rocker and came near me. "Sly Otto is good with the sly horse. Gustav said to let them be sly. They can slink into the shadows together."

A smile played at the corner of my mouth as I wondered how it would work.

"And Gustav says the big guy with the tall hat could be yoked to the oxen every time you come to a halting place. Let him think he is threatening you while you let him do the work. He watches you. You watch him work."

I laughed out loud.

"And he said to keep what you know about them under *your* hat."

"But you don't w-wear a hat," declared Sophie.

Kurt laughed. "But maybe she should. I'll give you one of mine in the morning to help you keep a cool head."

We bedded down for the night in a jovial mood, but as I closed my eyes I thought of Emil and his order to stay away from the crazy Oma Gunkel and her long-dead husband and wished for Mutter to help me instead of Oma. What would Mutter do? I longed for her to hug me and help me.

A shiver ran down my back, and tears came to my eyes. Mutter might be dead.

Right now Gustav's advice was nearer than Mutter or Emil. I hadn't seen Gustav, but he made me laugh.

Chapter 11

During the night the wind whipped into a cold frenzy. Wondering how it could be so cold in summer, I found extra cover for Sophie and struggled to tie down the canvas wagon cover. Stinging, cold rain pelted us the next day, turning the wagon trail into boggy ruts. Mud clung to my long skirt, made heavy clumps on my underskirt, and oozed up to the tops of my brown shoes. The lopsided, wide-brimmed hat Kurt had offered saved my head and face from the pounding rain but, like a drain spout, water collected in the brim and gushed out, drenching my already wet clothes. Weighted, I could scarcely struggle along fast enough to keep up with the oxen, energized by the cooler weather.

The wagon train halted for lunch only long enough to water the horses and oxen. We dug into our food baskets for quick food that didn't require a fire. Baya, tethered to our wagon, trailed at the end of his rope, balking when possible until the rope had cut into his neck. Sophie fed him sympathetic words and some of her cold cornbread. By way of thanks, Baya butted her into the bin on the back of the cart.

"I h-hate you," Sophie shouted. "You're a m-mean horse!"

"He is just being himself, Sophie." I sighed. "Brett said horses have feelings, too. He is tired like the rest of us. And see, he has caked mud all over him and the rain is washing it down in big streaks."

"I'm t-tired, t-too," whined Sophie. "I m-miss M-mutter and Emil. And when will we see Vater?"

"Soon, I hope." I lifted Sophie into the covered cart out of the rain. The answer haunted me all the way to New Braunfels as Sophie asked over and over, "A-Are we t-there yet?" and "How m-much longer until we see V-vater?"

⚬⚭⚬

"Remember, we're watching you," Otto whispered as he led Baya away that night.

I watched the back of his brown suit as he pushed, pulled, and yanked Baya toward the water. *They deserve each other*, I thought. I felt myself smile. *I'm watching you work, sly Otto, you funny little man leading my funny little sly horse.*

"I'll help you," growled Lucas as he lifted the oxen's yoke out of my hands.

"Oh, no, thanks. I can do it." How could I sound sincere? Would he fall for it?

There was threat in Lucas's voice. "I am going to help you. Just you be careful with your words to anyone." Lucas yanked the yoke from my hands.

"Thank you. I will be careful," I promised. He followed Otto to the creek, his big, black hat dripping water and his huge boots making a sucking noise in the mud.

Gustav, you old dear, I thought, *your advice was perfect. How could you be so wise and so dead?* Clutching Sophie's hand, I moved my exhausted body toward Oma's wagon.

"Are w-we w-watching them, or are they w-watching us?" asked Sophie.

❦

The rain didn't dampen Gustav's spirit when we sat huddled near the sputtering, meager fire that night. Oma said Gustav had two messages for me: He asked what had become of my lovely singing voice. *How does he know about my singing?* I asked myself. Then he said I could travel lighter if I would shorten my skirt and leave off my petticoat.

"No respectable young woman goes without a petticoat," I objected.

"What respectable young woman walks in mud beside two frisky oxen?" asked Oma. She had the scissors in her hands and made the first cut before I could resist. When she finished, the blue skirt looked cleaner and felt lighter, and I felt giddy. I stepped out of my muddy petticoat and threw it in a heap by the wagon.

The thought of shortening my skirt and throwing off my petticoat because a ghost told his wife it was a good idea tickled something funny inside me, and a giggle stuck in my throat until Sophie and Kurt laughed. Then the giggle escaped, and I laughed and laughed, feeling it come from way deep inside. The situation was so ridiculous that I exploded in more laughs until finally tears rolled down my cheeks. Was it relief that somewhere on this trail there might be something funny?

It was a turning point. Laughing at the shortened skirt and the clear view of those horrible brown oxfords put things in a new light that made me carefree and daring. Reaching under my loose blouse, I pulled out the reticule, opened it, and unwrapped the satin dancing slippers and held them happily to the firelight. Only slightly damp from the rain, their satin bows and rosettes gleamed in the light.

"One day soon there will be a place for dancing. I will be ready," I said.

Sophie gasped. "B-but M-mutter s-said to leave t-those."

"She didn't understand," I said.

"B-but you dis-o-obeyed Mutter!" Sophie's eyes grew wide in disbelief. "What will she say?"

Could I tell her that Mutter might not be alive? Should I tell her that I had become an adult, even unwillingly in charge? Not now. Not in the spell of howling laughter. "I'll think about it next week," I said between giggles.

❦

For two days we learned about Texas weather. Every morning a slight, cold, summer rain chilled us to the bones and kept the wagons sliding in the surface mud. By afternoon when the sun came out, the mud hardened into rough ruts that rattled the tubs and hanging pans on our wagon. And the baking sun burned our skins and quickly dried the wet animals. Steam rose from their bodies, and they made low moans of protest.

Catherine and Phillip, again riding with Sophie, thought the steam funny. "They're on fire," called Catherine. "Look at the smoke!" The three of them doubled over, laughing.

"No, they're boiling," said Phillip. Entertained, they hardly noticed the heat.

People called good-natured comments to each other and knocked the heavy mud off moving wheels and off their boots, using sticks that made a cheerful staccato. Suddenly the wagons stopped, and everyone turned silent. My heart pounded, and I coaxed the oxen to halt. Desperately, I looked behind us for the dreaded Karankawas, but only redwing blackbirds darted down to the ruts for insects.

Then I saw why we had stopped. In front of a small group of trees to the right of our trail were six crude wooden grave markers. Nearby, the dark body of a woman was propped against a tree. Around her were strewn clothes, food baskets, and other personal belongings. Her wagon train had moved on without her plague-ridden body. The shock of her slumping body scared me, and I had to turn away.

Then I knew I had to look at her. I had to know. Who was she? Why was she left here? Was she alive when the wagon train abandoned her?

Stomach churning, I looked away again, but a strange fascination made me look back. I had never looked squarely at death. Would we end up like this? What would I do if Sophie became sick and contagious? Even as I thought the question, I knew I would never leave her. We would perish together if necessary. I rushed back to the wagon, pulled her down to me, and held her close for a long time. Catherine and Phillip jumped from the wagon and came to throw their arms around me.

"It's all right," I murmured. "It's all right. We will stay together. I promise. I'll never leave you behind like that."

"It's h-horrible," wailed Sophie.

How could I console three children too young to have seen this terrible sight? *Is Mutter alive, or is she also dead?* What would she do if she had three horrified children clinging to her? "Find a way," she would say. "There's always a way."

I hugged the children and waited. Then I stroked their heads, waiting for inspiration. A prayer entered my mind. *Help me, God. I can't do this by myself.* I waited. The air was silent, but my mind was clear to make an explanation.

"That person has gone to be with God," I said. "That person has no fever and no chills and is not tired and hungry. God is loving that person. There is a part of us that never dies, even when the body has no breath. It's called spirit. That person's spirit is with God."

I gulped down air to still my dizzy head. "Look, Catherine and Phillip, your mother is taking a sheet to cover the lady, and your father and other men are going with their shovels. They are honoring her body with burial, but her spirit is already with God."

"How do you know that?" asked Phillip.

"I learned from my mother. And I was taught it at the church. Do you go to church, Phillip?"

"Yes, but I never knew what spirit meant."

"Well, Phillip and Catherine and Sophie, this woman has taught you and me a valuable lesson." Silently we watched, now more awed than afraid.

The wagon train moved on. The unnamed woman had made life seem precious, too special to put into words. She had also made death seem as near to us as our skins. Everyone on the wagon train was lost in thought. The only sounds we could hear as we moved away from the new burial site were the squeaking of harness, the grinding of wheels on axles, and the gentle clinking of pans and tubs moving against the outside of the wagons.

After our cornbread and dried vegetable stew that night, we settled back to wait for Gustav. Oma tilted her tiny eyeglasses to clean them as if that way she could see him better. Expectantly, I watched her and cast a curious look at Kurt, who grinned at me and winked. He was a ghost nonbeliever, and his grin reminded me not to take the ghost too seriously.

Nevertheless, Gustav's advice had been valuable. What would he say tonight about the unnamed woman we had buried? The sight and silence of her were seared into our thoughts.

But Gustav chose not to comment on it. Oma reported that he had only two sentences: "Life is fleeting. Life is fun."

"Fun?" I exclaimed. "He calls this fun?"

Sophie answered. "It was f-fun to watch the oxen b-boil."

"Herr Schmidt says we will get to Gonzales tomorrow. That could be fun," said Kurt. "If there's a dance floor, you might unwrap your satin shoes."

Kurt had remembered the shoes! A place for dancing was too much to hope for, but I needed to hope. "You may be right."

"I'd be in a bad mood, too, if I had my head tied up against a wagon where I couldn't see anything," Kurt said the next morning as he checked the yoke on the oxen. "Let's tether Baya on a long rope to the side of the wagon and give him some freedom."

Baya thanked Kurt by butting him over on his face as he walked away. Kurt picked himself up, gave Baya a whack on the neck, and said, "You *Dolt!* Do that again, and the wagon train will eat horse stew for two days!"

"S-stew you, Baya," giggled Sophie. "S-stew you, S-stew you."

It sounded like a song to me. I improvised music and words.

> *"Wild Baya stew,*
> *big enough to feed a wagon crew,*
> *wild Baya stew."*

I began again, "Wild Baya stew, enough to" and stopped.

Two things had happened at the same time.

Sophie had joined in with sweet, bell-like tones. . .*and she didn't stutter.* Her face glowed as she continued on and on.

And when I stopped singing, Baya rushed to the end of his tether and nudged me with his head. He nudged again. I sang, and he quit nudging. I stopped. He nudged me.

Baya liked my singing! And Sophie could sing without stuttering! I felt as if the sun had come up again. My spirits lifted. At least something positive was happening on the trail.

More silly lyrics popped into my head, and I sang them, echoed by Sophie with her newly found gift of singing plainly.

> *"Spanish speaking stew,*
> *cooked in a pot with chiles very hot,*
> *wild Baya stew.*
>
> *Wild Baya stew.*
> *A horse in a huff has to be tough,*
> *so we eat stubborn Baya stew."*

We repeated ourselves until we could sing no more, but when I stopped, Baya again rushed to the end of his tether, nudging me with the tip of his wet nose. I began singing again, then stopped and broke out laughing. Was I actually singing for a Spanish-hearing horse who liked my German singing?

The Roths in the next wagon started a medley of German songs that wafted to the front of the wagon train, and we all sang as we moved along, accompanied by the rhythm of the many pots, pans, and buckets clinking in our wagons.

The sight of Gonzales, a small town on the Guadalupe River, brought cheers from everyone. It was rumored to have a barber shop, bakery, and general store, where those with money could replenish their supplies. And, as Kurt had told me, there was to be a dance that night.

The town was a bitter disappointment. The war had left nothing standing except the skeletons of a few barely habitable houses into which several families crowded. There were some tents and a shell of a store with mostly bare shelves. The bakery had sold their last three loaves of white bread to someone at the front of our train.

When Otto and Lucas came to take Baya and the oxen for water that night when we camped, I learned who bought the bread. Otto shoved a beautiful loaf of white bread at me. "Here, we bought this for you."

"I can't take a present from you," I said, in spite of the fact that I could almost taste the bread. I hoped my mouth wasn't visibly watering.

Lucas grabbed my wrist. "Take it, and be quiet."

The minute they were out of sight I ran to Oma and showed her what would be on the evening menu. She laughed until tears ran off her nose and she had to wipe her glasses. "They are watching you and taking care of your animals, and they are feeding you, and we just love it."

Gustav did not appear that night. We were busily getting ready for the *Hopsa* that I had learned would not be on a wooden floor but on packed dirt. Once more I kept my satin slippers hidden away. But I had a good time even in the ugly brown oxfords since Kurt turned out to be an energetic dancer. We won applause for our rendition of "The Pigeon's Wing" and "The Double Shuffle," and somehow I managed to make the ugly shoes move fast enough to keep up with him on "Wired"—that was more body movement than dancing. The one walz Kurt saved for Oma, whose cute, tubby body bounced and moved skillfully and effortlessly.

Just out of Gonzales, the Guadalupe River we had been following from Victoria received a shallow, clear blue partner river. Into it flowed the spring-fed, peaceful San Marcos. It looked harmless, but Herr Schmidt pointed to the high dirt walls on each side and told us how floods had washed impassable baby canyons at many points. We would, he said, have to detour upstream a day's ride to a place where the banks were low and where washed-in gravel had created a shallow-water crossing.

The detour put a damper on the giddy expectations we had developed as we got closer to New Braunfels, but our wise wagon master had guided us safely so far, and we trusted him. Grudgingly, we set off in the hot morning sunshine.

The day was miserable. Damp heat pressed into our skins, and the wagon wheels threw dust from the dry prairie grass into a cloud around us. Being last, my wagon was engulfed in the choking cloud, and we had to pull back to let some of it settle. To make matters worse, grasshoppers, disturbed from the tall grass, jumped up my skirt. I in turn jumped up and down, trying to escape the scraping and stinging of their rough legs.

Sophie, clutching Gloriana, laughed and pointed and laughed and pointed to my dance. Finally, she took Gloriana to shade under the wagon seat, and I heard her laughing amidst pretended conversations with her doll. Oh, to be young and playful again. And riding instead of walking.

High-stepping through the tall grass disturbed fewer grasshoppers and seemed to take less effort, but by late afternoon, I could no longer lift my tired legs. Dragging my feet along, I left a mashed-down trail in the tall grass. Tired as I was, I didn't notice the trees along the river. Just as I couldn't move one more step, there were calls of "Water! Water!"

With one last burst of energy, I abandoned the oxen, Sophie, and everything, and dragged my heavy feet to the water. I plunged in, clothes, shoes, and all. What did it matter? My clothes were soaked with sweat. The water was so freezing cold it felt like it burned my skin. What did it matter? My skin was already truly sunburned. I sat down in the shallows and splashed water on my face, my hair.

Only then did I look up on the riverbank to see people lined up, laughing at me. What did it matter? I asked myself.

With a whoop, Kurt jumped in, then Oma, then Herr Schmidt. "People first," he called, "then animals."

Soon the calm, shallow river came alive with splashes and the foam of fun. Mothers clutched babies as the cold water made them catch their breaths. Fathers grabbed their children under their arms, swinging them in great splashing circles.

As we chilled down, the laughing calmed, and with our teeth chattering and our bodies tingling, we climbed out of the water, wrung out our clothes, and stood chattering in the sunshine, waiting for our clothes to dry. It didn't take long.

Herr Schmidt and some of the men wandered away to begin the arduous task of guiding, pushing, and pulling the teams and wagons down the dusty river bank and across the shallow gravel bar. Each team was paused in the middle long enough for them to drink. Kurt handled the oxen for me, and, for once, a thirsty Baya cooperated.

Only that night, when we camped near the river, did Baya go skittish again. He pumped his head up and down, bumping the wagon again and again when lightning flashed across the sky and thunder boomed in the distance. That's when I learned that animals sense weather trouble.

We spent the night camped inside our wagon after tying everything securely. Daylight came gray, and with it came winds that tore at the canvas of our wagons and blew sand and dust into our eyes and the animals' eyes. They strained restlessly against their tethers and stamped and snorted.

All morning the storm raged. The air turned cold, and we wrapped ourselves in blankets. Baya pumped his head over the back of our wagon under the cover of canvas and stood stoically while small hail bounced from his back. The hail got bigger, and soon we could hear fist-sized pieces whistling down from the sky. One huge piece ripped through our canvas wagon cover and bounced off a barrel. Then the rain came in torrents, pouring into the wagon from every direction and bringing with it wet green leaves that stuck to everything. The wagon rocked in the shrieking wind as Sophie and I also shrieked under our blankets.

When it was over, and we all crept out of our wagons, everything was silent. Awed, we looked at the changed world. The canopy of trees under which we had camped now stood barren of leaves. The leaves were plastered on our wagons and animals, giving everything a green tinge. The Bleiders crawled safely out of their overturned wagon. Behind them, a tornado had touched down in the woods, clearing a wide barren path all the way to the river. Toppled trees were everywhere, including one next to my wagon.

As people hugged each other and touched their animals, I was reminded of our landing on the mosquito-ridden beach at Indian Point, where we all had reassured each other by touching, including Wilma, the Kesslers' cow.

Otto and Lucas hitched our animals, and we pulled away from the now rain-swollen and roaring San Marcos River. The placid river of fun from the day before had become an angry mass of brown, roiling water spreading into the meadow behind us. We moved quickly out of its way.

All day rain pelted us, and by nightfull, when we again joined the path of the Guadalupe River, it also was swollen and still rising. We camped well away from it on higher ground.

⁂

The next day the wagon train moved on toward Seguin, and in spite of light rain still falling, spirits soared. In a day or two we would arrive at New Braunfels, and I would be enfolded in the hugging arms of Vater. At last, a bed to sleep in. Finally, school and church and family routine. At last, the warmth of Karl's smile and conversation with someone my own age! Long forgiven was Karl's abandoning us when Mutter got sick. Over and over I replayed Karl scenes from Indian Point—the funny lopsided hut he built for Oma, our funny songs on the beach, the stubble of dark beard first thing in the morning, his selfless purchase of the wagon and livestock, and his endurance when I refused to help on the trip. The Muellers owed him a lot, and I intended to apologize for my behavior.

As the sun came out, drying my wet clothes, I walked alongside the oxen, picturing our entry into New Braunfels. Over and over I played the scene: how word would spread, and welcoming friends and family would crowd around the arriving wagon train to reach up and touch their loved ones' hands even before they could hug and hold them. Now that the trip was almost over, I began to forgive Vater for bringing us to this awful place. I would welcome his hugs and smiles. The happy scene made me determined to overcome the fatigue, sunburn, and hunger that overtook me in the middle of the day.

Trying to buoy my sagging spirits, I tried to sing. Soon celebration songs popped into my head and I had to sing. I was flattered when Baya, on his long tether, nudged my elbow every time I stopped singing. That's when I realized how much I had changed. What normal singer would care if a horse cared? I needed people, not horses. I needed Vater and Karl for reassurance, and soon.

Otto and Lucas took the livestock to the edge of the swollen Guadalupe River when we halted in Seguin. The idea that had been nagging at me made me bold, so I went to their wagon for a quick look for their stolen money. They seemed to be traveling lighter than the rest of us, with few supplies except food. I did notice two guitars and a mandolin, and was about to look at them when I heard Lucas behind me.

"Poking around, are you?" he asked.

"Just waiting around," I said while trying to act nonchalant.

"For us?" Otto wanted to know.

"The white bread you gave us was delicious, and I just wanted to tell you what a treat it is." I proudly bluffed along, expecting them to buy my story.

Lucas leered at me. "Stay away from our wagon. You know the saying about curiosity killing the cat."

"Are you threatening me?" I yelled at him.

"Maybe." Lucas stalked away.

"Don't mind him, Rika. He talks big. I would never let him hurt you or Sophie. Do you know that I was once a schoolteacher?" Otto seemed almost kindly without Lucas.

That night, Oma said Gustav had only two things to say. "Don't trust Otto," he said, and "Help Oma."

"What kind of help do you need, Oma?" asked Kurt.

"I need a place to stay in New Braunfels until I can get a house built," she said.

Kurt puzzled over her words for a minute. "I don't have a place to stay, either. I can't help, but you are welcome to camp with me while I get settled."

Sophie, so excited she jumped up and down, said, "O-oma, O-oma. W-why don't y-you stay with us?"

"What do you think, Rika? Would it work?" Oma asked.

"Yes, yes! Without you, Sophie and I wouldn't even be here. I'm sure Vater would want both of you to stay at our house until you get settled." I felt proud to be able to repay in some small way.

But as soon as the words escaped my mouth, I knew Vater would not understand about Gustav. I could never make him understand how Gustav's bits of humor and wisdom had driven my determination to make it to New Braunfels. If Gustav became known in New Braunfels, Anna, or Oma as we called her, would become the butt of jokes and a lot of ridicule. Karl and I had laughed at her. Kurt and I had enjoyed a private wink at some of her antics. But I couldn't bear it if the whole town made jokes about her. Kurt and I would have to keep a close watch and protect her from herself and gossip.

Before I went to sleep, I had a lot to worry about besides Gustav and Oma. What had become of Emil? Could he be alive and well? And what about Mutter? Could she be alive?

As our wagons rattled and thumped across the flatland closer to New Braunfels, I gave a lot of thought to Oma and her determined but lonely trek from Germany to a new home in a foreign country. For all her funny little quirks, she had survived the trip in heroic style with good humor, and she had helped change my outlook and my self-confidence.

As we neared New Braunfels, there was a mixture of jubilation and curiosity. In the distance we could see scrubby hills, and even in the midday sun they had a mysterious foggy, lavender haze over them. Golden-tan prairie grass tall enough to reach the oxen's bellies changed color in the wind, blowing like whitecaps on sea waves. Soon we could actually see the small buildings of New Braunfels in the distance, and there were questions and chatter and excited observations among the immigrants.

But, to our dismay, we discovered that the town was on the other side of the flooded Guadalupe River. A few on the wagon train knew of this problem, but no one had told me. Never in a thousand years would I try to swim or drive the oxen across such turbulent water.

Chapter 12

I should have trusted our competent Wagon Master Herr Schmidt, who knew where to go. He even knew that at the convergence of the Comal and Guadalupe Rivers, Adolph Wedemeyer, an immigrant from Hanover, had built a flatbed ferry, powered by the rivers' currents. The ferry, made of closely fitted wooden planks and with sturdy wooden railings on each side, was guided by steering ropes attached to taut cables anchored to trees on opposite sides of the river. The ferryman stayed in a little shanty and was called by a horn hung to a tree on each side. During normal times, the ferry operated safely and serenely, Herr Schmidt told us, but because of the dangerously high water we would lighten the weight for each trip by crossing one family and livestock at a time.

After his instructions, Herr Schmidt ordered everyone to stay together for prayer. Men took off their hats; women bowed their heads after gathering children to their skirts. Noise of the rushing water drowned out most of the prayer, but genuine thankfulness seemed written on all faces even as, during the prayer, everyone stole glances to the opposite shore, searching for faces of loved ones. After the amen, Master Schmidt assured us we were in no danger, and going across to New Braunfels would be orderly. But confusion reigned, and in it, our wagon, having been last for 200 miles, suddenly became number one to cross the turbulent river on the small raft-like ferry.

I guided the oxen to the edge of the roiling, muddy waters. They stalled, and so did I. Cold sweat trickled down my face, and jagged fear ran between my shoulders as I balked at the brink of the raging water. How could I ever cross this deep, muddy, fast-moving water that tossed the little ferry to and fro?

Then Aunt Matilde's voice appeared in my head: *"You are strong, and you can make it."*

The ferryman, von Lochmann, shouted encouragement and directions, and, although my brown shoes felt weighted with lead, I reluctantly guided the balky oxen onto the wet, slippery wooden floor. The ferry teetered under the unbalanced weight of the wagon, then careened wildly, throwing Sophie against the footboard. She screamed for help, and Kurt ran on and snatched her out of the wagon and carried her back to solid ground. Other strong arms ran to grab the tiny ferry's railings and hold it steady against the riverbank so I could get the wagon straightened behind the oxen. Then Kurt, carrying Sophie, led Baya onto the ferry.

Even though during the crossing extra strong arms held our bobbing boat straight with the guide ropes and my head knew we were safe, my heart beat wildly as the ferry lurched, its edges dipping crazily into the cold, dark water.

Finally, the ferry touched muddy ground on the New Braunfels side, and many hands reached to steady and guide the oxen and wagon. Kurt handed Sophie into strong arms but held to Baya's reins with proud determination. The crowd cheered as they inspected the strange horse, the even stranger wagon that had come so far, and the thin, sunburned girl wearing a strangely short skirt who was in charge of it all.

"Welcome," called a tall blond man. "Who are you?"

"Frederika Mueller," I declared proudly.

"You were very courageous," said the handsome man.

"I'm basically a coward pressed into service," I replied. "I'm looking for my father, Sebastian Mueller."

The tall man looked around. "He was here earlier, but I don't see him now. I know where he lives, though, and will take you to his house. My name is Lux Buechner." Lux had comfortably large shoulders with muscles large enough to be seen through his faded blue shirt sleeves. On his head he wore a typical German brown, round flat-on-top cap from which blond hair trailed in back. Unusual for his blond hair and blue eyes was his deep tan. I remember thinking that he must work outside in the sun, but I was really preoccupied.

"I am pleased to meet you," I said while still scanning the crowd for Vater's familiar face. "Thanks for the offer, but I do think he is here."

"I c-can't find Vater." Sophie had been darting among the crowd expectantly.

"He will be here," I promised, believing it. I searched from face to face in the crowd, but he was nowhere to be found. Sophie and I clung to each other for support. We had expected joy and congratulations, even hugs of welcome from Vater or at least friends, but neither was here.

"Is your mother still alive?" Lux asked.

"What do you know about my mother?" I asked indignantly of the man I barely knew.

"It is a small community here, and everyone knows you left the trail with your sick mother. What happened to her?"

"I left her in Victoria to be cared for. I don't know if she is dead or alive." A cloud had been pulled over our arrival.

I turned away to watch the Schmidts loading for the return of the ferry. Water lapped the edges of the boat as their heavy wagon and large family loaded. A gasp went up on both sides of the rivers, but strong arms moved them ahead and steadied the animals. The Schmidts, unlike some others on the wagon train, had been friendly from the beginning and now felt like family. I was surprised at the joy I felt for their safe arrival. I hadn't known I was so attached to them.

As more wagons arrived, a wagon jam forced me to move quickly, so I accepted Lux's offer to help me find Vater's house. We pulled the wagon toward town and waited for Oma and Kurt. Then, with Lux leading the way, I guided the oxen down the muddy streets of New Braunfels, some of them nothing more than wagon trails. Baya, tethered to the side of the wagon, balked and tugged against his rope, dragging against the tired oxen. Lux walked to Baya and swatted him on the flank, yelling for him to move on.

"*¡Andele!*" I called to Baya. "This is a Spanish-hearing horse," I said to Lux. "He doesn't hear a word of German."

"No joke?" Lux asked in German.

"And he has s-sharp t-teeth. He will bite your s-shirt b-buttons off," called Sophie. "B-be careful."

Lux stepped quickly away, but not before Baya made a half whinny, pumped his head up and down, and gleefully butted Lux over into the mud.

I called, "*¡Andele!*" and Baya moved forward, leaving Lux in a heap in the mud yelling, "*Dolt*," after the insulting horse.

When Lux caught up to me next to the oxen, he said, "You are even more courageous than I first thought when I saw you come off the ferry. How did you ever get hooked up with that strange horse?"

"If I told you the story, it would take all day. Another time, maybe."

The story of my trip faded into the background as I watched men along the road working on houses or building stake fence. They called welcomes or cheered as we passed, and I had a feeling that this place, so different from the unfriendly climate of Indian Point, would soon feel like home.

"Lux, all the houses are so little and each is different from the other," I complained.

After all that had happened to us, still I carried in my head a picture of our large, brick house in Delmenhorst with its big south windows letting in the warm winter sun. During the cold rain on the trail and in the burning heat on the prairie I had pictured myself arriving at a nice house with steps, an open door, and the welcoming arms of Vater.

"The town is young, and people just need a roof over their head," said Lux, moving off the road toward a shack. "Besides, no one knows what is the best construction for this climate. We do the best we can." Lux sounded defensive.

"Are you a builder?" I asked.

"Almost," Lux said. "I am a carpenter who mostly builds furniture, but sometimes I help lay the logs when the builders have trenched for a foundation or help with the cedar corner posts. It's heavy work."

We walked on down a muddy side street.

"Here is the Mueller house," he said proudly.

My mouth gaped open in disbelief. It was no house, just a shack. . .something Germans would have housed geese or pigs in. Built flat on the dirt, the tiny, one-room house was made of wooden staves driven into the ground and had straw and mud filling in spaces between the wood. Sophie charged to the closed front door, flung it open, and called, "Vater, Vater!" with such enthusiasm that Oma and Kurt clapped their hands. The crestfallen expression on Sophie's face as she came back out the door told us the house was empty.

"Lux, are you certain this is the Mueller house?" I asked.

"Positive. Sebastian hired me to build a table here next week."

"But w-where is Vater?" whined Sophie. She began to cry.

Over and over again, as I had walked miles and dreadful miles, I had pictured our arrival in New Braunfels. It would be the day I handed the responsibility for Sophie and all our possessions over to Vater, taking the heavy yoke from my shoulders much like unyoking the oxen. Now, once again, I felt the weight breaking my shoulders. What could I do with my wagon and that of Oma, livestock, hungry mouths to feed and, most of all, a sister crying into my skirt?

Mutter would say, "Find a way," Frau Kellerman had said, "You can do it," whatever "it" was, and Aunt Matilde had said, "You are strong, and you can make it." I had thought she meant muscles and bones, but maybe she also meant emotions. Only I could decide what to do here.

I lifted Sophie up, hugging her close. "Sophie, just put your head on my shoulder and rest while we sort this out." With a sob, she rested her head. "Now, Kurt, pull Oma's wagon to one side of the house and unhitch your horses. I will pull our wagon to the other side and unhitch the oxen. Lux, will you make sure Baya can't reach the tree over there?"

Solemnly, everyone did as they were asked, and we managed to find some posts for tethering the animals and a barrel of water for them. Even though it was only midafternoon, we invited Lux to stay for supper and fell into our usual camping routine of fire building, eating, and resting around the fire. From her wagon, Kurt brought Oma's rocking chair and she began to really enjoy herself.

"Yes, we have arrived. All is well." Keeping to her usual method of communicating with Gustav, Oma laughed, adjusted her spectacles, laughed some more, then pronounced that Gustav had a message for everyone. "He said to tell you to be glad."

"That's all?" I needed specific advice.

"That's a lot," said Oma.

"Who's Gustav?" Lux asked.

We thought it over. How could we say it? Finally, Kurt said, "Gustav is Oma's departed husband. He er, er, ah, makes his presence known sometimes."

"Oh," said Lux with a lifted brow.

"Oh, yes," said Oma. "Gustav has given us much good advice on this trip, hasn't he? It was his idea to have Otto and Lucas take care of the oxen and the horse."

Lux looked puzzled. "Are Otto and Lucas also from the spirit world?"

We all laughed when Oma said, "We wish!"

⌘

Long after Lux had gone home, and all of us were placing our sleeping pallets out of doors, Vater was brought home by Fritz Haffner, a single man I had seen on our wagon train. In the dusk, as they walked down the road toward us, it was hard to identify the two men, and I knew it was Vater only because he called my name. Once clean-shaven and almost plump, Vater now wore a beard much darker than his blond hair, and he had lost so much weight that his rough, homespun trousers bunched around his belt and his shirt hung limply from his shoulders. When I hugged him, his sharp bones made him feel fragile, and when he reached to pick up Sophie, she darted away, taking time to walk a circle around him, inspecting his clothes and listening to him speak before jumping into his arms.

Later, as we sat facing each other on the cool ground, talking into darkness after Sophie had fallen asleep, disappointment crept into bits of conversation, then finally drenched everything we said.

That's when I discovered that Vater had joined the group calling welcomes to the wagon train across the raging waters. But when he saw me crossing without Mutter, he had fled. Bitterly disappointed that Mutter had been left in Victoria, Vater accused me of abandoning her, pointing out that we didn't even know if she was alive. I told him about Black Peter, the huge burial pit in Town Square, death in the air, my lack of money, my abandonment by Emil and Karl, and finally Aunt Mathilde, who encouraged me to be strong by making a decision.

After a while, Vater sighed, muttering, "You should not have left her."

"But Vater," I insisted, "Sophie and I could be dead and all the possessions I brought would have disappeared. You would have nothing."

His head dropped, and he seemed not to hear. I waited for him to say thank you or at least to acknowledge that he understood what I had been through.

But there was only silence.

A numb feeling started with my feet and moved slowly up my body until it reached my chest. Vater had changed. The brutal truth stabbed at my heart. Disappointment spilled onto everything I had done, the terrors I had overcome, the unsought weight of responsibility, the corpses I had seen, the bone-grinding fatigue I had endured, the taunting jeers about the strange girl on the stranger horse and the girl driving an oxen team, and the self-doubt and Indian fears that had engulfed me every night before I went to sleep. Foolishly I had thought my wonderful Vater would look at me like a hero, would reward me with his love and approval. I wanted to yell at him, shake him, tell him to wake up and look at what the trip had done to me. I wanted to say hurtful words.

But the soft voice of my Mutter seemed to whisper in my ear, "Silence is golden."

I left Vater sitting there and took myself to bed on the pallet next to Sophie, positioning myself with my back to Vater. He had turned his back on me. I was no longer his special friend, confidant, fellow musician, and favorite daughter.

⌒∞⌒

A great ground vibration shook me awake. Around me people began to come to life. From a tent down the way emerged a large woman, who as she walked, removed her mobcap, letting her long hair tumble down over her shoulders.

"What was that?" I called.

"Just the wake-up cannon. Happens every morning," she called back.

I could see men walking down the rutted, mud street carrying buckets. They seemed not to notice us in our night clothes. Sophie and I fled to the house and got dressed. Vater had made strange-tasting coffee from parched barley. He informed us matter-of-factly that the men were going to Henry Burkhart's slaughterhouse to claim their meat rations, and he would join them. Meat bucket in hand, he gave me another bucket with instructions to walk down to the spring for fresh water.

In a moment he was back. "Who are these strange people parked in our side yard?" he growled.

"That's Oma Gunkel, who helped me on the trail. I told her she could camp with us until she gets her assignment."

"You did that without asking me?" Vater shouted.

"No one could find you, Vater. Besides, I couldn't have survived on the trail without Frau Gunkel. I'd still be sitting at McCoy's Creek waiting for any wagon train to take me along. It was very difficult for a woman to get on a train."

Unexpectedly, Sophie rushed to defend me. "D-don't be mad, V-vater. Rika was b-brave. And O-oma helped us. K-kurt, too."

"Yes, yes. I understand, but they can't stay. Food is rationed. We have to carry water from the spring for ourselves and the animals. Besides, I asked Fritz Haffner to stay with us until he finds his place."

"Fritz from the wagon train?" I asked. "Where is he?"

"Still sleeping over there behind the chest."

⁂

Fritz became a fixture behind the chest, almost always sleeping. Nothing bothered him, even the reunion the next day when Karl came shouting noisily into the house, greeting me with a hug and huge smiles. Sophie jumped into his arms, then dragged him by the hand outside to see Oma, who hugged him around his middle, the part of him she could reach. We all became giddy, trying to talk all at once, laughing at things that weren't funny and telling things in bits and pieces until they made no sense. Even when Karl called Kurt "the little guy who helped you," I couldn't put a damper on my good humor, although I should have defended Kurt, who had become a good friend and so many times rescued me.

Karl told us he excelled in the local militia, a requirement of all able-bodied men of the right age, and he described the boring odd jobs he had picked up just to make food and lodging money. When Oma asked him if he would go back to soldiering now, he told her that last night he had taken a well-paying job in a tobacco and swap shop that would be opened by a huge guy with lots of money. My eyes met Oma's, and she asked, "Is his name Lucas Beck?"

"How did you know?" asked Karl.

Sophie chimed in, "R-rika l-let him h-help us on the t-trail."

"Helped her, yes, but she is afraid of him," said Kurt.

"Why?" Karl wanted to know.

Kurt scraped his heavy boot in the dirt, looked at the ground, and said, "I don't know, but if I were you, I'd be very careful. He and Otto are shifty and threatening."

"Well, Rika, what do you say about them?" asked Karl.

"Nothing. I just don't like them. You met them on the ship and again at Indian Point. Remember I told you then I didn't like them?"

"I thought the big guy looked familiar. Don't worry, though. I doubt they would harm a soldier."

Karl didn't take our concern seriously, but I dared say no more. Although the threats of Lucas and Otto kept me silent, I resolved to find the money and turn them in even if it took a long time. Only then could Sophie and I be safe.

My resolve was tested the next day when Vater showed me the new pipe given him by a new man in town, Lucas Beck. He handed me a bag of flour sent by Lucas to me and said he had invited Lucas and Otto to eat supper with us. Most women would have been overjoyed by the gift of white flour, a scarce commodity, but with my limited ability in cooking, I didn't know what to do with flour, and I certainly didn't want to fix it for two thieves.

"Please could we have them later after I learn how to cook?" I asked.

"Don't question me, Rika. I have already asked them." Vater's tone was disapproving. It was futile to argue.

"Oma can help me cook," I said.

Vater became more indignant. "I told you she has to go. There are no supplies for her here, and we need the space. Fritz will help you."

"Vater, she can go after we have our company. She is a good woman, and Fritz is no help to anyone. He sleeps all the time. Mutter would say that his limbs are very stiff."

"Why is that?"

"Have you forgotten the German proverb: 'Work makes life sweet. Laziness makes your limbs stiff'? Fritz doesn't understand the sweetness of life."

At the mention of his name, Fritz stirred, but he got up three hours later when he came looking for something to eat. He draped his long arm around my shoulder and asked if there was any coffee. The only romantic man in my life was Karl, and Fritz's arm on my shoulder was repulsive. I ducked from under his arm and dashed outside to Oma.

It seemed danger lurked everywhere in Texas, even in my own house.

Chapter 13

The supper wasn't entirely a disaster, partly because Oma helped me cook on the stove that had been delivered by the Mexican driver who had named me "Baby Dragon." When he heard that I had arrived safely, he came by to wish me well and find out if the stove still worked. Transactions were in Spanish, smiles, handshakes, German responses, curtseys, and head shakes that I hoped said "Thank you," with a smidgeon of being a contrite dragon. The driver's concern and friendliness encouraged me. Perhaps this place would prove better than I expected.

The stove, a heavy cast-iron creature with a fat belly and flat surface for pots, had a side oven also heated by large amounts of burning wood. Getting the right amount of wood inside to the right place required constant trips to the woodpile outside the back door. My challenge was to learn the stoking technique while also learning how to cook anything besides the vegetable gruel, corn porridge, and tough cornbread I had mastered on the trail. In front of me was a huge hunk of beef, and next to it was a bag of white flour. Rummaging through our half-unpacked trunk, I found Mutter's recipe packet, a few pinches of herbs in an envelope and a large, heavy skillet with an equally heavy lid. Dismayed by my ignorance, I sat staring at the pot, wondering what to do with it, when a cheery voice called from the doorway.

"Rika, are you there?"

Turning I saw Frau Kessler and Marie standing in the door. "Oh, wonderful! Welcome, welcome, and come in." I hurried to clear two chairs. Marie handed me a bowl of butter.

"Thank you. Wilma is doing well, then?" I asked.

"Better than we are," said Frau Kessler, holding out her dress to show she had lost weight. "Wilma has plenty of grass, good spring water, and is fat and contented, whereas I am having trouble cooking the food we have here. So much beef. Ach!"

"And corn! Ach!" said Marie. "It's for pigs."

"I have finally learned to make cornbread," I announced, hoping they hadn't heard that my cornbread had the reputation of rocks.

We talked of the trip, welcoming families, strange customs, and building styles. Marie, two years younger than me, told about the school held under the seven trees. Since she spoke the Hessian dialect it was difficult to learn to always speak in the correct High German, a requirement of the schoolmaster, Herman Seele. This news excited me since I spoke High German, a product of strict upbringing and the two schools I had attended. Marie described the planks set on posts that served older students as seats and desks, all set under a cluster of trees. She told about her studies in reading, nature study, and arithmetic that had to be done in her head since she had no slate. She laughingly described interruptions to class time when the supply wagons arrived and townspeople hurried through the classroom on their way to the Verein hill, where supplies would be distributed.

The school sounded strange, but I loved school and couldn't wait to get started. When I asked about going with Marie, who lived only a short distance from us, Frau Kessler said I would have to pay the half-dollar tuition first. My heart sank. Money did not exist in our family.

"Don't worry, Rika. Something will work out," said Frau Kessler when she read the disappointment on my face.

"I can teach you what I learn," suggested Marie.

Had Marie heard of Voltaire, Goethe, Schumann, or Mozart? Had she ever composed a song? She had no idea of my superior education or talents, and I could never tell her without sounding haughty. "Thank you, Marie. It would be fun to get together. I could use some social life."

"There is a developing social life here," said Marie. "You're invited to a quilting party next week at Elissa Fink's. It's on Tuesday. Please say you'll go."

"Yes. Yes. Yes." The idea made my heart sing. "But I don't know Elissa Fink."

"You will. She lives nearby," said Marie. "She is a *Giggle Cat*, very stylish in her way, and very friendly. We helped her finish the quilt she started in Germany, and we will celebrate."

Long after Marie and Frau Kessler were gone, as I hustled to keep the stove stoked with wood and learn how to cook meat from Oma, happiness bubbled inside. I was invited to a party. With plenty of spring water for washing, I could see myself with shiny blond hair and a clean dress. I couldn't wait. The invitation buoyed me through the rest of the day. Somehow in the cramped house, Oma and I got supper together and found enough pewter plates for everyone. Since we had only a plank for a table, some of us would need to eat off our laps.

Lucas arrived on time, bringing with him a gift pouch of tobacco for Vater's new pipe. Otto came later, bearing a gift for Sophie, folded paper strips in a small, wooden cup.

"Sophie, these are for when you are old enough to light your father's pipe. Meanwhile, you can lay them out on the table and use them to practice counting and addition and subtraction." Otto beamed at Sophie. "I can't help being a teacher," he explained.

"T-thank y-you," Sophie said.

The supper scene played itself out, looking like a happy family having company. Vater, Otto, and Lucas ate on the plank, and Oma, Kurt, Sophie, and myself perched on any available flat spot. From time to time I got up to serve more meat and dumplings or pour water, and each time, Oma rose to put herself between myself and Lucas, who watched me with satisfaction. His threats had worked, and now he had Vater admiring and thanking him. Then came the surprise.

"I plan to hire that young carpenter, Lux, to build me a handsome house near the Comal River. I have a scenic spot and will ask him tomorrow."

"Oh, just too late," chuckled Oma, reaching in front of Lucas to pour water. "I have hired him to begin work immediately on my house in Comaltown. It will take some time. In fact, we will be moving over there as soon as the ferry can take our wagon."

"My dear lady," said Lucas in a condescending tone, "your little house will take no time and be nothing compared to mine. I can start later."

Oma held an unwavering gaze on my father. "I haven't asked Herr Mueller for this favor, but I hope Rika can fix lunch for us every day, using my supplies, of course."

Vater could not refuse. After a slight pause, he said, "Er, ah, I suppose it will be all right if Rika gets her work done here at home."

Even with her short legs and hefty frame, the sly fox Oma could always stay six steps ahead of anyone. I dared not giggle, but it seemed to me that Gustav was laughing from under the plank table. This plump little lady we had thought crazy, who was shunned by Emil, and who had spoken out for me and helped me along the trail, had now plotted to get me out of Vater's dark little house every day, and had saved Lux from entanglement with the dreaded team of Lucas and Otto. At least for the moment.

But Vater would have the last word. "Rika will have a lot to do here at home. We all know the German three *k* requirements: *Kuche, Kirche, Kinder*. Kitchen, church, and children are important, but right now kitchen and home seem most important since there is so little to do with and so much to be done."

Otto cleared his throat, apparently gathering the courage to speak. "I watched Rika on the trail. She is a very hard-working girl. She can do home and later even have time for church and school."

"There will be no school for Rika. Not here." Vater changed the subject quickly. "Here, Otto, have more dumplings."

Was this the same father who had encouraged me in school in Germany and had fervently taught me music? Was this the same man who urged his music students to higher and higher levels? What had happened to the man who shared ideas with me, the man who had urged me to do something important with my life?

Vater had changed, and the changed man was definitely in charge.

The next few days found me cooking on the strange black stove, unpacking the trunk, and crowding the contents of the wagon into the little house. Everything was scarce, including space. Behind the chest and always in the way was the ever-sleeping, lazy Fritz.

By the time Sophie and I had a small bed in a corner, the house was so crowded Vater decided the leering Fritz should go to the boardinghouse. Reluctantly, Fritz gathered his belongings, and with a reminder that he would come visit me, trudged toward the boardinghouse at town square. I had dodged his advances more than once and hoped he would never come back. After all, Karl had already stolen my heart.

Lux was another story. I caught myself thinking about how the tall, handsome stranger had helped me at the ferry in his authoritative but gentle way. He talked to me as an equal and was one of a few men who thought me courageous for surviving the trip. I hoped he never discovered how I had acted at Indian Point when, as Sophie said, I was the old "pain-in-my-neck," and I looked forward to Tuesday, the day he came to build our table.

Lux arrived pulling a loaded handcart from which he took sawhorses for holding lumber, a wooden tool tray heavy with tools, and lumber that he set by the back door, where he began his carpentry. I was in and out to the woodpile, so we had a chance to talk. As he worked, he told me about the cypress wood planks he was using for our tabletop, how he had cut and cured the wood, the special planes he used for smoothing the wood and the oiled finish he would use. I could tell as he spoke that he loved wood and took great care to make the furniture he built sturdy but beautiful. Each time I went outside for more wood for the stove, he added bits of information until, finally, I closed the damper on the stove, set the soup pot to the back, and just went outside to talk.

As he worked, Lux asked me questions about the trip, and I found myself telling him about Emil, who was sick then gone to war, and how Karl had bought us the wagon and livestock but abandoned us when Mutter became ill. Lux questioned me for details about our hardships at Indian Point and on the trail. As I described Black Peter and the Town Square in Victoria, then our visit to Aunt Mathilde and the wrenching decision to leave Mutter behind, I found tears on my cheeks. But I went on to tell about the snakes, seeing the dreadful corpse, watching for Indians, the aching with fatigue, and finally ending with Oma's nightly vigils with Gustav.

"Sounds like Gustav kept you all entertained and going with good advice. Blessing, eh?" said Lux.

"A blessing, but he is dead. How do you explain that?"

"Don't try. Some things you just accept." Lux sounded like he had experience. "You left out Big Lucas and Little Otto."

I dared not explain. "Let's just say that I'm afraid of them."

"Why so?"

"They're dishonest. I'll tell you about them someday."

Conversation ranged on about the oxen, the strange horse, Baya, his antics with me on his back and my trouble feeding him even now. I told him how I longed to go to school and how much I feared becoming just a *Housefrau* when I really wanted to teach music and do something important with my life.

Lux stopped his hammer midair. "Rika," he exclaimed, "don't you know the important thing you have just done for your family? Your family has survived because of you."

"Perhaps. But life seems out of balance, Emil is in the army, and Mutter is either ill or dead in Victoria. I worry about her all the time. And here I am, unable to go to school or study music or sing."

"You will do all of those things. I promise you, in time, you will find a way," said Lux.

A tall shadow fell on the wood. "Do what things, Rika?" Lucas sneered a smile at me as he walked closer. His eyes stared into mine. "You must be careful what you want." Then he turned to Lux. "I had trouble finding you to talk about building my house."

I ducked into the house, grateful that it was almost time to get ready for the quilting party that afternoon.

⦾⦾⦾

The party began with giggles and moved to more giggles as we sipped grape juice and talked about the quilt. It had been started in Germany by Elissa, and her friends in Texas had helped her put it in a quilting frame with scraps of cloth, then quilt it. The group had become like a club, and I wondered how I would fit in. I confided to Marie that I'd never held a needle in my hand.

"Don't tell, and don't worry. You can learn," she whispered.

"The design is beautiful," I said. "What do you call it?"

Elissa fingered the embroidered flowers in the center. "It's called Garden of Music."

All I had seen were the flowers. Now I noticed the subtle light yellow musical notes dancing out of the flower clusters. My spirits danced. Such a simple thing, just to see musical notes and hear the musical laughter of friends.

The afternoon went by too fast, and soon we were eating pecans and wonderfully salty popcorn. I heard news of Frau Kellerman, who now lived on a farm, and of Engel Mittendorf, whose parents had hired him out to live with people in the country and build fence. I told stories about Frau Mittendorf and her chicken-like squawking at Engel, how he flapped his wings and met me secretly behind the wagon to tell me about Frau Kellerman. More giggles as everyone imagined the outgoing Engel doing his chicken imitations.

Spirits soaring, I walked home to find Karl sitting in the shade of the one tree in our yard. He often stopped in the yard as Sophie arrived home from school. Today he looked especially handsome in his German army uniform, and he had polished his worn boots and wore a huge smile that said he was glad to see me.

Although Vater had heard that Karl lived with us in Indian Point and in fact had bought the wagon, oxen, and horse that brought us to New Braunfels, he had not been able to repay Karl the money. Word had been passed that they were for sale, but so far only the oxen had been sold. The hungry, cantankerous horse still lived with us, and we still owned the wagon, which we used to store what would not fit into our tiny house. So Karl had very little money. He had eaten a couple of meals with us and had helped Vater split cooking wood, but he had not asked permission to court me. In my mind was the mouth-tingling, body-jangling, good-bye kiss at Spring Creek. My mouth wanted more, but rules of conduct were different in New Braunfels, and Karl and I merely talked to each other, always when other people were present.

Today Sophie played around the yard, running occasionally to talk to Baya or get a drink from the big bucket at the back door.

"You look happy," Karl said as I came into the yard.

"I've come from Elissa Fink's quilting party. It was exciting. We talked about her quilt and giggled a lot, trying to guess whose good or bad quilting was where. There was grape juice and popcorn and pecans. I had almost forgotten about that kind of food and fun."

"I know. Don't I know. Try being a young bachelor who works in a tobacco shop where customers are mostly old men."

"Sounds calm," I said.

"More than calm. Try boring. I feel like a Housefrau. I have to dust the boxes and cases and sweep the floor. It's terrible." Karl pounded his fists in the air.

"Poor Karl. And you came here for adventure and excitement. I'm so sorry you have to feel like a tobacco shop Housefrau. I'm a Housefrau, too, and I hate it."

"I know you do." Karl reached for my hand and held it. "Rika, will you run away with me?"

I was speechless. Finally I asked, "Run away to where?"

"I have joined a militia group moving out to scout Indian territory."

"You what?"

"You heard me. I couldn't take one more day of that boring shop. Before that I was a wild game hunter for Dickie Madam's boardinghouse. It's no use pretending I can do civilized work. I can't cook or build fence or farm. I'm a soldier. I need excitement and adventure. Please say you'll come with me. We can have this adventure together."

"But, Karl, I'm a woman."

"I noticed." We both laughed. I guessed he was remembering the kiss.

"Karl, women don't go out scouting for Indians," I said.

"But, Rika, you're different. You can ride. You brought a wagon and a crazy horse 200 miles by yourself. And you hate keeping house and cooking. You've certainly had plenty of practice at watching for Indians. You would be good company on the trail. Do it." I couldn't believe Karl was serious.

"A woman wouldn't be welcome, and you know it. Besides, I'm needed here. Don't go, Karl. You could get killed," I pleaded.

"We could both die of boredom here," insisted Karl.

Sophie had come out of the house carrying Glorianna. Now she inserted herself between us. "W-who's going to d-die?"

"No one, Sophie," I said. "Please take Glorianna inside where she won't get dirty."

"N-no." She planted her feet firmly next to mine.

"Then be quiet," I ordered her.

"Karl, please don't do this," I pleaded.

"D-do what?" Sophie wanted to know.

"Be quiet, Sophie!" My voice reached an impatient pitch.

"It's already done. I have signed up, and we leave in the morning. There will be five of us. Please make it six."

"Karl, even the request is scandalous. The answer is no. Think about what you are asking."

"I respect your wishes, but I'm not sorry I asked, scandalous or not. In the past, you haven't seemed to mind doing the controversial thing."

"Karl, you know I was forced by necessity to do whatever you think scandalous, like riding astride and driving oxen. I can't go, and you shouldn't either. Please don't go. It is very dangerous." I felt like a flower wilting down to the ground, all the fun and excitement gone out of me.

A quiet settled between us.

Karl leaned stiffly forward and kissed me on the cheek.

"It's already done." Turning, he walked briskly away.

I put my hand to the tingling place on my cheek where he had kissed me and watched his back disappear as he turned the corner behind a house.

"W-what's he already d-done?" Sophie wanted to know.

I could barely bring myself to say it. "Karl—is—going—away."

"Again?" asked Sophie.

Chapter 14

Karl's leaving left a hole in my life, and his quick, almost angry departure over my refusal to go with him worried me. A gray fog engulfed me the next several days. I smoldered with anger at Emil for joining the army. Then I moved to remorse for leaving Mutter in Victoria. Could she be dead? If alive, why hadn't we heard from her? Not going to school was the final insult. Nothing was going my way.

As with most immigrants, Vater had taken a job to provide cash for daily existence, and in a few days he earned enough money building fence to pay tuition for Sophie's schooling. But he still refused my request to go with her, saying my place was Kuche. It was more than a place. Kitchen represented a way of life, one that kept me in "my place" of responsibility for all that happened in the household, which came to include feeding and watering the animals as well as cooking and laundry. Just the thought of becoming a fat Housefrau, as Karl had jokingly suggested more than once, made my hands shake and put a weight of dread in my heart. However, for now there would be compensations. At least when Sophie and Vater were gone most of the day, if I hurried my chores, I'd have some privacy, a time when I could sing and compose music. And I'd have time to take lunch to Comaltown every day.

It wasn't far to Comaltown from New Braunfels, but I had to cross the Comal River on a narrow footbridge each day. The bridge had been made by cutting two pecan trees, one on each bank, to fall onto a small island in the river, so the bridge was really a nonbridge, just a passable narrow convenience. My heart beat wildly as I crossed the bridge. The flooded river had gone down, and what had been an ugly muddy, roiling mess was now calm and beautiful, but the pecan logs were high above the water, and if I fell in, I could be swept downstream in a matter of seconds. For once I thanked Mutter for making me wear the heavy brown shoes that seemed to keep me firmly grounded on the logs.

Safely across the bridge, I admired the Comal. Surrounded by large trees that were reflected in the clear cool water, the river shimmered in sunshine and sparkled as it bounded over rocks cascading into quiet, green pools and eddys. Near the edge of one of these pools beyond the island, I spotted two Indian squaws whom I hoped were Lepans. The women were small but squarely shaped and wore moccasins and leggings topped with yellow leather tunics with fringe that danced as they moved. I could hear their laughs above the gurgle of water. I had been told the Lepans were friendly to settlers but had also been warned that they were not to be trusted since in perfect good humor they might take anything they wanted. Quietly I turned away, clutching the basket of food I was carrying.

Comaltown, situated between the fork of the Comal Spring and the Guadalupe River, wasn't so much a town as a tiny, growing community. Laid out in fairly inexpensive lots very much resembling a German village, the few scattered houses were surrounded by trees and overgrown grasses. From Oma's double lot near the spring I could hear the continuous roar of water, and the air was slightly moist. In shady spots it was filled with mosquitoes.

I found Oma sitting next to her wagon under a canvas canopy that served as a roof for her campsite. Next to the campsite she had erected a tent that held supplies as well as her bed. "The climate and bugs here are strange," she said as she swatted mosquitoes on her arms and mopped her sweaty, flushed face.

"But your house site is beautiful, and you are making progress," I said.

Behind the tent a huge rack of oak logs, each flattened on two sides, stood ready to create walls for Oma's house. Beyond the logs, Lux had already built a small corral for the horses, using staves of oak driven into the ground. Between the staves he had strung lengths of rawhide. When the house was finished, Oma told me, a permanent split-rail fence would be built.

Oma walked me around the area explaining the dimensions of the rather large house with its south-north opening doors allowing for air circulation. One corner of the house would be the kitchen and there would be a combination bed and living room opening on to a porch that would later lead to an addition to the house. As we walked, I tried to stuff down the green envy seeping into my soul, for Vater seemed to have no plans for enlarging what he called our tiny starter house.

"Rika, can you help me?" Lux called from the trench. His face and arms glistened with sweat from digging the foundation holes.

I walked over the piles of dirt. "Of course, but I'm not good with a shovel."

"Don't need your muscles. I need your brain."

Puzzled, I tried to read his expression. Why would he ask a woman? Mutter's whisper in the back of my head said, "Silence is golden. Men don't want women telling them what to do." I knew I might regret it, but I let the reminder pass. "Of course I'll help."

"The foundation holes are almost finished, but there is a place where a big layer of rock is near the surface. I can't dig there. Do you have a suggestion?"

After doing mathematical calculations on moving the foundation and how that would change the walls of the house, we decided to flatten the rock with a pickax and use it as part of the foundation.

"You are a smart woman, Rika," said Lux." "Not many women could do the mathematics, and they were hazy in my mind. I'm sorry you won't be able to finish your schooling, but you can educate yourself. In fact, tomorrow I will bring you some of my books."

"I can't accept gifts from you," I murmured, but I really wanted those books.

"No gift. Read and study, then return them to me."

Later, as I crossed the pecan walking bridge toward home, I felt like I was floating. Lux would bring me books, but most of all he thought I was smart. Besides, he was tall, muscular, and very handsome. I was thankful for a new friend.

I thought of Karl, also tall, muscular, good-looking, and gone now for several days. Had his group found Indians? Was he captured or injured? I missed Karl's good humor and crisp military walk coming down the street toward me. Lost in thought, I stumbled near the end of the bridge and almost fell.

"Watch your step, Rika," a gruff voice called. "And just keep your sister happy and keep our secret." Lucas leered at me for a minute, then silently walked on.

My feet froze to the dry dust at the end of the bridge. Terror grabbed at my hammering heart, and cold shivers shook me. By the time I thought to answer, Lucas's huge threatening body was halfway across the bridge. He could easily have nudged me off the bridge to drown in the river, and it would have seemed like an accident. He could easily run his horse over Sophie under the guise of an accident. I had to find a way to get rid of Lucas and Otto or at least get rid of their hold over me, and I had only one clue about how to do it.

After church service under The Elms the previous week, I had overheard Vater and other men talking about large amounts of counterfeit money circulating in New Braunfels. Brokers tried hard to keep up with the confusing mix of piastres, which Prince Solms used, and the red back paper money and depreciated paper treasury notes. Bewildered money changers reported vast amounts of currency in paper money were fake, and that it had to come from a big spender rather than a poor colonist and they could not locate the source. I knew who had large amounts of money. It had to be Lucas. In my mind I had spent hours thinking about where the money could be. My clue came the next week when I saw Lucas and Otto at a Musikfest.

The settlers in our community, all Germans, brought with them a heritage of music. It was part of everyday life. Anyone who played an instrument brought it to play at a musical gathering under The Seven Elms, where benches served for school and church. Anyone who liked to sing came to join in, which included some folks who should have stayed at home as they couldn't carry a tune in a straw basket, but they came anyway, participating with gusto. We sat up front, where Sophie could watch the brass instruments, joining in on the songs that were familiar. I noticed Vater, who had a strong baritone voice, did not sing.

"Vater," I whispered, "you have a great voice. Why aren't you singing? What's the matter?"

"Without Anna and Emil, the joy is gone from me."

I put my hand over his. "One day soon we will have word from them," I assured him.

"We don't know that," he whispered.

Sophie nudged me. "C-come on, R-rika. Sing."

I glanced toward the band, seeing many friends and acquaintances doing their very best, not too successfully, to play the songs in tune. However, their zest was contagious, and I threw myself into the beat. It was then I noticed that Lucas and Otto, who had been carrying musical instrument cases on the boat and on the wagon train, had no instruments and were merely singing lustily. In an instant I figured out where their stolen money was. They had come to a community band concert without their instruments. They had money in the cases they had left at home!

The very discovery made my heart sing. I broke into song in my best high, clear voice, hardly noticing that people around me quit singing to listen. I continued, lost in my own joy of singing until at the end of the song people around me clapped, others joined in, then more until everyone was clapping and cheering for my singing. I felt myself go pink with embarrassment.

"T-that was g-good," said Sophie.

"That was shameless," said Vater. "A real lady never shows off." Vater got off the bench and stalked away into the darkness.

People around us whispered to each other and half-heartedly muttered encouragement to me. I was innocent of showing off. And I wasn't shameless. But I did feel proud. Bewildered, I longed for Germany, where a woman could perform without reprimand. Did the culture of German Texas have strange rules that kept women in their place? Or was it just Vater's idea that my place was in the kitchen, not singing? So far, I wasn't willing to stay in that place. Dragging Sophie by the hand, I fled into the darkness in search of Vater.

"Wait Rika, wait!" Lux hurried from across the crowd, catching up with us at the edge of darkness.

"I have to catch up with Vater to apologize," I said.

"S-slow down, Rika. M-my legs are too s-short," Sophie complained.

But Lux and I hurried on, catching Vater quickly.

"Wait, Vater," I called.

He slowed to a walk.

"I'm sorry. I didn't mean to embarrass you in public," I said. "I won't do it again."

Vater stopped and turned toward me. "Of course you won't. You will not be going with me again."

Sophie came to my defense. "D-didn't you l-like h-her b-beautiful v-voice, Vater?"

Lux stepped closer. "She is very talented, sir."

"You stay out of this, Lux. And, you, Rika," he ordered severely, "go home." Vater paused in thought a second and grabbed Sophie's hand. "Sophie and I are going back to the music." His stern voice showed determination to punish me for embarrassing him.

A rustling of skirts and hands clapping for attention announced that Oma Gunkel had followed and heard everything. "Wait, Sebastian."

We all stood motionless, except Vater, who stepped back toward the musical gathering.

"I said, wait!" Oma Gunkel blocked his way. "You've been browbeating Rika for weeks, and I don't like it. I learned to admire and appreciate her at Indian Point and on the wretched trip to New Braunfels. I want to tell you why. So stop!"

Vater stopped. "Make it quick. We're missing the music." The out-of-tune band played in the distance.

"Here's why I admire her. She didn't want to come to Texas, but you made her. She did not want to ride a mischievous horse that played pranks in trees and bit her constantly, but she did. Although taking care of her sick Mutter had been difficult, she didn't want to leave her behind, but she did so she and Sophie wouldn't starve and so you could have the supplies she brought. She did not want to walk 200 miles next to oxen in the rain, cold, burning sun, and mud that made her feet heavy and exhausted her, but she did." Oma stopped and took a deep breath. "She did not want to be afraid of the Karankawas or frightened by snakes or left behind by the wagon train because of overheated oxen."

Sophie tugged at Oma's skirt. "D-don't f-forget the s-storm."

Oma clapped her hands together. "You are so right. That was terrifying, but you made it together, didn't you, Sophie?"

"Uh-huh."

Oma pointed her finger at Vater. "She did not want to explain rotted corpses to Sophie, but she did."

"S-she d-did, t-too," said Sophie.

"She has seen more death and sickness than you have, Sebastian. She has overcome fears you don't even know about. She did not want to cross a flooded river on a tilting ferry, but she did. She expected a joyful reunion with you when she got off the ferry. You were not there." Oma paused for a quick breath and took a step closer to Vater. "She is a brave woman who has met every challenge. All the way here she told us how happy she would be to see her wonderful father. You have not been that man. You have been unkind to her, and I don't like it. She is going home with me tonight. I shall pamper her and enjoy her company."

Oma grabbed my hand and whisked me away into the dark amidst whining calls from Sophie for me to stay with her. Vater stood silently staring at the ground. Everyone waited for him to say something, anything. When he didn't, Lux followed us to Oma's wagon, helped us load, and said he would see us the next day.

"This nightgown should give us some laughs," Oma said, handing me a wide, faded, pink gown with tattered shreds hanging from the hem. It was also measured to fit Oma's broad and less than five-foot height. I put it on my tall, thin body, inspected myself in the tall, oval standing mirror, and laughed until I cried. I laughed because I looked strange. I laughed because I was standing in the kitchen of Oma's still unfinished house, looking at myself in a mahogany oval mirror standing on its gracefully curved legs next to a cold, black cookstove. I laughed because someone had stood up for me. I laughed because coming to Comaltown by crossing the ferry at night had meant total fear, and I had cheated death. When we finally stopped laughing, I wanted to cry, but there were no tears. I felt like someone had died, and I was unsure about who it was.

"We're laughing for different reasons, Rika," said Oma.

"I do look silly in your old gown." I wrapped it around me twice.

"I am also laughing because I finally got to tell Sebastian one or two things to set him straight. I've been wanting to do that ever since he didn't welcome you at the ferry."

"Thank you for sticking up for me. You're the only one who understands what happened to me, but I'm not nearly as great as you made me sound."

"Come on, Rika, forget the bad stuff. You made it."

Quietly we got ready for bed, then sat down for milk and cornbread. I sat at the table, and, as usual, Oma sat in her rocking chair. "Is Gustav coming tonight?" I asked.

"Gustav doesn't come anymore."

"What happened to him?"

"Nothing happened to him. He is well and happy, I'm certain," Oma said. "What happened is to me. I'm here. I'm safe. I'm well. I have friends. I don't need to pretend that he tells me things. He is dead. Dead people don't really come and tell you things. All I have is memories, and they are wonderful."

We sat in silence while I tried to absorb it. I had enjoyed knowing the dapper Gustav, the wise man who danced with Oma, the smart man who always knew what was happening to me. "I shall miss him, Oma. You and he gave me good advice and made the trip to New Braunfels bearable. Thank you."

"Gustav and I say you are welcome," said Oma.

"Is this a new you, the Oma, independent and sure of herself?" I asked.

"Independent, I'm certain. Sure of myself, I'm not so certain. We all make mistakes and suffer for them. Sometimes I get sick of the suffering. For example, this cookstove is four times too big and eats wood like a monster. What was I thinking when I bought it?" She laughed and got into her bed on the other side of the cookstove. "I can't wait until Lux finishes the rest of the house so I won't have to sleep in the kitchen." She chuckled. "On the other hand, the minute I wake up, I'm prepared to cook breakfast."

Oma reminded me of Mutter who always said, "Find a way," and she always did it cheerfully.

It was hard for me to be cheerful. Long after she was asleep and I was comfortable on my pallet, I tried to find the truth in my situation. My dream of an education and music had been shattered when I was forced to leave Germany. That was truth. I had lost Emil to the army. That was truth. Texas had made my dear Vater change into a hard, selfish man. That was truth. I'd just have to accept what I had suspected for weeks and learn to live with it. His harsh words tonight had proved it, and he would never forgive me for leaving Mutter in Victoria.

It was true. I had left her. Doubt crept into my thoughts. Could he be right? Could I have chosen otherwise? Had I done the right thing to leave Mutter behind? Could she be alive, or had she been one of the bodies on Black Peter's wagon? Again, as I had done so many times before on the trail, I played the conversation with Dillman's Aunt Mathilde over and over. Before I could get to sleep, I told myself that I had made the right choice. I had not abandoned her but had left property to pay for her care. Leaving her had been the only chance for us to stay alive and get the supplies to New Braunfels. I missed her, too.

Oma wrestled wood into the giant stove, lit it, and started breakfast. When I smelled the coffee, I jumped up.

"You have real coffee?"

"Yes. Straight from New Orleans. And I have real cream for it and lots of sugar." Oma reached for the blue-flowered sugar bowl on the table. "Gustav may be gone to the spirit world, but his money stayed behind to keep me comfortable."

While the coffee perked, I looked at myself in the big oval mirror. Vater's tiny mirror showed only bits of a face, and seeing myself all at once came as a surprise. During the trip, my blond hair had grown almost to my waist, my face was sun-tanned, and I looked mature, a bit like Mutter, as if I had suddenly grown up.

"You're beautiful, you know," said Oma, looking over my shoulder.

"You think so?"

"Pretty as a picture, even in the funny short gown."

"I thought a lot about being pretty in Germany, but after we got to Indian Point, I never thought of myself that way. The sand and sunburn and bugs and lack of water made me give up. I'm just sort of. . .um. . .me."

"That's nice. You know the saying, 'Pretty is as pretty does,' and you have been doing some pretty nice things for your family, and you have helped me a lot."

I hugged Oma. "You make getting up in the morning a pleasure."

Oma poured me a cup of coffee and laced it with thick cream and plenty of sugar. "Lux will be here soon, so enjoy this fast and get your clothes on. You know he is smitten with you, don't you?"

"With me?"

"Anyone else present?" Oma chuckled. "And don't act so surprised. I have eyes, you know."

"But I miss Karl so much. How can I like both of them?"

"Does Karl encourage you? Has he stayed with you? Is he dependable?" She lifted an eyebrow.

"No, but he has kissed me twice, and both times my whole body went all jangling. I couldn't get my breath. Is that love?"

"That's part of it, but there is more to love than jangling. Gustav and I were partners in everything. He was exciting, steady, spontaneous, and dependable. He allowed me to feel like a queen." Oma looked me in the eyes while she was talking, and I had the feeling she was giving me motherly advice that she expected me to seriously consider. "Now, get dressed. Lux will be here any minute."

∽∾∾

But it wasn't Lux who pounded on the door a couple minutes later. I heard Oma and

Vater talking in hushed voices, and Vater was invited in only after I heard Oma say, "Agreed?" and Vater answered, "Yes."

Vater came into the kitchen as I tucked my blouse under the broad band of my skirt.

"Oma says I can come in only if I apologize. Do you accept my apology?" Vater's hair was uncombed, and he had dark circles under his eyes as if he hadn't been to bed. For a moment I felt sorry for him until I remembered how his words had hurt me.

"Not really, Vater. You aren't really sorry. You have changed into someone I don't know. Someone who doesn't like me anymore, and he would only say he is sorry so I would come home and cook and take care of Sophie."

Vater looked at the floor for a long time as he admitted the truth to himself. "Perhaps you are right, Rika. Consider, also, that you have changed."

My heart beat faster, and I felt my face go red with anger. "I have changed because you forced me to come to Texas when I wanted to stay in Germany and study music. Because of you, I have become who I am. I am not a child. I am not your Housefrau. I am a strong woman with calloused hands, unkempt hair, and outgrown clothes."

Trying not to falter in speaking my mind, I took a deep breath and plunged on. "But I am also a young girl whose dreams are gone. I can't come home with you just because Oma told you to apologize."

My knees felt so weak I had to sit on Oma's bed to keep from falling to the floor. From under the bed I imagined Gustav saying, "Atta girl." What other wise sayings would Gustav have for a foolish young girl who had just insulted her father by telling him the truth?

I sat quietly, trying to know what to say to soften what I had deliberately blurted out.

Chapter 15

Vater turned to leave, but Oma blocked the way. "Sebastian, you foolish man, come back to the table and drink coffee while I fix the oatmeal." Oma led him by the arm, put him in a chair, and poured coffee into a big mug.

"Real coffee!" Vater looked stunned.

"Cream and sugar?" she asked.

"No thank you. I just want to savor the flavor." Vater leaned back and relaxed. "I haven't had real coffee for over a year."

Oma stirred the oatmeal as she talked. "So, Sebastian, you had hard times. Tell us about settling in when you first arrived."

"My story is just like all the others." Vater picked up his cup and sipped coffee.

Oma persisted. "But we haven't heard their stories."

"It's not a pleasant tale," he insisted.

"So, tell the good with the bad. Come on, Sebastian." Oma went back to stirring the oatmeal.

"Well, er, ah. . .I was seasick all the way over, so my condition was miserable when I got here, and the weather was miserable, too. It rained and rained and rained." Vater sat back and drank more coffee as if the story was finished.

"Don't quit. Tell the rest," Oma urged him.

I also wanted to hear what had happened to him, to change my Vater into someone I no longer knew. I had asked before, but he had always shrugged and said it had been bad.

"I moved inland from Indian Point with a nice family who let me ride their wagon and carry a few supplies. Each night I slept on the ground. When it was too cold or wet, I camped in a tent I bought at Runge Store in Indian Point. When we got to New Braunfels I camped in it while I cut wood for our cabin. I wasn't good with wood. My hands blistered, and my back ached, and I was slow. As you know I signed up to come to Texas, saying I was a farmer, just to get land. A music teacher doesn't fare too well cutting wood. Finally I gave up doing it myself and took a job building fence for the Schmidts. That way I could buy the wood."

Oma placed steaming bowls of oatmeal in front of us and set a pitcher of milk and a sugar bowl on the table. "Sebastian, however did you eat?"

"Mostly the kindness of friends and lots of beef roasted on a fire in front of my tent. But you notice my old clothes hang on me like a scarecrow. Since Rika came, I have put on weight." He looked at me and smiled. "Thank you, Rika."

My heart leaped for joy. "You're welcome. But we both know I'm a terrible cook."

"Oh, no. You are doing well."

I was totally surprised. "But you never said so."

"He says so right now. That's good news." Oma helped herself to a second bowl of oatmeal. "What was the hardest part for you, Sebastian?"

"I'd have to say worry about my family. Were they all right? Why didn't they arrive? Then Karl came, telling me that Emil had joined the Texian army. I had left Germany partly so Emil wouldn't have to serve in the army in one of the state's endless wars. I had counted on Emil to help with the building and the work, and now he was gone, perhaps injured or dead. That was a low point for me."

I studied Vater for a minute. He sat in a tired slouch, disheveled clothes hanging on his gaunt frame. His haggard face, with its sunken-in cheeks, told much about his struggles.

"I'm sorry you had such a hard time," I said.

He had told me we were leaving Germany for new political freedom in America, but I didn't know about Emil's possible conscription into the state's army.

"The next low point was when Karl told me that Anna had cholera. Every time a group of people arrived from Indian Point, I'd hurry to the ferry looking for her. Then, disappointed, I'd go back to working on the house. I wasn't equipped for carpentry. I was terrible at it."

"Couldn't Karl have helped you?" Oma handed Vater more oatmeal.

"I couldn't ask. After all, he had already spent his money for the wagon to get my family here, and he thought I'd repay him when he got to New Braunfels. Instead he found a destitute, sad, skinny man living in a tent next to the few walls of a house."

Oma took my empty bowl and spoon. "But you persevered. You finished the house."

"With help from friends. Thank God for friends. Even after the little house was built, it felt huge with no family to fill it. And yet, oh, it's nothing." He fell quiet.

"Come on. Tell." Oma reached over and patted his bony shoulder.

A stricken look came over his face. "I knew the house was tiny, and I-I felt embarrassed to bring my family to such a place with a dirt floor. They had been accustomed to many rooms with polished wood floors and sparkling windows with curtains and fresh wallpaper and paint. Some nights I didn't go to sleep for worry over how they would feel about the dark little house." He put his head in his hands. "It was the best I could do, but it isn't good enough."

I felt sorry for him, but he was right. The dark, dirty, crowded little house just wasn't good enough.

We sat in silence while Oma took the steaming coffee pot from the stove and drained its contents into Vater's mug. As if she had read my mind, she said, "Now Sebastian, the house is little, dark, and dirty feeling, but it's also cozy, warm, and filled with Sophie's laughter and funny observations. It's home. And when Anna and Emil come, you will make it cozier and happier, and you can add on a room and another room. In a short time you will have a grand house, and all this trouble will be forgotten."

"If they ever come." Again, he looked downcast.

"They will come. I'm sure of it," I said, my chin firm in determination.

"Sure of it?" asked Vater.

I sighed. "To tell the truth, Vater, I'm not certain. I just hope they will come. I'm worried, too. But it's important to hope. And Mutter would say to 'make do,' so we will."

"You are very much like your Mutter, Rika. Will you help me 'make do' until Anna comes?" He sounded sincere, but I felt uneasy about how he had treated me.

I had my mouth open to answer, but Oma stood in front of Vater, blocking my answer. "You still owe this young woman an apology for last night. Make it right and sincere this time."

Vater looked clearly at my eyes. "I am sorry for what I said last night, Rika. Please forgive me." He sounded like the Vater I knew before Texas.

"Yes, Vater, I forgive you."

"Last night taught me something. I have become a different person in Texas, one who is hard and unemotional, as if all the music is gone from life. This is a harsh land, and we have all had to do hard things to survive." Vater bowed his head as if embarrassed by speaking his discovery.

I nodded. "That's exactly what Aunt Mathilde told me."

"And she is?" Vater wanted to know.

"She is Dillman Mantz's aunt in Victoria who is caring for Mutter."

"Tell me about it as we walk home. Sophie will be awake soon, and I need to be there."

"You left her alone?" I was surprised.

"No. Lux came early to shore up the animal shed for your impossible horse. You will be glad to see him, I suppose."

∞

After Vater and I started talking to each other, slowly my home life changed. Although there wasn't much variety in food, with the help of a neighbor I improved my cooking and learned to make watermelon preserves. Marie Kessler visited with me on Saturdays, often bringing milk or butter. Now, more than ever, Marie said, their cow, Wilma, had become the most valuable member of the Kessler family.

Sophie was still a pest but seemed to enjoy the German mottos it was my job to teach her. Because of her speech stutter, she learned them by chanting in a sing-song voice, finding that she spoke plainly, which made her proud and me as the teacher look good. One morning as I swept the hard dirt floor of our house, it dawned on me that except for not being a fat Housefrau as Karl had suggested, I had become exactly what Karl said I would: the three ks of German womanhood: Kuche, Kirche, and Kinder (kitchen, church, children). My hopes and dreams were only dashed, not gone, yet Karl's prophesy had come true. What had become of him? Why had there been no word from the scouting party? I longed for the excitement of him, the fun of being with him, and the tingling feeling of his touch.

Our family's new beginning spurred me to renew my dream of becoming a musician, and in my precious moments of spare time I took music from the big trunk and fingered it, using my imagination to hear the piano notes. I kept hearing notes in my head that wouldn't go away until I wrote them down, so I used all the paper we had and margins of other music to write down the chords and melodies. This became my new form of amusement as I did the mathematical and musical notations in my head. Vater even took one of my compositions to band practice after he spent precious money for paper to arrange parts for different instruments. The piece was applauded at rehearsals, and I looked forward to hearing it sometime at a band concert.

My new beginning even seemed to affect Baya, who settled into routine feeding and watering without nipping me with his teeth. I wondered how an animal could know the difference in my attitude, but laid it to his extra attention from Lux, who was almost finished making the shed secure against the coming winter.

I asked myself if this strange horse could know Lux worked hard for him. Don't be ridiculous, I answered myself. But then I remembered how Baya liked for me to sing and had made his wishes known on the trip.

When Lux came to work every morning, we discussed philosophy and geology, cooking and economics, the weather, and anything else we could think of. The German proverb, "Ignorance is great darkness" took on new meaning when I realized that exchanging remarks and learning from Lux made me feel like the sun shone on me.

The most fun, though, was the gossip he brought from some of his other jobs and from the saloon on Market Square. Built on wooden pillars, the saloon had a broad gallery where men gathered to drink. The men, he said, were having difficulty finding drinks that suited both their pocket change and the climate. Whiskey made from distilled corn was not only the cheapest drink, but it loosened tongues. The gallery, he said, was blessed with many stories. He told about a spotted jaguar at the edge of town and about Reverend Ervendberg, who wanted to build an orphanage for the twenty or so orphans now housed in tents. He said the men argued about the fairness of the required two years of service in civic jobs as well as the conscription of men in the militia.

"What do you think of conscription, Rika? Is it fair?" Lux asked.

"Someone has to keep us all safe." I answered quickly, glad that someone wanted my opinion.

"Right. But there are exceptions to who has to serve. Judges, ferrymen, officials, notaries, postmasters, mail carriers, owners of public mills, and teachers are exempt. Is that fair?"

"No," I answered. "Wait a minute! It sounds unfair, but business would be disrupted if they had to leave."

Lux stopped pounding and looked at me. "Now you know why the men argue about it. There are several ways to look at it."

I frowned. "When Karl comes back, will he have to serve in the militia?"

Lux started hammering again, this time very hard and showing his anger. "Him again? Rika, you should write him off. That expedition hasn't been heard from for over two months, say men at the gallery."

A cold web closed around my heart. *Write off the only man I ever kissed? Forget the person who made it possible for us to have a wagon and team?* "I can't do that, Lux. I can't believe he is dead. That would be dreadful. Your gallery news is morose." I turned to go back in the house.

"Wait. I apologize. Of course you should hope your friend is all right. Besides, there is good news!" Lux followed me a few steps.

"What is it?"

"There's to be a dance, and it will be on a wooden floor. Will you go with me?"

I tried to remain demure as a lady should, but I couldn't seem to help myself. "Yes! Yes! Yes!"

"Had to talk you into that, did I?" He laughed. "Is it the dancing company that excites you or just the chance to wear the secret satin shoes?"

"Who told you about the shoes? Kurt or Sophie?"

"Neither. It was Oma Gunkel. She told me how you carried them all this way hidden in the bottom of that ridiculous reticule. They must be very important to you."

"At first it was just the shoes and the idea of a secret that Mutter didn't know about, but I think now it's not the shoes. It's the idea that somewhere in this awful place people are civilized enough to dance on a real wooden floor. In Gonzales, Kurt and I danced on a dirt floor to a comb and funnel band."

"This time it will be wood. Lucas Beck has hired me to make a smooth wooden floor, and he will pay me well. I'll make it very smooth," said Lux as he fastened a peg into the door hinge.

"Lucas Beck?" I shouted.

"Yes." Lux nodded.

"Don't trust him, Lux. He is trouble!"

"Seems nice enough," insisted Lux. "Why don't you like him? I have noticed that before."

"I can't tell you, but please don't get involved with his money. You could get into trouble."

"What kind of trouble?"

"Yes, what kind of trouble?" Vater, coming out of the house, overheard me.

Dare I put myself in danger by telling them? And what about the threats against Sophie? I waited for an answer from myself. None came. But I had started this, so I had to go on. "There's counterfeit money everywhere. You've heard about it."

Vater looked squarely at my eyes. "What does that have to do with Lucas Beck?" I stayed silent.

Lux encouraged me. "You might as well tell us, Rika, so we can understand."

"Sit down on the ground and come close so no one can hear." After they sat, I leaned toward them, speaking softly. "I overheard Otto and Lucas onboard ship. They robbed a bank in Oldenberg and smuggled the money to Galveston, where Otto exchanged it for American dollars. They know I know." I talked faster and faster. "They threatened to throw me overboard if I told."

"Oh, no!" Lux and Vater said at the same time.

"They keep threatening me and telling me they will hurt Sophie if I tell."

Quickly Lux got up. "I'll go take care of them right now."

"Wait! There's more. A lot of counterfeit money is circulating right now, both Texan and Mexican. I believe Otto and Lucas were cheated in Galveston and are exchanging fake money without even knowing it."

"How do you know this? Any proof?" asked Lux.

"I think it's in the mandolin and guitar cases they carried on ship. When they came to the Musikfest, they didn't bring the instruments they had been so careful about on the trip."

"Anything else?" asked Vater.

I laughed. "Yes. Part of their threat was to watch me like a hawk all the way to New Braunfels. In spite of my protests, they watered and fed Baya and the oxen every night, hitched them every morning, and even bribed me with delicious white bread in Gonzales. At first, I was scared to death until Gustav told me to use them every day and to be sure to protest. It worked. You can't imagine how much help they were."

"And Gustav is?" asked Vater.

"Gustav is. . .er. . ." I waited. Did I dare tell him this secret? Would he, like Emil, think Oma crazy?

"Well?" Vater became impatient.

The time for secrets is past, I told myself. "Gustav was Oma Gunkel's long dead and departed husband."

Vater was shocked. "You've been keeping company with a ghost?"

Lux laughed. "Rika, you are the most amazing, unbelievable woman I ever met. In spite of a despicable Spanish-hearing horse, two threatening bank robbers, and a ghost that gave advice, you made it to New Braunfels. My hat is off to you." Lux took the round cap from his head and placed it on mine. "I crown you either courageous or foolish woman of the day. Take your choice."

Vater was not impressed. "You know we do *not* believe in ghosts. That belief is evil. You traveled with a strange, evil woman. What about her? She must believe in ghosts. What a foolish woman!"

"Not foolish, Vater. When Oma pretended that Gustav was still with her, the un-bearable trip became bearable. You can't imagine how impossible it was for a woman traveling alone. Gustav's gone now. Not needed. We all knew he was imaginary, but Oma's memory of him was wise as well as entertaining. And, Vater, in choosing to travel with Oma Gunkel, I used something Aunt Mathilde, the one I told you is taking care of Mutter, told me. She said, 'Which consequences are most promising?' The consequence of not traveling with what you call a foolish woman, Oma Gunkel, was to stay at the McCoy Creek Encampment for weeks waiting for the next wagon train. Remember, I was alone with no money. It was more promising to travel with a crazy lady and the ghost of her dear but not departed husband than to go hungry waiting for another wagon train."

"You made the only right choice. Desperate situations call for desperate deci-sions," declared Lux.

"Lux!" I fairly shouted at him. "That is exactly what Aunt Mathilde said."

Lux looked quizzical. "Was she German?"

"Yes, Dillman took me to her because she spoke German, and I could make her understand about Mutter."

"It's a German saying. They do come in handy."

"One other thing about Gustav," I said. "He was rich. That's how Oma helped me, and how she has a house with floors and coffee with sugar and cream. That's how she hired Kurt Kessler to help with her wagon on the trail."

"Is she rich enough to pay for a wooden dance floor?" asked Lux.

❦

The question was innocent enough, but it got me in a heap of trouble when Lux told Lucas that Oma would pay him more to build the dance floor than their agreed price. It made Lucas so mad he came to our house pounding on the door so loud our neighbor heard it and stuck her head out the door.

I let Lucas inside, and he started yelling at me. "I know you are the cause of this disgrace. Everyone knew I was the donor for the dance floor. Now everyone wants to know why someone else is doing it. You told, didn't you?" He drew back his hand to hit me. "Admit it. You told! I warned you. Otto warned you!"

I stumbled backward to escape his arm, but he moved forward into striking range. A loud voice from behind me yelled, "Stop, or I will shoot you!"

Lucas dropped his arm.

"Now, come to the table and sit down," said the loud voice.

Lucas didn't move. I stared incredulously at my Vater, then at the gun he held in his hand. Never had I seen my father with a gun.

"I said move to the table and *sit*," Vater shouted again.

Lucas moved to the table and sat on a bench.

Frightened, Sophie had taken refuge under the table. Now she came out crying. I hugged her, told her everything was all right, and told her to go outside while Vater bravely took care of the trouble. Glad for escape, she fled, slamming the door behind her. I sat at the opposite end of the table, safely away from Lucas.

"Rika kept your secret until last week. You did a good job of threatening her, but you have made your last threat. If you ever strike or even threaten Rika or anyone in my family, I will find you and shoot you in both legs. I shall do the same for Otto. Do you understand?" Vater waved the gun toward Lucas's knees.

Lucas nodded.

Vater shouted, "Say it. Say, 'I understand'!"

My heart beat faster and faster as Lucas crouched above the bench, and I feared he intended to snatch the gun from Vater. Then the fight went out of him and he slumped back on to the bench. "I understand," he mumbled.

Vater waved the gun again. "What did you say?"

"Yes, I understand," Lucas shouted.

Vater dismissed me by using my full name. "Frederika, will you make us some coffee? Lucas and I have some business to transact."

While I measured the dried ground beans into boiling water, I listened to every word. Vater had obviously spent the last days deciding how he would handle a confrontation and had determined the right approach. After telling Lucas not to interrupt, he explained the freedom enjoyed by everyone in Texas, showing how easy it is to start over in a new country. With that freedom, Vater said, comes responsibility for our neighbors, not only to help them if they are in trouble, but to treat them fairly, being careful not to cheat them. Honesty is required. Passing counterfeit money is cheating everyone because the fraud is passed on and on and on.

At that point, Lucas, who had been fidgeting since he first sat at the table, could contain himself no longer. "Wait, Sebastian. You have it all wrong. I didn't know I was passing fake money. I gave honest money for the counterfeit I was given in Galveston."

"How do you mean honest money?" Vater asked. "You stole that money in Oldenberg from people who had worked hard for it."

Defeated, Lucas sat back down. "True. What are you going to do about it? I don't want to go to jail."

From the cookstove in the corner, I shouted, "You deserve to go to jail!"

"Rika, this man may not get what he deserves. Here is my plan. Lucas, burn what's left of the fake money. Tell no one. You can never go back and collect what is in circulation."

"I didn't know it was counterfeit when I started spending it," said Lucas.

"Part of your punishment will be to watch your friends struggle with their money. It is an evil thing you have done, but what's done can't be undone. You will stop it in its tracks. I will see that you burn the money. I mean, I want to watch the flames to make sure you do it. As to the bank in Oldenberg, German state law cannot touch you in Texas, but I am your watchdog, your sheriff, your constable looking over your shoulder. In New Braunfels, you will be honest with your neighbors. One false step and I let your secrets be known."

I took cups of the bean-smelling drink that served as coffee to the table.

Vater held up his hands. "Hold it. Before we drink, are we agreed on what to do?"

Lucas's curled lips betrayed his true feelings. "Do I have any choice?"

Vater narrowed his eyes. "Absolutely not."

"Then I agree." Lucas reached to shake hands with Vater, who pulled his back.

"This is a three-way agreement," said Vater. "Rika, you must put your hand on ours in agreement. You are the one who has suffered most."

Lucas looked at me in denial. "I never laid a hand on you."

"You have kept her in fear for months and terrorized her over your threats against Sophie. She has to agree to let you stay free, or the agreement is dead."

I put out my hand. "I agree. You must start over."

The three of us shook hands.

Vater stood. "Leave my house. You are not welcome here, nor will you ever be welcome. My daughter needs to be free of you."

Silently, Lucas left, closing the door quietly behind him.

I was too stunned to speak. My mild-mannered piano teacher Vater had just pointed a gun at the bad man and struck a hard bargain. In sticking up for me he had appointed himself my watchdog, constable, and sheriff.

Vater came around the table and took me in his arms. "I meant what I said to him, Rika. He will never be allowed to bother you again." Then he laughed nervously and sank onto the bench. "Let's not waste terrible coffee. Get Sophie in here, and we will drink up."

Sophie was full of questions and babbling about the gun on the table.

"Where did you get the gun?" I asked.

"Bought it the day after I found out about that pair of crooks." Vater lifted Sophie onto his knee and placed the gun squarely in front of her. "This gun is like fire that you are not old enough to touch. We have explained that fire could hurt you or burn our home. You are never, never, never to touch this gun. Guns kill or maim. When you are old enough, I will teach you to use it, but for now, it is my gun to be touched only by me. Do you understand?"

Sophie's eyes never strayed from the gun. "Y-yes, Vater."

"Promise me you will never touch it."

"I p-promise," Sophie said solemnly.

Vater picked up his coffee. "You are such a big girl to promise, I will let you have a sip of grownup coffee." He put the cup to her lips.

She took a sip. "O-oh y-yoik!"

Vater and I laughed.

I smiled at her. "I guess you're not ready for coffee just yet." I tilted my head toward Vater. "You surprised me by the bold way you handled Lucas. You're very brave standing up to him, but you surprised me when you gave him a second chance to be a good neighbor. Why did you do that?"

"Make no unnecessary enemies." He drank from the cup.

"Is that a German proverb?" I asked.

"No, my dear. It's a Texas proverb." He chuckled.

We laughed together as I told him another Texas proverb and how Frau Kellerman found me leaning against the wagon crying over Mutter and had said what might be another Texas proverb, "Texas is hell!"

Vater was appalled. "Rika! Watch what you say. Little pitchers have big ears."

I looked at Sophie and knew with certainty that I would hear Frau Kellerman's words again.

Chapter 16

The night of the dance was warm with just a hint of October cool in the air. Unpredictable Texas weather surprised all of us who at home in Germany by October would be wearing woolens. What to wear to the dance had been the main topic of conversation for days. Should it be summer clothes or something warmer? Practically no one could afford a new dress, so we determined to spruce up what we would wear. My summer calico for church and special occasions dress looked good after I trimmed it with extra lace cut from a night gown. Considering that I didn't know how to sew and had stuck my fingers with the needle over and over, it turned out well, and I enjoyed getting dressed for the dance.

"How could this happen?" I shouted at myself. "Just when everything is beautiful!"

Sophie came running. "W-what's the m-matter? Oh, you l-look b-beautiful!"

I thought so too—at least the part of me I could see in Vater's tiny mirror. My hair, pulled back into a bun and shiny from washing, looked exceptional. Then I looked at my feet, the ones that had walked 200 miles in wide, heavy, brown oxfords. They had spread out. Once again I leaned over and felt the smooth satin pumps with bows and pleated rosettes, the ones I had secretly carried all the way from Germany, the ones I had saved for this very special occasion. The ones that were now so tight on my feet that my toes felt like they were on fire. "Oh, Sophie, the shoes are so tight it feels like my feet are burning. What shall I do?"

"S-suffer," Sophie decided after a minute.

It was Sophie's new word. These days she picked up everything like a bath sponge I had once seen. After she had objected to eating the same menu day after day, I once told her to just suffer, and then I'd heard the word for days, not always used in the proper way. This time she was right. I'd just have to suffer pinching shoes. The thought of wearing my ugly brown oxfords made suffering desirable.

I forgot the tight shoes later when I saw Lux looking handsome in what he called his funeral suit, made of dark homespun with a dressy shirt and strange-looking necktie. As we walked toward the party, my feet felt light as feathers.

The town square danced with lights and shadows from dozens of lanterns hung on posts and trees. In the center lay the elegant, smooth wooden floor that Lux had so carefully assembled on top of thin, rough-hewn logs. Along one side of the wooden floor, a row of tables decorated with trumpet vine and ferns held lamps, bowls of popcorn, and pitchers of juice. A few people arrived with delicacies that they proudly placed on the table. Hardly any families had white flour, and even fewer had enough to share, but some generous persons had used their flour to make molasses bars and nut cookies. Oma brought plates of gingerbread for the table and was immediately surrounded by families who hadn't seen such a treat for months.

People gathered at the edge of the dance floor waiting patiently for the musicians to begin, and a flurry of feet flew into action at the first note. Joy seemed to fill the air.

I had waited so long for this moment, my heart beat wildly, and I kept thinking to myself over and over, *I can't believe it! Is it real? I can't believe it.*

With toes scrunched up inside the tight satin shoes, as if by magic my feet flew, barely touching the floor as Lux and I danced the "Double Shuffle" and "Wired." He even taught me how to cut the "Pigeon's Wing" so fast it seemed splinters flew from the floor as everyone got into a frenzy. When I took a turn with Kurt, we laughed about our dance in Seguin on the dirt floor and how people with shoes had let those who were barefoot borrow them so they could move faster. During the waltz I danced with Kurt, a strange feeling came over me when I saw Lux over Kurt's shoulder. He had paired with Elissa Fink, holding her a little too close, and I thought, they were both smiling a bit too brightly. I shuddered slightly with the realization that I had become jealous for no reason at all. After all, Lux was only a friend. My special beau, the only one I had ever kissed, had gone off on an Indian expedition. Then I remembered no one had heard from the expedition. Karl could be dead.

Engel Mittendorf asked me to dance with him, and when the harmonica music started playing the "Chicken Dance," we laughed so hard we couldn't dance. In both our minds we could see him flapping his wings behind the wagon each time his mother hen clucked for him to come climb on the wagon "right this minute." We stood to the side of the floor laughing and talking as Engel told me about hard work on the farm to which he had been hired out, and I told him how I had learned to cook, carry water from the spring, and take care of Baya.

"Does Baya still biteya?" He grinned at his own joke.

"Believe it or not, that animal is getting better." I told him about how I discovered Baya liked my singing, and he laughed when I told him how astonished I was when I thought about singing German to a Spanish-hearing horse and even caring that the horse liked it. Still laughing, we wandered back to Lux and Elissa.

The gentle voice of a woman spoke from behind me as Engel handed me back to Lux. "I told you that you could do it."

I turned to see a very pregnant Frau Kellerman and her husband, Herman, who had so graciously shared oatmeal with me in the dark. My heart leaped as I stood mute, studying her. Gone was the gaunt, sad woman from the wagon trail. Here stood a beautiful woman with braided, shiny blond hair and pink cheeks and wearing a blue-flowered dress that could not disguise her condition.

"Where have you been? I have looked everywhere for you," I said.

Then we flew into each other's arms.

"You were right about everything you told me, Frau Kellerman. All those dreadful miles, I kept hearing your confidence in me. 'You can do it! What you must, you will!' and I just kept walking and walking and doing what I had to do." Then I leaned close to her ear, whispering. "And, yes, Texas is hell."

She looked surprised. "I had forgotten I said that."

"Said what?" asked Lux.

Embarrassed, Frau Kellerman said, "Sorry, it's a lady's secret."

"Lux, this is the lady who taught me how to take care of Mutter," I said.

Lux shook her hand and bowed. "Thank you for that."

"Rika, we have found Texas to be a little bit of heaven," she said.

Herman held out his hands palms up, proudly displaying many thick calluses. "When you are establishing a farm, heaven can be heavy work. But it is ours, and we love it."

Herman and Lux talked farm talk while Frau Kellerman and I talked about the baby that was due in only two months. Hesitantly she asked about Mutter. I guess my face must have darkened into a frown.

"Don't worry, Rika. No news is really good news. Your Mutter is probably on her way to New Braunfels right now."

With promises of visits, the Kellermans moved on to the dance floor and were lost in the music, and Lux and I swirled, glided, and shuffled until people drifted away toward their homes and we joined them.

As Lux and I wandered quietly down the dark streets toward home, I felt excited, yet strangely comfortable with Lux. My first official date seemed like something from a fairy tale, and I didn't want it to end.

Apparently Lux felt the same. He walked slower and slower, occasionally stopping to face me to ask my opinion of the dance floor he had built and how I thought he ranked as a dancer. He even stopped in the middle of a street to tease out the secret Frau Kellerman and I shared.

"That's for me to know." I laughed. "A lady keeps secrets."

We moved on into the cool night that seemed to take on a golden glow. "Apparently, Rika, you have several secrets. You didn't tell me Kurt and Engel both had moon-eyes for you." Lux reached for my hand.

I took his hand. A tingling came into my fingers, and I felt my face get warm. The golden glow around us seemed brighter.

"Rika?"

"Yes."

"Thank you for being beautiful and for making the dance so much fun."

"No need to thank me, Lux. You were a wonderful companion."

An instant later a man and his son ran from the shadows past us. "There's a fire," the man said, pointing.

Lights came on in houses around us, and I realized the golden glow I thought was romance had turned to red. People hurried past us, carrying buckets and calling to each other. "Hurry. Hurry." Calls of, "Get your bucket," and "Tell John to hurry," echoed around us. A woman's voice called, "Bring the water pail. It's the Muellers'."

"Fire! Lux, my house is on fire," I screamed.

We ran with Lux still holding my hand and dragging me along, my tight shoes pinching with every hurried step. Just as we got to the corner, the wind suddenly fanned the low-burning fire into huge flames that licked tongues of red into the dark sky.

The crackle of dry wood burning roared in our ears and the acrid smoke filled our lungs as the wind blew it our way. People ran in and out of the door carrying things, and from a distance I heard Sophie screaming.

Vater yelled for the neighbors to bring water, and people appeared from everywhere carrying buckets. I didn't know that I had stood frozen in one spot until Lux grabbed my hand and dragged me toward the burning house to search for Sophie. I found her clinging to Baya's halter, her eyes wide with terror. As she screamed, Baya pumped his head up and down, his eyes wide with terror also.

"It's okay, Sophie. We are all safe," I called. Back at the door I yelled to people carrying things, "Get the trunk! Get the trunk!"

Mounds of belongings grew in the yard as people dropped what they had rescued and headed back for more, but the flames were too much. I heard Vater yelling for them to stop, that it wasn't safe. People yelled directions to each other and ran for more water, but it was hopeless. Despite their best efforts, fast, hungry flames consumed the house. Slowly, as we watched, unbelieving, the roof caved in, and our home burned itself into a pile of useless, black rubble with only the iron cookstove visible in the red, burning ashes. By the light of hot coals, our friends and neighbors murmured to themselves about the tragedy and congratulated each other that no one was hurt and everyone accounted for. I hugged Vater, whose soot-covered face had clean trickles down his cheeks from watering eyes.

"Oh, Vater," I said, "you worked so hard to build our house. I'm so sorry. How did this happen?"

"Sophie knocked the lamp. . .Rika! Where is Sophie?"

Her screaming had stopped long ago, but in the noise and confusion we hadn't noticed.

"She got out of the house. I put her by the horse shed and told her to stay there." Vater raced inside the shed, returned shaking his head, then ran around the yard calling her name.

"I saw her there hanging on to Baya," I said. "Where is Baya?"

He was found behind the shed, sheltered from the layer of smoke settling to the ground.

Frantically we searched the garden behind the shed, the piles of furniture and odd belongings, and the word went out: "Find Sophie."

People scattered every direction calling her name. Others pounded on the doors of distant neighbors who hadn't been awakened by the fire, and in every house a light appeared and sleepy people turned out with lanterns forming themselves into groups to search the streets and woods. From my seat on the ground next to the burning embers I could hear them calling in the distance. For hours the calling continued as men of New Braunfels turned out to look for Sophie.

Toward morning people wandered back to report failure and gathered fearfully next to the still-hot ruins of our home, trying to plan how to make an extended search on horseback along the riverbanks.

Our greatest fears deepened, and I put my aching head on my arms, trying to think where Sophie might have gone. Poor Sophie must be scared to death and well hidden to avoid punishment, or she might be lost and wandering in the woods amidst wild animals. Or had she fallen in the river and been swept away?

From behind me I heard, "Psst. Psst."

I turned toward the sound. At the edge of the dark ring of bystanders, half hidden by a big yaupon bush, stood Otto.

"Rika," he whispered, "come quietly. Your father has said he would shoot my legs if he ever found me here."

Quickly I got up and went to where he stood half hidden. Draped across his arms was the sleeping form of Sophie, her dress dirty and torn with little holes burned in it, one shoe missing, her whole body covered with soot and her face streaked from tears and soot. Otto gently thrust Sophie into my arms and disappeared into the darkness.

People around me turned and shouted to pass the word along. "She's found. Sophie is found. Sophie is safe." Cheers broke out, and everyone crowded closer to touch the child they had been looking for.

Sophie stirred and mumbled, "I-m s-sorry."

Vater ran to take her from my arms. "It's all right, child. Go back to sleep." He turned to the crowd, telling them of his immense thanks and praising them for their diligent search.

After everyone was gone, I told Vater that it was Otto who had found her.

The surprise made him thoughtful. Then he smiled at me. "My new motto, 'Make no unnecessary enemies,' has paid off. Just think, Rika, if we had sent Lucas and Otto to jail, this might have had a different ending. Tomorrow we will give him proper thanks."

∞

By daylight Vater, Lux, and I had sorted out some of the more badly scorched things to stay in the yard and stashed our remaining belongings inside the horse shed. The precious flat top trunk and heavy contents including my music had been saved and would serve as a table for the few pewter dishes we had left, and some bedding heaped in the corner held the still sleeping Sophie. There were two chairs, two cooking pots, a clock, and three books with singed corners. I felt like singing as I had on the trail from Indian Point, "Praise God from whom all blessings flow," for all of us were safe and, thanks to Lux and his careful work to winterize the horse shed, had a snug roof over our heads.

Then I remembered the winter coming on and looked at us in a dark horse shed wearing sooty, half-ruined clothes. How would we ever make it through the winter without clothes? How could we cook? Then I remembered Vater cooking meat over a fire in front of his tent. There was hope. He had made it. But our food and our seeds for next year's garden were gone, as were most of our blankets. Sophie's school slate would have to be replaced, and she needed shoes. Our winter coats hanging on pegs in the house had probably been the first things to burn.

"Vater, how will we ever make it?"

He looked awful. His hair was singed, and below his rolled-up shirt sleeves little crisp pieces of skin had blistered around the edges. His trousers, already loose from weight loss, hung in fire-streaked folds around his hips. Shoulders drooped and head bowed, he dropped onto a chair and stared blankly at the scorched trunk. "I have no idea, Rika. It was so hard. How can I do it again?"

"This will help you get started." Elissa Fink walked briskly through the open door carrying a metal bucket that she set on the trunk. From the bucket she unloaded

448

a jar of hot bean-coffee, two cups, and a plate stacked high with hoecakes. "It's not much, but we can spare it. Keep the bucket and the cups. Sorry, Lux, there are only two cups, but there are enough hoe cakes for you." Hoe cakes, the Texas equivalent of German pancakes, were made with ground cornmeal mixed with water and salt then fried in a skillet. Although corn was plentiful, it cost money to have it ground. Almost no one had extra cash and time, so the hoecakes came as a Fink family sacrifice.

Vater, too dazed by the fire to move, just nodded to Elissa, but I jumped up to hug her. "Thank you. Thank you. Thank you."

"You're welcome, welcome, welcome." She laughed. "By noon, I expect you will be surprised to see how everyone helps. See you later." Then she was gone.

Lux grinned. "People will help out. I know they will."

Remembering Indian Point and how everyone kept apart, barely speaking to us, I doubted it. "Those who have little, share little. If I learned anything at Indian Point and on the trail, it is that when food is scarce, family comes first. Except for the Kesslers and their cow, Wilma, no one gave us anything. I will be surprised if by noon we have anything."

My first surprise came within the hour when a tired-looking young soldier rode into the yard on a worn-down horse. Covered in grime and dust, the soldier seemed all the same color from his uniform cap to his boots and his faithful horse. Behind him were bulging saddlebags and bedding rolls. At first glance, I thought it might be Emil, but when he spoke, I was disappointed.

"Is this, er. . .was this the Mueller house?" he asked.

Lux helped the soldier from his horse. "Yes, it was until last night."

"I'm sorry." He eyed the smoldering embers. "Was anyone hurt?"

I offered my hand to shake. The soldier wiped the grime from his hand onto his even dirtier pants and shook mine. "I'm Rika Mueller. And no one was hurt, thank God."

"I am a friend of Emil."

My heart sank, fearing the worst. "Is he hurt?"

"No, he's fine. He sent messages and gifts. We did some shopping along the crazy border. There wasn't much to buy, but we got some wool blankets, and he sent you a couple. It seems our army pay was held up, and they paid us for three months all at once, so we spent some of it rather than having it stolen later." The soldier untied rawhide strips holding baggage behind his saddle and removed two tightly rolled Mexican blankets that he handed to Vater. "You must be the Vater I've heard so much about."

Vater and I were completely speechless. Perfect timing for the day: News that Emil was all right and two blankets for the winter!

Lux filled in the silence. "I think they are overcome, but say thank you. By the way, I'm Lux Buechner, a family friend." Lux offered his hand.

"I'm Conrad Melitz from Bockhorn. My family was on the first ship of the Verein. I joined the army from Indian Point." Conrad seemed very polite. Quite properly he shook Lux's hand. "Emil also sent you some money." He pulled out a little cloth bag and handed it to me.

I clutched the weight of coins. "Conrad, never has anything been so appreciated. As you can see we lost almost everything, and with winter coming on we had no blankets or food. But a neighbor has brought hoecakes and coffee. . .well, almost coffee. Would you like some?"

Conrad's good manners ended. He was on to the hoecakes like he hadn't eaten in days. We watched in amazement as he wolfed down most of them before he took a long breath. Finally he noticed our amazement and stopped eating. "Oh. Sorry. I haven't eaten in two days except for Guadalupe River water. My stomach was caved in."

We murmured our understanding as he continued to apologize for losing control. He sat next to Vater on the ground and began telling him about Emil and how they fought house-to-house and hill-to-hill. He told of food shortages, ammunition shortages, blistering heat, victory celebrations, eating well when welcomed by farmers, their difficulty in learning Spanish, and his own discharge from the army after his sixth month. And the best news of all, he told Vater that Emil would be discharged in one more month and couldn't wait to get home. After a while he seemed eager to leave, asked directions to Comaltown, where his family had settled, and climbed on his tired horse. "I probably shouldn't ask, but where are your Mutter and Sophie? I have heard a lot about them from Emil."

I explained about Mutter, and as if on cue, Sophie appeared from the horse shed rubbing her eyes and appearing lost.

Lux stepped near the horse. "As you can see, she is very much all right. Conrad, I will walk you to the shortcut bridge over the Comal River and point you toward Comaltown. See you later, Rika. Good-bye, Sebastian. Good-bye, Sophie."

The second surprise of the morning was a double surprise. Engel Mittendorf's mother, the woman who avoided me and had chicken-squawked Engel away from me at every opportunity, strode down the road, eyed the mess of ashes for a long time, and completely without ceremony thrust a cloth-covered item into my arms. "It's an extra and not beautiful," she said in her gravelly voice, "and it is a Necessary. I hope you can use it."

I uncovered a cracked, brown crockery chamber pot. It truly was ugly, but it would do. I smiled at her. "You are wonderful to share. Is this a loan, or would you like it back?"

This seemed to upset her. "Of *course* we don't want it back." Her voice softened a little. "Rika, I never approved of what you did. It was outrageous for a woman to drive a wagon and undertake such a trip, but you did it. Engel watched out for you, you know."

"Yes, I know. And I appreciate it. Thank you for coming, and thank you for bringing the Necessary." I placed the chamber pot on the dirt floor of the shed and offered my hand for her to shake.

For a moment she looked at my grimy, soot-streaked hand, as if considering not shaking it; then she offered hers. After she shook my hand, she wiped the soot on her skirt and said in her gravelly, chicken-squawk voice, "Good luck to you." Then she was gone. As I watched her back disappear down the road, it occurred to me that people are just themselves, and that inside her squawking exterior lived a person trying to be generous.

Throughout the morning a succession of wagons stopped in front of the smoldering ashes of our house. First was Herr Schmidt with Elise, Phillip, and Catherine who unloaded some packing crates and a hammer. When they left, Sophie was on their wagon and on her way to a good lunch.

Next came Frau Kellerman and Herman, who unloaded a saw, tripod cooking pot, and a tub of oatmeal. "I'll need the tub back, but we had extra oatmeal," Frau Kellerman said.

Carlos, the Mexican driver who had followed us on the first part of our trip, brought hot tortillas and a bucket of cornmeal. "Poor baby dragon," he said in English with a grin. Then, through gestures of fanning flames and scrubbing with his arms he told me that when the fire cooled he would help me clean the cookstove.

Otto came bearing money, and with a grin told Vater that he figured his gun had melted down in the fire, so he wouldn't be able to shoot him in the legs. Vater was overcome with gratitude, thanked him over and over for finding Sophie, accepted the money, and asked him to stay. Otto refused, saying he just wanted to make sure Sophie was all right.

Marie Kessler brought me a skirt and blouse. "They're old and may not fit," she said, "but they will be a change." She looked at my flowered dancing dress with the now tattered and singed lace and said, "If you will change into the skirt and blouse, I can take that dress and wash it for you."

Kurt had come with her bringing a worn but polished pair of black boots. In them he had stuffed a pair of socks. "I'm so sorry that your secret satin shoes got ruined," he said.

The satin slippers, once the focus of my ambition to dance on a civilized floor, had been completely forgotten. Now on my feet they were black and damp from dousing water, and the rosettes had wilted into soggy blobs. The shoes suddenly lost their importance.

"What about your reticule, Rika? And your diary?" Kurt had watched me write in it many times.

"They're gone."

Marie put her arm around my shoulder. "I'm so sorry, Rika. All those memories lost."

Guiltily, I remembered that one of my first thoughts after Sophie's safety had been the loss of my diary. I looked everywhere for it, suspecting that it was doomed since I had hidden it under my bed behind a basket of sewing. "Every event of this trip is seared into my brain in pictures. I can even remember the color of the surf at Indian Point, the sight of wagons leaving me behind, the jingle of harness as Lucas watered the oxen. I remember the storm on the meadow by the San Marcos and crossing the Guadalupe at flood stage. I'm amazed at what I clearly remember without the diary. "

"Why don't you write a book? I'll read it."

This from Marie, who hated to read, made me laugh. "I think I will, maybe as soon as I buy a pencil and some paper."

Kurt laughed and laughed. "Be sure to include the brown shoes that you loved so much. Describe where they have been and tell about this funeral pyre. I'm sure you will miss them something awful."

"Now there is one thing to be thankful for." I laughed. "The boots you brought are a godsend. Thanks."

After I changed from my charred, tattered dress into the skirt and blouse Marie had brought, Kurt and Marie said their good-byes and wandered down the street carrying my once pretty dress rolled into a laundry bundle. When they thought they were out of sight, I noticed they were walking close together holding hands. I carried Kurt's boots back into the shed and placed them under a pile of bedding. Even in their grimy, ruined state, I was reluctant to take off the dancing shoes. Somehow they seemed a triumph of my spirit.

The unexpected trickle of friends, acquaintances, and even complete strangers who brought us gifts dumbfounded me, and in the midst of grime and gray ashes, I felt my spirits lift in gratitude. People shared what they had. The Englemans brought two potatoes. Gessina Eberts brought a head of cabbage and a knife to slice it with. Franz Holm loaned Vater a razor that was a family heirloom. Someone left a worn but serviceable washboard and a bar of soap. A woman I didn't know dropped off a half-burned candle. Christoph Hahn, one of Vater's special friends, pulled his wagon near the shed and unloaded hay and firewood. Christoph lived near Comaltown in a half-finished house, so we knew the wood was sacrificed from his cookstove.

Chapter 17

Just at twilight, Christoph Hahn returned driving his hay wagon and hurrying his team of energetic black horses. We heard him calling from the distance. "Sebastian! Sebastian!"

We ran to meet him at the edge of our yard, prepared to go with him if he needed help. Christoph, a bulky man fattened on his wife's famous apple streudel, never showed emotion. If he ever got excited, no one knew it, so his shouting in the distance meant something was very wrong.

As he came closer, we could hear a rattle and see that he was carrying boxes. And someone was sitting down on the flatbed of the wagon.

"Sebastian! Rika! Look who I found at the ferry? Come quick!" Christoph pulled his sweating team to a halt in front of us. In the dim light we saw her.

"Oh, my dears," she said simply as she struggled to stand on the unsure footing of loose hay.

"M-mutter! M-mutter!" Sophie screamed. She leaped on the wagon and tangled herself around Mutter's legs before Mutter could climb down. Mutter's hands stroked the top of Sophie's head, caressing her hair and pressing her head lovingly against her own thin body.

Stoic Christoph kept swallowing and finally looked away, so overcome by the reunion he didn't know what to say. Finally, he said, "She crossed with Harriet and Adam Haas from the wagon train. I was there waiting to go the other way."

I knew that at least two of the crosses marking graves along the Indian Point wagon trail had belonged to Christoph and Hilda Hahn's children and that the Hahns had comforted Vater when I arrived without Mutter. Christoph was genuinely excited about delivering Mutter to us. He unloaded her cloth satchel and two boxes with great satisfaction while Mutter disentangled herself from Sophie and climbed from the wagon.

We were so surprised and happy we didn't know what to do. I just kept saying, "Oh, yes, yes, yes! Oh yes, yes, yes!" over and over because I couldn't think of a way to say the joy I felt. Vater hugged her close, refusing to let go.

Christoph clambered back on the wagon and guided his team toward the ferry, leaving our family joy to play itself out. At long last, Vater turned loose, and Mutter turned to look at me. For a moment, fear froze me. What if Mutter was angry that

I left her behind? Would she hold it against me forever? But there was no anger in her face as she inspected me head to toe, her eyes finally coming to rest on the secret charred satin shoes with their melted rosette blobs.

"Rika, you have changed so. And whatever happened to your beautiful shoes?" Then she took me in her arms. As I hugged her, the frail, thin body with its bony shoulders reminded me of Frau Kellerman, and I noticed that from under the knitted cap she wore, there was no hair.

"Mutter! You also have changed. But you are alive! What happened to my shoes was a fire. Look behind you. Our house is gone."

Slowly she looked at the ruins, now mostly white ashes with only a few red coals leaving curls of smoke in the wind. "Oh, my," she said simply. "It just happened, then?"

"Just last night. I'm so sorry, Anna." Vater's voice was sad.

Silently, we walked around the ashes of our home, recognizing only the messy form of the cookstove buried in them. "Carlos will help me clean the stove," I said. It was the only encouraging thing I could think of.

"Was there nothing saved?" Mutter asked.

Vater could not look at Mutter's eyes but looked at the ground. "Only the few things left in the horse shed."

Disappointment caught like measles. Sophie began to cry. "I-it was m my fault," she sobbed.

Vater picked her up, holding her close to his face. "Look at me, Sophie, and remember this. It was not your fault. It was an accident. "

Sophie calmed enough to lead Mutter inside the horse shed to show her the pile of covers on which she had slept. "M-my b-bed," she proudly proclaimed.

"Your bed is beautiful," Mutter said.

I could see her taking inventory of what was left, much as we had done on the small boat before landing at Indian Point. She looked inside the mostly empty trunk. "Oh, my," she said with a sigh. She walked around touching things, looking for missing items, and trying to let the sight sink in.

Vater kept touching Mutter's shoulder. Sophie bounced silently on her covers, and I stood mute by the shed door, the joy of seeing her suddenly gone sour. "Whatever will we do?" I asked.

Without a moment's hesitation, Mutter said firmly, "Why rebuild, of course." There was a familiar ring to the "of course" since she had stood in the boiling sun on the docks in Indian Point waiting for the arrival of our crates, and she had answered my question of "Where will we live?" by saying, "Why build, of course."

"Building this house was the hardest thing I ever did. I don't know if I can do it again." Vater's shoulder slumped and he leaned against the door, apparently overcome with the trial of it all.

"I'm sorry," began Sophie. "I p-promised you I w-would n-never touch f-fire or the g-gun."

"You have a gun?" Mutter's voice was incredulous.

"*Had* is the better word," said Vater.

"You have never owned a gun. Is it that dangerous here?" Mutter asked.

"It's the b-bad g-guys," piped in Sophie.

"Mutter, we have lots to tell you, and you have much to tell us. Let's find a way to settle in for the night and talk. Frau Kellerman and Herman brought us oatmeal, and we have plenty of hot coals to cook it. Frau Kellerman is the one who helped me nurse you, Mutter."

∽

After eating, we closed the door against the autumn chill and arranged ourselves in the small shed the best we could with Sophie in the corner on the bedding, Vater and I sitting on the trunk, and Mutter as guest of honor on a chair. Bitterly I thought we hadn't made much progress since we were similarly crowded into the tent shack at Indian Point. Then I saw the beautiful smiles exchanged between Mutter and Vater, and I knew we had come a long way.

"Tell us how it went in Victoria," Vater said.

Mutter wasn't ready. "First tell me about Emil. Is the news good or bad?"

We described the arrival of Conrad Melitz and the news that Emil would be coming home soon. We showed her the bag of money he had sent and brought out the two Mexican blankets. She draped one of the blankets over her knees, fingering it like an old friend since Emil had no doubt fingered it when he folded it.

Mutter held the blanket to her cheek and looked from Sophie to Vater to me. "Now my joy is complete. I can hardly believe it."

In the midst of the stench of burned out coals and the darkness of the crowded horse shed we sat in silence for a minute, just feeling the joy of balance back in our lives.

But Vater still wanted the story. "Now will you tell us about Victoria?"

The story took a long time. Aunt Mathilde, true to her reputation, had nursed and nourished Mutter through the crisis of cholera and the rattles, rales, and fever of pneumonia. Mutter told of vile-tasting herbs, weak tea, flavorsome broth, unpalatable gruel, and finally solid food. During the last stages of her recovery, she had helped care for other patients.

Mutter reported a love-hate relationship with Aunt Mathilde, who became a relentless taskmaster in their care, especially in the area of hygiene, an area that, in addition to herbal medications, probably saved Mutter's life. The washing and drying of linens and the patients' clothing had been an offensive, arduous task for Mutter, but in looking back on it, she said it meant she had gained strength for the trip to New Braunfels.

To her surprise, on the day she left, Aunt Mathilde had given her a present in a rough, wooden box, one she now opened. Folding back the layers of soft cloth, Mutter produced Emil's treasured trumpet. We all sucked in our breaths in awe. One of the Mueller family's favorite treasures, it was the one thing Vater could never understand my leaving behind. Aunt Mathilde, it turned out, had a soft spot for the Muellers, and although she had kept the pewter dishes, had generously returned this part of the fee she had earned as a boarding nurse.

It had been Dillman Mantz, assistant to Black Peter and friend of Karl, who offered to drive Mutter to the McCoy Creek Station, where she could wait for a wagon train going north. Apparently I had quite a reputation at the station, for when she told Bart Creedon who she was, he had immediately laughed and said, "You are the mother of the courageous girl wearing the strange skirts and riding the strange horse." Bart sent his regards and wondered if I had learned Spanish swear words for the strange horse, Baya.

Mutter sent me a questioning look. "And did you?"

"Oh, I learned them, all right. I just didn't use them. Well, perhaps once."

Sophie chimed in. "B-but she says T-Texas is h-h—"

I cut her off. "Come on, Sophie. That was a quotation. And it described the trip when no other word would fit." I was unable to meet Mutter's glance.

"So, Rika, tell me about the trip." Mutter shifted her weight in the chair.

We lit our half candle, and on into the evening I told the story of the trip beginning with the time Mutter became ill, for I knew she would not remember that terrible time. I told about Frau Kellerman with a hand missing, whose children had died at Indian Point and how she had taught me ways to nurse Mutter and had encouraged me to take her to Victoria. Truthfully, I told about my disappointment when Karl had gone on with the original wagon train. I recounted how Oma Gunkel vouched for me as a strong person of character getting me onto the wagon train; how Gustav had entertained us; how Otto and Lucas had threatened me and, in order to watch me, had taken care of the animals; how I was too tired to go on.

Sophie jumped up and down. "D-don't forget about the s-snakes and the d-dead woman."

So those stories were told, along with the wise mother of the wagon master who let Phillip and Catherine ride with Sophie so we wouldn't be truly left behind by the rest of the wagon train.

"S-swimming in the r-river and the s-storm. Tell it!" Sophie was excited to relive the trip that now seemed to her just an adventure.

"You tell it, Sophie," I said.

In her stuttering way, Sophie told it and added on the telling of our crossing the ferry at flood stage. She ended the story by saying that I was verrry b-brave to cross the r-river.

"Sophie," I said, "I didn't know you thought I was brave."

"L-lux told m-me," she said simply.

"And who is Lux?" Mutter asked.

How could I answer? My wonderful friend who had taken me to the dance? The person who sent shivers up my arm simply by holding my hand? The man who encouraged me to stretch my mind and use my intellect?

Vater spoke up. "He is a young carpenter who built our table and built this snug shed for the winter, not for us of course, but for Baya. He is also building a house for Oma Gunkel."

"Oh, yes. I remember Anna Gunkel. Wasn't she a strange one? The one you said helped you on the trail." Mutter was obviously reaching back in her memory for events before her long illness.

The telling and re-telling went on and on with the pace gradually slowing as the candle sputtered out and Sophie fell asleep in the middle of a stuttered sentence. Mutter nodded off during a telling until finally Vater took the blanket from her lap and placed it on the floor, making a bed against the chilly night. I crowded onto the covers piled in the corner next to Sophie and turned my back to my parents. With a feeling of contentment, I went to sleep hearing my parents whisper lovingly to each other.

During the night, wind whipped trees and rattled the door, lightning flashed, and crashing thunder made the thin walls vibrate. Rain pounded against the shed. The air turned even colder, and Spanish-hearing Baya kicked the wall next to where he was tethered, saying in any language, "I want my shed back." Little rivulets of muddy water crept under the door, snaking their ways on the floor to where Mutter and Vater had been sleeping. When the cold water touched their blanket they began to scramble, ending up crowded onto Sophie's bed, fitting spoon fashion with me, yet spilling arms and legs from under the edges of cover. In my half-awake state cramped in the bed, I closed my eyes only to see the terrible fire, playing each scene over and over.

When we looked out the door at a soggy daylight, we were silent and numb. All we could see was mud and the liquid ashes of our home seeping into the muddy ground. Around the edges, looking like blobs of cold gravy on a plate, sat soggy piles of unidentifiable objects.

Finally, Mutter spoke. "We will find a way."

Couldn't she see the desolation? Didn't she understand the shattered work of the tired, thin man standing next to her? With winter upon us, what could be the way? A churning took hold of my hungry stomach. What way was she talking about?

"W-what w-way, M-mutter?" Sophie clutched at Mutter's waist as we stood peering out the shed door.

After a long time, Mutter turned from the door. "Don't look out there. Look in here. We have each other. We have a roof." She gestured heavenward. "Thank You, God. We will all find a way." She fixed her determined gaze on each of us. "The beginning is this: First food. Emil has sent money. We buy food. Then we take care of ourselves. Warm clothes from somewhere in these piles or from a store. Then while it's raining we plan our new house. Then we figure how to build it."

Baya's renewed hoofbeats against the wall reminded us that he had needs, too. Vater said, "I'll use the packing crate lumber to build a lean-to for Baya, and it can cover the firewood Herr Schmidt brought, as well as the hay."

"Tether Baya opposite the firewood, or the hay will be gone by dark. He is one greedy horse," I said.

Chapter 18

But before the words were out of my mouth, a clatter of wood startled us. Lux, covered by a big black coat and a dripping, wide-brimmed hat, pulled a team to our shed and began unloading scraps of wood. That finished, he came inside carrying a basket from which he unloaded a coffee pot. "Sorry, it's not real coffee, but it is hot, and Oma gave me sugar for it. She sent bread, too. The Kesslers sent some of Wilma's butter. My neighbor, Andine, sent you a jug of honey. She needs the jug back, please, when you're finished."

Sophie ran to hug Lux. "O-oh y-yuk, y-you're wet."

"Mutter, this is Lux," I said.

Surprised, Lux stopped unloading the honey. "Pleased to meet you." He shook her hand. "With all the excitement about the fire, word of your arrival hasn't gotten around. This is a strange welcome, but you are definitely needed here."

Mutter rested her hand on Lux's arm. "Welcome to our shed, Lux. I understand you built it just in time for the fire. Thank you. And thank you for the food, and. . . just everything."

"You're very welcome, but I need to quit dripping more mud and water on your floor. I intend to build you a lean-to for Baya and the firewood."

"It's entirely too wet for you to work outside, Lux," I said.

He met my eyes. "All the more reason to get it done. It's way too cold for Baya. How would you feel about having the lean-to over the front door, sort of like a porch? You could have the stove under cover. Rain or shine, Carlos says he will be over to clean your stove and get it set up in a dry place. Is the front a good place for the lean-to?"

"An excellent idea, Lux. Herr Schmidt also brought a hammer, so I can help you." Vater reached for the hammer by the door.

"You eat first, Sebastian, while I get started. Remember that this is scrap lumber, so the lean-to won't be beautiful, but it will serve its purpose."

Into my mind popped the picture of Oma's house at Indian Point built of scraps of lumber by Karl, who knew nothing about building. I giggled as I pictured the lopsided door tall enough only for short Oma.

"What's so funny, Rika?" Lux wanted to know.

"I just remembered a lopsided door built of scrap lumber at Indian Point. It was short, and the door was shaped like Oma."

Lux laughed. "That would be a challenging shape. No comparison here. This won't even have a door."

Mutter had seen the Indian Point house, too. She stifled a laugh. "And I understand this young man is a real carpenter. Down there, we were all amateurs." Mutter tactfully didn't mention that Karl had been the builder, for which I was grateful.

We ate breakfast to the sound of thumpings and poundings and yells for Baya to move out of the way.

"A very strange horse, but a very nice young man," said Mutter. "How did you meet him?"

"He accidentally met us. When we crossed the Guadalupe River coming in to New Braunfels, Vater wasn't there, and Lux brought us to the house. He has helped us a lot," I said.

Sophie piped in. "H-he is s-sweet on R-rika."

"Well, Sophie," Mutter asked, "is Rika sweet on Lux?"

"Y-yes, I t-think s-so." Sophie helped herself to a bit of butter with her finger.

"Sounds to me like lady talk coming up," said Vater. "I'm out of here to help Lux while you decide about him. If I were you, I wouldn't talk too loud." He grabbed the hammer and stepped out into the rain.

Mutter pointed her finger at Sophie's nose. "Sophie, this is lady talk. If you are big enough to be a lady, you are big enough to keep secrets. This talk stays between the three of us. Do you understand?"

Sophie was wide-eyed with surprise. "I'm b-big enough."

"Promise?" I asked.

"Y-yes. P-promise." She held up her hand as a pledge.

"Now," said Mutter, turning to me, "tell me about Karl."

"That's hard to do." The words stuck in my throat. "He may be dead."

"Oh, no!"

"Adam Haddenbrock came in from the country saying that a scouting party was killed by the Comanches near Fredricksburg. I think he was in that party."

"So sad!" exclaimed Mutter.

"H-he w-wanted Rika t-to go w-with h-him. Y-you'd b-be d-dead now, too," declared Sophie.

"Is that true?" asked Mutter.

"Yes. He did ask me." I apologized for him. "He had no idea what he was asking. He just wanted me to run away with him."

"Such a foolish request, Rika. Not responsible at all," Mutter said.

For some reason I felt the need to defend him. "He spent all his money on our wagon, oxen, and Baya, so when he got here, he had nothing. He hated working at regular, boring jobs, so he wanted to escape to an adventure."

"Taking a young woman into the wilderness with a group of men is still not a good idea, Rika. It was a reckless request," said Mutter.

"It was because he loves me."

"Has he said so?" Mutter asked.

"No, but he said I was special, and he kissed me twice." I could feel myself blushing. "Once at Spring Creek and the other time when he left here with the scouting party. Both times it took my breath away. And I felt all tingly."

"And both times he abandoned you," Mutter murmured.

"That wasn't it at all," I said defensively. "Karl is special. Or Karl *was* special. I wish I knew if he is alive. He must be. He must be."

"Hang on to that hope. He seems indestructible. Now, tell me about Lux," Mutter encouraged. "Just call it a mother's curiosity."

"H-he looks at h-her with m-moon eyes," Sophie declared.

I rolled my eyes at my sister. "Lux is a friend," I explained. "He built our table and this shed, and he is helping Oma build her house over in Comaltown. He brings me books and discusses them with me. He values my opinion. He says I am smart. And he stood up for me when Vater wasn't nice to me. And. . ."

Mutter interrupted. "When he what?"

"V-vater was m-mad at Rika for l-leaving you, and h-he said R-rika w-was s-showing off," stuttered Sophie.

"Showing off?"

"S-singing t-too l-loud. S-she w-wasn't. Everyb-body stopped s-singing to l-listen," said Sophie. "S-so R-rika went home with Oma."

Mutter expelled a long breath. "My, my, my, a lot has happened to all of you."

"L-Lux t-took R-rika t-to the d-dance, and s-she wore the s-secret shoes." Sophie covered her mouth. "O-oops. T-that w-was a s-secret."

"My dear, everyone has a secret. That one slipped out, and I will pretend I didn't hear," Mutter said. "So, is Lux a good dancer, and was the party fun?"

"Yes, it was fun, and, yes, Lux is a good dancer, but toward the end of the evening it felt like my knees turned to jelly."

"Attraction! A fun sign. Enjoy it." Mutter smiled. "Are there any other young men in your life?"

"E-engel a-a-and K-kurt," Sophie added helpfully.

"And they are. . .?" asked Mutter.

I explained Engel with the flapping wing imitations after his mother hen and how Kurt helped Oma and helped me at the same time. I told her he had given me a cap and that we danced on the dirt floor in Gonzales.

"So you and your charms have been busy in my absence," Mutter declared.

"Not charms, Mutter. I was a strange-looking girl on an even stranger-looking horse and a dirty, tired girl needing help. Engel and Kurt were kind."

Mutter pursed her lips. "No doubt smitten, also."

Smitten was a new idea to me, and I had to take time to soak it in. During the trip, I had thought of myself as a grimy, demanding person, not a young woman with prospects. Mutter had a new point of view, but I didn't agree with her.

"Not smitten at all," I reasoned. "They both knew about Karl. They are just important friends."

"Enough talk about men. Sophie, come sit on my lap. We need to tell Rika something." Sophie climbed on Mutter's lap, and Mutter whispered something in her ear.

"T-thank y-you, R-rika," Sophie said.

"For what?" I asked.

Mutter cleared her throat, seeming to choke back emotion. "For doing something extremely important. Keeping me alive until Victoria, making the long trip on your own, taking care of Sophie—for all those things, thank you. You did something important and you were very courageous."

"I just did what I had to do," I said calmly. I felt my heart beat faster. I was thinking that during most of the trip I had resented what I had to do.

"It was more than having to do it. You learned to cooperate with life. That was a hard lesson." Mutter smoothed Sophie's tangled hair.

"Yes," I replied, having no idea what she meant. Cooperate with life? Wasn't it just getting along? Most of the time it meant putting one heavy brown shoe in front of the other.

"And I understand you have become the model *Housefrau*." Mutter said it as a compliment. "You've learned to cook and clean and do all the house chores besides feeding Baya. Sebastian says you never complain."

"Everyone makes sacrifices. The best I could do was take care of the cooking and cleaning. At first I hated it. Now *Housefrau* is merely something I need to do. Besides, I tried complaining that I couldn't go to school, but it got me nowhere. I may still complain about that. I have other ambitions besides being a *Housefrau*."

"All in good time, Rika. Anyway, we thank you for all the sacrifices you made for us, don't we, Sophie?" Mutter nudged Sophie, who nodded.

Appreciated at last, I felt pleased and important. Becoming a guardian, wagon master, and *Housefrau* had changed me forever, and the change felt good. After a minute I could say it sincerely. "Both of you are welcome." And they were, but I had just told them I had other ambitions, and neither had asked what my ambitions were.

Noisy hammering and sawing on the other side of the wall began again, and we quit trying to talk and set to work reorganizing the shed so we could sleep more comfortably. As we worked, a sadness danced around me because no one understood about my music. It was more than ambition. My head was so filled with music, it felt like it would explode and crack like a gunshot. High, clear singing came out of my mouth at the strangest times. I stopped in the middle of moving the trunk. The music had me; I didn't have it. As long as I lived, I'd be malcontent unless I could sing and compose music. Had Bach felt this way? Beethoven? Mozart?

I longed to talk to Oma Gruenwald, who told me that I was exceptionally smart and deserved a good education, who had seen to it that I was trained in music and math. She must have known that a smart woman in a man's world would have to struggle. Even in New Braunfels, a land of new freedom, only a man could collect the day's ration of meat, and Lux and Vater earlier had laid down their tools and set off in the middle of the morning to buy rations and get our meat. My role in the community was very disappointing, yet at the moment, I was buoyed by Mutter's appreciation and admiration.

Sophie and I spread out half-ruined linens that had been stacked around the cinders of our burned-out house. Damp, black ashes stuck to our skin and hair, and the smell of charred wood stung our noses, making our eyes water. Sophie's blond hair turned gray with black streaks, and her face looked peculiar with sweat streaks in the black. I pointed to her face and laughed. She pointed at mine and giggled until more tears streaked down her cheeks.

"Y-you l-look f-funny." Sophie pointed to my hair.

"Not as funny as you do, Sophie. Your mouth has a white rim set in your black face. We are so funny!" Fits of laughter took over. Every time we stopped laughing, another spell broke us up.

"It may be funny, but I've never seen you looking worse," said a voice behind me.

My knees went weak, and my heart pounded wildly as I recognized the voice and spun to face him. "Karl!" I raced toward him, arms outstretched for a hug.

Karl ducked away from me. "Whoa up there, Rika. You're a mess, and I just had a bath and put on clean clothes."

"Sorry," I said while I tried to absorb my rejection.

Sophie ran to Karl and impulsively threw her arms around Karl's waist, the part of him she could reach. "I-I'm g-glad!"

"Sophie," Karl said sternly, "you're getting me dirty." He pushed her away, then said softly, "I'm glad you're glad, Sophie."

Sophie raced inside the shed, calling, "M-mutter, M-mutter, c-come s-see! C-come s-see!"

"Oh, Karl, I thought you were dead. I'm so happy to see you." I tried dusting off some of the ashes that covered me, but it was futile. Reluctantly I stood at a distance.

"The Comanches also thought I was dead, so they left me behind. I was lucky they didn't want my scalp." He paused, looking down at the polished toes of his boots, the memory obviously painful. "Only two of us survived."

"I'm sorry for the others, but I'm so glad you are all right."

Karl inspected the ashes of our house. "Looks like the house is dead. What happened?"

Sophie danced ahead of Mutter coming from the shed. "M-my f-fault."

"There's no blame, Sophie. It was an accident," I said.

Karl walked the perimeter of the soggy ash pile, carefully avoiding anything that would get him dirty. He stood tall and straight, still wearing the now faded and worn but starched and ironed uniform of his German state, probably his only clothes. "There's a stove in there," he declared. "Anything else?"

Sophie's sooty hand grabbed Karl's scrubbed clean hand and dragged him toward the back of the shed. "T-there's B-baya."

"The contemptuous horse?" he exclaimed.

Something in the way he said it made me clench my fists. Baya was a trying horse, even disgusting, but one that had carried me miles and miles through heat, cold, and rain. Every morning when I carried his water, he applauded my singing with a nudge to my arm. I could tell by the nudges that he preferred opera to German folk songs. Perhaps he was becoming domesticated. He had even quit biting the buttons off my blouse. *Oh, dear,* I thought. *I actually like this horse.*

"The horse really belongs to you," I said, remembering the moment I had been lying in the gulf water with my eyes shut and had opened them to look into the strange face of Baya.

"I'll talk to Sebastian about that later. For now, I'm going to buy supplies while you get cleaned up. Afterwards we can have a proper visit. I have a lot to tell you." Karl turned away.

Mutter called to him, "Karl, eat supper with us. Simple German food, but good company."

"Of course," he said. "Thank you. About five?"

"Fine," Mutter said.

"Bye, Karl," called Sophie.

"I'm glad you're back. Good-bye, Karl," I called.

He nodded and walked down the street, picking his way carefully around puddles of mud.

"W-what's the m-matter w-with K-karl?" asked Sophie.

"We're dirty, and he's tired," I said. But I wondered, too.

"Remember that his friends were killed. Give him time to be his old self. Meanwhile, you sooty folks clean yourselves." Mutter pointed her finger at Sophie's smudged nose and the damp soot on her dress and began laughing. We caught the laughing like measles and couldn't stop, for when one person stopped laughing, someone else started. I noticed Baya's head pumping up and down, and once in a while he kicked a hoof against the shed.

"Sophie, look." I pointed at Baya and laughed. "Horses can laugh, too."

"Not all horses," Mutter chimed in. "Baya is very special—strange but special."

We giggled our way through trying to wash off the soot with water from the kitchen, making no difference in the color of our faces, then tried more water from the horse barrel. Finally we went to the spring, taking with us a bar of homemade lye soap. Splashing the cold water on our arms and legs brought on more giggles and squeals, but they turned to shudders when we tried to wash our hair in the frigid water. Having no towels, little rivulets of gray water crept down onto our dresses, and we were suddenly sobered by remembering that we also had no dry clothes. They had burned.

What followed was frantic activity by Mutter, who propped our damp clothes in front of a fire she built. Meanwhile, she admonished us about what she called our grimy giggles and the folly of getting ourselves in such a mess. She put us under warm covers in the shed.

But when late afternoon sun warmed the shed, our clothes became dry enough to shake out the charred dust and Mutter added to the fire and put a pot of stew on the ashes. Ecstatically I kept repeating, "Karl's home! Karl's home!"

༺☙༻

"The dress is a mess, but you look pretty anyway." Karl took my hand and rubbed it against his freshly shaved cheek, a possessive gesture that made Lux glower from across the trunk that served as our table.

For supper, in addition to bread, Mutter had created a delicious stew using spices from the trunk and leaves from the sage bush in the yard. Elissa Fink had called Lux from his work on our porch to get a freshly baked loaf of brown bread and deliver it to Mutter, who had noted that Elissa had, as Sophie called it, "moon eyes" for Lux. Our meal had been free and easy with discussion about the burned house, the add-on porch, stories of Mutter's stay in Victoria, and questions from Vater about Karl's adventures with the scouting party. The Comanche raid that brought about the death of most of his companions was told in a somber voice I had never heard from Karl. It was very touching, but I noticed the old Karl swagger to the rest of his tales. Whatever had bothered Karl in the afternoon seemed gone, and as we cleared away the odd collection of dirty dishes, he took my hand, pulling me toward the door.

"We are going outside for some privacy," he announced.

Indecision held me back. I should help with the cleaning up, and besides, Karl had announced, not invited me. I looked at Mutter for a clue.

Mutter nodded at me and said, "First, help me finish collecting the dishes. I'll wash them later."

I did as she asked, being very careful with the few dishes we had left. Even the hated pewter plates now seemed precious.

Karl watched me work. "I believe you have become good in the kitchen."

"She is good at many things," said Lux.

Again Karl clasped my hand, tugging me toward the door. "You've done your *Housefrau* duties. Now we are going outside for some privacy."

I hung back. He had *told* me what to do. A gentleman would invite a lady outside, but I was so happy to see Karl safe and sound that I gave in.

Lux quickly got out of his rickety chair and followed us outside, stopping in the doorway to observe rather than intrude.

The autumn chill made me pull Mutter's shawl closer around my shoulders. Karl put his arms tightly around the shawl and said, "How's my girl?"

He had never called me that before. No one had ever called me that before, and the idea made me feel warm inside. I basked in the warmth without answering.

"Well," Karl insisted, "how is my girl?"

From the doorway came an unexpected answer as Lux cleared his throat and loudly said, "Rika is not your girl. She is my girl if she wants to be. It's her choice."

Karl quickly dropped his arms from my shoulders, spread his feet apart in a formal military stance, and crossed his arms on his chest as he stared at my face for a clue. When I didn't answer, he said, "Well?"

Whirling through my head came memories of kindness and kisses, challenges and abandonments, his swagger and cockiness. So many things whirled through my head I couldn't think clearly.

Then, suddenly, something happened like a wind blowing clear air in after a rainstorm, and I knew.

"Karl, you have been my special friend and the only man I have cared for since we met at Indian Point. You are exciting, and your life will always be filled with adventure. But I can't go share those adventures with you."

"Oh, but you can," Karl insisted.

"Oh, but I can't. You ask me to take dangerous chances. If you loved me, you would want to keep me safe." I hated to hurt his feelings, but it had to be said.

"Rika, you have lived dangerously ever since I met you." Karl's voice became louder.

"The dangerous things I did were forced on me by circumstances. They changed me. Don't you see that my life has changed, and while you were gone, I grew up? I also grew to cherish Lux." Saying it out loud made me feel as if a weight had been lifted from my shoulders. How long, I wondered quickly, had I been struggling with this realization?

"Lux! I can't believe it. How dull. You will never be happy with the German traditional life of *Kuche, Kirche,* and *Kinder.*" Karl stomped his foot.

Evenly Lux said, "Rika will not be in the kitchen all the time unless she wants to. She will have a cook, and instead of the three ks, she will be doing the four ks of her own choosing: *Klingen, Kirche, Klub, Kinder.* You know, music, church, socials, and children."

The strange declarations on my part and those of Lux left me breathless and speechless but strangely lightheaded. Lux stared warmly and deeply into my eyes. It seemed for moments that sparks flew between us just in the look.

Karl shouted, "It will never work. You'll see."

Lux stepped toward Karl. "You can come see for yourself. Will you come to a musical social? That is, if you are in town."

Indignantly, Karl turned and stomped away. Even in the twilight, his cocky military swagger was unmistakable.

Lux pulled me close and whispered in my ear, "I love you, Rika."

The admission that Lux was my choice had suddenly revealed to me that admiration and friendship had bloomed into love. The surprise sent sparks through me. "Lux, you knew it all the time, didn't you? You knew I loved you!"

"Of course." Lux hesitantly then firmly put his lips on mine.

A shivery tingling coursed all the way from my head to my toes as our kiss lingered, and I was enveloped in his strong arms.

We pulled away only when Vater opened the door to the shed.

Vater simply cleared his throat and said, "Ahem. A later time."

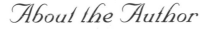

About the Author

Naomi Mitchum, a writer and public speaker, has degrees in Christian education and a special interest in disabilities, acting as Coordinator of Special Needs Ministry at a large church. For over 35 years, she has published mainstream and religious magazine articles, curriculum and teaching packets for teenagers, adults, and teenagers (Graded Press), online articles concerning special needs, children, and worship (Methodist General Board of Discipleship), plays (most recently, *Help Me! I'm Bent!* At Houston Country Playhouse), and books, including *Harps in the Willows: Strengths for Reinventing Life* (used in Salvation Army counseling centers after 9/11) and Abingdon's Intergenerational Programs and *Fun with Drama* and *More Fun with Drama* (Abingdon).

She often writes from her vacation home in the Texas Hill country, where she first became interested in the German settlement history of the area when she heard men speaking German at their morning coffee *Klatsch* at a local restaurant. "I visited Indian Point, Rika's point of Texas entry, and traced the wagon trails to New Braunfels. Along the way I experienced mosquito hordes, ankle-deep mud, beautiful landscapes, and visited the point of the long-gone Guadalupe River Ferry," Naomi says.

naomimitchum.com
www.oaktara.com